The Herring Summer

Also by Agnes Short

The heritors (1977)
Clatter Vengeance (1979)
The Crescent and the Cross (1980)
Miss Jenny (1981)
Gabrielle (1983)
The first fair wind (1984)
The running tide (1986)
The dragon seas (1988)
Silvercairns (1990)
Rainbow Hill (1991)
Willowbrae (1992)

under the name of 'Rose Shipley'

Wychwood (1989)
Echoes of Wychwood (1991)

under the name of 'Agnes Russell'

A red rose for Annabel (1973)
A flame in the heather (1974)
Hill of the wildcat (1975)
Target Capricorn (1976)
Larksong at dawn (1977)

Agnes Short

The Herring Summer

Constable · London

First published in Great Britain 1997
by Constable and Company Limited
3 The Lanchesters, 162 Fulham Palace Road
London W6 9ER
Copyright © 1997 Agnes Short
The right of Agnes Short to be
identified as the author of this work
has been asserted by her in accordance
...igns and Patents Act 1988
...9 474640 0
...on Palatino 10½
...et, Cambridge
...Great Britain
...dsbury Press Ltd
...munds, Suffolk

A CIP catalogue record for this book
is available from the British Library

PART I

CHAPTER 1

1881

The sun woke her, slanting through the newly hung screen at the tiny window, and filled her with joy, though she could not think why.

She lay savouring her excitement, feeling her pulse beat high and her heart sing: then the warm body beside her mumbled something incoherent, heaved itself on to its side and thumped a firm-muscled buttock into Elissa's back, almost pushing her out on to the floor. That was not Aunt Sarah, who was thin as a plank with bones that stabbed no matter how many layers of flannel she wrapped her modesty in. And that window was not the window into the Square. It was the wrong shape, for a start, and there was no plant-pot on the ledge. No ledge at all. Puzzled, she turned her head to escape the light, and the bare walls sent confusion flying.

Of course. She was in the herring-gutters' hut, in Shetland. And the warm body that pushed against her was Jessie Bain, from no. 23 North Square, more than two hundred miles away, in Aberdeen.

Today, at last, she was free.

Aunt Sarah did not approve of freedom for young, unmarried girls. As she did not approve of many things, including drink. Remembering, Elissa marvelled again that she was actually here, in a bunk with Jessie Bain, and with her aunt's full knowledge. And all because of that forbidden drink.

The blurred pictures sharpened and fell suddenly into place. Her aunt's protests. Endless warnings and instructions. Do this. Don't do that. The roped kist. The sea crossing. Some of the girls had had whisky with them 'to settle the stomach' but Elissa had not touched it. She had not been seasick either, though many others had.

The first glimpse of the island on the horizon, her own gathering excitement as the shadowy outline lifted slowly out of the sea to become a low spread of land nibbled by the tides into headlands and little creeks which the Shetlanders called voes. Then Lerwick harbour, crammed with Fifies, Zulus and luggers, their decks cluttered with drift nets and bladder floats, and so many of them that it was a wonder there was any room at all for the Aberdeen boat to tie up. And people everywhere: noisy, busy crowds calling to each other, laughing, some in foreign languages and strange dialects.

Ashore, narrow cobbled streets and white-painted houses with neat black borders to their windows, and what seemed in memory to be mile after mile of wooden curing sheds and jetties, and an invading army of wooden barrels. In fact, the girls had walked a mere two miles to their own 'station' at Gremista, one of the coopers leading a cart-horse beside them, with a swaying cartload of their wooden travelling chests.

And here she really truly was. Free.

Blissfully she lay listening to the dawn: the soft lap of tide on shore, a sea bird, crying high, a land bird, singing; and all around her inside the hut the rise and fall of steady breathing, like the sough of another sea. It was a small hut, like all the others; maybe twelve by fifteen, with wooden walls on three sides and on the fourth, the chimney-piece of brick, its last year's whitewash flaked and peeling. But they would soon see to that. She looked upwards to the rafters where at home she would have seen fish nets, baskets, the 'skulls' in which the coiled and baited lines were carried for the sma'-line fishing, with maybe bunches of dried herbs, onions, smoked haddies and even a ham, neatly sewn by Aunt Sarah into a cotton winding cloth. Here the rafters were bare, marching from door-end to hearth-end in parallel, regular rank, and on the side of each rough-hewn beam she could just make out a scratched Roman numeral, 'I', 'II', 'III' right through to 'XII' above the fireplace. There were white bird droppings on number five, and a dark blur where the beam joined the wall. A swallow's nest?

She turned her face towards the window, wondering idly how a bird could fly in, with the huts closed and only newly opened up for the summer season. Jessie's father and brothers, like her own, were fishermen and all of them would be somewhere at sea this very moment, catching the herring that Elissa and the hundreds of other girls like her would gut and salt and pack away while the men took off again to catch the next night's harvest. Last summer, and the one before that, when the menfolk followed the herring, Elissa had stayed impatiently at home with Aunt Sarah and the married women of the Square, while all the girls she had been at school with took off, in giggling excitement, for the distant curing sheds and a life of freedom.

Now, at last, she too had taken the curer's arles and was hired for the season.

The sleeping Jessie stirred and from beyond her came a muttered 'For God's sake, keep yer knees to yersel.' That was Ina, Jessie's younger sister, but in no way in awe of her elders. Before the

8

inevitable tussle, Elissa gave up all claim to her third of the bunk and swung bare feet to bare wooden floor.

But at least it was clean wood, she reflected, feeling the boards still damp under her toes from last night's scrubbing. She stretched her arms above her head to shift the cramps and tingles – the bed was hard and awful narrow for three – then ran her fingers through her long, thick hair, shook it back from her face and spread her arms wide. The first day of a new life. She spun round once, on her toes, in sheer joy and would have shouted aloud had it not been for the others.

They were still sleeping, three in the top bunk, two in the lower, where her own space had already been taken over by Jessie. Their wooden kists stood ranged along the wall under the window: Bethany's with the lid open and its untidy contents spilling over. As she raised her arms to twist her hair into a tight coil for the day, Elissa could see the little inner box or shottle, its hinged lid also open to show a tangle of cloth bandages and what looked very like a gutting knife, point upwards and with no protective leather sheath. Elissa shuddered at the older girl's carelessness, but dared not interfere. The other chests, her own included, were neatly closed, most topped by a little folded pile of clothes. Last night Meg, or was it Suffie, had stood on one of the kists to hang the screens, but she must have been tired after her journey, or just weary with cleaning the place, because she had hung the screen squint. Which was why that shaft of sunlight had struck so bright. Her hair firmly secured, Elissa moved silently across the narrow space, reached up and adjusted the folds of clean cotton till they hung straight. She liked things to be orderly and neat.

Then she turned back to survey the room and her exhilaration drained away. Suppose she failed them? For a moment, panic gripped her, but there was no going back. Home was an ocean away and she had taken the curer's arles.

As a fisherman's daughter, with fishermen brothers, she could split mussels, bait hooks, clean and mend nets, knit any garment you chose to mention, in several different patterns and all from memory, and could gut a herring with the best of them, but that was at home, with her own family. A packer was a different matter. And it was Jess's and Ina's packer who had fallen suddenly ill with the fever the day before they were due to go to the Shetland curing yard and Elissa only getting the place because she was tall and her father was drinking with Jessie's father when the news came.

In the winter months, when they worked the small-line fishing, Elissa's father drank at the Crown and Anchor with the other skippers and all the Square except Aunt Sarah knew it. Elissa suspected that

Aunt Sarah chose not to know it, for the peace of her teetotal household. When James Downie came home singing, with the smell of whisky still strong on his breath, she didn't see how else her aunt could be so unaware.

This time, he had come home with a job for his daughter, and no amount of protests from Aunt Sarah would shift him.

'The lass is seventeen. Should have been at the herring two years back. Where else is she going to find herself a man? Besides, the Bains are in a fix and our Elissa's a clever lassie. And tall enough.'

You needed to be tall to be a packer, or you couldn't reach down into the barrel to lay the important bottom layer all neat so that the black backs of the herring showed. Buyers could choose a barrel at random, Jessie said, and rip them open any way they chose, even as far as taking all the planks away. If the layers were well packed, then the fish stayed just where they'd been put: if not . . .

Elissa's heart turned over with apprehension. If not, then the barrel would be rejected, the team lose its pay and all because of her. She knew she was an expert at the gutting, but what use was that to Jessie and Ina? It was a packer they needed, especially as they were little taller than a barrel themselves. And though Elissa knew from Maggie Bain's hasty teaching how to lay the herring in layers, this way and that – 'and see you do it just so, or the foreman will send you home and shame us all' – it was one thing to know it, to practise at the last minute with a few fishes in a tub on the kitchen table, and quite another to do it for hour after hour, with your two gutters throwing herring faster and faster and the team paid by the barrel. And from something her father had said, Elissa suspected that Jessie and Ina had wanted someone else to fill the empty place.

Oh God, she prayed, please help me not to let them down.

On an impulse, Elissa turned back to that little window and lifted a corner of the screen. Beyond the stony headland the sun's first rays lanced low across the water, assorted gulls bathed and strutted in the shallows and over the horizon, out of sight, the fishing fleet would be turning their bows towards home. Hundreds of little boats, Fifies and Zulus and yoles, perhaps even a handful of Shetland's own sixareens, their brown sails spread and their prows proudly slicing a silken bow wave through the shimmering water. Her father's thirty-footer would be among them, with the Bains' boat and the Nobles', bigger, newer, but on the same contract with the curer as her father's. And somewhere in that returning fleet would be the unknown fisherman she had dreamed of, and who had dreamed of her.

For a moment, she allowed the beauty of the scene to envelop her: then she dropped the corner and cut off the light – she dare not risk waking Bethany before the morning call – but she was smiling again, her optimism restored. She would unpack that blue and white cloth her aunt had given her for the table, and with the girls' kists they'd have plenty seats to sit on. Later, she would find beeswax and polish them till they were gleaming. Then, with the door standing open and the sea breeze blowing the place would not seem nearly so fusty and small. And wasn't it what she had dreamed of for as long as she could remember? A summer at the herring-gutting?

She reached for her clothes, neatly folded on the lid of her kist, but the sight of it reminded her of Aunt Sarah and as she pulled the first petticoat over her head, her face clouded. Why had her aunt agreed so suddenly? Emptied her own wooden chest and given it to Elissa? Why had she embraced Elissa, a thing she had not been known to do since the day of her arrival in the Square? And, moreover, hugged her so close the girl could feel her aunt's ribs, hard as the school railings in St Clement's Street? With a twinge of unease, Elissa hoped Aunt Sarah was managing all right without her: then she pushed the thought aside. She was a herring-girl now, one of a team, with duties and obligations. Besides, she had already written a note to her aunt, telling her of her safe arrival, and she would see her father or her brothers on Sunday. If not this Sunday, then surely the next, and they would pass on any news from the Square. Meanwhile, it was her turn to make the meals today and she had work to do.

Again she felt that secret thrill of adventure which had been with her since the Shetland boat pulled away from the quay in Aberdeen harbour and she had watched her aunt's grey figure dwindle and disappear into the busy background of the town. Her waking instinct had been right: today would surely be the day.

She had already slipped on her flannel petticoat and the old blue drugget dress which Aunt Sarah had made over for her out of a gown of her own. It was faded and patched, but still serviceable, 'And you'll not be wanting to spoil your good clothes at the fish.' Now, she rolled up her sleeves to the elbows and tied a large striped apron over the skirts. Stockings and boots she'd add later, when it was time to go to work, and the long, all-enveloping oilskin apron, but for the moment she wanted to feel the cool grass under her feet. Last night Meg and Suffie between them had curtained off a corner of the hut, with a basin and ewer for washing and a chamber pot, but this morning Elissa preferred the open air. Besides, she had washed all over, as her aunt had taught her to do, before she went to bed last night. Cleanliness is next to Godliness.

Silently she raised the latch, eased open the wooden door and pulled it to behind her. Then she was outside in the cool dew of early morning, with larksong from the heathland at her back and in front of her, beyond the scrubby stretch of trodden earth and bent grass, the calm summer sea. To the north, in the distance beyond the huts, the land spread low and flat under the sky, with no church spires or

11

chimneys to break the silken thread of the horizon, and in the dawn light land and sea merged into one. Close at hand beside her were two sleeping rows of huts identical to hers and not a chimney alive. She turned her head to the right and saw in the two-mile distance the dark smudge that was Lerwick town. And between huts and town, the long curve of the bay, with the landing stage, curing sheds and quay.

Several different curers had set up 'stations' in the years since the herring shoals had come back to Shetland. These shoals moved up the west coast past Scalloway and Hamnavoe, to Flugga, Balti and Fetlar in the north, then south again down the east coast past Skerries, Lerwick, Bard and Mousa until the herring were 'spent', thus providing a generous livelihood for the hundreds of sailing luggers that trapped them in their drift nets: Shetland boats, Scottish boats, and strangers from as far away as Lowestoft and Holland. But the boats needed shore stations to deal swiftly with the perishable catch, and the curers provided them. It was in their best interests to do so and business arrangements between landowner, curer and fisherman were well established.

The Aberdeen firm of Sinclair and Gibb had several curing yards, on west and east coasts of mainland Scotland and the islands, including the yard at Gremista, in Lerwick bay. Easton Sinclair dealt more with the export side of the business, shipping the finished product to Germany and the Baltic ports, but Edward Brodie Gibb moved with the work-force from curing yard to curing yard, and kept a close and calculating eye on every detail. A tight-fisted bachelor, he was reputed to be first up and last to bed and to keep such a close eye on his business that every herring scale was counted.

Remembering her employer's reputation, Elissa scanned the shadowed yard with anxious eyes, but there was no sign of movement. If she was quick, she would be first at the pump.

She filled a pail with ice-cold water and splashed face and hands in it before carrying it, slopping and spilling, to her own hut door. The ground was so dry that the water rolled on the surface in glistening, dusty globules and already Elissa could feel the sun's heat on her back. In spite of the sea breeze, it would be hot work today at the curing sheds. Her nose wrinkled in anticipation of the reek from the slithery bucket-loads of fish-guts and the different, sharper reek from the filling barrels. They would have to work at breakneck speed if the fish were not to go off before they were salted.

She pushed open the door with her shoulder and carried the pail inside. Filled the big black kettle, making as little noise as she could, hung it from a hook and chain on the iron sway, struck a light and touched it to the pyramid of paper, sticks and coal which she had laid

12

ready the night before. Coal was provided by the curer and was essential for the cooking of their meals, all of which would have to be prepared and cooked over this open fire in what time they could snatch from the gutting.

Elissa crouched on her knees before the simple brick fireplace and blew till the flame took hold, then sat back on her heels and watched, waiting for the exact time to swing the kettle into place without dousing the flame.

The others still slept and for a few precious moments Elissa had the one-roomed wooden hut to herself and her dreams. No matter that the hard floorboards were chafing her knees, that it was not yet five in the morning and she had not got to bed till two. No matter that Jess had pushed her half out of bed and that the mattress itched and scratched. She was here in Shetland at last, and somewhere out there on the morning sea was the young fisherman she had dreamed of. Tall and strong, with eyes like a highland loch in summer, he would come ashore and . . .

Her day-dream was shattered by the sound of knocking from the direction of the curing sheds, and a loud, reverberating cry.

'Get up and tie your fingers!'

There was a groan from one of the bunks; muffled swearing from another. Elissa scrambled to her feet and hastily set out plates and cups on the scrubbed table top for their first, meagre breakfast. Jam, brought from home. A loaf of bread which she sliced quickly into six thick slabs. The big, earthenware teapot, set on the hearth to warm. The crunch of boot on dry earth warned her before a heavy fist battered the door, and a man's voice roared, 'Get up, my lovelies, and tie your fingers.' Then, in a softer voice, 'Unless ye'd like me to come in and wake ye with a kiss, Beth Noble?'

'B . . . off,' came a drowsy voice from the upper bunk, then, with more vigour, 'What makes ye think it would wake me anyway? More like the kiss of death from a poisonous rat like you, Will Masson.'

There was a cheery laugh from outside and the sound of receding footsteps. Will Masson. One of the coopers who had sailed with them from Aberdeen and had helped them with their travelling chests.

His voice came clearly through the closed door.

'Some folk don't know what they're missing, lass, but suit yourself.'

'Aye. I will. And I don't need your permission, neither,' shouted Bethany after him. 'What's the matter with you, Lissa Downie? Never seen a pair of drawers afore?' This as she swung her legs over the side of the bunk and dropped to the floor, her flannel bodice stretched tight across fat breasts and stained under the arms with half-moons of dried sweat.

Hastily, Elissa dropped her eyes, but not before she had seen that

13

Bethany's bare white arms were muscular as any man's and, below the elbow, well-tanned, though marked here and there with the scars of old sores and wounds.

'Well, you wouldn't have, would you?' the older girl added. 'Not with you being well brought up and modest, like. Probably have to shut your eyes when you get undressed, in case you see your own legs.' Bethany shrieked with laughter at her own joke, then, taking the sides of her open drawers between finger and thumb, as if the garment was a skirt, she said, 'Take a good look, lassie, while ye can,' and began to execute a bizarre kind of jig. Her calves were well shaped and surprisingly pale, compared with her forearms, and in spite of her bouncing breasts, she was light on her feet. But not for long; after the first delighted giggles, she lost interest and stopped suddenly, planting her bare feet squarely on the ground and breathing hard till she got back her breath.

'Well, Lissa Downie? Did ye like that wee dance? The Lissa Downie jig, that was, invented special. Well, don't just stand there gawping like a dummy. Did you like it or didn't you?'

'Leave her be, Beth,' called Jessie from behind the screen in the corner. 'She's the breakfast to get ready or we'll all be late.'

'There's no rule says you can't talk while you're making breakfast. Anyway, it's nought to do with you, Jessie Bain, so keep your ugly face out of other folk's affairs. It's you I'm talking to, Lissa Downie, and when I talk to folk I expect an answer.'

Elissa was bending over the oatmeal sack, at the same time trying to hide her blushing cheeks and to undo the top, to get meal for the day's porridge. She opened her mouth nervously to answer, but before she could find anything to say, Bethany was off on another tack.

'And there's me thinking you was brought up to be civil to folk.' She plunged head and arms inside a faded blue garment, struggled and swore and struggled again before her head emerged triumphantly through the neck hole. 'I told Ma this dratted thing was too small, but she said she wasn't going to waste good money on new clothes for the fish to spew their guts over, so I tellt her. If my seams rip, I said, and me standing naked on the quay for all the world to see, then it's your fault, Ma.' She thrust one arm through a sleeve and, as if on cue, there was an ominous tearing sound. 'Hell! That's your fault, Lissa Downie.' She whirled on Elissa. 'Staring at folk when they're getting dressed. And there's me thinking you was such a holy wee lassie without a sin to your name. Well, you can stitch this tear for a start, and you'll not get your dinner till you've done it.'

'She's cooking our dinner, Beth,' pointed out Ina from the lower bunk. 'Take no notice of the silly cow, Elissa. She's always picking on folk.'

14

Bethany, ignoring the interruption, said, 'Is it true what they say, Lissa Downie? That you're not allowed to take your clothes off, ever, but have to get washed with them on, like in a tent, and feeling about with the wet soap underneath?'

'I . . . I . . .' But she could not in truth deny it. Aunt Sarah did not allow nudity and even the daily all-over washing had to be done without removing one's shift. But it was not something to be jeered and sneered at. In a two-roomed cottage, which was home to four grown men as well as Elissa and her aunt, it was no more than Christian modesty. Standing upright, a ladle of oatmeal in one hand and a basin in the other, she looked Bethany in the eye and said in a voice that was almost steady, 'How I wash is my business. Not yours.'

'Hoity-toity la di da! Pardon me if I breathe.' Bethany sat down on the edge of Elissa's bunk, hauled her skirts up to her crotch, and pulled on the first of her thick woollen stockings. 'We've got a right one here, lassies. But then the whole Square knows her aunt's that strict she'll choke herself on her own virtue one of these days. Knows the Bible inside out and upside down, and even chants it in her sleep, Maggie Bain says. It's no wonder the quine's touched in the head, having that one for a ma.'

It was thirteen years since Elissa's real mother had died, taking with her the new-born son who had killed her. Small though she had been at the time, Elissa could still remember the tears and the black solemnity that had enveloped the house for days; still recall the empty, lost feeling in her own heart, and the sight of her father's and her brothers' tears. When the men were away at the funeral and she was left with Mrs Bain, that motherly woman had given her a doll, with a stuffed body and little painted hands and feet. Mr Bain had got it from a sailor on the quay and said it came on one of Mr Sinclair's ships from across the sea in Germany. She had clutched it hard to her chest, burying her face in its beautiful, silky hair, but all she had really wanted was her ma. Instead, she got Aunt Sarah.

Sarah Downie Robertson, a childless widow, had answered her helpless brother's call, as her Christian duty required her to do. Without complaint she had taken over the running of his household, the baiting of his sons' lines and the upbringing of his motherless daughter. James Downie's house was hushed and sober under her firm teetotal rule, but, thought Elissa with a rush of loyalty, in spite of her strictness and her piety, Aunt Sarah was always fair. She might have rules, but they were good rules on the whole, and you knew where you were with her.

You did not, Elissa was fast learning, with Bethany Noble, who could be laughing one minute, swearing in fury the next, and changing her mind with every breath.

15

'Take no notice of Beth,' yawned Ina, swinging her legs over the edge of the bunk and scratching her scalp with both hands. 'She's always in a foul temper when she wakes, that one.'

'Only when fools with nought better to do stand gawping with their eyes hanging out on stalks,' retorted Bethany and pushed past Elissa with unnecessary clumsiness to get to her open kist and the tangle of discarded clothes. 'Where the bleeding hell did I put my other stocking?'

Elissa did not answer, but set aside the measured oatmeal and busied herself with preparations for the midday meal. In future she'd try to have everything set ready the night before, but last night, what with scrubbing the place out and unpacking bed-rolls and pots and pans, there hadn't been time. Then Bethany had wanted to get to her bed. 'And I'm not wanting you lot clattering about and disturbing folk.'

Of course she had known Bethany before they all met up on the Lerwick boat, as she knew everyone in North Square, but only by sight and from a distance, as one of the Nobles who owned two fishing boats of their own, not leased to them by someone who took half the profits, but fully paid for, and who lived in the only house in the Square with an upper storey. Bethany was four or five years older than Elissa and, said Maggie Bain behind her back, 'should have been wed years back, only no man's brave enough to take her on'. She was bold and comely, with unruly chestnut hair and gleaming eyes, and Elissa was a little afraid of her. Especially now, when Bethany's team and her own were to share the same hut. She was glad she had Jess and Ina for support.

Trying to ignore the bustle all around her as the other five girls scrambled to get ready in the limited space available, Elissa tipped potatoes into a tin basin, added water and picked up the kitchen knife to begin scraping them. If she was quick, she could get them all done before the kettle boiled. Then, her hands moving deftly over the potatoes, she risked a glance in Bethany's direction. Fully dressed now, the girl was standing with her back to Elissa, scratching.

'My, but yon mattress is itchy. Reckon there's bedbugs.'

'It was clean straw,' protested an unseen voice from behind the screen. 'Aye, it was,' added another. 'Reckon it's you as has lice, Bethany.'

'If I have, they've jumped off you, Meg Duthie.' She barged the girl hard with her shoulder. 'Get away from me afore I catch a few more. And get a move on while you're at it. You know what a cantankerous old devil yon Brodie Gibb can be some mornings.'

'Like someone else I know, not a mile from here,' giggled Ina. 'You'd make a right pair, you would. Mr and Mrs Cantankerous Gibb . . .'

'At least we'd be rich,' retorted Bethany. 'Which is more than you'll ever be, Ina Bain, even if you do find a man daft enough to take you.'

'Hark who's talking,' jeered Jess. 'You've been looking long enough, Beth Noble, and still single.'

'Aye, I reckon we'll all be wed before you,' said Ina, from the safety of the other side of the table. 'Even young Lissa.'

'Maybe you will, maybe you won't,' said Bethany with a shrug. 'Some folk will take anybody. Me, I've got standards. Have you finished behind there, Suffie Lennox,' she bellowed in the direction of the curtained corner, ''cos there's other folk waiting in case you didn't know.'

'Is there indeed? Well, I'm glad to hear it,' came Suffie's sarcastic voice and Ina, who was tying up the first of her fingers with a long strip of torn calico, the end held firmly in her teeth, said gleefully, 'The lass is right, Suffie. You'd best hurry. There's some folks around here as is strangers to soap and water and it's time they was introduced. I'll be needing a clothes peg, else.'

Bethany aimed a blow at Ina, who ducked. 'Mind your manners, fish-head. Was you never taught to respect your elders and betters?'

'Aye, I was. But I don't see any around here.'

'You cheeky young – ' but at that moment Suffie emerged from the corner and in the scramble for who went next, the argument dissolved into giggles and good-natured shoving and pushing.

All around her the room filled with activity as girls dressed, set the bunks to rights, clattered water jugs, tossed slops on the ground behind the huts, tied hair up in scarves and linen squares and generally prepared for the day ahead. Bethany's antagonism forgotten, Elissa tackled the last of the potatoes with returning happiness: it was nothing malicious after all, only the routine grumbling and banter of early morning. The important thing was that they were a team: two teams, Beth and Meg and Suffie in one, with Jess and Ina and herself in the other. The comradeship of the team would sustain them.

The kettle lid rattled in a hiss of sudden steam. Elissa dropped the last potato into the waiting pan, dried her hands on her apron, quickly spooned tea into the pot and poured on the boiling water. 'Tea's made, when anyone wants it,' she called and turned her attention to the porridge pot. Breakfast proper would be around eight thirty and if she banked the fire and put in the right amount of oatmeal and water, it ought to be ready by then. She did so want to get everything right this first morning. She was a good cook, her aunt said so and her aunt always told the truth, but she wanted the girls to say so too, especially Bethany.

'You not tied your fingers yet?' challenged Bethany through a mouthful of bread and jam. 'You'll make us all late you will, Prissy

Lissa. And this tea's like dishwater. How many spoons did ye put in?'

'Shut yer mou' and move over, you greedy cow,' said Jess with a good-natured shove. 'There's other folks wanting tea even if you're not. But Beth's right, Lissa. You'd best get a move on.'

Hastily Elissa gave a last stir to the porridge pot, hurried to her kist and pulled out the long strips of torn cotton which her aunt had prepared for her, washing and boiling the flour bags before tearing them into suitable-sized pieces.

Bethany gave a shriek of delight. 'Wait till she tries to put her boots on. You've got a right turnip-head there, Jessie Bain.'

Blushing furiously, Elissa dropped the calico strips and pulled on stockings and boots, before tying the voluminous oilskin apron over her clothes. She was bundling her hair up in a cotton scarf when Suffie opened the door to leave. A plain, angular girl, her strong arms bare to the elbow and her fingers, as Elissa's should have been, bandaged at the ends, she was the other team's packer.

'Come on, lassies. We'd best be off. It doesn't do to get in yon Gibb fellow's black books the very first day.'

'You not ready yet, Lissa?' called Jess.

'I'll catch you up,' Elissa mumbled through her teeth. She was trying to tie the knot on her bandaged forefinger and still with the other hand to do.

'Right. See you on the quay.'

They had gone before Elissa could ask whereabouts on the quay, but she knew she must tie her fingers before she left – otherwise she'd be marked for ever as a useless novice and all her careful practice would be worthless. The bandaging was easy, it was the tying that was difficult: but she managed it somehow, slammed the door behind her and sped down the rough dirt track after the disappearing girls. Not only her own hut-mates, but dozens of others from the surrounding huts, all with their backs to her, all moving in a purposeful mass down the dirt track towards the quay.

She knew she was the last, the alien, the outcast, and suddenly wanted more than anything in the world to belong. She scooped up her skirts and ran, bounding over the dry earth with the grace and speed of a roe deer, until she caught up with the stragglers, thrust her panting way through them and spotted Suffie's bright-checked scarf. Half a head taller than her companions, she was easily visible and, with a gasp of relief, Elissa saw Meg Duthie beside Suffie, and, nearby, the small, round shape of Jessie Bain, her arm linked with her sister Ina's. Elissa was pushing forward happily to join them when she heard someone say, 'You're a dumb-head, Jessie Bain, you know that? No man'll look at you two with her around.' And Jess said, 'Who says we're wanting men? It's money we're after, and our team'll beat yours any day, see if we don't.' Then another voice, Bethany's, said 'With that daftie? She'll likely fall into the first barrel and stick there, with her legs in the air and her bum showing.' 'You'll get plenty men around then,' sniggered someone else and in the shriek of laughter that followed, Elissa felt her cheeks flame with mortification.

In that moment she made her resolution. She would show Bethany Noble which team was best: she would make the Bain girls glad they had chosen her, and on Sundays, she would bake the best scones in Lerwick so that the men for miles around would beg to be invited to their hut for tea.

Before her nerve should fail, she pushed forward and linked her arm through Jessie's free one.

'There. I caught you up in time. I haven't missed anything, have I?'

She was pleased to see that Jessie blushed.

CHAPTER 2

Brodie Gibb surveyed the army of girls through narrowed eyes. Half of them he knew already, from Stornoway, Wick, Fraserburgh or Yarmouth. The regulars who followed the herring four or five years in a row. Till they tired of the work, found a man they fancied, and stayed at home to rear his kids. Then they'd send their daughters, at fifteen or sixteen, to repeat the process. There were one or two older women in the crowd: widows maybe, spinsters, people without obligations. And the usual rash of novices. One in particular caught his eye: a tall, slender girl with delicate features, unusual in a fisherlass. Then, in the group beside her, the one he was looking for: the bright-eyed and buxom figure of Bethany Noble.

Twenty years ago, at the age of fifteen, Eddie Gibb, as he was known then, had been put out of his father's two-roomed croft in the wilds of Dinnet moor, pointed in the direction of Aberdeen forty miles away and told to seek his fortune. As the third of twelve children, on a croft scarcely big enough to support two, it was understandable, but during that forty-mile walk, behind his fear and resentment, young Eddie had had time to think. The conclusion he had come to was a simple one: for life to be at all bearable, it was necessary to be rich.

For the ordinary working man like his father, marriage meant children, and children meant poverty. For the rich man, on the other hand, and here he had his own feudal landlord in mind, marriage meant more riches, for like inevitably chose like. And the third son, instead of being shown the door, would be groomed, like the rest, to marry money, and thus swell the family coffers. Eddie had left it too late to be born rich, but he was strong and healthy, and he saw no reason why he should not correct the balance by his own efforts. And eventually marry money himself, if he chose.

By the time he reached the bridge over the Dee at Potarch, he had resolved to die a rich man. He paused at the riverside to draw breath and rest his bruised and shoeless feet and as his eyes lingered on the welcoming walls of the Potarch Inn it came to him with all the force

20

of an empty stomach that a rich man would be welcomed there with open arms. A rich man would be given a seat by the fire, more logs would be heaped on it for his comfort, and ale would be poured down his parched and rasping throat while they hurried to bring him roast beef or venison pie. Except that a rich man would not be footsore and parched: he would ride in comfort, on the best horse money could buy, with his feet shod in handmade leather boots and his throat soothed from the silver flask at his saddle.

Eddie wondered whether to try his luck at the door, but fate guided him to the river instead. For it was when Eddie lay down on the bank and hung his head over the water ready to scoop up a handful and drink it that he saw the fish. It glared at him, its round eyes bulging and its silly pursed mouth opening and shutting in outrage, like Miss Ogilvie at the village school when they'd hidden a frog in her desk, and it was at that moment that the first small idea came.

When he reached the tranquil fields of lower Deeside and glimpsed the misty outline of the city where river met sea, the idea was triumphantly full-grown and he had chosen his path to wealth. The river flowed to the sea and the sea belonged to no man. Its harvest, unlike that of his father's croft, needed no laborious sowing and tending: it was gloriously abundant and free to all who chose to gather it. All it needed was the means.

By the time young Eddie Gibb limped on to the quay at the Inches, his bare feet blistered, his threadbare garments grey with dust and his nose burnt red by the sun, he knew exactly what he would do.

That had been twenty years ago, and during those years he had worked his way up from the humblest yard-boy on the Inches to one of the best-known and most successful fish-curers in the business. What if he was known as tight-fisted: folk who threw their money about got nowhere. And folk who were soft-hearted and sentimental only got themselves swindled for their pains.

But fish-curers needed more than fish: they needed salt for the curing and wood for the barrels which were made fresh every year. They needed freight for the finished product and why pay someone else to import and export something one could handle oneself? Brodie Gibb, as he was by then known, had acquired shares in a shipping company which imported salt and timber and had recently gone into partnership, at advantageous terms, with a local fish merchant who exported extensively to Europe, the Baltic and Russia. Easton Sinclair, a decent, honest man who had worked hard for his wealth. Unlike his son Hugh. Hugh was supposedly learning the business, but he was an idle wastrel, who regarded his father's wealth as his own god-given right. Gibb could not abide idleness, or waste. Which was why

21

he still lived in the same tenement room in the Shiprow that he had occupied for fifteen years, though he had more than enough in the bank to move into a mansion if he chose – and to take a wife.

Brodie Gibb had no desire for a mansion, but he was prepared to concede that one small tenement room might not satisfy a wife, and in the past year he had decided that it was time to marry. Not for any fleshly lusts – on the rare occasions when he felt the need they could be satisfied for ready money – but because he wanted a son. Someone to carry on the business after him. What was the use of his riches if he had no one to leave them to when he died? His family didn't deserve anything, not after putting him out on to the bare hillside. He could endow a charity: the Edward Brodie Gibb Hospital for orphans and the deserving poor. But, watching the tilt of Bethany Noble's head, the swing of those sturdy hips and the way her hair bounced under the scarf with every step, he thought a wife might be preferable. A healthy wife, with good child-bearing hips. A strong, biddable wife who knew the business as he did and would work alongside him; not sit around at home in the parlour, drinking tea and gossiping all day. Or expect to drive a carriage and have servants to wait on her. Someone his own class, used to hard work, but someone with a bit of style about her. And money. Old Gideon Noble, Bethany's father, had money and to spare.

His eyes slid back to that new girl, standing beside Jessie Bain from North Square. It must be the girl with the fancy name, James Downie's lass. Now, she had style, and the Downies were a respectable, hard-working family. It might be worth his while to keep his eye on her as well; see how she shaped up. He was in no hurry and it would not do to make the wrong choice.

But the girls were clustered on the quay now, and matrimony could wait. As it was the first morning, they'd had no topping up to do, but Davie Koss the foreman would have kept them busy till breakfast, filling salt tubs and the like. Moving barrels. Putting everything ready for when the first boat came in.

Each of his boats was contracted to bring him two hundred crans of herring the season and he kept a close eye on every catch. Some boats were ahead of contract already, some way behind. But it was the best herring he wanted, not the 'spent' or spawned ones, and if the slackers were not up to the mark by the end of the week, they'd earn a warning. If reports were anything to go by, this season promised to be even richer than the last: he hoped he'd contracted enough gutting teams to deal with the daily catch, but it was always a risk: too many and they stood idle, too few and the fish perished till they were fit for nought but fish manure, or dumping back into the sea.

From the corner of his eye he caught a flurry of movement and did not need to turn his head to know the first boat had been sighted.

'Right,' he bellowed over the general chatter. 'Listen carefully, for I'll not say it twice. For those of you that haven't been to Gremista before, over there's our landing jetty and the boats are due any minute. These are the farlins you'll be working and when the catch is landed, our fish'll be tipped in here. Then it's up to you. Right, Davie?' he called across to one of the coopers, a cheery fellow with short blond hair and a moustache.

'Aye,' called Davie, with a jerk of the thumb and a grin. 'Leave it to me, Mr Gibb. I'll see they don't slack.' Then he turned to the nearest girl and said, with a wink, 'Or it will be round the back of the sheds with you, lass, for your punishment.'

Before Elissa could think of an answer, Bethany jeered, 'Mind your tongue when you speak to Holy Lissa. She's not used to mixing with rough folk like you, Davie Koss, and you a married man. Now if it was us you was speaking to . . .' and she winked at her immediate neighbours, 'we'd maybe listen. Though you're a randy wee devil, Davie, and we lassies was wondering – if that's our punishment, what's our reward?'

In the laughter and the back-chat that followed, Elissa played no part. She had turned her head away in embarrassment at Bethany's jibe to find her attention instantly caught by the activity on the jetty where men were making ready to receive the first of the herring boats. Anxiously she watched what was happening, needing to learn all she could. The crowd of waiting coopers and gutting teams was growing increasingly restless as the boat neared shore and Elissa felt her own excitement rising. Then, through a sudden gap, she saw clearly jetty, fishing boat, bustling men, everything – and in the stern of the half-decked thirty-footer a young fisherman standing, thigh-deep in shimmering silver. He was leaning on a long-handled herring-shovel, his cap pushed back on his bright, burnished hair, and his face half turned away from her. She saw his strong, clean-shaven profile clearly outlined against the dark heaps of drift net behind him. He wore a hand-knitted jersey of an unknown pattern, and his traditional flap-fronted trousers of heavy serge disappeared into the longest thigh-boots she had ever seen. Then someone shouted, he turned his head, and in that moment she was lost.

'Did you hear what the mannie said?' urged a voice at her side.

'Yes, Jessie,' said Elissa, though she had not heard a single word. The crowd moved across her vision, parted again, and she saw the boat tied to an iron ring and the unknown fisherman shovelling herring into the first basket in an effortless silver stream.

'Then get a move on,' said Ina, with a friendly shove, and abruptly the scene was lost. 'Yon farlin's ours.' She indicated the nearest rectangular wooden tub around which Jess and the others were already waiting, empty barrels grouped behind each team. 'And here comes the first basket. The sooner we start the sooner we'll finish.'

Ina took up her position beside Jessie at one side of the wide wooden farlin as the first basket was upended and a cascade of salt-sprinkled fish slapped into the trough. She had the first one gutted and in the tub behind her so fast that Elissa hardly saw the knife blade.

'That's one for the bottom. And another. And a third.'

Elissa reached for the tub.

'Not yet, mutton-head,' warned Jessie with hardly a turn of the head. 'We've to rouse them again first.'

'Just be ready to shift the moment we say.'

'But mind you call him when you've packed your first layer.'

Another basket-load flashed into the farlin, and another, in a spray of flying salt and sea drops.

'Call who?' managed Elissa, confused by the sudden movement, the shouting and general clamour all around her and by the flashing speed of the girls' knives.

'Davie Koss, you daft quine. Who else?' said Bethany from the adjoining side of the farlin.

There were half a dozen teams round the rectangular trough, two teams on the long sides, one each on the short, and Bethany's cloth-bound fingers were flashing as fast as Ina's over the salt-sprinkled herring. If you had a cut, the salt stung like the very devil, but it kept the fish fresh and made them easier to hold. In with the knife, rip, twist, toss guts one way, fish another: Bethany, like most of them, could gut a herring a second once she got into the swing of it, spattering blood, salt and scales as she did so.

'Told you you'd got a right one there, didn't I, Jessie?' she added with a grin and not a pause in the gutting rhythm. 'You'll be lucky if you get a barrel a day out of that dummy.'

'Unless she's acting dumb on purpose and it's Davie she's after. Round the back of the sheds,' giggled Meg Duthie beside her, as she nimbly ripped the guts out of one fish, tossed it behind her into one of the waiting barrels and slit open the next, in one unbroken movement. As if she has four hands instead of two, thought Elissa in nervous awe.

'Take no notice, lass,' called Jessie, half over her shoulder. 'They're just jealous, what with our team being the best in the yard.'

'Aye,' said a passing cooper, a young lad with freckles and an engaging grin. 'As well as the best-looking.'

'You need your eyes sorted, Fergus Mackie,' jeered Bethany.

'At least they're nay green like yours, Beth Noble. Green wi' envy

24

o' your betters,' grinned Ina and neatly dodged the fish Beth flung at her, and both girls without a pause in the gutting.

'Aye,' added Jessie. 'We'll beat them easy, if you just take it steady and do as you're told, Lissa lass. Hey, Davie Koss!' she bellowed in a surprisingly penetrating voice. 'Come over here and show the quinie what's what, before she's led astray.'

In the good-natured laughter that followed Elissa forgot her awkwardness and paid close attention to the foreman's guidance: sorting, Jess and Ina's responsibility, rousing which Elissa helped them with, then the packing which was hers alone and vital. No matter how well gutted, he said, how perfectly matched in size and colour, if the fish weren't packed properly, in those intricate, interleaving layers, and pressed well down with salt between each layer, then the barrel would be rejected. It was an awesome responsibility. But Davie Koss was a kind and patient instructor and later, when he had moved on to the next team, having approved her packing of the vital bottom layer, she allowed that picture of the unknown fisherman to creep back into her thoughts and colour the tedium of the endless herrings – layer after salted layer of them, seven hundred to a barrel if they were 'fulls' or 'large fulls', up to a thousand a barrel if they were 'matties' or 'sma's'. Once, she even dared to lift her eyes and look about her, but in the constant movement and confusion she knew she had no hope of seeing him, except by blessed chance, and the interruption broke her rhythm, so that she had to scramble twice as fast to catch up. She wished she had noted the lettering on his boat: then at least she might have known his port of origin. It might have been L something? Lerwick? Or Leith? Or perhaps a B or an F? Then she gave up even that speculation as the fish heaped higher in the farlin, scales and blood spattered everywhere, guts overflowed their tubs to slither and squelch underfoot, gulls wheeled and screamed, snatching up beaks of entrails and showering the unsuspecting, and it was her job, and that of Suffie and the other packers, to make order out of chaos and produce perfection in a barrel, over and over again.

For after her first bewilderment, the pieces soon fell into place and the natural rhythm of the process took over, with little time for thought or rest. After that first wee boat, from the unknown port, the herring boats came thick and fast, jostling for position at the wooden jetty where the catch was unloaded by basket into waiting tubs, and each basket counted. Four baskets measured one cran. As the fish were tipped into the tubs, they were sprinkled with salt, or 'roused', to help keep them fresh, then the tubs were manhandled across the yard and emptied into the large wooden farlin around which the gutting crews stood.

Each girl had a small wooden coug beside her, for the guts, and a barrel nearby in which to empty the cougs when full. Besides that, each crew had five or six tubs arranged at their backs to hold the different sizes of fish. Most crews, like Elissa's own, gutted and sorted in one movement, knowing from the feel of the herring in the hand whether it was for the 'sma's', matties, matt fulls or the biggest of all, the large fulls, and tossing it behind them into the correct tub without a backward glance, though any mistake would be spotted by the coopers soon enough and the girls chastised. Damaged and 'spent' herrings had a separate tub and were sold off cheap. Elissa had no part in this sorting process, but as soon as the tubs were full she helped Jessie and Ina carry them, two at a time, to the special rousing tub, where they treated each size separately, until it was thoroughly tossed about and salted. Then Elissa was left to pack the results, again in separate barrels according to size, and with more salt, while the others resumed the hectic pattern of the gutting, and Elissa strove to keep up with the constant supply. She learnt to shout over her shoulder for more salt before the salt-tub was empty, to call for the cooper when her barrels were full, for as well as the girls, a small army of coopers and the like worked among them, shifting fish, heaving tubs, replenishing salt supplies, laying tops on the newly packed barrels, while the fishermen set about mending any torn drift nets, re-coiling ropes and generally preparing their boats for sea. Some went up into the town, others strolled the shore, smoking pungent clay pipes and exchanging back-chat with the girls, some tipped hats over eyes and settled down in a convenient corner of boat or shore to snatch much-needed sleep. And the girls worked on.

Elissa soon found that packing was back-breaking work. That there was no time to admire the design of the essential bottom layer where the black backs of the herring were displayed at their best. No time for pride or thought or anything but the work in hand. Until midday brought dinner time and blessed rest.

Except that she had to race up the headland to the hut to make everything ready before the others arrived. The fire had almost died, and in spite of all her frantic efforts the soup was lukewarm, the potatoes underdone and the mince still pink, but only Bethany had the energy to grumble.

'Thought you said you was a good cook? I wouldna serve this muck to a starving dog. Next time give us bread and cheese. Even a dummy couldn't spoil that.'

Elissa was close to tears at the failure of her ambitious meal. Her back ached, her head swam, her hands stung with the constant salt, she felt grimed from top to toe with salt and sweat and her whole, fish-reeking body was strained to jangling, snapping point. She had hardly the strength to lift her spoon to her mouth.

Bethany, on the other hand, seemed as full of energy as ever. 'I

26

reckon we'll have our photos taken Saturday. What do you say, Jess? Better still, if we work twice as hard, we'll maybe have time to go into Lerwick today before the mannie shuts shop.'

'You go if you like,' drawled Ina, leaning back against the wooden wall and closing her eyes. 'I like to be scrubbed clean and dressed in my best if I'm paying that sort of money and I don't see Moneybags Gibb letting us off early.'

'Not on the first day,' added Jess, helping herself to more mince. 'You and Meg and Suffie go on your own.'

'And pay double? You know fine we always go two crews together.'

'We could go straight from the yard,' suggested Meg. 'That photographer mannie likes to do pictures of fisherlassies in their working clothes, so Willie Masson said, and we'd maybe get it cheaper.'

'Besides,' pointed out Suffie, 'come Saturday all the lassies in the place will be pushing and shoving to get to the mannie first, and he'll be able to charge us what he likes.'

'I'm not wanting a picture of me with my fingers tied and my clothes stinking, you daft quine,' said Bethany. 'Nor of you lot neither. I can see you like that any day of the week, and free. We're wearing our best clothes or we're not going.'

'Then we're not going today,' declared Jess and Ina together. Jess added, as an afterthought, 'What about you, Lissa?'

But Elissa had barely the energy to shake her head. The thought of walking the two miles to Lerwick and all the way back again, today or any other day, and all for a photograph, was too much for her. All she wanted was to fall into bed, dirty as she was, and cry herself to sleep.

'Suit yourselves,' said Bethany, unabashed. 'Me and Meg and Suffie could have managed it fine, what with our team being the best this side of Yarmouth, but we'll just have to make allowances. We'll go Saturday, if you peely-wally dumb-heads still have the energy to crawl out of your beds by then.'

But neither Jess nor Ina took up the challenge. There were other things to do with the precious rest hour than waste energy on ritual squabbling. As for Elissa it was all she could do not to dissolve into tears of exhaustion, and she still had the pots to stack and rinse, the kettle to fill and the fire to bank.

Then it was back again to the yard. A handful of salt, a layer of fish, a handful of salt, a layer of fish, over and over, faster and faster, up and down, from the black-backed bottom layer to the silver-bellied top, then plunge to the floor of the next barrel and start all over again. Seven hundred to a barrel, three barrels an hour. That was the goal she had set herself and by the end of that first, endless day, Elissa had almost reached it.

'Twenty-seven barrels. Not bad, for a beginner,' said Jessie and Ina added, 'Aye. We'll make a packer of you yet.'

Elissa's eyes brimmed with tears at the unexpected praise: tears of relief and gratitude and sheer exhaustion. She brushed them away with a forearm and then, with a flash of joyful memory, looked towards the little jetty and the harbour.

The boats were gone and his boat with them. Put to sea again and she had not even noticed. Her shoulders sagged in utter dejection.

'Cheer up, lassie. You've done a fine job,' said Davie Koss, patting her kindly on the back as he did his rounds of the yard. 'Now away home to your tea all of you. You've earned it.'

'Aye, I'm that hungry I could eat a horse,' said Bethany. 'Leastways, I could if it was cooked proper. What are you giving us tonight, Lissa?'

Oh God! The tea. She had forgotten all about it.

'Herrings, of course,' said Jessie. 'I've kept these back, special.' And Ina added, 'Fried, like we always have. Isn't that right, Lissa?'

Then they linked arms with her, one on either side, and led her home.

Later, in the darkness, on the drowsy edge of sleep, Elissa thought of that moment as the happiest in her life. Then at last, her mind cleansed of the day's drudgery and her body of its filth, she took out, like a secret talisman, the memory of the young fisherman in the morning sunlight, and knew with absolute certainty that he was hers. Fate had sent him to her: tomorrow they would meet. Then nothing and no one would stand in their path. Tomorrow. Or the next day.

An owl called its warning to the pale summer sky, but Elissa was already asleep.

CHAPTER 3

No one knew what made the herring shoals bless one stretch of sea one year, another the next. It might be the abundance of plankton, the favourite food of fish that swim near the surface, or the vagaries of the sea currents, or merely the direction of the prevailing wind. It might be a combination of all three. No one knew.

Some folk said the interaction of waters from the Atlantic, the Baltic and the North Sea had something to do with it; others the water temperature in the spring. But whatever the reason, as long ago as the 1600s Dutch boats had fished for herring off the coast of Shetland. For a while the Shetlanders had taken little interest, except in the trading opportunities these visiting ships provided, but the Dutch and Napoleonic wars changed their attitude. The government offered attractive bounties which discouraged the Dutch fleets and kindled new interest among the locals.

It didn't last. Those who ventured into the new fishing were soon disheartened by the loss of the West Indian market. Slave owners had been large-scale purchasers of herrings, but emancipation changed all that. The next blow came when the government withdrew that enticing bounty. Four shillings a barrel had been worth fishing for. An uncertain market was not so attractive, especially when the herring shoals themselves did little to help, being capricious and unpredictable. Within ten years the fluctuating shoals had disappeared, storms and treacherous weather had pounded the little undecked sixareens which the Shetlanders were using and even the stranger boats from Scotland and beyond had had a hard and unprofitable time of it. After a run of poor seasons most of the would-be herring fishers decided to return to the more traditional line-fishing and leave the herring to foreigners, the Scots included.

And then suddenly the elusive herring reappeared, in shoal after generous shoal, and this time the signs were more promising. The boats were decked and larger, their catching power greater, and the shoals themselves proved full and faithful. By 1874 eleven hundred barrels were cured ashore in Shetland from a fleet of fifty small boats.

Now, seven years later, it was almost sixty thousand from a fleet five times as large and the figure was still rising.

But that fleet was by no means restricted to Shetland boats: they came from both west and east coasts of Scotland and from as far south as Lowestoft and Yarmouth, with a sprinkling of foreign boats for good measure. The boats themselves were as varied as their ports of registration and though there were still a few of the local Shetland sixareens and yoles, most were the larger Fifies, some as long as sixty-five feet, from the Edinburgh and Aberdeen coastal villages, with the smaller Scaffies from further north. Even one or two of the new hybrid Zulus, which combined the straight stern of one with the raked stern of the other and promised to outshine them both. With the English luggers and a hotch-potch of foreign vessels too, they made a colourful and motley band.

To see the herring fleet set sail on a summer's evening, their sails like drifting coloured swans' wings, brown and red and black and golden against a fading sky, and to watch them return in ones and twos, low in the water and flashing silver with the sun behind them, was a sight Elissa learnt to watch out for with excitement and pleasure. Somewhere among those boats was her fisherman. Somewhere, one day, she would meet him.

She had hoped to see him on Saturday, on their visit to Lerwick, but though the town was thronged with fishermen as well as groups of fishergirls, newly arrived as they were and on their first adventure of the week, his face had not been among the many who had grinned, shouted greetings or blatant invitations, exchanged back-chat and generally filled the afternoon with exhilaration and a sense of new freedom. For Elissa anyway. Her arms linked with Ina's and Jessie's, she had felt both safe and confident, and even the long session with the photographer, in the stifling studio which smelt of beeswax, macassar oil from the men's hair and the fish-reek, faint but persistent, which permeated the entire town, had not drained her spirits.

Against a background of a draped velvet curtain and some sort of fern in a brass pot, the six of them stood, sat, smiled, held posies, put a hand on another's shoulder, held an open book in a demure lap; over and over until at last the photographer was satisfied. Three at the back, standing; three at the front seated, not a smile among them and all with the same expression of cautious pride. A band of sisters, together against all comers. Bethany with one hand on Meg's shoulder beside her, the other on Elissa's, seated in front with a bunch of artificial flowers in her lap. Beside Elissa, Ina, with, on a higher seat, Jess, and behind Jess, Suffie Lennox, her hand resting on Jess's shoulder, the other invisible behind her back.

'I'm not wanting my hands showing,' she had protested when the photographer told her to let one hand hang naturally against her thigh. 'Not with my fingers swollen and chapped already with the salt. What'd the neighbours think?' The photograph was destined for pride of place on the dresser when the season was over and must do everyone credit.

Each of them had her hair brushed back and coiled tight into a shining knot. Each of them had on her Sunday best, high-necked bodice, fitted tight, with long tight sleeves and a row of little buttons from neck to pointed waist. Suffie wore a fitted jacket over her dress and Ina had a white fichu and white frills at her cuffs. Meg wore a cameo brooch and Bethany's skirts were of best quality French merino. Aunt Sarah did not believe in self-adornment and suchlike vanities, but the sober, respectable gown which Elissa wore on Sundays was as well made and as becoming as any. In a soft shade of blue, the light woollen material fitted the curves of her young body to perfection, and the points of the bodice emphasised the smallness of her waist. She had no brooch or fichu, but the row of buttons, covered in the same material as the dress, followed the outline of her bosom and guided the appreciative eye from narrow waist to slender, graceful neck, and back again.

During the afternoon, Elissa attracted many an eye, though she herself was unaware of it, assuming always that the winks and smiles were directed at her companions, not herself. Certainly it was Bethany that Mr Gibb raised his hat to, with a solemn 'Good afternoon, Miss Noble', when they met him by the town hall, and Ina that Fergus Mackie greeted near Victoria pier, with a wide grin and the offer of a glass of lemonade. And when they strolled up and down the quayside, pretending to admire the rows of boats tied up for the weekend in the harbour, and pretending equally to ignore the vocal admiration of the fishermen who sat about on steps and bollards, smoking their pipes, or strolling up and down as the girls were, all Elissa could think of was her fisherman.

They met Bethany's brother Joseph, Suffie's brother Wallace, her own brother William, with various of their crew; even Will Masson from the yard, with a crowd of boisterous coopers in tow. Later, they went to a café for tea, then looked at the shops in the narrow paved street which ran the length of the old town. In one of the closes off the main street, Elissa saw a shawl, beautifully knitted in the finest of Shetland wool, which she determined to buy for her aunt when she had enough money. Then at last she turned reluctantly for home. But though she checked every face between Lerwick harbour and their own jetty at Gremista her fisherman was not among them. It didn't matter. She knew that she would meet him one day soon.

It was towards the end of the second week, a Thursday, before she saw him. For some reason they were ahead of the catch, the early landings being already gutted and packed and the later, from the

31

more adventurous boats, not yet landed. Usually, at a slack time, they took their knitting on to the hill behind the hut and sat enjoying the rest and the sun, the sparkling view across the bay to Bressay and each other's company. All of them had menfolk to knit for – fathers, brothers, cousins – who needed a constant supply of thick woollen jerseys, or 'ganseys', and stockings, and when the men were supplied, the women needed stockings too. Besides, idleness was unknown to them and hands were used to work.

But on this particular morning there was not time. The first of the later boats was newly arrived, its catch being measured, and the girls, enjoying their enforced idleness, brief though it would be, were waiting in position around the empty farlins and passing the time in half-hearted back-chat with the coopers, or in lazy gossip, one eye always on the jetty. Then someone, somewhere and for no apparent reason, began to sing. *Guide me, O Thou great Jehovah, pilgrim in this barren land.* Within seconds the whole curing yard had joined in, Elissa with them. She lifted her voice in the surging beauty of the music and, weariness and all self-consciousness forgotten, sang her happiness to the summer sky. *Bread of heaven, bread of heaven, feed me till my want is o'er. Feed me till* . . . Then her voice faded and died as she saw him, not three yards away, behind Meg Duthie's shoulder. His cap was pushed to the back of his head, burnished hair bright in the sunshine, eyes blue as harebells, skin weather-tanned and healthy. His black hand-knitted gansey was frayed at the cuffs and strained across the chest, as if knitted for a smaller man – or for him before he was fully grown – but his thigh-length leather boots were splendidly new. He spoke to Bethany, but his appreciative eyes were on Elissa.

'Aye, aye, lassies. Holiday today, is it?'

'Mercy, look what the tide's washed in!' cried Bethany. 'Adam Grant, as large as life and twice as ugly. Well, aren't you going to give a lass a birthday kiss?'

'Didn't know it was your birthday, Beth,' said Meg. 'You should have tellt us, so's we could pull your hair.'

'It isn't,' giggled Ina. 'She's just desperate for a man.'

'A man maybe. But not a wee sillock like Adam, still wet behind the ears.'

'. . . *he's young, but he's growing* . . .' sang Jess and Ina together and Adam grinned. It was obvious to Elissa that they all knew him well already and her spirits sagged with dejection as the amiable banter continued.

Then she heard him say, 'But I see you've a new wee packer. The hungry lassie with the golden voice. Aren't you going to introduce me?'

'You mean Lissa?' said Suffie Lennox. 'She's Jess's and Ina's. Their

Eppie Guyan went and caught a fever the day before the steamer sailed.'

'Maybe it was the thought of seeing you again that turned her stomach?' giggled Meg, with a wink at the others.

'So Lissa came instead. Not knowing no better,' finished Suffie, with a grin.

'But before you try your tricks on her, laddie,' said Bethany, 'I'd best warn you. She's shy of talking to strangers.'

This time when Adam grinned at her, Elissa, to prove Bethany wrong, smiled and opened her mouth to speak. But before either of them could say anything, Bethany planted herself squarely between Adam and everyone else and said, 'You took your time coming, laddie. I was beginning to think you'd forgotten us.'

'See? She's thinking of me still, for all her pretending.' He ducked to avoid Beth's swinging hand and, grinning, stepped out of range. 'But I was needed elsewhere. James wanted the nets barked and there was this dogfish ripped a great rent in one of them and it took us forever to mend.'

'You still with that James Hay?' demanded Bethany. 'I thought you said you was leaving the old misery. Going to buy your own boat, you said, and be your own master. With all that money you was going to make last year.'

'It's nice to know you're thinking of my welfare, lass, but next time, do your sums proper. It takes more than one season's earnings to buy the sort of boat I want.'

'You after one of they steamboats, then?' teased Meg.

'Maybe, one day.' He winked at Elissa. 'And when I do, I'll take all you lovely lassies for a cruise.'

'You, in a steamboat!' jeered Bethany. 'You couldn't boil a kettle, Adam Grant, let alone get one of they steam engines going. Besides, steamboats cost money, and more than you'll ever see. Or keep, if you spend it all on fancy boots.'

'Do you like them?' Thumbs hooked into his braces he looked down at the boots in question with obvious pride. 'Handmade, they were, in Aberdeen. They're the devil's own job to put on, but a fisherman can't go to sea without a good pair of boots and these'll last me years if they're oiled regular.'

'Like their owner,' giggled Ina and Jess snorted, 'Aye, at the Crown and Anchor.'

At that moment there was a stir of activity at the jetty and Bethany said, 'You'd best take yourself and your blessed boots elsewhere, Adam, before you're sent packing. Brodie Gibb doesn't like to see folk idling and getting in the way of other folk's work. Will we see you Sunday?'

'Maybe. Maybe not. Depends who's doing the cooking.'

'Suit yourself,' said Beth with a toss of her head. 'There's plenty men queuing up and you'll not be missed.'

'It's Lissa's turn on Sunday, so you needn't worry,' said Ina. 'Not that a bumpkin like you'd know the difference between a griddle scone and a cow-pat.'

'There's no difference when it's Beth's cooking,' said Suffie, with a straight face, and in the ensuing scuffle Elissa thought that Adam Grant had gone. Then a soft voice spoke behind her.

'And are you really called Lissa? It's a new name to me, but then yours is a new face, for I swear if I'd seen it before, even for a second, I'd not have forgotten.'

Before Elissa could find words to answer, there was a shout from the direction of the jetty, followed by another from Bethany.

'You stop pestering Lissa Downie, Adam Grant, or you'll have Jessie after you, with a gutting knife. She's work to do like the rest of us, even if you haven't, you lazy, skiving . . .'

But at that moment the next load of herring slapped into the farlin in a slithering silver heap, spray and salt crystals spattering everywhere, with the familiar waft of fish-reek and sea water, and Beth contented herself with an expressive gesture of her own gutting knife before using it viciously on the first fish.

'I'll be off then,' said Adam, to no one in particular. Then he bent close and murmured, 'See you on Sunday, Lissa Downie with the angel's voice.' She was almost sure he added, 'And an angel's sweet face to go with it.'

For the rest of the day she worked in a confusion of bliss, hope and anxiety. Once, she even dared to ask Jessie, 'Who is Adam Grant and where's he from?'

Jessie shrugged. 'Just a fisherman. An orphan laddie from Buckie or thereabouts. Nobody special.' She glanced quickly to either side to make sure she could not be overheard, then added in a half-whisper, 'Take my advice, Lissa. Forget Adam Grant. *For your own good.*'

But Elissa could not forget. As to her own good, what did Jessie know about that? When she saw the fleet put to sea and later, between salting the top layer of one barrel and starting on the bottom layer of the next, watched the last sail pass over the horizon into the dying sky, Elissa felt excitement sparkle inside her till it filled her aching body with jubilation. He had spoken to her. She knew his name. And he was coming to tea on Sunday.

Sundays were always days of rest. Not merely because Sundays were for God and church-going, but because the herrings needed a day of rest too, to collect their strength and multiply. First, scrubbed clean, hair shining, and everyone in their Sunday best, there was the two-mile walk to church, the two-hour sermon and the two-mile walk back again. Then, there was nothing to do until Monday, except knit and chat and generally relax – and entertain visitors.

On the first Sunday these had been mostly family: two of Bethany's brothers, Joseph and Peter, Meg Duthie's father, Suffie's brother Wallace and some Bain cousins. Elissa's own brother William had looked in for a while, 'Just to check you're managing, like.' When she assured him that she was, he had said, 'I'll be off then, lass.' She must have shown her disappointment too clearly, for he had added in a confidential aside, 'I'm courting a lassie from Eyemouth and she's giving me my tea. Don't tell Davie, though, or he'll likely go after her himself.' Elissa's youngest brother Davie had a reputation with the girls.

'Is Davie coming? Or Tom?'

William had shrugged. 'Maybe, maybe not. But they're fine and Dad says to say so is Aunt Sarah so you're not to worry. Though Dad said she'd maybe like a wee note from you, Lissa, when you can find the time.' Then he had gone.

Others had come later, including the young cooper, Fergus Mackie, invited by Ina. Meg said, 'Reckon that's Ina fixed up with a man, anyway,' and Suffie, in her usual down-to-earth way, commented, 'Aye. Pity he's not a fisherman, but it can't be helped. And at least he'll not drown and leave her with rows of kids to bring up on her own.'

Will Masson had come too, after an offhand half-invitation from Bethany at the church door. 'Come if you've nought better to do, but don't expect anybody to take notice of you.' Though once he was there, Bethany had treated him to the same rough-edged banter she had served out to all the men. Except one.

For Mr Gibb himself had arrived at their door uninvited in mid-afternoon, his whiskers trimmed, his stiff collar dazzling, his Sunday shoes mirror-bright under the pressed exactitude of his Sunday suit.

'Ten shillings and ninepence from Alexander's in Broad Street,' Ina had whispered behind her hand. Jessie had pinched her, hard, and for once Ina had not retaliated.

'I called to see how you are settling in,' Mr Gibb had announced into the astonished silence. Then he had drunk one cup of tea, eaten one griddle scone with jam, and taken his leave. The sigh of relief that followed him could have shut the door by itself, as Fergus Mackie said, when they dared to speak normally again.

But this Sunday, thought Elissa in happy anticipation, would be different. It would not matter if none of her family came to visit her: her brothers were all much older than she was, with lives of their own to lead, and her father could get news of her through Jess's and Ina's father, Isaac Bain. The only visitor she wanted was Adam Grant and he had promised he would come.

Once the Saturday morning catch was landed, those fishermen who could went home for the weekend, but these were mostly Shetlanders. The greater part of the fleet came from too far distant to make the journey feasible, especially when no one would sail during the twenty-four hours of Sunday. But the girls had soon made friends among coopers and fishermen alike and the huts at Gremista would not lack Sunday visitors.

Elissa scrubbed and swept and polished; picked wildflowers from the headland and filled three jam jars with them. Unfolded her aunt's blue checked cloth and spread it over the rough deal table. She would have liked to bake oven scones or bread, but there was no oven: only the open brick fireplace. Instead, she had beaten up a bowl of batter for griddle scones and set it ready, covered with a clean linen cloth. She greased the iron griddle and was spooning jam into a pretty china dish when she heard a voice behind her.

'My, but you've made the place look real pretty,' said Bethany, coming in from the headland where the rest of them were sitting about on the grass, knitting, and discussing whom they had spotted in church, who was wearing what, and similar happy topics.

Elissa looked up with a smile, but Bethany's next words sent happiness flying. 'Who is it you're expecting then, Prissy Lissa? The Minister, maybe?'

Bethany was standing in the middle of the small hut, looking round her for all the world like a queen inspecting her kingdom, her fingers all the time moving over the inevitable knitting. One needle was stuck into the leather pouch at her waist, to hold the weight of the garment – a jersey for one of the Noble menfolk – and the spare wool protruded from a pocket. It was as if the knitting proceeded independently of its owner, whose thoughts were obviously on a quite different matter.

'Though it's maybe not the Minister after all, him being a married man with children and you knowing the Ten Commandments. Thou shalt not this, thou shalt not that, on and bleeding on.' She cast her eyes deliberately over the hut, turning slowly on her heel till her eyes had combed every inch of the four plain walls and the plain wooden floor. 'But it seems to me, Lissa Downie, that you wouldna go to all this trouble for one of your poxy, plain-faced brothers with no more life about them than a drawer of cold porridge. No, I think ... I think ...' and here she dropped her voice to a malicious whisper, 'I think little Miss Lissa is hoping for a follower.'

But at that moment the doorway darkened and Ina said, 'My, my, wonders never cease. Here's Bethany come to help out. And we all know why, don't we, girls?' This last called gleefully over her shoulder. 'She's expecting Mr Gibb again.'

Bethany lunged for her in fury and dislodged the knitting from its belt. 'Damn and bleeding damn. Look what you've made me do, you – '

'Language!' warned Ina, stepping quickly out of range. 'What would Mr Gibb think if he heard his intended sullying her sweet lips with . . .'

'I'll sully your bleeding lips, you daft cow, if you don't shut your mouth and keep your pig's snout out of other folk's affairs. Just look at this bleeding tangle.'

'Protest till you're black in the face, Bethany dear, but it won't convince us, will it, Lissa? Who was it saying only last week that she wanted a man, a grown man, and it didn't matter who as long as he was rich?'

'Will you shut your stupid face and help me sort this, for pity's sake. They'll be here directly.'

'Aye, and we know who "they" means, don't we, Lissa,' teased Ina. 'We reckon Mr Gibb has his fishy eye on you, Beth Noble, and you've baited your hook to catch him and his moneybags before someone else does.'

Bethany decided to ignore the gibe. She turned her back on Ina and said, to the room in general, 'Some folk have nought else to talk about but men, but that's usually 'cos they're too fat and ugly to catch one of their own.' Then, looking straight at Elissa through narrowed eyes, she said with deliberation, 'You and me was talking about higher things, wasn't we, Lissa. We was discussing the Ten Commandments and the punishment folk gets for breaking them. That one about coveting, for instance. Wanting what isn't theirs to have. The fourth, is it?'

Elissa moistened suddenly dry lips and managed, 'The tenth.'

'Say it for us, Lissa.'

'Leave her be, Bethany,' said Jess, pushing past Ina into the room. 'She's work to do before the men come.'

'B . . . off. I'm speaking to Lissa, not you. *Say it!*'

In spite of her fear, which was making her limbs tremble and her heart beat uncomfortably fast, Elissa set her jaw and turned away. 'It is wrong to mock the Scriptures,' she managed. 'Especially on a Sunday.'

Not for the first time, she expected to feel the sting of Bethany's hand across her ear, but at that moment someone cried, 'They're coming! Is the kettle boiling?' and the rest of the girls crowded into the room, on a gust of happy chatter.

'Just you remember,' warned Bethany, gripping Elissa's upper arm and digging in her fingers so hard she bore the bruise for days. 'Though shalt not covet – and that means keeping your hands off other folk's property. Or else.'

The last two words left Elissa in no doubt as to Bethany's meaning. As to the nature of the 'property' Bethany had so violently defended, the afternoon soon enlightened her.

CHAPTER 4

At first Elissa was kept so busy filling teacups, turning scones on the griddle, spreading jam, handing plates of bread and cheese, or of buns bought specially yesterday in Lerwick, that she had little time for chat with their visitors, but she managed in spite of that to keep one eye on the door and with each arrival her heart quickened, only to fall back again into steady expectation. He had promised, and he would come.

Many of last Sunday's visitors reappeared, with one or two new ones, though Mr Gibb was not among them, to everyone's relief. In a moment's respite while Elissa waited for the freshly filled kettle to boil, she poured herself a cup of tea and leant against the wall near the fireplace to drink it. All the kists were in use as seats and all occupied, by girls or visitors or both, and, as it was a fine afternoon, the overflow was already spilling out through the open door on to the grass outside. She saw Ina laughing with Fergus Mackie, Jess and Suffie talking with one of the Bain cousins and a pair of fishermen she had not seen before. Meg Duthie was with Suffie's brother Wallace, and Bethany in animated conversation with a group of men Elissa knew by sight, but little more. One of them was Will Masson. Bethany, she was fast learning, liked to be the centre of attention, especially of the male kind. But Elissa did not mind that she was the only one without a companion. Soon he would come. Soon.

'I've been watching you,' said a voice at her side and she turned her head in surprise to see Bethany's brother Joseph beside her. 'You have done nothing but work since I arrived.'

'But it is my turn,' said Elissa, and added before she could stop herself, 'and I do so want everything to be special today.'

'Is there any particular reason for that?' She had known Joseph most of her life, for he was her brother Tom's friend, and though Aunt Sarah's rigid teetotal regime meant that there was little of the boisterous hospitality of other houses in the Square, Joseph did call now and then, when Tom was at home, though they usually went out again together as soon as they decently could. Aunt Sarah's tea was something of a penance.

Now, his voice reminded her of her brother Tom, and when she looked at him, she saw his eyes were the same warm, reassuring brown. Tom was her favourite brother. Her most vivid memory of her mother's funeral was of Tom taking her on to his knee, and comforting her. She remembered him saying how happy her mother would be when she got to heaven, but that if Elissa cried it would make her sad again. Then he had given her a sugar mouse, with a long string tail. Her eldest brother George was not at the funeral, because he and her brother James were at sea, and they never saw them again. There was a sudden storm in the Baltic and they were both drowned. But she had three brothers still: William and Tom and Davie.

But the thought of brothers reminded her that however sympathetic a companion Joseph Noble was, he was also Bethany's brother, and caution curbed her tongue.

'No particular reason,' she said and, knowing that he did not believe her, added, 'except that it is my first season here and I want to do everything right.'

'I don't think you need worry on that score,' he began, but she was no longer listening. Her eyes were fixed on the open doorway and the tall figure silhouetted in its frame.

'Well, if it isn't Adam Grant, turned up like a bad penny,' cried Bethany. 'And about time too. Come over here and sit with me, laddie, while Lissa fetches your tea. Hey! Lissa! Move your lazy bum and get a move on with them scones, will you? There's folk starving over here. She's new, see,' she said to Adam, 'and not just right in the head, what with it being stuffed to the gills with religion, but we make allowances, don't we, lassies, and she's learning. Well, sit down, now you're here,' and she patted the space on the seat beside her. Adam took no notice.

'New. Then I must introduce myself properly.' He pushed through the crowd and the next minute he was taking Elissa's hand in his and looking into her mortified eyes.

'Adam Grant, at your service,' he murmured and flamboyantly kissed her hand. 'But we have met before.'

'I . . .' The back of her hand where his lips had touched the skin seemed to burn and she could think of nothing at all to say.

'On the quay? On Thursday? Surely you can't have forgotten. I know I haven't. But then it isn't every day a man sees someone as pretty as a mermaid and with a voice to charm the hardest-hearted seaman on this earth.'

'And the smoothest-tongued,' growled Joseph Noble. 'Don't believe a word the rascal says, Elissa.'

'Not believe me when I tell her she's pretty? You're an even bigger fool than you look, Joseph Noble. And a blind one, too, if you cannot see I'm speaking the plain truth. Which is that young Elissa is the best-looking lassie in the whole of Shetland.'

'I can see you're making a nuisance of yourself, laddie,' muttered Joseph. He spoke the work 'laddie' like an insult. 'And not for the first time, neither.'

Elissa watched in dismay as they glared pugnaciously across her in what was obviously an old, familiar enmity. Fortunately at that moment the kettle lid came to a spluttering and overflowing boil and with a quick, 'Excuse me,' Elissa pushed her way between them and busied herself at the fire. When she had made fresh tea, dropped spoonfuls of batter on to the hot griddle for a new batch of scones, and topped up the kettle again with cold water from the pail, her alarm had quietened, and Joseph had gone. She saw him on the far side of the room, his back to her, and apparently deep in conversation with Will Masson.

'Your scones are bubbling,' said a soft voice and she spun round to see Adam Grant, holding out an empty plate and grinning. 'And your watchdog's gone. Turn them over, there's a good lassie, and fill up the plate, before I die of hunger.'

Elissa bent over the fire to hide her joy and turned the golden, bubbling pancakes one by one, to brown the second side. He watched while she slipped them deftly on to the plate, then spread them with butter. The smell was wholesome and inviting, the little pancakes cooked to perfection. Happily, she offered him the plate.

'Please help yourself, Mr Grant.'

'Thank you.' In one fluid movement he lifted two scones with one hand and with the other took the plate itself and handed it to the nearest girl. 'Here, Suffie. Stir your bones and help out for a change.'

'Cheeky devil,' muttered Suffie, but she took the plate and moved away.

'And now, my busy wee lassie,' he said, putting the first scone into his mouth whole and offering her the other which, shaking her head and blushing, she declined. 'Where have you been all these years while I've been fishing the length of the east coast and the west too and not a sight of you till now?'

In the bliss of the moment Elissa was tongue-tied, her glowing eyes fixed wonderingly on his face. He was young, as Bethany had said. Maybe younger that her brother Davie, who was twenty-two. His face was brown and laughing, his eyes a glorious blue, and his voice, when he spoke next, had a soft, caressing timbre which seemed to melt her bones.

'I tell you this, Elissa, and it's the gospel truth. If I'd so much as glimpsed you, I'd not have forgotten. Are you from Aberdeen way, like Bethany?'

Before Elissa could answer, Bethany called, 'Enough of your smooth

40

talk, Adam. It'll get you nowhere with that one, so leave the lass alone. Besides, you'll frighten her standing that close, and her a well-brought-up young lady who's not allowed to talk to coarse menfolk, especially when she's work to do. Isn't that right, Lissa?'

'Ignore her,' murmured Adam. 'She's a silly cow, sometimes.'

'Did you hear me, Lissa Downie?'

'Take no notice,' urged Adam. 'You'll only make her worse.'

But this time there had been a note in Beth's voice that Elissa recognised all too clearly. Nervously, she took up the teapot and held it protectively against her front.

'Aye well, and about time too,' said Bethany. 'The service in here is something dreadful today. Now that that's sorted, and Lissa's pouring our tea,' she went on, tipping her head invitingly, 'you can come over here and sit with me, Adam Grant. If you've nought better to do.'

Bethany patted the seat beside her and Elissa noted that her bosom seemed more prominent than usual, her eyes greener and her hair more bright.

'We haven't had a chance for a blether yet and it was me as asked you. You don't get fed for nothing, remember.' This time there was a glint of malice in her eyes and at the same time a hint of something intimate which made Elissa blush and look away.

Adam turned to Elissa and shrugged. 'You see how it is: but then a lad can't help being popular, can he?' He leant closer and whispered, 'We'll talk again, lass, when there's no one else around.' Then, with lazy ease, he moved across the space between and sat down beside Bethany on the wooden chest. 'There now. I've come to sing for my supper. Satisfied?'

Elissa moved obediently among the nearest guests, pouring tea into empty cups, but she could not help noticing, with pain, that Bethany had left too small a space for him to sit so that they were pressed close together and he had to put an arm behind her for support.

'The thing is, Adam,' said Bethany, deliberately loud enough for Elissa to hear, 'I'm responsible for her. With her being no more than a child, really, and me being the eldest. Her aunt asked me to keep an eye on her, like. See she came to no harm . . . She's awful strict is her aunt.'

'Is that so?' Adam caught Elissa's eye and winked. She blushed and turned her back, but too late.

'See! What did I tell you? And all you did was wink at her. But in Lissa's book even winking is wicked, on a Sunday. It's a good job you didna laugh or you'd have been out of that door and straight to damnation. Isn't that right, Lissa?'

Elissa's face was scarlet, but she said nothing.

41

'Pay no heed,' said Joseph from the group beside her and held out his half-empty cup. 'My sister's in one of her showing-off moods, that's all.'

Gratefully, Elissa filled his cup, glad of the opportunity it gave her to hide her face and shelter in his company. Willie Masson and Joseph and another man she did not know were discussing the new steam trawler being built at Grimsby and the threat it represented to the line fishermen. The old steam tugs which had been adapted to pull a beam-trawl presented little threat, being unreliable, of a short range and not the sort of vessel in which to tackle the North Sea. A specially built trawler was something different.

'Ninety-eight feet long and a speed of nine knots,' said the awed owner of a thirty-foot sailing lugger.

'They reckon on catching four times more fish than any sailing vessel.'

'Aye, and they'll sweep the sea-bed clean while they're doing it.'

'That means a fortune for some.'

'And ruin for more.'

'There's talk of building a steam drifter, at Leith.'

'A drifter? After what happened in Fraserburgh and Wick? The propellers will foul the nets again and there's a season's profits gone before you've even started.' The trawlers dragged the deep sea-bed for white fish like haddock and cod, but herrings were caught by drift nets, on the surface.

'They're maybe working on a new design.'

'For the nets?' jeered another. 'Or the drifter?' But Elissa heard the anxiety behind the scepticism. What chance would sailing boats have against steam?

'Would a steam drifter be a bad thing, Joseph?' she asked, remembering Bethany's mockery of Adam at the farlin. He, she had said, planned to buy a steamboat.

But apparently it was her turn to be mocked today and Bethany had not finished with her. Her voice rang loud across the room.

'Holy Lissa, we calls her in the Square. That aunt of hers fed her on religion, see, 'stead of food. To keep her skinny and flat-chested so she wouldn't be tempted to sin. And Jess and I, we promised her aunt we'd keep her that way, didn't we, Jess?'

'Speak for yourself,' said Jess and added, in a loud aside, 'She's mad, that one. Barking mad.'

'It's maybe something in the tea,' giggled Ina. 'Give her another cup, Lissa, and they'll lock her up.'

But Bethany was not to be deflected. 'Not that we have to worry,' she said, sipping with exaggerated daintiness from her teacup, though above the rim her eyes were bright with malicious glee. 'She's that holy you dinna need to say your prayers when she's around, what

42

with her being full to the gills with psalms and that, and her knowing the Bible inside out. I reckon there's enough prayers stuffed into Lissa to do the whole quayside for a year. That's why we chose her for our hut. For good luck – and to save ourselves time.' She leant back against Adam's arm and looked up at him, her green eyes gleaming. 'So's we'd be free for other things.'

A moment's silence greeted this outrageous performance, before Jess said, 'You want to watch what you say, you daft cow, or you'll get thunderbolted, you will. And on a Sunday, too.'

'You're lucky Mr Gibb isn't here,' added Ina. 'He'd be right put off you, and him a God-fearing kind of a man. You ought to be ashamed of yourself, blaspheming and carrying on, and picking on our Lissa for no reason except plain jealousy. Just 'cos she's better looking than you'll ever be.'

'Aye, maybe,' said Bethany, 'if you call a pig's arse good-looking. But with that aunt of hers bringing her up so strict, she wouldn't know an arse if she saw one. Oops, pardon me. I said a naughty word on a Sunday. Reckon that's another prayer used up.'

'Shut up, Bethany,' said Suffie Lennox. 'We've guests, remember.'

Some of the men were shuffling their feet in embarrassment, others looking studiously at the floor, but Joseph, deliberately turning his back on Bethany said, as if his sister had not spoken, 'That's an interesting question, Elissa. Steam could make lifting the nets from the sea much easier, of course, though on the other hand . . .'

But Elissa did not hear him. Her face was burning with humiliation, her chest choked with anger and unshed tears. How dare Bethany shame and belittle her in front of everyone, especially Adam Grant. That she might perhaps have borne, but how dare she sneer at Aunt Sarah and her faith? Elissa heard her aunt's voice, loud and clear: *The third rule of Christian living is loyalty.*

She took a deep breath and said, in low, fierce tones which, in spite of her trembling, reached every corner of the room, 'My aunt is a good, kind woman and it is wicked to make fun of someone's religion. Wicked and cruel and ignorant.' She was aware of Adam's eyes regarding her with surprise, and Bethany's with something more complex. But she stood her ground. 'And it is wicked to take advantage of someone's innocence and trust. And wicked to tell lies. You are a . . . a . . . *stupid* woman!'

Then she flung the teapot to the floor, spattering tea and tea-leaves everywhere, pushed blindly out of the hut, and ran.

Joseph found her, half an hour later, huddled up in the lee of a dry-stone dyke on the headland above the harbour. There were wild-flowers in the scrubby grass around her and, stretching behind her to

43

the west, the moorland wastes were softened to misted mauves and blues in the fading summer light. Shetland had never looked more beautiful, but Elissa saw none of it.

She was gazing, desolate, across the sea to Bressay and beyond where the water lay in slate-grey ripples under a dove-grey sky, and her face was blotched and smeared with tears. Joseph wondered if she knew how long the journey would be from the curing station to Aberdeen, with so many intervening ports to call at before the season was over for the year. If not, he could not tell her.

A breeze stirred the dark tendrils of hair at her temples but it was the only sign of movement in the slim, still figure. She did not turn her head when he spoke.

'Elissa?' Quietly, he folded his long limbs and sat down beside her, then, legs outstretched and ankles crossed, he leant back against the dyke and waited.

The silence lengthened, and gradually Elissa felt the pain drain out of her as the warm presence beside her seemed to soothe and heal. At last, she turned her head to glance at him and saw that he was gazing out to sea, as she had been, his face thoughtful and a little sad. He must be her brother Tom's age, she supposed. Twenty-five or twenty-six. Old, anyway. Brown-haired, clean-shaven, he looked altogether ordinary. Kind, but ordinary. Not like ... Abruptly, she bit her lip.

'You must not mind too much,' he said quietly. 'My sister likes to be outrageous, though unfortunately she does not always think of the effect on others. If that effect is hurtful, it is not through intention, merely through thoughtlessness. My parents have often spoken to her about it, but you know Bethany. She never listens.'

His voice was strangely calming and though the words themselves meant little to her, being, as she thought, merely brotherly loyalty, Elissa's shame began to ease.

'You take things too much to heart, Elissa. Everybody knows Bethany, and nobody believes a word she says. They will think none the worse of you.' When she made no answer, he went on gently, 'You were brave to speak up as you did. Brave and loyal and honest. I admire you for it.'

But what would *he* think? cried Elissa in silent anguish. Bethany had ridiculed her and belittled her for ever in his eyes. She could not say this aloud, not to Joseph, even though he was her brother's friend, so she said nothing.

'You were right, you know,' he said after a moment. 'My sister is a little ... stupid. But Bethany will not bully you again. You stood up to her, and passed the test. Besides, I have spoken to her and she understands me.' He paused a moment to let the implications of his words sink in, then said, in a different voice, 'But you asked me a

44

question and I did not have time to answer you. Whether a steam drifter would be a good thing or a bad?'

Elissa had forgotten everything in the shame of Bethany's onslaught, but she managed a bleak-eyed nod. Joseph was obviously trying to soothe her back to normality and she was grateful to him, though it would do no good. Only one person could heal her hurt, and he had not come after her.

'The good points are the speed and power, the bigger boats that could be used, the weight of nets that could be cast and lifted.' Joseph spoke thoughtfully and as if he was rehearsing old arguments, to make things clear in his own mind as well as for Elissa's benefit. 'And, of course, the bigger catch. But a steam drifter would cost four times as much as a simple sailing lugger and who could afford money like that? Not fishermen such as myself. No, it would be the capitalists on shore who would put up the money – and collect the profits.'

In spite of her misery, Elissa was interested, at first because if Adam Grant really was thinking of a steamboat then she wanted to know all she could about it, and then, as Joseph talked, because the subject seemed increasingly important to all fishermen, her own family included. Not just the rich skipper-owners, but every member of the crew, from the most experienced to the newest, unskilled laddie. Under the present system everyone got a share of some kind at the end of the season, and the better the season the bigger the share. But before she could ask her question, Joseph answered it.

'Look what is happening with the steam trawlers. They cost a fortune to buy and as much again to fit out and so will the drifters. Where are the likes of your brothers and mine going to find money like that? It will be the end of the old share system and the shore capitalists will have the last word. We will be nothing but paid deck-hands before we know it, and the so-called pay will be as little as they can get away with.'

'But surely the sailing luggers will still be able to fish the sea?'

'Aye, maybe. But what will they get for their catch? With the steam drifters flooding the market the prices will likely come down, and the merchants will all be contracted to the big fellows and not want to buy from the little man.'

When Elissa said nothing, being too dismayed by his words to speak, he confided, 'It worries me, Elissa. When I hear what is happening in the deep-sea fishing – steam trawlers scraping the sea-bed clean so there will be no fish left to breed and all to fill the pockets of the shore-based owners – I weep for my fellow fishermen, and for the future of our livelihood.'

Something in Joseph's voice moved Elissa to sympathy and for a moment she forgot her misery: until she remembered their own curer who had hired both fishermen and gutting teams for the season.

45

'Do you think Mr Gibb will buy a steam drifter?'

'If he thinks he can make money out of it, yes,' said Joseph with bitterness. 'Though the opposition threatens to be strong and violent. Men fear for their livelihoods as I do. And for the fish.'

'But . . . surely the sea is full of fish?'

'Aye, lass. But man's greed will empty it fast enough, given the means.'

The sadness in his voice echoed her own despair and Elissa retreated once more into silence. Together they gazed across the darkening sea to the paler outline of Bressay and the haze beyond, each lost in private thought, until Joseph said quietly, 'I hoped to cheer you up and reassure you. Instead I have depressed you further. I am sorry.'

'No. If that is the future, then we must face up to it.'

'But not accept it,' he said, with a vehemence that startled her. 'Not without a struggle. *And there will be one . . .*'

Elissa felt a shiver of fear at his words, but after a moment, he said more quietly, 'You must be tired, Elissa. I should not have burdened you with my troubles. Please forgive me?' When she made no answer, he added, 'When you are ready, I will walk you home.'

But it was a long time before Elissa found the courage to leave the safety of her little headland and the calming beauty of the sea. Too many turbulent thoughts churned in her head, not least the memory of Bethany's spite, for though Joseph had succeeded in diverting her mind for a while into other channels, the hurt was still there and the shame.

In the harbour, under a thicket of bare masts and rigging, the huddled boats were sleeping, awaiting the end of Sunday before they could put to sea again. The unaccustomed stillness was strangely comforting, as were the dark rows of wooden barrels, motionless and unattended. There was no one in sight. Even the sea birds were quiet, the sounds from the little harbour town below them muted and faint.

'Are you warm enough?' asked Joseph, as the last light left the sky and a chill wind rose from nowhere to stir the grasses and tease the hem of her Sunday skirt. Elissa nodded, but when, a moment later, she shivered, Joseph removed his jacket and put it round her shoulders. In her misery, Elissa left it there, with a hardly audible, 'Thank you,' and when Joseph put his arm around her too, and drew her close, to shield her from the wind, she was content to feel his warmth and strength and to draw comfort from it.

But at last Joseph took her hand in his and drew her reluctantly to her feet. 'Come. Unless you plan to freeze us both to death, we must go back.'

'Oh! I am so sorry, Joseph, I did not think.' She shrugged his jacket quickly from her shoulders and thrust it towards him. 'Quick. Put it on while it is still warm.'

'Warmed by you,' he smiled. 'For me.' Then he bent down and kissed her gently on the forehead. Before she could take fright, he pulled her arm companionably through his and said briskly, 'Now we must make fast for home, for I smell rain in the air.'

Lights were burning in the row of huts. They could see the blurred squares of yellow below them when they rounded the corner of the headland path. Then a new wedge of light was flung suddenly across the grass from an open door. The sound of voices drifted up to them and a girl's quick laughter before the light was cut off again, with a thud. Male shadows moved away along the path.

'Don't worry,' said Joseph at her side. 'Everything will be all right.'

She thanked him, but she did not believe him. Not even when he held open the door of her hut for her, five minutes later, and she saw that everything had been swept and tidied, the pots washed and put away. Even her blue and white tablecloth had been neatly folded and laid on the lid of her kist.

'We thought you'd best put it away yourself, Lissa,' said Bethany demurely, 'when you came back from your stroll.' If there was sarcasm behind the words, it was well hidden. 'Not wanting you to think we was prying.'

Even when Jess said, 'Remember it's me doing the tea in the morning, Lissa,' she felt no better. And Ina's well-meant 'Hope you've not been leading Joseph Noble astray' could not raise the smallest smile.

For the first time in her life, Elissa's faith in the world had been sorely shaken. Even the firm foundation of the fishing was under threat, if Joseph was to be believed, but in the circumstances it seemed no more than appropriate. She had done nothing wrong. Nothing. Yet Bethany had picked on her, deliberately, and set out to humiliate her, for her own amusement. Worse, she had done so by making a mockery of God. If there was any justice, Bethany would surely be punished for that one day, but whether she was punished or not, Elissa would never forgive her. Never, as long as she lived.

Later, in the twilight of the summer darkness, with Jess and Ina asleep beside her, her mind picked over the details of those humiliating moments for the hundredth time or more, and at last a small shred of comfort surfaced. She remembered those whispered words of Adam Grant and felt hope come creeping back. Certainly he had spoken them before Bethany's outburst, but he had spoken them: *We will talk again, lass, when there's no one else around.*

*

But in the life of the curing yard there was always someone else around. Even on Mondays, which, because of the Sunday rest day, followed a different pattern. There were few fresh landings and the day was given to topping up, to the sealing of matured barrels and the tally. Without the hectic pressure of the gutting and the race to keep abreast of the day's catch, it was more relaxed and leisurely work, and often finished early. This meant time for the girls to catch up with housework, washing and mending, and if the weather was fine, to sit outside the huts and knit, chatting and exchanging gossip; even singing if the mood took them.

For the fishermen, Mondays were equally useful. Their gear needed constant attention, and there was always plenty to do. The herring nets would be carried ashore and spread out on a convenient stretch of ground and checked for rents and tears. One dogfish in a net could cause tremendous damage, as well as the weight of a heavy catch and general wear and tear. As each boat carried a drift of forty or fifty twelve-fathom nets, there were plenty to check, as well as the ropes, the floats and buoys. Then the boat must be maintained and the hull inspected for barnacles, while the men's leather boots needed constant care to keep them supple and as watertight as possible. Some rubbed in oil, others grease, but whichever the method it was a tedious and necessary job.

It was the boots that caught Elissa's attention. Jess, whose turn it was, was busy cleaning out the hut, and Ina was helping. The others had drifted off to one of the neighbouring huts, 'for a wee news', and to keep out of Jess's way. Elissa had carried a pail of water out on to the grass and was kneeling beside it, her sleeves rolled up and her hands immersed in suds as she scrubbed her last week's flannel petticoat and stockings with a bar of Hudson's soap. On the grass beside her, awaiting their turn, were the calico strips she used for tying her fingers. Then suddenly, from the corner of her eye, she saw the oiled toe of a boot, followed the long leather upwards to serge, flap-fronted trousers, ragged gansey and Adam's beaming face.

'Busy as always, Lissa? Would you wash a shirt for me if I asked you nicely?'

Blushing, Elissa scrambled to her feet, wiping her soapy hands dry on the front of her apron. 'Yes, Mr Grant, if you . . .'

'Don't be daft, lassie,' he grinned. 'I was teasing. And call me Adam. Everyone else does.' He looked around him, chose a spot and sank to the grass, folding his legs neatly under him as he did so. 'You carry on washing whatever it is you're hiding under all those suds – and if it's something I shouldn't see, I promise not to look. Then maybe we can have that wee chat that you promised me yesterday, before you remembered something urgent you had to do elsewhere.'

Elissa blushed in embarrassment. 'I'm sorry.'

'Whatever for? It was time someone told Bethany a few home truths and a rare treat to see her face when you called her "stupid". I don't blame you for wanting peace and quiet after all that rumpus. I was going to come after you, but Jessie said you'd maybe rather be alone, and with me being still a stranger . . .'

There was something in the way he said the word, as if it was almost a question, that made Elissa look up at him.

'But I hope we'll not be strangers for long, Elissa.' He picked a blade of grass, reached out and very gently brushed a strand of hair from her forehead with it. 'There. I can see you properly now. And,' he added with a mischievous gleam in his eyes, 'I like what I see, little Miss Singing Bird. But then I liked it the first time I set eyes on you, and you've been singing away in my mind ever since. So, now that we have a private moment, may I ask you formally to be less of a stranger and more of a . . . friend?' There was an infinitesimal pause before 'friend' which somehow managed to suggest a great deal more.

'Oh yes,' said Elissa with simple happiness and in that moment all her troubles and anxieties vanished, swallowed up by one small word. She lifted the dripping petticoat from the pail and wrung it out while he made a great pantomime of putting his hands over his eyes and averting his head. Somehow the laughter and the action together were delightfully intimate. She wrung out her stockings and the rest of her small wash, then tossed the water away on to the grass. 'There. You can look again. But I must fetch more water, for the rinsing.'

'Allow me, madam,' and he took hold of the pail handle. In doing so his hand brushed hers and sent excitement dancing through her veins. Together they walked to the pump and back again with the brimming pail between them and while she rinsed her few garments and wrung them out again, he sprawled on the grass nearby and watched her.

'If we are friends,' he said after a moment's thoughtful silence, 'will you ask me to tea on Sunday? And promise not to run away and hide this time? Or at least, if you do run away, to take me with you? We could walk on the headland, maybe, or down on the shore.'

'I would like that,' she said, her eyes shining.

'Good. Because I can't stay long today. James is set on sailing early so as to get to the shoals afore the rest of them.'

'Is James your skipper?'

'Aye, but only for the season. He's been a sort of uncle to me for years, ever since my ma died, and I can't just walk out and leave him, can I? Not till he's fixed up with someone else.'

'But I thought . . .' Elissa faltered to a stop, remembering Bethany's jeers.

Adam remembered them too, for he said, 'You don't want to listen to what Bethany says about me. I'd best tell you now, before someone

49

else does, that at one time, a year or so back, she and I ... well ... let's say we walked out together.'

Elissa turned her head away so that he could not see her face while she wrung and twisted the garment in her hand till she almost tore it in two.

'Only for a week or two. Not long. Just long enough to know we weren't suited.' He shrugged and grinned engagingly up at her. 'Now we're just friends, like anybody else, but Bethany has a malicious tongue when she puts her mind to it, as you and I both know. A man can't save enough to buy a boat in one season, whatever she says, and a fisherman needs a good pair of boots. This pair will last me years. Aye, I'll be skipper of my own boat before these wear out. Maybe even standing on the deck of my own steam drifter.'

'Some people think steam will be a bad thing,' ventured Elissa, remembering Joseph's anxieties.

'Some people thought the same about gas light, and the railway. There's always fuddy-duddies afraid of progress, terrified of anything new. If we listened to them, we'd never get anywhere, Lissa lass. And I mean to get somewhere. Aye, I'll have a boat of my own by next season, you'll see. A fifty-footer maybe. With so many folk wanting that new Zulu boat, there's plenty good bargains to be had on the east coast of Scotland if you know where to look, and I don't mind taking a second-hand Fifie, just for a start. Then, when I've made a bit, I'll trade her in for a better, and after that, who knows? But I'll not get anywhere if I'm late back.' He grinned suddenly, unfolding to his feet. 'James won't wait and I don't want to be left stranded. Mind you,' he added, holding out his hand for Elissa to take and pulling her to her feet so that they were standing close, 'I wouldn't mind being stranded with you, Elissa.' Then, his eyes on hers, he lifted her hand, palm upwards, to his lips and kissed it, closing her fingers over the place. 'That's to be going on with,' he said softly. Then he called in the general direction of the hut, 'See you on Sunday, lassies.' The next moment he was striding jauntily down the grass towards the jetty.

'Cheeky young sod,' said Jess from the doorway. 'Pestering you, was he?'

'No,' said Elissa. She turned her back to hide her happiness and made great play of spreading out her washing on the grass to dry. 'Just passing the time of day.'

'You watch that one, Lissa. And don't believe a word he says. He's a smooth-tongued rogue, as half the lassies in Lerwick know to their cost.'

'But if you must speak to him,' added Ina, tossing a bucket of dirty water on to the grass, 'do it when Bethany's not looking. She's a jealous cow.'

50

CHAPTER 5

But in the days that followed there was no chance to speak to Adam Grant. He appeared briefly now and then, between unloading and putting to sea again, waved, called a greeting, but no more. It did not matter. He had asked her to be his friend, had kissed the palm of her hand and promised to see her on Sunday. No matter what Jess and Ina said, she knew he had meant every word and from that moment the herring summer was everything that Elissa had dreamed of, in a world sparkling with happiness and promise.

She glimpsed him often across the crowds, for she had learnt to identify the small brown lugger with the red stripe on her hull long before he reached the shore. Then she would follow the glint of his fair hair as he moved among the curers and fish buyers, watch his progress along the quayside towards the Whaler's Arms, note when he spread his nets to dry or examined them for rents.

But there were long hours when she dared not take her eyes from the salt tubs and the endless herring, lest she fall behind with the filling of barrel after barrel of interleaving fish, packed down with salt and the strength of her pressing hands, bent double over the empty barrel, and slowly unwinding upwards till, blessedly, the barrel was full. On bad days her hands stung unbearably from the penetrating salt and her back ached and creaked till she feared she would never be able to stand straight again. Then, with the harbour empty and the boats invisible somewhere beyond the horizon, only the memory of his teasing eyes and those precious, whispered words kept hope alive.

She liked the early mornings best, after the first cup of tea, but before breakfast proper, when they went down to the curing yard for the topping up of the previous day's barrels. The fish settled overnight and each barrel had to be topped up with fish of the same size, from the same day's catch. That done, the coopers fitted lids and helped the girls stack the barrels at the back of the yard, in rows three layers high. There the barrels rested for ten days, before it was time for the next stage in the process, which, because of Sunday's enforced idleness when the fleet did not put to sea, was usually dealt with on

Mondays. This time the coopers cut bungholes into the barrel's side and the girls drained off the brine. The barrels were opened, topped up with more fish, the lids refitted, and finally the brine was poured back inside by means of a funnel and the bungholes were closed.

After that, all that remained was the official inspection though that was perhaps the most harrowing part of the process: each crew felt personally responsible for the quality of their barrels and to have a barrel rejected meant public shame. If all was well, the barrel was christened with the official stamp and from that moment was no longer their concern.

Without the hectic pressure of the gutting, where everyone was racing everyone else – and racing time as well – and without the noisy crowds that accompanied the landing of the day's catch, the early morning topping up was a strangely tranquil operation. Elissa's naturally tidy nature found satisfaction and a sense of achievement when, the work finished, she stood back and surveyed her barrels all topped up and lidded and stacked away at the back of the yard, and the new day's barrels, empty and redolent of clean-cut wood, set up ready in position, a pile of wooden lids close by. Old barrels were never used for herrings: only new, which was why so many coopers were required as well as gutting crews.

A little before that final, satisfying point, the girl whose turn it was would hurry back to the hut to make everything ready so that when the rest of them returned for half an hour or so they could relax over a bowl of well-earned morning porridge, with more bread and jam, in the knowledge that all was ready for when the new day's catch arrived.

So the weeks passed, measured from Sunday to Sunday – bleak when Adam did not come, blissful when he did. The first time he took her walking on the seashore, he held her hand. No matter that half the gutting yard were also on the seashore or on the headland above. His hand was in hers and that was all that mattered. The next time, he slipped his arm around her waist and, later, kissed her. Though they always began the afternoon stroll in a happy crowd, boys and girls soon paired off and Adam seemed to know all the secluded places in the neighbourhood, from little secret coves to grassy hollows where they could sit on the soft turf together, murmuring and kissing until every unawakened nerve of Elissa's body yearned into life. She told him of life at home with Aunt Sarah and how she had longed for freedom; of her brothers and father whom she loved, but who were so much older than she was; of her loneliness and dreams. He told her his mother was a fisherman's daughter, who worked as a housemaid at the big house. His father, he said, was a nobleman, up from London for the fishing and gone again long before Adam was born, though his mother, he said, had refused ever to reveal his name, and now she was dead and it was too late. He was a penniless orphan with his way still to make in the world and no one to help him but himself.

'And me,' she promised, kissing him.

'And you,' he murmured, his hand on the warm curve of her breast. Then she longed for the world to empty of everyone but herself and Adam; or to be alone with him in the darkness of the box bed at home, with Aunt Sarah away and the doors firmly closed. But always someone interrupted – Ina calling from the headland, or Jessie from the path. Sometimes Elissa suspected they had a pact together to prevent her being long alone with Adam, but when she said as much they told her not to be so daft.

'Though you watch yourself, Lissa. You may have stars in your eyes and can't see clear, but your lad's like all the rest. Give him an inch and he'll take a mile, the randy young stirk. But we set out together and it's best we all go back together,' they said. 'Folk will talk, else.' Then they would link arms with her and, the menfolk following a discreet distance behind, they would stroll back to the huts, singing.

Then one precious Sunday, in a sun-warmed hollow near the sea's edge, Adam told her he loved her, longed for her, needed her; slipped a hand inside her bodice, kissed and caressed her till she ached unbearably for him.

'Soon we will find a way, my darling,' he murmured. 'Soon. Or I will die with longing.'

'We can be married in November,' she said, her eyes bright with happiness. 'When the herring season is over. We will have money then.'

There was a silence, in which the soft soughing of the sea on shingle was the only sound. He lay back on the sandy grass, his eyes closed. When he spoke, his voice was flat, without emotion.

'But not enough.'

'Enough for what?' said Elissa, puzzled. 'We will have each other, and the skill of our hands. And the herring money will be plenty for the Minister's fee and the party. Why do we need more?'

'Because...' but before he could elaborate she kissed first his eyelids, then timidly his lips.

'I love you as you are, Adam. I want nothing more.'

'But I do!' He pushed her away from him, rolled over, face hidden, and groaned aloud. 'Oh God, Elissa, I want you so much. More than I have ever wanted anyone. But...'

'But my love is not enough?'

The small, bleak words cut him to the heart. He sat up, pulled her

53

towards him and, his arm around her shoulder and holding her head against his chest, said, 'Listen to me, my darling, and I will try and explain.'

He looked down at her anxious, loving face, pushed the hair away from her eyes and said, with no trace of his usual light-heartedness, 'It is because I love you, truly love you, that a season's paltry takings are not enough, for you or for me. I confess, though I think you know it already, that I have been with other girls . . .'

Elissa bit her lip on the jealousy which stabbed through her with heart-stopping pain, but said nothing. Eyes lowered, she merely nodded agreement.

His hand caressed her hair, gently stroking away the pain. 'But there was no one like you, my love. When I saw you that first time, standing by the farlin, singing so sweetly, I knew you were the lass I had been searching for ever since . . . ever since I felt the first yearning way back when I was sixteen. Do you understand that?'

'Oh yes,' murmured Elissa, happiness returning. 'I felt the same.' Though she had never been with other men, would never have dreamed of doing so.

'So you see, my little singing bird, when I marry you, I want it to be more than a salt-herring-and-whisky affair. More than the dreary hand-to-mouth existence my mother had. I want to carry you over the threshold of our own house. Not your father's house or my uncle's house, but our own. A grand mansion house like my father owned – '

'But Adam,' protested Elissa, 'I do not want a mansion house. It would be too big and – '

'All right, my darling. No mansion. A small, dry cottage with two rooms and a good hearth will do to begin with, but later, when I make my fortune, I will buy you a grand mansion house, whether you like it or not. A house like the one where my mother worked and should have had herself if my father had been the gentleman he claimed to be. A house with lawns and flowers and upstairs a bedroom with a soft and secret four-poster bed and curtains to draw close around us, to keep the whole world out, like this.' His arms tightened protectively around her and she felt the pulse beat warm and strong in the curve of his neck.

'My mother had nothing,' he went on, talking freely now, without deception or striving for effect. 'Except the love and trust she gave to my father. My father had everything – and kept it all to himself. She did not say so, for she was loyal to the last, but we saw nothing of the money that set him so much above her, only the pittance she earned at the gutting yard. Until I was old enough to earn my bit. He certainly sent no sovereigns to help out. Not even when my mother's employer dismissed her, for expecting a child when she had no husband. His own house guest's child. If I had known who my father was I would have sought him out and demanded recompense for my mother's hardship and suffering. But she would never tell and it is too late. Otherwise we might have been rich . . .'

'What do riches matter, my darling?' She looked up at him, her hand caressing his cheek, turning his averted face towards her. 'Do not worry so much, Adam. Your poor mother is at peace now and as for me, I want nothing except your love. We will work together, you and I,' and her soft lips brushed against his, 'and save and save until . . .'

But her warm and yielding contact was too much for resolution. Before she could finish the sentence he stopped her words with a kiss, a deep and lingering one which swept her mind of everything except her love for him and her wish to please him, always. At that moment she would have done whatever he asked of her, but the first warning call came fluting over the dunes behind them. The other girls were preparing to go home.

Reluctantly, he moved a discreet space away from her and said, his blue eyes grave and intense, 'I love you, Lissa Downie. Never forget it. But riches matter as well as love. If you had seen my mother, working her heart out so that she and I could keep alive, you would understand.'

'Your poor mother . . .'

'Aye. So when I marry, I'll have none of that. I'll have money to buy leisure and fine clothes for my wife so she can stay the lovely young creature that she is now.'

He scrambled suddenly to his feet, pulled her up to stand beside him, and said with a return of his old teasing good spirits, 'If you will not let me buy you a mansion, my thrifty wee darling, then I shall buy a splendid ship instead, a steamer fit for a king, with deep plush carpets and chandeliers and crystal glasses to drink from. A cabin with mahogany furniture, just like in a house, and a soft, panelled bed just big enough for two. Then I will catch you up in my arms like this,' and he swung her suddenly into the air where she clung to him, laughing while he murmured close into her ear, 'and carry you aboard my fine new ship, like this,' and he walked the few steps from their hidden hollow to the cliff path, 'and sail away with you into the sunset. Then what nights of loving we will have.'

'But I love you now, Adam,' she said with such unashamed simplicity that he would have forgotten all propriety had not Ina's strident call from twenty yards away brought them back to cold reality.

'Put the lass down and keep your hands to yourself, Adam Grant, if you know what's good for you. Unless you're wanting her brothers to teach you respectful behaviour.'

'Soon, my darling,' he murmured in Elissa's ear before setting her down on the sandy path. 'Soon we will find a way, I promise.' Then he turned to face the others with a defiant grin. 'I was just showing the lassie the strength of my arm, that's all.'

'Aye well, William Downie will show you the strength of his if he hears you've been making free with his sister. And there's two more brothers and a father if you overstep the mark. You remember that.'

'Spoil-sport,' grinned Adam, unrepentant. Then he winked at Elissa and strolled off to join the men.

The next time they managed to escape the others he took her by a dodging, roundabout route to the latest hide-out he had found – a ruined cottage, roofless, but with two walls still standing. The corner where these joined was sun-warmed and private and it seemed only natural to fling themselves down on to the soft turf together and laugh at their successful escape. The grass was warm and springy under her back, the sky so bright she had to close her eyes. He kissed her eyelids, then, very gently, her lips, and his caressing hands moved over her awakening body and stirred her to willing, loving, exultant life. This time no dreams of riches intervened. This time no one called her name.

Afterwards, thinking about it, she supposed there must have been a moment when she could have said no. When his hand loosened her bodice, perhaps, and exposed one round breast to the sun, or when his questing fingers found the soft, bare skin at the top of her stockings. But it did not occur to her. She loved him, with all her heart and every tingling, longing nerve in her body.

Aunt Sarah had forbidden her many things, but if ever men were mentioned her aunt had turned away in embarrassment, or said, 'Remember, Elissa. A good girl saves herself for her husband.' Somehow, if she had thought of it at all, she had confused this with collecting wedding linen or crockery. But now, in secret, Adam was her husband. Elissa knew he could not officially marry her until the herring season was over and she did not expect it, but after that . . . He said he had his way to make in the world first, but he did not really mean it and when they were married, she would help him. A fisherman needed a wife. She even understood why Adam wanted to keep their love secret.

'I want you all to myself for a while, my little singing bird,' he had told her. 'In a secret world of our own. Without folk teasing and jeering all the time and asking when's the wedding.'

Adam was quite right. Already folk were teasing Ina and Fergus Mackie about marriage and families and Elissa did not want her own affections made such public property. She feared the intrusion into their private happiness, but also she admitted to herself with a shiver of apprehension, she feared what Bethany Noble would do when she found out. It was easy for Adam to say it was all over long ago between him and Bethany, but suppose Bethany felt differently? Most of all, she remembered Ina's threats of what Elissa's brothers might do to Adam if they heard he was 'making free' with their sister. But now that she and Adam were hand-fast, in the eyes of God she was his wife. She could wait. And while she waited, she could love him, as he loved her, with this new, intimate abandonment and blissful, draining passion.

Afterwards, they lay together, arms around each other and eyes closed, murmuring loving nonsense while the sun blessed them, and they slept until eventually, from somewhere in the distance, the usual warning call thrust through their drained contentment, and it was time to go back.

He helped her to tidy her hair, refasten her little buttons, straighten her skirts; kissed her on the eyelids, the tip of her nose, then on her loving, parted lips. She put her arms around him and held him tight, whispering something to herself, but when he asked, she would not tell him what.

'I hope it was something loving,' he said, lifting her chin with a forefinger and looking into her eyes.

'Oh yes.'

With a whoop of triumph, he swung her high in the air, then let her slide slowly down again, kissing the buttons of her bodice one by one until he reached the warm skin of her slender neck and finally, blissfully, her mouth.

'You are a beauty, my little singing bird. Did you know that? A delicious, secret, passionate wee beauty, and I love you.'

Then, whistling and with a swagger in his step, he led her back to a changed and brighter world. For even the simple huts looked different to her, bathed as they were with an aura of new happiness, and the gutting yard was no longer a malodorous sweat-shop of toil and filth, but a place of happy companionship and fulfilment. He had told her he loved her and she . . . she carried the memory with her, as she carried the intimate, precious bruises, to sustain her through the days ahead.

Elissa glowed with happiness, sang at her work and met all Bethany's bad temper with serene good humour. She had feared Bethany's jealousy on the Sundays when Adam took her 'strolling', and now was doubly fearful, lest her happiness show too clearly in her eyes. But fortunately Bethany had interests of her own. Brodie Gibb had taken to calling regularly on Sundays, and it was soon known throughout the curing yard, with varying degrees of incredulity, that he had Bethany Noble in his sights. But Bethany was a different woman in his presence, putting on a veneer of respectful courtesy and behaving with astonishing decorum. She toned down her natural belligerence to just the right amount of plain-speaking good sense and ordered the others around for all the world like a capable young housewife with important guests. Out of loyalty, and devilment, the girls backed her up, straight-faced, as long as Gibb was there, but though they teased her unmercifully behind his back and at the farlin, Bethany refused to be drawn. If he chose to come visiting, that was his business. She hadn't invited him, but she was not going to stop him and while he was there, she'd see everyone behaved themselves.

Then suddenly and for no apparent reason, the herring flocked to the nets as never before. Every evening the harbour mouth was jammed as the two hundred and fifty or so yawls and Scaffies and Fifies, some a mere thirty feet, some fifty or more, jostled and pushed for position in order to reach the slipstream and the passage seawards to the fishing grounds. Then, as one by one the brown sails unfurled and the wind took them, the fleet swirled and dipped like a myriad fragile moths in the evening light until sea and sky together engulfed them and they vanished. In that northern sea, at the height of summer, the night was barely night at all, merely a brief blinking of the sun's eye, and under a clear sky a man could see to cast a net, or a girl to gut a fish, at eleven at night or three in the morning. The day's catch doubled, the hours lengthened with scarcely time for rest or food, and every morning the fleet raced home in twos and threes to unload at speed, and every boat full to overflowing.

For two whole weeks the gutting crews were at work from six in the morning till after ten at night. With more barrels filled each day even the early morning topping up took longer till the breakfast break shrank to almost nothing. The curers, Brodie Gibb included, sent urgently to the mainland for more salt. As stocks of barrels rapidly dwindled, the coopers were kept as busy as the gutting crews, knocking up fresh ones, with the hundreds of newly fashioned barrel lids which soon littered the yard in precariously balanced piles. Some of the more high-spirited apprentices bowled them across the quay to each other with whoops of encouragement, but not for long and increasingly rarely as the glut continued.

For though the girls valiantly sang at their work and joked and laughed with the lads as they always did, there was exhaustion in the air and no energy for anything at the end of the fifteen- or sixteen-hour day but to fall into bed and sleep. Sunday was a blessed respite, but all too short a one and fraught with tensions. Many stayed away from church, preferring to sleep on in their beds or on the open heathland, and many of those who did summon the effort to dress in their Sunday best and walk the hot miles to the kirk were chastised from the pulpit, men and girls alike, for sleeping during the sermon. Even the afternoon tea-time was affected as, up and down the rows of huts, exhaustion drove normally sweet-tempered girls to snap at their best friends or, worse, their suitors.

For as well as the endless cascade of herring to be dealt with, at faster and ever faster speeds, the sun blazed and made speed even more imperative if the silver riches were not to putrefy under their hands. As it was, and in spite of all efforts, the tubs of spoilt herring multiplied until even the processing plant called a halt and refused to take more.

Inevitably, tempers began to fray and small grievances became large ones overnight. A crew from Buckie took to blows over a dropped herring: a gutter from Peterhead drew her knife on a cooper who called her 'slow'. Several girls fainted in the heat, to be revived with brutal efficiency by their crew-mates, lest the crew fall behind and drastically reduce their day's earnings.

And still the herring poured in, in relentless, shimmering rivers, till Elissa prayed that the salt supplies would run out or the barrels split – anything to earn them an hour's rest.

Then miraculously the pressure eased, there was time to breathe again, and men began to talk of moving south to the mainland, to Wick or Fraserburgh or Peterhead, some even of going home. The herring shoals followed a regular pattern throughout the season, appearing on the west coast in early May, then in the Minch and northern waters round the islands until by July they were to be found further south, off the east coast of Scotland. Whether it was the same shoals that swam round the northern tip of the Scottish islands and south again, or a succession of different shoals appearing in sequence, no one knew, but year after year the pattern remained the same. Though some boats followed throughout the season, many took the opportunity to go home for a spell, to help with the haymaking or harvest. Some of the gutting teams did the same, depending on family circumstances and the terms of their hiring: for there were social events such as the Nairn games and the Aberdeen races to look forward to, as well as the harvest.

By October the herring shoals would be in English waters, off the coast of East Anglia, and, the harvest safely gathered in, those boats and gutting crews who had taken a summer break would follow, the former by sea, the latter by the special trains the railway provided. By the end of November the herring season would be over and she and Adam could marry.

That dream was Elissa's precious, guiding star, but in the mean-time, while part of her still yearned occasionally for the comfort and safety of the Square at home, especially at the end of yet another relentless, back-breaking day when she was, as usual, last at the

59

wash-stand and so weary she could hardly lift the cloth to her sweat-drenched, salt-encrusted face, another part of her wanted the herring fishing to go on for ever. So that she could see Adam Grant. Not merely for two seconds across a crowd of herring barrels, but properly, blissfully, on a long Sunday afternoon, alone and private in a sun-warmed hollow on the headland, or in a little, hidden cove with the sea gently lapping and the gulls high overhead.

Occasionally, something Bethany Noble said, or did, would remind Elissa of that dreadful, shaming Sunday when she had run away and Joseph Noble had found her, tear-stained and desolate, gazing out across the sea towards home. But the memory no longer stung. Joseph had been kind and comforting, and she had been grateful. She still was, when he came to tea on Sundays, presumably to see his sister Bethany. Sometimes he talked to her about the new developments in steam power and his fears that the bigger, more powerful boats would alter the balance between the fisherman and the shipowner, between what the sea provided and what men took out of it. Then Elissa would try to answer him sensibly and he always listened to what she had to say with respect and genuine interest.

'But it's not only the steam that's a threat,' he told her one Sunday. 'The new cotton nets certainly make it easier for men to cast and draw in again – the old hemp ones weighed a ton – but some men are misusing them already. Making the mesh smaller so the wee sillocks are caught as well as the matties. The curers won't like that, if it spreads. They contract for quantity, believing the fish will be of a proper size. If too many of them are not, then there'll be trouble.'

'And fewer wee fish left in the sea to grow bigger?'

'Aye, lass. But greedy folk think only of their own immediate profit, not of the future. If we net even the small fry from the sea, what will be left for our children? Where will their livelihood be then?'

But Joseph was not always so gloomy. Last Sunday afternoon which until then had been bleak with Adam's absence, Joseph had taken her to see a pair of lapwing chicks he had found on the heathland behind the huts, and picked a bunch of wild orchids for her to take home.

Nevertheless, she wished it had been Adam who had found the chicks and given her the flowers. As she wished it had been Adam who had followed her on to the hillside after Bethany's taunts; who had found and comforted and reassured her. She yearned for Adam every moment of the day and would have peopled all her memories with him if she could. But truth was truth and he had not followed her. He said Jess had not let him, but perhaps it had been Bethany?

The memory of Bethany and Adam together still had the power to stir her with unease. Bethany liked to be the centre of attention, and

Adam was too easygoing to cause any trouble. Yet sometimes Elissa wished he would not be quite so willing to answer Beth's imperious summons when she said, 'Come and sit with me, Adam,' or 'I havena seen you for a whilie, Adam laddie. Come over here and whisper me your secrets.' She was not exactly jealous, she told herself, for Adam loved her, and her alone. He had told her so, when she mentioned it.

'But it's best not to annoy her, lass. Believe me, I know. Bethany can be right vicious when she chooses and if she found out about you and me . . . It would be you who would suffer, my darling, and me away fishing and not at your side to protect you.'

Elissa did not say she suffered already: it sounded unloving and she loved Adam with all her heart and soul. Nevertheless, Elissa grew to welcome Mr Gibb's arrival, for that was usually the signal for several of the men, including Adam, to slip quietly away. And though she could not always follow, at least it kept him safe from Bethany's greedy eye.

She had not seen Adam for several days, even at a distance, and was beginning to frighten herself with the fear that he might have taken off already for his next port of call, maybe in a hurry and James Hay not giving him time to say his goodbyes, when a voice spoke behind her.

'I've come to say I'm moving on, Elissa. If it is Elissa under all that skirt.'

The voice made Elissa start with pleasure. She had completed ten barrels already that day and was bending over the eleventh, of which the bottom was barely covered with its first layer of matt fulls, but his words made her straighten and turn in one fluid movement, a salt-crusted herring still clutched in each hand.

'Oh yes,' she said, her eyes bright with joy. 'It's me.'

'Won't you introduce me to your friends?' he teased, and smiling she turned and bent quickly over the barrel to lay them in place. He put his hands on her waist and when she shot upright again in alarm he swung her up and round to set her down in front of him.

'Nay, lass, there's no call to take fright,' he said softly, his eyes looking straight into hers. She saw intimate memory and promise together, and his voice was warm as a caress. 'Not with you and me knowing each other so well.'

His hand lingered at her waist and it cost the greatest effort not to move forward, to fit her hips to his, in the loving, giving way he had taught her, to reach up and kiss him in full view of all the yard. But Bethany was not ten yards away and she contented herself with putting her hand over his and keeping it there for a blissful moment on the curve of her hip.

Then, with a private smile which told her he remembered every-thing that she remembered, he withdrew his hand and said, deliberately loud, 'I was merely rescuing you from a fishy fate, Elissa. Jess and Ina don't want to wake up one morning and find their wee packer's pickled herself in her own herring barrel. There's no saying where you'd get posted to, with Brodie Gibb up to his gills in shipping orders and that ass of a Sinclair laddie snarling them up the moment they get sorted.'

Elissa had seen the Sinclair 'laddie' from a distance, a dashing young man in bright city clothes. His father, Mr Gibb's partner, had sent him to Shetland, word had it, to learn the business, though word also had it that the only business he'd learnt so far was that of the drinking house, the gambling club and worse. But Elissa would never have dared refer to young Mr Sinclair in the familiar terms that Adam used. She looked up at him with admiration and a touch of awe. Then her happiness faded as she remembered what his first words had been.

'Are you really moving on, Adam?'

'Aye, lass. As soon as James Hay gives the word. Our boat landed what we're contracted for days ago and with the glut we've had lately there's not a decent price to be found anywhere for the surplus. We've had the best catch ever and all of us counting the profit, then Gibb won't buy them. James says we might as well give them away, or throw them back in the sea.'

'But why won't Mr Gibb buy them from you? Surely he can sell as many as he can provide to those merchants in Germany and Russia?'

'Aye. And he'll take them off our hands "as a favour" if you argue long enough. But he won't pay. Leastways, no more than a pittance.' Adam's usually cheerful face was sombre and he aimed a kick of frustration at the nearest barrel. 'And why should he, when he knows none of the other merchants will pay either, not with them all having contracts already for all the fish they want. You work hard, fish hard, and then you can't sell what you've caught because the likes of Brodie Gibb hold all the cards.'

'But that doesn't seem fair,' faltered Elissa.

'Aye, well. Life isn't fair. Leastways, not for the likes of us.'

At that moment Jessie called over her shoulder, 'That barrel filled yet, Lissa? We're nearly ready for the next rousing.' Then she saw Adam.

'What the bleeding fish-head are you doing, Adam Grant, pestering Lissa and interrupting when we're set fair to win "best crew in the yard"?'

'You? Best crew?' jeered Meg Duthie from further down the farlin. 'Only if the rest of us drop dead.'

'That's not a bad idea,' crowed Ina. 'Afore you get beaten.'

Suffie Lennox snatched a fish from her half-packed barrel and hurled it at Ina, catching her smartly on the ear. 'Mind your manners, cloth-head. There's plenty more where that one came from and we can spare them. Being way ahead of the likes of you.'

'Go sling your hook, afore we sling it for you,' retorted Ina, one hand to her smarting ear. With the other she scooped up a handful of fish-guts and threw them at Suffie, missing her completely and spattering Bethany instead.

'Right, that does it,' glared Bethany. 'Come on, Meg.'

'Ladies, ladies,' grinned Adam, ducking as a fish hurtled past his ear. 'I just called round to pass the time of day, though if I'm not welcome I'll move on.'

'You do that – or we might just help you on your way,' crowed Ina. 'How about it, lassies?'

But Bethany and Meg had picked up a filled tub of matties and were already moving ominously in Adam's direction.

'Right, I'll be off then,' he grinned, retreating a step. 'Likely we'll all meet up again in Wick, God willing. Or in Yarmouth.' Then he bent his head and murmured in Elissa's ear, 'Tonight? Behind Gibb's office? I'll be waiting for you.'

She looked up at him in returning happiness, impervious to the commotion and movement around her. All she saw was his bright hair and smiling eyes and his handsome, well-loved face.

Then, over Adam's shoulder, she saw Bethany and Meg Duthie coming fast towards them with a tub of gutted herrings swinging between them and said in a rush, 'I'll be there, I promise. As soon as – '

Her words ended in a gasp of pain as Bethany crashed into her, pushing herself and the tub between Elissa and Adam. The tub caught Adam across the knees and in the same movement knocked Elissa back against the hard rim of the salt-tub. She flung out an arm to save herself and gasped again as pain ripped through her wrist. Her head seemed to spin, her eyes clouded, she had a momentary vision of that upturned knife point in Bethany's wooden kist – and knew before the blood welled what she would see.

CHAPTER 6

'Watch out, you clumsy cow!' cried Adam indignantly. 'You could kill someone, ramming into folk like that. And you've ruined my new boots.' The left one bore a long, deep scratch across the calf.

'That's not all I'll ruin, neither,' glowered Bethany. 'Poking your nose where you're not wanted. I thought I told you to leave our Lissa alone,' she snarled, barring Adam's way. Then she dumped the tub in his path, turned her back on him and said, 'I warned you, Lissa, to keep away from that one. Always pestering folk and hindering their work. And don't say he wasn't because I'll not believe you. You're not the first, by a long chalk, nor the last neither. Pesters all the lassies till he gets what he wants. Then when he's got it, he's not wanting it any more, see?'

Her eyes were hard and bright, like twin blades of the same steel knife and Elissa's heart thudded with fear and pain and outrage. She moistened her lips to say, 'What business is it of yours?' but Bethany forestalled her.

'Well, what are you waiting for, Meg? Get a move on. We've work to do.'

But Jess and Ina blocked Bethany's path. 'You all right, Lissa?' demanded Jess, one eye on Bethany.

White-faced and shaking, upper teeth biting hard into lower lip, Elissa held her left wrist tight in her right hand and fought against the pain which seared her arm from shoulder to fingertips. Her eyes clouded over and she swayed. Jess pushed Bethany aside and put a hand under Elissa's elbow, to steady her.

'Why can't you look what you're doing, Bethany? You've hurt her.'

'It was an accident,' blustered Bethany, glaring round her in defiance. 'Folk shouldn't stand in other folk's way.'

'Some accident,' snarled Adam. 'Let me through.' He tried to push his way through the open barrels and the crowding girls to Elissa's side, but the girls closed ranks to prevent him.

'You keep out of it, Adam Grant,' said several voices together. 'You've done enough harm already.'

Meg said, with a nervous giggle, 'The tub was heavy and it sort of ran away with us. You all right, Lissa?'

'Of course she's not,' cried Jess indignantly and Ina added, 'And nor would you be if you had a great tub of fish rammed into you by two clumsy – '

But Suffie Lennox had shouldered her way to the front. 'Is your wrist bleeding, lass?' The alarm in her voice quieted even Ina. 'Here. Let me look.'

Suffie took Elissa's hand in her own capable ones and forced away the cotton-bound fingers, which were already blood-soaked, to show a two-inch gash through which the blood welled up and spilled on to the ground. In a second she had whipped the scarf from her hair and bound it round the cut, drawing the edges tight together. 'Hold your hand high, like this, lass. To stop the bleeding.' Then, still gripping her wrist to stem the flow, she turned accusingly to Bethany.

'You clumsy fool, Bethany. I've told you a dozen times to keep that knife safe. It could have been fatal.'

'Well, it's not fatal, more's the pity. And anyway it's her own fault, getting in folk's way. Blethering instead of getting on with her work and letting me do mine.'

'Well, you've certainly stopped her working today,' said Suffie with a worried glance at Jess. 'I doubt she'll be able for the packing now.'

'I'll get you, Bethany Noble, see if I don't,' glared Jess, 'ruining our team.'

'If the devil don't get you first,' added Ina. 'And all because we was winning.' But her fresh face was clouded with concern. 'Will she be all right, Suffie?'

It was Adam who answered, looking straight at Bethany. 'As right as anyone who's had her wrist slashed with a gutting knife.'

'I never,' protested Bethany. 'Did I, Meg? It was an accident. I stumbled, that's all. Slipped on some of yon guts Ina Bain was throwing about. If it's anybody's fault, it's hers, making folk . . .' but her voice faded as she caught a warning frown from Meg.

'Is there some sort of trouble here?'

At the ominous voice there was instant silence. Brodie Gibb had noticed the disturbance and come to investigate. It was not unusual for squabbles to break out among the girls, especially after a spell of particularly arduous hours, but he had found by long experience that the sooner they were stamped out, the better for all concerned.

'Oh no, Mr Gibb,' said Bethany, moving deftly in front of Elissa to block his view. She added, with her best smile, 'Leastways, nothing I can't handle. An argument over a few spilled herrings and a wee scratch, that's all. But we're well up to schedule. Like we always are. I see to that.'

'I'm glad to hear it.' He regarded her thoughtfully from under the dark thicket of his eyebrows, noting the bright hair, fresh, healthy complexion and strong build. A comely lass even in her work clothes; comely and capable. Her crew was one of the best in the yard. Hers and Elissa Downie's. Elissa was behind Bethany's shoulder, the Bain sisters close by, with Bethany Noble's crew-mates, the plain girl with the ginger hair and freckles and the tall one with the sharp tongue. All in the same hut, he remembered. A loyal, hard-working bunch, controlled most competently by Bethany. Reliable. Always polite. And they served a very good tea.

Briskly he recalled his position. There were coopers and fishermen in the crowd as well as the gutting crews and discipline must be maintained.

'Then if there is nothing wrong, I suggest you get on with your work.'

When he was out of earshot, Bethany let out a sigh of relief, then turned on Elissa and the Bain girls. 'You heard what Mr Gibb said. There's that barrel not full yet and another tub ready and waiting to be packed and you boasting you're the best! You'll get us all the sack, you will, Lissa Downie. Standing about talking when you should be working.' Then, seeing the expression on Suffie's face, she added grudgingly, 'Sorry, Lissa. It was an accident, like Meg said. But you'll need to learn to do as you're told and keep out of folk's way. Tell you what, when we've dealt with this tub of ours, we'll help Jess and Ina with the rousing while you have a wee rest and get your breath.'

'Aye,' growled Adam. 'That's the least you can do. In the circumstances.'

'You still here, Adam Grant?' said Suffie. 'Then you can make yourself useful. Take Lissa straight over to Mrs Koss, to get a proper dressing on that, before the poison sets in. I'd take her myself, but we're a packer short already. See you hold your wrist up, Lissa, like I showed you, and don't forget to bring my scarf back. I might need it to strangle our Bethany with.'

'And if they ask, say you did it accidental,' warned Bethany. 'For it's the gospel truth.'

As Elissa moved off obediently towards the little hut on the quay, she heard Adam say, 'You wouldn't know the truth, Bethany Noble, if it leapt up and hit you smack between the eyes. Which I've a mind to do myself if you don't leave the lass alone.'

Then he was at her side, his hand gentle under her raised arm. 'You'll be all right, lass. It's only a wee cut and Mrs Koss'll soon put it right. She's a wonder with the ointment and you'll be right as rain in no time. Bethany should be locked up for a raving lunatic, cutting you like that.'

'It was an accident,' faltered Elissa, but they both knew it was no such thing.

'You are a loyal wee soul, and I love you for it. But she doesn't deserve it. I'd best not hold you any closer, my love,' murmured Adam, as she stumbled on a rock. 'Not with folk looking. Especially Bethany. You watch that one, Lissa. And if ever she tries anything like that again, and me too far away to defend you, tell her brother Joseph. He'll sort her out.'

And me too far away ... Her eyes brimmed with sudden tears. 'But you will see me again, Adam, before you go? Tonight ?'

'Tonight, my love, I promise. I'll be waiting for you.'

But they had reached the wooden hut which served as first-aid post for the curing yard. Adam bellowed into the open doorway for someone to 'Come and see to a lassie who's cut herself'. Then he bent his head, whispered, 'Be brave my little singing bird. And fly to me soon.'

She looked up at him, her eyes bleak in her dead-white face: he glanced quickly to either side, kissed her on the lips, and left.

'You'll be lucky if that doesn't go septic,' said Mrs Koss, the head cooper's wife, as she tipped whisky liberally into the gaping cut. 'What sort of barrel you was tripping over to get a gash like that beats me. Though it's not as bad as I thought now it's cleaned up. Just a scratch really. Long enough, but shallow, and the edges will knit up real neat if you're careful. I've seen plenty worse in my time. Nay, lass, keep still. The whisky will stop stinging in a minute and you don't want to get blood poisoning, do you?' She tore a long strip from a piece of clean linen and began to bind up Elissa's wrist. 'I'm doing it tight, like, to stem the bleeding and close the cut. A pretty girl like you doesn't want a great ragged scar on her arm, does she? Aye,' she continued conversationally, 'cuts is bad things to have around here, so you take care. A septic hand and it'll be home for you on the next boat, and no more herring-gutting for the season. There now. That should see you right,' she finished, tying the frayed ends tight. 'Mind and keep the bandage clean and if your fingers go blue, then you'll need to loosen it a wee bittie, but not too loose or it'll bleed. Now I'll make you a nice cup of hot tea to put the colour back in your cheeks while you sit there by the fire and rest.'

Obediently, Elissa sat, but while her eyes roved restlessly over the simple room, so like her own house in the Square at home with its plain wooden furniture and whitewashed walls, her mind picked over and over what the woman had said. A septic hand and no more herring-gutting for the season.

Perhaps that had been what Bethany wanted? For however much she protested that her foot had slipped, that it had been an accident, Elissa knew it was not true. Either she had barged into her because Elissa's team was winning, or for other, more personal reasons. One or the other. Perhaps both. But it was no accident.

'There you are lass,' said Mrs Koss, putting the steaming mug into her hand. 'Drink it up while it's still hot. I've put plenty sugar in it, and a wee drop of whisky, for your strength.'

Whisky. Whatever would Aunt Sarah say? But the reminder brought home the reality of the threat. Only last week a gutter at the next farlin to theirs had been sent home with a septic finger and the poison running up her arm in an ominous red line. What better way to get rid of a rival?

She drained her mug and set it down. 'Thank you, Mrs Koss. I feel much better. Now I'd best get back to my work before I lose it.'

But I will not lose it, vowed Elissa under her breath as she threaded her way across the crowded yard. I will not get blood poisoning. I will work my contract and go to Wick with everyone else. And I will see Adam again. Tonight and any time I please. No one, and certainly not Bethany Noble, will stop me.

From the doorway of the shipping office a young man in a well-cut frock-coat, striped trousers and a dashing cravat of which he was particularly proud hooked a thumb into the pocket of his buff waistcoat and watched her with appraising eyes.

'Who is that woman?' he asked of the man beside him. 'I've seen her before somewhere.'

'Very likely,' said Brodie Gibb. The lad was even stupider that he had thought. 'She has been working for us all season. A respectable girl from Footdee in Aberdeen.' He laid just the right amount of emphasis on the word 'respectable'.

'Really?' Deliberately Hugh Sinclair watched her out of sight, before he turned back into the office and closed the door.

It was easier to slip away than Elissa expected. Word had spread around the curing yard that the fleet would soon be moving on. There was a restlessness in the air, a toing and froing between the different huts, and outside one of these huts, on the foreshore, a group of girls from Buckie had lit a brushwood fire and they were sitting around it with their menfolk, singing. Bethany and some of the others had drifted over to join them. Elissa, pleading tiredness and the discomfort of her cut, stayed behind. But as soon as they were gone, she found her plaid, clutched it tight about her shoulders, and crept away under cover of the general camaraderie.

She kept in the shadow of the huts as long as she could, then she was on the familiar path to the quay and the denser shadows cast by row after row of herring barrels, piled three barrels high. The evening sea was calm. She could hear the waves sucking and drawing at the shore with no more than a soft susurration, and when she reached the wooden quay and jetty of the curing yard she heard the water lapping gently round the posts of the wooden structure.

Beyond where the jetty protruded into the sea fishing vessels crowded together at anchor, all with sails furled and nets stowed, all rocking in the same motion as the sea gently rose and fell, all in darkness. They would not put to sea again till the Sabbath was over. She wondered which one was Adam's and whether he was aboard. There was no sight or sound of movement.

A sudden wind blew from nowhere and she shivered, pulling her plaid tighter about her shoulders. She hoped Adam was already there, and waiting. She hurried quickly across the yard, threading her way between empty farlins, skirting empty barrels and full, until she neared the neat wooden edifice of Mr Gibb's office. A small office, with a single window and a corrugated iron roof, it was built away from the shore, on the firmer land just below the road to Lerwick. A flight of shallow steps led from the office up the short slope to the grassy verge of the high road. Elissa knew that Mr Gibb always arrived and departed that way and had chosen her own route accordingly. Mr Gibb was renowned for the late hours he kept, and made others keep, in the business interests of Messrs Sinclair and Gibb. But surely even he would have packed up and gone home by now? She moved carefully towards the darkened building, hoping to see Adam waiting in the shadows.

Though there was no moon, the night sky was still pale enough for her to make out the details of planking, window frame, steps. The office was in darkness, the door locked. Perhaps Adam was waiting in James Hay's boat? If so, he would see her and come. Again she shivered, suddenly aware of the emptiness, the lurking shadows, the sense of being entirely, helplessly alone.

The sea sighed and moaned, a boat gently creaked, and somewhere in the night sky above her she heard the whirr of feathered wings and a faint mewing cry. An oyster-catcher?

Then through the silence, over the beating of her own heart, she heard a new sound: footsteps on the road above her. Approaching footsteps. Adam must have been into Lerwick for some reason and be hurrying back to meet her. She drew back into the shadows of the office wall and waited, her heart full with loving expectation, her eyes on the headland at the top of those steps. A black outline was silhouetted briefly against the sky before shrinking, step by step, as he descended towards her.

She waited, quivering, until she could bear it no longer, then started forward with a joyful cry. 'My love, I thought you would never come!'

'Well, well,' said a soft, well-spoken voice. 'I had not expected such a charming welcome. And from a stranger, too. But perhaps it is a highland custom?'

Elissa looked up, appalled, at a pale-haired gentleman in evening finery complete with opera hat and soft kid gloves.

'Do not be afraid, my dear. I am merely fetching something I inad ... inadvertently forgot.'

Oh dear God, thought Elissa. He is drunk. But before she could speak, or move, he had reached out a gloved hand and gripped her firmly by the forearm, where her sleeve concealed Mrs Koss's bandage.

'Brandy. The very best. You shall share it with me.'

With a strangled gasp of pain and fear, she tried to pull away, but he held her fast.

'No, my dear. I insist. After all, it is not every day fortune blows such a charming prize my way.' He held her away from him so that her face caught what light there was from the night sky. 'Let me look at you, my dear. Why, I do believe it is Worthy Gibb's "respectable" lassie from Aberdeen. A remarkably pretty lass, too, and all alone. As I am.' His voice slurred on the s's and her heart raced with new fear.

'No,' she pleaded, struggling as his grip tightened. Behind his shoulder was empty headland, to her left, the darkened office, to her right empty quayside, and the dark mass of shipping asleep in the bay, masts so many bare twigs against the night sky. There was no movement anywhere, no sound but the sea's sighing and her own heartbeat; not a soul in sight. She felt sick with pain and terror, but she must not panic. She must talk to him calmly, sensibly. 'No, sir. You ... you misunderstand.'

'Do I?'

'Yes. I am waiting for a friend who ...' but he did not seem to hear. Instead, he was forcing her into the shadow of the office building, forcing her until her back was against its bare wooden wall.

'You were looking for company, I think. As I am.'

There was blown sand under her feet, the familiar tang of fish on the night air and still no sound but the sea. If only Adam would come! But, she saw with gathering horror, the whole world remained empty of everyone but herself and him. His breath smelt of cigars and old brandy and as he leant towards her she caught the incongruous scent of eau-de-Cologne.

70

'No. Please . . .' She tried to slip sideways, under his arm, but he pushed her back against the wall and pinned her there with the hard thrust of his body.

'But I say yes. Please.' His voice was low in her ear and his eyes glinted with an excitement which filled Elissa with terror. Behind the blinding fear, she heard her aunt's voice in embarrassed warning: *If ever a man attacks you, bring up your knee, hard.* But she could not move her knee. Either of them. Instead, she put her hands flat against his loathsome, scented shirt and pushed with all her strength, but he merely laughed.

'Pretend virtue if you must. Indeed, I like a token struggle. But it makes no difference. Respectable girls do not linger in darkened doorways, alone.'

'I was not lingering,' she protested, writhing and struggling against his tightening strength. 'I was waiting for a friend. He will be looking for me.' In the darkened landscape she thought she glimpsed a movement and said wildly, 'He will be here at any moment.'

That was a mistake. She knew it the moment the words were spoken, for it seemed to light an excitement in his eyes that had been merely dormant before. 'Then he can wait his turn. While you and I, my dear, get closer acquainted.'

Though his voice was slurred, she knew his mind had hold of a single, dominating idea. He was the master and entitled to whatever he wanted, whenever he wanted it. And he wanted her. Dear God, if only Adam would come. Now. Before it was too late.

'I said I wanted to talk to you.' His voice was menacingly soft, and he paused between each word while his greedy eyes took in her eyes, her lips, the fullness of her breasts under their plaid. When she did not answer, but stared defiance at him from eyes made round with fear, he suddenly ripped the plaid from her shoulders. 'And to look. May I not look at my own employees?'

'I work for Mr Gibb,' she managed, 'who always treats me, as he treats all the girls, with respect.'

'More fool him. Doesn't know what he's missing. You're a lovely lassie. Lovely, toothsome lassie.' His fingers were at the neck of her blouse. 'Less look and see how lovely . . .'

'No!' She twisted, ducked, and might have escaped had he not caught her by an arm around her waist.

'Got you, you little vixen.' He was angry now. 'And mean to keep you. But less go inside . . . warmer . . . brandy too . . . then we'll see just how respectable you are.' One arm still clamped around her waist, pressing her hard against him, he fumbled at the door behind her, trying to fit a key into the lock. 'That's right, my dear. Wriggle and fight me. I like that. Like it very much.'

His whole body weight was pressing her against the wall, one knee forced between her unwilling thighs, while he fumbled with the lock. Then she heard the key turn. With the strength of terror, she fought one hand free, her good hand, drew her nails hard down the flesh of his face and screamed, 'Adam! Help me . . .'

CHAPTER 7

A hand clamped over her mouth. He struggled to drag her bodily through the doorway, swearing with pain and fury. Then miraculously the oaths changed and time assumed a different pace. In slow motion she saw a new figure erupt out of the darkness, grip her assailant from behind with an arm round the neck. And wrench. Heard Sinclair gasp as his throat was compressed. Felt her own head strike the doorpost as his grip loosened, dragging fingers tearing at the cloth and the flesh of her arm. Pain burned through her as it had done at the farlin when Bethany's knife had cut, but this time a blessed, cleansing pain. Then she was suddenly light and free while outside in the night two figures struggled in a gust of gasping oaths and grunts. For a moment they separated and she saw them clearly outlined against the night sky: two men of equal build and height, confronting each other with deadly venom and gathering breath. Then one of them summoned the backbone of privilege.

'What the hell do you think you are doing, you oaf? Striking a gentleman on his own premises? I'll have you for assault and trespass. I'll – '

Adam hit him full in the supercilious face; and hit him and hit him till he slumped groaning to the ground.

Elissa crouched where she was, on the floorboards of the open doorway, her head in her hands and her whole body shaking. She felt sick with shame and disgust and terror.

'Are you all right, Elissa?'

She looked up to see Adam's ashen face. There was blood on his cheek, more on the knuckles of his right hand and his shirt was torn open at the neck.

With a quivering sob she flung herself into his arms. 'Adam, Adam my love. I thought you would never come. He tried to . . . to . . .'

'Hush, hush, you're safe now. I'll not let him touch you.' He soothed and comforted her until the shuddering calmed. Then he held her away from him and studied her face. 'Tell me exactly what happened, Elissa. No lies. No evasions. I want to know everything.'

'He . . . I heard him coming, but I thought it was you. Then when I saw it was not, it was too late to run. He said . . . he said he needed company. When I struggled, he said he . . . he liked it. Oh Adam, I was so frightened.'

'Did he . . .' Adam swallowed, and when he spoke again his fingers dug so hard into her shoulders that she almost cried aloud. 'Did he rape you?'

She shook her head. 'But if you had not come when you did . . .' She buried her face against his chest and felt the warm, restoring strength flow into her.

'I would have killed him,' said Adam quietly, and she knew it to be true. With that knowledge came a different fear and her heart thudded fast and high in her throat. She looked past Adam to the motionless heap at the foot of the steps. No sound. No sign. Suppose he had already killed him? Oh God.

Then as she watched she saw the head move, the face slowly lift, the blurred eyes clear in the blood-streaked mask and stare straight at herself and Adam: Adam with his strong arm protectively around her shoulder, the other ready to beat back all attackers, and herself clinging to Adam in open love. Behind them the darkness of the wooden shed, its door standing fruitlessly open. It was no wonder that hate consumed that bruised and battered face.

'I'll get you for this. One day.' The voice was slurred and blood-choked, the words unmistakable. 'I'll know you again, wherever you try to hide. Breaking and entering. Assault when I tried to stop you. I'll see you swing, you bastard. You'll not escape me.'

He attempted to rise, struggled to one knee. Elissa snatched Adam's hand and ran, pulling him after her. Ran till the office building was far behind them, with the curing yard and the jetty and the herring barrels neatly stacked and ready for transport. Ran till they reached the curve of headland under the first of the dormitory huts, where the spring tides had eaten away the shore and made a little sheltered cove. Here they collapsed on to the soft white sand and drew long, shuddering breaths until their hearts slowed and their lungs could breathe again in quietness. There was blessed silence: the sea's whisper, the night's cool air. Only now and then a voice from one of the dormitory huts or from further along the shore where the Buckie girls had had their fire. The tang of wood ash still lingered. And inside Elissa's head, those terrible words, over and over. *I'll see you swing, you bastard. You'll not escape me.*

Adam's arm was around her shoulder, her head against his chest. She felt his heart beat slow and strong, but when he bent his head to kiss her, she turned to him with fear in her face, fear for him, not herself.

'You heard what he said, Adam. You must go, now, before it is too

74

late. Find another curer, another town. Quick, before he puts the law on to you.'

'What, and stand accused of trying to rape one of his workers? He wouldn't dare.'

'But you did strike him, Adam, and though I thank you with all my heart, it would be his word against ours. Who do you think the law would believe? They would hang you, Adam, and I could not bear it. Or send you to prison.'

Adam shrugged. 'He'll have to catch me first. And prove it. But maybe you're right. We were leaving anyway. What's another day?' But he had caught the urgency in her voice and it sobered him. 'You'd best keep well out of that villain's way, young Lissa. Promise? And I'll do the same. Just till things have blown over. He maybe won't remember much anyway. It was dark, after all, and he'd had a bottle or two.' Then he grinned with sudden glee. 'He'll have a fine pair of shiners in the morning or I'm not so good with my fists as I used to be. I wonder how he'll explain those away to his friends?'

'Oh Adam, my love, I am so frightened for you. Promise you will take care?'

'I promise. I could grow a beard, as a disguise,' he teased. 'Will you still love me with a beard?'

'You know I will, Adam. I will love you always and for ever. Whatever happens.' She looked up at him with such transparent truth that he was instantly sobered.

'Don't look so troubled, my sweet, serious love. Beard or not, he will never recognise me, Lissa, not with it being dark and him completely fou' with the drink. Don't worry, my sweet.' Then he kissed the tears from her eyes, murmured love and promises and kissed her again until the dawn light nudged at the horizon and Elissa knew he must go. For herself she did not care, but Adam must escape, quick, while there was still time.

'I'm not much of a hand with the pen, Elissa, so you're not to worry if you hear nothing from me. But we will meet again, my wee singing bird, very soon. Wick's a fine, big place, with room for everyone, and I know where Gibb's curing yard is. He's bound to go there next, like all the rest, and when he does, I'll find you, my love.'

'Are you sure it will be safe? Won't he come looking for you?' They both knew 'he' was not Brodie Gibb.

'If he does, he'll not catch me. Don't worry, Elissa. I can take care of myself, and of you. And if Gibb goes somewhere else instead of Wick, then we will meet in Yarmouth. Somehow we'll be together again before the season's over, I promise you.'

'Truly?' She looked up at him with brimming eyes.

'Truly.' He took her hand in his, kissed the palm and curled her fingers over the place. 'That's to remind you, my sweet one.'

'Now you must go, Adam. It is not safe to linger.'

'I'll go. When I've watched you safely into your own hut.'

She turned in the doorway, saw the still figure at the shore's edge raise a hand in farewell, and stepped resolutely inside.

It was only afterwards, as she bound a clean bandage round her throbbing wrist, that she remembered it was Sunday.

That last week there was a new air of frivolity over the curing yard as well as increased competition between Bethany's team and her own. Elissa worked faster than ever in spite of her bandaged wrist – or, when she saw Bethany looking at her, because of it – topping up barrels, adding brine, drowning her fears in physical exhaustion and feeling safe only when she was bending over her herring barrels, face out of sight. For suppose Hugh Sinclair came looking for her? Scoured the faces of all Gibb's employees, searching? Summoned her to his office in front of everyone and locked her inside? With him? Oh God. Her imaginings terrified her: but when she thought of what he might do to her precious Adam it was ten times worse. Yet she must smile at the others' jokes, pretend she was as excited as they were to be moving on, no matter where, and work even faster than her best. But whatever her speed, Suffie Lennox matched her.

'Working like the very devil she's been,' said a young fisherman whom Elissa recognised from a Sunday visit a while back, John Barron from South Square at home. 'I told her if her team didn't beat yours she'd get no goodbye kiss.'

'Cheeky devil,' grinned Suffie.

Elissa said quickly, 'Goodbye? When do we leave?'

'End of the week. Maybe sooner. Brodie Gibb says it's not worth staying now the fish are moving on so when all the topping up's done, we're off.'

Elissa's heart was thumping hard with anxiety, but before she could ask, Suffie told her.

'To Wick. It wouldn't be my choice, but Gibb's got a wee curing yard there and if you're feed to him for the season like the rest of us, you'll be coming too. Though rumour has it Gibb's leaving his golden boy behind.'

'Sending him home in disgrace, more like,' grinned John Barron. 'Fell down a flight of steps, dead drunk, so they say, and old Gibb finding a store of brandy bottles hidden in the office desk and put through the books as "sundries".'

'I heard it was a wager, in a gentlemen's club,' said Suffie. 'Something about a pugilist.'

'A punch-up more like,' sneered Bethany. 'Probably over a whore.'

In spite of her joy that they were to go to Wick, where Adam would be waiting for her, and that Sinclair would be left behind, Elissa felt her cheeks burn with guilt, but fortunately no one noticed. Yard gossip was too interesting.

A black eye anyway. And a broken nose. Might be an improvement really. Take the sneer off his face. Though he did have the decency not to show himself in church. Or anywhere else, come to that. Cowardice. Vanity more like.

As she listened, Elissa's fears calmed and hope came creeping back. They were going to Wick and Mr Sinclair was not. And he had not reported Adam after all. If he had, the whole island would have known it by now. Adam was safe, for the moment anyway, and perhaps for ever if he kept out of Mr Sinclair's way.

Aye, vanity. Reckon it's spoilt his precious profile for ever and him always preening in the nearest window-glass. He'll not forgive that. I pity the fellow who landed the blow. If it was a blow. He'll not sleep easy in his bed till he's a thousand miles away and out of reach.

The words jolted Elissa's new confidence, but only for a moment. They would be safe from discovery in Wick. Then perhaps they could run away together? Emigrate? To Canada or America or even Australia? Adam would know what best to do. With his loving arms around her all would be well: she could hardly bear the waiting. But there was work for her hands to do.

In the rush to be gone, everyone helped with the topping up, the draining of pickle from the bungholes and the pouring in again, while the coopers moved along the rows, fastening down the lids, checking the inspector's stamp on the side of the barrels and noting the packer's mark on the bottom, for the final tally. Completed barrels were loaded on to trolleys and restacked on the jetty for transport, uninspected ones lined up and the inspector summoned, unused ones stacked away with salt-tubs and the fish baskets that would travel with them to the next station. Then there was the totting up of barrels for the reckoning, and the scores of the individual crews. Bethany's and Jess's team were equal best, to the former's annoyance and the latter's delight.

'Who said we were dummies to pick our Lissa?' she crowed and Ina added, 'Aye, and she's brought us good luck in more ways than one.'

Ina smiled up at Fergus Mackie behind her and Elissa saw him slip an arm round her waist. It was their last afternoon and they were on the grass behind the huts: girls and menfolk together, gathered for a last celebration before the curing station closed and they all moved on. As she poured tea and handed round scones and slices of fruit bun, she thought only of Adam, who should have been here, with the rest. *Remember I'll be waiting for you*, he had said. Only a few days more, a week at the most, and they would be together again, his arms

77

around her and ... The thought made her weak with longing and excitement and love. Dear, brave Adam who had rescued her and put himself in danger. Please God keep him safe. Please God let Sinclair forget Adam's face. And hers. Please God keep Sinclair out of their lives. For ever.

Yesterday, she had walked into Lerwick with half a dozen other girls and bought wool for a gansey, as well as a beautiful shawl for Aunt Sarah, worked in gossamer navy wool. Now, she sat on the headland with the others and cast on the first of the stitches that would one day clothe her beloved Adam. She knew the measurements from the measure of her arms around him and though, with every stitch she knitted, her wrist burned and ached she welcomed the pain and yearned the more for Adam, pouring all her love for him into the garment and finding solace in the making of it. It reminded her of his love for her, kept loneliness at bay. Soon she would be with him again. Very soon. She held his promise in the palm of her hand.

She was still there an hour later, dreaming of Adam, half-listening to the chatter around her and working her steady way round the needles, when she saw her brother Tom approaching. He was walking fast, his face grave, and when he saw her he came straight towards her without a pause.

'Elissa, there's a message come from the Square at home. Aunt Sarah's ill and you're needed at home.'

To her shame, Elissa's first thought was for herself and Adam. Adam, who would be waiting for her, with love and expectation. Then she put the thought aside.

'Is she very ill?' She knew as she asked the question how futile it was. They would not have sent for her otherwise.

'Aye. Maggie Bain says she's failing fast and you're to go home on the first ferry tomorrow. Here's money for your passage,' and he gave her coins. 'You'd best pack your wee kist tonight, and I'll get one of the coopers to take it into Lerwick for you first thing. You'll likely get a lift on the cart as well.'

'But ... but ...' With a dismay that was turning rapidly to despair, Elissa saw her meeting with Adam recede into the distance and vanish. She would never see him again. Never. How could she when he dare not show his face in Aberdeen harbour for fear of Sinclair and she was to be bound to the confines of the Square?

She saw Tom looking at her with concern. 'I'm sorry, lass. I know it's a shock to you, but she hasn't been well for a while now. It's a pity the news came too late for today's ferry. I know you'll be counting the hours.'

With an effort she collected her thoughts. 'What will Mr Gibb say? And how will Jess and Ina manage without me?'

'They'll sort something out between them. You just get that kist packed, and say your goodbyes. I'll arrange the rest.'

There was much sympathy for Elissa and genuine regret – she was well liked in the yard and her worth recognised – but it was their last day in Lerwick and after the first flurry of concern, the company split up into twos and threes, some going into the town for a last look around; others strolling on the headland, or in the countryside behind the huts. Elissa was collecting plates and cups, her shoulders drooping and her heart fighting against despair, when she heard Joseph's voice at her side.

'I've heard the news and I'm sorry, Elissa. We'll miss you. I know you have to pack, but first will you walk with me a while?'

She was too distracted and too polite to say no, though all she really wanted was to throw herself on to her bunk and weep with loneliness and loss. But when Joseph turned northwards, towards the open countryside, she hung back. She had seen several couples heading that way, including Ina and Fergus Mackie not five minutes ago and she had no wish to intrude, or to remind herself so painfully of what she had lost.

'I would rather walk into Lerwick, Joseph, for a last look round.'

If Joseph was disappointed he did not show it. 'As you wish.' He tucked her arm under his, asked solicitously about her cut wrist and how it was healing, expressed repeated regret about her aunt's illness, sorrow that Elissa was leaving them, promised to look in and see her the next time he was in Aberdeen, and then, as they walked the familiar road into Lerwick, talked about the profits of the season so far and the prospects for the months to come.

'Our family boats are our own, fully paid for . . . we plan to change one for a bigger next season . . . a Zulu of fifty or sixty feet, with new, lightweight cotton nets . . . negotiate a loan with Brodie Gibb . . .'

Elissa, not listening, murmured something appropriate from time to time, but her mind was elsewhere, with Adam. Had he reached Wick in safety? Was Mr Sinclair really being sent to Aberdeen, and if so for how long? For the rest of the season, or only for as long as it took his bruises to heal? *Spoilt his precious profile for ever – he'll not forgive that.* Suppose he was sent to Wick after all, and Adam not suspecting anything? While she, Elissa, was a prisoner in the Square of the city which Adam must avoid at all costs, and was powerless to help him. She would ask Ina to give Adam a message. Tell him where she was. But suppose he thought she wanted him to come to Aberdeen, to see her? And Sinclair was waiting? Her thoughts darted this way and that, finding no comfort and no peace.

But they had strolled as far as the south end of town, where a number of houses seemed to be built into the sea. Joseph was explaining that they had once been loading piers, before the harbour

79

was made, when he suddenly stopped, cleared his throat and said, 'Elissa, may I visit you in North Square?'

'Of course.' He had done so often enough in the past, being her brother Tom's friend. But the mention of the Square reminded her. 'It is time I went home, Joseph. I have packing to do.'

He opened his mouth to speak, changed his mind, and instead took her arm and walked her home in silence. When they reached the hut, the other girls were not yet back, but she did not invite him in. He said goodbye to her at the door, kissed her hesitantly on the cheek, wished her a safe passage and promised to visit her soon, in North Square.

Elissa watched him out of sight, but instead of Joseph she saw in her mind's eye Adam Grant, burnished hair gleaming, thigh-boots supple with oil, long limbs vibrant with animal warmth and vitality. So lost was she in her day-dream that she willed him to turn his head, just once, so that she could see his dear, beloved face. At the dip where the headland curved round to the shore he did: only it was Joseph's face that looked back at her, not Adam's.

She turned abruptly away and stepped into the hut where her open kist awaited her. It was a matter of minutes to fill it and rope it securely. Now all that remained to do in the morning was to roll up her bedding, say her goodbyes, and leave happiness and the herring summer behind her, perhaps for ever.

CHAPTER 8

Elissa had forgotten the Square could be so quiet. Some of the menfolk, like the Downies, Nobles and Bains, were away at the herring fishing; some at the traditional long-line fishing which kept them at sea for days in a row. Others were pilots in the harbour, worked in the shipbuilding yards on the quay, or in the smokehouses, fishmarket or other fish-related trades. They left home in the small hours and were away all day, and though many of the wives and children remained, it was a far cry from the bustle of the gutting yard.

Elissa missed it, missed the company of Jess and Ina and the others. Even of Bethany. Missed the warm constriction of the hard bunk bed and the constant fight for sleeping space. Missed the cheerful, hectic, relentless routine. Most of all, she missed Sundays and the sweet privacy of heathland or shore, with Adam.

Instead, she had a cold truckle bed in an empty room and the company of the living dead.

Aunt Sarah, as Jess's mother Maggie Bain explained in a sepulchral whisper, had had a wee shock. 'Left her half paralysed, poor soul, and lucky for her the door was open and Bessie Guyan saw her fall. And lucky for us she was skin and bone already or we'd not have been able to lift her into her bed. We called the doctor laddie, but he said it was too late and there's nought he can do. If the shock doesn't kill her, the wasting disease will. So we sent for you. He said to put her in the hospital if you couldn't manage.'

'I'll manage.'

'Aye, we reckoned you would, being a good wee lassie and your aunt bringing you up like you was her own child. She's not wanting to die in a hospital bed, among strangers. And there's always folk to help out if you need.'

Bessie Guyan's Eppie, well recovered from the fever which had cost her her packer's job, had taken the next train north to Wick, to take Elissa's place, and would go with the rest of them to Yarmouth when the time came. The thought was almost more than Elissa could bear.

It was the loneliness she found hardest to endure. The loneliness and the smell. Not the familiar fish-reek of the curing yard, but an insidious sour and sickly smell which caught the breath in her throat and curled her nostrils, no matter how hard she strove to conceal her distaste. The fire's warmth did not help, nor the animal smell of drying wool as the blankets steamed in front of the grate, and increasingly she found reasons not only to keep the door standing open, but to step outside for a breath of clean air.

On either side of her were neat, one-storey houses like their own; in front, across the little gardens and wooden sheds, more houses. Fisherfolk, like herself, bound together by custom and tradition, by ties of blood and of trade: boats shared, work shared, lives shared. An enclosed world, offering no escape.

North and South Squares had been built by the Council at the beginning of the century, to house the fisherfolk of old Footdee when their land was needed for harbour development. New Footdee was regarded by the Council as a model of town planning, each Square consisting of four sides of one-storey terraced cottages built with no doors or windows on the outer walls so that all backs were turned to the elements and the outside world, all fronts to the inner Square and each other. Footdee folk liked to keep themselves to themselves.

Inside the Square and safe from townsers' eyes, little gardens had sprouted over the years, with flowers and shell-patterned paths, wooden huts for smoking fish or storing nets, and the busy life of the fisher community carried on, much as it had done in Old Footdee. Most cottages housed a family of eight or nine and sometimes two families under the one roof, so life inevitably spilled out into the Square and privacy was rare.

As her eyes ranged over this familiar, crowded cage Elissa ached for the headland above Gremista, for the clear skies of Shetland and the clean wind, for Adam's arm at her waist and the close, enveloping warmth of his skin against hers.

Instead, she had Aunt Sarah with the smell of death in her bones, and these kindly, suffocating neighbours.

'She's not been right for a while now,' they told her. 'Thin as a rake and not eating and that cough of hers, on and on all night. Mrs Duthie next door says it fair drives her wild.'

Mrs Bain, mother of five daughters and as many sons, took up the tale. 'Last Friday it was and the sun shining, and everyone with their doors open and having a good sweep out, when Mrs Guyan says to me, "Look over there, Maggie. What's that Robertson wifie doing?" and I looks and there's your poor aunt, leaning on her besom and swaying and then she falls, thump, to the ground.'

'Thump, to the ground,' echoed Mrs Guyan with cheerful relish. A thin, black-haired woman, with no front teeth, she had given birth to

82

a dozen children, and lost eight of them before they reached adolescence, but remained uncomplaining and always ready to help out a neighbour, especially with a birth, or a death.

'Well, we gets her into her bed,' continued Maggie Bain, 'and my Nellie fetches the doctor. A wee shock, he says. Not fatal, but it has affected her limbs, he says, and she'll not be able to look after herself. Then he says, quiet like, fatal or not, with the consumption so far gone in her chest she'll not see the summer out. We'd best get her into the hospital, he says, but you could see she was set against it and who wouldn't be. No, she keeps saying, when she's collected her wits and found the use of her tongue again. I'll go to no heathen hospital. I'll die in my own bed, she says, over and over. In my own Christian bed. So we sent a message to your father, to send you home. We reckoned it was what your aunt wanted and what you would want too, when you knew.'

Over and over they told her the same story, as if to compensate her for not being there herself. Over and over till Elissa feared if she heard the tale one more time she would scream. Yet somehow she managed to say, over and over in reply, 'Thank you. You did quite right.'

'She's awful weak, mind, and barely able to leave her bed,' said Maggie Bain, 'but we'll give you a hand, lass, any time. My Jess and even my Ina, wee devil that she is, say as how you're the best packer in the yard and they wants you back, soon as you're free. But I told them: she's a good wee lassie, that one. She'll not put her poor auntie into any hospital to die, no matter what. So if ever you want a wee minute's peace and quiet to yourself, or a trip up town to the shops, me and Bessie Guyan will come in and sit with her.'

But her aunt's illness and her own misery were not for the Square to see and she would manage alone. She owed it to her aunt, and it was her duty.

For Aunt Sarah was clearly dying, her life ebbing slowly away on an inexorable tide which no one could halt. Instead of the ram-rod strength of rectitude and the unbending guidance along the straight and narrow path which had characterised Sarah Downie Robertson for as long as Elissa could remember, there was a frail and utterly dependent bundle of bones whose anguished eyes, if they were trying to command, did not succeed, and whose tongue was pitifully hampered and unsure.

But Elissa talked to her in the same respectful tones she had always used, read a passage of the Bible to her every day, washed her, spooned gruel into her, brushed and combed her hair, while the bones grew more brittle and the skin withered until she was little more than a skeleton and Elissa could easily lift her unaided from the sodden bed. Then she would peel off the damp and acrid nightgown, sponge her aunt clean, with embarrassed apologies and reassurances that there was no one in the house to see her nakedness, dress her in fresh linen, tuck the shawl which she had brought from Lerwick round her pitiful shoulders and prop her up with cushions in a chair beside the fire while she stripped the bed and made it up again with dry blankets and fresh bed-sheets.

Then, when her aunt was settled back into bed, Elissa would heave the basket of soiled bedclothes on to her hip and carry them out to the shed at the foot of their small strip of garden. Every house in the Square had a garden, most of them ending, like the Downies', in a wooden shed of one kind or another. The Nobles' shed had a constant plume of smoke from its lum, with the scent of smoking haddock on the air. The Bains' had a whole jaw-bone, filched from some long-ago whale carcass and set on end to form an arch over the gate. Old Isaac Bain's father had been a whaler in his time. Other strips had roses, marigolds, forget-me-nots, carnations. Paths edged with scallop shells. One, China Christie's, had conch shells and coral. Yet others were festooned with herring nets, or cluttered with baskets of coiled lines – small lines for the winter fishing, long lines for the summer – and their sheds housed bundles of horsehair for the tippens, or hanks of rope. Elissa had moved her father's and brothers' lines out of the way, since her aunt's illness, to make more room for her wash tubs. There was a strict rota for the wash-house itself, with its copper boiler and great iron mangle, and she could not always slip in an extra turn. So she managed as best she could, with hot water from the kettle and cold from the pump.

In the middle of the Square, towering high above this jumble of gardens and garden sheds, stood the Mission Hall where for many years Aunt Sarah had instructed the younger Sunday school children in the Catechism. As often as possible, Elissa left the house door open, officially so that her aunt might see this inspiring building and hear the voices of the women gossiping over their knitting, or mending the fishing nets or any other of the never-ending tasks their lives involved. Unofficially, to clear the fetid air, though sooner or later a neighbour would say, 'You'd best close that door lass, for the wind's awful cold today,' and once she overheard, 'Trying to kill the old besom off, likely, and who could blame her.'

The washing was her best excuse. It was hard work, but Elissa welcomed it. The air and the soap suds seemed to scour her body of the sickness which permeated the very walls of the cottage and turned her own stomach increasingly queasy. She welcomed the steam, the caustic sting in her nostrils from the carbolic soap, the clean shock of the icy rinsing water, the whole, exhausting process.

When it was her turn at the wash-house, it was easy. Someone would have been before her and left the fire under the copper already burning. Often, the copper itself would be filled and waiting, and there were always women around to give a hand with the huge iron mangle. But for the rest of the time, she managed alone, in the privacy of her own garden shed.

Then, Elissa fetched water from the pump, carried out the boiling kettle to pour into the tub, refilled and replaced the kettle over the fire, checked that Aunt Sarah was comfortable, fetched more water for the tub where she would do the rinsing, scrubbed the soiled linen with a bar of carbolic soap, rubbing the cloth against the ridged wood of the washboard, before poking it down with a pair of long wooden tongs till the suds frothed. She would go back to the house to see if her aunt needed anything, then settle down to the hard work of what had become the daily wash. Scrubbing, soaking, rinsing, twisting, and finally taking the wash out on to the green behind the houses to dry.

'I cannot help it, Aunt Sarah,' she explained to the skeletal woman in the box bed. 'I know you worry what the neighbours will think, but we have not enough bed-linen to last the week and I will not have you lie in damp sheets.' Then, to counter what she knew would be her aunt's objections, she added, 'Suppose the Minister were to call?'

But she could not do the blankets alone and usually Bessie Guyan or Maggie Bain helped her. They would take one end of the dripping blanket each and twist and twist till the blanket resembled an anchor rope and they could squeeze not one more drip out of it. Then untwist it, shake it vigorously by the corners and spread it out on the grass if it was fine; if not, string it up in front of the fire.

'You'll need to buy more rubber sheeting,' said Maggie Bain one morning, after a particularly heavy wash-load. They were standing on the green behind the cottages, with the blankets and sheets spread out around them on the sandy grass and weighted with stones at the corners against the fresh sea wind. Just over the rim, not twenty yards away, was the clean sand of the shore. A wide, fresh sweep of it, for the tide was out. Sea birds strolled about the glistening sand, inspecting the scattered debris of beached seaweed and scoured scraps of driftwood. Others paddled in the shallows, or rode lightly on the curving water. Far out on the skyline she could see the outline of a fishing boat.

Adam, where are you? Come and rescue me, Adam, my love, my husband.

'You'll get it in Pratt's or Campbell's.' Mrs Bain's motherly voice dragged her back to reality. 'One shilling a yard, Bessie says, and I reckon a trip up into the town will do you good, with you looking peely-wally and sick these last few days, and that cut on your wrist not healed properly even yet. And not like to heal with your arms forever up to the oxters in soapy water. So away you go, lass. Bessie and I'll easy watch your auntie for you till you get back. And while you're there,' she added, casting her eyes in the direction of the Downies' open door and lowering her voice, 'you could get yourself a nice bit of black crêpe, for it'll not be long before you're needing it.'

That last sentence checked temptation. 'Thank you, Mrs Bain, but I couldn't leave her. Not when . . .'

'Suit yourself,' shrugged Mrs Bain, but she was clearly offended.

'It's just that if she died while I was out . . .' faltered Elissa.

'I know, lass, I know.' Offence forgotten, Mrs Bain put a kindly arm round Elissa's shoulders and for a brief and blissful moment Elissa hid her face in the woman's aproned chest and let the tears spill over. Then she straightened and brushed the back of her hand impatiently across her eyes.

'I am sorry, Mrs Bain. I'm tired, I suppose, and . . .'

'There's no need to explain, lassie. The whole Square knows how hard you work and a few tears are nothing. And if you'd rather stay with your auntie, then my Nellie can easy nip up into the town and do your wee purchases for you, no bother. But just remember, the offer's always there.'

With that thought to sustain her, Elissa fought down her revulsion and resumed her nursing: washed and tended her aunt, read the Bible to her, prayed, spooned warm milk between the bloodless, wrinkled lips, changed bed-sheets and linen, brushed the long grey wisps of hair and plaited them up again into a braid which was thin as a candle's wick. Aunt Sarah submitted to everything with a silent, angry pride which wrenched Elissa's heart.

When the fishing ended at Wick, several of the men, including James Downie and his sons, came home for a brief respite. 'And to see how you're managing, lassie.' They would go north again in a couple of days, to join the rest at Fraserburgh, where they could be easily reached – the implication was, for the funeral – before the autumn migration south, to Yarmouth. It took all Elissa's self-control not to pray that she would be free by then, to go with them.

But she welcomed their brief visit as a breath of pure, life-giving air and though the house was hushed in deference to the invalid and dutifully teetotal, for two short days there was a little life and light about the place again, instead of brooding death. She listened intently for mention of Adam, or of James Hay, but heard nothing, and dared not ask.

Neighbours looked in for a chat, no longer in hushed murmurs on the doorstep, but at the fireside with James Downie, Davie, William or Tom, and though they invariably bore the men away with them, about some unspecified 'business', they drank tea first and exchanged family news. William was to marry his Eyemouth girl at the end of the year, Ina Bain was engaged to her cooper laddie and if the herring

86

season was as good as it promised to be, they would marry too. Suffie Lennox's brother Wallace was courting Meg Duthie. Gideon Noble's second cousin had moved to Grimsby, to be skipper of a steam trawler. Gideon Noble himself did not approve of steam trawlers: the works of the devil, he called them, that would bring only misery and damnation. He had brought his boat home, like the Downie men, for essential work on the nets and to see his family, and on the second evening Joseph Noble called to collect Elissa's brother Tom, and lingered to talk.

Steam was uppermost in their conversation, for the gossip was that work was afoot to form a syndicate in the town to buy a steam trawler that would operate out of Aberdeen. Easton Sinclair was behind it with that fellow Gibb, though with the profits they were making from the herring it could only be greed that drove them. The steamer would trawl for white fish, but everyone feared that if the power of steam was successful there, then the herring drifters would be next. The money would be put up on shore, a captain and engineer hired on a profit-share basis, and the rest would be no more than hired labourers.

'And where's the satisfaction in that?' demanded Joseph, whose own boat had been one of the highest earners of the season so far, and whose own crew had shared equally in the profits. 'I know my men wouldn't stand for it, and nor would I.'

Others apparently had no choice. Rumour had it that many of the trawlers down south scoured orphanages and remand homes to find a crew when honest fishermen refused. It was a sobering thought, but the power of steam meant greater catches and far greater profit. A steam-driven trawler could range much further afield than a sailing boat, even as far as Icelandic waters, and be away from home not for one or two weeks only, as at present, but for months at a time.

'And what are the women supposed to do, with their menfolk away half the year?' demanded Maggie Bain, who had looked in 'in passing'.

'Make the most of it when we come home,' grinned one of the men and there was a shout of laughter, before an anxious 'Ssh!' from Elissa reminded them and they dropped their voices accordingly.

Joseph was upholding the virtue of the share system which operated in the herring fleet and which rewarded hard work with hard cash. Into the pockets of the men who had earned it, not those of the idle bosses ashore. And the herring catches were good this season. Over a hundred and forty thousand barrels so far. There had been a bit of trouble here and there over the small size of some of the fish and Brodie Gibb had refused some boats, but they had been over their quota anyway and the trouble had blown over. Elissa tried to listen with full concentration, but it took all her will-power not to grab Joseph's arm, shake him into silence and demand, 'Where is Adam?'

She resisted, and the need to keep one eye always on her aunt was a help, but even so, when he stood up to take his leave and her brother Tom went off to look for his jacket, she could not help herself.

'Do you ... have you seen anything of ... of Adam Grant?' They were standing on the doorstep, waiting for Tom. She had turned her face to the life-giving breeze and did not see the sudden darkening of his brow.

'I heard he went south,' he said carefully.

'Who?' demanded Tom from behind him, one arm in his jacket sleeve.

When Joseph did not immediately answer, but instead stepped outside into the Square, Elissa, who had meant to say, 'No one,' heard herself say, 'Adam Grant.'

'James Hay's laddie? He went somewhere, certainly, and he went in a hurry, but no one knows where. I know James Hay wasn't too pleased about it. No one wants to lose a good crewman in the middle of the season and whatever else he was, young Grant was a good fisherman.'

Adam, gone. Oh God, how would she find him again?

'There's no need to look so dismayed, Lissa lass. That kind always fall on their feet and he'll have found himself another berth soon enough. He's likely in Yarmouth already, waiting to be first off the mark when the season opens.'

'What do you mean, "that kind"?' Elissa had not meant to say anything, but even in the relief of hearing the word 'Yarmouth' she could not stand by and let her own brother slander Adam.

'Nothing, Lissa lass,' soothed Tom. 'I meant nothing. Only that he's a sociable, high-spirited sort of a fellow who likes his dram.'

'As do most men,' said Elissa, her voice deadly quiet and trembling with the effort of keeping control as a new fear seized her. Suppose Sinclair had tracked Adam down? In a bar where he was enjoying himself, all unsuspecting, with his friends? And had ... had ... but she could not put her worst fear into words, even unspoken ones.

'Tom meant no criticism, Elissa,' said Joseph Noble, misreading her expression. 'All young men get high-spirited now and then and forget themselves. I'm sure I did so myself at his age.'

Elissa found this difficult to believe, but she was grateful to Joseph for taking Adam's part.

'Aye, that's all I meant,' agreed Tom. 'A wee bit happy-go-lucky and carefree. Young Grant's likely fixed himself up with a new boat already – and is gambling the shirt off his back in some Yarmouth quayside pub at this very minute. Which reminds me, Joe,' and here

88

he winked at Elissa, 'we have a bit of business to see to down the road. Are you coming?'

The men were not home long, and most of the time was spent outwith the house. There were things to see to: nets to be treated, old nets to be checked over and put away, new ones taken out and inspected. There were always new nets for Yarmouth.

'And with you being busy, lass, with your aunt, we knew you'd not have the time to mend them for us,' her father had told her. 'So we came home to see to them ourselves. And to see her,' he added, lowering his voice and with a jerk of the head in Aunt Sarah's direction. 'All you have to do, Elissa lass, when the time comes, is to tell Maggie Bain to get a message to her Isaac, who'll tell me.' Then her father had said, 'You're a good wee lassie,' and put his arm briefly round her shoulder in the nearest he ever came to overt affection.

Then the men were gone again and she and Aunt Sarah were once more alone. The house was colder and bleaker without them, her aunt more pitifully frail. But soon Elissa found she had more than pity to contend with. For the weaker and more dependent her aunt became, the clearer and sharper grew her tongue. It was, after all, her only weapon against the shame.

'I am sorry, Aunt Sarah,' said Elissa, fighting back the tears of exhaustion as she struggled to change the drawsheet under her aunt on a late afternoon a week later. 'But you taught me yourself that cleanliness is next to Godliness. And I know that nakedness is wicked in your eyes, but you cannot lie in a wet nightgown. Suppose the Minister were to call?'

But this usually soothing argument only produced a new anxiety, and though the querulous words were daily more faint and dis-jointed, Elissa had grown adept at translating.

'Is the floor swept and the dresser polished? I did not see you black-leading the grate this morning. Do it now, quick, before the Minister comes. And the brass candlesticks are awful dull-looking. Are you sure you polished them?' It did not matter that Elissa said yes to every question: her aunt had always another waiting.

'The window-glass could do with a shine, and have you scrubbed the step?'

'Yes, Aunt Sarah,' said Elissa with weary calm, though it was all she could do not to scream aloud. 'I have scrubbed the step.'

'I didn't see you do it. Are you sure?'

'Of course I'm sure. There!' and she flung open the door, as much for air as anything else. 'You can see for yourself.'

'There is no need to shout, child. And shut the door. You are always trying to freeze me to death. I'll die soon enough without that.'

Elissa bit her lip hard to quell the hysteria which threatened to overflow at any moment and almost fell out of the house, but by a huge effort of will managed to close the door quietly behind her. Then she stood, filling her lungs with clean sea air and praying over and over for patience, before she crossed the little strip of garden to the shed and her wash tub. And was suddenly, unexpectedly sick.

When she returned, her aunt greeted her with, 'I don't know what's come over you, Elissa. You always used to be such a helpful child. Now it is nothing but rudeness and impatience.'

Elissa said nothing, being too drained and weary to do anything except sink into the chair beside the hearth and close her eyes. But upbringing was too strong. Within a minute, she had picked up her knitting and after the first leaden stitches, worked steadily until the tension drained out of her and her spirit calmed. South, Joseph had said. To Yarmouth. Adam had gone early, so as to be first at the herring fishing. It would be like him to do that. And if he had left James Hay, it was because Mr Sinclair was in Wick and it was not safe to stay. She wished he had written to her, but he was not much of a one with a pen, he had said so himself, and he had told her not to worry.

Adam had gone south to find himself a new berth and to work and save so that they could be married. And as soon as she was free, she would go to him, to work and save as he was doing so that in November, when her brother William married, and Ina Bain and the others, Elissa would be married too. To Adam Grant whom she loved, and who loved her.

Comforted by the thought, she knitted quietly on as the light left the sky and a twilit silence settled over the cottage. She heard voices in the Square outside. Laughter. A child crying. The thud of booted feet. A door closing. All the ordinary sounds of ordinary life, while here in the cottage there was only an ill old woman who filled the air with the scent of death.

Adam where are you? Come and rescue me, my love. Take me back to Yarmouth with you. I want life and laughter again, and love. I am knitting the secret patterns of love into your gansey, here, where it will lie across your heart.

She held the woollen garment briefly against her cheek to find comfort in its soft warmth, drew a long breath of faith, then set it aside. Adam loved her. One day they would be together again.

She rose, lit the lamp, stirred the pan which was simmering gently at the side of the fire, then tasted the milky gruel. She ladled a little into a wooden basin, put the basin on to a cloth-covered tray and carried it to the bed.

'Time for your bedtime gruel, Aunt Sarah. Let me lift you a little higher in the bed.'

Compassion flooded through her as she slipped an arm under her aunt's shoulders and felt the shoulder-blades sharp under the parchment skin. The old woman weighed so little, her body frail as an autumn leaf.

'It's not too hot, Aunt Sarah. I've tasted it. So open your mouth.'

'I'm not a child,' the old woman grumbled, but she did as she was told. After three small spoonfuls she pushed the bowl away. 'Enough. I'm not hungry.'

'Please, Aunt Sarah? Just one more spoonful? For me?'

'Go away, for pity's sake. Leave me alone.' She fell back on the pillows, eyes closed. Elissa hesitated, then picked up the tray and was about to slip away when she heard her aunt speak.

'I'm sorry, child. You have always been a good lassie and I know you do your best. If I snap at you, it is the illness talking, not me. Promise you will remember that?'

'Of course I will, Aunt Sarah. Now I'm going to say a wee prayer for you and turn down the lamp, so you can sleep.'

Weary to exhaustion with the tensions of another endless day, Elissa washed, brushed her hair, and slipped into the narrow truckle bed in the next-door room. The room was her father's and brothers', when they were not away at the fishing, and was cold with their absence, especially now when they had so recently been home. But she could not bear to sleep ever again in the same room as her aunt, in spite of the firelight's comfort. For nothing could obliterate that all-pervasive smell of death which caught at her throat and made her gorge rise no matter how she fought against it.

Remembering, she savoured the cool, slightly musty air of the bedroom with particular pleasure, picking out the dry scent of wicker baskets, the oil of rope, the faintly fishy odour which always clung to the nets no matter how well they were redded. The other room had a whitewashed ceiling – her aunt had insisted – but not this one. Above her in the rafters she could make out the shapes of the rolled nets, newly put away, the wicker skulls which held the coiled lines for the winter fishing, and all the paraphernalia of the fisherman's life. It was a comforting sight and the rafters reminded her of the gutting hut at Gremista. And of Adam Grant. She fell asleep smiling.

She woke reluctantly and too soon, jerked out of sleep by a voice calling her.

'I'm coming, Aunt Sarah.' She wrapped a plaid around her and padded into the next room, to see her aunt lying rigid in bed, her face turned to the wall. With the usual sinking of the heart she recognised the signs.

'Why didn't you call me sooner, Aunt Sarah, so I could help you on to the chamber pot?' But her aunt only averted her face, staring angrily at the wall. Elissa glanced at the window: the short summer night was already over, the sky golden with dawn.

'I'll just finish dressing, then I'll be back.'

But when, fully dressed and clean-aproned, she bent over her aunt's bed to strip the wet nightgown from her, her nostrils filled with the acrid smell of urine and she felt her stomach heave. She clapped a hand to her mouth and ran into the little back scullery where she retched over a pail until the nausea passed. Then she rinsed her mouth, splashed her face with cold water, took a deep breath and went back into the room.

Her aunt was no longer studying the wall in shame, but stared straight at her niece with a new expression, from hard, accusing eyes.

'I'm sorry, Aunt Sarah. I don't know what came over me,' said Elissa, attempting a smile. 'But I'll have you clean and comfortable again in no time. Now let me see if I can take off your nightgown with the blanket still covering you. To keep out the draught.'

It was a fiction Elissa had invented for the sake of her aunt's modesty, but when Elissa bent over her aunt to undo her nightgown buttons, the old woman's hands flashed upwards, grabbed Elissa by the collar and pulled her close. Her eyes glittered like granite as she spat out the words.

'*You have been with a man!*'

CHAPTER 9

For a terrified moment Elissa thought her aunt demented, or caught in the clutch of death, then as she understood the words she smiled with relief.

'Yes, Aunt Sarah,' she said, with happy innocence. 'His name is Adam and he is a fisherman. You will like him. I know you will.'

Her aunt struck her hard across the face, then fell back gasping on to the pillow. But though her body's strength was exhausted, her eyes still held their blazing fury.

'I never thought it of you, Elissa. You have disgraced me. And yourself.'

Elissa stared, one hand to her stinging cheek. 'But I don't understand,' she faltered. 'How have I – '

'Not understand? You harlot!' She tried to strike Elissa again, but her hand fell weakly back on to the blanket. Instead, she channelled all her venom into words. 'Fornication and wickedness. Sins of the flesh and of the devil.'

Apart from the bright red weal on her cheek, Elissa was white-faced with shock and a growing indignation born of a lifetime's dutiful and always virtuous submission. 'I do not think you should speak such words to me,' she said, very quietly. 'Adam and I are to marry – '

'Are to? Are to?' The old woman's voice was half scream, half croak. 'You fool. Where is the fellow now, tell me that? Over the seas and far away. And there he'll stay.'

Elissa's heart chilled at the words, then swelled hot with outrage. Adam was far away, just as she said, but for the best of reasons. The moment it was safe to do so, they would meet again. He had promised.

'I cannot let you say such things about Adam. He is a good man, Aunt Sarah. When the season is over, he will marry me.'

'Good? Good men don't lie with women before they're wed.'

'But he does not! He – '

Her aunt's shriek ripped like a gutting knife through Elissa's defence. 'Good men don't marry whores.'

93

'Hush, Aunt Sarah,' warned Elissa, alarmed by her aunt's agitation. 'You must not excite yourself. And you misunderstand. Adam loves me, as I love him. That is all there is to say. Now let me – ' She reached out a hand to continue with the shaming business of changing her aunt's sodden nightdress, but that demented creature clutched the bedclothes to her skeletal chest and screamed, with all the breathless weakness of her wasted lungs, 'Keep away. Don't dare to touch me, you whore of Babylon.'

'But I only want to – '

'Whore! Get out of my house. You'll not give birth to your bastard under my roof.'

Elissa's patience snapped. 'My father's roof, not yours. I have as much right as you to be here and here I'll stay. Until my father tells me to leave.'

Her aunt's face was the colour of death. 'How dare you speak such words to me,' she gasped, fighting for breath. 'I'll not let ... I'll ... dis ...' One hand still clutching the blankets to her chin, with the other she fumbled in growing agitation at the side of the bed, fingers plucking and probing at the mattress edge.

'What is it you want, Aunt? Let me get it for you.'

But as her niece took a step towards the bed, the old woman cried out, 'No!' and the blazing fury in her eyes pinned Elissa where she stood.

'It's only me, Aunt Sarah,' she soothed, while her heart thudded fast with fear. The woman's eyes were evil. Twin blades, stabbing and turning. But she forced herself to speak, with gentleness and calm. 'I am your niece, Elissa. I want to make you more comfortable, that is all.'

Deliberately, she made herself reach out an almost steady hand to peel the bed-sheet back, but the old woman snatched it and herself away, clawing like a crab backwards in the tumbled sheets, her eyes still nailed to Elissa's face.

'Keep ... away ... you wh ...' She struggled in vain to force the word out, opening and shutting her mouth on a travesty of gurgled speech, fingers clutching at her breast. Then suddenly the eyes rolled upwards, the hands twitched and jumped, and Aunt Sarah fell back on to the pillows, one arm outflung in accusation.

Elissa stared at her aunt in horror, while the skeletal head with its wisps of grey tipped sideways to face the wall and a thin trickle of spittle whitened the corner of the open mouth and slid slowly towards the chin.

Silence spread over the room; a silence thick with awe and freedom and emptiness and pity. The fire stirred suddenly, a flame spurted

94

and settled, and Elissa felt her eyes prickle with unwilling tears as a sense of helpless outrage caught her by the throat. Suddenly, she could not bear the continuing accusation of that outflung hand. What had happened between her aunt and herself was private, too unjust and shameful for the public gaze. She must move it before they saw. Lay it peacefully on her aunt's dead breast.

Nevertheless, it seemed a lifetime before she summoned the courage to touch that terrifying hand. Suppose it grabbed hold of her and . . . Elissa shuddered. She counted ten – and touched.

The skin was cold, the hand lifeless. Overwhelming relief flooded through her. She wanted to laugh and cry together. She was free. And her poor, suffering aunt was at peace at last.

Carefully, she lifted the dead leaf of a hand and laid it on her aunt's thin chest beside the other. Like the hands of an effigy. As if her aunt had been saying her prayers. That was better. More dignified and fitting. Now the eyes. She took a deep and steadying breath. They must be closed, Bessie Guyan said, or they would stay for ever open, staring . . . Oh God. She shuddered in remembered horror.

But it must be done. She took a deep breath of courage, leant over the twisted figure – and started back with a cry of terror. Two granite eyes gleamed with undiminished venom from the speechless, twisted face.

Elissa never knew how long she crouched, shuddering, by the damped-down fire. How long it was before she drove herself to open up that fire, add more coals, fill the kettle and swing it into place over the hottest flame. To mix water and oatmeal for porridge. Make tea. Drink one scalding cup. Pray over and over for strength.

But no matter how she forced herself, she could not approach that bed. She knew she ought to do something, wash her aunt's face, change the drawsheet under her, smooth the pillows, comb that wisp of hair. Ought to make her decent for the doctor and the Minister. But she was powerless to do any of these things. If she managed to summon even a shred of courage, she had only to glimpse the bed with its venomous, damning burden for fear to paralyse her once more.

It was her neighbour, Mrs Duthie, who broke the spell.

'Is everything all right, Lissa lass?' she cried, with a knock at the closed door. 'I thought I heard shouting a while back.' When there was no answer, the woman pushed open the door.

'And there was the poor lassie, crouched by the fire, shivering and shaking and fair paralysed with shock,' she told the ladies later. 'So I sits her down and feeds her hot tea with a good peck of sugar to it. I'd have put in whisky too, if I could have seen any, poor wee lassie.

95

There, there, I says to her, it's a shock, I know, but a happy release, and not before time. But the lass just stares at me with those big eyes of hers, all innocent and frightened. Your auntie's suffered enough, I says, and is at peace. I thought she was dead, see. But when I goes to look at the old wifie, there's her eyes staring like one of the devils in hell. It fair chilled my bones. No wonder the lass was feared. So I shouted for my Billy to fetch Mrs Bain and Mrs Guyan, quick.'

Those capable women instantly took over. 'Away home with you, Ina,' they told Mrs Duthie. 'You've a family to see to and we'll easy manage here. But you'll maybe look in again later.' Then they closed the door behind her, cutting out light and life and all the busy normality of the Square.

They washed her aunt's face, tidied the pillows, straightened the blankets on the bed. 'Best not to do more till the doctor laddie's been,' they told Elissa. 'We'll strip the bed and tidy her up after.' Then they sat with Elissa and drank tea while they waited.

The doctor came and went again, leaving no hope and little cheer.

'Only a matter of hours now. Nothing more to be done, Miss Downie, but constant care, of course. Constant care.'

'As if she hasn't given the old besom enough already,' murmured Bessie Guyan, 'and the poor wee lassie half dead with the strain.'

The Minister came, said a prayer, and left again. Elissa made more tea then put milk into a pan to warm. Somehow she would find the courage to hold it to her aunt's lips. Somehow. Behind her back, the women whispered together, and when she turned to refill their cups, she saw their kindly faces beaming.

'We've been thinking, Bess and me,' began Mrs Bain. 'You've had a heavy time of it, lass, since you came back from Shetland, and not a day's rest.'

'And nothing but these four walls for company,' added Mrs Guyan, 'and up all hours of the night. And don't deny it for we've all seen your lamp lit when you should have been long abed.'

'And now a shock like this,' resumed Mrs Bain. 'So Bess and me, we're packing you off for the afternoon, up into the town, for a wee break, while we give your auntie a good tidy up and put her bed to rights.' She dropped her voice to a loud whisper. 'I've sent my Robbie for fresh chaff for the mattress, so we can burn it after.' Then, aloud, 'And this time we'll not take no for an answer. You'll have a hard time of it soon enough, one way or another, and your aunt will be fine with us for an hour or two.'

'She'll not be going anywhere,' grinned Mrs Guyan, bare gums gleaming, 'and we'll have her real nice for when you get back.'

Nice? Elissa shuddered. She dreaded her aunt's company, dreaded those stabbing eyes, dreaded the return of speech to that wicked, wounding tongue. *Over the seas and far away*, her aunt had said, but it was not like that. Adam had to go for his own safety. And to go where the herring went. He had to earn money so that he and she could marry. Her aunt had no right to say otherwise. It was a wicked, cruel slander.

'There's plenty shops to gaze at,' urged Mrs Bain, 'and carriages and folk in fine clothes to cheer your spirits and you'll maybe see something pretty to buy for yoursel'.' She added, with a wink, 'For after. So away you go, lass, before we change our minds.'

'Thank you, Mrs Bain, Mrs Guyan. I would like that.'

'Good lass. I'd offer my Nellie to go with you,' said Mrs Bain, 'but I reckon it's peace you're needing, not a pesky wee quine to keep in order.'

'No, please. I would like her company,' said Elissa. 'To keep my mind off . . .' but she remembered in time that they had not heard her aunt's damning words.

'Then I'll away and fetch her,' beamed Mrs Bain, 'while you make yourself smart, for the town.'

Elissa took the child's hand and almost ran out of the Square. It was wicked of her. She ought to have stayed at her aunt's bedside. Except that her aunt did not want her. Those terrible eyes made that plain enough. She had accused Elissa of such sinful things, with a venom that brought the shivers to Elissa's spine even now, outside in the clean sea air. But it was her slanderous slurs on Adam's character that hurt the most. Adam who had saved her from Sinclair's attack and, because of that, was in hiding for his own safety. How dare the woman condemn him out of the spiteful mire of ignorance and prejudice. Adam was a good man, whatever her aunt said. A good man who loved her. Elissa clung tight to that idea and fought down all others. She would not let her aunt's words tarnish her faith. It had been the illness speaking, that was all. She had not meant it. Had not known what she was saying. Sick words, from a sick old woman.

Then suddenly they were in the wholesome bustle of York Street with Hall's shipyard on one side, the blacksmith's forge on the other, and the cheerful shouts of workmen all around her. The window of Wee Jeanie's was bright with jars of pear drops, humbugs, cupid's whispers and treacle dabs, and the caramel scent of boiling toffee billowed out from the open door as she hurried Nellie past temptation.

'Later,' she said in answer to the child's wails of protest. 'I'll buy you sweeties in the town.' But she was smiling. After weeks of gruel and invalid slops the wholesome smell of boiling toffee was like nectar, or the milk of Paradise.

If only she did not have to go back. She could go to the quay where the fishing boats berthed; beg passage to where the herring fleet was operating. Find out Jess and Ina and ask for her job back. Mrs Bain had said they wanted her. Then she would be with Adam again. For ever.

'Will your auntie be dead when we get home again?' asked Nellie cheerfully.

'No, I don't expect so.' But please God make it soon.

'Are you scared of dead folk, Lissa?'

'No. They are at peace. In heaven.'

'I'm scared of them. I'm glad your auntie's nay going to be dead in my house. Billy Duthie says dead folk haunt you if you've been bad.'

The whole Square knew there was no love lost between Nellie Bain's gang of mischief-makers and Sarah Downie Robertson.

'Well, I am sure my auntie will have better things to do with her time.'

But Nellie's words had reminded her painfully of what she strove to forget. Whatever her aunt had said, Adam loved her. She would hold fast to that central truth and refuse to be shaken. She would put Aunt Sarah out of her mind. And she would stay in the town until every last shred of doubt had been blown away and she was whole again.

'Come on, Nellie. Let's see who is walking on the Plainstanes today, then you can choose where we go next.'

Nellie Bain was cheerful company and her non-stop chatter seemed to require few answers as they made their way up into the town and joined the busy crowds in the Castlegate, at the sea end of the mile-long vista which was Union Street. Hansom cabs stood about, waiting for custom, their horses munching patiently from canvas nosebags, or merely dozing on their feet. Water carriers, messenger boys, horsemen, housewives, vegetable sellers and fish sellers, a knife sharpener, an old woman selling broken biscuits, a melodeon player, a candy stall, eggs and chickens and cheeses, even a Glasgow doctor in top hat and frock-coat selling quack medicines. Elissa had forgotten what variety there could be on a market day in a big city and soon found herself caught up in the unexpected excitement of it all.

She bought a candy apple for Nellie and a quarter each of best tea for Mrs Bain and Mrs Guyan, with a fine piece of honeycomb from the bee wifie. It was crusted with honey and, Nellie pointed out with squealing delight, had a dead bee in it. The wifie, straight-faced, said bees was extra, and Elissa, happily joining in the game, countered that the bee took up honey-space that she had paid good money for,

98

and where was her change? They parted, laughing, and the wifie gave Nellie a broken corner of honeycomb to eat there and then.

They strolled the length of Union Street on one side of the road and all the way back again on the other, taking as long as they could to make their small purchases and looking in every shop window in the process. But at last, and reluctantly, Elissa decided it was time to go home. It was unfair to keep Mrs Bain waiting and they had been away long enough. They were dawdling at the windows of Ellis's for one last admiring look at the latest fashions in millinery, the artificial flowers and feathered ornaments, when Elissa felt her arm tugged hard.

'Look at her,' breathed Nellie, her eyes wide with wonder as she indicated someone beyond Elissa's shoulder. 'She looks like a princess.'

In her own plain dress and the Shetland shawl she had bought for her aunt, Elissa had felt elegant enough until now, but the lady who was alighting from the private carriage at the door of Ellis's sent her simple ideas of elegance flying to the four winds.

'Do you think she is one of Queen Victoria's daughters?' whispered Nellie in awe.

'I don't think so. Not out by herself,' said Elissa, though she was as interested as Nellie in the gorgeous sight: a young lady little older than herself, carrying a white lace parasol, her golden hair in curls across her forehead under a little yellow straw bonnet on which waved an enormous ostrich feather. The feather appeared to be secured to the hat by a bunch of flowers, and an even bigger bunch was suspended among the folds of yellow silk which hung like pairs of windless sails – 'On her behind!' whispered Nellie in awe. Then, with returning mischief, 'What happens when she sits down?'

Elissa did not answer. The girl was not alone after all. There was a young man with her, tall, slim, impeccably clothed in dark morning suit with discreetly striped trousers. It was the glint of gold under the black top hat that had caught her attention. His back had been turned to them as he closed the door of the carriage, but now he put a hand under the girl's elbow to steer her towards the open shop door. As he did so, she saw his face – a face she had last seen blood-streaked and venomous, in the dark on the sands at Lerwick.

Her heart lurched with remembered fear, but before she could gather wits enough to escape his eyes caught hers and before she could look away, his face twisted again in an intimate, insolent smile and he touched the brim of his hat with a pale-gloved hand. Elissa blushed furiously, turned her back, snatched Nellie's hand and dragged her away round the corner into Market Street, her heart pounding with shame and dread.

'But I wanted to see,' wailed the child. 'I wanted to see the lady.'

'Another time,' said Elissa, almost running in her haste to reach the harbour and the safety of the quay. Please God he would not follow her; or send one of his men after her. Please God keep her safe. 'We're going to see if the fishing fleet is back. Jessie and Ina might be there.'

Then they were on the quay with the usual hustle and bustle all around them: shore porters, horse-drawn carts, open hatches, derricks loading cargo or unloading, tea-chests, barrels, travelling trunks, crates. In these familiar surroundings the agitated thumping of her heart began to ease. *But how dare the man look at her like that, as if she were a dockside whore.*

Suddenly, a cold wave of memory washed through her and brought her to shocked and quivering attention. Whore, her aunt had said. And something else.

'Lissa, Lissa!' Nellie was tugging at her arm. 'Which one is the London steamer?'

Elissa did not answer. Did not even hear the child, nor the sailors shouting, nor the constant noise and chatter all around her. Only her aunt's condemning words, ringing over and over in her head: *You'll not give birth to your bastard under my roof.*

Could it really be true?

'Lissa!' wailed Nellie. 'Tell me where's the London steamer?'

'Over there,' said Elissa automatically, while the idea swelled and grew till it filled her whole being, driving out all other thoughts, except the urgent need to find Adam. 'But never mind the steamer. Help me to look for the fishing fleet.'

As well as the London steamer they picked out the Shetland boat and a dozen different coastal vessels, steam and sail, with the usual crop of fishing smacks and yawls, and even the *Louise* embarking passengers for Brisbane in Australia, but however hard they looked they saw no sign of the herring fleet. They were still in Fraserburgh, as Elissa had known they would be. And Mr Sinclair was here in Aberdeen and would surely stay here, when the fleet moved on to Yarmouth? Where Adam would be waiting for her with impatience and love.

Spirit, and hope, restored, she took the reluctant Nellie firmly by the hand.

'Time to go back, Nellie. Your ma will be waiting.'

Five minutes ago Elissa had been as reluctant as the child to leave the quayside and the beguiling bustle of the harbour, but now the world had changed and she with it. She was a woman, with new responsibilities. Besides, she owed it to Mrs Bain, and she had promised.

Determinedly she hurried the child past the London Steamer Office, the iniquitous Crown and Anchor, the Seamen's Mission and the Harbour Board, up York Place and round the corner into York Street.

They threaded their way back between trundling wooden hand-carts and whistling message-lads, past Hall's shipyard and Hall, Russell's with their great double doors and cheerful shouts, and on again, past Fiery Dod the blacksmith's and Wee Jeanie's sweet shop. The same pear drops and cupid's whispers and treacle dabs, with fresh trays of fatty bannocks and sticky London buns.

'How's your poor auntie?' called Wee Jeanie, a wizened woman with eyes like blue diamonds, from the open doorway.

'No better, thank you. But I can't stop . . .'

Wee Jeanie's voice trailed after them, calling, 'Tell your auntie I was asking for her,' as they hurried on again, past pantiled houses and bleach greens and the arches of whale jaw-bones, with the noise of the sea washing louder now against the harbour wall and the long blade of the north pier. Gulls wheeled and squabbled over the shore line and the sea wind buffeted the harbour reek of fish and almost triumphed.

Then they were at the entrance into North Square, the four-square enclave of smoking chimneys and neat gardens, collective backs turned to the outside world, collective fronts ever watching each other. Here, Nellie tugged her hand free and went skipping off towards her own house where a gaggle of squealing siblings greeted her with demands for 'Sweeties!' Elissa watched the child until she disappeared into the open doorway, then straightened her back, drew a long breath of courage, and stepped forward. Into the open Square. Along the east row. To the door of the two-roomed prison which had been home for all of her seventeen years.

And stopped abruptly on the threshold.

Inside, she saw a tableau which was to stay imprinted on her mind long into old age. By that time it would have taken on the sepia haze of all old photographs, the edges blurred, the savagery dulled, but on that gusty September afternoon, with the sun on her back, the cleansing salt air in her lungs, and the bustling normality of the city's streets still colouring her spirits, the tableau struck like a guillotine.

At first glance the room was as it had been when she left it, a mere three hours ago: neat, well-swept and dusted, the two framed photographs of her two dead brothers in their usual symmetrical places on the dresser. The rag rug in the exact centre of the hearth. Her aunt's chair on one side, her father's on the other. The fire burned as it always did, with quiet reliability, the kettle simmered, there was a clean cloth on the table, cups and saucers set out, just as she had left them, the teapot warming on the hearth. But the bed . . .

It was like a picture Elissa had once seen, in a shop window in Union Street, of a poor invalid on a couch, his torso bared to the surgeon's knife, and standing round him a group of interested onlookers. A medical class, learning the art of surgery, said someone

101

behind them, but before she could hear more, her aunt had hurried her past the offending window to another, safer, displaying Mazawattee tea. Nudity was forbidden and male nudity unthinkable.

But as her eyes adjusted to the dim light inside the cottage, Elissa saw that the figure on the bed was not, as that oil-painted patient had been, mother-naked, but wrapped from neck to bony wrists in bleached white linen. Her aunt's face was the colour of candle wax, her hair a thin white web on the pillow. Her skeletal hands lay immobile on the stretched white sheet which had been turned down over the brown blanket. There was an unfamiliar bag on the bed, just out of reach of those resting claws; a small bag, tied with faded blue cord. And between bag and claws ran a line of invisible tension, bright and hard and dangerous as steel.

On the periphery of vision, her eyes registered two figures, motionless, but comfortably substantial, and for a wild moment she thought her aunt was dead, and already laid out. Then she caught a flash of movement in that alabaster face and the steel eyes fastened on hers with an intensity that made her draw in her breath. It took all her strength of will not to turn and run.

'It's all right, lass,' said a comforting voice and the larger of the two neighbours stepped forward into the light cast by the open doorway and held out her arms. They were plump and red, sleeves rolled to the elbow, and Elissa allowed herself to hide in their wholesome warmth for one, brief shuddering moment. Then she straightened, pushed a strand of hair back from her forehead and, with a nervous glance towards that accusing figure, murmured, 'What happened, Mrs Bain?'

Maggie Bain took the girl by the arm and led her nearer the fire. Then, with her back to the bed, she said, 'Mrs Guyan and I thought, seeing as how it was a fine blowy kind of a day, we'd have a real clear out, like, with the bedding.'

'Aye, we did,' put in Bessie Guyan, beaming.

'Take off all the blankets, we thought, and give the mattress a good airing,' continued Mrs Bain. 'Maybe burn it, and fill a new one. But when we went to lift your auntie into the chair, she carried on something dreadful. Wet herself again, too. You're a wicked wee wifie, I tellt her. What'll your niece say when she comes back and finds you all in a mess? And the poor wee lassie looking after you so well.'

Elissa made to speak, but Maggie Bain interrupted her. 'No, lass. I know what you're trying to say, but the whole Square knows how you slave and scrub and wash and cook and never a word of complaint. The old witch couldn't be better cared for if she was a new-born baby. And don't shush me, Lissa Downie, for it's the plain truth I'm speaking and the whole Square knows it. Cantankerous old besom that she is.'

'I'm sorry if she was a nuisance, Mrs Bain. I should never have gone out and left her.'

'Nonsense. Best thing for you. And for her. She'll maybe appreciate what you do for her now.'

'But . . .' Elissa glanced over her shoulder towards the bed, and quickly away again. Those eyes were still stabbing, piercing and turning in her flesh like that surgeon's knife in the picture. Pray God she would not speak. 'You haven't told me what happened.'

'We found a – '

'No, Bessie. Let me tell it. You're missing out things. We took off her clothes, see – '

'We had to, with her being – '

'And what a carry-on that was,' said Mrs Bain, firmly overriding her friend. 'You'd have thought we was a pair of ruffians trying to rape her the way she fought, and us both grown women like herself. But no matter. We got her cleaned up and dressed respectable, then we wrapped her in a blanket and propped her in that chair, see.'

'Her own chair,' put in Bessie. 'We made certain of that.'

'Then I sent our Annie to get the boiler going for the water while we stripped the bed. Well, what a carry-on. She was gurgling and twitching like a mad woman and when we went to lift the bottom mattress she shouted, "No".'

'She did,' echoed Bessie, with awe. 'And her not speaking a word till then.'

'We took no notice, but when we lifted yon mattress to carry it outside . . . show her what we found, Bessie.'

Bessie Guyan crossed to the bed, picked up the little cloth packet and held it out to Elissa.

'We found this.'

There was a strangled sound from the bed and Maggie Bain said, 'Take no notice, Lissa lass. She's been carrying on like that ever since we found it. But we haven't touched it, have we, Bessie? We thought we'd best leave it for you to open, when you got back.'

Elissa reached out a hesitant hand to take the packet and was surprised by its weight as it lay in her cupped hands. She looked from Bessie to Maggie to the bed: three pairs of eyes staring at her, two pairs with eager curiosity, the third . . . But this time she dared to confront that venomous gaze.

'Well, go on, Lissa,' urged Maggie Bain, and Bessie Guyan added, 'Open it.'

With careful fingers, Elissa unpicked the knot, eased back the ridged cord and finally unwrapped the envelope-type packet, fold by fold. The material had once been striped blue and white drugget of the kind used for fishergirl's skirts, but it was dull now and threadbare at the folds. Elissa felt inside and pulled out a folded square of paper, then a small suede leather pouch. She did not need to open it to know that it contained coins.

'Gold sovereigns,' breathed Bessie in awe, when Elissa slid them out on to the tablecloth.

'At least a hundred pounds,' added Maggie Bain. Then, with instant generosity and not the smallest envy, 'Reckon you've earned them, lassie. Ten times over.'

But Elissa did not hear. She was staring at the words on the paper which trembled in her hand.

'Go on, lassie. Read it,' urged the women together, and one of them added, 'Out loud.'

'For my niece Elissa Downie when I am gone,' began Elissa in a hesitant voice. There was a sound from the bed that could have been encouragement or curse. Elissa's voice strengthened. *'In token of her obedience, piety and good companionship. She has always been a credit to me. May God go with her.'*

Elissa looked up from the paper, her face bright with gratitude. 'Thank you, Aunt Sarah. I did not realise you . . .'

But as her niece approached the bed, the old woman's mouth opened, her thin throat worked convulsively, and she shrank back against the pillows, her eyes never leaving Elissa's face.

'Wh . . . who . . .'

'I am Elissa, Aunt Sarah. Your niece, Elissa, remember?' Deliberately, she made herself touch the nearest wizened hand, but with a final effort the old woman snatched it and herself away.

'Who . . .' She struggled in vain to force the word out. Then with a triumphant outrush of breath she loosed one long-drawn-out, accusing 'Whoooo . . .' The terrible eyes lost their power at last and she fell back, dead.

CHAPTER 10

Slowly Elissa straightened. The two older women stood at the table, beside the spilled riches of Aunt Sarah's hoard.

Mrs Bain was the first to speak, in a low, reverential voice as befitted the company of death. 'A merciful release, God rest her soul.'

'Poor old wifie,' said Mrs Guyan, criticism forgotten in the solemnity of the moment. 'But she went quick, and that's a blessing.'

'Aye, it is. Couldn't even recognise her own niece at the end,' said Mrs Bain. 'And Elissa always so good to her.'

'Who, she kept saying. Who. As if she'd never seen the lassie instead of bringing her up from a wee bairn.'

Elissa listened to the ritual dirge while her own heart thumped hard and strong. They thought her aunt was dottled. They thought her aunt was saying 'Who?' because she didn't recognise her. But Elissa knew better. Knew why her aunt had struggled to keep the packet secret. Knew why those fingers had clutched and twitched in torment, powerless to unwrite what was already written.

Knew beyond all doubting that that poor, unuttered word was not a harmless 'Who?' but a shrieking and accusing '*Whore!*'

She heard again her aunt's venom as she destroyed Elissa's innocent, tender memories, trampled them in the mire of her own repressions, smeared and tainted and warped and condemned. Tore him to worthless shoddy. Reduced her own golden loving to dross. Even damned her innocent, unborn child.

'Don't take it hard, lass.' It was kindly, misguided Maggie Bain at her side. 'She had a long life and little pleasure in it. She'll rest easy now, poor soul. She was a hard taskmaster, that one, but you always did your best by her. And you've the comfort of knowing that she appreciated it, at the end.'

Elissa was silent, truth urging her to put the record straight, while every other instinct told her to hold her tongue. What had passed between herself and her aunt was private, whether it had been the illness talking or not. Private and shameful and cruel. But there were decencies to be observed.

'Shouldn't we say a prayer?'

105

'The Minister will see to all that,' said Mrs Bain, with a return to her normal brisk cheerfulness. 'You're best leaving it to him, with him knowing the right words.'

'But I . . . There must be something I . . .' She broke off and buried her face in her hands.

'There, there, you cry if you want to, lass, and leave everything to us. We'll send a message to your da and your brothers and my Nellie can go round to the Minister. She went straight home, like I tellt her?' Elissa nodded. 'Good. Then after she's fetched the Minister, we'll get your auntie laid out proper. But first, Bessie's making a pot of tea for us and I reckon as it's such a solemn occasion, we'll add a wee droppie of whisky, for our strength.'

Bessie Guyan was already at the fireside, spooning tea into the pot, but stopped, spoon suspended, at Mrs Bain's words.

'Whisky? In this house? The poor wifie will turn in her grave.'

'Well, she's not in her grave yet, is she?' said Mrs Bain with a wink, then with the matter-of-fact efficiency of much practice, she reached across the bed, closed Sarah Downie Robertson's eyes and drew the sheet up over her face. 'There. What the eye don't see the heart don't trouble itself over. She'll be fine there till we've had our tea. There's biscuits in that tin, Bessie. I brought them over specially.'

'I'm sorry,' said Elissa, startled out of her reverie. 'I should have thought. But with Aunt Sarah not eating and the men away . . .'

'Don't you trouble yourself, Elissa. You've had enough to do, the Lord knows, without worrying about biscuits. Bessie, nip round to my kitchen, will you, and tell Nellie to give you the whisky jar. It's on the dresser – and mind she doesn't upset the lamp while she's at it. She's a clumsy wee quine, that one.'

When the woman had gone, Mrs Bain put a comforting arm around Elissa's shoulder and led her to a chair by the fire.

'You sit here, lass, and relax. I know it's been a shock, but I reckon it's for the best and she was a fair age. Now, before Bessie comes back,' she said, with a brisk change of voice, 'I've something I want to ask you. Was anything said between you and your aunt? I wouldn't ask, only Mrs Duthie next door said she thought she heard shouting. It's not like Sarah Robertson to shout, and not like you to give her cause.'

Elissa looked up into the woman's kindly face and said, with bleak honesty, 'She told me to leave her house.'

'Her house indeed! Since when has James Downie's house been that?' The woman's breast swelled with indignation. Then curiosity took over. 'Why?'

For a moment Elissa was tempted to confide in her, but the memory of what had passed was too shaming, not only for herself, but for Adam.

In all her seventeen years Elissa had never knowingly told a lie, and it did not come easy.

'She said . . . she said I had not cleaned the step properly.' That at least was partly true. 'She called me a . . . a slut.'

'The cantankerous old besom.' Maggie Bain was outraged. 'And you such a good wee lassie, working all the hours God sends to keep your wee house spotless and your auntie likewise. Don't think we haven't noticed it and all of us admiring you for it. You'll make some lucky lad a grand wife one day and I could name someone who'd take you tomorrow, if you'd have him. So pay no heed to what your auntie said. She didn't mean it, lass. It was the illness talking, that's all. The pain and the shame and the helplessness. You remember that, Lissa love. Complaining about the doorstep indeed. And in the middle of the night! I reckon your auntie was dottled . . .'

Elissa was saved from confessing the truth by the arrival of Mrs Guyan, red in the face from her exertions and clasping an earthenware jar in her arms.

'I told your Nellie to find the Minister and tell him what's happened,' beamed Bessie, uncorking the jar and tipping whisky liberally into three cups. 'Reckon we've got time for this, though, before he comes. Are you wanting tea with yours lass, or will you take it neat?'

'With tea, please.' Elissa sat in a daze, while the two women fussed over her, poured tea, laced liberally with whisky, made her drink it. She had told a lie to Mrs Bain. The first lie of her life. And she did not regret it. She would tell it again and again – for her beloved Adam's sake. And for their child. Her lips moved in silent prayer.

Oh God, please keep Adam safe. And help me to find him.

There was the sound of running footsteps, the door burst open and the skinny, freckle-faced and dishevelled figure of Nellie Bain skidded to a halt on the threshold. She had discarded her town plaid with her shoes and her bare feet were already dusty to the ankles.

'I tellt the Minister, Ma, and he's coming directly.' Nellie Bain's eager face brought a gust of refreshing reality to the sombre room and when, after a nervous glance towards the bed, she added, in a whisper, 'Can I have a biscuit, Ma?' all three women smiled.

'Away with you, Nellie, and see to the broth-pot,' said her mother, thrusting two into the child's hand. 'I'll be along directly. Bessie, rinse out these cups quick, and put the whisky jar out of sight in the scullery. You'll maybe have need of that later, Elissa, when the visitors call.'

Then her eyes lighted on the money bag, still lying on the table where Elissa had left it.

'Take my advice, lass. Put that away safe, before folk see it and ask questions.'

107

'Aye, do as Maggie says,' urged Mrs Guyan. 'We'll not breathe a word to a soul.'

Elissa hesitated, remembering her aunt's accusing eyes, but Maggie Bain's common sense prevailed.

'Take it, lass. You've earned it. And whatever she may have said at the end, your auntie meant it for you.'

The funeral was a brisk affair, soon over. Not so the refreshments afterwards.

Though Sarah Downie Robertson had been a haughty kind of a woman, keeping herself to herself and looking down her righteous nose at other folk, especially drinking folk, the house was full for the tea, in Aunt Sarah's honour, and the whisky for her grieving family and neighbours. Elissa had excelled herself in a penance of house-cleaning so that even the poker shone, and the white-laced table top was crammed to overflowing with food. Cheese and ham and sliced cold beef, little pies steaming hot and rich with gravy, oatcakes, fruit cake, even slices of cloutie dumpling.

'More like a wedding than a funeral party,' said one gleeful neighbour, helping herself to another plateful.

'Elissa's done the old besom proud.'

It was not only duty that had driven her: that hidden pouch of sovereigns had weighed heavy on Elissa's conscience. But when, in spite of Mrs Bain's advice, she had offered it to her father, he had refused.

'Nay, lass, your aunt left it to you, and you've earned it ten times over. Take good care of it, mind. You'll maybe have need of it one day. When you find the right man. Or he finds you.'

He had smiled and put his arm briefly round her shoulder, with a quick hug of affection. Elissa could number the times he had done such a thing on the fingers of one hand. James Downie spent little time at home, especially in the herring season, and was not a demonstrative man.

But he was a conscientious father and though he had left Elissa's upbringing to his sister Sarah, he had always done what he thought best for his only daughter. Elissa knew that he and her brothers, especially Tom, had plans for another herring boat and could have made good use of the money, but he had not given it another thought.

They were talking about herring boats now, with old Gideon Noble and his son Joseph. The men had come home specially, and would go back tomorrow, but with the fishing virtually over at Fraserburgh they would be home again at the weekend, for good. At least, until Yarmouth.

Elissa moved about the room, filling cups, offering plates of this

108

and that, murmuring thanks for condolences. The first time someone said, 'You'll miss her, lass, with her being like a mother to you all these years,' she had not been able to answer: merely lowered her eyes and nodded.

Would a mother cry, 'Get out of my house'? Turn her own daughter and grandchild out into the street? But it was the illness talking, not her aunt. The illness. If she clung fast to that idea surely the pain would ease? *Oh Adam, why aren't you here, to help and comfort me?* Except that if he was, she would be terrified for his safety, with the vengeful Mr Sinclair in town.

But the teapot was empty again. She moved over to the fire, raised the lid of the kettle to check if the water simmered, replaced the lid, took up the poker and stirred the coals into flame. Then she carried the empty teapot out into the scullery, tipped water into it, swirled the tea-leaves round to loosen them, emptied them into the bucket. Was James Hay's boat still at Fraserburgh, and if so, did he know which skipper Adam had signed up with, and how to get a message to him?

She dare not ask her father, because of the suspicion it might arouse and she knew what the reaction of any normal father would be in the circumstances. She may have led a sheltered life, but some things had penetrated even Aunt Sarah's virtuous stockade. She could not bear the idea of her father and brothers hunting down Adam and bringing him to heel like a whipped and cowering dog, as the Cowie menfolk had done for that lassie in South Square.

'Need any help, Lissa?' called Maggie Bain from the doorway. The noise level was steadily rising as, the courtesies of condolence over, the whisky circulated and conviviality spread.

'Thank you, Mrs Bain. If you could see that everybody's plate is full . . .'

Mrs Bain, armed with a platter of sliced ham and another of black bun, pushed her way cheerfully back into the crowd and a moment later there was a shout of laughter, in which at least one of the Downie men joined. Elissa slipped quietly round the edge of the company and back to the fire. Poured hot water into the teapot and stood cradling it in her hands while the warmth spread through the earthenware.

Wherever Adam was, he would find her, if she did not find him first herself. Then she would see his face light up with joy when she told him, feel his arms protectively around her as he led her proudly to the Minister.

'I am sorry about your aunt.' The quiet voice made her start and turn her head. Joseph Noble was standing behind her, his face grave. Firelight touched his dark hair with gold and showed up the line of cheek-bone and chin. He had good features, strong and honest, and in the unfamiliar formality of his Sunday best, he looked almost handsome. 'She was a good woman.'

'Yes.' She bit her lip and looked away. He saw only the outline of her hair against the firelight, the slender neck, the soft curve of her shoulder, and it was all he could do not to put his arm around her as he had done on the headland at Gremista, to comfort her, to feel her head resting on his shoulder, the soft touch of her hair under his lips. Soon, he told himself. Soon.

'In another week, we will be home again,' he said. 'I will call to see you, if I may?'

'Of course, Joseph.' She turned to look at him, her eyes dark with anxiety. 'Joseph . . . if . . . if I asked you to . . .'

Joseph had never seen her more lovely. She seemed suddenly mature, as if her aunt's death had removed the last traces of childhood. Mature and sad and achingly vulnerable.

'Anything, Elissa. I will do anything you ask me.'

But there was something in his eyes that brought the blood rushing to her cheeks. She turned her back, snatched the tea-caddy from the mantelshelf and spooned tea-leaves into the pot.

'What is it you want me to do?' His voice was low and measured, and it was as if there was no one else in the room but Joseph and herself.

She poured water into the teapot, swung the kettle back over the flame, and said, not looking at him, 'Would you . . . would you . . .' But the words would not come. When he looked at her like that, how could she ask him to take a message to Adam for her?

'It doesn't matter, Joseph. I will manage.' Holding the teapot like a breastplate in front of her, she fled to the safety of the crowd.

Afterwards, when everyone had gone and the menfolk were asleep in the next room, she lay wide-eyed and sleepless in the box bed which had until so recently borne her frail and dying aunt. The bedding was clean and lavender-scented, the mattress new, nevertheless in spite of everything the memory of Aunt Sarah lingered to undermine her faith. *Over the seas and far away.* But wherever her beloved Adam was, they would find each other and before it was too late. She held his promise in the palm of her hand.

On the platform of the railway station, she hugged her friends again, her eyes brimming.

'Thank you Mrs Bain, and Mrs Guyan, for all you have done for me. And you too, Mrs Duthie.'

'Nonsense, lass,' said Mrs Guyan and Mrs Bain added, giving her a hug, 'You've a new life ahead of you now. So away you go to

110

Yarmouth, and find yourself a man. And when you do, you can tell him from me he's a lucky fellow.'

'Come on, Lissa,' called Ina from the train. 'Or I'll give your seat to some other quine.'

'Away you go, lass,' urged Mrs Bain, pushing her towards the open doorway. 'You don't want to have to stand all the way to Yarmouth. And see you behave yourself, Ina,' she called to her daughter, who was leaning out of the carriage window, waving to various of her friends on the platform. 'You can tell that lad of yours that I'm not wanting any seven-month bairns to explain away to the neighbours.'

'How about a six-month one?' called Ina gleefully, from the safety of the carriage, and there was a shriek of laughter from the other girls who crowded the compartment all around her. The 'fish' train was packed with women, mostly young, but several older among them, all bound in the usual crews of three for the herring fishing at Yarmouth. The luggage vans were crammed with wooden kists, roped bundles and assorted baskets and more spilled over into the compartments where the girls crammed tight as the herrings they packed, with lunch bundles and knitting and all the happy parapher-nalia needed to make life tolerable in the eight or ten weeks they would be away.

The menfolk had sailed already: Elissa had gone with the rest of the women to the long arm of the north pier to wave them on their way. Across the water and reaching towards them was the shorter south pier at Torry. To their right, the safety of the harbour, to their left beyond the harbour mouth, the choppy, foam-frothed waters of the open sea. Gulls wheeled and screamed above the green hump of Torry hill, more swooped over the fleet of fishing boats as they eased their way slowly out of the sheltered waters. The Noble boat slipped past them, close under the pier where they stood, with Joseph at the helm, too busy negotiating the harbour bar to have eyes for anything else, for which she was grateful. Beyond the Nobles, the Guyan boat with Bessie's eldest son Eddie at the helm. Beyond them, the Bains. Then her own father's boat, with her three brothers, a Downie cousin, and Suffie Lennox's little brother Matt, just turned fourteen and proud as a peacock to be taken along as cook. Other boats followed, some large, some small, all with sails dipping to the wind before billowing full and free.

High above the gulls' screams she heard Nellie Bain's shrill voice.

'Goodbye, Da. Bring me back a sweetie!'

Beside her she heard Maggie Bain murmur, 'May God bring Isaac and my boys safe home again.' Other women's lips were moving in similar prayers and Elissa had felt her own heart lurch as she realised that each frail craft held a family's menfolk, fathers and sons together,

111

at the mercy of wind and sea. *Dear God, please keep my father safe, and my brothers. Keep watch over Adam, wherever he is, and bring him safe to me again.* It was the first time she had felt such a bond with the other women.

Now she climbed the step into the already crowded compartment, Ina pulling her arm to hurry her, Jessie shoving, Meg and Suffie calling goodbyes over her head to their families on the platform while they pushed her further into the carriage until the door slammed behind her. Instantly heads filled the open window, calling goodbyes, while others pressed faces to the window-glass. Through a gap over Jessie's shoulder Elissa saw young Nellie Bain jumping on and off the empty railway cart that had dragged the girls' kists on to the platform and waving excitedly to any face she recognised among the many which lined the open windows of the special train.

Nellie's sisters were in the compartment with Elissa, together with Suffie Lennox, Meg Duthie and a handful of other girls, most of them scrambling on the seats and crowding at the windows. The train gave a sudden lurch and Elissa fell sideways on to someone's knee.

'Move your fat bum, Lissa Downie,' said a familiar voice. 'You're squashing my jammy piece.'

'Is that what you call it now?' jeered her neighbour and Elissa, to her own astonishment, joined in the laughter as she found her footing again. Bethany Noble looked up at her with a venomous glare, but Elissa merely grinned.

'Sorry, Beth. But I'm glad it wasn't your knitting needles,' which prompted more laughter. She was too excited to concern herself with Bethany and her jealousies or with what Bethany's reaction would be when she found out Elissa's precious secret, as everyone must do sooner or later. So she was unprepared for the stab when it came.

Somewhere a whistle blew, then another. Doors slammed up and down the length of the train. A green flag waved, Nellie Bain squealed with excitement, sparks cascaded from the engine where an already black-faced boilerman was shovelling coal into the blazing furnace, steam escaped in a triumphant shriek and the heavy wheels ground slowly into motion.

'Goodbye! 'Bye, Jessie. 'Bye, Ina. 'Bye, Lissa!'

'And you can take that smug look off your face, Prissy Lissa,' snarled Bethany under cover of the general excitement. 'A lot can happen when your back's turned and you've missed your chance. So keep your thieving hands off what's not yours and never was. Unless you want another "accident".'

With a huge effort of will, Elissa ignored her. 'Goodbye, Nellie,' she cried, her voice joining cheerfully with the others. 'Goodbye, Mrs Bain. Goodbye, Mrs Guyan.'

Then the train curved round the long bend southwards, waving figures and station disappeared from view and Aberdeen slipped away behind them. Her companions shoved each other playfully to move up and make room, scrabbled in baskets for knitting or apples, stood swaying on tiptoe to root about in the assorted bundles in the string luggage net overhead. Elissa waited for the commotion to ease, then turned her face to the sea wind that streamed in through the open window and felt Bethany's threats blow away like so much thistledown. Bethany did not know Elissa's secret. Adam loved her and her alone and she was carrying his child as living proof. She could have sung aloud with joy.

At last she was on her way to Yarmouth, and to Adam.

CHAPTER 11

Nothing had prepared Elissa for Yarmouth. The low-lying flatlands, the long, straight blade of sea front, with bathing huts and restaurants and seaside hotels, even the shingle beach, had a foreign air to them: and though she knew the sea that soughed and sucked at the shore line was the same sea that pounded the Girdleness at home and crashed against the north pier in a fifty-foot arch of ice-green foam, it had a different, alien air. As if wary of outsiders and prepared to send them packing the moment they overstepped the mark. Even the sky was different: wide and flat, like the strange flattened vowels of the local people and the different rhythms of the local tongue.

The town was busy in the summer months, for it was a popular resort for holidays, with plenty of entertainment on the sea front and invigorating sea-bathing for those brave enough to attempt it. By late September the holiday season was over, but as one set of visitors left the town, another of a different sort took their place. For with the opening of the herring season, thousands of fish-workers flooded into the town, to serve the vessels of the herring fleet.

At the southern end of the sea front, where the Yare met the sea, the land curved in on itself and back again, like the open mouth of a shark, and all along this inner shore were the fish-curers' sheds and the quays where the herring boats unloaded the daily catch. Hundreds of vessels, of all shapes and sizes, from the length of Britain.

Between fish quays and the parallel sea front was a long spit of land crammed to the old town walls with houses, 1,811 of them, in seven miles of interwoven alleyways, row after row and some so cramped that the houses on either side almost touched. Passageways too narrow to be called streets, running parallel from sea front to estuary and from east to west. The narrowest was only twenty-seven inches wide in the middle, though it opened out a wee bit at either end. It was easy to see why the Yarmouth barrows or troll-carts were made so narrow: otherwise they would never have been able to negotiate a passage.

The Rows, as they were known, were numbered, from 1 to 145, and many had names as well, Adam the Barber's or Sailmakers or Money Office Row, but even so it was easy enough to lose one's way, especially in the gloom of an autumn evening after a wickedly cold and exhausting day in the open air, with the sea wind stinging and the salt crystals knife-sharp on the skin.

Their Row was narrow enough, but they were lucky in one way: instead of a street door to their house, they turned under an archway into a tiny courtyard, and entered that way. Which was lucky, because they had to leave their boots outside on the step, with their oilskin aprons. Mrs Jolly had too much care for her furnishings to allow them in the house. With the same care, she had pinned clean oilskins of her own over the bottom part of the whitewashed walls of their room, and removed the carpet, as well as most of the furniture. She did not want fish scales all over everywhere, and her with her summer visitors to think of. But she brewed a good cup of tea.

Ina, Jessie and Elissa shared one room, Bethany's crew the room next door and up the stair in the coom-ceiled attic, Eppie Guyan shared with a pair of lassies from South Square at home: Bella and Jeannie Cowie, second cousins of Eppie's father's sister-in-law. Elissa felt a moment's guilt about that, but it passed. Her place was with the Bain girls, everyone said so, and they were set fair to be best crew already. Besides, Eppie did not seem to mind and the girls got on together well enough.

But the place was noisy and cramped. If Elissa opened the little latticed window it almost touched the one opposite and if she leant forward far enough she could see into the other room. Three girls from Buckie lodged there, with three more crews crammed somehow or other into the tiny house and everybody's conversations could be overheard several doors away.

But after the silence of her last weeks with Aunt Sarah in the Square at home, Elissa thrived on it. Her shyness gone, she breathed in the cheerful camaraderie of the fishergirls as if it were pure oxygen; laughed and chattered with them, slipped back effortlessly into the rhythm of the gutting crew and packed her barrels faster than ever. In that first week every day dawned with the bubbling expectation of looking up from her work to see Adam beside her, with his splendid leather thigh-boots and laughing, loving eyes.

By the second week, with one precious Sunday behind them, her mood was less ebullient. By the third, fear had a toe-hold in her heart.

That first Sunday had been happy enough, with the usual crowd of menfolk in attendance, though with Mrs Jolly's hawk-eyed vigilance to contend with, there had been no entertaining in the Row. Instead, they had met on the promenade and spent the afternoon there, a happy crowd of men and girls which had shifted, as the afternoon progressed, into a pattern of natural pairing: Ina and her Fergus,

115

Suffie and John Barron, Meg Duthie with Suffie's brother Wallace, Jessie and her man, until only Bethany and Elissa were without particular partners. In Bethany's case it was because she had kept at least four men around her, playing one off against the other with her usual mixture of coquettishness and jeering contempt. In Elissa's, because she was too busy searching the crowds for the one face she yearned to see.

She had not noticed that Joseph Noble had fallen into step beside her until he asked, for the second time, 'Are you looking for someone in particular?'

'No.' It was surprising how easy it was to lie once the first step had been taken. 'Just looking about me. It is all so different from Shetland, and from the Square at home.'

'Yes. But once you are at sea, the fishing is the same, and the herrings look no different for being English herrings.'

'That's because they're not. They have travelled as we have, all the way from their native Scotland, to find food.' Elissa's voice had been light and teasing, but her eyes had still scanned the faces all around her.

'Perhaps, perhaps not. They may be different shoals, appearing in their season, but swimming always in their own part of the sea. Some people think . . .'

But Elissa was not listening. What did it matter whether the same shoals circled the British Isles, one step ahead of the herring fleet, or whether a necklace of separate shoals lived and bred and died in one place, while the fleet culled them, one by one? To the herrings it might matter, but not to the fishing boats. Not to Adam.

Adam should have sought her out by now, or sent a message. Brodie Gibb's curing shed was there for all to see, squashed in among the others on the quay of the Yare estuary, with the name 'Sinclair and Gibb' painted in letters a foot high over the office door. The curing yard was not, as some were, under cover, but out in the open, as it had been in Shetland, with the farlins and herring barrels and gutting crews packed tighter together than in Shetland, but still in full view, still threaded by a constant stream of coopers and, when the fleet was in, by fishermen. Adam had come south early, they had told her, for the season. But only a week of fishing had passed: he could not have packed up and gone already. Had Sinclair found Adam after all? Had him punished? Arrested? But if so, surely she would have heard?

'You are not listening, Elissa. Is something troubling you?'

'No. At least . . . I was just thinking . . .' It was twelve weeks since she had seen Adam. Fourteen since that first, blissful Sunday. Why, in all that time, had she not heard from him? For the first time, her faith had faltered. Dear God, keep Adam safe.

116

'What about?' Joseph's voice had been low and gentle and she had turned her head away so that he should not see her face. When, her sight blurred, she had stumbled, he had taken her arm and drawn it firmly under his.

'If you are still grieving for your aunt, you should not. She was in great pain and suffering and you did your best for her. No one could have done more.'

Elissa, to her own shame, had not corrected him. She would not voice her fears to anyone, not even to Joseph whom she had known all her life. To do so would be to give them substance and they had *none*.

They had walked on in silence, behind the laughing group of their friends from the Square, so far away beyond the horizon to the north. A chill onshore wind lifted the hems of skirts, the fringes of shawls, and rattled the doors of the little wooden bathing huts on the boundary between promenade and pebbled shore. On the pier, a thin-faced Italian man with a wooden barrow and a shiny bowler hat was trying to sell ice-creams, though the wind snatched at his hat so persistently that he had to hold it on with one hand and manage barrow and ice-cream with the other. The wind was strengthening and the curling waves seemed bigger than they had been, and topped with pale green froth.

Joseph drew Elissa closer in an attempt to shield her from the wind. 'Hardly ice-cream weather. If the wind doesn't drop overnight, there'll be stormy seas.'

Stormy seas. That was it. Why had she not thought of that before? Adam had been fishing away from the main fleet and had put ashore somewhere, maybe Lowestoft way, to shelter. It had been windy yesterday, and on Friday. Or perhaps he was fishing for a Lowestoft curer, ten miles down the coast? And word had not reached him yet that the fishergirls had arrived? Hope suddenly restored, she had turned to Joseph with a smile.

'Not ice-cream. But a cup of tea would be warming. Look, the others have the same idea. Ina! Meg! Wait for us!'

There had been no glimpse of Adam in the crowds on the pier, on the promenade or in the main thoroughfares of the town. No sight of him when they walked home, arms linked, in the blustery evening darkness, past the charity school and along King Street, with the richer, more spacious houses of the wealthier citizens on their left hand and on their right, the massed humanity of the Rows. They counted the numbers as they went, groups of girls breaking off as they reached their own Rows, shouting their goodbyes before disappearing in single file down one or other of the cobbled alleys, to their spartan quarters and their shared beds.

But though the Rows were narrow and the accommodation

cramped, the air was wholesome enough blowing as it did from the sea to the river and back again. Even the all-pervasive smell of fish was tolerable, though on a bad day the smell of boiling shrimps from two doors away and the competing smell from the pie shop on the corner made Elissa bite her lip hard and fight to quell the nausea. Then she would make an excuse to get outside: or, if she was outside already, would turn her face to the sea wind and breathe deep till the feeling passed.

It was hard work on the Denes; harder than in Shetland, for the October wind had a bite to it and a habit of seeking out every crack and cranny, not just in clothing, but in split and weathered skin. Then they envied the girls whose curers had rigged up sheds for them, or overhead covers to keep off the rain. But it was no use expecting Brodie Gibb to part with good money in any such cause. Where was the harm in a drop of honest rain or a good sea breeze?

By the middle of the second week Elissa's hands were split and stinging in spite of the calico strips which covered her fingers, and, as the weary days crept past and still she could find no sign of Adam, her spirits drooped, with her health. Till, in spite of a twelve-hour day of relentless work, at the end of which she could barely summon the energy to climb the stairs to her room, she found she could not sleep.

'East is the wind! East-north-east. Past two on a cloudy morning.' Wide-eyed she heard the nightwatchman's cry from several Rows away; heard doors open and close in neighbouring alleys, with the sharp echo of booted feet, as one or another skipper or pilot or inshore line-fisherman made his way to the harbour. In the hard bed beside her, Ina slept soundly, though from time to time she giggled in her sleep and once said loudly, 'Don't, you cheeky wee devil.' Jessie snored softly in perfect peace. But though her body was weary to exhaustion, Elissa's mind would not let her rest. Round and round went the question, on and on the arguments and reassurances.

She had found James Hay on the first free afternoon, but he was uncommunicative.

'Don't you mention that fellow to me,' he had growled. 'One day he's here, the next he's not. Disappeared without so much as a goodbye. And good riddance to him, ungrateful devil. Drinking and picking fights in bars.'

Elissa had been too shaken to press for details, though in a slack moment in the gutting yard she had plucked up courage to ask Suffie Lennox, when Bethany was out of hearing.

'Adam Grant? Ask Bethany, if you dare. Though he's maybe run away from her in self-defence.'

'But where to?' persisted Elissa.

'I did hear something a while back,' offered Meg, 'but no one's seen him for weeks. Took up with a pair of lads from England and went south, someone said. To make that fortune he was always on about, likely. Take my advice, Lissa lass, and forget the fellow.'

But how could she forget Adam, when she loved him and he loved her, and when she carried his child inside her? They had agreed he should lie low for a while, for his own safety, but Sinclair was in Aberdeen. Had been for weeks. She knew that if Adam was making his fortune it was for her and their future together, but it was no longer the future that concerned her. Oh God, it would not be long before someone noticed and if she had not found Adam, what would she do then?

'Five o'clock of a brisk morning,' came the distant cry. Elissa swung her feet to the ground and prepared to face another day in which hope was inexorably dwindling. She was almost dressed when nausea overwhelmed her. She thrust Ina away from the wash-stand, clutched the rim of the enamel basin and was unashamedly sick.

'Watch your manners, you . . .' began Ina indignantly, then her voice died away as she exchanged one startled, incredulous look with her sister Jess. Too many bairns had been born into the Bain family for them not to recognise the signs.

'You all right, Lissa?' asked Jess. Ina tipped her head towards the window and held up a warning finger. No point in broadcasting your private troubles to the whole of Buckie.

Elissa straightened, managed a weak smile, and faltered, 'I'm sorry. I must have eaten something that . . .' But she did not bother to complete the useless sentence. Jess and Ina pulled her down on to the bed between them.

'Who was it?' 'How many weeks?' 'You'd best tell us. We can't help you else.' Their low voices were full of concern and friendship, and an urgency which Elissa did not at first understand.

'Adam and I . . .' she began hesitantly, looking down at her hands. 'We are to marry, but . . .' Suddenly she gave up the struggle. 'I have not seen him, or heard anything from him, since I left Shetland to go home to nurse Aunt Sarah. He said he would meet me in Yarmouth. I thought he would be here.'

There was a moment's silence before Jessie said carefully, 'Are you saying it was Adam Grant who fathered that child on you?'

'And you the pride of the Bible class,' breathed Ina in awe. 'Who would have thought it?'

'How dare he,' said Jess with such whispered venom that Elissa flinched. 'How dare he take advantage of an innocent like you. I swear I'll kill the bastard when I get my hands on him.'

'You'll have to find him first.' Ina's voice was grim and Elissa's heart flinched under the implied accusation. But *Adam loved her*.

After a moment Jess said, in a different voice, 'Right. Now we

119

know where we are, we'd best get a move on. There is one way out and you've still time.' She exchanged a look with Ina who shook her head. 'But that's for quines who want to lose their babies and you'll not be wanting that.'

'No!' Elissa wrapped protective arms around her waist. 'It's Adam's child and . . .'

'And no Adam,' completed Ina. 'So if you're set on keeping the baby, we'd best find him for you, before it's too late.'

'Another month and you'll not be able to hide it,' said Jessie. 'There's too many sharp-eyed besoms around to miss a juicy bit of gossip like that one and we wouldn't want it to get back to the old biddies in the Square. Leastways not until you're safely wed. Good job your auntie's dead, Lissa, or your life wouldn't be worth living.'

'Her father's not dead,' pointed out Ina. 'Nor her brothers.'

'Don't tell them,' cried Elissa before she could stop herself. 'I don't want him hunted down like a . . . like a criminal.' But suppose he already had been? By Sinclair? In secret? *Reckon it's spoilt his precious profile for ever . . . he'll not forgive that . . . I pity the fellow who landed the blow . . . he'll not sleep easy in his bed till he's a thousand miles away . . .*

But the noises in the narrow alleyway below had increased till they filled the length of the Row: the clatter of many boots, girls' voices. 'Are you coming to work today Ina Bain? Or have you ordered your breakfast in bed?'

Another voice, sharp with mischief, called, 'You'd best hurry, or we might tip something nasty into your boots.'

Ina snatched up the water jug and leant out of the window. 'What was that you said, Bella Cowie? I didn't quite catch it.' There was a shriek from below as Ina made to upend the jug.

'Come on, Ina. We'd best shift ourselves,' said Jess, 'before Mrs Jolly slams the kitchen door on us. I canna face a day at the yard without a good cup of tea and a jammy piece inside me.'

'Me neither.' Ina closed the casement window and dumped the jug on the bare floor. 'And don't worry, Lissa lass,' she added, her arm around Elissa's shoulder. 'We'll stick by you. We'll put the word about, secret like, so as not to scare him off and we'll find your Adam for you somehow, or my name's not Ina Duthie Bain. Now shift your lazy bones, lass, or we'll all be late for work.'

Another week passed, another Sunday came, and still no Adam. The Bain girls were apologetic, but not downcast.

'My Fergus says there's a man he knows over Lowestoft way who says a lad answering Adam Grant's description was seen there two or three weeks back,' reported Ina. The description they had put about was 'Tallish, fairish, a swaggering sort of a laddie and impudent with the lassies', but they had not told Elissa that.

'And Suffie's brother's friend's da heard of a Scots laddie and two friends flashing their money around in one of the town bars. The landlord noticed them because it was before the herring fleet arrived.'

'And because he was throwing dice and betting what he hadn't got.'

'Lissa's not wanting to hear that,' frowned Jessie, shaking her head at her sister, who took no notice.

'Yes, she is. She's wanting to hear everything, aren't you, Lissa?'

Bleakly, Elissa nodded. 'Yes, I am. Whether it is the truth, or malicious lies.'

Behind her back the sisters exchanged glances.

'Lies or not, we've at least found out something,' said Jessie with an attempt at cheerful encouragement. 'And we'll find out more. Wallace's friend is courting a lassie in Lowestoft and she's putting the word around among her friends.'

'That's our best bet yet,' said Ina. 'If the lassies haven't seen him, no one has.'

'Come next Sunday,' put in Jessie quickly, 'you'll likely see him yourself, Lissa. Here in Yarmouth.'

But there were six bleak days to be endured before Sunday came, and nothing more tangible for Elissa to cling to than Ina's ambiguous optimism, Jessie's encouragement and her own determined faith. Thank God Jess and Ina had kept their promise to be discreet and Bethany Noble had not heard: Elissa had a fear of Bethany which she could not explain. All she knew was that Bethany must suspect nothing until she and Adam were together again, and safe.

The days seemed endless, the sleepless nights the same, while her breasts grew tight and she felt her waist inexorably stretch. Sometimes she fancied the girls at the farlins looked at her differently, with pitying sympathy; sometimes she feared they were laughing at her. Gossiping behind her back. Maligning Adam. And she could not defend him. Could not tell anyone the real reason Adam had gone into hiding. For fear of Sinclair and the law. Once she saw Bethany and Meg whispering, their heads together, and when they burst into a crow of laughter, for a moment she was sure it was at her expense. But Bethany had made no mention, dropped no hint, and Bethany could not have helped doing so if she really knew. So Elissa reassured herself that it was all her own imagination; that even if it was not, it did not matter. Nothing mattered except her child and her child's father, who was a good man, whatever they said. A good, brave man who loved her. She refused absolutely to lose faith, or hope. Soon it would be Sunday again and this time *Adam would come.*

CHAPTER 12

On that fated Friday of 14th October, 1881, the storm blew up out of nowhere.

Wednesday night had been calm enough: nothing to worry about. Thursday morning the same, with a good catch of herrings to deal with, and the wind that whipped the salt spray into unprotected faces and snatched at the red sails of the Yarmouth luggers and the brown of the Scottish Fifies and Zulus was nothing out of the ordinary for October. Nothing to keep the fishing boats from putting to sea as usual in late afternoon.

But by the small hours of that dark Friday morning the south-west wind was a screaming hurricane. Any vessel that was not already in harbour made for the nearest as best they could against the howling fury of wind and sea. Those that could make no headway called on prayer and expertise to help them ride out the storm. Hailstones lashed like grapeshot against straining canvas and unprotected faces, bounced off tipping decks and swirled in crunching drifts against the bulwarks. Sea water churned through sluices, slopped knee deep in hold and cabin, while frenzied oilskinned figures bailed out, reefed sails, tied down hatches, secured straining ropes, and fought against fate to keep themselves and their vessels afloat.

By mid-morning the tempestuous sky was grey with lashing rain. The wind had veered round to the east and was driving the sea with pounding fury against the shores of the eastern seaboard, from the Shetland islands to the southernmost tip of Kent. Ships lost cargo, rigging, crewmen overboard; fishing boats capsized; drift nets were torn from their moorings, sails from their masts, men from the wreckage they clung to.

In Aberdeen, danger lights were hoisted at Torry, at the mouth of the harbour, and kept there throughout the storm. The sea ran mountains high, waves dashed continually over the south breakwater and the north pier was awash with spray. By 4 a.m. on that terrible Friday a handful of ships had successfully made for harbour and even as late as seven the *Jane Douglas* fought her way into the shelter of the inner basin, though not without great difficulty and much

122

anxiety in the watching crowd. After that, no other vessel dared attempt the passage.

Palmerston Road from the railway bridge to the fishmarket was flooded a foot deep. Shipbuilding sheds in York Street oscillated violently in the storm and had to be roped to the nearest firm support and shored up from inside. Several brick walls in Footdee threatened to give way under the force of the hurricane and were swiftly strengthened with wooden supports. Slates flew from roofs, chimney pots toppled to smash on pavements, or on unlucky passers-by. Several windows were blown in by the force of the winds and a glass panel in one of the side doors of the County Buildings was smashed. The mails were late and the telecommunication line cut. Railway lines were blocked by fallen trees. And in North Square the Footdee women, with countless other women up and down the coast of Britain, prayed with desperate anxiety for their absent menfolk, at the mercy of wind and sea.

In Yarmouth, the wind howled down the Rows with banshee fury, the seas thundered on the shore, lashed the foundations of the pier, surged in swelling tumult up the estuary of the Yare, tearing dinghies from their moorings, rattling the roofs of the curing sheds, snatching every kind of debris and whirling it skywards, or hurling it smashing to the ground.

All work at the curing yards was suspended, except that of securing anything loose, battening down anything open and generally trying to save what could be saved from the thieving wind. Plaid-wrapped and shivering, the girls huddled together in groups, in whatever shelter they could find, and waited for news. Some battled their way through the Rows to the eastern shore and the promenade, from where they hoped to see the fishing fleet fighting its way home. Others to the mouth of the estuary. Others clung to the familiar curing yard and the quay, believing news would come first from there. Some, numb with cold and terror for their loved ones, sought the shelter of their lodgings and the hot comfort of tea laced with whisky, only to emerge minutes later, drawn inexorably to the terrifying sight of those mountainous seas.

By early afternoon the fury of wind and rain had begun to ease; by three the rain stopped; by six the wind had changed direction and blew again from the south-west. The evening quivered into calm, though the sea still heaved and rolled, and broke over the breakwater in wave after wave of spectacular surf. The roar of shifting pebbles as it drew back before the next onslaught was like the roar of an attacking beast.

That night, no one slept. Everyone was up and dressed again before the watchman's call and Mrs Jolly, whose own husband and two sons had drowned five years ago in a freak squall at the harbour mouth, had strong tea ready and waiting for them. 'It's a bad business,' she said. There was no need of more.

During that Saturday, news trickled slowly in. No herring was landed that morning, but they went to the yards just the same. There was tidying up to do, barrels to be checked, lids to be retrieved from where the wind had blown them and stacked neat again. Anything to keep them occupied. Whatever scrap of news came anyone's way was quickly spread. And one by one the stricken vessels limped home.

The Noble boat had lost all its nets, but nothing worse. The Guyan boat had lost one man overboard and had a hole a foot wide in its hull. Seven other fishing boats had lost one or more men overboard and most had lost nets and valuable gear. There was no word of James Downie's boat, or of the Bains. In the face of their shared fear, Elissa's private plight was for the moment forgotten.

Soon the harbour was full of damaged vessels and they continued to arrive, many from ports miles away, up and down the coast, and blown off course by the storm. News came from Lowestoft: one boat had lost two men overboard and a large number of smacks were still unaccounted for.

On Sunday, the churches were crammed to overflowing. There was grief in the air itself, laced with despair and dogged, pleading hope. Men had been lost from a score of east-coast fishing villages and many more were unaccounted for. One village alone had lost forty-five fishermen.

On Monday, the news arrived that the Bain boat had come ashore at Cromer, badly damaged, but all hands safe. Jess and Ina had hardly finished their tearful prayers of thanksgiving, when more news came. One hundred and twenty-eight men were now lost or despaired of from the Scottish fishing village of Eyemouth. Elissa's brother William's girl was distraught and had to be held down lest she throw herself into the sea to join her drowned father and her four drowned brothers. To add to her anguish, the Downie boat had not been heard of, with William himself aboard. Though Elissa did her best to comfort Katrine, her own heart was sick with dread, for her family and for Adam. What made it worse was that she had no idea from which port or in which boat Adam had been sailing.

But on Tuesday morning early, when she and the Bain girls were threading their way down the shadowed alley towards the pale morning light on the quay, they found their exit blocked by a familiar figure.

'William!' Elissa flung herself into his arms and buried her face in his chest, before looking up with sharp anxiety at his weathered, weary face. 'And the others? What about Da?'

William shook his head. It seemed a mountainous wave had caught them broadside on and though they had fought to right her again, and managed it, the sea had swept James Downie from the deck, and with him young Matt Lennox, Suffie's brother, whom he had been trying to help. They had searched for hours, but in vain.

She knew the answer, but she had to ask. 'Is there any hope for them?'

'I fear not, Lissa. They might come ashore eventually. That is ...' He hesitated, but though her face was ashen, her gaze was steady, her composure resolute. 'Their bodies might. But I doubt it. We were far out to sea. There will be a memorial service of course.'

'Poor Father. He was always good to me.'

'Aye. He was a good man. But you've still got me to care for you, Lissa, and Davie and Tom.'

It appeared that after her father's and Matt's drowning, they had been blown William did not know where, but after thirty hours of fighting to keep their battered craft afloat they had eventually come ashore south of Lowestoft. Tom and Davie and the cousin had stayed with the boat, to get her seaworthy again and, as he put it, 'keep her safe from the wreckers', but William had come back as fast as he could.

'To see you, Lissa. And Katrine. How is she? I heard about Eyemouth.'

'She will be so much better when she sees you, William,' said Elissa, her eyes brimming. 'Poor lassie. She feared she had lost you too.'

'And you, Elissa? Will you be all right?'

Elissa nodded. Though with so much grief to contend with, she could see no glimmer of hope for Adam, or herself.

'Good lass.' He put his arm round her shoulder in a quick hug. 'Now I must go to Katrine. I will see you again later.'

There were few herrings to gut, the battered fishing fleet not having settled back into its daily pattern, though every day another patched-up boat put doggedly to sea. But once the day's catch was dealt with, the yards closed and the work-force drifted away, some to help their menfolk patch and mend torn nets or tattered sails, others to comfort the mourners, to help where they could.

Elissa moved as in a dream, a dreary, relentless dream of doom and despair and guilt. But at least her father had been spared the sight of his daughter's shame. And it would be shame, if the father of her child was not found in time to marry her.

'I am so very sorry, Elissa.'

She looked up from the herring barrel which she had been topping up with automatic efficiency while her mind wandered now into

125

memory, now into a grey future unlit by hope. Joseph Noble was standing beside her, his face haggard, as most of the men's were since the storm, but soft with sympathy.

'William has told me about your father.'

Elissa bit her lip and turned her head away. What was there to say?

'I know it is so much worse without a proper funeral. But there will be a service.'

It was uncanny how he had read her thoughts. 'Thank you, Joseph. It was kind of you to find me.'

'Not kind,' he said, in a voice of startling intensity. 'You know I would do anything to . . .' But his sister Bethany had come up behind him.

'Sorry about your da, Lissa,' she said, with curt sympathy. 'And you losing your poor auntie only four weeks back. Bad luck, that is.'

'Thank you. How is Suffie?'

'Angry. She liked that wee loon, and for a brother he was not as bad as some.' She flicked her eyes scornfully at Joseph and away again. 'But she's got her John to support her. He's lucky, that one. Not a man lost, not a scratch on his boat, and three cran of herrings still in the boat when he landed. Suffie will survive.'

And so will I, vowed Elissa, behind Bethany's departing back. They shall not shame me or my child. We'll hold our heads high and defy them all. But it took all her strength to remember her vow as that terrible week dragged on. Then on Wednesday night a strong wind sprang up from the east and by Thursday morning word spread that wreckage was being washed up on the shore, including the sea-sodden carcasses of sheep, the cargo of a cattle steamer sunk some weeks before. The sea-bed was delivering up its dead.

Elissa went with the others, though her legs would hardly carry her and her heart thumped hard with dread. Wreckage from the damaged bathing huts and the pier had been cleared up days ago, but now for the length of the six-mile promenade, from the estuary point to the northern distance, the pebbled beach bore a wavering fringe of destruction: debris of all kinds tossed up at high tide and left there as the treacherous seas receded. Already a swarm of barefoot local urchins scavenged along the tide-line, collecting kindling and other treasures as they picked over the flotsam. Seaweeds, barnacles, crab shells and razor shells, flecks of bubbling foam trapped in the tangles of trailing weed and torn rope; drowned sea birds, fish with their bellies torn open, sodden lumps of sheep's wool, a fisherman's hat, an enamel mug which one of the urchins pounced upon, a torn and sea-soaked Bible, an oatmeal sack with a sour and glutinous lump still clinging to one corner, an orange, a sailor's oilskin 'dopper' with J.A. stitched under the collar. And wood in abundance.

126

There were bits of broken spar, an oar, all kinds of splintered planking, half a mast with the yards still attached, a sodden piece of sail, a tea-chest with its side split open, the remains of a wooden kist, and, in the fringes of water as dusk was falling, a dark shape rising and falling with the sea's motion, sometimes under the water, sometimes breaking the surface. Five or six feet in length and tapering. A large fish, perhaps, or a small whale. Then as it came inexorably closer, they saw that it was neither of these, but a man's drowned body.

Men waded out into the shallows to carry the body ashore. Straightened the sea-battered limbs; laid their burden reverently on the shingle, made it as decent as the ravages of storm allowed. The clothing was in shreds, the hair matted with seaweed and sand, the features a blur of bone and battered flesh. Contact with rocks or with hungry sea creatures had made the face unrecognisable. After the first appalled sight, Elissa shut her eyes on the horror, only to open them again a second later, unable to resist the urge to look and look again for some dear point of recognition, in the hope that she would not find it. But in that brief interval someone had spread a clean kerchief over the ruined face, for decency's sake, and for compassion.

Elissa searched the battered shoulders, then the chest for traces of the familiar woollen gansey, but the threads of sodden wool could have belonged to any man, their pattern unravelled and lost to the obliterating waves. What remained of the breeches likewise. She was beginning to relax into renewed hope, when her eyes moved on past the hips to the drowned man's legs. She had expected more of the same reassuring anonymity, but instead saw something that set her heart pounding with dread. For to those lifeless legs a pair of thigh-length leather boots still clung with sea-defying tenacity. The once-gleaming surface was dull with slime, the leather sodden, and on the left boot, below the knee and clearly visible, a deep, disfiguring scratch. Sea water trickled slowly out over the cuffs and into the sand.

'Should have kicked them off, poor bastard.' 'Likely didn't have the time.' 'It would be overboard and straight to the sea-bed with the weight of them. Look at they metal studs.' 'They'll maybe tell us who he is, poor devil.'

Elissa knew the maker's name before they found it. Knew what initials the owner had proudly stitched inside the cuff.

A.G. Adam Grant. The father her child would never know. With a moan of despair she slipped senseless to the ground.

PART II

CHAPTER 13

In the upstairs office of a building on Waterloo Quay, on a morning in late November, a number of men sat round a heavy oak table of the refectory type. Cigar box, blotting pad, pens and papers and notebooks lay neatly ranged in front of them.

The gloom of dark timbered floor, panelled walls, heavy roll-top desk and leather-bound ledgers was lightened at regular intervals by gilt-framed paintings of ships at sea, and, in the place of honour above the fireplace, a portrait of Alexander Christie Sinclair, one-time Provost of the city, founder of the firm of Sinclair's Fish Merchants and father of Easton Sinclair. Shrewd-eyed, grey-bearded and impressive in the full splendour of civic ceremonial, he was a constant reminder of what the ordinary man could achieve by determination and sheer hard work.

The shutters of the two tall windows were folded back to let in what winter sunlight there was and dust motes danced in the slanting rays. In the captain's chair at the head of the table, with an uninterrupted view to the far wall and the heavy-panelled oak door through which each man must enter, sat Easton Sinclair, a grey-haired, grey-whiskered man of fifty-five who as the years passed bore an increasing resemblance to his father. Now, as he waited, he glanced from time to time at the portrait over the fireplace, or through the nearest window to the crowded shipping in the inner basin and over the massed masts to the fish quays, knowing he had no cause for shame. He had not wasted his inheritance, as some sons did, but had used it to expand and prosper. And would continue to do so, as long as his health, and the good Lord, allowed.

Hugh Sinclair, on his father's right, thought the Lord's indulgence had lasted far too long already: the sooner the old man handed over to young blood, i.e. himself, the better. He'd soon get rid of the dead wood and the mould, the jumped-up little autocrats and petty dictators, the people like Brodie Gibb who thought they could order their betters about merely because they had spent their lives knee deep in fish. As if that conferred some sort of automatic superiority. He glanced across the table and away again. The new suit, made for

Gibb on Easton Sinclair's insistence, by Ellis's most experienced tailor and in best worsted cloth, succeeded only in making the oaf look uncomfortable.

Hugh deliberately tipped back his chair so that it balanced on two legs – a habit which infuriated his father – and hooked one thumb lazily in the pocket of his elegant, blue brocade waistcoat. He hated board meetings and usually avoided them, but this one promised to be more interesting than most: besides, he did not trust his father not to cut him out of the profits behind his back.

Faint sounds drifted up from the quayside: men shouting orders, the creak of a derrick, the squabbling of herring-gulls. His father drummed the fingers of one hand impatiently on the polished wood while Hugh inspected his own fingernails and buffed them, one by one, on the sleeve of his jacket until at last came the sound of hurrying footsteps on the stairs. The door opened and swiftly closed again.

The last man had arrived: Captain Glennie, who had made a fortune in the tea trade and invested the proceeds in a flourishing rope factory, a tappie-tourie mansion in the west end of the city and an elegant young wife half his age. She, if rumour was to be believed, was no doubt responsible for the man's late arrival. Hugh made a mental note to call on the lady some time, when her husband was out.

Ironically, his success with the ladies had vastly improved since that business in Shetland, especially since he had hit on the dashing explanation of bare-fist boxing. His father had not swallowed that, of course, but he was a suspicious old bastard at the best of times and with Gibb whispering poison into his ear-hole morning noon and night it was only to be expected.

He ran a finger lightly down the flattened ridge of his nose, a habit he had developed lately. Though the lump where the bone had healed was no longer tender, the wound to pride and profile still rankled. For in spite of nose straighteners, countless ointments and the expensive attentions of three private doctors, the damage had proved irreversible. He felt the usual rush of vitriolic hatred for the author of his downfall, though this time it was tinged with satisfaction.

He had taken most agreeable revenge on one of the perpetrators and as for the other, there was plenty of time. Besides, anticipation was sweet.

But old Sinclair, as his son privately thought of him, was whacking the table top with the company gavel: the meeting was about to begin. Twelve of Aberdeen's most influential businessmen, and Hugh included himself in the description, had gathered to plan their momentous step into the future: a syndicate to commission the first steam trawler to operate out of Aberdeen harbour, and in so doing to make themselves a fortune. But first there were the ritual expressions

132

of sympathy and grief for those drowned in the recent terrible storms, the arrangements for charity for the widowed and orphaned, acknowledgements of donations, the usual . . .

Hugh listened impatiently, as they ran through figures of herring catches, barrels exported, profits in Russia and Germany; the advantage the railways had brought to the fishing industry; and finally the development of the new screw-propellered steam-driven trawler which could lift bigger catches and work much further afield.

'In short, gentlemen,' said Easton Sinclair, 'we already have a splendid harbour, and a flourishing white-fish trade. With the right investment, we could lift that trade to a full-scale industry as big as any in the land and make ourselves a fortune.'

'There will be trouble,' warned Brodie Gibb and nodded an expressive head towards the window. 'The local fishermen won't like it.'

'But the local smokesheds will,' said a burly fish salesman, who owned one himself, 'and the gutters and curers and fish merchants and railways, not to mention housewives the length of the land.'

Brodie Gibb was silent, remembering the mutterings of discontent he had heard among the herring fleet whenever the question of steam arose. What chance, they said, would the little sailboats have against a boat driven by steam? Steam did not depend on the vagaries of wind and weather. Steam could range further and longer afield. Steam was big and powerful and greedy. Steam would scoop the sea clean of fish and leave nothing for the little boats. And though the new steamers would trawl for white fish, if they were successful it would be herring next. Bethany Noble's brother had been particularly outspoken about it and he was no idle agitator. Old-fashioned perhaps, but a solid reliable fellow.

The reminder of Bethany deepened the frown lines on his brow. What with opening up the curing yard and then the storm he had had no time to spare for courting. He didn't want to lose the advantage he had so laboriously worked for in the summer months, but on the other hand, business must come first and perhaps a little uncertainty might work to his advantage? And though her brother was set against steam, that did not mean that she would be, too. Once this syndicate was set up and running he would think about resuming his discreet pursuit.

But the thought of Bethany threatened to divert his attention into inappropriate channels and he thrust it aside. Smokesheds had been mentioned, and had reminded him that the firm of Sinclair and Gibb owned a smokeshed of sorts on Pocra Quay, a dilapidated wooden structure by the old boilhouse. If business was going to increase so rapidly it might be time to expand the smokeshed side of things.

The syndicate having been duly formed, a deputation chosen to

133

visit the Clyde shipyards to choose a suitable vessel, Lawyer Forbes instructed to draw up the necessary agreement and the meeting concluded, Gibb said as much to Easton Sinclair.

'We'll walk round to Pocra now,' said Easton, with the decisiveness which had made him so successful a businessman. 'To inspect the place. See what needs to be done. You will come with us, Hugh. I understand from Gibb that you are not happy in the curing yard: a smokeshed in Aberdeen harbour might be more suited to your talents.'

Hugh Sinclair, who had his own plans for the rest of the day, opened his mouth to protest but thought better of it. Best not to antagonise his father so soon after that other business. Besides, if a fortune was indeed waiting just around the corner, he didn't want Brodie Gibb grabbing it all when his back was turned, and at least he would be at the centre of things in Aberdeen.

'Yes, Father,' he said, with a suitably solemn expression.

The visit would give him the opportunity to run his eye over the female workers. If, as the old man hinted, they were to be Hugh's workers, then he could take his pick. Droit de seigneur and all that. He adjusted his hat to a more jaunty angle and, with returning insouciance, followed his father out into the street.

Joseph Noble saw them from Pocra Quay, where he was working on the upended hull of the family boat. The storm damage had proved more extensive than they had thought and, the herring season over, he had taken the opportunity to careen the hull and repair any splintered planking with new. His father and brothers were already at the long-line fishing, in the family's second boat, but Joseph had opted to stay ashore. He had served his time as a ship's carpenter and was better qualified than the others for the job, but that was not his reason. Ever since that fellow's body had been washed up on the Yarmouth beach and he had heard the news his heart and head had been in turmoil.

The Downie girl's lover . . . drowned before they could be wed . . . and the lass expecting . . . The whispers had crept into his mind like poisonous venom and he had fought against them furiously as malicious lies: until Bethany's outburst of screaming grief and fury. After that, he knew they were true.

But in spite of his revulsion, his jealousy, his heart-wrung torment and condemnation, he could not help himself. She was no longer the innocent maiden he had worshipped. She had rejected him, given herself instead to that smooth-tongued rogue. Yet he could not see her valiant, desolate figure without yearning to put his arms around her and comfort her, to kiss the grief from her eyes, to . . .

But she was carrying another man's child.

That was something no man could endure. No man.

Even so, he rose early so as to be there, on the quay, when she passed on her way to the smokesheds. Worked all the daylight hours God gave so that he would be there when she emerged in the evening to make her weary way home. Followed her at a discreet distance to see that no harm came to her. Watched her safely inside her own door. He knew, because Tom had told him, that her brother William only tolerated her under his roof because of what the neighbours would say if he turned her out. And because she was useful. Knew that once home she would face William's preaching and Katrine's reproachful mourning. That she would don a clean apron and tackle the cooking, scrubbing, cleaning that Katrine should have done but had not, because Katrine was grief-shattered and, in William's word, 'delicate'. That after that there would be nets to mend and lines to clean. That it would be one or two in the morning before Elissa crawled into bed, and that bed a chaff-filled mattress on the floor of the room where her unmarried brothers slept when not at sea. William and his new wife had the box bed now. Joseph had vowed never to see Elissa again; never to set foot in her house. But the moment Davie and Tom Downie came home from the fishing, he would go round to the house, to collect his friend Tom and carry him off for a pint or two in the Lemon Tree or the Crown and Anchor. And to watch Elissa.

She wished he would not. She knew well enough what he thought of her; could read the revulsion and censure in his face. When he called at the house she was careful not to meet his eye, to speak only when spoken to, to draw no attention to herself. It was the policy she had adopted as the only one to make her life endurable while she lived in her brothers' house. The only time she spoke out was if one of them insulted Adam in her hearing; then she flew furiously to his defence, though she knew it did her no good. She would have liked to leave, but she had nowhere to go: besides, Katrine needed her. But the days were long and weary and she felt tiredness like a heavy garment weighing her down.

It would be different when her child was born. Then she would take out Aunt Sarah's money, count her savings and plan what was to be done. In the meantime, the smokeshed filled her days, and her brothers' house the nights.

Sinclair's smokehouse was a simple affair: one large room with a great slab of a table at one end and a pair of wooden cupboard-structures at the other. Corrugated iron walls that rattled in the wind in spite of being reinforced with wooden uprights, one skylight in the roof, a dirt floor. But it was indoor work and warmer than the yard at Yarmouth.

135

The haddock were carried in by the male fish-workers, in huge wicker baskets. The women gutted the fish, flattened them out, strung them on spits ready for smoking. The spits were hung in the wooden cupboards, over a smoking fire of soft peat and white-wood sawdust, for up to nine hours, until they were golden yellow and gleaming. Then they were carefully wiped over with a cloth soaked in warm sea water, and tied by the tail with dry rush, in batches of three. This last was Elissa's job and she soon grew adept; also at packing them carefully into baskets or flat wooden boxes, for the various orders which the foreman pinned to one of the wooden uprights with a nail and a swift blow of the hammer. The foreman's name was Thomas Anderson, but he was known everywhere as Bervie Tam. He wore a black bowler too small for his polished head, and his moustache reminded Elissa of a Border terrier. He would stand, feet apart and thumbs in waistcoat pocket, watching them for half an hour at a time, occasionally barking out, 'More heat on the left, Alex,' or 'Nay so much sawdust. Keep the smoke steady.' Or he would walk slowly up and down behind the women, watching every move. Elissa found it unnerving, till, like the other women, she learnt to ignore him. If he criticised, it was usually with reason, and he was on the whole a fair man. The hours were long, the pay small, and Elissa's spirits desperately low, but it was better than suffering William's endless reproaches and she was grateful to Mrs Bain, whose daughter Annie worked there, for finding her the place.

She was packing the last of the day's baskets on a gloomy February evening when the door to the yard unexpectedly opened and she looked up to see a man's figure outlined against the murky sky. For a wild moment her heart skipped with the old excitement, only to subside again into the usual grey misery of loneliness and grief. Only another month and her child would be born. What would become of them then?

She did not look up when she heard the foreman say, 'Good evening Mr Sinclair.' Mr Sinclair often visited the smokehouse these days 'to see how things are going'. Took no notice when she felt a presence behind her, watching. Only Bervie Tam, as usual.

But it was not Bervie Tam. For a different, educated voice said, 'You tie those bundles beautifully, if I may say so, Miss . . . ?'

'Downie,' she supplied, and immediately wished she had held her tongue. For when she glanced half over her shoulder, expecting to see Mr Easton Sinclair, she saw instead his son. Bervie Tam had moved on and was already yards away.

'Downie,' he repeated with a half-smile. 'How very appropriate.' His voice was disturbingly intimate and she flushed.

'Certainly. As it is my father's name.' She spoke with all the cold hauteur that she could muster and turned her back. But not before she had seen his eyes take in the line of her bulging apron with that same look of insolence and something more which had so frightened her on that evening in Shetland.

'Not your husband's name?' The words were soft, but full of a meaning which filled her with shame and impotent fury. How dare he think that because she and Adam had . . . For the first time she understood something of her aunt's thinking. Only whores behaved as she had done because when respectable girls behaved so, men treated them as whores. As Hugh Sinclair was doing now.

She summoned all her strength to stop her hands from trembling, to lay the smoked fish at just the right angle, to bind the tails at just the right tension so they neither slipped through the loop, nor snapped. To freeze him into shame. It seemed a lifetime before she trusted her voice to say the one frigid word, 'No.'

But Bervie Tam had joined them. 'Elissa's one of our best workers, Mr Sinclair. Fair shifts them along, and handles them so gentle you'd think they was babies in a cradle. Not a snapped tail yet. Now let me show you where we smoke the fish.'

'Well done, *Elissa*,' murmured Hugh Sinclair as he moved away after the foreman, and the way he pronounced her name sent a shudder down her spine. Why couldn't Bervie Tam have kept his mouth shut?

Her child was born in mid-March. The cramps came on her in the small hours of the morning, but she rose, did her normal tasks, and left for the smokehouse as usual. Mrs Bain had told her what to expect and she would work as long as she could, if only to avoid Katrine's unsettling company. Katrine had a fund of tales of women who had died in childbirth, suffered agonies, given birth to weaklings or worse. She always finished with the mournful hope that 'You, Elissa, will be spared such agonies, in spite of your . . .' Katrine never actually spoke the word sin but she did not need to. It permeated the very air. The clean fish-reek of the smokehouse was far preferable.

Elissa endured until late afternoon; thought she would manage till the end of the shift; but the fear of giving birth there, in the smokehouse, was too strong. Annie Bain, Nellie's sister, helped her home, then fetched their ma and Mrs Guyan. Those capable women bundled Katrine next door to Mrs Duthie's, with a whispered suggestion to 'Give her something strong in her tea', and took charge. If the menfolk appeared, they'd be sent packing. Not that they'd need the telling, being a weak-stomached bunch in Mrs Bain's opinion, and 'more trouble than they're worth'.

Elissa had meant not to make a sound, not to cry out as the pain burned and forced, and certainly not to scream 'Adam!' with heart-rending entreaty as the final pain ripped through her.

'Poor wee lassie,' murmured Mrs Bain. 'I'd kill the bastard if he wasn't dead already.'

'So would plenty others,' agreed Mrs Guyan. 'But you're doing fine, Lissa lass. One more push . . .'

The child was healthy, pink-skinned, perfect, with a down of soft gold hair. Elissa closed her eyes in exhaustion and thankfulness and grief. If only Adam could have seen his little child.

'A girl,' said Mrs Bain with satisfaction. 'That'll keep your brother happy. At least she'll earn her keep.'

'Aye, he'll have her taking tea to his wife in bed before she's three,' giggled Mrs Guyan.

'When she's finished splitting the mussels, for bait.' The two women grinned, but Elissa did not. She held her precious daughter to her breast and as the baby nuzzled and sucked, she felt overwhelming love flow through her, and knew she would fight to protect her child against the whole world, if necessary. Certainly William would not be allowed to exploit her. Or to choose her name.

But when the time came, she had not the strength.

'Sarah,' he decreed. 'After a virtuous and godly woman.'

You'll not give birth to your bastard under my roof. The words rang clearly through Elissa's brain.

'I had thought Margaret,' she ventured, looking down at the tiny scrap at her breast. 'After our ma.'

William, as always when she put the child to the breast, had his back to her, but she did not need to see his face to read the tight-lipped disapproval.

'As head of this household, I think I know what is appropriate.'

Think? He'd never doubted it! But Elissa dare not go against him. Not yet. Not while she was still weak and her child helpless. Even so she opened her mouth to protest. And closed it at his next words.

'Aunt Sarah, in her trusting innocence, left you her money. Money to which you have no moral right.'

It was the first time any of her brothers had mentioned Aunt Sarah's money and Elissa was shocked into close and anxious attention. Did William want it for himself? If so, she would resist him with all her strength. That money was hers, for her child.

'That matter is between yourself and your conscience, Elissa. But I trust the name Sarah will be a daily reminder to you of the depth to which you have sunk. And will inspire you to seek forgiveness and to follow the path of virtue in the future.'

Oh God. He does want it. This is the beginning.

'Then Sarah it shall be,' she said demurely. But she was glad when

138

her brother Davie kissed her affectionately on the cheek, said, 'Congratulations, Lissa lass.' Then tickled her baby under the chin and said, 'Hello, young Sal. Where's a smile for your Uncle Davie?' Tom did the same, and before the week was out, William and Katrine were the only people in the Square who called the child Sarah. To everyone else, she was Lissa Downie's Sal.

Jess and Ina Bain came to visit her; Ina three months married and already pregnant. Suffie and Meg and even Bethany called, to drink tea and inspect the baby. 'A healthy-looking lassie,' said Bethany grudgingly, 'though with that fair hair she'll likely have eye trouble later. But it's a good job she's not a boy. Your William wouldn't like that. I'll have more tea if you can spare any, Lissa, though it's awful weak and tasteless. And pass them scones, Ina, afore you eat the lot.'

Elissa's visitors were still there when her brother Tom arrived home, with Joseph Noble.

'Congratulations,' said Joseph, his face expressionless. 'I trust you and the child are both well.'

'Yes, thank you, Joseph. As you see.' She had been suckling the baby and still cradled her in her arms. But Joseph had already turned away.

'We just looked in to see if Davie was here,' explained Tom. 'There's a meeting at the Lemon Tree, but he's likely there already.' Then they left. Joseph did not say goodbye.

'No manners, some folk,' said his sister airily. She added with a malicious gleam, 'But then he's got more important things on his mind than a new wee bastard in the Square.'

Last month news had broken of the steam trawler that Easton Sinclair's syndicate had bought. Rumbles of anger had spread through Footdee and groups of fishermen had met to air their fears and grievance. When the new vessel steamed into Aberdeen harbour it had been showered with stones from north and south piers alike. The crew the syndicate had hired to man the new trawler dared not go ashore. A week after Elissa's child was born there were jeers when news got about the town that the first trip of this much-vaunted steam trawler netted a mere three boxes of haddock. Then someone suggested changing the first fisherman for someone who knew what he was doing. After that, catches and profits improved.

So did the opposition. Every day, bar Sunday, the trawler steamed out of Aberdeen in late afternoon, trawled the bay from Collieston in the north to Muchalls in the south, then steamed back again in the morning, whatever the wind or weather. It was a daily provocation to the families of the line-fishermen of Footdee and of Torry across the water. They showed their disapproval by hurling stones or abuse, though the wiser knew even then that it was futile. They had only to see the trawler, bigger, more powerful than their Fifies could ever be, cut through the heaviest seas at the harbour mouth without a falter to know that steam would one day drive out sail. But they opposed it just the same.

There was talk of sending a deputation to the Provost.

Meanwhile, at Sinclair's smokehouse rumours of expansion grew.

When, in April, Elissa resumed work, little Sal spent her days at Mrs Bain's house, for, decreed William, Katrine's nerves would suffer otherwise. So Elissa left her there on her way to the smokehouse in the early morning, collected her on the way home, and at intervals during the day young Nellie Bain would bring the baby to the smokehouse door so that Elissa could hold her to the breast, in a quiet corner somewhere out of sight. Those were the most precious moments of her day.

It was a cold month with late snows in the hills. Some mornings, when she left for work in the chill half-light, frost gleamed on the cobbles of New Pier Road and the haar hung thick over the harbour waters. On those mornings, she wrapped her plaid tight around herself and her precious baby, until she handed Sal over to kindly Mrs Bain and felt the warm air billow out from the crowded kitchen. Then Annie Bain would join her, the door close, and there would be only the haar and the cold and the dreary prospect ahead.

But when the herring season started, Annie would go with the others. Only she would be left, to work on at the smokehouse or one of the curing yards on the quay, while someone else looked after her baby and there was nothing left from her meagre earnings to save. And no one to help her. Or to love her. On those mornings she would yearn for Adam with unbearable longing.

The men sent a deputation to the Town House to put their case: the steam trawlers were taking away their livelihood, filling their great trawl-nets with so many fish the sea would soon be empty. The steam trawlers were bigger and stronger than any sailing vessel, cost more than a humble fisherman could ever hope to afford, and must be stopped. Otherwise the future, for Footdee and similar villages all round the coast of Scotland, was ruin and starvation.

'And what was our precious Provost's advice?' fumed Tom Downie, when he returned from the Town House. '*Go and do likewise.*'

Elissa, from the shadows of the bedroom where she had retreated to feed her baby in privacy, heard the outcry. William, evidently, was dispensing whisky, which meant the situation was serious. She heard the clink of glass on glass. She half rose to join them when another voice spoke and she changed her mind.

'He heard all the arguments,' said Joseph Noble with bitterness, 'then pointed out the profits steam was bringing to the city, the new business for rope works and salt factories and all the rest. And he had the nerve to tell us it was good for us, the fishing families. With steam, he told us, we could land our fish, sell it in twenty minutes, and be home for breakfast.'

'Maybe we could. If we was millionaires.' That was Tom.

'I cannot help but feel that steam is against God's purpose for us.' Who else but William was in God's confidence? But he sounded worried.

'Our precious Provost does not think so,' said Joseph. 'The sooner you lads are into steam, the better, he said. And showed us the door.' Joseph, it seemed, had been a member of the delegation.

·Elissa remembered those conversations they had had in Shetland about the share system in the traditional sailing vessels and the shore-based owners who ran the steam trawlers, for their own profit. People like the Sinclairs.

'What are we going to do?'

'What can we do? Except fight them?'

'And make the most of the herring fishing while we have the chance.'

After that, more men arrived and left again, with the Downie men in tow, to continue the discussion elsewhere. It was a measure of the seriousness of the issue that William went with them.

It was a week later, a moonless night and the haar lying so thick over the harbour that a man could see scarcely a yard in front of his face. For the past week the menfolk had been working on the herring boats at every spare moment. Nets had been tumbled out of lofts, spread out and checked. Some were new, some ancient spares, much mended, for last autumn's storm had left its mark, but the vessels moored at Pocra Quay were uniformly spick and span.

Tonight, however, they were invisible in the mist, only a mooring light glinting here and there as the water stirred. Lamplight glowed in yellow blurs from lighted window and doorway, and from the lighthouse in Greyhope bay the foghorn sent out its mournful warning. Elissa shivered and drew her plaid tighter round her shoulders as she stepped out into the gloom. She was the last girl to leave the smokehouse, having stayed on to finish tying a particularly heavy order, and behind her Bervie Tam had already doused the light. Now he closed and barred the heavy double doors.

'Goodnight, lass. And watch you don't walk off the jetty on your way home. The haar's that thick you can scarcely see your own feet. Maybe I'd best walk with you a step, to see you right?'

'I'll manage, thank you. It's not far. Goodnight, Mr Anderson.' She heard his steps receding in the direction of York Street and the town. She could have walked with him to the corner, and found her way to the Square that way, but it was not yet time for Sal's evening feed, and she valued every minute she spent alone. Between the smoke-house and Katrine's complaining she had few enough.

She stood a moment, savouring the silence. In front of her, ten yards or so away under the concealing haar, stretched the waters of the lower basin, with, somewhere, those waiting herring boats. Another week and they would be in Shetland, but even if she went with them, Adam would not be there. She could hear the sea water swirling and heaving against the timber supports of the quay, with the soft slap of wavelets when a tug-boat or some other vessel passed somewhere out there in the channel. The mist against her face was damp with the chill of death and her eyes stung with sudden tears of loneliness and despair. *Adam, my love, my darling. Why did you leave me? We had so much loving still to do together* . . . She hugged her arms tight around her waist and moaned with loss and desolation.

But it was time to collect Sal and go home. Katrine would be waiting for her, wanting tea or chicken broth or a cold compress on her forehead. She would have let the fire die and the kettle would be empty. Or stone cold. The vegetables would be unpeeled, the broth not made. Then William, without a spoken word, would manage to lay all the blame on Elissa's head, and would read aloud an improving text while Elissa reminded herself over and over that she must endure, for her child's sake, and must above all things hold her tongue. For she was afraid that if she spoke one word of protest, all her grief and pride and hurt defiance would burst out and her brother would have the excuse he needed to do what she knew he longed to do and turn her out. Without Sal. He would keep her baby to be brought up by himself and Katrine, as was their Christian duty, in the straight and narrow path from which Sal's mother had so disastrously strayed.

With a shiver, Elissa turned away from the quay and made her way eastwards through the swirling mist to the corner of Sinclair's smokehouse. There she paused, tempted to walk straight on, as she often did, into Pilot Square and so to the north pier and the harbour mouth. She would stand at the easternmost tip of the pier and look out to sea while her heart yearned for Adam to share her burden and support her with his love, and she fought against the urge that was always with her to step over the edge and join him in those all-obliterating waters.

But as Mr Anderson had said, the haar was thick as brose and she could not see the pier. Besides, she had her baby to think of. For herself, to walk into the sea's oblivion would be nothing: but what would become of her helpless, orphaned daughter? So, at the corner of the smokehouse she turned dutifully left into the murky silence of New Pier Road. Here there were no lights to guide her. Only the high blank walls of Sinclair's on one side and on the other, through the blurring mist, the lower but equally blank walls of South Square. For some reason the muffled silence unnerved her and she quickened her steps towards the end of the smokehouse wall where there was a strip of rough ground before the timber yard and the old boilhouse building on her left, and on her right, somewhere in the shrouding mist, the narrow entrance which led to North Square.

She reached the end of the guiding wall, stepped forward, and found her path suddenly blocked by a shadowed figure in a greatcoat and hard black hat.

'Excuse me,' she gasped, attempting to avoid him, but he stretched out a gloved hand and took her by the arm.

'Not so fast, my dear. It is Miss Downie, is it not? Elissa? One of my best workers?'

She had forgotten the door at the back of Sinclair's, on the corner beside the timber yard, and saw with dread the predatory face of Hugh Sinclair, saw the diamond glint in his shirt front, the gleam of silver from his walking cane.

'It is a most inclement night for a young lady to be out alone. Allow me to escort you.' His smile was courteous, his eyes cold steel.

'No thank you.' She tried to pull away, but his grip tightened.

'But I insist. For your own good. I have just finished an inspection of our building,' he went on, as if she had made no protest. 'Sadly dilapidated in parts, but that need not concern us now. However, it is thirsty work. I had in mind a glass of wine, if you would care to join me?'

'No, I would not.' Elissa rooted her feet firmly to the spot and with all her strength resisted the increasing pressure on her arm. 'I am afraid I cannot,' she amended carefully as she saw the expression in his eyes. 'Not tonight. I must go home. They are expecting me.'

She fought to keep the fear out of her voice, to keep her voice calm and reasonable, to speak as one civilised person to another. But Hugh Sinclair was not civilised: his rules, if he had any rules, were to take what he wanted, when he wanted it. Oh God, how was she to escape? *Adam! Help me, Adam!*

'You forget, Miss Downie, there is unfinished business between us. You were discourteous enough to refuse my invitation on the last occasion. This time, I insist. My carriage is waiting in York Road.'

This time. Oh God, he did remember. And would take his revenge. She saw it in his vicious, gloating eyes. Yet she still resisted, pitting all her strength against that relentless grip on her arm.

He lowered his voice to a threatening snarl. 'You had better do as I say, woman. Unless you want something *unpleasant* to happen to your family? As it did to your hot-headed friend?' Then, having allowed the threat to sink in, he switched to blood-chilling persuasion.

'Come now, my dear, we both know you are no shy virgin. We

143

could spend a most enjoyable hour together, you and I, in all sorts of ways. You are an attractive girl, Elissa, and if you please me, you will be well rewarded. Shall we say five shillings?'

Elissa let her arm go limp, head meekly lowered in apparent submission, while her mind raced with fear and outrage and an appalled realisation of what he had said. But there was no one in sight, no one to help her, no possible escape. To attempt to run would be futile. To scream for help useless. No one would hear, or if they did hear it would be too late. But she would not give in to him. She would not. Not without a fight.

Miraculously, she felt the grip of his fingers slacken as he assumed victory. On the instant Elissa snatched her arm away and slapped his odious face with all her strength. She should have screamed for help while she had the chance, but it was too late. Of course he grabbed her wrists, forced her back as he had done that other time, back till she felt the hard stone of the smokehouse wall against her shoulders.

'Still a girl of spirit, I see?' His mouth wore a smile, but his eyes were hard and bright as glass and lit with an exultant, twisted lust which terrified her and at the same time made her furiously angry. How dare he lay one finger on her . . .

'But that is what I liked about you last time. I like a little spirit in my women. It can be put to most pleasurable use, as you and I will find out together, very soon my dear. And do not act the innocent. It does not – '

Elissa rammed down her heavy working boot with all her strength on his handmade kid shoe and in the same movement ricocheted her knee upwards into unprotected groin. He yelped, doubled up, she twisted sideways, broke free and ran. Straight into waiting, outspread arms.

'Was that gentleman annoying you, Elissa?' said Joseph Noble, his left arm protectively around her shoulder, his right fist ready and waiting, his eyes fixed warily on Hugh Sinclair's furious face, mere yards away.

'I . . . I . . .' but Elissa could not speak for fear and relief and gratitude. Then she lifted her face from Joseph's shoulder and cried out in new terror. 'No! Get back!'

Joseph leapt aside just in time, pulling Elissa with him as the blade flashed, and she realised the wall that was behind them now was their own wall across the street from Sinclair's, with, somewhere close, the narrow entrance into their own Square and safety. But Hugh Sinclair was advancing upon them, his face mottled with humiliation and pain and venom. His fine top hat had disappeared, fallen into the dirt somewhere, his pale hair was awry, the ends of his cravat flapping like washing in the wind, but he still had the walking

144

cane. He flicked the handle, raised it to strike again and Elissa saw the glint of steel.

Before she could stop him, Joseph sprang forward, there was a brief tussle, a clatter of wood on cobbles, then a moment's stillness as the two figures faced each other in the mist. Spittle flecked the corners of Sinclair's sneering mouth and blood spattered his fine buff waistcoat. Joseph's blood. She saw the knife-slash on his hand as he flexed his fists for the next bout.

'No!' she gasped, clutching at Joseph's arm. 'Please, no. It is Mr Sinclair.'

He shook off her hand. 'I swear I'll kill the bastard, whoever he is.'

But Sinclair had backed out of reach. 'If you do, you will swing for it.'

Eyes never leaving Joseph's face, he stooped on one knee, felt about for the walking cane, retrieved it and stood upright. 'But don't trouble yourself. One whore is much like another. If this one is yours, you are welcome to her.'

This time Elissa managed to hold Joseph back, though his face was dark with fury. 'No, Joseph. Please, no more.'

'Joseph? I'll remember that. Touch me again, *Joseph*,' said Sinclair with all the sneering authority his ruffled arrogance could muster, 'and I will have you deported. Better still, hanged. An unprovoked attack on a gentleman. Intention: robbery.'

'Spoken like the liar and the coward you are.'

Sinclair flushed, but hung on to his tattered dignity. He adjusted the cuff of first one kid glove, then the other. 'Uttering threats, too. The magistrates shall be informed of dangerous footpads in the area. Be warned: I do not forget the names or the faces of those who displease me. Ask your little whore, if you do not believe me. You will pay for this one day, like the other one did, I promise you.'

Then he turned on his heel and strode off into the mist.

With calculated insult, Joseph called after him, 'You've forgotten your hat.' And kicked the battered object after its owner, with as much force as if it had been Sinclair himself.

She heard the steps recede, then, in the muffled distance, the sound of hooves on cobbles, and the faint rattle of carriage wheels. They faded. Died away. And there was only her own heart's pounding and the burning, drowning agony of shame.

Joseph Noble stood a little apart, motionless, staring into the mist which had closed over Sinclair's receding back. He did not speak.

Elissa bowed her head, her whole body shaking with shock and humiliation. Sinclair had treated her like a common whore to be picked up in the street, for money. *If this one is yours, you are welcome to her.* She would never be able to look Joseph in the face again and because of her, he was now a marked man. She had ruined him and

145

herself. For how could she go back to the smokehouse when any moment Sinclair might appear? And how could she not go back, when William would demand to know the reason? And if she told him? Oh, God, would her penance never end? Or that of her innocent, hapless child?

Suddenly, into her mind crept a new terror: what was it Sinclair had said? *Unless you want something unpleasant to happen to your family, as it did to your hot-headed friend.* He meant Adam. What had he done to Adam? Into her mind came that terrible image of the drowned, disfigured, sea-battered body on the beach. But suppose it had not been the sea which inflicted those terrible injuries after all? Oh dear God! And he had threatened her family. Her baby. And she had no one to help and protect her. No one.

Then Joseph's arm was round her shoulder, drawing her close till her head lay against his chest. With his free hand he stroked her hair, gently, gently, till she quietened and the shivering stopped.

'Hush,' he murmured. 'Hush . . . you are safe now.'

'I am sorry. I have caused you trouble.' She brushed the back of her hand across her eyes and straightened. 'But I am all right now. And thank you.'

She reached up her arms to put her hair to rights; adjusted the plaid which had slipped from her shoulders; attempted a smile.

'I must go. Mrs Bain will wonder where I am.'

'Elissa . . .' He stopped, and when he spoke again it was in the carefully impersonal voice he had used ever since Yarmouth. 'If there is anything, anything at all that I can do for you, you have only to ask.'

Like a beacon light blazing through the darkness, she saw the solution. She hardly dared to ask it, but shock, her own loneliness and the thought of her precious, fatherless child gave her the courage.

'There is something you could do for me, Joseph.'

'Of course. Only ask, and I will do it.'

She drew a long and steadying breath. 'Would . . . would you marry me?'

CHAPTER 14

Looking back in sober reflection on her encounter with Hugh Sinclair and her rescue, as she could only describe it, by Joseph, Elissa felt a bewildering tumult of emotions from shame and fury, to gratitude, humility and a burning mortification. How could she have asked Joseph such a thing? As she busied herself over the fire, stirring the broth pot, boiling the kettle for hot washing water, ministering to Katrine and later to her brother William, the question pounded over and over in her head, alternately burning her cheeks with shame and blanching them with anxiety as to how she could ever look Joseph in the face again. To propose to a man! It was shameless, outrageous, unheard of. Especially when she did not love him. Could never love him, as he himself must know. Oh God, what was she to do?

When he had promised to help her, he could not in a thousand years have meant marriage, yet when she asked him, he had accepted. To be sure he had turned the colour of grey granite first, had closed his eyes and made the sort of sound a man might make who had been thumped hard and unexpectedly in the softer parts of his anatomy, but when he had opened his eyes again it had been to look into hers with an intensity that frightened her. She realised now what that look had signified: that she had trapped him by his own sense of honour. He had given his word and must keep it. But at the time, she had been merely nervous and though she had managed to look calmly back at him, it had taken all her strength.

Then he had given a small nod, cleared his throat, and said, 'I will. If that is what you wish.'

'I do wish,' she had said, still borne up by the fears of the moment and the constant undercurrent of anxiety which had run through her ever since Adam's drowning: not for herself but for her child. Anxieties multiplied now into real fear by Sinclair's wicked threats. *What had he done to Adam?* Afterwards, during that endless, sleepless, tossing night of mortification and memory she knew she should have added, 'But only if you truly wish it too.'

By morning, it was too late. When she opened the door into the early April air, little Sal wrapped tightly to her breast, his dark, motionless figure was waiting for her, and to her shame she felt a rush of relief. If she had been able to find a plausible reason for not going back to the smokehouse she would have done so, but the thought of William's probing disapproval blocked that particular line of retreat. That, and a returning spark of defiance. Why should Hugh Sinclair be allowed to cost her her job? His threats might be empty air. After all, everyone knew Adam Grant had been drowned. Perhaps Sinclair had meant only that fate would punish? But she was not convinced and, in spite of all her scruples, the sight of Joseph was unexpectedly welcome.

He stepped forward, put a hand under her elbow, and escorted her in silence to the Bain house to leave Sal, and then to the door of the smokehouse. There he kissed her forehead, his lips cold against her colder skin, and said, 'Goodbye. I will be waiting for you, tonight.'

And he was. Whether merely as her escort and protector, or for some other reason, she was too embarrassed to ask. As it was, they spoke hardly a word on the way home. He stood back and waited while she collected her baby from the Bain house; put a steadying hand under her arm when she stumbled on a broken cobblestone; and said not a word. But when they reached the door of her house, instead of turning away, he followed her inside, 'To speak with your brother William, when he comes home.'

Elissa, outwardly calm but inwardly in turmoil, settled Sal into her crib, made tea, answered Katrine's idle questions, spread tablecloth and plates in preparation for the evening meal, while Joseph sat in renewed silence in the fireside chair that was usually William's, big hands cupped incongruously around the blue and white patterned teacup, eyes staring at the iron kettle on its chain over the fire, or out of the small-paned window. Anywhere, it seemed to Elissa, to avoid meeting her eye. For her part, in spite of all the obligations of hospitality, she could think of nothing at all to say.

It was William's reaction which broke the awkwardness between them.

'Marry Elissa? Are you mad, Joseph? You know as well as I do that she has borne a child out of wedlock. That she has disgraced herself and her family, has sinned before the Lord. And with a drunken, gambling, blaspheming – '

'That is enough,' interrupted Joseph, to Elissa's gratitude. 'The man is dead and beyond your censure. As to Elissa, if she has sinned, she has suffered for it, and not least at your hands.'

'A sinner must make recompense,' declared William, his face flushed with righteous annoyance. The two men were on their feet, facing each other across the patterned hearthrug. William had a hand on the back of his wife's chair where she sat to one side of the simmering fire, pale hands idle over a flurry of white sewing in her lap. Joseph stood opposite her, having risen from his chair when her husband arrived home, and now her pale eyes moved anxiously from one antagonistic face to the other. Elissa, standing rigid beside the table, clutched the edge of the wood with white-knuckled hands, one ear as always tuned to any sound her precious baby might make so that she could quiet her quickly before William could complain, and all her attention on the contest between the two men. She heard Katrine's small moan of 'Oh dear' somewhere in the background, but ignored it, as they did. William was speaking again.

'I have told Elissa time and again that God requires of all sinners repentance and humility, of which she has so far shown regrettably little. If her aunt were still alive . . .'

'You would not be master in this house,' supplied Joseph and for the first time for weeks Elissa smiled. It was not a wise thing to do.

'Do not mock me, woman,' glowered her brother. 'I see you are as unrepentant and as steeped in sin as ever. You have lured this honest man into a promise of marriage which, for my conscience's sake, I will not allow him to keep.'

'But – '

'Hold your tongue,' thundered William. 'You will not leave my house until you have shed this sinful obstinacy and developed a chastened and a contrite spirit. A spirit suitable to offer to a husband.'

'Besides,' put in Katrine whom everyone, including her husband, had forgotten, 'who will bring me my tea in the morning?'

There was a moment's pause, before William said, looking hard at a point somewhere above Elissa's head, 'There can be no question of any marriage until your child is weaned. Let us say, a year from now. Then you may go. The child, naturally, will stay with us.' He laid a reassuring hand on his wife's shoulder. 'When that time comes, we will send for one of your sisters to help you and the child will grow soon enough, Katrine dear. With a proper Christian upbringing, safe from evil influences, I have no doubt that she will prove a dutiful help and a comfort to you.'

Elissa stared at her brother in astonishment and a disbelief which turned rapidly to fear: William's motives were plain to her, but what of the man who was to be her husband? Did he think as William did about her child? She searched Joseph's face for reassurance and found it unreadable, his eyes fixed intently on William's.

'That is settled then,' said William, with the satisfied air of an executioner who had chopped a particularly difficult head off with one clean blow. 'No man wants to live with a daily reminder of his wife's . . . unfortunate . . . past. As the good Lord has not yet chosen

149

to bless my wife with a child, it is obviously His will that Sarah shall supply that lack. And she will soon earn her keep. A year from now,' he went on with a benevolent nod in Joseph's direction, 'you shall have Elissa, unencumbered. That is what you wish, is it not?'

Joseph stared at William for a long assessing moment, then turned to Elissa, took both her hands in his and drew her close. He looked down at her and she saw gentleness, concern, and something else which set the blood burning in her veins. 'I am not sure I can wait a year. Can you, Elissa?' When she did not immediately answer, but looked anxiously into his eyes, he knew the question before she asked it. 'And I think our home would be an empty and a soulless one without young Sal. Sal's mother agrees with me,' he said to William. 'We intend to marry as soon as a licence can be obtained. With your permission, if you choose to give it. Without it, if not.' Then he slipped his arms around her and deliberately kissed her on the lips. For a startled second she held back, but as the warmth of his lips covered hers and she felt the pounding of his heart hard against her breasts she forgot William and her months of misery and remembered only the comfort of a man's strong arms around her and the joy of giving. Her lips parted under his and she kissed him willingly, with gratitude.

'Really!' exploded William. 'Have you no shame? Oh, I see now why there is such haste for the wedding. Shame on you, Elissa, for a harlot and a whore. And your first bastard not three months old.'

'You have a mind like a sewer, William Downie,' said Joseph quietly, his arm protectively around Elissa's shoulder. 'And always have had, since you were a grovelling, tale-bearing little prig of six whose sole ambition was to be teacher's pet. If you were not Elissa's brother I'd do what I've always longed to do and upend you here and now in the nearest midden, where you could sniff out muck to your miserable heart's content.'

Katrine gave a strangled giggle which threatened imminent hysteria.

'Be quiet, woman!' roared her husband, forgetting his usual tender solicitude, and Katrine clutched a handkerchief to her mouth and cringed back into the chair, her eyes huge with outrage.

'I'm not deceived by your insults, Joseph Noble. They're no more than a malicious smoke-screen to hide your real motives. It's her money you're after, isn't it?' William stabbed the air with an accusing finger. 'The money which she has no right to keep. Her aunt would never have left it to her if she'd known. Is no doubt turning in her grave and cursing her at this very minute. Well, let me tell you this, Joseph Noble. That money is family money, for family use. Not a dowry for a whore.'

Elissa broke from Joseph's restraining arm, whirled on her brother and slapped him hard across the face. He started forward, hand raised, but a movement from Joseph stopped him short and he stood trembling, the long fingers of one hand pressed against his flaming cheek and his eyes glaring venom.

Elissa glared back, undeterred. 'You've wanted that money ever since Aunt Sarah died, haven't you? Wanted it for yourself because you can't bear the idea of anyone else having it. Aunt Sarah left it to me because she loved me and I loved her, which is more than you ever did. You couldn't get out of the house fast enough when she was ill and dying, could you? But the moment she's dead and no more trouble, you want her money. Well, I've a written will and witnesses that the money is mine; *and I mean to keep it.* For my children.' She reached behind her, searching for Joseph's hand, and clutched it tight. 'And for my husband.'

'If he is fool enough to marry you. But after the way you have spoken tonight, the sooner you take your sin from under my roof, the better it will be,' glared her brother. 'Now get out.'

'We will go,' said Joseph, with ominous quiet, 'when you have apologised.'

At that moment the door burst open behind them, letting in a gust of chill evening air and Tom Downie, smelling agreeably of wood-smoke and ale.

'So this is where you've got to, Joe, you old rascal.' He clapped Joseph cheerfully on the back and grinned. 'Thought you'd escape me, did you, and you owing me an evening's free ale after watching yon cockle-shell of a boatie for you till all hours. But now I've found you, you'll not escape me again. So come on, lad. What are you waiting for?'

'For your brother William to apologise.'

'Then you'll be here till doomsday, Joe laddie. Holy Willie's never apologised for anything in his life, have you Willie? It's against his principles.'

'He will this time. My father is Session Clerk, remember, and William's not wanting to be up before the kirk elders, for slandering his neighbour and bearing false witness.'

'Then hurry up about it, Willie lad,' said his younger brother with cheerful disrespect. 'Joe and I have business to attend to, on the quay.' A thought struck him, and he turned to Joseph. 'What did he say?'

'Something which he regrets.' Joseph looked steadily at William who fumed and glared, then withdrew into a white-gilled hauteur which was infinitely more chilling than rage.

'If I said anything amiss, I apologise.'

'Well, did you, or didn't you?' demanded Tom cheerfully. 'I don't know what you're arguing about, but for pity's sake get it sorted before someone downs my pint. Ma Cameron won't guard it for me for ever.'

'I apologise,' said William as though speaking through broken glass. Into the waiting silence he dropped another icy word. 'Unreservedly.' Then as the silence stretched, 'To both of you.'

There was an audible loosing of held breath before Joseph said, with satisfaction, 'Thank you. And now, Elissa, if you pack your kist, Tom and I will carry it round to my father's place. Under the circumstances I think you'll be more comfortable there. You can move in with my wee sisters till we're wed. I've spoken to Ma already and she has no objection.'

'Wed?' cried Tom in astonishment. Then he seized Elissa round the waist, swung her into the air, plonked her down again, laughing, and gave her an exuberant and brotherly kiss. 'That's the best news I've heard this side of Christmas. You sly old devil, Joe, and me not guessing a thing. But away and get that kist packed, Lissa. Joe and I have some celebrating to do and we canna hang around here all night, can we, Joe lad?'

Twenty minutes later, Joseph and Tom manhandled her wooden kist over the threshold and into the Square, while Elissa followed, a wicker basket of assorted possessions on one arm and the precious bundle which was Sal in the other. But she could not leave her lifetime's home without some sort of farewell. On the threshold she turned back, her eyes ranging over the box bed where Aunt Sarah had died, the dresser with her dead brothers' photographs in their polished silver frames, her father's chair beside the fire, the familiar table with her aunt's checked blue and white cloth, and the supper plates laid out as usual; the whole familiar well-worn scene. She saw her own chair, now, as always lately, occupied by Katrine, and standing beside it, the unbending figure of her brother William. Summoning all her courage, her sleeping baby held tight against her breast, she crossed to the chair.

'Goodbye, Katrine. I will look in to see you now and then, if you would like me to.'

Katrine glanced nervously at William's closed face and gave a little shrug. 'Perhaps.'

Elissa bent and kissed her sister-in-law's unresponsive cheek. 'Goodbye.' She hesitated, expecting some sort of response, if only of accusation, but there was none. Straightening, she saw her brother William's cold eyes upon her and was sparked to defiance. Fate had taken charge and she had nothing now to lose. Deliberately she stood on tiptoe and kissed his cheek.

'Goodbye, William. You will be welcome at our wedding if you choose to come.'

He did not reply.

A week later Joseph Noble and Elissa Downie were married, in the front room of the Noble household, a room set aside for important family occasions and exhumed from its dust-sheets for the purpose. William and Katrine did not attend, though Tom and brother Davie did, with several of their neighbours and as many of the Noble family as could squash into the room, including Bethany who, to everyone's astonishment, arrived back at the house after some unspecified errand on the arm of Brodie Gibb.

'And why not?' she glared at the younger members of her incredulous and for the most part derisive family. 'There's no law against friends coming to folk's weddings. Leastways not that I've heard of.'

'Since when has Brodie Gibb been anyone's friend?' muttered one of her brothers but a sharp clip on the ear stopped that particular line of questioning. Bethany sailed majestically across the room and deliberately sat in the second-best chair, immediately beside her mother. 'And she'd have sat in the best one if her ma hadn't bagged it first,' said Ina Bain, who, with her mother and sisters Jessie, Annie and Nell, the last holding baby Sal in her arms, stood crammed into the open doorway. 'And that Gibb fellow tied to her apron strings so tight he couldna move without her permission.'

'Reckon she thinks a wedding will give him ideas,' giggled Ina. 'Seeing as he hasn't any of his own.'

'And seeing as the lass he really wanted is being wed to another,' contributed Jess. 'Remember how he used to watch our Lissa at the packing? Like a starving tom-cat eyeing a bowl of cream.'

But at that moment Gideon Noble ushered in the Minister and everyone had to make room for them to pass as they pushed their way to the clear space in front of the fireplace. A hush fell on the company, followed by a sudden flurry of whispering. The room was so full of people that it was difficult for anyone to move, what with the potted palm on the jardinière by the window, the polished mahogany dresser with its tombstone of a clock flanked by two massive brass candlesticks, the cabinet containing, among other treasures, Mrs Noble's best china teaset, a pair of ornate Japanese vases and the collection of carved ivory elephants which a Noble uncle had brought home from the East. There were more candlesticks on the mantelshelf, flowered china ones this time, and another clock and, against the inner wall, Mrs Noble's especial pride, an inlaid mahogany upright piano, never used, with a row of family photographs on its chenille-covered top. Chairs had been bundled together somehow in what remained of the room and a space left for the chief performers in front of the small, brass-fendered fire. Gideon Noble stood to one side, beside a small table on which rested the family Bible, open at the flyleaf. Someone had put a jam jar of daffodils on the mantelshelf, and the sight brought unexpected tears to Elissa's eyes.

'I wonder what my sister is up to now?' murmured Joseph to Elissa, as Bethany settled noisily into the chair immediately behind them. Whatever her motives, she was too close for comfort. Especially as Bethany had decided the occasion required what smelt like half a gallon of violet oil to overlay the usual lingering fish-reek. The smell was overpowering and cloyingly sweet in the already overheated room. Elissa hoped she would not faint.

Elissa and Joseph stood side by side before the Minister who, his back to the fire, was absent-mindedly lifting his coat-tails and warming his behind until it was time for the simple ceremony to begin. Elissa, stiffly correct in her best blue dress, hair neatly coiled under a plain straw bonnet, stared straight ahead of her at the jar of daffodils on the mantelshelf and did not answer. Bethany had plagued her enough in the week she had spent under the Noble roof, and no doubt would continue to plague her, wedding or not. Bethany had not forgiven Elissa for, as she saw it, 'taking' Adam, and, as she accused on one particularly cruel occasion, 'driving him to his death, poor devil. Maybe that's why Joseph fancies you, out of spite? He never could abide Adam. He was always going on at me when Adam and I were . . . but you're not wanting to hear about that, are you?'

It was as if Bethany was determined to spoil any memories Elissa had of Adam and their love. 'If you must speak to Adam,' Ina had told her that day outside the hut at Gremista, 'do it when Bethany's not looking. She's a jealous cow.' Jealous and vindictive, as Elissa had learnt to her cost. And now Elissa would have to live under the same roof as her tormentor for the foreseeable future. Or until one of them moved out.

But that problem could wait, with all the others. Elissa's head was too full of the awful knowledge that she was about to vow her life away to the well-scrubbed stranger beside her, whom she did not love and who did not love her, and all because of one moment of helplessness and fear. In the last week she had tried more than once to release Joseph from his promise, but he was an honourable man who had given his word. And meant to keep it.

Any minute now the ceremony would begin, and there was nothing whatsoever she could do to stop it.

*

154

When the food was finished, the drinking over and the visitors gone, taking most of the Noble menfolk with them, Mrs Noble shooed Elissa away from the sink with instructions to 'Take that new husband of yours up to your room and get on with it, lass. He'll be away to the fishing with the rest of them soon enough. And you can leave wee Sal with me if you like, just for tonight.'

Elissa thanked her, but declined. She was nervous enough as it was without parting with the one companion who gave her reassurance. Besides, as she explained, the child needed a night-time feed and . . .

'And you're not wanting anyone interrupting ye?' grinned Mrs Noble, a small, black-haired woman who, with a mixture of well-aimed wallops and much humour, kept her extensive family under tyrannical and apparently effortless control. 'Quite right, lassie. And if any of you wee rascals are thinking of getting up to your tricks,' she warned, glaring round her assorted family, 'you can think again. You too, Beth lass. Or I swear I'll skelp your backsides so hard you'll not sit down for a week.'

'Goodnight, Ma,' said Joseph with only the hint of a blush. 'And thank you.' He kissed her lightly on the brow. 'For everything.'

'Away with ye, lad. It's past your bedtime.' But she looked pleased.

'Goodnight, Mrs Noble,' said Elissa, avoiding Bethany's eye.

'Goodnight, lass. Sleep well.' She grinned, and the wink she gave Elissa was unmistakably lascivious. 'If you must.'

The Noble house, unlike most of the others in the Square, boasted an upper storey and it was one of the two upstairs rooms that had been given to the newly married couple, to be their home until such time as they outgrew it. The other room, across the wooden landing, housed the younger Noble males, all five of them, and on the landing and in the space above were stored nets, baskets, coils of assorted fish-hooks and other paraphernalia of the line-fishing trade, as well as spare drift nets for the herring and anything that could not be stored elsewhere in the teeming household.

But the room Mrs Noble had prepared for them was clean and neat, with plenty of space. Elissa saw that someone had moved her kist upstairs from the room she had shared for the past week with Bethany and her two young sisters. There was also a wickerwork crib for Sal, and crisp, clean linen on the bed. Someone had polished the brass knobs on the bedstead till they shone like four bright oranges and a faint scent of lavender hung in the air. The floorboards had been scrubbed and polished and there was a small rag rug on either side of the bed. Elissa bit her lip with a mixture of gratitude and shame. She did not deserve such kindness when her heart was . . . was . . . But she no longer had a heart; she had given it unreservedly to one man and that man had died, taking her heart to the grave with

155

him. At least, she amended, that part of her heart which could love a man: she had love enough for her baby, and affection for her family and friends. But for the man she had apparently married, before witnesses, that very afternoon, she felt nothing, except a guilty awkwardness and a shyness which made her seek refuge in her baby. She had known Joseph for as long as she could remember, liked and trusted him, but it made no difference. She could not think of one thing to say.

But there came a time when even Sal was satisfied, and she had no more excuse to cradle her protectively against her breast. She rose from the side of the bed where she had been sitting in the half-light, her back to Joseph, while she suckled the baby, and walked on bare feet across the room to the cradle. She laid the child carefully down on the clean linen, tucked the bedclothes around her, marvelling as always at the miniature perfection of cheek and eyelid and delicate, fragile little hands. It was as she lingered, checking that Sal was really asleep, that she sensed a movement on the other side of the ill-fitting plank door. She turned her head and saw that Joseph, who had been sitting quietly in his shirt-sleeves on a rush-bottomed chair under the skylight, had sensed it too. He was across the room and had flung the door wide before she could raise even a questioning eyebrow. The next minute he was laying about him furiously with a pillow in a clatter of pan lids and what sounded like a whole playground of squealing children. In reality it was no more than half a dozen and Bethany who, grinning from a safe distance, found it not so safe after all as the whirling pillow caught her full on the side of the head and knocked her back on to a skull of coiled fish-hooks, from which she leapt up with a roar of outrage.

'Thank your lucky stars I didn't choose a boat-hook, you prying wee devils,' panted Joseph. 'As for you, Bethany,' he finished, straightening and giving her a look which she obviously understood, 'your memory must be slipping. But I might forgive you, this time. *If you get back downstairs this instant*! And you can untie that string of pan lids before you go. You'll wake the baby. It's a wonder you haven't done so already.'

Surprisingly, Bethany went, herding her siblings meekly in front of her down the narrow stairs.

'And you can tell Ma from me to get on with that skelping she promised you,' called Joseph after them. 'If one of you so much as sets a toe on the stair.'

'I hear you, Joseph,' came his mother's voice from below. 'And when your da gets back from the bar, he'll be happy to give me a hand.'

Joseph closed the door and leant his back against it, but he was

156

grinning. 'You need not worry, Elissa. They're only kids and they mean no harm. They'll not come back.'

She nodded, blushing. After a moment, he said, offhand, 'We'd best go to bed, lass. There's work to do in the morning.'

She crossed to the bed, sat nervously on the edge of it, shook her hair free from its pins and resumed unbuttoning her bodice, but the buttons were small and her fingers clumsy with nervousness. She sensed Joseph moving about behind her but dared not turn to see what he was doing. The light which slanted through the small rectangle of skylight was fading but not enough; moonlight made the room silvery with shadows. If only a cloud would obliterate the moon so the darkness could hide her. Then she felt the bed springs give under his weight and bit her lip hard.

'Elissa?'

She turned her head reluctantly at the unspoken command in the too-soft voice. He was lying back on the pillows, naked to the waist – and below for all she knew, for the blankets were discreetly high – and his eyes were dark caverns in the eerie light; dark with something that sent a quiver through her tensed and nervous body.

'Yes?'

'Are you deliberately driving me distracted – or is that button really stuck?'

Her cheeks flamed and she turned her back. But she managed the last button and pulled the garment smoothly over her head.

Not looking at him, she drew the blanket cautiously back a little on her side of the bed but he reached out a hand and gripped her wrist with a strength that made her gasp.

'Why did you ask me to marry you, Elissa? Was it to get a father for your child?'

She blushed and tried to shake her head, but the lie would not come.

'Wanted a protector, maybe? To see you home safe in the dark?'

'No, I . . .'

'Someone who would beat off the predators?' he continued, with an edge of bitterness to his voice. 'Someone safe and reliable who would be no trouble to you? A well-trained guard-dog who would keep his distance and do as he was told?'

That stung her. 'No, of course not. How can you say such a thing, Joseph, when you know I . . .' She stopped, embarrassed by the intensity of his gaze which was travelling hungrily all over her as if . . . as if she was mother-naked instead of decently covered in her best linen shift. She folded her arms tight across her breasts.

'Don't do that, wife,' he said, very softly. 'Hold your arms wide – now high above your head.'

157

Trembling, she obeyed – and before she realised what he meant to do, he had seized the hem of her shift and peeled it neatly up and over her head. In the same movement, he tossed it to the far side of the room and lay back again on the pillows, hands comfortably behind his head and his eyes ranging over every curve and roundness of her body.

'I knew you would be beautiful, Elissa.'

Dark hair falling loose to her waist, she stood naked, her eyes lowered. Then she raised them, saw the expression on his face and was suddenly quivering, though not with cold.

'Forget the question. It does not matter now.' He spoke so softly she could hardly make out the words, while his eyes looked deep into hers and she could not look away. 'I know I was not your first choice. I know you do not love me. But whatever your reasons, you asked me to marry you. I accepted, for reasons of my own. Now, as your lawful husband, I expect you to share my bed. Is that too much to ask?'

She shook her head. He was right and it was all her own doing. She remembered an old adage from school-days – she had made her bed and must lie on it. The aptness of the saying added an edge of hysteria to her nervousness.

'Well then.' His hand flicked back the blankets in invitation and she slipped obediently under them, lying stiffly on her back, not touching him, but burningly aware of his nakedness and of her own, a mere hair's breadth apart. *I must remember this is for my child's sake. She needs a father and a protector.*

Then his hand was on her cheek, turning her face gently towards him, and her eggshell resistance shattered. It was not disloyal to Adam, how could it be, when Adam was dead and she was alive and lonely? Besides, it was not the same. She had loved Adam in joyous innocence. Now, in her maturity, she was merely giving her husband what was his right. And, she recognised with a shock of surprise and wonder, what was his burning, passionate need. When he kissed her, drew her closer till they folded naturally together as one body, she buried her face in his neck, at first to her shame pretending he was Adam, then not pretending. Knowing she was giving him all and more than he had dreamed of, and feeling, deep inside her, the first flicker of a treacherous flame of pleasure. As the flame blazed exquisitely higher, she could have cried aloud to the stars in the tiny skylight, had it not been for the listening ears below. But whether in pleasure or in guilt and apology to her dead love she could not tell.

Moonlight flooded the simple room, turning the gold orbs of the bedstead to silver. Silver apples of the moon. Beside her, Joseph slept, his body still twined with hers, but Elissa lay bleak-eyed and mourning. Adam was dead. It was a betrayal of his memory to go to bed with another; an equal betrayal to find even a moment of pleasure in it. And a worse betrayal of her new husband to think of her old love on her wedding night. Remembering her vows of the afternoon, before a Minister of the Church and a score of witnesses, she knew what she must do. For Joseph's sake, and for her child's.

She lay a long time, staring wide-eyed into the night sky, saying her final goodbye. Then she closed her eyes and fell asleep with her husband's head against her breast.

A long time later, with the first dawn light slanting through the misted skylight, she struggled up from the dreamless depths of physical exhaustion to see Joseph standing beside her, clad only in a long flannel shirt and holding her baby awkwardly in his arms.

'I think our little daughter is hungry.' He placed the child carefully against her mother's naked breast.

Joseph had said 'our' and, after the first moment's suspicion, she realised that he meant it, without sarcasm or reproach, from his own honest heart. She looked up at him with a shy smile of gratitude. Afterwards, when the child was replete and swathed in a clean napkin, he carried her back to her crib.

'Is it time to get up?' murmured Elissa, listening for sounds of movement from the house.

'Not yet.' He peeled off his shirt and slipped back into bed, then folded his arms around her, drawing her into the warm curve of his body and cupping her breasts in caressing hands. 'But that does not mean we have to go back to sleep, Mrs Noble. Does it?'

The next time she woke it was to find Joseph gone and his sister Bethany shaking her shoulder.

'Ma says here's a cup of tea for you, Lissa, and you're to help her with the smoking soon as you feel fit. In ten minutes' time. Just 'cos you're married to my brother doesn't mean you can lie around all day being waited on,' she said, with an air of righteousness which put Elissa instantly on guard. 'There's work to be done in this house, same as in any other.'

She put the teacup into Elissa's hands then without warning whipped the blankets back and out of reach over the foot of the bed, leaving her exposed and naked in the tumbled sheets.

'Well, well,' said Bethany with a grin of what looked like triumph. 'And there was me thinking your aunt brought you up never to be naked. And in a man's bed! Shame on you, Lissa. What would Aunt Sarah have to say about that? Or your precious Adam? Well, don't just lie there gawping like a stranded haddock. Drink up your tea and get moving. I told you, there's work to be done.'

In the doorway, she turned to put in the knife. 'And with me and the other girls leaving for Lerwick any day now, you'll be doing most of it.'

Then she clapped a theatrical hand to her forehead, said, 'I'll forget my own head next,' and drew a crumpled, much-folded paper from the pocket of her apron.

'A fellow on the quay gave me this a while back. Lad from one of they whalers, or maybe the Grimsby steamer, a foreign sort of a laddie anyway, not from these parts. What with your wedding and all I clean forgot. Hope it wasn't important.'

She tossed the crumpled scrap on to the bed and left with a flounce of what looked suspiciously like triumph.

Elissa reached out a tentative hand and unfolded the paper, smoothed the creases as best she could and stared at the sea-stained but still legible words.

To Miss E. Downie, North Square, Footdee.
I have to go away for a while, but do not forget our promise. I remember it, always.

There was no date and no indication of where it came from. Only the signature in careful, schoolroom script. *Adam Mackenzie Grant.*

It was the first and only letter he had written her and it had come too late. She covered her face with her hands and wept.

Joseph had decided Elissa was not to return to the Sinclair smoke-house once they were married. He didn't trust Hugh Sinclair, especially while Joseph himself was away with the herring fleet, and Elissa could help his mother in the family smokeshed in the Square instead. His distrust was proved justified sooner than he expected.

For Joseph Noble, on reporting as usual with everyone else to the Sinclair-Gibb yard on Monday morning, met with an unexpected shake of the head.

'Sorry Joseph, but we've no need of your boat this season.' Brodie Gibb looked evasive, but firm.

'And why not?' Joseph inquired, with ominous quiet. 'Wasn't last year's performance good enough for you?' He knew the answer, as did everyone else, for the Noble boat invariably delivered top-class fish in prime condition and more than fulfilled the contract.

'Apparently not,' said Gibb with a level glance and the slightest tip of the head which Joseph read rightly as an invitation for a word in private.

'I don't know what you did, lad,' he told Joseph later, 'but I have orders to cross you off the list, permanently. And before you ask, the orders came from the top.'

'Easton Sinclair?' Joseph was surprised: Sinclair senior never interfered in the operation of the curing yard.

'Aye. And when he orders, whatever I think on my own account, lad, and I have the highest respect for you and your family, I obey. And so do you.'

Joseph drew a long, steadying breath, then shrugged. 'It wasn't Easton, but no matter. I'll tell you this, though, in friendship. Watch out for young Sinclair. He's hoodwinked his father and spun him some lie or other. But I'll tell you the truth.' And he did.

Gibb, to his credit, offered to go against orders and sign Joseph for the season, but Joseph declined. 'It would only lead to trouble. Besides, I reckon this is the opportunity I need to start out on my own, but thanks for the offer.'

Afterwards, the two men had shaken hands and though the family didn't understand, they had taken Joseph's word for it that 'Brodie Gibb couldna help it.'

That did not stop the fellow being in bad odour in the Noble family, all the same. At this late stage of the hiring Gideon and Joseph and the others would have to find another curer to take on the Noble boat, or take a chance and hope to sell in the open market.

'I don't know what Gibb's thinking of,' grumbled Gideon Noble, glaring round the family table. 'If he's by way of courting Bethany, as your mother seems to think, then he's a queer way of going about it.'

'It's not Brodie's fault,' said Bethany, in her most refined accent and several of the smaller children sniggered, whether at the accent or the use of old Gibb's Christian name was not clear. The accent slipped. 'Shut your mou' Zach, you pesky wee tyke. You too, Sam and Abel, or I'll knock your stupid heads together. Jeering at your betters.'

'Who's that then?' dared Saul. 'Old Gibb or you?' Another eruption of glee which Gideon Noble promptly quenched.

'Quiet, all of you,' he thundered. 'I will have respect at my table, respect and good manners, or by God you'll feel my belt across your arse. And that goes for you too, Bethany, make no mistake about that.'

'No, Father.' Bethany sat, eyes demurely lowered, for perhaps twenty seconds, then resumed, 'What I was going to say was that it's not Brodie's fault our boat lost the contract. He was just doing his job, like anyone else, and obeying orders. If it's anyone's fault,' she went on, her gleaming eyes suddenly fixed on Joseph, 'it's that precious wife of yours, Joseph, and you not wed and bedded a week. Lissa Downie's brought you ill luck already, and I reckon she'll bring plenty more afore she's finished with you. And us.'

'Hold your tongue, Bethany!' ordered her father, his hog's-bristle eyebrows meeting across his nose in rage. 'Remember Elissa is your sister-in-law and a member of our family. I insist on family loyalty above all else.'

'Yes, Father. I know that and I apologise. Please forgive me.' But in spite of the honeyed words and apparent submission, Bethany managed to direct a look of malicious triumph at Joseph, and to include Elissa in its wounding orbit.

'I am sorry,' said Elissa, when they were alone together. 'Bethany is right and it is all my fault.'

'Rubbish. You did not ask to be molested, and it was I who struck the fellow.'

'But to lose the contract, for your family . . .'

'Who support me absolutely. So there's an end to it.'

But Elissa had turned her back and was bending over the open lid of her kist where she had hidden that precious scrap of paper which had caused her so much torment. If only she knew when Adam had written it and where. But she knew it was hopeless to question Bethany who was quite capable of concealing the letter for months, perhaps for ever, had not the opportunity to taunt her rival with it proved too tempting. No doubt she had waited deliberately till Elissa was safely married to Bethany's brother and there was no turning back.

But why should she even think of turning back when Adam was dead and she needed a husband and a loving father for her child? She snatched up what she was looking for, straightened and held out a small, folded canvas packet.

'Take the money, Joseph. I want you to. Please?'

Joseph's face closed. 'I will support my wife by my own efforts. That money is yours, and Sal's. Put it away.'

'But you and your father can use it to – '

'*Put it away, woman.*'

She bit her lip, turned her back and did as he had ordered her. Ordered her. That was what hurt. Adam had never ordered her about in such a way. Adam whom she had vowed never to think of again. Then she felt a hand on her shoulder. A gentle hand.

'I am sorry if I spoke harshly. Forgive me, Elissa?'

She nodded, not looking at him. But he turned her towards him, lifted her chin till she was forced to look into his eyes, then kissed her.

'We will not quarrel, wife, and certainly not over money. Is that understood?' Then he kissed her again, more slowly this time, and by the end of it her resistance had melted away. He picked her up in his arms and carried her to their bed. 'Another week and the fleet will be sailing, we Nobles with it. I think we have better things to do with our time than argue about nothing, don't you?'

But if family loyalty was strong in the Noble camp, it was less so in the Downies', at least where William was concerned. Far from commiserating with the Nobles, he could not conceal his satisfaction.

162

Any misfortune that fell upon wrongdoers, in this case Elissa and her misguided husband, was God's proper punishment and the agent responsible merely acting out God's predetermined will. This was a useful philosophy which allowed him to enjoy other people's misfortunes with a clear conscience. And he was certainly enjoying the latest. It went some way towards compensating for the domestic inconvenience of Elissa's removal. When one of Katrine's numerous sisters arrived to fill that gap, his satisfaction was complete, except for one niggling doubt about the infant Sarah.

But he quieted his conscience on that point with the thought that if he saw the slightest sign that his niece was being led down the same path of wickedness her mother had followed, he would exercise his Christian duty and remove the child from danger. That would serve Elissa right.

CHAPTER 15

The Square emptied with the herring drifters. Younger sisters took over from older sisters who had married since last season and a rash of new widows joined the work-force. Bethany took her sister Phemy, barely fifteen, but big for her age, to replace Meg, who, married to Suffie's cousin Wallace and four months pregnant, stayed behind like Ina Bain. Wallace agreed with Fergus that a curing yard miles from home was no place for a decent wee babe to be born. Annie Bain filled Ina's place and she and Jessie found a new packer, Liz Christie from South Square.

There were changes in the boat crews, too. Some of the older vessels had suffered too much of a battering to be made seaworthy for the long voyage to Shetland and their crews had split off to man newer, more reliable craft. The previous winter's storm had left its mark. On top of that, some of the younger dissatisfied men had swallowed the lure of the new screw-driven wooden steamers which, so rumour had it, caught four times as many fish as any sailing trawler, and had been enticed as far south as Grimsby. Including one of the Noble boys, young Zeb, who hoped to find out his father's cousin and get himself a bit of useful patronage.

He was going to need it, for Gideon Noble, on hearing the news, had sworn a solemn oath on the family Bible that any son of his who so disobeyed him and deserted to the enemy – i.e. steam – had no further claim on family loyalty or support. He had even, to Elissa's horror, drawn a thick line in black ink through Zeb's name on the flyleaf of the family Bible where the births of all the Noble children were recorded, from 'Joseph born 1855', with his marriage added two weeks ago, right through to the fourteenth, 'Millicent, 1878', and the deaths of four of them. Five now, for that black line was as good as a death. Mrs Noble had not said a word, her face impassive, but later Elissa had found her in the smokeshed at the end of their strip of garden, her face buried in her apron and her shoulders heaving with stifled sobs. Elissa had put an arm round her in silent sympathy until the older woman had straightened, dried her eyes on her apron and smoothed it flat again. But she had murmured, 'Thanks, lass,' before taking up the pail of water and sprinkling it on the smouldering sawdust of the fire, to produce the required amount of smoke.

It was only a wee shed, nothing like the size of the Sinclair-Gibb smokehouse: an enclosed chimney, like a cupboard, to hold the tenterhooks of smoking fish, a fire at the foot of it and doors to keep the smoke in, a scrubbed deal table and buckets of various sizes, for mixing the pickle and treating the fish before stringing them up in pairs, tied by the tail. But it was Mrs Noble's pride and one more job that Elissa could help with, and did. Her conscience troubled her enough already on the matter of the Nobles' lost fishing contract: she had no wish to be accused of not earning her keep.

The Noble boat had found another curer to take them on, though on less favourable terms and only, vowed Joseph, as a temporary measure. Like his younger brother Zeb, he had grown restless.

Change was in the clean salt air, tainted more and more now with the smoke from the new steam trawlers. Old Gideon Noble called steam the enemy: others called it the future. Certainly, after the first lumbering hiccups, the Sinclair-Gibb steam trawler had settled into a pattern of steady profit. Out in the afternoon, a night spent fishing Aberdeen bay from Collieston to Muchalls, then home the following morning, fish sold by private bargain or sent by rail to Glasgow and London and a morning free to count the profits. Which, if rumour was true, were mounting steadily from two hundred pounds in the first month to almost double that by the third. Then, at the end of May, a week after the herring fleet had sailed, came the news that the trawler's catch had been sold for the first time by auction. Change was definitely in the air.

There was change in the curing yard, too. For Easton Sinclair, after a private consultation with Brodie Gibb from which he had emerged black-browed and resolute, had removed his son Hugh from the Pocra smokehouse and posted him north the next day, though the season had not yet begun. When it did, he was to take charge of their curing yard at Gremista. Sinclair senior had obviously decided his son could do less harm in Shetland than at home. Elissa was relieved for herself and Sal, but frightened for Joseph.

'You will take care, Joseph?' she pleaded. 'Remember how he threatened you, and he means it.'

'Don't worry, my love,' said Joseph, kissing the tip of her nose. 'I'll keep well out of the fellow's way, I promise you.'

Elissa was unconvinced – look what had happened to her beloved Adam, whether by Sinclair's hand or fate's – but she kept her fears to herself.

At the end of July, the herring fleet came home for a week before taking off again for the east-coast fisheries. While Gideon Noble mourned the passing of the old ways and prophesied doom with a group of similar-minded friends, Joseph and Elissa's brother Tom had more productive discussions in the Crown and Anchor with a crowd of younger men including Fergus Mackie. Since his marriage to Ina and the promise of a wee son before the year was out, Fergus had developed ambitions beyond being merely one of a band of coopers at the beck and call of an ignorant upstart like Hugh Sinclair, under whose arrogant and despotic rule the Sinclair and Gibb curing yard was no longer the fair, efficient and smooth-running enterprise it had once been.

With the success of the new steam-trawling venture, it looked as if Easton Sinclair had decided the herring-curing side of the business must fend for itself, for with only Hugh Sinclair in charge it amounted to the same thing.

'Which,' said Joseph, looking round the group with a new gleam in his eye, 'is an open invitation to the competition.' He tipped back his chair and called across the smoke-filled room to the barman to 'bring the same again', then pushed a space on the cluttered, ale-spattered table in front of him and leant forward, elbows spread. 'I tell you, lads, between ourselves, I'd give a lot to wipe the arrogance from young Sinclair's face.'

'It would cost you dear if you tried it,' warned Tom.

'Aye, by the usual methods.' Tom, like most people, was ignorant of Joseph's confrontation with Hugh Sinclair, and Joseph was dropping no hints. 'But no one gets deported for business competition. Leastways, not if it is honest.'

'Best thing would be for all of us to sign on with some other curer next season,' said someone. 'That'd fix him.'

The impromptu conference was interrupted by the arrival of the barman with refills, but the moment he was out of earshot, Fergus Mackie took up where they had left off.

'If I can raise the money to get started, lads, you can sign on with me. I've been wanting to set up on my own for a while now and I reckon I could do a better job than the Sinclair laddie with my eyes shut and one hand tied behind my back.'

The rest of the evening was spent in happy speculation: the look there would be on Sinclair's face when no one signed on with him, the profits Fergus would make, and share with the rest of them: the bright, independent future without the shackles of folk like Sinclair and Gibb: even, one day, steam for the drifters so they could make the fortunes old Sinclair was making with his steam trawlers.

'Though you'd best wait till your da's passed on, Joseph,' warned someone, 'or you'll get disinherited for tangling with the devil.'

'For a steam drifter maybe,' grinned Joseph. 'But I reckon even my da would be in favour of a curing yard – especially if it took Hugh Sinclair's business away from him – and hiring suitable land should

166

be easy enough and not too costly. There's always a bit of shore going spare. If you're serious, Fergus lad, I might come in with you. I've enough brothers waiting to fill my place in the family boat.'

But they would need money for the farlins and jetty, money to hire gutting crews – at least three – and the girls wouldn't come without arles. On top of that they'd need salt and wood for the barrels as well as money to fee the herring boats to catch for them. And an extra cooper or two to help with the everyday running of the place. With the listing of practicalities, euphoria died.

'We've a bit put by, Ina and me,' said Fergus, suddenly dejected. 'But we'd need as much again, and more to set everything up.'

'I haven't much,' said Tom. 'William gives most of it to Katrine and I reckon I drink the rest. But what I have, you're welcome to.'

'Keep it, lad. You'll likely need it yourself one day.'

Most of the others were in the same situation as Tom, or with families of their own to support and little enough money to live on, let alone save.

'We could maybe borrow?' suggested Joseph, but without conviction. After the losses of last year's storm many, including themselves, had been forced to borrow to pay for repairs and some loans were not yet paid back. Besides, the enterprise, if it ever took off, was to be theirs alone, not funded by some shore-based capitalist, like the Sinclair-Gibb steam trawler company. If they couldn't borrow from the bank, or the family, then they must wait till they could raise the money themselves. Of course there was one source Joseph could tap, but that was out of the question.

'Maybe by next spring you'll have saved enough?' suggested Tom, with his usual optimism. No one answered. Though they all, for different reasons, wanted to shrug off the old way of working and take on the new without delay, they all knew that even the most skilled of fishermen had no control over the sea, or over the sea's bounty.

But when the fleet came home at the beginning of September for a brief respite and to prepare nets and vessels for the Yarmouth season, though plans for the project had been worked out down to the smallest detail, the two men were no nearer finding suitable backing than they had been in July.

Joseph could not hide his despondency from Elissa and when she asked the reason, he told her.

He had sought her out, as usual at that time of the evening, in their own room. She was sitting in the chair under the skylight, to catch the best of the evening light, mending some small garment of Sal's while the baby lay in a wicker basket on the floor beside her, waving arms and kicking plump legs in gurgling joy at her own prowess and howling in annoyance whenever her little cotton bonnet slipped over her eyes, as it frequently did. Elissa liked to spend time alone with Sal whenever she could, and to be in their own room when Joseph came home. She was still ill at ease in the maelstrom of the Nobles' family life, especially if Bethany was about, and in the days since the girls had returned from the curing Bethany had resumed her particular brand of torment. Sometimes it was a reference to the Noble family's loss of the Sinclair-Gibb contract 'and we all know why that was', sometimes to 'more mouths to feed and nay even our own kin', and once, Bethany had come up behind Elissa in the kitchen where she was ironing Joseph's Sunday shirt and whispered, 'A year ago today your auntie died.' As if Elissa did not know that already: she had fought long enough with her conscience and her fear that very morning, before buying flowers on the green to lay on her aunt's grave. But Bethany had not finished.

'The Duthie wifie says there was rare goings-on that night, screaming and shouting. Maybe you helped the old besom on her way? Maybe she'll come back to curse you?' Then she had crowed with laughter before posturing in front of the looking-glass above the dresser to adjust her bonnet. A new straw bonnet she had bought in the town that morning, for one and sixpence.

'Do you think Brodie will like it?' she asked, rolling her eyes like a coquette at her sister Phemy, who was watching the broth pot from a low stool by the fire while her fingers knitted an indeterminate-looking undergarment in bleached wool.

'Aye,' said Phemy, grown bolder after her first spell at the curing. 'It'll remind him of a herring basket.' She wrinkled her nose and added, 'Smells the same, too.' In the ensuing scuffle, Elissa escaped upstairs to the comfort of her baby and the attic room which was home. The trouble with Bethany's words was that, behind the malice, they always held a needle of truth. She and Sal were extra mouths to feed. Joseph had lost that contract because of her. As for Aunt Sarah . . .

Now Joseph's words gave her the excuse she needed to set everything right.

'We'll not find backing before the spring, if then,' he told her. 'With the trawlers flooding the market with cheap white fish, there'll be little enough profit for the line-fishermen this winter and if we miss the start of the season, the lads will sign on with someone else. And the lassies too. There must be a solution somewhere, Lissa, but I just can't see it.' He subsided on to the edge of the bed and held his head in his hands.

'I can. It is my fault that your family lost their usual fishing contract. They have never reproached me for it and I am grateful. So if you cannot find it anywhere else you must use the money Aunt Sarah left me. It is yours, Joseph. Please take it.' She looked up at him with a smile in which he saw affection and pleading, but he merely glowered.

'And give your brother William the satisfaction of saying "I told you so"? I'd die first.'

'Then if it is merely a question of male pride, I give up,' said Elissa, with a shrug. 'It is a pity, though. When Ina's son is born, and ours, they will have no more to look forward to than working for the likes of Sinclair and Gibb.'

Joseph turned pale. 'Did you say "ours"?'

'I did. Though of course it might be a daughter.'

He snatched her to his chest and held her for a long, shuddering moment, and when at last he set her free she saw his eyes were glistening with unshed tears. But all he said was, 'Daughter or son, I shall be equally happy. And I promise you our child, children, will have the best future I can give them.' Then he kissed her. He was still kissing her when the door burst open and one of his smaller siblings skidded into the room. Six-year-old Zach whom Elissa could only distinguish from brother Abel by the state of his front teeth. This lad's were missing.

'Ma says the stew's getting cold and the tatties like to burn and she'll not save any for folk who don't help and don't come when they're called.'

'Where's Beth?' demanded Joseph, his arm protectively round Elissa's waist. He knew as well as she did that Elissa more than pulled her weight.

'Dunno. Ma said to tell her, but I couldn't find her, so I tellt you instead.'

'Next time, knock before you come barging into folk's rooms. And tell Ma we're coming!' he called after Zach who had scurried prudently out of reach and down the stair. 'There, the message was not for us at all,' soothed Joseph. 'But we'd best go just the same. Have you told Ma?' he whispered as they reached the kitchen.

Elissa shook her head. She and Mrs Noble rubbed along well enough together, but not on terms of sufficient intimacy for Elissa to confide in her. Though Joseph's mother had never mentioned the subject, she must, like everyone else, be aware of Elissa's past: 'shameless' to the likes of her own brother William, 'unlucky' or plain 'sad' to the more sympathetic. Elissa still had no idea which word Mrs Noble used in the privacy of her thoughts.

The family kitchen was stiflingly hot, as usual; the window closed and the fire in the iron range blazing under the great iron stew-pot and the smaller, of potatoes. The five younger children were already crammed together on the long bench on one side of the table, the youngest, Milly, with her chin at table-top level. She and Joseph took their places on the other side, beside Phemy and nineteen-year-old

Pete, and the empty place which was Bethany's. Mary Noble presided at one end of the table, Gideon at the other.

Elissa waited, eyes lowered, for Gideon to finish the grace. Longer than usual today: talk with his friends had been particularly depressing, especially when a group of swaggering trawlermen had erupted into the bar and, in Gideon's words, 'taken over the place'. They had spent indecent amounts of money and boasted of the fortunes yet to be made. By them. The crowning insult had been that they came from 'down south'. Aberdeen's importance as a trawler port was obviously spreading.

But even Gideon's eloquence dried up at last. Mary Noble ladled out large helpings of stew to the menfolk and suitably graded ones to everyone else, and the meal began. Bethany's place remained empty, for which Elissa was grateful, though her absence had led to three minutes of extra praying from Gideon, and a particular tightening of the lips from his wife.

When Joseph's plate was empty, his mother rose to offer more, but he stopped her.

'Later maybe. First, Elissa and I have news for you.'

Mrs Noble's face lit up with joyous expectation. 'She's not . . .?'

'She is, Ma.'

But at that point the door opened and Bethany sailed in, her face flushed and her hair dishevelled, a gleam of triumph in her eyes.

'Who is what?' She made her way straight to the hearth and began to help herself to stew.

'Put that plate down,' ordered her father. 'I'll have an apology from you, before one morsel of food passes your lips.'

'Suit yourself,' shrugged Bethany. 'Sorry I'm late. This stew smells good, Ma,' she went on, ladling more on to her plate. She slipped into her seat and, after a warning frown from her mother, closed her eyes and gabbled something that finished with a loud 'Amen'. Then she took the first, greedy mouthful. 'Now what were you talking about? Who is what?'

'Are you sure, Joseph?' said Mrs Noble, ignoring her.

'Yes, Mrs Noble.' Elissa answered for him, encouraged by the obvious joy of the older woman.

'What did I say, Gideon?' cried Mary Noble looking at her husband in delight. 'You may as well know, Lissa lass, that Gideon wasn't at all sure about our Joseph marrying you. But I said the lass couldna help being widowed and that dead lad of yours wasna the first to try for a child afore the wedding and won't be the last. And at least we knew you weren't barren. There's some lads marry and wait years for a bairn, but not you, Joseph lad. Aye, you made a grand choice when you chose Lissa here. She's a fine worker and good, healthy stock.

Just think, Gideon, we'll have our first grandchild afore we know it. When's it to be, lass?'

'In the spring,' said Elissa, blushing. 'April maybe.'

'You didn't waste time, did you?' said Bethany, staring hard at Elissa. 'It's not a year since you was heart-broken. What'd your precious Adam say if he could see you now?'

'Mind your tongue, woman, and leave the lass alone.' Gideon Noble rose from his chair, an unheard-of occurrence in the middle of a meal, and moved to the door. 'I think the occasion demands a small dram, don't you, Joseph? I'll not be a minute.' He crossed the narrow entrance hall to the door of the best room and they heard the clink of glasses.

'Best make it a large dram, Da,' called Bethany after him. 'So's you can kill two birds with one stone. Brodie and me's getting married, soon as he's found us a house.'

When the first uproar had died and Gideon had filled their glasses, Bethany, delighted at having stolen the limelight, looked round the company with a mixture of condescension and triumph.

'Brodie, I said, I'm not living in one poky room, with folk all over the place, prying and listening at keyholes. I'm having a place of my own, I tellt him, or I'm not getting wed. Anything you say, my dear, he said, so long as you will be my wife. So he's away to look for a place for us. He said he'd best find it afore he spoke to you, Da, but I tellt him you'd say yes. What with Brodie being a partner in yon trawler company that's doing so well and the house here full to bursting. I fancy one of they new places in Marine Terrace. There's two trawler captains have houses there, and other rich folk from the town. It's a fashionable area is Marine Terrace and nay so common as Trinity Quay and the Shiprow.'

'Why not go for the west end while you're at it,' jeered Phemy. 'Though they'd maybe not stomach the fish-reek so well in the Queen's Road, it being for gentlefolk.'

'Keep a civil tongue in your head when you speak to me, Euphemia, or I'll clout you one,' glared Bethany. 'I'm going up in the world, I am, and you'd best remember that, if you know what's good for you. Brodie's making the sort of money you couldn't even count, 'cos you'd run out of fingers and toes afore you'd half begun, and there'll be more once the ice factory is . . .' She stopped, deliberately tantalising, then said to the room at large, 'But you're not wanting to hear about me. It's Joseph and Elissa we was toasting. To the wee grandchild.' She raised her glass. 'If it's a girl, I might even be her godmother, if you was to ask me. Though with me likely being a married woman by then, and awful busy, you'd need to ask well ahead.'

171

'We'll remember that,' said Joseph, his face expressionless, but he sought Elissa's hand under the table and squeezed it in reassurance. Elissa, however, did not need it.

'I am glad you are to be married, Bethany, *at last*. And with a house of your own, too, so there'll be no more need to listen at keyholes. Not unless you have folk to stay. Are you planning to do much entertaining?' she went on quickly before Bethany could gather breath. 'I've heard Brodie Gibb is a solitary sort of a man who keeps himself to himself, and sups off a mutton pie and a pint on the quay. But you'll likely change all that, being the accomplished cook and hostess that you are.'

There was a moment's astonished silence, then Mrs Noble gave a great shout of laughter in which first her husband, then everyone else, except Bethany, joined. 'Well said, lass,' she managed at last, wiping the tears from her eyes. 'Joseph fair knew what he was doing when he chose you. You're a lass after my own heart. If you could have seen your face, Beth . . .' and she collapsed once more into laughter.

Bethany fixed Elissa with a stare that told her battle was by no means over, but Elissa did not flinch. Mrs Noble's laughter had shown her as nothing else could have done that she was accepted, and not just because she carried Joseph's child. Besides, if Bethany did marry Brodie Gibb, she would soon be out of the house and far away, with children and interests of her own. As married women they must both put thoughts of Adam Grant behind them. She had said her own goodbyes on her wedding night; now Bethany would say hers and they could forget past rivalries for ever. One day, in the age of miracles, they might even be friends.

'Enough of this foolery,' said Mrs Noble through her laughter and pushed back her chair. 'I've a fine cloutie dumpling bursting to be eaten. Give a hand, Phemy, to clear the plates away, then Lissa can help me serve. And if you're planning all this fancy entertaining, Beth lass, you'd best copy the recipe, so's you can feed your man proper. He's a peely-wally look about him sometimes, that Brodie Gibb, and he'll need to keep his strength up if he's to father a bairn. With him being not as young as he was. Not that age has ever stood in your father's way!' and she laughed so much that Phemy snatched the pudding dish from her in case she dropped it.

At the head of the table Gideon Noble grinned. Then he reached for the whisky bottle and refilled the glasses.

'To my grandchildren. May there be plenty of them.'

Elissa, raising her glass with the others, caught Bethany's eye and faltered. But only for a moment. If it was to be war, so be it.

172

CHAPTER 16

1887

The city of Aberdeen was in a state of happy turmoil. Once it had been decided which Saturday in June was to see the official cele-bration of the Queen's Jubilee, shopkeepers, tradesfolk, business-men, councillors, everyone with a spark of patriotic blood in his veins and many others who were fuelled purely by the love of a holiday, entered whole-heartedly into the task of dressing up the streets for the occasion.

Even the heavens joined in, sending sunshine and summer breezes soft enough to lift the spirits without tearing the bunting from the lamp-posts or stripping shop fronts and civic buildings of their banners, transparencies, loyal slogans and strings of coloured lights. Seven hundred of them on the Crosshouse alone and as many more on the Town and County Buildings and the North of Scotland Bank. It was a pity certain disruptive elements had lit the civic bonfire two days early, in spite of its padlocked protective railings and personal watchman, but the damage was soon remedied and the pile replaced. On the evening of the great day the Jubilee bonfire would blaze, as planned, on the headland of Torry on the south side of the harbour, while on the north the city would answer with a constellation of coloured lights.

The harbour itself was crammed with vessels, their masts and yards bright with bunting and each vessel vying with the next to show the city folk they hadn't the monopoly on patriotic fervour. Or at least, that they knew how to put on a good show. Even the black-funnelled steam trawlers had scrubbed their smoke-grimed decks and made an effort of sorts to dress up, while the entire herring fleet was in harbour, spick and span, anything that could be polished, polished to sun-dazzling brilliance and many vessels bright with new paint. They would be off to the east-coast herring fisheries again on Monday, but in the meantime, the city was in festive mood, and the fishermen with it.

Many of the shipowners and other prominent businessmen had

173

been invited to the banquet in the town hall and Bethany Noble Gibb, in a purple merino walking outfit and a straw bonnet tied under the chin with sky-blue ribbons, had called on her mother in the Square the previous week to make sure everyone knew that Brodie had been invited too.

'Your Joseph's not going?' she had asked archly of Elissa who merely shook her head and continued to fold the linen which she had newly fetched in from the drying green. She had spread an ironing cloth over one end of the kitchen table and was sorting the linen into different piles while Mrs Noble worked amicably away at the other end of the table, sleeves rolled to the elbows and arms white with flour.

'We're not all important city folk with money to burn on fancy food and fancy clothes,' said Mary Noble with amusement and no trace of envy. 'Some of us have work to do and mouths to feed. Some of us still think birds should live in trees and not on top of folk's heads. Some of us still have the sense we was born with.' She winked at Elissa who smiled.

'No, Bethany,' said Elissa. 'Joseph is not going to the banquet. He will spend the day with me and the children. There are so many exciting things to see and do together, and then there is the procession.' In five years of marriage, and the setbacks and tribulations of Joseph's struggling curing yard, Joseph and Elissa had grown close in friendship. With Joseph so often away with the fishing fleet, the rare times spent together with Sal and Gideon Joe were precious to them both. Besides, all eight thousand of the city's schoolchildren had been invited to tea at the Lord Provost's house and were to process school by school behind their heraldic shields through the city streets to Devanha. And five-year-old Sal was to march with them. The pleasure of that spectacle far outweighed any civic banquet, even had Joseph been asked.

'What a pity,' said Bethany, preening. 'All the city's successful businessmen will be there. You tell your Joseph if he's ever to get on in the world he'd best mix more with the right folk.'

Elissa went over to the range, picked up the flat-iron which was warming there, held it an inch from her cheek, then with a shake of the head, replaced it. 'Not hot enough yet.'

'Don't see how you can tell without spitting on it,' said Bethany, forgetting her status. 'I do. Leastways, I did before I had servants to do it for me.'

'La di da,' crowed her mother, who was kneading bread dough on her half of the kitchen table. 'I knew you was grand, Beth lass, but I didna know you kept servants to do your spitting for you. You have come up in the world.'

Bethany chose to ignore her. 'I mean it, Lissa,' she said, adjusting

174

her bonnet in the looking-glass over the kitchen dresser and arranging the bits of dead bird to better advantage. 'It's time your Joseph did better for himself, then you could have smart clothes like me. This is a real kingfisher, all the way from London. Just for morning calls, like. I've ostrich plumes on my best bonnet. And so could you have, Lissa, if that man of yours stirred himself a bit more, made himself more sociable. You tell him, lass. My Brodie would be happy to advise him, any time.'

'I reckon it's your Brodie needs advice,' said Mrs Noble, thumping the bread dough harder than necessary before dividing and shaping it into two. 'You've been wed near on five years and no sign of a bairn. And there's your sister Phemy with two already. You tell your Brodie to ask around at his precious banquet for a hint or two. And if there's oysters on the menu, to eat the lot. Then if the old Queen, bless her, survives another ten years you'll maybe have a bairn of your own to cheer in the school procession.'

'We've a business to run and our way to make in the world,' snapped Bethany. 'Time enough for bairns when we're well settled. That reminds me, Lissa. What with yon wee curing business of Joseph's not doing so well as it might, and him refusing all offers of help though the Lord knows he could do with some, I was thinking. I've an old gownie or two I'm not needing and with Phemy away to Buckie with that lad of hers, maybe you'd like them? Call round any time and I'll tell Nessie to let you have them. They'll do you fine for the fish. Or cut down for that lassie of yours.'

Elissa didn't bother to reply. She was so used to the barbs and condescensions that she no longer noticed them. Or if she did, it only made her pity Bethany the more. Marriage and money had not mellowed her sister-in-law and now, watching her smirk and spread her city skirts in the homely clutter of the Noble kitchen, Elissa glimpsed discontent behind the vainglory. Ever since Bethany, in her own words, had 'gone up in the world' she had been acting a part and sometimes Elissa thought it must be a dreadful strain, in spite of the new clothes and the new house in Marine Terrace, from where she could look down over the harbour 'and count the ships my Brodie's company owns and the factories he's got shares in'. Rope and salt and, the latest, ice – essential for the increasing fish trade. But Elissa would rather dress Sal in flour bags than in Bethany's cast-offs and though Joseph's business was, as Bethany had said, not doing so well as it might – too many doors were closed against him, too many contracts refused, or overpriced – it was doing well enough. Fortunately, when the slump in the herring market came, only a year after he and Fergus had set up their curing yard together, they were operating on such a cautious scale that their losses were few and containable.

Not like some. With the curers contracting, as usual, for quantity, when the glut came, they found themselves deluged with undersized and poor-quality fish, no use at all for curing. As Joseph had feared, too many fishermen used smaller meshes in the hope of gain and the curers carried the burden. They were contracted to pay and pay they had to, even though what they paid for was worthless. Young Hugh Sinclair lost his father a deal of money that year; though Sinclair senior had had the foresight to keep the curing separate from the trawling side of things and the loss was contained. But the result, apart from banishing Hugh Sinclair to their Grimsby office, was the closing down of the Sinclair-Gibb curing business altogether.

'Good,' said Joseph with satisfaction. 'That leaves the field wide open for us.'

Now, three years later, he and Fergus were employing six gutting teams instead of three and the old system of contracting had gone for ever. Fish was sold the moment it was landed, to the highest bidder, usually by salesmen for the fishermen to agents for the curers. Joseph and Fergus acted as their own agents, but Tom, after some disagreement with his brother William about the meagre profits of the family boat, had taken his small share and set himself up as a fish salesman. Under the old engagement system fishermen had not needed such a middleman, but now with the daily catch to be sold at auction, the easiest arrangement was to hire someone on a regular basis to do it for them. Tom had seen the opportunity and, being a cheerful, fast-talking and persuasive lad, had found it suited him. He knew the product and he knew the market, and had quickly acquired a score of clients all happy to pay him five per cent to dispose of their catch. Only his brother William thought he should do it for nothing and Tom soon disabused him.

'Five per cent or nothing,' he said cheerfully. 'Suit yourself. But if it's nothing, you sell your own fish, Willie lad. I've plenty other clients.' Then he had strolled out of the house, whistling.

Tom was doing well, and was walking out with a healthy, sensible lassie from South Square. A cousin of Meg Duthie's on her mother's side. Elissa's brother Davie was married to Jess Christie, with a child due in a month's time. The three brothers still lived together, more or less amicably, in the house they had been born in, though Elissa suspected Tom would move out when he married: Tom's lass was not as easygoing as Tom and made it plain to everyone that she couldn't abide William Downie.

Elissa sympathised. She bore William no ill-will – after all, he was her brother and family loyalty came first – but no one could call him forgiving. In his eyes she was and would always be a sinner and that was that. As a result, Elissa seldom visited her old home, and never, if she could help it, when William was there, but she liked to keep in touch with her family and she got on well with Davie's Jess. Also, as time passed, with Katrine who became almost a friend. Once, she even asked after Sal and hoped she did well. The next time, Elissa took her children with her, and had it not been for William's determined aloofness, which even in his absence she sensed in the very furnishings of the house, she might almost have felt at home.

But home now was the Nobles' house. It was as crowded as it had ever been, for though Bethany and Phemy had left, Joseph's nearest brother Peter had married and brought home a wife, Elspeth. They had the room across the landing from Elissa and the sound of their quarrelling and the endless wailing of their baby kept her awake for hours, though Sal and Gideon Joe slept peacefully enough, and Joseph too when he was home. Elissa did not like Peter, who had little of his brother's straightforward honesty and reliability and none of his gentleness with children. Or with women. Already old Gideon Noble had warned him about his behaviour, and secretly Elissa hoped he would take his family and go. At least it would ease the over-crowding. But Peter had as much right to be there as Joseph, and said so – more, he claimed, for he was not the one to desert the family boat for a piddling little shore-based curing yard – and Elspeth was another pair of much-needed female hands, if not a particularly willing pair.

The younger boys would not reach marriageable age for a while yet, but suppose the errant Zeb came home, with a wife? The trawling industry was thriving from Grimsby to Aberdeen and for the lucky ones, fortunes were being made. For Mrs Noble's sake, Elissa hoped Zeb would return, but how then would everyone fit in? Increasingly Elissa yearned for a home of her own – not a smart terraced house in Ferryhill, like Bethany's, just an ordinary tenement would do, in York Street or St Clement's. She remembered her dear Adam's dreaming on the heathland above Gremista when he had promised her a grand mansion with a fine four-poster, curtained bed and beautiful gardens, and she had insisted that a two-roomed cottage would do to start with. Now she would willingly settle for two tenement rooms and a shared wash-house on the green. She promised herself that at the end of the next herring season, if profits were good, she would mention it to Joseph.

She did not want him to think that she was dissatisfied, but she felt increasingly oppressed and only in dreams did she find any comfort. She knew it was wrong of her but increasingly she let Adam into her dreams; talked to him, asked his advice – and was ashamed of her disloyalty. But there was so much work to do and so little time in which to do it and since Phemy had left, the burden had grown heavier. In winter, when the men resumed the small-line fishing and the women the endless baiting of lines, she had hardly gone to bed before it was time to rise again, and even when they were away at the herring fishery, the household tasks seemed endless, what with washing and cooking and cleaning, the smokeshed to be tended and the fish sold, and always the ceaseless knitting. Some days Elissa felt so tired she had hardly the strength to comb Sal's hair or lift the spoon to feed Gideon Joe, but she could not let Mrs Noble shoulder all the work and Peter's Elspeth was, in Mrs Noble's words, 'a lazy wee besom'. As for Milly, the youngest of the three Noble girls, she was a mere schoolgirl of nine and a frail, undersized little thing. She did her best, especially with her young cousins, but it was a small best and she was easily tired.

Then Elspeth's baby took ill and Elissa's real fear started. Suppose it was scarlet fever? Or cholera? Suppose her precious Sal caught the disease, or little Gideon Joe? The baby recovered, thanks to Mrs Noble's brisk administrations, but Elissa's fear remained. She determined to keep an eye and an ear open for any suitable tenement to rent, and when she found it, to speak to Joseph. That was what Adam would have wanted her to do.

She had no fears, however, on that bright June morning, only happiness and expectation. Sal, spotless in a neat clean apron over her neat clean school dress, her black boots polished like mirror glass and her little scrubbed face pink with pride, was leaping up and down with impatience while Elissa tied the laces of Gideon Joe's little boots. Joseph was already downstairs and waiting, dressed in his Sunday best like everyone else, and discussing the latest gossip from the harbour with his father who remained adamant that steam was the devil's work and equally adamant that he must hear every detail of its growing power and influence, so that he could curse it afresh. Joseph indulged his father in his obsession, though Peter called him, behind his back, a bone-headed old fool and, to his face, suggested he 'leave fishing to the young folks, who know what they're doing'. But this morning Peter and Elspeth had gone on ahead with their baby, taking family friction with them.

Mrs Noble bustled here and there, banking up the fire, checking this and that, chivvying one or other of the remaining children and finally lining them up in a row for inspection, before pinning on each child the commemorative medal they had been given in school the day before. Then she called up the stair, 'Are you ready, Lissa? We're off now.'

'My medal, Ma,' cried Sal, frantic with anxiety. 'I want my medal.'

'And you'll get it, Sal, when we're ready,' said Elissa, crouching on one knee in front of Gideon Joe who was perched on the stool his grandfather had made for him and kicking his legs with exuberance.

'No, she won't. She didn't say please. She never says please till you tell her, does she, Ma?'

'I do so! I do say please. And you're a tittle-tattle tell-tale *baby*.'

'I'm not a baby. I'm four and – '

'That's enough from both of you. Gideon, keep still till I've tied your lace or they will go without us. Yes, Sal? Did you say something?'

Sal, who hadn't, said in a small voice, 'Please may I have my medal now, Ma?'

'Of course you can, my love. There. Doesn't it look splendid?' Then she took each child by the hand and hurried downstairs to join the others.

When the younger children had been safely delivered to the school and into their teacher's care, the others were to disperse, or stay together, as they chose. All the shops were open, for what was the point of a holiday if there was nothing to buy, and with the sun shining and the city decked in party clothes, there was plenty to see and do and friends to meet everywhere. Elissa and Joseph, with Gideon Joe skipping between them till his legs grew tired and then riding on Joseph's shoulders, strolled along Union Street, admiring the shop windows, the decorations everywhere, the clothes of the passers-by, while the sun shone from a cloudless sky and the new peal of bells in St Nicholas's steeple clanged discordantly overhead.

The schools were to muster at Robert Gordon's College in School-hill, at the back of St Nicholas, where a horse-drawn carriage waited to carry the lame children who were not up to walking the mile and a half south to Devanha House. When the first sound of the flute band floated over the crowds in Union Street there was a sudden wave of movement, like the turn of the tide, as hundreds of mothers and fathers moved towards the sound, and their invisible offspring. Windows overlooking the route through the town suddenly filled with onlookers, crowds milled and pushed and Elissa and Joseph made their way to their agreed vantage point, on the corner of Schoolhill and St Nicholas Street. From there, as soon as the St Clement's contingent had passed, they hoped to take a short cut through St Nicholas's churchyard and see the procession again as it passed along Union Street, though when she saw the density of the crowds, Elissa's optimism faltered. However would they make their way through that solid mass?

But for the moment they had a good view and Joseph hoisted young Gideon Joe on to his shoulders again so that the lad could see something more than the skirts of the woman in front. He himself could also be seen above the heads of the seething crowd and because of that, Fergus and Ina were able to join them, and a few minutes later, Tom, his arm firmly linked with that of a fresh-faced, smiling girl of a solid build.

'I told you Kate was a determined lass,' he said cheerfully, raising

179

his voice above the surging noise around them. 'Ploughed her way through the crowd like yon steam trawler of Brodie Gibb's in a force ten. Here Ina, let me give wee Mackie a view from the crow's nest,' and he lifted the infant high above his head until the one-year-old let out a howl of indignation. 'Don't you want to see your big brother marching, then? I don't blame you. You see more than enough of him at home, likely.' Grinning, he restored the child to Ina just as the first school came marching proudly out of the gates of the College, their school shield in heraldic red and gold held high in front of them and the flute band of the Junior Oddfellows leading. The music of the band was almost drowned by the cheers of the spectators, which grew louder as the children approached. The flutes grew louder too and the general surge of noise and happy exuberance brought tears of emotion to Elissa's eyes. The children looked so innocently proud, so vulnerable and young.

School followed school, the cheering swelled to greet each new shield and ebbed as they passed from view, swelled and ebbed like the beating of waves on the shore. Then came the shield they were waiting for – St Clement's school. Three hundred and fifty children and in the very front row, with the youngest, were Sarah Noble and Ina's son Fergus. Elissa's eyes filled with fresh tears of love and pride. Her little daughter was so straight and clean and trusting, so bright and brave. So beautiful.

'Our wee Sal's the best of the lot, bless her,' murmured Joseph at her side and, looking up, she saw that his eyes were suspiciously moist too. She squeezed his arm in understanding and gratitude. Then turned to Ina.

'Your wee Fergus is a fine-looking laddie. And just like his father.'

'I know,' said Ina, 'but don't say it so loud. His head is big enough already.'

'But the child can't possibly hear over the . . .'

Ina and Fergus laughed, and the others with them.

'She means this Fergus's head, my love,' said Joseph and put an arm around his wife's shoulder. 'And she's right. I know. I have to work with him.'

Elissa did not hear the back-chat and teasing that followed: she heard only those two unguarded words, 'my love', and felt her heart quiver into life after its long constriction. This was surely the happiest of days.

But St Clement's school had passed and a new school had arrived in its place. 'Quick! We must hurry or we'll miss them.' The others caught her urgency, Joseph lifted Gideon Joe down on to his own two feet and Elissa grabbed tight hold of his hand while Joseph endeavoured to drive a way for them through the throng. In a tight group the others followed and together they pushed their way up Schoolhill the short space needed to reach the gate into St Nicholas churchyard. Then they were stumbling and running, weaving between the tombstones, round the end of the kirk, with the new bells ringing in deafening discord overhead to mark the hour. Others had had the same idea as they had; yet others followed with the mindless instinct of sheep and in moments the kirkyard was almost as full as the streets outside. Elissa was separated from Joseph, though she still clutched Gideon safely by the hand, and though she could see Ina's green plaid ahead of her in the press, she could not reach her. No matter. Once they gained the south side of the kirkyard and the great granite-pillared façade that divided it from Union Street she would find them all again.

She lifted Gideon up on to the low wall which supported the columns of the façade, told him to hold tight to the iron railings while she herself, clutching the railings with one hand, the other holding tight to her little son's belt, found a footing on the narrow plinth the better to see over the heads of the throng. She looked left and right, then over the crowd in front of her to where she thought she could see Ina and the others at the kerb's edge. Joseph was turning his head this way and that, searching for her, then he half turned to look behind him, caught her eye and waved. But at that moment the sound of the familiar pipes came skirling towards them from somewhere to the left and all heads turned towards the corner where St Nicholas Street emerged on to Union Street, to continue straight over and down, as Market Street, to the harbour.

'They'll come in a minute, Gideon Joe,' said Elissa happily. 'And we'll see fine from here. There'll be the band first, then you can wave to Sal again. And to Fergus. After that, we'll wait for your daddy to come and find us. Just watch that corner, over there.'

There was a big crowd outside Ellis's on the corner and more people streaming in from all directions to see the fun. There were coloured lights over the shop doorway, with garlands and a huge banner proclaiming 'Loyal greetings to Queen Victoria on her Golden Jubilee'. Suddenly into Elissa's mind came the shameful memory of a carriage stopping at that same entrance on just such a busy afternoon, a lovely lady in elegant clothes alighting from it, followed by the odious figure of Hugh Sinclair. He had accosted her even then, stripping her naked with his lascivious eyes. She shuddered and slammed the door hard on the flood of other memories that threatened to follow – from Aunt Sarah's illness and death-bed cursing, to her last encounter with Hugh Sinclair, in the fog and darkness of New Pier Road. But Hugh Sinclair had not been seen in Aberdeen for many months – banished to the firm's office in the trawling port of Grimsby, 'where he can do least harm,' said Bethany's Brodie with satisfaction, and if he did appear in his home town from time to time, he was soon gone again, to everyone's relief, including Elissa's. For she knew he had not forgotten, knew he was merely biding his time until he could take his revenge, undetected and unpunished, knew he had meant every word of his threats: to herself and to her family.

She dreaded meeting Sinclair unawares; dreaded what he might do to harm Joseph; dreaded the turmoil he might stir up in the tranquil waters of her life. And they were tranquil: she had done her best to bury the dreams of her youth, with her dead lover, and over the years, despite her memories, she and Joseph had built up a happy enough relationship. It had not the passion of her first, wild love, but nothing could ever match that; and she and Joseph were content with each other, and with their children, Sal and Gideon Joe. For Sal was Joseph's child, as he had promised, and he made no distinction between her and his little son, unless possibly to favour her more. She was a bright child, quick and loving, and she adored him in return. In spite of Sinclair, all was still well with her family.

Optimism restored, Elissa dismissed memory and returned to the happy present: any moment now St Clement's school would come round that corner with the childen of all her friends and neighbours and in the midst of them, her own precious Sal.

But for a moment the crossroads was empty, one school having turned the corner and marched past them up Union Street, the next, St Clement's, yet to appear. In that moment of suspended expectation Elissa's eyes flitted over the waiting crowds, checking idly for a familiar face. And found one. Her own face lost all colour and she trembled so violently she had to step down on to firm ground lest she fall.

But it couldn't be. Her eyes were playing her false. It was the distance. The excitement. The sun blinding her vision.

'Ma! What's the matter, Ma?' Gideon Joe's face crumpled into tears of anxiety. Wailing, 'I fall . . .' he let go of the railings and reached out his arms to her.

She managed to catch him safely, clutched him tight against her, murmuring reassurance, until he was quiet again and her own heart slowed its frantic thudding. It couldn't have been him. It was impossible. It was her memory intruding, her day-dreams, that was all. She should never have allowed herself to look back into the past. Suddenly into her pounding thoughts came the different rhythm of marching feet and the cheerful trill of flutes. She tried to push her way into the press, to find Joseph and safety, but the crowd was too dense.

'Here, lass, I'll lift the laddie for you,' said a kindly man beside her and whisked Gideon up on to his shoulders. 'Now you climb up on the wee wall beside us and the both of you'll have a fine view.'

Too agitated to argue, Elissa obeyed and was in time to see Sal march past once more, still proud, little blonde head held high. She saw Ina's wee Fergus still stepping out valiantly, and Milly and Zach and the others. Saw them with her eyes, while beside her Gideon Joe squealed delightedly and waved, but inside her head all vision was overlaid by the silhouette of the figure she had seen – had thought she saw – on the corner of Market Street. A group of sailors, trawlermen newly up from the harbour and one of them ... But it was impossible. A trick of the light, that was all. A mistake.

The last of the St Clement's contingent passed, amid cheers and much waving of handkerchiefs from the windows overlooking the route. The thud of another band, with accompanying pipes, drifted towards them from the direction of Schoolhill and the crowd around them began to shift, in the way crowds have; some people pushing to the front, others turning away to seek another vantage point. With an effort, Elissa collected her thoughts.

'Come on, Gideon Joe,' she said, retrieving him from the man's shoulders with appropriate thanks. 'We'll go and find the others. They can't be far away.'

Holding his hand firmly in hers, she began to move slowly along the clear space near the railings, her eyes searching the dense and shifting crowd which churned like a turbulent river between her and the procession. This still marched relentlessly westwards, to the cheers and waves of the happy townsfolk. The vanguard would have turned into Crown Street by now; might even have reached the gates of Devanha. She was impatient to follow, so that they would be at hand to retrieve Sal when the ceremony ended, but was reluctant to go on ahead without Joseph. He had seen her at the railings and she ought to stay there, until he came. Besides, she needed him, wanted the reassurance of his kindly, honest face. She found it impossible to keep still.

'We'll walk to the end of the little wall, then back again,' she told her son, 'until Daddy finds us.'

They reached the last granite column of the façade, turned to retrace their steps, and found their way suddenly barred.

Elissa looked up into the face of a blond and bearded sailor in a fine brass-buttoned coat, black knitted gansey, flamboyant scarlet neckerchief and with a black bowler hat tipped jauntily over one eye. His clear blue eyes were jubilant.

'Lissa Downie, my own true sweetheart! I knew it was you the second I clapped eyes on you from way across the street. But then I'd have known my little singing bird anywhere.'

Before she could speak or move so much as an eyelid he caught her in his arms and kissed her on the lips.

She struggled, gasped, fought and protested until, laughing, he held her away from him, his smiling eyes greedily studying her face.

'Are you so outraged to see me after all these years? Have you forgotten our loving and our promises? And me keeping the thought of you always close in my heart, like a talisman through all the bad times? Didn't you promise to wait for me, my darling, and didn't you hold my own promise safe in the palm of your hand? And here I am, Lissa, and you looking lovelier than all my dreams.' He took her face in his hands and looked deep into her eyes. 'Tell me you have missed me as much as I have missed you. That you love me as you did on our little beach in Shetland, that you . . .'

But she was staring at him from horror-filled eyes that grew large and black as doom. His arms fell to his sides and the light left his face.

'What is the matter, wee one? Don't you recognise me? And you promising to know me anywhere, even with a fine blond beard? I will shave it off this instant if it displeases you.' When still she said nothing, dry lips opening and shutting, but making no sound, he added uncertainly, 'Surely you cannot have forgotten? I have come back to you as I promised I would, my sweet one. Look at me, Elissa, and tell me that you remember me. I am Adam Grant. Your hand-fast, promised husband.'

'You can't be.' Elissa backed away from him, her whole body shaking with outrage and dread. It was some trick of Mr Sinclair's. Thank God Sal was not with her, was safely out of sight. But even as she thought it, a cold terror rose and rose inside her till she feared she would drown. Or scream.

'What is the matter, Lissa? Have I changed so much?'

His voice was anxious, tinged with sadness and an unfamiliar cadence which she could not place. Her Adam had not spoken like that. She studied his face, searching for the trick, the mistake that would give this impostor away. The beard had not been there before, but it was short and fair and little barrier to the set of the face. The eyes were as she remembered, though perhaps not so intense a blue, the height and build almost the same. She could see just where her head had rested against his collar-bone, where her hands had . . . But it was impossible. Six whole years had passed since she had stood at his graveside and imagination was playing tricks with her.

'Who are you?' she demanded. Then, more strongly, 'Move out of my way.'

But when she tried to push past him he stopped her, with an arm across her shoulder. At the familiar touch a shudder ran through her and she looked up at him, her face stripped of all emotion but an appalled, despairing recognition. Before she realised what he meant to do, he bent his head and kissed her again, this time like a lover, as if she were young again on the heathland above Gremista instead of a respectable married woman.

'Ah . . . just as I remembered,' he murmured with relief, 'my own sweet love, at last.'

But Elissa recoiled in horror and struggled out of his grasp.

'You are dead, Adam Grant,' she managed through dry lips. 'I saw you myself. Drowned.'

'Do I look drowned?' he asked in astonishment. Then he laughed. 'Maybe I am, lass. Drowned and in heaven. Which is where I've found you. And now I mean to keep you, always.'

He reached out a hand to take hers, but she leapt back.

185

'No. You must not. I tell you I saw you dead. They pulled you from the sea and laid you on the shingle. I saw you. It was terrible.' She covered her face with her hands and her shoulders shook. 'I saw your poor dead face, all eaten away by the sea, and your ... your body rock-battered and your clothes in sodden shreds and ... and ... your beautiful boots full of sea water, but your initials were still clear as day ... Oh God.' She closed her eyes against the pain. 'You were dead, Adam. We buried you and my heart was broken.'

His face was suddenly white, all joy gone. 'But ... Oh dear God, there has been treachery somewhere. Treachery and evil, I swear it. Darling Elissa, you know who I am, Adam Grant, alive and come back for you at last. I could not come before, believe me I had no choice. But the moment I was free I took the first ship home and ... look at me, my sweet one. Do not turn away.'

He reached out a hand to her cheek and suddenly, for no reason, Gideon Joe began to cry. When he put his mind to it, the child had a voice 'fit to wake the dead' as his father said, or to stand in for the Greyhope foghorn. His wail was certainly desolate and remarkably penetrating.

'Hush, my wee one,' soothed Elissa, snatching him up in her arms and clutching him like a shield against her breast. The child put plump arms round her neck and clung tight, still sobbing, though quieter now.

'Who is the wee loon?' asked Adam. 'A friend of yours?'

'My son.' Above the downy softness of the child's hair, she looked with desolation into Adam's eyes. 'You are too late.'

Slowly he shook his head in disbelief. 'I thought you would wait for me, like you promised. I thought you of all people would keep your word. It was the thought of you that kept me sane all these years when I ...' He stopped and finished, with bitterness, 'And you forgot me the moment I was out of sight.'

That was too much to bear. 'You were dead,' she cried. 'Dead and buried.' Her voice rose dangerously high and he put out a hand to calm her.

'Don't touch me!' She turned her back and pushed her way through the press, not caring which way she went, wanting only to escape. She felt his dear hand on her shoulder, twisted away with a cry of anguish, plunged through a gap in the crowd and found herself suddenly held tight in strong, familiar arms.

'Joseph, thank God,' and she buried her face in his chest.

'Hush, Lissa lass, hush. It's all right now. Hush ... You'll frighten the wee loon.' Then he looked over her shoulder and she felt his body go rigid.

'You.' Joseph's face held the same horror as that which raced through Elissa's veins, filling her with a boiling turmoil of emotions.

186

But his next words confirmed what she dreaded to hear. 'What hell-hole has spewed you up, Adam Grant?'

'I'm newly arrived from London, by the packet steamer, though I doubt the skipper would agree with your description.'

'That's of no concern to me. But what is of concern, laddie, is that you *keep away from my wife.*'

That wiped the smile from the fellow's face, as Joseph reminded himself over and over in the days that followed, dreary, silent, blighted days divided only by darker, blighted nights when they lay rigid, not touching, each pretending sleep. Adam Grant's return had blighted everything, even the air they breathed. Even the happy, joyful air of the Devanha picnic.

Elissa had smiled and laughed with Sal at the fireworks and balloons and the little gingerbread cake that each child was given at the gate of the Provost's grand house. Joseph had smiled and congratulated Sal on her marching, and had insisted on carrying her on the last stretch home, while his father Gideon carried his small namesake and Elissa walked, arms linked, with Mary Noble. If anyone noticed the tension, they put it down to the strain they all felt after a long, exhausting day. But the news had not yet reached them.

'You're tired, lass,' said her mother-in-law kindly, when they had put the younger ones to bed, made tea and set out bread and cheese for those who wanted it. 'Best take her up to bed, Joseph.' Then she winked. 'You'll be away to the herring soon enough.'

But in the darkness of the bedroom, there was nothing to say. Only a gulf between them that grew wider with every minute a dead man lived. Elissa knew what Joseph must be thinking: that he had been trapped into marriage; that if she had known Adam was alive she would never have married Joseph. *I know I am not your first choice,* he had said on their wedding night. *But you asked me and I accepted. For reasons of my own.* She still did not know what those reasons were: but whatever they were, he must regret them bitterly. Must suspect her of wanting to leave him and go to Adam. But she was married to Joseph, for better, for worse, for ever. And he to her. They lay side by side, not touching, like two frozen effigies on a granite tomb.

Word was round the harbour soon enough, and all over North and South Squares. Adam Grant had come back from the dead. Fell into bad company, seemingly, gambled his boots away in a Yarmouth alehouse, with most of the clothes on his back, and still owing enough to keep a family of ten for a year. There'd been some sort of fight and next thing he knew he was on one of they emigrant ships to Melbourne. That was one tale: others elaborated freely with talk of press-gangs, debt collectors, irate and murderous fathers, jealous

187

women with gutting knives. But whether he had jumped or been pushed, all agreed on one point: Adam Grant had landed in Australia, on the wrong side of the law, and had been there ever since. At first because he had no choice, then, in his own words, because he was 'working his way up' and from the way he swaggered and boasted and drank himself senseless on his first night in harbour, you'd think he was skipper of half a dozen ocean liners instead of one small, dirty-chimneyed cargo boat. A pipe-stack, likely, and money still owing on it.

But whether he was millionaire or pauper was immaterial. He should have been dead and was alive. For some, especially late at night in the quayside bars, this was a matter of absorbing interest. For Elissa it was torment. To see Adam again had been shock enough; to feel his touch and remember what had been between them, to hear his soft, beguiling words of ... but here she stopped herself. How could it be love after six years of silence? Six years in which she had married and grown used to someone else?

'If you'd done as we said and told folk you and Adam were married,' said Ina, waylaying her friend on the washing green on Monday morning, 'you could have gone back to Adam no bother, and everything legal. But with you not even telling folk that you was hand-fast, that's a different kettle of fish. With you wedding Joseph before a Minister and witnesses, I reckon Joseph's your legal husband, whether you like it or not. Though you could always elope,' she added and her voice was not altogether sarcastic. More as if testing the water and with some anxiety.

Elissa did not, dared not, reply, lest the tight band of rectitude she had fastened round her heart should slip, or snap apart. She had asked Joseph to marry her: how could she free herself, unless he wanted freedom too? But from the moment he had ordered Adam to 'keep away from my wife' she had known that Joseph would fight to keep her, whether from pride or the old antagonism to Adam or some other, private reason she did not know. As for Adam himself, she yearned to be with him, to find their old, sweet intimacy, to hear all that had happened to her lost love since that far-away parting in the half-light of a Shetland morning. Not third-hand and garbled from the mouths of quayside gossips, but from Adam's own lips, in blessed privacy. Wanted to know why, if he loved her as he said he did, he had not come for her till now. Wanted above all to be with him.

But she was Joseph Noble's wife 'till death do us part', and that was that.

So she argued against and fought down the great swell of longing which rose inside her for the man she had mourned as dead. Reminded herself that, in spite of his return, he was still dead to her.

Dead for ever. She was married to Joseph, the father of her child. But dear God, how long would it be before someone told Adam about Sal? And when they did, what would he – and Joseph – do? Part of her wished for such a cleansing confrontation: at least it would force Joseph to do something. But most of her crouched in fear, dreading the inevitable.

Bethany was jubilant.

'Who'd have thought it?' she declared, spreading her rustling skirts with her usual vanity and settling back in her mother's chair at the Noble fireside two days later. 'And there was everybody thinking he was dead. I wonder he didn't hear about it, and with that fine headstone on his grave, too. He'll need to get the name changed on it. I tellt him. Adam, I said, there's some poor drowned laddie lying there with your name stuck on him and him maybe the pride of the kirk and innocent as the driven snow. He's not wanting the name of a skiving no-good philanderer stuck on him for ever, is he? What'll St Peter say at the Gate when he turns up wanting entry? Tell me that, I said.'

'And did he tell you, Beth?' asked Milly, when no one else commented. Elissa had her back turned and was pouring boiling water into the teapot, while Mrs Noble was mending a long tear in her husband's work shirt and had a mouth full of pins.

'Aye, he did, but it's not repeatable in polite company. He's a devil, that one, and no better for six years where he's been, neither. But it's a wonder we didn't hear from him in all that time. Now if he'd written a wee letter and it had arrived in time, Elissa might not even have married our Joseph, might she?'

This time even Milly made no comment, but concentrated hard on her knitting.

'Six years, just think,' went on Bethany, enjoying every twist of the knife. 'If he'd been married to some lassie before he vanished, she might have married someone else in that time, with him being officially dead. Then where'd she be when he came back? Seven years and she'd be all right, but not six. She'd be a bigamist and her children would be bastards, even if they weren't already. You should have stayed away longer, I tellt him, just to make sure and do you know what he said? There's plenty lassies as would wait twenty years for me, he says, grinning. Arrogant bastard. Are you going to be all day with that teapot, Lissa, or must I pour my own?'

Elissa wanted to stop her ears so that she need not listen to Bethany's barbed chatter, and at the same time longed to hear everything, though she knew that most of it was lies. Only Adam could tell her the truth and he had avoided her. She could not seek him out behind Joseph's back. It would not be right. But she ached with doubt and anxiety and curiosity and longing: for the Adam of

189

her youth and love, in that herring summer on the headlands of Shetland.

What hurt her most was his accusation of faithlessness. Apparently she should have known the drowned man was not Adam, in spite of the boots, and certainly should not have married. Only by telling him the truth about Sal could she justify herself, yet every instinct told her to guard Sal's secret. She owed it to Joseph, for all the love he had freely given the child. Elissa had feared from the moment the news reached her sister-in-law that Bethany would gleefully stir the pot and tell. Unaccountably, Bethany said nothing.

Listening to Bethany's chatter, Elissa puzzled and puzzled, but could see no explanation: except the simple one that Bethany wanted to keep a hold over Elissa, to be able to torment her secretly, as she was doing now. For Bethany couldn't have forgotten, though others apparently had. Somehow over the years Sal had become Joseph's child; not only by his own deliberate decision, but by common acceptance. If anyone in the Square remembered the particular circumstances, as they surely must, no one was telling. Joseph was a Footdee man and popular, and Footdee folk did not hold with bumptious strangers thrusting their way into the Square and interfering in what was none of their business. But no such considerations would have stopped Bethany if she had set her heart on mischief. If she kept silence, it could only be for her own ends. So, as the brief days of public celebration passed and the ordinary rhythm of the summer herring fishing resumed, Elissa worried and watched and tormented herself with yearning while Joseph remained silent and aloof.

It could not last. On the morning of the day the fleet was to sail, a note arrived at the Nobles' door. It was addressed to 'Mrs Noble' who promptly opened it, then folded it again and slipped it into her apron pocket.

'What is it, lass?' asked old Gideon who, with his younger sons, was just leaving for a last overhaul of the family drifter before they sailed for Shetland on the evening tide. Joseph was already round at Fergus Mackie's, checking stores for the curing yard.

'Just a recipe I asked for,' said Mrs Noble. 'A cough syrup which the Minister's wife reckons is better than mine.'

'Dinna believe it,' growled Gideon. 'And you the best cook this side of Edinburgh. Besides, if it's that good, why is the Minister always coughing his lungs out and the half his peely-wally family with him? If you're brewing up good lemons and sugar, you use the recipe you always use, woman. We don't want needless waste.' Then he slammed out of the house, taking the menfolk with him.

Mrs Noble wiped a hand across her forehead, said, 'Remind me to make lemon syrup, would you, Lissa? And to speak with the

Minister's wife come Sunday? And you'd best take care of this for me,' she said, glancing at Milly out of the corner of her eye.

Elissa held out her hand for the paper, opened it, and felt her face go hot, then deathly pale. *I must see you,* she read. *Alone if possible. If not, then with whoever you choose to bring with you. But I cannot live until we have settled things between us. Name a place and time and I will be there.* It was signed *Adam Mackenzie Grant c/o the* Hopeful, *Albert Quay.*

'And if you have a moment,' went on Mrs Noble, as if the world was its normal untroubled place instead of a sudden maelstrom of turbulence and rainbow possibilities, 'I'd like your opinion on that new sawdust we've been using for the smoking. I'm not convinced it burns steady enough. Watch the bairns for a wee minute, Milly, will you? We'll be back directly.'

In the privacy of the little smokeshed at the end of the garden strip, Mrs Noble looked steadily at Elissa. 'Well, lass? I read yon note in mistake, for it said only "Mrs Noble" on the outside, but I'm glad I did. What is your answer to be?'

'I am glad you read it, too,' said Elissa, 'for I want no secret meetings and I cannot speak of it to Joseph. But I will meet Adam. I must. It is all I have been able to think of since . . . since he came back. I want to know, you see. To know what happened. I cannot go behind Joseph's back, but at the same time I dare not ask his permission. He wouldn't understand and he . . .'

'And he is sour jealous and black-browed enough already? Aye, lass, and there's no help to it that I can see until you and that Adam laddie sort things out between you. So away you go and write him a note. You'd best say three o'clock outside the Northern Tea-rooms. What you do then is your own affair, but be home before the men leave, lass, or there'll be talk. It's a sorry business and no one's fault that I can see. So you must do what you think best.'

Elissa's eyes brimmed with tears of gratitude and she hugged the older woman with quick affection. 'Thank you for understanding.'

'Away with you,' said the other, adjusting her apron and busying herself unnecessarily with the fire shovel. 'You're a good lass.' Elissa thought she finished, 'and I'll miss you,' but could never afterwards be sure.

They did not go into the tea-rooms. Instead, Adam took her hand, led her to a waiting hansom cab and told the driver to take them to the west end of town, where the buildings ended and the countryside began. 'Somewhere where a man can walk with a lassie in peace and quiet.'

Fairfields, it seemed, was such a place. Where the town road gave way to a country one and that in turn became a rutted track, there was a stone gateway and a drive into some large private house, out of sight beyond the rhododendrons, and surrounded by trees and a dry-stone wall.

'Come back for us in one hour,' said Adam, then, taking her hand, he led Elissa along the grassy bridle path which skirted that boundary wall on the southern side. The wall, with the ground at its foot, was untidy with trailing ivy, numerous mosses, yellow stone-crop, purple foxgloves and even, here and there, the heavy scented blossoms of a rampant climbing rose. Behind the leafy barrier was unknown territory, but the bridle path ran across open countryside, with heathland, whin and clear skies. Behind them, the sounds of the town fell away and apart from the steady hum of bees and occasional bird-song in the trees overhead, there was silence.

When they turned the first corner of the wall, town and townsfolk vanished, and there was only green space with, in the far distance to the west, the soft violet outline of the mountains. They turned to face each other. Elissa had meant to tell him straight away, to keep him at a respectable arm's length, to ask so many questions about his life since they parted. Instead they kissed.

Elissa thought her very bones would melt with the bliss of that moment as the intervening years fell away and she was alone again with her own true love and the sky a blessing overhead.

'We have an hour, my darling,' he murmured. 'One short hour after so many wasted years.'

But his voice had broken the spell, brought reality cruelly back to taunt her. 'I should not be here at all,' she said. 'It is wrong of me. And I should not have kissed you.'

'On the contrary, my little singing bird. You owe me years of kisses, and more than kisses. How can you ask me to cancel such a debt?' His dear voice was what she had dreamed of in her loneliness, his hands gentle and loving. His arms around her were treacherously persuasive and her own body the worst traitor of all. But she was no longer an innocent of seventeen. With a cry, she pushed him away.

'No, Adam. I loved you once. I still love you. I think I always will. But I have a husband.'

'That is what I do not understand,' he said, his voice suddenly cold and dead. 'How could you do such a thing to me? I wrote to you. I told you I had to go away. Why did you not wait, as I waited for you? Waited and worked and saved, as I promised you I would do.'

'I told you, Adam. You were drowned and all the curing yard saw you dead on the shingle beach. Drowned in that terrible October storm of '81 that killed my father and so many others.'

'*But not me.* There was villainy somewhere, Elissa. There must have been. I didn't want you to know, but how else can I explain so many years away? *I was serving a jail sentence, behind bars.* Don't look so horrified, Elissa. Believe me, to this day I don't know how it happened, or why. One minute I was drinking in a bar with people I thought my friends, a pair of English lads who knew a man with a fine drifter to sell and wanted a share ... I can't remember the details but we were to go into it together, the three of us. We were laughing and joking, then ... I can't remember anything else however hard I try. The next thing I knew was that I had a terrible headache, every part of me that could be bruised was black and blue, and I was a prisoner below decks on some sort of ship, bound for Australia.'

Elissa was appalled. 'But that is dreadful, Adam.' Her mind raced over the possibilities and finished, as always, with Hugh Sinclair. *Or something unpleasant will happen as it did to your hot-headed friend.* 'You should have written to me, told me where you were. At least I could have sent you letters, to cheer you.'

'I told you. I did write. I sent a note by one of the sailors.'

How long had Bethany kept that scrap of paper to herself? And would it have made any difference?

'The only note I had came after I was married, and before you accuse me of faithlessness, Adam, there is something you should know.'

They were still standing close under the wall, with the scent of flowers wafting over the moss-encrusted stones from the hidden garden beyond, Adam leaning against the pitted stones and Elissa a careful distance from him, on the grass of the bridle path. Now she reached out a hand to take his.

'Listen carefully, my love, and do not interrupt me or I might lose my courage.'

Then she told him about Sal, her own loneliness and misery in her brother William's house, her fears that he had designs on both her baby and her money, then of Hugh Sinclair's pestering. 'You told me once that if you were not around to protect me, I was to go to Joseph Noble. So when he saved me from Sinclair, and asked what else he could do to help me, I said ...' She gulped, looked Adam firmly in the eyes and said, 'I said he could marry me. It was for Sal's sake as well as my own,' she went on quickly, 'and he has been the best of fathers to her.'

'Which I have not.' His voice was heavy with ... what? Elissa searched his face, fearful of what he would do or say. But even so he took her unawares. He caught her in his arms and crushed her so hard against his chest that she gasped in pain. Then he pressed his cheek against hers and she felt the tears, hot on her skin. She put her own arms around him, murmuring comfort, soothing, reassuring until he straightened, rubbed his eyes with the back of his hands, and managed a small smile.

'One way and another I have failed you in just about everything, haven't I? Courtship, marriage, fatherhood. I've messed up the lot.

But I promise I'll make it up to you, Lissa. I know I was a wee bit feckless as a lad, but I'm older and wiser now. Richer, too. Did I tell you I own my own cargo boat? I could not come back to you with nothing and that was to prove I could succeed if I tried. That's only the beginning, Lissa. I'm on the way up now, and with you to work for I promise I'll be the most responsible, sober, law-abiding husband you could possibly wish for, and the most responsible of parents. I have reformed already. No gambling or excessive drinking. I confess I did drown my sorrows several fathoms deep on that first night, when I thought I had lost you for ever, but that was a solitary lapse and won't happen again, I give you my promise.'

Elissa tried to interrupt, but he would not let her.

'It is my turn to speak now, lass, so listen.' He took her hand and led her slowly along the path. 'When we reach that far corner,' he said, pointing ahead of him, 'I will lift you up to peep over the wall. After that, you have permission to speak. Not before.'

She walked obediently beside him in apparent calm while her mind churned with arguments and possibilities. Adam took it for granted that she would go to him. But she had been married to Joseph for five years and could not leave him just like that; on the other hand Adam had a rightful claim on his own daughter and on the woman who would have been his wife if fate had not intervened. Besides, she longed with all her loving body to go back to Adam, to lie down with him here, now, in the fresh grass of the meadow and to find the innocent rapture of that first time, in the herring summer in Shetland.

To go back. That was the trouble: suppose she was just yearning for what she had lost? Chasing a dream? She and Adam were six years older than when they parted, with six years' different experience separating them. She knew nothing about this older Adam, and he knew nothing about her.

'So you see I have money now,' he was saying. 'And though my little steamer is not the smart vessel I mean to buy for you one day, it has a cabin for the captain, with a brass lantern and a brass-rimmed table and a mahogany panelled bed that is comfortable enough for one, and will be just as comfortable for two and a hundred times more friendly. The profits are good too, and promise to be better with every voyage. But here is the corner.'

He turned to her with such happiness in his eyes and such suppressed excitement that she could not speak for the knotted lump of pain in her throat.

'See this wee jutting stone here? Put your foot on that and I'll heave you higher. There now. What can you see?'

Elissa clung to the top of the wall as Adam told her, balancing with one foot in the precarious toe-hold while Adam steadied her with firm hands at her waist, and she looked through the tangled mass of ivy across flowerbeds and a green lawn to a stone terrace with urns and geraniums and, behind it, a row of tall windows in a granite façade. There was another row above the first and above these, at attic level, were three more smaller windows in the roof itself, each under its eyebrow of slates.

Hastily Elissa slid down again to ground level, her face pink with embarrassment.

'It was someone's house,' she said.

'I know. Did you like it?' His hands were still at her waist, but he had turned her to face him and had drawn her closer. She should have resisted, but her heart wouldn't listen.

'Yes, it was beautiful, but . . .'

'Then you shall have it, my love. One day I will buy it for you, for you and me and Sal and the rest of our children. I give you my solemn promise.' Then he kissed her again. She allowed it, exulted and gloried in it, held his dear face in her hands and kissed him back with all the lost love of that far-off summer. And knew in that moment of longing and pain that it was her final farewell.

'Goodbye, Adam,' she said. 'We cannot meet again. It would not be right.'

'Why not, when you are the mother of my child? Of course it is right.' He tried to draw her down on to the grass beside him.

'No. Oh, God, I should never have come. I thought we could talk quietly, sensibly . . .'

'Talk? When I have waited for you so long, with such love and longing? Come, my love, no one will see us and we have time. I know you love me, want me as much as I want you . . .'

'No!' She pushed him away and shook her head in anguish and confusion. 'I mean yes, I love you. Yes, I want you, but no, no, *no*. I made my marriage vows before God and I cannot break them. Only death can do that.'

There was a long silence in which Elissa saw all the jubilation drain out of Adam as it had drained out of her. When he spoke it was as if a dead man spoke.

'And what of my daughter Sal?'

'She will stay with me and with the man she calls Father. It would be cruel to make her do otherwise.'

'And you? Do you love this Joseph?'

'Not in the way I love you, Adam, no. But he is a good man and a good husband and I hold him in . . . in affection.'

'Affection? A wishy-washy emotion. If you really loved me, you would come away with me now, today. Listen Elissa,' and he seized her hands eagerly in his. 'I will take you to Australia. We can make a good life for ourselves there. You and me and Sal. People would understand.'

'And what of Gideon Joe, my little son?'

'He can stay with his father. That will be fair. Then you and I can – '

'God would not understand,' said Elissa with bleak finality. Then she turned her back on Adam and all happiness and walked back along the bridle path beside the long, high wall of the forbidden garden, towards the far corner and rectitude.

'I'll not give up. I'll make you change your mind.' He ran after her, snatched her roughly to him, tried to kiss her into submission, but she froze under his hands, became an icy, unrelenting block of virtue, and he let her go again.

'That villain Sinclair has certainly had his revenge,' said Adam bitterly. 'On both of us. I wish I'd killed him when I had the chance.'

'No, you don't, Adam. Not really,' though for a moment her own heart had echoed Adam's wish. She dared not look at him in case resolution faltered and stared instead at the rough stone of the wall so close beside her, at the little clinging mosses, a sudden frond of ivy, the pink and gold and green mottling in the stone. The grass was damp and springy under her feet. 'You could have found no peace with murder on your conscience.'

'And I'll find no peace now, with you married to that fellow and refusing to leave him. I might as well have stayed in Australia.'

'I think you had better go back there,' said Elissa, walking resolutely on towards the corner of the endless wall round which would be the stone gateway and escape.

'Perhaps I will. I am obviously not welcome here.'

Goaded beyond caution, Elissa turned on him. 'Stop behaving like a spoilt child, Adam. You and I are no longer children to take what we want when we want it. We are adults with responsibilities. And mine are to the man I married and to our children. Suppose the situation was reversed. Suppose I had married you. Would you have me turn round and walk out of the door because a man I once loved suddenly reappeared after six dead years and beckoned me?'

'But you still love me. I know you do. As I love you.'

'That has nothing to do with it!' cried Elissa in despair and fled before he could touch her and change her mind.

Glowering with frustration and bitterness, Adam followed. 'Don't think you have won the argument, because you haven't. I have business to see to in London and a return voyage to Australia, but I warn you, I will be back. I don't give up as easily as that, especially now I know I have a wee daughter. I will not forget you, Elissa. Or Sal. I didn't forget you all those years in prison and I'll not forget you now. Not ever.'

'You must.' It was all she could trust herself to say, but he took it as encouragement.

196

'I know it has been a shock for you, a confusion.' His voice was suddenly gentle again, loving and persuasive. He even tried to take her arm, but she shook him off. 'Don't be frightened, my love,' he soothed. 'I have been too impatient and I am sorry. I should have realised you need time to think about things calmly and properly. And so do I.' He attempted a smile, though Elissa's eyes were still fixed firmly ahead, her steps quickening. 'I knew I had, or thought I had, a sweetheart, but I never dreamed I had a daughter. We must think about her, too. Not make any rash decisions. Burn any boats. I have rushed you too fast. So make no decision now. Not until you have thought carefully about what I have said.'

'I have thought,' she said, her eyes on the patch of deep pink willowherb which marked the corner of the boundary wall and safety. '*I have thought of nothing else.*'

'Think how we love each other,' he persisted, lengthening his stride to keep up with hers. 'Think of our daughter. Then decide. Not in a hurry, but carefully, remembering we were separated through no fault of our own, but by outright villainy.'

'Or fate.'

'No. Unless Sinclair is fate in person. But I will have my revenge on that villain one day, I swear it. Even if I have to wait a lifetime. But I will wait, as I will wait for you. Listen, my love. I sail for London in two days' time. For Melbourne a week after that. Come with me, Elissa? I beg you?'

'Please, Adam. Don't try and make me.' She was pleading now, her eyes brimming tears.

'Why not? When I know you want me?'

'Because . . . because I can't, Adam. *I have a husband.*'

'Who should have been me.' His grip on her arm tightened. 'If you don't leave him, Elissa, and come to me, I swear I will . . .'

But they had reached the corner and she rounded it with a gasp of relief for there was the hansom cab, waiting as ordered beside the great stone gateposts, the horse quietly nibbling the grass of the verge and the driver apparently asleep in his seat.

Adam's voice changed from threat to urgency. 'You need not decide now. Send a message to the *Hopeful*. Or come to London to join me. If you miss this voyage, there will be another, and another. I swear I will not give up until you change your mind. You will marry me one day, I promise you, Lissa Downie. One day . . .'

She walked on, not looking at him, giving no answer beyond a small, despairing shake of the head.

'I will write to you from London,' he persisted, still close at her side. 'I'll not give up you or my daughter. You love me, I know you do.'

But the driver had heard them approaching, had jumped down on to the grass and was waiting to help madam up the step.

'Yes, I do,' she said bleakly. 'But I cannot come with you. Ever. Goodbye, Adam.'

Elissa turned her head away to hide her sudden tears and stepped up into the waiting cab. 'The gentleman has decided to walk. Please drive me back to the Castlegate.'

Back to reality and North Square, to the crowded life of the Noble household and a husband who would not speak to her.

The fishing fleet sailed, as planned, with nothing said between them, except the formal farewell of a wife to a sea-going husband. Joseph kissed the children goodbye, said, 'Be good, till I come home again,' but when Elissa stood waiting in the doorway, as she always did, for her turn he brushed past her without even a token kiss on the cheek.

Dutifully she took her children to the north pier with the other women, to wave the herring fleet on its way, but her heart was leaden and with every hour her loneliness grew harder to bear. She had turned away her lover like a faithful wife ought to do and now her husband wouldn't speak to her. Had he heard of her meeting with Adam? Soon, it began to seem so.

Though in the past Joseph had often managed a weekend home in Footdee, now his absence stretched into weeks and when he did return, between leaving one curing station and setting up the next, she hardly saw him and then only when he looked in to say goodnight to Sal and Gideon Joe and to mutter, not looking at her, that he was going to spend the night on board the *Optimist*, on Pocra Quay. The *Optimist* was the converted Fifie that he and Fergus Mackie had bought together three years ago, when everyone was after the new Zulus, to convey the essentials of the curer's trade from one station to the next, as well as serving a useful purpose in the herring fishing when required. Again, Joseph had not kissed her, or said goodbye, and loneliness closed round her like a cold shroud.

Adam had gone, was presumably at this very moment somewhere on the high seas between London and Melbourne. Though it had cost her every ounce of moral strength and fortitude that she possessed, she had not written after him, and would not. But with every hour her loneliness grew harder to bear. Joseph had told her nothing of his plans and she did not expect him home again until September, when there would be the big preparations for the Yarmouth season.

In this she was wrong. He arrived one Saturday morning in late August, saying they needed new salt supplies urgently as the Fraserburgh landings were unexpectedly good. He was out most of the day organising this, and came home in the early evening, looking grey-faced and drawn.

Elissa longed to ask what worried him, for the anxiety of Sinclair's threat in the mist of that long-ago night by the deserted smokeshed still haunted her, intensified as it had been by the discovery that Adam Grant had been hoodwinked, imprisoned and banished for no reason, except the obvious one. *Or something unpleasant will happen as it did to your hot-headed friend.* And it was no good reassuring herself that Sinclair had already taken his revenge when he banned the Noble boat from the Sinclair curing yard; or that Sinclair was no longer in Aberdeen or the curing business: if he had paid others to act for him where Adam was concerned, he could do the same again. In Adam's case they had played on his weakness for conviviality: that would not work with Joseph, but what were her husband's weaknesses? In the present atmosphere of his forbidding disapproval, she could think of none.

The barrier that had sprung up between them had become impenetrable and the longer it persisted, the worse it became till she began to believe her husband actually wanted her to leave him. He had married her 'for reasons of his own': perhaps these same reasons now drove him to wish her gone? Since the day of the Queen's Jubilee he had said nothing about Adam's reappearance and, though she had tried on several occasions, she found that her mouth dried and she trembled so violently that she could not raise the subject. It was Sal who raised it for them.

The evening meal was not quite ready and when Joseph had lingered in the family kitchen, his mother had sent him upstairs 'to say hello to those wee bairns of yours while you're waiting. You see them rarely enough these days.' He had had no choice but to obey and now they were together in the upstairs room that was home, Joseph in a chair by the empty grate, which, as it was summer, was filled with a fan of paper which collected dust no matter how often Elissa shook it. Sal, who, under her mother's careful tuition, had already learnt to read, sat on a stool beside him, *Alice in Wonderland* open on her knee. She was laboriously reading aloud the well-known words to Joseph while Gideon Joe crawled on all fours round the floor, pushing a little wooden engine which his grandfather had carved for him and muttering 'Choo, choo' under his breath. Elissa sat on the chair under the skylight, knitting a gansey for Joseph, though every stitch was an effort as the tension between them tightened. Then Sal stumbled over a word.

'Da, what does con . . . conver . . . sation mean?'

'Talking together,' said her father.

'Like you and Mummy used to do?'

Elissa looked up from her knitting and watched his face.

'Yes,' he said, not looking at her, and her shoulders slumped in despair.

'Choo ... choo,' chanted Gideon Joe, pushing his engine over Joseph's foot and round behind his chair. 'Daddy doesn't talk to Mummy any more. Choo ... choo ... Daddy doesn't kiss Mummy any more.' He gave a loud, whistling noise to imitate the engine's steam, then scrambled in a mad race across the floor till the engine crashed into the bed-leg. 'Station!' he cried. 'Everybody out.' Then he flopped spreadeagled on the floor in mock exhaustion. After a minute he said, 'Why don't you kiss Mummy any more, Daddy? Don't you like it? The hell-hole man did.' Delighted with his own vocabulary he began to chant 'Hell-hole, hell-hole'.

'Quiet!' thundered Joseph and at the unexpected rebuke, Gideon Joe's face crumpled into frightened tears. He scrambled to his feet and ran to his mother, to bury his face in her skirts. Without speaking, she scooped him up and rocked him gently in her arms.

'What is a hell-hole?' inquired Sal, unafraid. 'Is it deep and nasty?'

'I expect so,' said Elissa quietly, but her eyes never left Joseph's face. When he neither met her gaze nor spoke, she continued, 'Why don't you ask Daddy to help you finish your reading while I wash Gideon's face and hands. Gran will be calling us soon, for your tea.'

When the summons came, reverberating up the narrow stairway from the kitchen below, Elissa bundled the two children out of the room with instructions to go straight downstairs to Gran, then before Joseph could follow she closed the door and leant against it. Her mouth was dry, her heart pounding so hard she thought it must deafen him, but she could not go on as she was and after all, what was there left to lose?

'Joseph, you have hardly spoken to me since the day of the Queen's Jubilee. What have I done to offend you?'

'Did that fellow kiss you?'

After Gideon Joe's revelation, what was the point of attempting a lie? 'Yes. Before I could stop him.'

'And did you want to stop him?' There was such pent-up passion in Joseph's voice that Elissa flinched away from him. She felt the wooden cross-piece of the door hard-edged against her back and straightened in defiance.

'Of course I did. He was a stranger.'

'Your lover a stranger? You have a short memory – or a fickle heart. Or both.'

'Neither,' flashed Elissa, stung to anger by the injustice. 'I remember a dead man on a beach. I remember my marriage vows to a live man whom I honour and obey. I remember his vows to me which he seems to have forgotten.'

'And love?' He gripped her by the shoulders, forced her back against the wooden door, and she felt his fingers dig hard into her flesh. 'I notice you do not mention love.' His eyes were hard and terrifyingly bright as he brought his face close to hers. 'But we both know why that is. The whole world knows that. Because Elissa Downie's lost lover has risen from the dead and come back to claim her and Elissa Downie cannot wait to jump back into his bed.'

If she could have moved her arm she would have slapped him with all her strength, but he held her pinioned. Instead, she put all her rage into her voice.

'That is a lie and you know it. I have given you no cause.'

'Do you deny he came to claim you?'

'Yes. No. But that is not the point. He cannot claim me, because I am married to you.' It was the wrong thing to say: she knew it the moment the words were out, but it was too late.

His face turned the colour of the polished granite columns of St Nicholas kirkyard's façade, and as coldly unyielding.

'Aye, I give you that. You keep your word.'

'Yes, Joseph,' she managed though she could hardly speak for dread. 'I do. And I gave my word to you.'

'Aye, in desperation and ignorance. But you'd given it before, hadn't you? If not your word, your body, which for you is the same thing.' His grip tightened on her shoulders and he quivered violently with the effort of self-control. If he had been his brother Peter she had no doubt he would have struck her. Her mouth dried with fear and she moistened nervous lips as his face came closer. 'That is how I know you want to keep your *word* as you call it to that villainous, lying scoundrel who has the brass-necked nerve to – '

'It's not true, Joseph!' gasped Elissa, white-faced with pain and desperation. 'Please believe – '

But he was beyond reason. 'You always were a loyal wee fool. You wouldn't hear anything against him if you saw him cheat and steal and fornicate with your own two eyes.'

'That is not what I meant ! I meant that – '

'Are you two coming down today or tomorrow?' cried a voice from below and suddenly the strength drained out of him.

'What's the use?' His voice was so low she could hardly catch the words. He closed his eyes and a long shudder ran through him. When he opened them he looked straight at her and she saw a stranger.

'Have you been seeing that fellow while I've been away?'

'No. He is at sea.'

'Did you see him before that, in private?'

'Yes.'

'And?'

'And nothing. He asked me to go away with him and I refused.'

'So you say. But then I have only your word for that, haven't I? And only your word that there was "nothing".'

'Do you doubt my word, Joseph Noble?'

He had the grace to look away, but only for a moment before the hatred flooded back. 'You can deny it till you're blue in the face, woman, but I know you want him. You've wanted him from the moment he reappeared, in spite of all your pious protestations. So go to him if you must. I'll not stop you. But when you go, you go for ever, and you go alone. The children, both of them, stay here. They are mine. Remember that.'

Then he pushed her out of the way, flung open the door, and she heard his boots on the wooden stairway, descending. Somewhere a door opened and closed again, with a heavy thud. The door into the Square. Joseph had gone.

Elissa drew herself up, straightened her back, adjusted the disordered portions of her clothing. She felt numb with a sense of hopeless injustice, and filled to the brim with a grief beyond tears. She had given up Adam for *this* ... But they were expecting her downstairs. She stepped to the small mirror under the eaves, tidied her hair, sponged her eyes with cold water from the jug on the washstand, made herself fit for company, and for her children. Joseph had gone. She knew he would not come back to her room or to her bed, but he could not turn her out. He was her husband and she had made her decision. She would stay in her husband's house and she would keep her children with her. *She had done nothing wrong.*

Armed with that knowledge, and with a new and lonely resolution, Elissa prepared to go downstairs to join Joseph's family.

CHAPTER 18

1890

The port of Aberdeen had grown rapidly in the years since the Sinclair and Gibb syndicate had bought and commissioned their first steam trawler, and the syndicate had grown with it. Two years after their first venture they contracted for a screw iron trawler to be built by John Duthie's of Footdee, with a boiler and engine from Hall, Russell's in York Street, and, playing safe, chose a design that could be converted into a tug if the trawling failed. But the trawling did not fail and the syndicate acquired three further vessels, all Aberdeen built, while the business of the port expanded: fish-curing sheds, ice factories, coal merchants, insurance brokers, ships' chandlers, rope and timber merchants, auctioneers and fish salesmen and, as more and more fishermen flocked into the town, houses for themselves and their families.

In 1889 the new fishmarket was opened on Albert Quay, to serve the new, larger trawler fleet. It was a structure on a grand scale: a huge length of quay covered by a weather-proof pitched roof supported on columns and with a string of gas lights overhead, essential for a trade that started as early as 3 a.m. Trawlers could unload straight on to the quay and into the market and from there it was a short step to the railway siding where the fish porters emptied their barrows directly into the trucks which would carry the day's catch south. Aberdeen was fast becoming the greatest white-fishing port in Scotland.

The firm of Sinclair and Gibb prospered, and the directors with it. Brodie Gibb was now a wealthy man, though he did his best to prevent his wife from knowing this and absolutely forbade her any kind of what he called 'show'. Bethany nodded, said, 'Yes, dear,' and did exactly what she liked, or could get away with. She filled her house in Marine Terrace with the latest furnishings and fashionable gadgets, fought over them when Brodie tried to send them back, and decked herself in the brightest and most flamboyant clothes Aberdeen could supply. She would have liked to buy her clothes in London, but on the one occasion when she had dared to suggest it, Brodie's reaction had been so violent that she did not mention it again. Instead, she took to inviting the more important of the firm's business contacts to the house for drinks, including several skippers of the Sinclair and Gibb fleet, and when her husband objected, pointed out that it was good for business, and besides if he thought she was going to sit twiddling her thumbs every night and listening to the clock tick, he could think again. So it was that the rumours started.

'Bethany had best watch herself if she doesn't want tongues to wag,' said Ina one morning in May when she, Jess and Elissa were working in the smokeshed on Pocra. This shed was Elissa's project, though no one knew that except Mrs Noble. When Elissa realised that Joseph was not going to come back to her, or forgive her, she felt insecurity chill her bones and knew she must have money of her own, as a bulwark against misfortune. Even, as a last resort, to pay her passage to Australia. She had sent Adam away and he had stayed away – but she knew he would welcome her if she went to him and she was increasingly hungry for affection, and love. She had given her small legacy to Joseph and willingly, but now in her loneliness she felt its loss. No doubt he would have paid her back had she asked him, but nothing short of her children's starvation would drive her to such an indignity.

Instead, the next time Mrs Noble grumbled, as usual, that her wee smokeshed in the garden was too small, Elissa suggested that it might be time for her to think of moving into larger premises. Since Sinclair and Gibb had opened their grand new smokehouse by the railway arches, the old smokehouse on Pocra had been standing empty. It was small and dilapidated, but larger than the Nobles' garden shed, and the roof was still rainproof. With Joseph away so often, Elissa said, she would like an occupation of her own while the children were at school and if Mrs Noble would like to go into partnership with her and could lend her the money for her share of the lease Elissa would guarantee to pay her back in a year's time and to work her heart out for the smokehouse. After all, she had learned a lot about the trade during her months with Bervie Tam in the Sinclair and Gibb smokeshed and what she didn't know, Mrs Noble could teach her. Mary Noble was cautious at first, then suddenly threw caution aside and allowed excitement to take over.

'It's what I've always wanted, lass, and I've money enough put by. I'll be sixty next year and if I could see my name over the door of my own smokehouse by then, that'd be the best birthday present ever.'

With the help of Samuel, Saul and the younger Nobles, they had gathered together what simple equipment they needed and Gideon Noble and Peter between them had patched the brickwork, repaired the walls and checked over the roof. The blackened smoke cupboards of the previous occupant had been broken up and burnt, but the menfolk built new ones at Mary's direction, and the wooden racks on which the curing fish would hang. Bervie Tam volunteered to run his eye over things for them, 'Just so's everything's as right as it should be, lass.' And three weeks after they had taken over the place, it was.

Samuel and Zach, who had a skill with the paintbrush, made the sign between them and all of them helped to nail it in place over the big double doors. 'Mary's Smokehouse' in green letters outlined in gold, with an emblem of three gold haddocks tied by their tails with green straw. They had toasted the new venture in whisky and those of the neighbours who were not busy elsewhere had joined in the celebrations. Only Joseph had been absent, on business in some distant herring station, and Elissa had been glad. The smokehouse was her private defence against an unknown future.

Elissa had secured several of her old friends to work for her. Pocra was a mere step away from the Square and convenient for Ina and the other women who had small children to care for and did not fancy travelling, as the unmarried girls did, to Shetland and the farther east-coast ports. On Pocra, younger Bain sisters or Duthie sisters could bring nursing infants to their mothers to be fed and carry them away again, replete, with little disruption to the work in hand. Ina's husband Fergus had gone north with the herring fleet, in company with Joseph and the others, but Elissa's brother Tom Downie was now a well-established fish salesman operating from the new fishmarket on Albert Quay and Elissa arranged with Tom to sell on the finished product for them.

'There is no need to mention it to Joseph,' she told Tom. 'This is Mrs Noble's own business and she wants to keep it separate, and private. She's afraid she'll not see the profit otherwise,' she had added, and managed a smile.

Tom had grinned. 'Silent as the grave, Lissa lass. I promise.'

Since the Queen's Jubilee, Joseph had made something of a reputation for himself. The whole harbour knew he channelled all his energies into the curing business he ran with Fergus, and, said Fergus to Ina in private, he had become obsessed with making and saving money.

'Not content with running the curing yard, and the Lord knows that's work enough with the crans to be measured, the barrels inspected and lidded down and manhandled every which way and the tallies kept, let alone packing the whole thing up and moving on when the shoals move, he has to put to sea with the rest of them and fish for herring all night. Folk reckon he's set his sights on buying a steam drifter one day, to beat yon Adam Grant at his own game, but at this rate he'll kill himself before he's forty.'

'Jealousy, likely,' Ina had replied, offhand, but she too had noticed the difference in Joseph and it worried her, especially when she saw Elissa grow thinner and more withdrawn. Ina and Jess knew the cause could only be Adam Grant's return. 'Like two stags fighting to show who's best.'

'Will Masson was seen round Bethany's place again last night,' Ina said now without a break in the gutting rhythm which she and Jess had quickly re-established in the old, easy pattern of those far-off Shetland days, though here the fish were beheaded, gutted, split open, cleaned and flattened for the smoke chimney. 'While her Brodie was over in Torry sorting some trouble at the ice-plant. Bethany always did fancy the lad.'

'But she is married!' cried Elissa, before she could stop herself.

'Knowing Bethany, I doubt she remembers that when her man's away,' said Jess, briefly turning her head. Last year Jess had married a widower fifteen years older than herself, a herring fisherman with four children under ten years old, 'And looking for a new house-keeper,' said Ina behind her sister's back. Jess, however, seemed content with George Black, in spite of the instant family that came with him, and was six months pregnant with her first child.

'Bethany'd best be careful though,' went on Ina. 'She hasn't given her man the heir he wants and word has it his patience is wearing thin. Even at the best of times, Brodie Gibb's not a man to cross.'

Nor, thought Elissa with the usual grey hopelessness, is Joseph. It was almost three years since that ill-fated Jubilee and still the barrier held between them. In that time Ina had given birth to a daughter and was pregnant again, in spite of the frequent absences of Fergus with the herring fleet whereas Elissa, through no choice of hers, slept alone. She had gone beyond hope long ago and had begun to welcome Joseph's absences, to pray he would stay away longer, to hope that a glut of herring might prevent his coming home for the weekend; had even, to her shame, after a particularly heart-tearing episode, prayed for bad weather to keep him away. For when he did come home, though he invariably slept on board the *Optimist* he ate at the Nobles' house and went through the motions of family harmony. Played with Gideon Joe, read stories to Sal, took them both to see the boat or to walk on the shore, but all without the smallest crack in the barrier he had built between himself and Elissa and always, always in company. If only she could have been alone with him, for a mere five minutes, she might have broken through that barrier, but he out-manoeuvred her every time until she found she could not bear his proximity and coldness; if she so much as touched his arm, his features set as if in granite and he stared straight ahead of him till she removed her hand. She and Joseph rarely spoke, and if they did it was of practical things: the children's progress at school, his mother's smokeshed, his father's line-fishing, the successes, or disappointments of the herring season, then he would turn to Gideon Joe or Sal and for the rest of his visit talk exclusively to them. He did not inquire what Elissa did with her time when he was away: the implication was that it was no longer his concern.

To make matters worse, two years to the day after his first reappearance, Adam Grant had returned, as he had promised, on a cargo boat from Australia: his own. Elissa waited in quivering expectation for him to contact her, but he did nothing. Three days of nothing while the cargo was unloaded, the vessel cleaned and restocked, and made ready for the return voyage. Then, on the fourth day, to her white-faced dismay, she was walking along Pocra Quay with Joseph and the children, on their way to the *Optimist* where Joseph was going to show Gideon Joe the wheelhouse, when out of a doorway not ten yards ahead of them stepped Adam Grant.

'Holy herring! If it isn't my wee Lissa with her new man and her wee laddie. Good morning to you, madam.' He gave an elaborate and sweeping bow, then repeated the bow to Sal. 'And the same to you, lassie. Whoever you are, I'll say this, and when did Adam Grant ever lie? You're pretty as a picture, so you are.'

'And you are drunk,' glared Joseph, thrusting his children behind him and squaring up to Adam.

'No, Joseph, please...' Elissa grabbed hold of his arm, but he shook her off. What might have happened next she imagined with varying degrees of dread in the lonely nights that followed: what did happen was that two of Adam's friends followed him out of the alehouse on to the quay, took in the situation in one glance, and solved it by taking his arms and frogmarching him briskly out of harm's way.

'Sorry about that, sir,' called one of them over his shoulder. 'No offence meant. He's had a wee bit over the Plimsoll line, that's all.'

Only Elissa knew it was a sham. She thrust the folded note he had given her deep into her pocket and fought down the surge of hope and longing.

'What's a pimsole, Da?' demanded Gideon, but Sal was watching Adam Grant and his friends stagger along the quay and round the corner into York Place out of sight.

'Stop staring, Sal,' said Elissa quietly. 'It is not polite.'

'Who was that man, Ma?'

Before Elissa could answer, Joseph said, 'No one we know, or want to know. Forget him.'

'But I thought he was nice...' began Sal, still preening because the stranger had called her pretty.

Joseph whirled round, took her by the shoulders and looked down into her face with such suppressed anger that the child paled and bit her lip.

'I said forget him and I meant it. If you see him in the street, you are forbidden to speak to him. Do you understand?'

'Yes, Da,' said Sal meekly.

They walked the rest of the way to the *Optimist* in silence.

The following day and quite by chance, Elissa came face to face with Adam in the usual bustling turmoil of Trinity Quay.

'Well, if it isn't my wee Lissa again. At last, and all alone this time.' He took her arm, to steer her out of the path of a shore porter's hand-cart, and frowned when she tried to snatch it away.

'I want an answer,' he said in a low, urgent voice. 'Quick, before we are seen. Did you read my note?'

'I did. And the answer is still no.'

'But why? He doesn't love you, anyone can see that, and I do. Come away with me. We sail at dusk tomorrow. If you say no this time . . .'

But she broke away from him and ran before his voice could beguile her and spent the next twenty-four hours in frenzied argument with her conscience and her heart. She read that crumpled note over and over: *I have a house with a garden now to offer you and a small fleet of my own, steam driven and profitable. I have money enough to keep a wife and a daughter in comfort – and love. Please say yes.* She could take Sal, leave Gideon Joe, take both children, leave both behind, and whatever she chose would be torment, one way or another. Would Adam's love be enough justification for that?

Now, a year later, in the familiar tang of her own smokehouse, a vivid picture sprang into her mind of the bothy in Shetland on a summer Sunday, of Bethany patting the space on the wooden chest beside her and saying, 'Come over here and talk to me, Adam lad. You don't get fed for nothing, remember.' Elissa had been innocent and trusting then. Like Sal. She was older now, and married, but she could still feel the pain of that moment as piercingly as ever. Oh God, she yearned for Adam as she had yearned for him then, all those years ago. Dear Adam, with his love and laughter. And she had sent him away. But if Joseph persisted in his hostility she might not have the strength of purpose to refuse when Adam asked her again. If he did . . .

Others as well as Adam were growing richer. The Sinclair and Gibb fleet continued to expand and their trawlers ranged as far as their greedy engines could be fuelled to take them, for hundreds of miles and for weeks, even months at a time. Their business grew with the harbour, and the town.

The losers were the few remaining line-fishermen, like Gideon

Noble, who obstinately stuck to sail and the old methods. But what chance had the old methods against the speed and voracity of steam? The beam trawls with their wooden jaws held open to suck in even the small fry from the ocean bed scooped up ten times what a line-fisherman could catch and in a tenth of the time. And in so doing, depleted the ocean's wealth, ruined the fishing, and took the livelihood from the mouths of honest fishing folk.

When the Noble boat came home at the end of the Shetland herring season, Peter Noble, made argumentative by excess of alcohol, pointed this out to a group of trawlermen in a quayside bar one night and in the resulting scuffle which spilled out of the doorway and on to the quay, fell into the harbour waters with two of the trawlermen for company. All three were eventually fished out again, but by that time two of them were dead. One was Peter Noble.

All the men of the family attended the funeral, including Brodie Gibb and Phemy's husband from Buckie, together with most of North and South Squares. The women stayed behind, to prepare food and drink for the men's return, and in a private moment Mrs Noble said to Elissa, 'I wish my Zeb was here.' There was so much grief and mourning in the older woman's words that Elissa put her arms around her and held her close.

Then Mary Noble pulled herself together, brushed her eyes with the back of a hand and attempted a smile.

'Thanks, lass. You're a good lassie and I've tellt Joseph so more than once, but he can be an obstinate fool when he puts his mind to it. I wish things were better between you.'

Elissa bit her lip to keep back the tears that sprang to her eyes. 'So do I,' she said.

'Aye, lass. I know.' It was Mrs Noble's turn to hold Elissa in comforting arms, but the arrival of the first of the black-clad and sombre menfolk put an end to that. Elissa moved among them, offering food, pouring tea, keeping a watchful eye on the children for signs of tears. Elspeth, Peter's wife, had shed none when she first heard the news, and shed none now. Instead she looked defiance on all of them.

'Arguing about scraping the sea-bed,' she said in disgust. 'As if he knew the first thing about it, the fool. Or cared. He'd have been into steam long ago, given the chance.'

'Aye, lass,' sighed Gideon Noble. 'I know that. But he was maybe sticking up for the likes of old fools like his father.'

No one contradicted him. If the idea gave Gideon Noble comfort, let him believe it. It was better for a man to think his son had died in an honourable cause, than from sheer drink. Brodie Gibb rose to the occasion.

'To Peter Noble, a brave and honest lad.' He raised his glass and everyone did the same, murmuring some sort of agreement, if only the name.

As if on cue, Elspeth's son, wee Georgie, began to howl.

'Poor wee laddie,' said Brodie, studying the child with interest. 'He misses his father, likely, and he has a fine pair of lungs.'

'More's the pity,' said Elspeth. 'Shut your mou', Georgie, for pity's sake, or I swear I'll clout you so hard you'll . . .' but before she could finish, Elissa took the child by the hand and led him away.

'Come with me, Georgie, and I'll find you a wee biscuit,' she said and his wail receded into the general noise of the room.

'Aye, a fine pair of lungs,' repeated Brodie. 'He'll be strong like his father, I reckon. What do you say, Bethany?'

Bethany didn't bother to reply. Brodie was always passing comments on other folk's sons: it was his way of reminding her she'd not kept her side of the bargain. What did he expect, the old fool, when he'd all the vigour of a dead cod? Her eyes ranged over the room for more exciting company and, finding it, she ploughed her way towards a middle-aged man with a short, grizzled beard and an air of natural command. 'Dycie' Paterson, skipper of the harbour lifeboat. Peter Noble had gone out with the lifeboat more than once, in an emergency, and would be missed.

'I hear you've put your boatie in a fine new shed by the lower jetty,' she said by way of opening. 'And hanging on ropes over the water, so's you can drop it in quick. Not like that time the tide was too low and you had to push and shove the old boatie off the north pier and took so long about it that all the *Comply* crew was drowned.'

'You don't know what you're talking about, Bethany,' said Joseph, joining them. 'It was black as pitch that night and a man couldn't see a yard beyond his own nose till the pilot sent up the flares. I was there. I would have been in the boat, too, if they'd had room for me.'

'You,' jeered Bethany, 'you're always somewhere else when you're needed. You canna man a Footdee lifeboat with a man who's in Shetland or Yarmouth. It must be awful hard work, though, for the brave folk who are here. Do you find it an awful strain, Dycie?' and she laid a sympathetic hand on his arm.

'It's my job,' he frowned, moving out of reach. Then he turned to Joseph. 'If you're ever around for longer than a day or two, come and see me. I'll show you how this new contraption works. If you're interested.'

Elissa saw Bethany shrug and wander off in search of more susceptible prey, saw the two men deep in conversation and felt the usual grey despair. Since he came home Joseph had not spoken to her, beyond the necessary politenesses, and if she had hoped that family grief might unite them her hope died. Joseph would leave with the others and she would sleep alone.

'Come on, Georgie. We'll go and find Gideon Joe, shall we?' and she led the child away.

The next morning Elissa was up early as usual, had made up the kitchen fire, seen to the porridge pot, boiled the kettle for tea as well as doing a dozen other household tasks, checked that her children had washed faces and hands and brushed their hair and was preparing to go to her work at the curing shed, when she noticed that Elspeth's child had been crying longer than usual. The pathetic noise drifted through the closed door and across the landing to where Elissa stood in her own doorway, listening.

Poor wee mite. Elspeth was maybe weeping so much she didn't hear him, what with being numb with shock since Peter's death. Elissa ran quickly downstairs, poured tea, and carried the cup upstairs again, for Elspeth.

She knocked gently on the door, then louder. When there was still no answer, she pushed open the door and looked in. Wee Georgie was alone, lying sodden and howling in his crib. The bed was unmade, the room in disarray, dust and untidiness everywhere, but the lid of the wooden kist stood open and when Elissa moved closer, she saw that it was empty except for a blanket and a handful of grubby garments among which she recognised a small shirt she herself had made for Gideon Joe and handed on to Elspeth, for wee Georgie. There was nothing of Elspeth's anywhere: not a shoe, not a plaid. Nothing.

Then she noticed a scrap of paper, pinned to the side of Georgie's wooden crib. *I've had enough. Georgie's yours. Goodbye.*

A week later Georgie's Aunt Bethany and Uncle Brodie took the child to live with them.

'He'll be a fine son for us,' said Brodie, beaming. 'George Noble Gibb.'

Bethany, who had had no say in the matter, merely grunted. But she didn't mind the child. He was no beauty, but no wishy-washy angel either. He was a lad of spirit, with a temper that delighted Bethany, and though Nessie, the maid of all work, bore most of the brunt of the child's tantrums, Georgie and his aunt rubbed along together well enough. She even, eventually, began to talk of him as 'my son' and to boast of his more disruptive escapades while Brodie Gibb visibly mellowed. He had a son, now, to work for. Someone who would take over when he himself grew too old. Meanwhile, it was important to make as much profit as possible, for posterity.

Joseph Noble, for his own bleak reasons, was also intent on profit. He came back briefly in early September, to arrange salt supplies and timber for the barrels, to check shipping contracts and collect new nets. That done, he sailed for Yarmouth to set up the curing station for the autumn herring fishing, leaving Fergus to follow later. Fergus and Ina had four children now and, watching them together, Elissa ached for the happy days with Joseph when her own two were young, before Adam Grant had reappeared and shattered their contentment.

But Ina's children were often in the Nobles' kitchen, with Jess's lot and various of the neighbours' young, and Elissa found comfort in their innocent, high-spirited company. It was not long before Bethany brought wee Georgie to visit – and left him 'while I take a trip up to the shops. I'm wanting a new hat and that Nessie can't do a thing with the wee horror today.' After that, the 'wee horror' became a regular visitor, but Elissa did not mind. Not until she realised, but by then it was too late.

Meanwhile, she had the smokehouse. 'Mary's' was doing well: they had doubled their profits in the first six months alone. Besides, Elissa's brother Tom was a big figure now in the fish trade and believed in family loyalty: 'Mary's' was never left with unsold smokies, never short of the raw supplies. And already Tom's wife Kate had taken to bringing their wee son to join the 'nursery' in the Square. All of this was some consolation for her loneliness, but never enough. As the savings mounted in the black tin box she kept under the folded linen of her kist, she knew she would have exchanged every penny of it for her man's love. But if that was not to be, she would save for the future, for herself and her children.

At first, Elissa had feared the competition of the larger firms, but she need not have worried. Profit was in the very air as the trawling industry boomed and with it the constellation of supporting ventures, and there was room for everyone, from the tiny, shoe-string ventures such as 'Mary's' to the large city-funded syndicates like Sinclair and Gibb.

The firm of Sinclair and Gibb had been in there from the beginning, and continued to skim off their share, but in that autumn of 1890 a chill draught of unease began to be felt in the board room. They were not doing as well as they had been, no one could pin down why. Several old members had died and new ones had not been forthcoming. Whether because of young Sinclair's reputation for arrogant mismanagement or because they had better offers elsewhere was not known. If a banker in London had not bought into the syndicate for one of his clients they would have been in trouble. But the worry of it had affected old Easton Sinclair's health, that and the worries over his son. He had hoped his son would marry and give him a grandson, but he would not wish the fellow on any girl (and he had one or two suitable ones in mind) until his whole attitude to life had improved. One day he would have to bring Hugh back to Aberdeen, to groom him for management, but it was a dispiriting prospect.

However, Easton Sinclair remained determined to make what was left of the syndicate as profitable as humanly possible while he still had the strength. He knew he could rely on Brodie Gibb's support and Lawyer Forbes was in favour of any profit going. He had a wife, five daughters and two sons to support, the youngest, Cameron, a mere child of six. It was his own strength that was the unknown factor, to others as well as to himself.

It was to discuss the situation and their mutual unease that Brodie Gibb and the lawyer arranged to meet on a dour afternoon some four weeks later. For Sinclair senior's health had visibly failed and he turned overnight from an alert and vigorous sixty-five-year-old into a tired old man.

It was common knowledge throughout Aberdeen that old Sinclair was ailing, and equally common knowledge that young Sinclair was 'a bad 'un'. The question which fuelled many a late-night debate in the commercial meeting houses of the town was whether the undoubted abilities of Brodie Gibb and the keen-eyed vigilance of Lawyer Forbes could steer the company safely through these rock-strewn waters until Easton Sinclair regained his strength. Or whether young Hugh would scupper the foundering vessel by some ill-timed idiocy no one could foresee or prevent. While Easton lived, the chances were good: but Easton might die at any moment, and shrewd businessmen preferred to put their money on a certainty.

As a result, Sinclair and Gibb's profits dwindled. A rival syndicate, London-based, had already poached three of their best captains, orders had fallen at the rope works and salt works, and even the ice factory was not making the money which the increased business in the harbour should have brought them. Someone, somewhere, was undercutting prices, but it was hard to pin down who. Public confidence had been undermined, not only by Easton's illness but also by a series of mishaps, most of which could be traced back to Hugh Sinclair. Orders promised and forgotten about, prices mis-quoted, late deliveries of urgent supplies, on one notable occasion to the biggest trawler in their own fleet, as a result of which two full days' fishing was lost and the profits with it.

'I regret to say this, but we have acquired a reputation for unreliability,' said Lawyer Forbes, on that dreich winter afternoon.

Brodie Gibb's parlour with its smoking apology for a fire and its unlit gas lamps increased his depression and the lawyer made a mental note to meet his business partner in one of the local hostelries in future and never mind the eavesdroppers. Besides, he did not care who heard his opinion of young Sinclair: it could do them no more harm than the fellow had done already.

When Brodie made no comment, Forbes added, 'But without the authority to throw Hugh Sinclair overboard I fail to see what we can do about it.' He stared morosely into his half-empty tankard, knowing it would not be refilled. Even his bitterest enemies could not accuse Brodie Gibb of squandering his fortune in lavish hospitality. 'Perhaps we could persuade the old man to tie his son's hands somehow . . .'

'Disinherit him? I wish to God he would. Or buy him out. That would solve all our problems, but I don't see Easton going that far. Not with his only son.' Having at last acquired a son of his own, Brodie thought he understood a father's feelings. 'A sleeping partner- ship, though. A non-executive salary. Something that would keep the fellow happy and leave the power with us. Surely there is a way that could be done? Legally?'

There was just the right length of pause before the last word to indicate that, in Brodie's mind anyway, legality was not essential.

'It's possible,' mused Forbes. 'Though I doubt Easton would agree. Besides, the fellow is greedy. He might ask more than we want to give. There is one other way, of course.' The lawyer paused, studying Brodie's face from under carefully lowered brows. He did not want to overplay his hand: but he had five daughters to consider. 'If a suitable wife could be found for the boy, Easton might agree to skip a generation.'

'You mean leave everything to the grandchild? It's possible, though you may be in deep waters there. I'll wager there are half a dozen "grandchildren" already, and in as many countries. We don't want a queue at the door.'

'The will would have to be specific: only legitimate heirs.'

'All fine and good, Forbes. There's only one thing missing. What self-respecting lass of any brains at all would take that profligate for a husband?'

Lawyer Forbes cleared his throat and went slightly pink. 'My eldest daughter is eighteen. A dutiful and obedient young lady . . .'

'Ahhhh.' Brodie Gibb lay back in his chair, legs outstretched and ankles comfortably crossed, and regarded his visitor with a shrewd expression and the smallest hint of a smile.

The two men were in the parlour of the house in Marine Terrace, a room over which many a domestic battle had been fought. The rag rug was Brodie's triumph (Bethany had wanted Indian), the dome of artificial flowers on the mantelshelf Bethany's. Similarly, though Brodie's own chair was the battered but serviceable 'captain's' chair he had brought with him from his bachelor lodgings, the chair in which Lawyer Forbes sat was the latest fashion in moquette, with buttons that stuck into the back of its occupant and an unyielding upholstered seat. The walls were papered in the latest ornately floral pattern, chosen by Bethany, but the curtains were Brodie's trophy: run up by Mrs Noble from an off-cut left over from one of the White Star line steamers and found via a ship's chandler friend.

'The stateroom curtains, likely,' mocked Mrs Noble and Bethany had been too furious to reply. She had wanted bright red velvet and instead was required to frame her windows with dung-coloured upholstery cloth. In retaliation she had marched out of the house, bought the brightest coloured pair of china dogs she could find and slammed them defiantly down on the mantelshelf, one on either side of the wax flowers.

'If we live in a junk shop,' she had snarled, 'I'm having guard dogs to keep out the tinks.'

Now Brodie regarded the two china animals with the usual annoyance, but underneath was a new satisfaction. Wee Georgie liked the dogs, and what Georgie liked, the lad should have. After all, he was Brodie's son. A ready-made son, he told himself, saving him the bother of a crying baby and all the upheaval and mess that came with such things. A fine, healthy four-year-old with a bit of spirit about him. George Noble Gibb.

But the reminder of his son brought him back to the present. Why should Lawyer Forbes think he could get his hands on Easton's share for his own grandson? What about Brodie's grandchildren?

'Ahhhh,' he repeated, and now the ironic smile was definitely in place.

Forbes sighed and mentally crossed that particular idea off the list. Brodie's exclamation said everything: if Lawyer Forbes thought he could feather his own nest via his own, sacrificial daughter, he could think again.

'A good enough idea, in theory,' said Brodie, when he had given the lawyer time enough to squirm. 'But suppose the fellow were to marry someone unsuitable? A gold-digger, for example, with a mind of her own?'

Before either man could pursue the thought, the outside door slammed, the inside door opened and Bethany pushed unceremoniously into the room.

'Drinking again? That's all you men ever do. It's a wonder there's any work gets done around here.' She tore off her bonnet, a bright blue object with yellow bits on it, and tossed it on to the chenille-draped table. Then she turned to the lawyer. 'You staying long? Only I saw your wife in town and she said she was wanting you. And the *Arrogance* is newly arrived and unloading, Brodie. You'd best get down to the quay and see no one swindles you. They can be light-fingered, some of they deck-hands, and the fish porters are no better.' The men exchanged glances, drained their mugs and rose to their feet as one.

'I'd best be going, right enough,' said Forbes.

'I'll walk with you some of the way,' said Brodie. 'Fetch me my hat, woman. And my stick.'

'They're in the hall, where you left them,' retorted Bethany. She crossed to the mantelshelf over the fire and began to adjust her hair with the aid of the gilt-edged looking-glass on the wall above. 'I left Georgie at Ma's,' she said, before Brodie could ask. 'He likes to play with Lissa's two and there's always Ina's or Jessie's lot around so where's the difference?'

'I will collect him on my way home.' He glared disapproval at his wife who took no notice. She knew he considered his son should be looked after in his new home, not his old; knew he expected her to teach the child to read and write. But she had better things to do than chant 'A, B, C' all day or the two-times table. And if Lissa would do it for her, why not?

'Don't bother,' she said now. 'I've tellt Nessie to bring the lad back when he's had his tea.' She omitted to add that she had also given her long-suffering maid the afternoon off.

Brodie muttered something vehement, wrenched open the street door and almost pushed his visitor outside.

'You should send your Cameron round to play at Lissa's, Mr Forbes,' Bethany called after them from the doorway. 'It's good for kids to play together and Mrs Forbes was telling me your son's a peely-wally kind of a laddie. More like a lassie really. I reckon Lissa's Gideon and my Georgie would soon put him right, and he'll get his tea free. Why else do you think Brodie lets wee Georgie go? Goodbye, Brodie darling,' she added with a trill of brittle laughter. Then she closed the door.

Only to open it again five minutes later.

'Come in, if you're coming. The coast's clear and he'll not be back for hours.'

'Is that so, Mrs Gibb? But best not to waste time, just in case.'

'Then what are you waiting for, you devil?' He lunged, she twisted out of reach and ran giggling for the stairs, with her visitor in lusty pursuit.

Bethany's words about his son set Lawyer Forbes thinking. Brodie's wife was a formidable woman at the best of times, and a downright harridan and foul-mouthed besom when she forgot she was aiming to be a lady. But there was a seed of truth in what she said about Cameron. The boy was a touch effeminate. His mother's fault of

216

course, and with five sisters to fuss over him as well Cameron hadn't a chance. They even called him 'Cammie', for God's sake. A lad of six should be mixing more with boys, not sharing his sisters' governess and playing with water-colours and crayons like a moon-struck girl. A spell in a household like the Nobles' might be the making of him. He'd ask Brodie to speak to Mrs Noble about it at the first opportunity.

So it was that Cameron Forbes joined the group of children that flowed in and around the Noble household outside school hours and at weekends. He quickly attached himself to Gideon Joe who, a year older, was an easygoing lad who grew to regard the spindly, red-haired Cameron as some sort of personal pet, to be tolerated or ignored as life required. Bethany's Georgie, though younger, was less tolerant and would have tormented Cameron unmercifully had not Sal kept a firm and schoolmistressy eye on him. Sal was maturing fast, with the natural authority of the first-born.

So, on a raw Saturday in late November with a glut of fish to be dealt with at 'Mary's' before the sacred hours of the Sabbath stopped all work till Monday, it was natural that Elissa should ask Sal to take Georgie home for her while she gave Mary Noble a hand. Cameron Forbes had already been collected, but Bethany's maid had not appeared, for whatever reason, and the night was drawing in.

'Take Gideon Joe with you for company,' said Elissa, 'and to see you safe home again. Milly can't go because of her chest, but you'll see to the supper, won't you, Milly love, for when your ma and I get back? And see you wear your thick plaid, Sal. It can be a raw kind of cold if the haar's about.'

The children had been to their Aunt Bethany's house on several occasions in the past, though only when they could not avoid it. They didn't like the dark rooms and the quarrelling and even the splendid view over the harbour did not compensate. Besides, Aunt Bethany was a hopeless cook and her maid Nessie no better. So Sal and Gideon Joe, dragging young Georgie between them, made what haste they could with the handicap of a reluctant, wailing child who, as he told the whole harbour at the top of his lungs, did not want to go home, not ever.

Along Waterloo Quay, Regent's Quay, Trinity Quay, with the exciting bustle of the harbour all around them, the ship's riding lights, the cheerful lights from open hatchways and warehouse doors flung wide. The sharp smell of salt spray and seaweed and the slap of water against quay as a bow wave from some new arrival or departure rippled the inner basin. Windows were lit up in the tall buildings that lined the quayside and more in the tenements of the Shiprow.

But their route lay south, round the curve of the harbour and the railway, till they were climbing the steep slope of Ferryhill Road to where the elegant row of terraced houses called Marine Terrace stood on a green eminence, looking seawards over the heads of lesser mortals and the jumble of smokesheds, railway sidings, brick and tile works, fishmarket and trawler-crowded harbour: all the distasteful but necessary paraphernalia which served to line the pockets of the terrace's residents.

'I don't want to go home!' yelled Georgie, with a final wail of rebellion, but his guardians dragged him up the steps to the closed front door and held him firmly between them while, in unison, they rapped on the door. A light shone from the basement of the next-door house and through the uncurtained window they could see a woman in a large white apron chopping onions on a wooden board. More lamps shone from other windows in the terrace, brightening the gathering gloom with welcome patches of light, but Brodie Gibb's house was in darkness, except for a small chink of what could pass as lamplight at the top of a shrouded upstairs window. The basement at the foot of the shadowed area steps was a black, uncurtained void: Nessie was obviously not back yet.

Sal and Gideon Joe exchanged glances: the door of the Noble house in the Square was never closed, let alone locked, but they knew better than to try the door of this house uninvited. The heavy brass knocker was made in the shape of a dolphin and elegantly curved. After a moment's hesitation, Sal lifted the polished head and let it fall, twice. When Sal stepped back to wait politely on the step, Gideon Joe could not resist gripping the dolphin's head himself and banging it down, once, twice and again for good measure.

A light gleamed through the glass panel at the top of the door and someone shouted, 'All right, I'm coming. You don't have to bang the door down.'

There was the sound of a bolt being drawn back and a chain, then the door was wrenched open to reveal their Aunt Bethany, her hair bundled up all anyhow and her skirt unfastened at the side. Her cheeks were red and became even redder as she glared at the trio on her doorstep.

'What the bleeding hell are you doing, hammering the door down as if the house was on fire? I thought I tellt you to stay at Lissa's till you was fetched, you disobedient wee tyke.' She aimed a clout at Georgie's ear but, well used to such assaults, he ducked nimbly out of reach and back down three steps to safety.

'Ma said to bring him home,' said Sal bravely, 'before it was dark. Nessie didn't come.'

'Of course she didn't come. She was tellt six o'clock.'

'Yes, but there's a haar threatening and Ma thought – '

'Well, you can tell your precious ma to mind her own flaming business and not think till she's tellt to or I'll give her something to think about, the sanctimonious cow.'

A door opened somewhere along the street and a wedge of light cut across the gloom. Bethany lowered her voice to a threatening hiss.

'As for you, Georgie lad, you'll come up those steps and through this door this minute, or else.'

Georgie clung tighter to the wrought-iron railings which edged the steps and opened his mouth to howl, but as Bethany lunged towards him a man's voice called from inside the house, 'Who is it?'

Through the half-open doorway they glimpsed black polished boots on the stairs, black-striped legs, white shirt with a frilled front, unbuttoned grey waistcoat. But the feet stopped with the head still in shadow. It made him look sinister and frightening.

'What are you staring at?' snapped Bethany. Then, over her shoulder, 'Get back in there and put your jacket on, before folks see.'

She was going to slam the door when she remembered her son.

'Well, come in if you're coming, Georgie.' She grabbed him by one ear and yanked him inside. 'And you two can get back where you came from.' She gave Georgie a hefty clout on the other ear and slammed the door.

Sal took Gideon Joe's hand and they ran back along Marine Terrace towards the town. Aunt Bethany was horrid and rude and that man was frightening. And they hadn't even been given a thank-you biscuit.

Near the end of the row of houses, the door which had opened earlier was still open, spilling light into the street, and when they reached the place they saw a figure leaning against the railings, waiting. He stepped forward as they approached. A tall man, with blond hair and a fine, brass-buttoned jacket.

'Don't be alarmed,' he said, blocking their path, but smiling. 'I heard voices and wanted to make sure you were all right.'

Sal looked up at him with relief. His face was kind and normal, not like that other man.

'I do believe it is the pretty little lady from the Noble household, and with her brother Gideon Joe. I thought it was you when I heard the voices. Voices carry clearly on a night like this. Good evening to you both,' and he solemnly bowed.

Sal stared at the figure while her face grew pink with embarrassment and pleasure. It was her mother's friend, the man her father didn't like. But Sal liked him, especially when he smiled at her with twinkling blue eyes, as he was doing now, and paid her compliments. But Gideon Joe was tugging at her hand.

'Come on, Sal. We must go home. Ma will be anxious.'

'Your brother is quite right, Sal. You mustn't upset your ma by keeping her waiting. Tell her . . . tell her that the *Singing Bird* is newly arrived from Melbourne – and waiting for passengers. You will see her moored at the quay, if you're going that way. Tell your ma if you come along tomorrow, I'll show you the engine room myself and the cabins: mahogany panelled, all of them. Just ask for Captain Grant.'

'Thank you,' said Gideon Joe and tugged hard at Sal's hand. 'Come on Sal, and stop gawping.'

'Goodbye, both of you, and don't forget my invitation.' He smiled again and winked, as if they were old friends.

CHAPTER 19

'Best not tell Ma,' said Sal when the two were back in the familiar bustle of the quayside. There, they slowed their steps to a stroll, to draw breath and look around them. There was a new ship, right enough, moored beside the London steamer. They had been hurrying too much to notice it on their way to Bethany's, but now they stopped and stared, noting the bright paint and gleaming brass.

'Why not?' Gideon, like Sal, had been brought up to tell the honest truth, as their mother had been before them.

'You know how cross it makes them if anyone mentions . . .' But Sal was too embarrassed to finish her sentence. Her cheeks were still glowing from the warmth of Adam's compliments.

Gideon had no such scruples. 'The hell-hole man! Da told you not to speak to him, didn't he? That's why I'm not to say. In case you catch it for disobedience. It's not because of Ma at all. You're a fibber, Sal Noble, and I'm going to tell. Besides, I want to see the engine room, like he promised.'

'You breathe one word and I'll kill you, Gideon Joe, do you hear me?' She grabbed his ear and twisted it, hard. She was half a head taller than he was and used to being obeyed. 'And I didn't speak to him, anyway. I never said a word.'

'You wanted to,' accused her brother, rubbing his ear and glaring at her. 'I saw you, blushing and smiling and – '

'Shut up!' Sal whirled on him in fury, but this time he leapt nimbly out of range, delighted at the success of his gibe . . .

'Sal loves the hell-hole man. Sal loves the . . . Ow!'

Sal had launched herself at her brother with a fury which took him by surprise, scratching and thumping and pulling his hair till he managed to fight free and take refuge behind a pile of tea-chests which had just been unloaded from the open hatch of the London steamer.

'Hit me again and I'll tell Ma,' taunted Gideon. 'Sal was fighting in the street. Sal was fighting in the – '

'Hey, you! Out of the way!' called an angry seaman as the arm of a derrick swung overhead with another bulging net of tea-chests swaying from its massive iron hook. Instantly the two forgot their quarrel and united against their adversary.

Gideon Joe jeered and gestured in derision, Sal stuck out her tongue, then they linked arms and strolled triumphantly round the nearest corner, where they collapsed against the wall in fits of giggles. Then, remembering, they ran quickly for home. Ma would be wondering where they were.

'You'll not say anything, will you, Gideon?' whispered Sal when they reached the door.

They both knew Sal didn't mean fighting in the street. That was a straightforward sin; the other was complicated with undertones neither of them understood.

Gideon shrugged. 'I won't if you don't.'

'Promise?' She pinched his ear in warning.

That was a mistake. Gideon pushed past her into the house, one hand to his burning ear, and said indignantly to the room at large, 'There was a man at Aunt Bethany's. He came downstairs with his waistcoat undone and no coat on and she was cross.' When no one spoke, he added defiantly, 'And the hell-hole man called Sal a pretty little lady and Sal *smiled* at him.'

Sal blushed crimson with fury and mortification as all eyes in the room were turned on them and the silence stretched and stretched. Old Gideon and Mary Noble sat on either side of the fire, Gideon with a tankard in his hand, Mary with her knitting. Twelve-year-old Milly had been setting plates and spoons on the table for the evening broth which Elissa had been stirring in the big iron pot on the range, but now all action was suspended. There was a warm smell of new bread in the room and a shiny yellow pat of butter on a brown dish in the middle of the table. And silence.

Gideon Joe glared at them all and added defiantly, 'Aunt Bethany had her skirt undone and her face was all red and she swore at us. It's wicked to swear, isn't it?' When still no one answered, he shouted, 'And she hit wee Georgie!'

Elissa found her tongue first. 'That is enough,' she said in the quiet voice they always obeyed. 'I will have no more tale-bearing. Come in and close the door, both of you. Sal, take off your plaid and help me serve the soup. Gideon Joe, wash your hands and sit down at table. We have been waiting long enough for you and your grandpa is hungry.'

There was general movement in the room as tasks were resumed and the two older Nobles took their places at the table. No one commented on the boy's outburst – the lads, even Zach the youngest, were all away at the fishing for which Elissa was grateful – though Milly whispered something into Sal's ear when she thought no one was looking.

Gideon Joe was outraged by the failure of his story. 'But she hit Georgie! Didn't you hear me, Ma?'

'I heard, and we will talk about it later. Now, you will do as you are told. Grandpa is waiting to say grace.'

Old Gideon's face was thunderous, though the words of the grace were the usual ones and, seeing his expression, Elissa knew that Bethany would not escape his punishment. As head of the family and clerk to the Session, he had no choice: the only question in her mind was whether another black line would be scored through a name in the family Bible.

When the children were in bed upstairs and Mary and Gideon had retired to their box bed off the kitchen and closed the doors, Elissa heard the low murmur of their voices, mostly old Gideon's, for some time until at last there was silence. He had decided Bethany's fate. She did not doubt that Bethany would blame her for it. Could hear her voice loud inside her head, taunting: *You're jealous, Lissa Downie 'cos I've a man in my bed, and you haven't.* There was a faint tap on the door and Gideon Joe tiptoed in.

'I'm sorry, Ma.' He buried his face in her lap and cried into her skirts until she soothed him into calm. Then he said, 'I didn't tell you the message. The man said to ask for Captain Grant and he'd show us over the ship himself. He said the *Singing Bird* was waiting for passengers.'

'Which man was that, Gideon Joe? The man on the stairs?'

"Course not. The . . .' He had been going to say 'hell-hole' but thought better of it. 'Sal's friend.'

When he had gone back upstairs to bed, Elissa sat on in the light of a single candle and what glow remained in the damped-down fire, her fingers moving automatically over her knitting while she tried to sort out the turmoil in her thoughts. Gideon Joe's outburst had shaken her more than she had realised. Not just because of the meaning behind the details her son had innocently chosen to report: red cheeks, unbuttoned clothes, the swearing, all indications that the children had interrupted Bethany and . . . and her visitor before they expected to be interrupted. But also because of Sal. *Sal's friend.* The phrase haunted her.

Elissa did not doubt that Sal was as innocent as her son about the scene they had witnessed. Neither child would dream that Bethany and whoever it was were doing anything they shouldn't. Certainly not committing adultery.

Thou shalt not . . . Which commandment was it? Bethany had taunted her once with the commandments, wanting her to repeat aloud *Thou shalt not covet.* Bethany had meant Adam. And now Adam was tempting Elissa to break a different commandment.

Adam. She spoke the word deliberately aloud, though softly, so as

223

not to disturb the sleepers. Adam whom she had loved with all her soul and being. Adam the father of her precious Sal. Adam who this very day had sent a message that he was waiting for her. And had sent it by her own children. By his own daughter.

For a moment memory flooded through her with unbearable sweetness and pain; to be washed away by a flood of cold anger. How dare they torment her, both of them and each as bad as the other. Joseph, using her virtue to punish her, on and on, for some imagined faithlessness, and Adam, refusing to give up, beguiling her daughter with compliments, trying to bribe Elissa with money and success. He had even named a steamer after her. If they loved her, couldn't they see what torment it was for her? Dear God, why had Adam Grant come back into her life? Hadn't he caused her enough misery already?

He should have stayed dead.

The moment the thought came into her head she was ashamed. It was wicked to wish someone dead and she did not mean it. Then slowly the revelation came. She had no need to wish Adam dead because he was. At least, the Adam of her youth, the golden-haloed hero of her innocence was dead. Dead, as the past was dead and could not be retrieved. She might have learnt to love the new Adam if she was free, but she was not.

She sat suddenly still, her hands idle in her lap and resting on the warm heap of the half-completed gansey. This one was for Samuel, now a grown man of twenty who had stepped into his dead brother Peter's shoes as second in command on the family drifter. She was fond of Samuel who was a kindly lad and, though not of the brightest intelligence was solid and reliable. He was a big lad, though, and the gansey was taking longer than anticipated. She would have to hurry if it was to be ready for when they came home from Yarmouth, in three weeks' time.

She remembered that other gansey she had knitted, long ago, for Adam. She had woven her love into every joyous stitch and had begged them to bury it with her dear, drowned lover: now it was rotting on an unknown corpse in a Yarmouth graveyard. The death of love.

Beyond the silence of the sleeping house she heard voices across the Square, someone calling 'Goodnight', then the closing of a door clear in the sharp night air. A dog barked briefly and stopped. Then there was only the distant rhythm of surf on shore. A sound she had lived with all her life. Inside the room, the iron kettle simmered quietly on the range, a coal stirred in the grate and somewhere behind her left shoulder the wag-at-the-wall ticked the minutes away with the slow pulse of eternity.

Carefully, wonderingly, she examined her heart, turning over affections and longings, vows, loyalties and love; and at last she saw her way clear.

In the sudden freedom of self-knowledge she knew that she had waited long enough. Her dogged virtue had not brought Joseph back to her, nor the years of slaving in the curing shed for some unspecified future. That future was worthless if she did not share it with the man she had vowed to love and cherish for ever. The choice had been virtue or sin: now it was to be a different choice. The time for meek endurance was past.

It was time to take matters into her own hands.

She was on the deck of the little coastal steamer, watching the ropes being cast off, when Bethany caught up with her.

'I'll get you for this, Lissa Downie!' she yelled from the quay. 'You jealous, tale-bearing cow. I'll get you one day . . .'

There was more, but the vessel was already in the channel and heading seawards. Elissa turned her back on Bethany's curses and her face into the clean sea wind.

CHAPTER 20

Great Yarmouth had altered little in the nine years since Elissa had last visited the place, though she herself had altered much. She remembered that innocent, nervous, excited young girl as a stranger. Remembered her unshakeable faith in her lover; her naïvety and absolute trust, in God and in her fellow men. The storm which had killed so many fishermen, including the father of Elissa's child, had been the end of innocence, the beginning of a more clear-sighted reality.

Nine years ago she would have gone blithely to the curing yards on the Denes, have asked everyone she saw for directions till she found her man. Now, age had taught her caution. If Joseph knew she was about, he would avoid her: no one must know her mission till it was over, one way or the other. She had had no choice but to confide in Ina and Fergus, and in Mary Noble who would have to take charge of smokehouse and children till Elissa returned, but she had extracted promises of secrecy from all of them and knew she could trust them. Officially, if anyone asked, she was going to Yarmouth to learn the East Anglian way of smoking herrings with a view to introducing it to the Pocra smokehouse. She travelled with Mary's blessing, with Ina's strong encouragement – 'It's time someone taught that stubborn bonehead sense' – and with Fergus's undertaking to do all he could to help her. At her request, he had found her lodgings in one of the Rows and had told her where Joseph's boat was usually moored.

That was an obstacle she had not envisaged: it was one thing to plan to brave Joseph in an upstairs room in Sailmakers' Row, quite another to attempt to do it on board a herring drifter, in full view of the entire harbour and with half the crewmen still aboard. But she might have known: Joseph came ashore in the morning to unload the catch, put to sea again with the rest of the fleet in late afternoon, and spent the intervening hours helping Fergus in the curing yard. If he ever slept, said Fergus, he must do it at sea, for he certainly found no time for such frivolities ashore, even on a Saturday. Sunday was her only chance. But how, and where?

While puzzling over the problem, Elissa set about making her

226

supposed mission in Yarmouth a reality. Her landlady directed her to where she would find 'the best kippers in God's universe': the landlady's cousin's smokehouse, next to the Seamen's Mission on the quay. It was a structure much like the one she had left behind on Pocra: a brick chimney with wooden walls, patched here and there with corrugated iron, and more of the same on the pitched roof. The wind found its way inside through the gaps round the big double doors, but it was a welcome wind when one met the wall of smoky warmth at the chimney end. Inside the doors, salt and brine and overflowing tubs of fish-guts; girls in rubber boots and long oilskin aprons, sleeves rolled to the elbow above scarred and red-raw arms; fingers bound up in sodden, blood-streaked rags. A dozen girls, locals mostly, engaged in splitting and gutting the fish which, explained the foreman, were then tossed into great buckets of brine to soak for half an hour. After that, they were taken out and hung on hooks on wooden rods. Two red-faced and perspiring men in long oilskin aprons suspended these in the smoke of the curing 'cupboard' to hang there for up to eighteen hours while a lad of fifteen or so fed the fire with oak chips and sawdust to regulate the smoke. It was all much as she had expected, much the same method that they followed at home. Of course the red herring was different, they told her. Steeped in salt for two days and then smoked for two or three weeks. Then there was the famous Yarmouth bloater. That was roused in salt overnight then lightly cooked in the heat of a smoking fire. The trick was to get the balance of heat and smoke just right. But she was not interested in bloaters or in red herrings. Only in Joseph.

She thanked the landlady's cousin for his help and left, closing the big double door behind her and leaning against it for a refreshing moment while the cold sea air blew the taint of fish-laden smoke from her hair and stung the colour back into her cheeks. She closed her eyes briefly, to savour the sea breeze and the salt tang of the spray which arched from the breakwater as the bow wave of a passing tug-boat slapped against it. Then opened them again. She must not lose her courage.

The harbour was busier than she remembered it: daily at least fifteen hundred drifters jostled for position in the roads and at the quay to unload their catch and put to sea again, while tug-boats and ketches and all manner of little sailboats scurried to and fro in the wind. There were even one or two steam trawlers, though the bulk of these – some two hundred – were further down the coast at Lowestoft where the harbour was more suited to their needs. Elissa was searching along the line of massed shipping for Joseph's boat when she noticed an unfamiliar vessel tied to the quay some twenty yards away from her, in among the herring drifters and the local ketches. A sturdy wooden smack of eighty feet with *Preach the Word* painted on the nearest bow. An unusual name for a boat. Her eyes paused for an interested moment, then moved reluctantly on.

On either side and beyond stretched the usual tangle of masts and rigging, of vessels crammed so tightly together a man could use them as a floating road on which to walk from one end of the quay to the other; so tightly crammed it was impossible to pick out one from another. Many had their sails still set and idly stirring in the breeze while the canvas dried: red and yellow and brown, like autumn leaves. The density of them almost obliterated the dun-coloured shore of the far bank, and the grey river in between. To her right, at the innermost curve of the estuary, lay the town, with the dense body of the Rows behind her on the jutting finger of land which separated river from sea. To her left, at the river mouth, was the lighthouse and from there, on the seaward side, curved the long blade of the sea front northwards, to the shingled strip of beach where she had once mourned the death of a drowned stranger.

But she could not see Joseph's boat anywhere in the crush, and if she had, would not have known what to do. She pulled her plaid tighter about her shoulders and turned towards the inner basin. She would seek out Fergus and see if she could be of use in the curing yard. If Joseph saw her there, then so be it. She could not spend another idle moment in this melancholy place.

She had not gone many steps when her eye caught a movement on the deck of the nearest vessel, not ten yards away. The *Preach the Word*. She turned her head to see emerge from the fo'c'sle hatchway a tall bearded man with the clothes of a fisherman and his arms full of books. As he reached the deck, he raised his eyes, saw her, and stopped. They regarded each other for a long, disbelieving moment, then Elissa spoke.

'Zeb? It is Zeb, isn't it?'

He dropped the books on to the deck, leapt over the gunwale on to the quay and flung his arms around her in a great bear-hug of welcome.

'Elissa. Who'd have thought it? And not a day older than when I last saw you, was it seven, eight years ago? Tell me, how is Ma? And my father?'

'Both well, but . . .'

'We can't talk here, lass. Come into the Mission and I'll buy you tea, then you can tell me all the news from home.'

The 'Mission' was the Mission to Deep-Sea Fishermen for which, Elissa learned, Joseph's brother Zeb had worked for the past six years. A solid, well-built and welcoming hut close to the smokehouse she had recently visited. Inside it was plain, but clean. A coal fire gave out a steady warmth into the smoke-filled atmosphere and there was a pleasant smell of toasted teacakes and frying bacon. Some half a dozen sailors sat at a table near the fire, all smoking pipe or cigarette, all drinking tea. They raised their hats politely as Elissa came in.

'I never met up with that cousin of Father's,' Zeb confessed, when they had found seats at a nearby table. 'Caught on my first night in Grimsby by a skipper's mate short of a crewman and carried off to the Dogger Bank on the filthiest, cruellest vessel imaginable. The boy I replaced had been murdered, the cook told me. Tormented and beaten till he was near dead on his feet, then pushed overboard to drown. "Swept" overboard, the report said, "by a freak wave." But everyone knew it was murder. The men had rowed over to the coper – that's the villainous ship that used to sell tobacco and alcohol to the trawler fleet – drunk themselves into a bestial stupor, and killed the poor boy for entertainment.' He shuddered. 'It is terrible to see what drink can do to a man.'

'And . . .' Elissa hesitated, but she had to ask. 'Did they ill-treat you too?'

Zeb did not answer. Instead, he called over his shoulder to the woman at the counter for more tea, 'And something to eat, Annie. Whatever you've got.' Then he turned back to Elissa, his face grave and his dark eyes older and wiser than his twenty-six years.

'I was eighteen. Four years older than the lad who died. But they were strong and vicious men when the drink was in them.' He paused, his face expessionless, but Elissa knew with a shiver of revulsion that he had suffered, and suffered badly.

'I'd been with them a year, maybe two. I know it seemed like an eternity. But I remember the day exactly. It was January and blowing half a gale. The fleet was somewhere off the Dogger Bank and the steam cutter had come to collect the day's catch. You know in a trawler the catch is gutted and sorted into boxes on board, not ashore like the herring drifters do it, then the boxes are rowed over to the steam cutter to take back to harbour. Well the sea was rolling and tossing something wicked. Smacking spray from the ship's side in twenty-foot fountains. Already we'd seen one boat lifted high into the air, turn a somersault and vanish under the next wave, fish boxes flying to the winds and both hands lost. When a man's clothes weigh twenty-five pounds and his sea boots fill with water, he's no chance of swimming, even if he knows how.

'But our skipper was a hard man. "Ours next," he says, meaning the boat, and when there was an outright mutiny it was me and the mate who had to go. Well, with a pile of loaded boxes five feet high amidships and the sea rocking our boat like a demented cradle, we thought we'd never make it. Him in the prow, me in the stern, rowing on our feet and praying the next wave wouldn't curl us over. Then we reached the cutter and what did it do? Rolled on top of us, smashed the boat to splinters and sent the fish back where they came from.'

'Dear God,' breathed Elissa in horror.

'So said I, and God heard me. He put a spar in my path and I grabbed hold and hung on till someone fished me out with a boat-hook, but I never saw the mate again. Nor my skipper, thank the Good Lord who was watching over me that day, as He does every day of my life. Well, they was asking me which ship I'd come from and all ready to post me back again in the next mad boat to reach the cutter, when this new, strange ship suddenly appeared in the middle of the fleet, a great blue flag flying from her mast, and everyone started shouting, "It's the Bethel ship." In the excitement, they forgot about me. Then when the boxes were all loaded and the sea settled, boats were lowered from all over the fleet and rowed to this Bethel ship. I went in one of them, and when I reached yon Bethel ship, I stayed. I knew the Lord had sent it to me.

'I've been with the Mission ever since, taking the Lord's word to the fleets, selling the men tobacco, writing letters for them, reading the Bible, holding prayer meetings and socialising over cups of tea. We've had many a man sign the pledge before he leaves us, and there's ships now in the trawl fleets that are sober to a man, and the better for it.'

Elissa had heard of these missionary ships and of the amazing transformation they had brought to what had too often been a brutal and vicious way of living. She said quietly, 'Your father would be proud of you, Zeb, and your mother has never stopped yearning for you and worrying, as mothers will do.' She did not ask why he had never written: remembering Gideon Noble and the family Bible, she did not need to. Instead, she said gently, 'May I tell them how you are?'

When he nodded, she told him that if he wished it, he could meet his brother Joseph that very day. Then, feeling the depth and sincerity of his understanding, she told him other things.

So it was that on Saturday evening Zeb took his brother Joseph back with him, to a rented room in Sailmakers' Row, and, saying he must speak to the landlady about something, left him there, quietly smoking a pipe and gazing into the flickering fire. Consequently, Joseph did not turn when the door opened behind him.

'All fixed up now?' he asked.

'Not yet, but I hope it will be very soon.'

At the quiet voice, he leapt to his feet with shock. Elissa closed the door behind her, leant her back against it and looked at him from grave, unwavering eyes.

'This has gone on long enough, Joseph. It is time for us to settle things between us. No,' she warned, as he took a step towards her. 'I'll not let you run away this time. You have avoided me for long enough. You will not leave this room until we have spoken properly together.'

Before he realised what she meant to do she turned the key in the lock, then deliberately dropped it down inside her bodice, between her breasts.

'If you want the key, you must take it from me yourself.'

The blood drained from his face. Abruptly he turned his back.

'My brother Zeb will be here in a moment,' he said, in a voice she hardly recognised. 'He will not expect to be locked out of his own room.'

'No. But Zeb is dining tonight with a friend, in Lowestoft. This room is mine.'

As the implications sank in there was silence. A cold, empty silence that filled Elissa with dread. It had been a mistake. All a terrible, humiliating mistake. But, she told herself defiantly, *through no fault of hers*. This was her last chance and she would take it, whatever further shame it cost her.

'Joseph,' she began, in a hesitant voice which grew stronger as she met with no interruption, though it was the empty strength of despair. 'I have to speak to you. There are things I must say to you in private, without children or family to hide behind. I am sorry you were tricked into coming here, but Zeb agreed with me. Zeb is a forgiving and compassionate man and . . . and it was the only way.'

She hesitated, hoping for some reaction from him, but there was none. So be it. She would speak anyway, even if it was into a hostile void.

'You are my husband and I love you. You may not believe it. You may not want to believe it. You told me once that you married me "for reasons of your own" but you never told me what those reasons were. If they are why you no longer want me, then so be it. But I love you. I believe I have loved you since the day you followed me on to the headland above Lerwick and comforted me while I wept over my infatuation with . . . with Adam. I loved Adam. I am not ashamed of that. Adored him with the selfless devotion of innocence and first love. He filled my life with laughter and joy. Then he died.'

Still there was no hint of response in the motionless figure. But now the averted back stimulated her to defiance. All was lost anyway. Why should she not speak her mind?

'I admit I asked you to marry me out of fear, loneliness, all sorts of

231

reasons. But it was you I asked, and no one else. Because I felt at ease with you, trusted you, admired and ... and loved you. Not the same love that I felt for Adam – how could it be the same – but love nonetheless. Quieter, sadder, more mature, but still love. I know it now, and have known it ever since little Gideon Joe was born. No, before that. Since, I think, our wedding night when you ... when you ...' But in the face of his relentless silence she could not go on.

She waited, hoping even now for some sort of reply, but his back remained rigid, his face averted. Whether from pride, jealousy, hatred or all three she did not know.

'Adam asked me to go away with him. Asked more than once. I refused, because I am your wife. But if you persist in setting no value on that, then I intend to leave you. But I will go because you send me away, not from my own choice. You have ignored me, punished me, for long enough.'

She paused for an answer which did not come and her control snapped. 'You are still doing it. You are worse than my brother William. At least he had good reason to condemn me. You have had none. Yet you are as implacable as he is. And as relentlessly unforgiving. What have I done that is so unforgivable? Turned away my love. Turned him away for ever. Yet here, in the privacy of my own room with no one to hear but ourselves you cannot even bring yourself to speak to me. Well, I have almost finished, Joseph. I have only one more thing to say. These last years have been torment while you kept me cruelly apart from you. I do not think I can bear it any longer. You are my husband. I have loved you faithfully, as a wife should do, but I have also yearned for you and wanted you till I thought my heart would break.'

When still he made no answer, her anger died away. She had tried and failed. She finished with quiet dignity, 'Perhaps it has already. So be it. I will leave you if that is what you want. But I know that all I want is to live in peace with my husband, and to have his love in return.'

In the stillness which followed she heard footsteps in the street under the window, the mewing of a cat, the murmur of voices from a nearby house, a burst of sudden laughter, and, inside the room, the rapid beat of her own heart. She was turning away, defeated, when she heard something else.

'Joseph?' She stepped towards him, put a tentative hand on his arm, and at last he turned to face her.

Tears blurred his eyes and more streamed down his cheeks in silent, glistening trails. He made no attempt to stem or to disguise them.

'Oh my love,' he managed through his tears. 'You cannot know how I have longed to hear you say those words.' He spread his arms in helpless entreaty, then closed them tight around her.

'I am sorry, my love,' he mumbled, his cheek against her hair. 'I thought . . . I thought you . . .' Then he broke down and sobbed.

She put her arms around him and soothed him like a child, murmuring endearments till at last he quietened. And drew away from her in embarrassment.

'I'm sorry, Elissa. I did not mean to do that, but I thought that you and he . . . that you only stayed out of duty.'

Elissa looked sadly up into his tear-streaked face. 'I know what you thought, and it was not at all flattering to me. Also, none of it was true. None of it. For an intelligent man you have let jealousy lead you ridiculously astray. But I forgive you. So let me dry your eyes and then we will talk of other things.'

But when she reached up to dry his eyes with her own handkerchief, he caught her wrist with one hand and with the other clasped her close against his chest. Then he bent his head and kissed her, crushing her so hard against him that she gasped for breath. Then forgot everything else in the overwhelming relief of finding him again.

'I am glad you locked the door,' he murmured some time later as he unfastened the buttons of her dress one by one until it slipped in blue woollen folds to the uncarpeted floor. The key fell with a clatter on the floorboards and they looked at each other, startled.

Then Elissa smiled. 'I locked the door not to keep my landlady out, but to keep you in. However, I have said my say. You are free to go now, if you choose.'

'I'll show you what I choose, woman.' With one foot he sent the key skidding across the floor, then swept her up in his arms and carried her to the bed.

Much later still he whispered, 'Whatever will your landlady say? Entertaining a strange man in your room.'

'I am glad you are entertained, Mr Noble.' Then she added, with a note of sadness, 'But you have been a stranger for too long.'

'Forgive me, dearest.' He kissed her eyes, her ear lobes, her throat, and as his lips moved downwards towards her breasts she knew she would forgive him everything. Even the destructive jealousy that had kept them apart for so long and that she knew, with a cold, warning part of her brain, was not entirely dead, and never would be. Pray God nothing would rouse it into life again. Then she forgot even that anxiety in the obliterating fire of Joseph's love.

The sound of booted feet in the Row below awoke them and for a moment Elissa thought it was morning, then she saw bright pinpricks in the black square of the window, heard the steps recede in a flurry of suppressed whispers and a sudden burst of drunken song and realised that it was still Saturday, still the day which had begun so bleakly, and had not yet ended. Her husband's arms were around her, his warm body still twined with hers. Though no longer sleeping.

'I think I should tell you,' whispered Elissa. 'My landlady understands that a woman needs privacy when her man comes home from the sea. I showed her my marriage lines,' she added demurely, 'and she will not intrude. Though she may bang on the door in the morning. She has promised us a "real fine breakfast", to keep your strength up. For a while,' she teased, though there was pain behind the words, 'I feared it would not be needed.'

Remembering the bleak misery of the last three years, she did not immediately respond when he tried to draw her closer. The *Singing Bird* would be sailing for Melbourne, perhaps had sailed already. Without her. Goodbye Adam, for ever.

'Please, my love,' he murmured. 'We have so much time to make up for.'

Shaking off memory, she turned to him. 'On one condition. Tell me, what were those private reasons that made you marry me?'

'Don't you know yet, you ninny? I loved you. I have loved you since you were a solemn-faced little schoolgirl with a ribbon in your hair and a starched pinafore over skirts that were always too long for you. I marked you out even then as the lass I would one day marry. I loved you when you were six, ten, fifteen, always. And I love you now. So much it tears my heart with the pain of it. If you only knew how much I love you, Elissa Downie.'

Then he set out to show her.

CHAPTER 21

1897

Elissa Downie's Sal was restless. Not just because the whole city was restless with the suppressed excitement of anticipation – another week and the old Queen's Diamond Jubilee was to be celebrated all over the kingdom with exuberant pomp and jollification – but for a score of other, more personal reasons. To begin with, she had had another of those mysterious and exciting presents which always made her father clamp his jaw tight and stare out of the window at nothing while her mother was too carefully calm and offhand.

'A brooch? In the shape of a bird. How kind of your godfather.'

'It is a dove, Ma. See?' and she held it out in the palm of her hand for her mother's inspection. 'A little gold dove with a leaf in its beak, and a little pearl for an eye. Please may I wear it on Sunday?'

'It is very pretty, Sal,' said her mother while her father, as she had known he would, puffed at his pipe with sudden concentration and studied the coal scuttle. 'But you are not quite old enough to wear such things, and certainly not to church. I will put it away for you, with the other gifts, until you are older.'

'But I am fifteen, Ma,' said Sal and would have stamped her foot in frustration if she had dared. 'If fifteen is old enough to work in Da's curing yard and your smokeshed, then it's old enough for me to wear my own brooch.'

'Watch your tongue, lass,' warned Grandpa Noble from his usual chair at the fireside. 'And don't answer your mother back. She knows what's best for you.'

'Sorry, Ma,' mumbled Sal, but with ill grace. Her ma did not know what was best for Sal. How could she, when she was a middle-aged woman with no interests outside her precious family and her precious smokeshed? Sal knew exactly what she wanted and it was not to spend the rest of her life on the fish quays of Aberdeen.

She wanted to meet someone: not just one of the fisherlads she'd known for as long as she could remember, but someone different. Someone clever, witty, utterly fascinating, someone who would whisk her away into unknown adventures: certainly take her away from the overcrowded house where she had to get up at all hours to help bait hooks or mend nets or smoke fish when she would much rather be at her books, and on top of that she had to help with the hundred other household tasks that Grandma and her mother had to do in the house in the Square where she had spent all her life. With her grandfather, father, four unmarried uncles and her own two brothers there was plenty to keep the women occupied, especially as Auntie Milly was not strong.

But whether or not Sal met a fascinating stranger here at home, she and Gideon Joe had decided long ago that one day they would go to Australia to visit Sal's 'godfather'. Australia would be full of strangers.

That was another mystery: how had the man who had been unmentionable as the hell-hole man suddenly acquired respectability as a 'godfather' she never knew she had? Respectability, but not friendship, for though he sent an annual present to Sal and she acknowledged it, neither her mother nor her father had any contact with him. At least, not that Sal knew of anyway. Sal had given up asking long ago, knowing she would never get an answer out of her parents, but that did not mean she had forgotten the question. And an incident that very morning had reminded her all over again.

The Diamond Jubilee was to be celebrated in the city with much the same extravagance of bunting, coloured lights, bonfires and feasting as had marked the golden version, and with the same exuberant high spirits, but there were changes. The bonfire, for instance, was not on dry land, but a floating one, in the harbour: old wooden boats heaped with an assortment of inflammable rubbish, roped together and ready to be torched. Symbolic, grumbled old Gideon Noble, of how the new generation felt about the old. There was a time when an old yawl would have fetched good money: not any longer, with the young folk greedy for steam.

It was when she and Gideon Joe had strolled down to inspect this floating bonfire that they had seen the new steamer. A splendid liner all strung about with bunting and loyal sentiments in flowers and flags, tied up in the deep-water harbour with a score of other vessels, but far and away the most impressive of the lot. The name, in blue and gold lettering so large that they could read it clearly from where they stood on Pocra Quay, was the *Laverock*. It must be the latest of the Scott Mackenzie fleet, the Melbourne-based company which named all its vessels after some sort of bird, usually a Scottish bird, or the Scottish name of a bird. The first had been the *Singing Bird* which they had been forbidden to visit, for no reason that Sal could see except prejudice. Because Grandpa Noble refused to budge from his opinion that steam was the devil incarnate, and in the Noble household Grandpa's word was law.

But it was not long after the *Singing Bird* had sailed, all those years ago, and her parents had come back from Yarmouth together, that the first gift had arrived from her 'godfather'. A little gold locket shaped like a heart. Her mother and father had looked at each other, then her father had nodded, and her mother had wrapped the locket up again and stowed it away in her kist, 'for when you are older'. Sal had then written an excited thank-you letter which her father had vetted before posting for her.

This year, as well as the official thank you which her father, as usual, had posted, Sal had written a secret letter of her own and had persuaded her best friend Adelaide Forbes to post it for her: she did not trust that busybody of a wifie in the post office not to tell her parents that Sal had been writing letters 'to foreign folk'.

So, though she knew it was impossible for her own letter to have reached Australia yet, Sal felt her insides churn up with excitement in case the *Laverock* had brought her a message, even perhaps her godfather himself? Daringly, on the morning of the celebrations, Sal challenged her mother.

'May I have my little dove brooch please, Ma? I would like to wear it today.' Then if she did meet her 'godfather' he would recognise her immediately. Sal thought her mother was going to refuse, but she suddenly smiled.

'All right. If you promise not to lose it. I see no harm in wearing it, do you, Joseph?' and she looked at Sal's father in that private way she had which always made Sal feel left out.

'I remember the last Jubilee, ten years ago now,' said Elissa, pinning the little brooch to the front of Sal's best dress. 'You wore a different brooch then. A medal, like all the other schoolchildren, and you were so proud.'

Sal did not answer. It was embarrassing to be reminded of your childhood behaviour when you were as tall as your own mother and almost a grown woman. Then, feeling her father's eyes on her, she said, 'Yes, Ma. But it is Daniel's turn to wear the school medal now.'

They both smiled, as Sal had known they would. Her little brother Daniel was the centre of their world and she had to admit he was a nice enough wee loon, for a brother, sunny-natured, bright-eyed and healthy. All the women adored him, from Ina Bain's two-year-old Maggie to Granny Duthie, the oldest and most cantankerous old wifie in the Square. Even Aunt Bethany who was usually bad-tempered and sometimes downright rude to Sal's mother admitted that 'he's not a bad wee loon, considering'. The only thing was, he took up all their attention and sometimes, though she knew she shouldn't, Sal felt a wee bit left out.

Today, the whole family set off for the town together, grandparents, parents, uncles and aunts, cousins, neighbours, children, friends; but in the crowds that thronged the town they were soon separated. It didn't matter. They would meet up again soon enough and as the whole of North Square was in Union Street and the whole of South Square too there was a friendly face of one kind or another wherever you looked. The grand parade along Union Street and the principal streets of the city was led by, of all things, a band of cyclists, mounted on an assortment of Stanley Psychos, Valkyries, New Rapids or Bon-Accords and cheered to the rooftops, with the horse parade of mounted police, harnessed cart and lorry horses following at a suitable distance, with the band.

'I wish I had a bicycle,' said Sal to no one in particular. 'Adelaide Forbes is going to get one. A lot of her friends bicycle into the country for exercise and take a picnic.'

'You get enough exercise, my girl,' said her grandma, 'without showing your legs on one of they contraptions. And if you want a picnic you can wait for the Sunday school outing.'

'But that is only once a year, Grandma, and Adelaide's friends go every week.'

'That's because they have nought else to occupy them. Ladies of leisure, they are, and not knowing how to use it when they've got it. Bicycling! If they want exercise, what's wrong with their own two feet?'

Sal and Gideon Joe exchanged glances behind Grandma Noble's back, raised their eyes to the heavens in mutual exasperation and quietly melted into the crowd behind them, out of range of her grumbling tongue.

It was easier than they had thought. They had been told to stay close, not to get lost, but, thought Sal in justification, if she was with her brother, no one could complain. Then Gideon Joe spotted a group of his friends from school, said 'You'd best stay with Ma, Sal', and the next moment was shouldering his way through the press to join them. Gideon Joe preferred the company of the lads above family any day and especially hated being seen with his 'big sister' who was a head taller than he was. He was a small lad for his age, but recently he had started to grow and he certainly pushed his way through the crowd with no bother.

Sal shrugged, noted out of one eye where her parents still stood on the edge of the pavement so that six-year-old Daniel could have a good view, and looked about her. Someone was leaning out of a first-floor window across the street beside what looked like a tripod with a black box on top. As she watched, the figure raised the window sash higher, stepped back and did something to the box. It must be the cinematograph which was supposed to take moving pictures, but

238

the general opinion, in North Square anyway, was that the only result of that newfangled contraption would be one long and gloomy blank.

Sal was not so dismissive. After all, if the Queen's message, 'From my heart I thank my beloved people. May God bless them', could speed all over the world by telegraph so quickly that within sixteen minutes of her gracious words being sent, the first replies arrived, then all sorts of miracles were possible. The old Queen might be in the fading twilight of her years, but modernity and change were vibrant all around her, and, on this her Jubilee day, Sal could feel it in the very air, hear it in the shrieks and laughter of the children and in the exuberant cheers of the populace. Great things were going to happen, she knew it. She spotted a group of girls from her old class at school further along the pavement and was moving towards them when suddenly, close above her, she heard a familiar voice.

'What glorious weather, and really the decorations are far better than Edinburgh's. Mr Forbes tells me those are quite ordinary.'

'Papa says even London's efforts cannot rival ours, Mrs Burnett.' Surely that was Adelaide?

Sal turned her head and saw behind her a tobacconist's shop front with a private door beside the shop door and on the first floor above it, a row of windows. One of them was open. Rented out to those who preferred to watch the procession in comfort. She remembered Adelaide had told her that was what her mother planned to do, 'so we need not mingle with the common herd'. Suddenly, with a rush of daring fuelled by the knowledge that she was looking her Sunday best, Sal made her way to that private door, checked the brass nameplate, opened the door, closed it behind her and ran up the stone-flagged, iron-railed stairway to the first landing. She hesitated only a moment before knocking, pushing open the door without waiting for an answer and stepping inside.

Across the narrow hallway the door to the parlour stood open and beyond the occasional tables, the potted palms and framed photographs and the hard-buttoned upholstered sofa she saw a row of assorted chairs at the window. A row of hats of diverse colours and diverse decorations turned as one and a row of disapproving faces stared. At least two of the faces raised lorgnettes the better to inspect the intruder.

Sal gulped, spotted Adelaide in the shadows of the second row, and said with all the charm she could muster, 'Good morning, Mrs Forbes. And what a glorious morning it is. I hope you will forgive my intrusion, but I heard Adelaide's voice from the street below and I felt I must just run up and say hello. I have not seen her for such a long time.'

Whether it was the extraordinary nature of the occasion, the effect of the Madeira wine which several of the ladies were drinking, or the fact that a stray shaft of sunlight chose that moment to pick out the gold of Sal's new brooch and reflect it with particular brilliance, Mrs Forbes decided to overlook the impertinence of her daughter's least suitable friend and to play the gracious lady.

'Of course Mrs Burnett will forgive you, Sarah. Just this once,' said Mrs Forbes with a languid wave of her gloved hand.

Just as if she was Queen Victoria herself, thought Sal, and dared not meet Adelaide's eye in case she spoilt it all by giggling.

'Sarah Noble is the daughter of the woman I told you about, Euphemia,' Mrs Forbes explained to a portly woman in purple half-mourning who seemed to be the occupier of the rooms. 'That kind Mrs Noble who helped Cameron with his schoolwork when he fell a little behind. A relation by marriage of Brodie Gibb. Years ago, of course. Cameron is quite the young scholar now. We have great hopes for him when the time comes to sit the bursary exam. Well, don't just stand there, Sarah. Come in and shut the door. You may sit beside Adelaide until the procession is past.'

Sitting demurely at the end of the second row, the girls spoke in excited whispers, for fear of reproof, catching up on news, making plans, while all the time dutifully watching what was going on in the street below them. The civic buildings and shop fronts the length of Union Street were splendidly decked with crimson cloth which stood out brilliantly against the silver granite. To this splendour were added whole forests of evergreen garlands, and so many flowers that every garden in the north-east must have been stripped bare. Rhododendrons, laburnum, bay laurel, roses, any and every variety of flower and plant that could add colour and scent to the summer air were massed in loyal profusion on balconies, window-sills, door-steps and porticoes: hung in scented festoons from lamp-posts and railings and even decorated the collars of the cab horses. The sun-drenched vista of the city's most elegant street quivered with colour and glancing light: a sight to lift the spirits of the citizens and of the thousands of visitors who had streamed in from the adjacent country-side to enjoy the holiday. The scent of flowers and warm dust filled the open window and mingled with the sweeter scent of Madeira wine and furniture polish inside the room itself. From a dozen different flagpoles the Union Jack and the blue and white saltire of St Andrew hung motionless but proud against the high summer sky and the air echoed with the sound of horses' hooves, church bells, distant pipe bands and flute bands and drums, and everywhere the particular chattering continuo of a huge and good-humoured crowd in holiday mood.

It was the people that Adelaide and Sal studied with greatest interest, searching for faces they knew, pointing out the most striking and elegant costumes or the most bizarre. Beside them, Mrs Forbes and her friends were apparently doing the same.

'I do believe that is the Henderson girl. Across the street beside the woman in purple. That masculine style of straw hat is most unflattering. I told her mother no good would come of letting her attend the university and you see the result before your very eyes. Unfeminine clothes and unfeminine attitudes. Believe me, no man wants to marry an encyclopaedia, especially in such a drab binding.'

'I heard a rumour the other day,' said a woman with the straightest back Sal had ever seen, a long hooked nose and a neck like a small giraffe, 'that Sophia Henderson is to marry a mathematics professor. A widower with several children, I believe.'

'There you are,' said Mrs Forbes. 'That proves my point entirely. For a second marriage, a man looks only for strength of constitution.'

'Though a good dowry helps,' said another.

There was the smallest of pauses before Mrs Giraffe-neck turned to Mrs Forbes and inquired, 'How is your daughter Madeleine? Is there any news of an engagement?'

'I sincerely hope not,' snapped Mrs Forbes. 'Madeleine is such a help to me and I would hate to lose her. But why don't you ask her yourself, if you are so curious? She is expected at any minute.' Mrs Forbes rose from her seat in majestic outrage.

Sal was wondering whatever had annoyed Adelaide's mother so much when that woman's relentless eyes fell on the intruder.

'It is time you left, Sarah,' she frowned. 'You have had ample time to say hello to Adelaide and your family will wonder where you are.'

'May I go down to the street door with her, Mamma?' asked Adelaide. 'I will come back directly.'

'Very well, but do not dawdle. You know we are expecting more visitors and I will not have you absent on such occasions. You must learn to practise social graces if you are to find favour. Remember that.'

'Phew!' said Adelaide when they reached the safety of the stairway. 'Mamma will be in a temper now for the rest of the morning.'

'What has your sister Madeleine done?'

'Nothing, except reach the age of twenty-five without finding a husband. Or rather, without accepting any of the awful suitors Mamma trots out for her inspection. The latest offering is dreadful. I can't think what Papa is thinking of to allow him over the threshold, unless there is a business deal involved somewhere. Thank goodness Maddy has too much sense to be hoodwinked. But never mind that,' said Adelaide, pausing at the turn of the stairs where there was a small landing and sitting down on the step. 'What did you think of Mamma's attitude to girls and university?'

241

Sal looked down at Adelaide, who was sprawling on the step like one of the fishergirls in the Square in spite of her white stockings and yellow sprigged skirts, her chestnut ringlets and pert, beribboned straw bonnet. She looped her own skirts carefully together and sat on the step above her friend. 'I . . . I don't really . . .'

'Grotesque, isn't it?' grinned Adelaide. 'Why are the old so set against any sort of change? But I will have to make her see sense. I can't possibly ask her when she's in such a temper, but I have absolutely decided to sit the bursary competition when I'm old enough. Then I shall go to university myself, like Sophia Henderson. If Mamma will let me. Why don't you do the bursary comp. too, Sal?'

'Do you really think I could?'

'Of course you could. Girls are allowed to sit the exams now as well as boys and though we will have to learn Greek and Latin or we haven't a chance, we can easily do that. Papa is going to get a tutor for Cameron in a year or so and when he does, we can borrow his books. Do say you will, then we could go to the university together?'

Before Sal could find words to answer, they heard the street door open below them and a languid male voice drifted up to them above the distant chatter of the crowd.

'God! Is it really up these disgusting steps? It's more like a jail than a private house.'

Hastily, the two girls scrambled to their feet and brushed the dust off their skirts.

'Who am I to argue with your superior knowledge,' said a contemptuous female voice. 'I have never seen a jail.' Adelaide, her back against the wall in the shadows at the turn of the stair, clapped a hand across her mouth and suppressed a giggle.

'It's my sister Madeleine with Mamma's latest offering,' she whispered. 'He's ancient. And awful.'

'Let's run,' urged Sal. 'Back upstairs, to the top landing.'

But it was already too late. They looked down through the banister rails at the ascending figures, though it was not Madeleine Forbes, unremarkable in lilac, that Sal watched with such fascinated distaste. The man was old, just as Adelaide said, but what a dandy.

Fair hair immaculately waved, a waxed and curled moustache with a minute triangle of beard beneath the lower lip, white wing collar, silk cravat with diamond stud, silver brocade waistcoat, dove-grey jacket and trousers, neat, handmade boots mounting step by supercilious step, as if picking his way through a midden. A pale-gloved hand and polished Malacca cane. And when he lifted his chin to look upwards, cold pale eyes, a twisted nose and a sneer of the lips which sent a shiver of revulsion down her spine.

She shrank back against the wall of the half-landing, making herself as inconspicuous and flat as possible, her eyes fixed determinedly on her own sensibly shod feet and trying her best to hide behind her friend. But the landing was small and Adelaide defiant.

'Hello, Madeleine. Mamma's been waiting for you for ages. You'd better hurry or the Madeira wine will be finished and there's nothing else.'

'Where are you going?' demanded her eldest sister. 'I thought you were supposed to be helping.'

'I am,' said Adelaide sweetly. 'I am speeding my guest on her way.'

'Sarah Noble isn't a guest,' retorted Madeleine. 'She's Lissa Downie's Sal from Footdee and she can see herself out. She's used to hawking her fish creel up longer stairways than this one.' Then she tossed her head and flounced on up the steps.

'Lissa Downie's Sal,' said a soft voice too close to Sal's ear. 'I hope we meet again, very soon. I never forget a name. Or a face. Especially not such a young and desirable one.'

He made the word 'desirable' sound both lascivious and threatening. He was as old as her father, every bit as awful as Adelaide had said, and his breath smelt of brandy. Sal pushed past him and fled down the stairs, almost tripping over her skirts in her haste, to where the street door stood blessedly open to clean air and safety.

'Sal! Wait for me!' cried Adelaide, scrambling after her, but Sal had reached the door into the street. Only to find her exit suddenly barred by a group of half a dozen young people, mostly men, and all of them laughing.

'Hey, not so fast,' said the nearest, spreading his arms to block Sal's escape, but this time when Sal looked up into her accoster's face she saw humour and friendliness in the laughter, and beyond his shoulder someone she vaguely recognised.

'Thomas!' cried Adelaide in delight, and Sal realised it was her friend's older brother. 'Mamma didn't say you were coming here.'

'Because she didn't know! Ben, put that nice girl down and behave yourself. But I told my friends we would get a much better vantage point from aloft. Ben here has a deadly aim with the catapult and young Alec is pea-shooter champion of Turriff. Isn't that right, Alec?' A stringy lad with a mop of bright red curly hair and more freckles than Sal had ever seen on one nose grinned at her and winked.

'Thomas, you *can't*!' cried Adelaide in delighted horror. 'Mamma has all her most disapproving cronies upstairs, sipping Madeira by the gallon with their little pinkies in the air and pretending alcohol never passes their lips.'

'Then we will convert them. Hey, Stuart!' he called into the group behind him. 'Be prepared to launch into your "Beverage of Hell" sermon the moment we open the door. Stuart is a son of the Manse and will be a Minister himself one day,' he explained to Sal who was listening open-mouthed to the general lunacy, 'so it will be good practice for him.'

A dark-haired boy with steel-rimmed spectacles moved them further down his nose, peered over them straight into Sal's eyes, and intoned in a deep and sonorous voice, 'Lips that touch liquor must never touch mine.' Then dissolved into helpless laughter in which everyone else joined.

Sal felt the last of her unease drain away leaving her clean again and bubbling with happy expectation. The one they called Ben was smiling at her, not in a knowing or suggestive way, but openly, in friendship. And they were not drunk, as she had at first thought. Unless one could be drunk with youth and good health and high spirits and hope.

'Move along there, you at the front,' called a female voice and Sal saw that it was the girl Mrs Forbes had been so disapproving of. The Henderson girl. Close to, she looked bright-eyed and intelligent, with an honest, downright sort of face that was certainly not beautiful, but was not off-putting either.

'Do as the nice lady says,' grinned Ben, taking Sal's arm to steer her back inside. 'You can lead the way, Miss Modesty. Forward, lads! To the lions' den!'

Sal wanted more than anything in the whole wide world to go with them and the thought of Mrs Forbes's disapproval alone might not have stopped her. But she remembered that other visitor who had passed her on the stairs and who was still up there.

'No, I can't. I'm sorry. I must go home.' Blushing, Sal pushed her way through them and fled.

But their laughter followed her into the wholesome sunlight of the holiday crowds and was still with her when she rejoined her family, who had not even noticed she had gone. While she listened to the harmless chatter around her the thought of them whirled round and round in her head like a joyful chorus of bird-song. Adelaide's brother Thomas was a student at Marischal College and all his friends were students. Ben and Stuart and Alec with the freckles. To Sal they had seemed demigods. No wonder Adelaide wanted to go to the college and from that moment it became Sal's ambition too. She could think of nothing else. Their confident, cheerful voices lingered in her ears above the commentary of her parents and grandparents, the back-chat of her school friends, the clumsy raillery of the boys from the Square. Whatever her parents said, one day she would go to the university with Adelaide.

*

On that evening of the Queen's Diamond Jubilee, with everyone in holiday mood, relaxing and laughing together, Sal took the first momentous step.

They were in the family kitchen, newly home from watching the fireworks on the Links, and everyone was reluctant to part company though it was almost midnight. Friends had joined them and, a rare occurrence, Elissa's brother William with his wife Katrine. Sal did not like Uncle William. She knew he disapproved of her mother and of Sal, though she did not know why. But Uncle William believed in family ties and family obligations, as he had told them on more than one occasion, though in his case that seemed to mean watching her mother and herself for signs of backsliding, reproving them for the smallest levity and pouncing on Sal unawares to demand a recitation of the Shorter Catechism, or the text from last Sunday's sermon. Sal dreaded his rare visits and became positively tongue-tied in his presence. But tonight the general bonhomie and the whisky had relaxed even his vigilance and he was actually laughing over a joke with his brother, Uncle Tom. The door stood open to the Square and the pale summer night and Elissa had unveiled the parlour to take the overflow as friends and neighbours joined them.

Leaning companionably against the kitchen dresser, whisky tumblers in hands, Joseph and Fergus Mackie were discussing the curing business, comparing this year's catch with last year's and grumbling about the price of matties and fulls on the expanding Russian market, but it was only token grumbling: the herring-curing business continued to flourish, or at least to jog along satisfactorily.

Privately, Gideon Joe complained to Sal that their father had no ambition. He worked hard enough, but he was always coming up against suppliers who wouldn't give him this, or charged him too much for that, or obstructed or lost papers or thwarted him. In Gideon Joe's opinion these were just excuses for his own failing to get on. Not like Captain Grant who had started from nothing and now had half a dozen ships of his own in Australia with a new steamer, so rumour said, being built for him in a Clyde shipyard this very moment. It was all very well for his father and Fergus Mackie to say they were doing fine, considering the competition, but it was small beer compared to Captain Grant. But the only time Gideon Joe had dared to say this to his father's face there had been such ructions that Sal shivered again just remembering them.

'Do not mention that name in my house!' her father had roared and for all her mother's soothing and reassurance and desperate diplomacy it had been days before peace returned to the family. The memory made Sal's determination falter: suppose her simple request were to cause such explosions?

In a corner of the parlour Grandpa Gideon was upholding the

merits of sail over steam as usual, and with some justification, for in spite of the overwhelming presence of the trawl fleet, the few line-fishermen such as Gideon Noble who continued to work from the harbour managed to do so with success and even profit. They did not have the massive overheads of the trawlers, explained old Gideon, and their fish found a ready market on their own doorsteps without having to be dispatched south with all the expense and palaver of ice-packed fish boxes and special trains. But it was a small market just the same, thought Sal. Small and outmoded. All right for Grandpa who had known no other, but not for his grandchildren.

Old Gideon's audience included his son Samuel and Jessie Bain's husband, George Black, though both looked as if they would have preferred to be across the narrow entrance hall with the group of menfolk, old and young, who were engrossed in an impromptu shove-halfpenny match on the kitchen table. Young Gideon Joe appeared to be winning.

Elissa and Ina Bain, Fergus Mackie's wife, were comparing notes on the day's events and keeping a collective eye on the various children while the other women gossiped lazily together and drank tea. Then Connie Black, one of Jessie Bain's stepchildren, said suddenly, 'I'll be sixteen soon and my dad says I can go to Shetland for the curing next spring.'

Sal's heart thumped suddenly faster. There were sighs of envy from the younger girls and of wistful reminiscence from the married ones, followed by a rush of 'Can I go, too, Ma?' from Sal's contemporaries.

Someone demanded, 'Tell us what it's like in Shetland, Aunt Ina,' and when she protested that she'd told them a dozen times already they turned on Aunt Jessie and Aunt Elissa and even old Mary Noble who was dozing contentedly in her chair beside the fire. At sixty-six she reckoned she'd earned a few hours off and they were getting on well enough without her.

But when several of the smaller girls clamoured around her knees and Connie Black said in her politest voice, 'Please tell us, Mrs Noble,' she roused herself enough to scoop the youngest on to her knee and said, 'Well now, where shall I begin . . .'

Sal heard her grandmother's voice clearly across the buzz of conversation – the wooden kist, the sea crossing, the scrubbing of the wee hut to make it home – and bit her lip against the flood of longing. She knew her own mother had gone with the herring-girls to Shetland when she was little older than Sal was now, and though she knew it was a hard life with long hours in all weathers Sal had until now taken it for granted that she herself would do the same. But how could she learn Latin and Greek if she was gutting herring all day?

246

How could she study with Adelaide if one of them was in Aberdeen and the other in Shetland or Peterhead or Yarmouth?

She remembered Adelaide's brother Thomas and his friends and unconsciously straightened her back while she considered her choice. On the one hand, what Uncle William would call family obligation and the curing yard. On the other, the new vista of university education. She was clever enough. Everyone said so. And if girls really were allowed to compete for a bursary . . . For some reason Sal turned her head, saw her mother watching her, gave a quick smile and looked away again, pretending to be engrossed in the tale her grandmother was telling. But in that moment Sal's decision was made.

'Sal, you will be sixteen too by then,' called Connie. 'We'll find one more lass and make up a team, shall we?'

'Me! Take me!' A chorus of voices clamoured at once, but Sal's voice cut clear and bright across the general din.

'I'll not be going to the herring, Connie. Next year or ever. I'm going to try for a bursary to the university.'

In that moment it seemed to Sal that all conversation stopped. Something made her look towards the parlour: Uncle William stood in the open doorway, Aunt Katrine beside him, and obviously about to leave. Her heart thumped so fast and loud she thought everyone must hear it, but she managed somehow to say, 'Are you going so soon, Uncle William? What a pity. Won't you stay and . . .?'

William was directing at her the full force of his forbidding glare and it took all her courage not to lower her eyes.

'Did my ears deceive me, Sarah? Or did you have the audacity to say what I thought you said?'

Forgetting manners in the terror of the moment, Sal said, 'I don't know what you thought I said, Uncle William. I was talking to Connie.'

William turned white with outrage, but before he could gather breath for the onslaught, Joseph intervened.

'So you were Sal, but naturally your uncle takes an interest in your future. A kindly interest.'

But William had found breath. 'Outrageous behaviour! Impertinence beyond belief. Pernicious and most damnable pride. Remember your Catechism, girl. Children, obey your parents in the Lord. Honour your elders and betters. And what does the tenth commandment forbid? *All discontentment with your own estate.* You are a fisherman's acknowledged daughter. You should be grateful for that, for it is more than you deserve. Oh yes, far, far more.' Leaving Sal quivering with bewildered terror, he swung round to fire instead at her mother.

'It is as I feared all along. Bad blood will out. Impertinence. Vain adornments. And now this. But I warn you Elissa, if you allow this ... this ... hubris, do not turn to me for help when the inevitable happens. *On your own head be it.'*

Then he gripped his wife by the forearm and marched her out of the house without another word.

'Ma?' said Sal in a small voice, but Elissa was trembling so much she could not speak.

'It's all right, Sal,' said Joseph, his arm around Elissa's shoulders. 'Uncle William is a bit of a pessimist, that's all, and it has been a long day. We will talk about it tomorrow. Your mother is tired and it is time for bed.'

But when the visitors had gone and the family settled down for the night, Sal lay awake into the small hours, worrying. Why had Uncle William been so angry? She had been impertinent, she saw that now, but she had not meant to be and surely a slip of the tongue was a very small sin? There had been something spiteful and revengeful in her uncle's voice, as if he hated her. Sal shivered and snuggled deeper under the blanket in the bed she shared with Aunt Milly. Aunt Milly was asleep or Sal would have asked her opinion; as it was, Sal went over and over in her mind what her uncle had said and every time the injustice of it struck her afresh. Why had he said it was more than she deserved to be a fisherman's daughter?

No. Slowly, wonderingly she corrected herself. Acknowledged daughter. That had been the phrase. And she had been told to be grateful for it. As if other fathers did not acknowledge their daughters. She was still puzzling over the question when she remembered the other, far more important one. This time she knew Uncle William was wrong. If everyone stayed content with their own condition, the one they were born into, no one would ever get anywhere. Look at Brodie Gibb, Aunt Bethany's husband. He had been born a poor crofter's son and look at him now: a house in Marine Terrace and a box at the theatre and Aunt Bethany boasting of all the folk they mixed with who kept their own carriages.

Sal didn't want to keep a carriage. But sometimes she thought it would be nice to have a bigger house so that everyone wasn't under everyone else's feet all the time. And she would like to go to the university. She knew it would cost money, even with a bursary, but her father had not said no and her mother had said nothing. Only that they would talk about it in the morning. And she must remember to ask them what 'hubris' meant. At last, hope restored, Sal fell asleep.

'Insolent pride,' said her father.

How dare Uncle William say it was insolent of her, or proud, to

248

want to go to college and learn? If Sal had had any lingering doubts, that information dispelled them. Her uncle was a bigoted killjoy and she would take no notice of anything he said. Especially as her father had agreed to talk to the teacher at the school and discuss her chances of being able to sit the bursary competition one day. If the teacher said she had a chance, then they would see what arrangements they could make for Sal to learn Greek and Latin and anything else she might need for the exam.

'We will find the money somehow, Sal,' said her father and smiled. 'I know you will earn what you can to help and I would be so proud of you if you went to college. So would we all. The first Noble to go to the university. What a triumph that would be. But you'll need to win a bursary to get there. It must be all by your own efforts, lass. Remember that.'

Sal was to remember that often in the months that followed: she had Greek lessons with the Minister and Latin lessons with the headmaster and in between she worked in 'Mary's' smokeshed or in the Noble household, so that no one, least of all Uncle William, should be able to say she was not earning the money for her tuition. Often the only time she had for studying was in the small hours, by candle-light, when everyone else was asleep. But Adelaide's brother Thomas said that twice as many marks were awarded for Greek and Latin as for French so it had to be done. Not that Sal knew any French anyway, though Adelaide did. Mrs Forbes thought French was 'ladylike'. But how slow it was and how lonely. It would take her years to learn.

Working away in 'Mary's' on a gusty day in September, she was thinking of Adelaide and how nice it must be to have all the time in the world to do what one wanted to do instead of gutting endless fish all day and stringing them up to be smoked, when she heard her Grandma Noble say something about 'that Sinclair fellow and Lawyer Forbes'.

Too many winters at sea had swollen Gideon's finger joints and knees to the point where no amount of flannel compresses or bowls of steaming skate bree could ease the pain or correct the clumsiness and two years ago, when he was seventy, he had given in to the family's united plea for him to hand over command of the family boat to Samuel. Though not until Mary Noble had lost all patience with him.

'Stay ashore, for pity's sake, you obstinate old fool. Before you send the lot of them to the bottom with your bungling.' Then, to ease the hurt, she had added, 'There's work enough for you to do ashore and me rushed off my feet in the smokeshed.'

So now the pair of them went off together at seven every morning, to spend the day in 'Mary's' where the heat of the fire did wonders for Gideon's knees and for his wife's peace of mind, though apart from shovelling sawdust on to the fire now and then, Sal couldn't see what work her grandfather actually did.

'He acts as watchman,' Elissa told her, when Sal asked, in private. 'With so many untrustworthy people about the harbour these days, we are lucky to have Grandpa to keep guard.'

By Sal's observation, keeping guard seemed to consist of gossiping with all and sundry, and, when there was no one else around, with Grandma, as he was doing now. Sal herself was doing the job she liked best: tying the newly smoked fish up in bundles of three as her mother had taught her to do, with a twist of straw around the tails, before packing them away in their basket, for delivery to a fish merchant in the west end of town. At one end of the shed, by the open doors, a group of girls stood around a thick wooden slab of a table, gutting fish, while at the other old Gideon sat beside the big smoke cupboard, a long-handled shovel beside him ready to add more sawdust, rake over the embers or otherwise adjust the components of the smoking process. In a chair opposite him, for all the world as if they were at their own fireside, sat Grandma with a mug of ale in her hands.

Sal's own table and wooden racks of smokies were in the middle, with bundles of straw for tying and a pile of flat baskets for the finished bundles. Sometimes another girl helped her, but she preferred to work alone. Then she could go over Latin verbs in her head, or chant the latest Greek passage she had been set to learn by heart. Or listen to her grandparents, as she was doing now.

'Courting the lawyer's eldest daughter, if you can call it courting,' her grandfather was saying. 'Likely hoping for a dowry to pay off his debts afore his father finds out.'

'There'll not be much of a dowry there,' scoffed Grandma. 'That lawyer mannie's already married off three lassies and they'll not have gone for nothing. Like a row of mealy puddings, those Forbes girls, except for Sal's friend. But then with a ma like that what can you expect? The eldest one's no beauty, so her da's maybe paying extra to get rid of her, though she's a good head on her shoulders for all that and she'll maybe refuse the fellow, like all the other lassies have.'

'Not all, Mary,' said Grandpa, as if he meant a whole lot more than he was saying, and Grandma sniggered.

'Aye, but he has to put out good money for them – and double rates now from what I hear, with him being shop-soiled merchandise.'

They both went into gales of laughter at that witticism and only stopped when one of the gutting girls went up to Grandma to ask her something. When she had gone again, old Gideon went off on another tack.

'He'll have to watch it, that Hugh Sinclair. Sails too close to the

250

wind from what I hear and there's too many folks know it. Keeps bad company, too. Brodie Gibb reckons he's angling for an engagement to pacify his father and if he doesn't get one, then Easton Sinclair will give him the chop. If it'd been me, I'd have done it years ago. No son of mine would carry on like that and get away with it.'

'No,' said Grandma and there was something in her voice that made Sal remember the family Bible. One name had been crossed through with a thick black line, though later, in different ink, someone had amended it to 'Zebediah – working for the Lord 1890–'.

'And no daughter of mine would be allowed to consort with yon Sinclair, neither,' growled old Gideon. 'I don't know what Lawyer Forbes is thinking of.'

'Currying favour with the boss, likely,' said Grandma. 'Or spying.'

'Hey! You! Out of there afore I skelp your backside!' roared Grandpa Noble and a lad who had slipped into the shed without Sal noticing yelped, skidded on the sawdust of the floor and shot outside again, showering the fish he'd filched in all directions. 'Varmints,' grumbled the old man. 'I'm needing eyes in the back of my head what with loungers and loafers pretending they're looking for work and eyeing up the place for easy pickings and a score of mischievous wee pests like yon darting in and out day and night, like thieving rats.'

'Away with you, Gideon. That was only wee Geordie Christie. There's bigger rats than him to worry about.'

And Grandma was right, as they were to find out soon enough.

It was a month later, the tail end of November, a dreary month at the best of times and on that Monday morning particularly dismal. Her father had come home early from the herring season, two days ago and by train, leaving the others to fish on without him. He had come home, he said, 'to see about a few things' and would return to Yarmouth once he had done what he had come to do. There was an air of suppressed excitement about him that everyone noticed, but he answered all questions with, 'Wait and see. You'll hear soon enough.'

He had spent the weekend around the harbour: Sal had seen him go into Hall, Russell's when she was coming back from the smoke-shed and later, when she been sent to the new fishmarket on a message from Grandma Noble, she had spotted her father deep in conversation with Uncle Tom. At home, her mother wore a secret smile when she thought no one was looking: obviously her father had told her, if no one else. Sal found the whole business intriguing, especially the secrecy, for usually her father said, 'I'm away to order more salt' – or nets or the flat measuring baskets called crans or stores for the drifters; even, occasionally, 'I'm away to the Crown and Anchor for a pint of relaxation.'

On Sunday evening, he took Sal aside and for a moment she thought that he was going to let her into the secret too, but all he said was, 'How are your studies progressing?'

'Slowly, Da. If I had more time I could . . .' then she remembered and said hastily, 'I mean, I learn all I can after my work is finished. But there is so very much I don't know. I wonder sometimes if I will ever catch up.'

'You will, lass. The Minister is very satisfied with your work. He told me so today. You still have a long way to go – but plenty of time for the journey. In three, maybe four years from now he thinks you might be ready.'

Three years. It semed like an eternity.

'You haven't changed your mind have you?' For a moment she thought he wanted her to say yes, but when she shook her head he smiled.

'Good lass. Everything worth having is worth waiting for. And worth working for. Remember that. I wish your ma and I could help more, but I reckon you'll have to do the best you can with those two lessons a week. For the moment anyway. Till the family's settled.'

That was the cue for Gideon Joe to start his nagging. 'I don't want to be cook on a leaky bath-tub of an old yawl, Da. I'd rather be in an engine room. If you asked Uncle Brodie, he'd maybe – '

'No. You'll start at the bottom, like I did and my father did and his father before him.'

'It's not fair, Da. Sal's getting to do what she wants. Why can't I?'

'Sal is working for the privilege and doing the work her ma did, and her ma before her. You will start as cook on the family drifter and work your way up from there. If you work as hard as Sal does, you'll soon succeed. So no more complaining. The food has to be good whatever ship you're on. Poison us on the *Optimist* and you're finished. Remember that.'

'I'd rather be on a pilot boat,' dared Gideon Joe. 'Or a tug.'

'Time enough for that, lad, when you can see over the gunwale,' said his grandpa. 'Until then, do as your father says or you'll have no trade at all. Unless it's yard boy on the Inches.'

'That's how Brodie Gibb started,' muttered Gideon, but prudently under his breath and only Sal heard.

'So did Piddly Guyan,' she whispered. He was the harbour down-and-out and drunk. Gideon Joe pushed her, hard, but he was grinning.

'I'm going to be a Zulu when I grow up,' announced Danny. One way and another, they all went to bed laughing.

Early on that Monday morning everyone in the Square was still asleep, except for those timid individuals for whom the blustering gale and the roar of the sea were too nerve-racking and those others who had stayed up until midnight was safely past in order to do essential work on nets or lines, work forbidden on the Sabbath. And, in the Noble household, Sal who had risen early in order to do her daily ration of studying by candle-light. She was crouching over her books at the kitchen table, bundled up in a plaid for warmth and trying not to singe her hair in the candle flame when a thundering on the house door shot her bolt upright and quivering with instinctive fear. She heard voices shouting, more hammering in the Square and another thunderous knock on their own door. The south-easterly gale was howling and rattling in the chimneys, while the noise of the sea roared louder than she had heard it in her whole life.

'Joe Noble! You're needed for the lifeboat.'

Sal wrenched open the door. A gust of wind whipped through the room, doused the candle, lifted her papers from the table and tossed them anyhow while Sal struggled to hold her plaid at her throat with one hand and keep the door steady with the other.

A sou'westered, oilskinned figure dripping rain from every crease put a hand to his mouth and yelled across the noise of storm and tempest, 'Shipwreck. Tell your da!' Then he was gone.

CHAPTER 22

Joseph heard the summons and was across the floor with the skylight flung open in a matter of seconds. The wind howled into the room and snatched his words away as he yelled into the tempest, 'I'm on my way.' Then the skylight dropped shut and curtains, bedclothes, fluttering papers subsided into peace. Joseph was already pulling on gansey and thick serge trousers, tightening braces, buttoning jacket. Biting back her fear, Elissa handed him one long woollen stocking, then the other, remembering every loving stitch she had knitted into them and praying over and over for his safety. Then he was jumping the stairs two at a time – Sal stood ready in the hall with his sea boots, his oilskins and sou'wester – and two minutes later they heard the heavy house door slam behind him.

By that time Elissa was fully dressed and, pausing only to tell Sal to 'Stay here and see to the others for me' she followed Joseph into the storm, pulling her thickest plaid around her as she ran.

'Milly can do that, Ma. I'm coming with you.' But Elissa had gone.

Other doors were opening all round the Square, other muffled figures fought as she was doing against the darkness and the buffeting wind, and all of them making for the pilot's station by the north pier. This could be clearly seen through the gloom, not only because of the rocket which shot its combined summons and warning into the lowering tumult as she stepped over her threshold, but because among the lifeboatmen, pilots, harbourmen and onlookers were a dozen carefully shielded storm lanterns in whose flickering and uncertain glow the anxious shadowed faces took on the expressions of souls in a variety of torments. By the time Elissa reached the huddle of onlookers, the lifeboat had been swung out over the water and lowered into the mounting turbulence of the harbour.

She had no need to ask: the news was all round the harbour already with the mysterious swiftness of disaster. A trawler, a twenty-three-tonner with a full catch of fish, had run ashore in the channel. One of Sinclair's fleet. The *Alice May*. Lit a bonfire of bedding and suchlike on deck to attract attention. With the seas running so high in the

254

south-easterly gale and driving her in one direction and her rudder straining so hard against it to keep her on course in the other, she had smashed her steering-wheel chains as she crossed the bar. Now those same seas were driving her inexorably towards the south shore. She lay floundering and rolling and yelling for help, on the far side of the channel, half-way between the old south breakwater and Poddie's Jetty, while the lifeboat fought to reach her across the distance between.

But the seas were rolling higher and with pounding force over the harbour bar and into the channel, and though the crew rowed their utmost, they could make no headway: every time they rowed beyond the protection of the lower jetty on the north side and fought to cross the channel to the south the surging force of the sea drove them back. Once. Twice. Three times.

Oh God, prayed Elissa over and over, clutching her plaid tight across her chest. Keep the men safe. Bring Joseph back to me, please God. Please. But while her whole body was tense with fear and gathering dread, a part of her was steadfast with pride. She would no more try to stop Joseph going out with the lifeboat than she would walk naked the length of Union Street. The sea was a treacherous master: men who lived by the sea could expect to die by the sea, and it was every man's duty to go to the help of his neighbour while he had breath in his body.

It was growing clearer by the minute, however, that were the lifeboat crew to launch themselves against that mountainous sea a hundred times they would not prevail.

'Ma? What's happening, Ma?' Elissa turned her head to see Sal beside her, wrapped as she herself was, in a thick woollen plaid. Grandma Noble's by the look of it. Then she saw an oilskinned figure behind Sal's shoulder. Gideon Joe.

'I told you to stay inside!' she raged at them, her face grey with strain. Then heart-thudding fear rose like a scream inside her till she thought her legs would crumple under her and her heart spill open on the glistening cobbles of the quayside. 'Where's Daniel?'

'Here, Ma,' came his cheerful voice from somewhere in front of her. 'Where's the lifeboat? I can't see . . .'

He stood on the very edge of the quay, peering innocently into the sea-tossing darkness of the void. But before she could move, or scream a warning, someone grabbed him, pulled him to safety, cuffed his ear in kindly reproof and shoved him towards her. She clutched his hand and gripped it so tight he gasped aloud.

'You're hurting me, Ma.'

'And I'll hurt you a lot more than that if you do such a stupid, thoughtless . . .' But she was shaking too much with relief and the inrush of new fear, for Joseph this time, that she could not finish.

255

There was no need, for a new excitement shot through the watching crowd.

'They're putting to sea again!' cried Gideon Joe. 'See, that's Da in the bow.'

Oh God, not all over again, thought Elissa, knowing it was inevitable. Who could stand by and not try to help with that poor afflicted trawler rolling rudderless and helpless in the turbulent sea and not even a flicker of moonlight in the cloud-ridden darkness. Only the pale glimmer of a lantern, the intermittent beam from the lighthouse at Girdleness, and the leading lights of the harbour mouth. The light-keeper and his men had fired two lines across the trawler when she first foundered, so the crowd told them, but the crew preferred to wait for the lifeboat.

'Who wouldn't,' shuddered Sal, 'with all that sea between ship and shore?'

'I could swim that, easy,' boasted Daniel, but his voice lacked its usual cheerful conviction and when no one answered, he said, in a subdued voice, 'Will they be all right?'

'They'd have been all right if they'd taken the lines when they were offered and hung on tight,' said a woman beside them. ''Stead of risking other folk's lives.' Elissa recognised the woman as mother of the youngest lifeboatman, a widow whose husband had drowned in the harbour mouth not two years back.

'Look,' she said, taking the woman's arm. 'They are fixing a hawser to the lifeboat. That will serve as a lifeline, won't it?' She had meant it as comfort, for herself as well as the poor widow. But a moment later she realised her mistake.

There was a general surge of movement in the crowd around her, then the strongest of the menfolk looped the hawser end around his middle, a dozen others lifted the rope and together they carried it at a trot along the quay to the north pier, down channel to the east of them. There they attached the rope end to a bollard, gathered up the slack and hauled till the veins stood out on their temples. '*Heave* . . . and *heave* . . . and *heave* . . .'

The lifeboat travelled fast and smoothly at first, till it left the shelter of the lower jetty and met the full force of the incoming, gale-driven billows.

'*Heave*!' yelled the anchorman on the pier and with each successful haul he looped another stretch of rope around the bollard while in the treacherous black water the lifeboatmen pulled on the oars so hard that Elissa thought she saw muscles stand out on neck and shoulder and biceps, saw heart strain against rib-cage, heard breath rasp in labouring throat. In reality all she could hear was the whine of wind in the rigging of ships safe at anchor in the inner basin, the rattle of a tin roof somewhere in York Street and the deafening crash

256

as wave after towering wave broke against the pier in a thunderous fountain of grey foam. Under the dark-shrouded sky, water glinted eerie orange where the lantern light caught it, but for the rest was a terrifying murky and unfathomable black. A man alone in that water would have no chance. If the boat foundered there would be no time even to shed boots before . . .

But Elissa closed her mind tight against that thought. Instead, like all the other watchers, she strained all her hope and encouragement and prayers towards that flimsy, valiant little lifeboat and her crew of volunteers as the hawser tightened, the boat arced and plunged and gradually the distance between pier and lifeboat shortened.

'What are they doing, Ma?' Sal, white-faced as her mother, tugged Elissa's sleeve, while her eyes stayed fixed on that perilously frail little lifeboat which careered up each oncoming wave and shot over into each churning trough, like a helpless beetle in a torrent.

'They are trying to position the boat so that when they loose the rope, the incoming sea and the current will carry her to the south shore, over there where the trawler has foundered in the shallows.'

'Oh.' The small sound expressed the appalled comprehension which had gripped each onlooker when they realised what was happening.

Then there was a shout, a sudden snaking line across the darkness, the group of men on the north pier scattered, collected themselves and re-formed in a tight and watchful group while somewhere in the darkness of mid-channel the lifeboatmen fought their battle unaided, except by the same sea which had dashed the trawler against the south shore. And which could, if the fancy took it, do the same for them.

The watchers on the north shore saw the valiant speck disappear half a dozen times, held terrified breath, and loosed it in collective relief as the little craft reappeared, and always nearer to the trawler and the opposite shore. To the east, the sky was paling as the winter sun strove to rise above the turbulent mass of cloud. Light glinted on the horizon, touching the sea with dull silver, and in the shelter of the harbour shadows sharpened into the reality of wall and window, roof and step. On the southern shore, the streets of Torry emerged as darker blocks against the murky hillside. To her right, across the inner harbour basin, Elissa could make out the long, low roof of the new fishmarket, and the tangle of masts and funnels which topped the shipping moored along Blaikey's Quay. Then her eyes traced the line eastwards again, past the houses of Torry where the trawlermen lived, and on to the patch of water near the old south breakwater where the trawler still lay at the mercy of each incoming, battering wave.

But the water was shallower there, the driving wind and water still too strong. Dear God, keep Joseph safe.

A gasp went up from the crowd around her. The indomitable little lifeboat had fought her way to within rope-throwing distance and a man was climbing precariously to his feet in the bow. They saw him draw back his arm, hurl something forward, and fall. But the cheer which rose from the distant trawler was instantly echoed from the crowd around her and Elissa knew the rope had found its mark, and that her man was safe.

The crowd watched the trawlermen climb into the lifeboat, one by one, saw the boat cast off and pull for the shore. The nearest shore, on the south side, at Torry.

'Ma! Can we see them land, Ma?' cried Daniel at her side. Gideon Joe did not wait for her answer but set off at a run for the inner basin, with Sal close at his heels.

Elissa grabbed her small son's hand and hurried after them.

They found the lifeboat crew hauling the boat above the water line, with a crowd of Torry folk milling around them and, in their midst, the rescued trawlermen. Eight men, sea-drenched, wind-battered, salt-crusted and exhausted, laughing and joking and blustering with relief, clapping their rescuers on the back, hugging and thanking them, over and over. A ninth man in a tweed hat and thick Inverness cape, with his back to them, was arguing with one of the lifeboat crew.

'I said, launch the bleeding boat again, damn you! Or I'll have you horsewhipped till you drop, you insolent rogue. There's valuable gear aboard that trawler as well as a night's catch of fish.'

'Launch your own boat. We're here to save men's lives, not to risk our own to line another man's pocket.'

Too late, Elissa put out a hand to hold Sal back. Then watched, appalled, as her daughter pushed through the crowd towards where Joseph and the gentleman confronted each other on the pebbled shore, the dawn sky lightening behind them and across the stormy waters the dark outline of the north pier and the rooftops of the Square. Joseph was drenched to the skin, sea water oozing in rivulets from every fold and crease of clothing, beading hair and beard and eyebrows, seeping over the rims of sea boots and squelching into the sand and pebbles underfoot. His face was weary with strain and fatigue, but there was a tenseness about him which told Elissa before she saw for herself that his fists were clenched and ready.

Who knows what might have happened next had not Sal erupted from the crowd at that moment and flung her arms around Joseph's neck.

'I'm so glad you're safe, Da. We thought ... we thought...' then she burst into tears.

'Hush, my wee one, hush,' soothed Joseph, but his eyes still glared their challenge over her bent head. Then Gideon Joe joined them, took in what he thought was the situation and squared up beside his father.

'Good work, Da,' he said, man to man. Then to the other, 'I reckon these men owe their lives to my father and the lifeboat crew. You should say thank you to him and to all of them.'

'Well said, lad,' called someone and someone else called, 'Say thank you, sir, like a good boy.' There was laughter and a sudden rush of invitations to trawlermen and lifeboatmen alike to warm their bellies by a good fire, with a dram and hot porridge to put the life back into them.

Hugh Sinclair bellowed, 'Stay where you are, men! I give the orders here and . . .' but in turning his head to shout he saw Elissa, still clutching Daniel by the hand and standing a mere yard away, behind him. The transformation was extraordinary to see.

He touched a gloved hand to the rim of his hat, bowed mockingly from the waist and said, 'Elissa Downie, I believe.' His eyes flicked towards Sal and back again as he added in a voice meant only for her, 'And Lissa Downie's delightful little Sal.'

Elissa tried to pass him but he blocked her way. 'You were once one of my best workers, until . . . but no matter. We can settle that small *disagreement* at a later date.'

In spite of the revulsion which gripped her with dread, Elissa managed to look him coolly in the eye and her voice was almost steady. 'You are mistaken. My name is Noble and I have no outstanding business with you now, or in the future. Please allow me to pass so I may speak to my husband.'

'Let the lassie through,' jeered a dozen voices and with a frown and a contemptuous sweep of the arm, as if throwing an invisible cloak at her feet to walk upon, Sinclair said, 'The highway is yours, Mrs Noble.'

But as she pushed past him she heard his menacing voice low in her ear.

'Do not think I have forgotten, *madam*. One day I will collect my debt. From you. Or yours.'

Fear stopped her breath, but she managed to push past him without a word to reach Joseph and her children.

'Are you all right, Joseph?' she asked, putting all her love and reassurance into voice and eyes. He looked at her with a brief nod, then away again, beyond her shoulder. But Hugh Sinclair had abandoned menace for cold sarcasm.

'And why should he not be, Mrs Noble? With his feet on dry land and his loving family around him? It is not his vessel lying helpless in the shallows, within reach of any thieving scoundrel who cares to

259

wade out to rob her. Though no doubt he will have the cunning to wait till my back is turned before he does it.'

Sal clutched her father's arm in warning and at the same time Elissa moved to block his path. But they had no need. The crowd was on their side and Sinclair had gone too far.

'You watch your tongue, mate!' 'That's a lifeboatman you're speaking to.' 'One more insult and we'll throw you into the sea.' 'Then you can launch your own bleeding boat and good luck to you.'

Sinclair surveyed them slowly, one by one, the sneer on his face etching deeper till it ran like a scar down one cheek. But if he thought to quell them by arrogance, he failed.

'When will we get our pay?' dared one of the trawler's crew.

'Aye, that's what we want to know.' The eight men, captain included, bunched together in a belligerent and dangerous group.

Sinclair adjusted the cuff of his handmade kid glove, transferred the Malacca cane from one hand to the other, looked at them with contempt and said, 'Pay? We do not pay men who abandon ship. However, when the cargo is unloaded to my satisfaction, I might reconsider the matter. I suggest you start unloading now.'

There was silence. The joy and relief of the rescue had vanished, leaving an atmosphere of crackling antagonism and threat. The dawn light was strengthening, but there was no warmth in it, nor in the wind which snatched at sodden garments, sent shivers through sea-soaked bodies and deadened fingers and toes to nerveless white, nor in the heaving grey sea whose treacherous waters sucked and snatched at their heels on the shifting shingle around the lifeboat.

Sal had unwound herself from her father's neck, and now stood close beside him, her arm through his, her anxious eyes moving from his face to her mother's and then with fascinated revulsion to Hugh Sinclair whom she had last seen on the stairs of Mrs Forbes's Jubilee apartment in Union Street. He was about her father's age, she supposed, but how different. Her father was forty-two, his hair iron grey, his skin creased and wind-beaten and his gnarled hands scarred and chapped under the fingerless mittens her mother had knitted for him, but his eyes were still honest, every line of his body wholesome and dependable. Whereas that other spelt idle decadence in every manicured and perfumed line of his languid frame. Decadence and threat. Sal doubted whether he knew what honesty was: there was certainly no trace of it in his ice-cold stare. No wonder her mother was afraid of him.

'You.' Sinclair jabbed his cane towards Joseph's chest and Elissa gasped, remembering the hidden knife, the deadly blade. 'Show them how to go about it. There's thirty boxes of good white fish aboard. Get that ashore in time for the market. Should fetch a good price today, the weather being what it is. Then and only then will we see what sort of pay-out there will be. Meanwhile,' and here a gleam touched the cold eyes, 'Mrs Noble and her daughter may give me the pleasure of escorting them home. My carriage is waiting.'

Someone in the crowd laughed, then another until a great roar of merriment rose from the quayside.

'Don't listen to him, lass. He's a lecherous, lying rogue. Besides, he'll need to sell his blessed carriage to pay his crew. No one'll get near the *Alice May* without a fishtail and a pair of gills! Look!'

All eyes turned towards the stricken trawler, and Sinclair's indrawn breath was like a snake's hiss. The trawler's bows tipped at a crazy angle sideways and upwards while the stern was already half submerged under the snatching, rolling waves. Before anyone could speak, with an almighty gurgling, dragging sound as of water draining from a giant bath-tub, the *Alice May* rolled over and disappeared. A moment later they saw the helpless hulk rise half out of the water only to be dragged down again in a swirl of foam and treacherous black water; this time, as the erupting debris told them, against a rock.

'*You will pay for this.*' The words were low and clear and though his glare encompassed the whole lifeboat crew, they were aimed directly at Joseph.

Then, without warning, his cane lashed through the air between them and would have struck home had not Joseph leapt backwards into the treacherous edge of the sea. Elissa watched in horror as Joseph sank before her eyes: waist deep, shoulders deep, till the water closed over his head. Only for a second before half a dozen men pulled him out again, but in that second Hugh Sinclair's face split in a rictus of cruel satisfaction. Then he turned on his heel and with his cape wrapped tight around him strode furiously through the crowd, striking a way for himself with venomous thwacks of his cane. He pushed the driver from the seat of his carriage, snatched up the reins himself and whipped the horse into a thunder of pounding hooves and rattling wheels, away towards the harbour basin and home.

'Why was he so angry, Da?' asked Gideon Joe, when his father had regained dry land. 'If the *Alice May* is insured, he'll get his money, won't he?'

'Money's nothing to the likes of him, lad,' said a bystander. 'He's put out 'cos he couldn't have his own way, that's all.'

It was not all, as they were to find out, but in the meantime the wreck stayed where it rested, stuck on the submerged rocks off the south shore. Some of the gear had been salvaged, but little enough, and the thirty boxes of fish which were going to make their owner's fortune, fed the herring-gulls instead. But Sinclair would survive, whatever the outcome. Folk like him always did. It was the honest folk who suffered. Folk like the lifeboatmen and Joseph, half drowned and soaked to the skin.

'You're shivering, Da. And you're soaked through,' said Sal. 'Come on home for a hot bath. Milly will have the kettle boiling.'

'Sal's right, Joseph. The sun is almost up and – '

'Don't fuss, woman. I'll not let that arrogant villain beat me. Dry clothes is all I'm needing. I've a list of errands a mile long and if I'm to get the project anywhere near the drawing board before I go back to Yarmouth I'd best do them quick. Before he thinks up a way to stop me. So home, all of you. At the double.'

Once at home, all Joseph would consent to was a rough towelling down and a change of clothes. Standing impatiently in the doorway, he gulped a bowl of porridge, downed a cup of steaming tea, wiped his mouth on the back of his hand and was out of the house again, a mere fifteen minutes after arriving home. The storm had died down and a gusty, penetrating rain had taken its place, but Joseph refused to be deterred. The frustrated fury of his encounter with Sinclair drove him into frenzied activity and he had urgent work to do before he could even begin to rest. It was well into the afternoon before Elissa saw him again and by then the heavens had emptied most of their rain into the heaving harbour and the first rumours were drifting in.

The *Alice May* was not insured after all. She should have been, but she was not. Brodie Gibb was apoplectic with fury and 'you'd think yon storm had swept in through the windows of the Sinclair and Gibb offices and out through the door with the turmoil the place is in,' reported old Gideon gleefully. 'Files scattered, papers tossing every which way, terrified clerks running in all directions. And it'll not die down till the culprit is caught. Then what ructions we'll see. Well, I'll away back and see what more news Mary's collected. Thanks for the tea, lass.' He picked up the tin can which Milly had filled with hot tea, stuffed the packet of bread and cheese into the pocket of his oilskin and left again, grinning. Life in the harbour had not been so exciting since that highland bull escaped from the cattle boat and got in among the passengers alighting from the London steamer.

'What are we going to do, Joseph?' asked Elissa, her face pale with dread. If Sinclair had known the *Alice May* was not insured it would explain his fury, and his venom. It had been plain to her that Sinclair's threat had been meant for Joseph, and for herself and Sal. She had wondered what vulnerability of Joseph's Sinclair could use to get at him and suddenly she saw.

Oh God, suppose he attacked Sal as he had once attacked her? Vulnerable, innocent, loving-hearted Sal? Lured her somehow, till he had her alone, undefended, then ... The unspoken fear whipped through her like a knife blade.

'He is evil, Joseph. Evil and vicious. I saw him look at Sal as if, as if ...' But fear stopped her putting the disgusting thought into words.

Joseph and Elissa had the room to themselves. Milly, well wrapped up against the November chill, had gone to visit a neighbour, the children were still at school and old Gideon and Mary at the smokehouse, where Elissa would have been herself, had she not seen her man half drowned and soaked to the shivering skin and too obstinate to do as he was told when he was told. Until Joseph came home again Elissa had run to and fro between home and smokeshed 'like a demented blow-fly', as Mary Noble complained. 'Away home with you, woman, before you drive us all mad with your buzzing about.'

Elissa had done so. Stoked up the fire to furnace heat, boiled kettles and pans for hot water and set the zinc bath ready on the hearthrug. Put out towels and a loofah, and clean clothes to air in front of the range. This time, when her man came home he was not going to escape.

So as soon as Milly was away she had made him strip and wrap himself in a blanket while she filled the zinc tub. The air was soon hot and humid as a Turkish bath, the window panes beaded with condensation, and steam rose in steady clouds from the garments Elissa had strung from the pulley overhead. Then she had rolled her sleeves above the elbow, tied on her largest apron, and when Joseph had stepped obediently into the bath-tub, had soaped his back and gently massaged the strain from his shoulders. After the work those muscles had put in at the lifeboat oars they would be stiff enough by evening. Then she had soaped and rinsed his hair for him, under protest, and would have washed him all over like a child if he had let her.

Instead, she stood warming a towel at the fire and worrying over how Hugh Sinclair might be plotting at this very moment to ruin their lives.

'Don't look so troubled, Elissa. We will be on our guard, and so will Sal. You could see from her face how disgusting she found him. It is not as if she would listen to his persuasions.'

'But ...' She had never told Joseph the true reason for Adam Grant's sudden disappearance all those years ago. He thought Adam had been imprisoned for drunken violence or grievous bodily harm or some such and she had feared the truth might rouse his doubts about Elissa's allegiance, and revive all that destructive jealousy. Now, for their own protection, he ought to know the truth. 'I did not tell you before because it did not seem necessary,' she said with a rush, 'but when Adam Grant was arrested he had done nothing except get on the wrong side of Hugh Sinclair. He was framed and set up by Sinclair's hired thugs.'

'A likely tale! Invented to soothe your suspicions and clean up his own reputation.'

'You had better believe it,' said Elissa quietly, 'for all our sakes. And don't frown like that. You have no idea how childish and ridiculous you look sitting naked in a bath of soapy water and glowering at the sponge.'

For a moment she thought she had gone too far, then the tension snapped and he grinned. Only to frown again in a different way. 'If you are right, then we must be vigilant.'

'I am right. I would have told you long ago, but I thought the threat was over. That blacklisting you with all the curing yards and suppliers Sinclair's deals with – and don't say he didn't because I know better – had satisfied him. Now, he will start all over again. I know it.'

'And now, so do I. Don't look so worried, lass. I'll keep good watch over all of us. And he'll not push me around again, I promise you.'

She held out the towel, warm from the fire, and wrapped it round him as he stepped out of the tub. But when she began to rub his back dry for him, he caught and held her tight against his chest.

For a long moment they clung together, without words. Then she said, with low intensity, 'I love you, Joseph Noble.'

'I know.' He looked into her eyes and said, with a bare simplicity that set her heart thudding with dread, 'If he sets so much as one finger on you or on Sal, I will kill him.'

Dear God, prayed Elissa inside her head, *don't let there be violence, Please keep my family safe.*

'Pass me my clothes, woman,' said Joseph with swift decision. 'I can't hang around the kitchen all day like a sick child. I've work to do. And before you ask, I'm going back to the shipyards, to speed up my inquiries. If young Gideon wants to ship aboard a steamship one day, I'd rather it was a new drifter, solid-built and seaworthy and me the master, than a sieve of a third-hand trawler like the *Alice May*. Wait, lass, I'll give you a hand to empty the tub. Then I'll be off.'

At the door, he stopped, came back into the room and hugged her. 'Don't look so anxious, Elissa. Everything will be all right, I promise you.' Then he kissed her. 'We will talk more about Sal when I get back.'

But by evening there was other news to talk about: the *Alice May* was registered in Grimsby, one of the fleet operating from the Sinclair and Gibb office where Hugh Sinclair was in charge. Not only was the *Alice May* not insured, word had it that she didn't belong to Sinclair and Gibb either. Not any more anyway. Had been pledged as collateral for a loan, under the combined signatures of Easton Sinclair and Brodie Gibb. What those two gentlemen had to say about the transaction was unrepeatable. But Lawyer Forbes had been sent for at the double. As for Hugh Sinclair, he had prudently taken the first train south, 'to handle things at the Grimsby end' though what he proposed to 'handle' was the subject of much ribaldry and insult.

But on two points opinion was unanimous: any firm that failed to insure its vessels was asking for trouble. And any man who set out to help himself to his inheritance prematurely, via the back door, deserved to lose the lot.

Late that Monday evening Joseph came home exhausted but satisfied with his day's work, and the news that met him on his arrival increased his satisfaction. With Hugh Sinclair out of town and, if things turned out as folk expected, likely to stay there, that was one thing less to worry about.

'I've settled the contract, Elissa,' he murmured, under cover of the general chatter. 'They're drawing up designs and specifications, then we can go ahead.'

Gideon and Mary were in their usual places at the fireside, Milly on a chair beside her mother and both women knitting. Sal and Danny were seated at one end of the table in a jumble of school-books while Gideon Joe was concentrating on the model fishing yawl he was carving out of a piece of driftwood and pestering his grandfather for advice with every breath. In a clear space at the other end of the table, Elissa had been ironing, but now she set the flat-iron back on the range and lifted the lid of the nearest pot.

'We saved you some boiled beef, Joseph, and Milly baked the bread fresh today. Sal, clear a place for your da while I cut the meat.'

'Stay where you are, Sal. Thanks, Elissa, lass, but I'm not wanting anything. It has been a long day and I'm weary. I'll just away to my bed.'

But Elissa made up a hot whisky toddy and insisted he drink it, 'to keep out the chill'. Then she filled an earthenware 'pig' with scalding hot water, screwed in the stopper, checked the rubber washer was not leaking and slipped it into Joseph's side of the bed. She had the ironing to finish before she could join him and the 'pig' would help to keep out the draughts.

It was the shaking that woke her. Her eyes jerked open and she lay watchful and listening. Faint moonlight gleamed through the uncurtained skylight, vanished behind a scudding cloud, gleamed again. Stars pricked the small glass rectangle: like moth-holes in the world's dark blanket, showing the bright heaven beyond. The brass orbs at the bed end gleamed silver, as they had done, she remembered, on their wedding night. Silver apples of the moon. Every line, every shadow was clearly etched in the silence, as it had been on that other, long-ago night which seemed now to belong to a different woman, in a different world. Then the brass orbs quivered and beside her, Joseph stirred.

'Joseph? Are you all right?' She raised herself on one elbow, peered into his face, then laid a hand on his cheek. The skin was hot under her hand.

The hot water 'pig'. That was it. The 'pig' had over-heated the blankets. She felt about with her feet and found warm earthenware. Manoeuvred it until she could reach it with her hand, slid it out from under the blankets and placed it carefully on the floor. But the 'pig' was no more than lukewarm. Almost cold. Then the shaking started again and to her horror she realised it was Joseph himself: shivering uncontrollably in great shuddering spasms that shook the bedstead and made those brass orbs quiver in the darkness. His forehead burnt like fire and her heart turned over with fear. Joseph was ill. Joseph, who had never been ill, not in fifteen years of marriage.

She slid out of bed, found her clothes, dressed with the speed of terror, and ran downstairs. Found a basin, filled it with water from the pail, sped upstairs again, added eau-de-Cologne. Then she lit the candle which she kept beside her bed and in its soft glow began to sponge her husband's forehead with gentle, murmuring care.

'Ssh . . . You will soon be well again . . .' At first light she would send Gideon Joe for the doctor.

'Is the window open?' The voice was barely above a whisper and painfully dry.

'No, my love. We do not want a draught to – '

'Open it! Do you hear me? Open it now.' He clutched her arm. The sponge dripped water on to the blanket and she could not pull away.

'Of course I will, my love, when you let go of my arm.'

He fell back on to the pillow, eyes closed. 'I need to see the moon. The herrings rise to the moon.'

She crossed to the window and raised the little skylight till it held on the first notch. The night air was cold, but she dare not close it again, not yet.

'There. Is that better?' Her own voice was dry now, with alarm.

'I must watch the sky. If we don't catch them when they rise, we'll lose them. Can you hear them rising?'

'Not yet.' *Oh God, he is delirious. I must find help.*

'Then I must listen for them, lass. I can always hear them first. Don't make any noise . . .'

Elissa slipped out of the room, ran downstairs and banged on the panelling of the box bed where old Gideon and Mary slept. It was almost time for them to rise anyway, but had it been a mere hour after bedtime she would have done the same. She had never felt so helpless in her life.

'Quick. Joseph is burning with fever. What shall I do?'

Mary snapped out of sleep to instant attention, said, 'Hand me my plaid, lass, and get back upstairs to your man. I'll be up directly. And rouse Sal on the way. She'll be needed.'

Then followed the nightmare days, the endless, nightmare nights. Tossing, groaning, fevered delirium, snatches of disconnected words. Occasionally he surfaced enough to say, 'I am sorry, Elissa. You have enough work to do already.' Then she would sponge his forehead, soothe and kiss him.

'There is nothing else I would rather do, Joseph. Nowhere else I would rather be.' And it was true. Not like when she had nursed her dying aunt. That had been one gorge-rising purgatory of dread and longing: longing for her lover to come and rescue her. Now she was consumed by a different dread: suppose Joseph were to die?

She spent every hour with him, only leaving for necessity and then not until Sal or Mary had taken her place. She reminded herself over and over that Mary Noble was Joseph's mother and entitled to share her son's nursing, but she guarded the bedside jealously just the same. As if she knew she had so little time. The children, Sal, Gideon, Danny, looked in to see him every day; just for a moment, for Elissa feared infection, but she couldn't deny them, or him, and they always came to say goodnight.

She slept in a chair beside the bed, if you could call it sleeping, for she woke at the slightest sound. That night, his voice woke her instantly. Moonlight flooded the room for he refused to have the skylight curtained. The brass orbs on the bed end gleamed silver and when he reached out a hand to find hers, his skin was white as wax.

'Elissa. Listen to me. The sailing drifter is finished.'

She thought at first it was the usual delirium, but when she looked into his haggard face, the dark eyes huge in their shrunken sockets, she saw the lucidity in their anxious depths. He was with her, speaking not in the confusion of fever, but with intelligence and firm purpose.

'Listen to me my love. You must remember for me, in case I forget. Remember, and act.'

'I will, Joseph. I promise. Tell me what it is you want me to remember.'

'The drifters. The Provost was right about steam. "Go and do likewise," he said. They are building a steam drifter in Lowestoft and no matter what my father says, the obstinate old devil, sail is finished. Promise you will remember?'

'Hush, Joseph, don't distress yourself. I'll remember.'

267

He clutched her hand tight, with both his, and though his voice was faint it was unwavering. 'Listen carefully, my love. I may not think straight for long and must make best use of it while I can. The past is for old Gideon and his generation. The future is for our children. Sal must go to college, if they will have her. Gideon Joe must learn to handle a steam engine as well as a sail. Danny . . .' he smiled at her with the love the boy's name always invoked. 'Danny will find his own way and be happy – and you, you must have that fine house you've always wanted.'

Elissa smoothed the hair from Joseph's forehead and said, 'Hush, my love. You mustn't tire yourself. It was only a day-dream, nothing serious.'

'No. You must have it, one day. I vowed when you came back to me that I'd give you everything *he* promised you and I will.'

'But – '

'Listen to me. About the drifter.' This time there was new urgency in his poor, cracked voice. 'We have money in the bank. If you need more, Fergus Mackie will buy out my share of the curing yard. But we have enough for the down payment, and I have placed the order with Hall, Russell's. A steam drifter. Ninety feet long. Rigging and engine. Bunkers for fifteen tons of coal. A good, deep hold. The bargain has been struck and they will honour it. Promise me . . .'

'Yes, Joseph?' She tried to keep her voice calm, reassuring, and almost succeeded.

'That if I am unable to see it through myself, you will do it for me?'

'But you will see it through, Joseph,' she said, the tears standing in her eyes. 'You will be well again. Look how you are tonight. You will be well again and strong.'

'Promise me!' He tried to sit up, fell back again, defeated, but his grip on her hand did not loosen. 'You are a lass who keeps her word. So promise me, as God is your witness.'

'I promise.' Then, when he still looked at her with those urgent, anxious eyes, she said slowly and clearly, 'I promise before God that I will carry out your plans.'

'All of them.'

'All your plans, as you would wish me to carry them out, if for any reason you cannot do so yourself.'

'Thank you.' With a long sigh of content, he lay back on the pillow, his eyes closed, and when he spoke again it was in the voice of the young man she had married, fifteen years ago.

'I love you, Elissa. I always have, since you were a solemn little schoolgirl and I was only your brother's friend. Forgive my jealousy and any hurt it caused you? And tell my daughter Sarah that I love her.'

'I will.' Elissa could hardly speak for the tears which rose in her throat to choke her. She bent over the pillows and kissed Joseph's forehead. He raised his hand and touched her cheek.

'Don't cry, my love. You are always so brave. Brave and straight and true. My heart's own love.'

'As you are mine.' She laid her face against his on the pillow, her tears on his cheek. His arm fell naturally across her shoulder, drawing her close.

'Hush, my wee one, hush.'

She did not notice the exact moment when the strength left his arm, when the troubled breathing ceased. Only a gradual, strengthening pain which wrung and wrung her as if she were a blanket being squeezed and twisted on the headland behind the Square, till out of the twisting torture rose a sound like the keening of the wind in the bent grass, followed by a long and desolate moan as of receding waves on the shore.

The moonlight had faded into the half-light of dawn before Sal knocked softly on the door and tiptoed in, a cup of hot tea in her hand.

'Are you all right, Ma? I thought I heard . . .' She stopped as Elissa rose slowly from her knees at the bedside and turned her face towards the open door. 'Ma? Is he . . .?'

She put down the cup, flung herself into Elissa's arms and sobbed like a little child.

CHAPTER 23

The men came back specially from the herring fishing and the whole of North and South Squares turned out for the funeral. It was the sense of the honour they were paying Joseph that kept Elissa's back straight and her eyes dry. She owed it to Joseph as well as to her family, for she knew that if her control showed so much as a hairline crack they would all give in to the dragging weight of grief which flowed over and around them.

Poor Gideon Joe had locked himself into his room and cried in secret for hours at a time; Sal was white-faced and silent, her eyes swollen with weeping.

But it was Joseph's father that Elissa worried about most. Old Gideon Noble had aged ten years on the day his eldest son died, and though he had four remaining sons – five if you counted Zebediah 'working for the Lord' – the life seemed to have died in him, with Joseph's life. Only six-year-old Danny could light any spark of interest in the old man and the child's uninhibited questioning – 'What is heaven like, Grandpa?' and 'What do angels eat?' – instead of deepening his grandfather's grief seemed to ease and lighten it, until Danny wandered off to talk to Milly or Grandma Noble.

Mary Noble, though bleak-faced as they all were, was stiffened by an inner fury that kept her vigorously alive. 'A severe chill leading rapidly to pneumonia' indeed! 'Not altogether unexpected after immersion in winter sea water.' That doctor didn't know what he was talking about. She knew what had caused her son's death all right. And who.

The four remaining Noble sons carried the coffin, with Brodie Gibb and Phemy's husband, and back at home, the Noble womenfolk set out the food and drink that would go towards lifting their menfolk's spirits after the sombre reminder of man's mortality.

'Only forty-two.' 'Never a day's illness in his life till now.' 'Survived the storm of '81 no bother, and plenty others after.' 'Been out with the lifeboat a score of times.' 'And capsized twice.' 'You never can tell . . .' The doleful phrases filled the house as more and more

270

mourners gathered to remember Joseph and comfort his family and each other with the warmth of companionship.

But Mary Noble refused to be comforted.

'It's all yon villain Sinclair's fault,' she raged, over and over. 'Keeping my laddie standing in the cold and the wet with his clothes as sodden as that cursed *Alice May*. But he'll pay for it, one day. Oh yes. He'll pay.'

As the food and the whisky, the warmth of the fire and the hot tea spread their soothing comfort, it began to look as though Mary Noble might be right. For Brodie Gibb was indignant: at the devious methods of Hugh Sinclair, at the loss of company funds, and most of all at the loss to his own pocket. After his third whisky, his tongue was loosened beyond the usual tight-fisted caution.

Apparently the *Alice May* was not the only one of their trawlers to be uninsured. Several more were in a similar state. The premiums were entered into the company accounts, the money paid, but somewhere along the line that money found its way into Hugh Sinclair's pocket – and out again as fast as it came in – and the insurance certificates proved to be false. That wasn't all that was false, either. Easton Sinclair's signature for one, and his own, *Brodie Gibb's own* signature. On promissory notes and loan guarantees. The fellow was clever, you couldn't deny that. Too clever by half. Those signatures looked genuine. Even Brodie himself couldn't tell the difference. But when had Brodie ever borrowed money, let alone signed away a trawler as collateral? If Hugh Sinclair dared to show his face in Aberdeen again he'd suffer for it. Oh yes, he'd suffer. They had tried to keep the worst of it from the old man, but with the harbour buzzing with rumour that would not be possible for long, though old Easton Sinclair would take it hard. Very hard.

By evening (when the funeral guests had dwindled to a handful of close friends and family) they learnt just how hard: on hearing the full extent of his son's dubious financial dealings, Easton Sinclair had been seized with apoplexy and had dropped dead at Lawyer Forbes's feet. Worst of all, he had done so before he could sign even the first draft of his hastily rewritten will.

On the day of Hugh Sinclair's arrival at the city's railway station to take up his new responsibilities, accompanied by a weasel-faced manservant and enough luggage to equip a five-year expedition to the interior, a letter was delivered to the Noble household in the Square. It was addressed to Mrs Elissa Downie Noble and was delivered by Lawyer Forbes in person.

Naturally Elissa, dressed soberly in widow's black, asked him in,

271

and, after he had expressed the sympathy of both himself and his family 'and especially Adelaide who feels deeply for her friend Sarah in the tragic loss of her father', offered him tea or something stronger. The family kitchen was both welcoming and warm, but Lawyer Forbes waved away her offers.

'The letter,' he insisted. 'Read it.'

Unsuspecting, Elissa opened the letter, assuming it to be a quotation of some kind relating to the proposed steam drifter. Instead, she found a formal solicitor's letter headed Messrs Williamson, Williamson and Forbes.

'As executors of the late Easton Mackenzie Sinclair it is our duty to inform you that under the terms of his will . . .' Elissa looked up from the paper in shock, and found Lawyer Forbes watching her, his face grave. He gestured to her to read on.

'. . . In recompense for the insult offered by my son Hugh to Elissa Downie, a virtuous and honest woman, and for the subsequent injustice done to her husband Joseph Noble in my name by which injustice the said Joseph Noble was deprived of his dignity and livelihood . . . I leave to the said Elissa Downie Noble the sum of five hundred pounds . . .'

Elissa stared at the lawyer in disbelief before saying, 'There must be a mistake.'

'No mistake,' said Lawyer Forbes, smiling.

It was not often he had the chance to bring such splendidly unexpected news to such a deserving house as the Nobles', and especially Elissa who had done wonders with his boy Cameron over the years and refused all offers of payment.

'No mistake at all, I can assure you. I drew up the will myself some months ago and it is perfectly legal and above board. Old Mr Sinclair, I can tell you in confidence, was appalled and much distressed to learn that his son had . . . er . . . fabricated slanders against you and authenticated them with, let us say, an unauthorised version of his father's signature. It troubled him much at the time and more so in recent years. Therefore he determined to make what private recompense he could. I know I need not ask you to keep the details to yourself? The money, if people should come to hear of it – and I know what prying eyes and gossiping tongues the town contains – could perhaps be explained away as insurance? Or even as your husband's unexpected savings?' He smiled encouragingly.

But Elissa's mind had already reached the door of his secret anxiety.

'Who else knows about this bequest?'

'No one. At present. I am informing each beneficiary in person of their own particular inheritance and of no other. However, should the heir wish to inspect the will . . .'

As he will certainly wish to do, thought Elissa with dread.

'. . . I have no powers to prevent it. However, you need fear no dispute over your bequest. It is, I assure you, legally binding and correct.'

It was not dispute she feared, but revenge. Before pride, or fear, made her refuse the money, Elissa said quickly, 'Thank you, Mr Forbes. It was most generous of Mr Sinclair, for whom I feel, felt, nothing but respect and now gratitude.'

'Well, between you and me he couldn't rest easy in his mind, poor man, till he'd done what he could to put right as many of his son's wrongs as he possibly could. Now,' he said, with a brisk change of tone, 'if I was you, I'd put that money to good use. Invest it. No, I don't mean in the bank or the Stock Exchange, but in something more tangible. Shipping, or ice – there's room for a new ice factory in the harbour with the business expanding at the rate it is. Or in your children's education? Send that son of yours to college, maybe.'

'I don't think . . .' began Elissa, still bowled over by the unexpectedness of her fortune.

'Or your daughter,' beamed Lawyer Forbes. 'A bright lass, that one, and I know she and Adelaide have talked about it often enough. You could send Sal along to our house to learn with Addie. Mrs Forbes was quite against it at first, and is still not altogether happy in her mind, but with three of our daughters married now and a fourth absolutely set on staying at home, in spite of more than one most acceptable offer,' and another, unacceptable, which fortunately never materialised, 'Addie persuaded her mother it would be rather distinguished and modern of her to be able to talk of a blue-stocking in the family.' Lawyer Forbes smiled with private amusement. 'Adelaide played her mother like a fish, the little minx. But if the two girls were to be bajans together, a "bajan" as I am sure you are aware, Mrs Noble, is a first-year student, that would quell any lingering doubt in my wife's mind. You, as a mother yourself, will know how nervous mothers of young daughters can be about any possible impropriety, and your legacy would more than cover any fees. In fact, I am surprised I did not think of it before. If Sarah were to share Adelaide's studies, and, of course, our house, it would be the perfect solution.'

'Thank you, Mr Forbes. You have given me much to think about,' said Elissa, then, remembering her promise to Joseph, she added, 'On a different, though related subject, perhaps you could tell me as much as you know about my late husband's negotiations for building a steam drifter? You see, I promised him, before he died, that I would see them through.'

Since then, in the dark days of mourning, she had wondered over and over and with increasing doubt how she, a mere woman and a widow, would ever be able to achieve that aim. Now, she saw that it might be possible: Gideon Joe would be so excited, Danny too. As for

273

Sal ... Elissa remembered Hugh Sinclair's face as he had snarled 'You will pay for this,' his 'invitation' to herself and Sal to join him in his carriage and that other invitation, all those years ago, when Joseph had rescued her and earned Sinclair's enmity, for all of them, for ever.

Except that she had earned it herself before then, when he had molested and tried to rape her. Adam had saved her, had broken her attacker's nose and had had his own life broken in return. Where was Adam? Suddenly she wanted him with a need that almost choked her. Joseph had died and left her vulnerable. And, she realised with a shock, free. She had not thought of that till now. But she had not heard from Adam for seven years, not since she had refused to run away with him on the *Singing Bird* and had gone instead to Yarmouth and her husband, Joseph. Adam had not forgiven her for that and she would not write to him.

But now Joseph, dear Joseph, was dead and could no longer protect her. She must protect herself. And Sal. Oh God. She knew Hugh Sinclair would be furious at his father's will, that it would inflame his vengeance afresh, that he would exult in Joseph's removal, and in her own and Sal's vulnerability. Here, in the harbour, they would be under his surveillance every day. But if Sal moved into other, higher circles? Into university circles? It was what Joseph wanted for Sal. And there was no longer any danger of her meeting Sinclair at the Forbes house: that gentleman had had his eyes opened wide on that score. Whether Sinclair's aim had been to spy, to ingratiate himself, to lull suspicion, or merely to steal a copy of the lawyer's signature for future use was immaterial: it had certainly not been matrimony, and Lawyer Forbes would not forgive the insult to himself, to his intelligence, or to his daughter.

But Lawyer Forbes was explaining the system of ordering a vessel from the shipbuilder's yard, the money required at different stages in the process and, for a steam-driven vessel, engine specifications and suchlike. With an effort, Elissa thrust her fears into the background and, for Joseph's sake, gave him her full attention.

'Thank you,' she said, when the lawyer had outlined the steps already taken and what remained to be done. 'If you could perhaps advise me from time to time ...?'

'Of course, Mrs Noble. Only too willing. An admirable project, well thought out and most opportune. Steam has made fortunes for the trawling industry. There is no reason why it should not do the same for the herring drifters, and for your family too. I know that was what your husband had in mind. As for this small legacy here ...'

'I accept it,' said Elissa quickly. 'With gratitude. It will be put to good use, I assure you.'

'And that little project I mentioned, for your daughter Sarah?'

'I accept that too. Sarah will be overjoyed, I know, to share in Adelaide's studies, and to start whenever you think fit.'

'Would tomorrow be too soon?'

Elissa would have agreed to send Sal to the Forbes house within the hour: anything to get her safely out of the harbour before Hugh Sinclair read the details of his father's will. And came to take his revenge.

'Tomorrow would be ideal.'

PART III

CHAPTER 24

The upstairs office of the Sinclair and Gibb company was not a happy place.

To the usually sombre atmosphere of dark panelled wood, heavy oak furniture and reproving, gilt-framed portrait of the firm's founder had been added an undercurrent of wariness, dislike and downright apprehension. Of those present, the only man completely at ease was Hugh Sinclair, in the seat his father had occupied until a month ago, at the head of the table. Scented, manicured, expensively outfitted and triumphant, Sinclair surveyed his adversaries with an air of wry amusement which deceived no one: for vindictiveness emanated from every fold of those elegant clothes, from the curled lip and twisted nose and the cold, hard, calculating eyes.

'Gentlemen.' Even that word was a sneer. 'The company will, naturally, honour all my father's debts.'

'You mean your own debts,' growled Gibb.

Sinclair ignored him. 'An old man, broken by ill-health and failing faculties, can be forgiven for making errors of judgement, but those around him cannot be excused for their failure to advise and guide. You, Gibb, should have overseen my father's dealings and prevented such wilful waste of the firm's resources. You, Forbes, should never have allowed the sentimental legacies to this or that nonentity which my father chose to add to his will. *In his dotage, when of unsound mind.*'

'His mind was perfectly clear,' said the lawyer with the cold calm his profession had taught him, though his face was unnaturally pale and strained. 'His will, as I have told you a dozen times, cannot be disputed on that ground. Nor on any other.'

'More's the pity,' said Brodie Gibb with venom. 'You should count yourself lucky not to be up before the court for forgery, and any more slurs on your father's name and I'll file a report to the Procurator Fiscal myself, you treacherous, lying little thief.'

Sinclair flinched, but only momentarily. 'The language of the gutter is only to be expected from one who was spawned there.' He leant back in his chair and inspected the nails of first one hand, then the other. When he looked up it was with a smile of cold contempt.

'You will remember that I run this company now. My father, in his loving wisdom, left me the manager's share. If you wish to keep your own puny toe-hold in the company, you will do as I say, when I say, and without argument. *Is that clear?*'

Brodie Gibb pushed back his chair and stood up. 'Aye. Clear enough to me. Though obviously not to you. But you'll find out soon enough. You've had your thieving hand in the till for too many years and not an honest day's work to your name. Now you can reap what you have sown. But I tell you this, laddie. If the news of your infamy hadn't killed your father, "in his loving wisdom" he would have cut you out of his will and stopped your thieving once and for all. Unfortunately an unsigned draft is not legal. Unless you'd care to "sign" your father's will for him, as you signed so many other things in his name?'

Sinclair regarded him from narrowed eyes before saying softly, 'I would not utter such slanders if I were in your shoes. You might find yourself . . . punished.'

'Aye, and so might you, laddie. I don't take kindly to having my name used without my knowledge. So you'd best watch your step, because other folk are watching you. Night and day. Are you coming, Forbes?' He jerked his head towards the door. 'I'm needing a breath of honest air.'

The lawyer stood up to follow him. Sinclair went even paler than he already was and smashed his clenched fist down on to the table. 'Stay where you are, both of you,' he ordered. 'The meeting is not over.'

'It is as far as I'm concerned,' said Gibb, and strode from the room. Lawyer Forbes stood for a moment in indecision, then snatched up his papers and scurried after him. As he closed the heavy door behind him something large crashed against the wooden door panel and fell to the ground with a thud. A ledger? Or something more lethal? Whatever it was, Hugh Sinclair could pick it up himself. Brodie Gibb and the lawyer had other things to occupy their time, and their thoughts.

In the board room Sinclair sat rigid in his father's chair, hands gripping the wooden chair arms, back straight, and eyes glaring at the door which had cut him off from his victims. He sat in the same position for a full minute without moving so much as an eyelid. Then with an oath he reached across the polished expanse of table and pulled towards him the one paper which the lawyer had left behind. A crackling parchment scroll tied with a length of new red tape. His father's will.

Thoughtfully, he unrolled the paper and began to read, pausing here, frowning there, rereading one passage, then another, until at last he came to the end of the infamous document. His devil of a father had planned to rob and persecute him even from the grave. Splitting up the company, forbidding this and that. A rightful son and heir could dispute those clauses, whatever that villain Forbes claimed. A son was entitled to his inheritance. But he'd soon sort that out. Show them all who was in charge. No, it was the smaller legacies that most infuriated him: gifts to fawning servants and swindling tradesfolk, sentimental recognitions of so-called loyalty and devotion. Where was the old devil's loyalty to his own son? That last calculated slur on Hugh's character was particularly villainous and to think that Lawyer Forbes had actually written those slanderous words with his own hand and the woman herself had read them!

In recompense for the insult . . . A virtuous and honest woman . . .' Lies, damnable lies. She was a whore like the rest of them. A scheming, lying whore. But he'd make her pay, one way or the other. He remembered her husband's reported death with pleasure – serve the villain right – and the punishment he had arranged for that other scoundrel, years ago. Perhaps he should remind her of what happened to people who thwarted him? Then the next time he invited her to join him she would know better than to refuse.

Thoughtfully, he rolled up the document and tied it so that the red bow of tape lay just so. Then he sat back in his chair and surveyed the length of the polished table, the unoccupied seats, the untouched water glasses, the unused blotters and newly filled ink-wells. One hand lay flat on the carved wooden arm, the other elegantly supported his chin in a manner which best revealed the heavy gold signet ring and tapered fingers. Unfortunately there was no one to see and envy. Even that blasted portrait above the fireplace averted its painted eyes.

'I will have my revenge on all of them,' he declared to the empty room. 'I'll make them pay for their sneering, scurrilous insults.' Out of long habit, his fingers explored the line of his ruined profile and suddenly the memory of that night on the sand rushed back in all its mortifying detail. He seized the gavel and crashed it furiously down on to the table.

'And I'll not pay five hundred pounds to a whore. Or if I do . . .' A gleam came into his pale eyes. 'I will extract value for money. From her. Or hers.'

CHAPTER 25

The New Year dawned bleak and cold with loss. Elissa wore black, though her grief had no need of such outward advertisement. It was visible enough in her suffering eyes, in the pale, taut lines of her face and the too-thin shape under the layers of winter warmth. In the tightly drawn-back hair, the colourless lips, the air of desperate determination. To do what was required, to endure, to survive, and to support all who depended on her. Not just support, but carry forward into a better future.

That was the task she had set herself: to achieve all that Joseph had hoped to achieve. She could only guess at the extent of his dreams, but she knew they began with a steam-driven herring drifter, paid for by the hard work of a seasonal curer's yard. Ina's husband Fergus had been Joseph's partner in that particular enterprise and when Elissa went to see him after Joseph's death they agreed that Ina's and Fergus's sons should take over the work Joseph had done, but that Elissa should keep his share in the business, with its small percentage of the yearly profits, 'just in case'.

In case she failed.

But she would not fail. Not only because she owed it to Joseph, had promised him on his death-bed, but because it gave her life purpose. Most of all, it gave her the strength to defy Hugh Sinclair. If he thought the death of her husband would cow her, then he would learn his mistake. With every nail she saw driven into the hull of the nascent vessel in Hall, Russell's shipyard, she felt her resolve strengthen. Joseph had told her the name the drifter was to be given, had made her promise to carry out his wish, and when that day came, she would declare her independence to the whole world, Hugh Sinclair included.

Meanwhile, 'Mary's' was her only livelihood and output must increase. Elissa took on extra girls for the gutting, had another smoke chimney built, trained one of Ina Bain's daughters to take over Sal's job, to tie the smoked fish in bundles and pack them for delivery. Sal lived at Lawyer Forbes's house now and Elissa was glad. Sal at least was safe and working hard to achieve her goal. As hard as they all

282

were, for even Gideon Joe, sobered by his father's death, had stopped complaining. As for Joseph's brothers, they continued to work the family fishing boat, the small line in winter, the herring in season, but that was still the modest family affair it had always been, where any profit after the household expenses went immediately into the upkeep of the nets and boat. Joseph's enterprise had always been separate and his own unaided effort: if Elissa was to carry it through it must be on the same terms.

So Elissa threw all her energies into expanding the business of 'Mary's'. She walked up into the town and called personally on several hotels and fish merchants to secure regular orders, while her brother Tom ensured she never ran out of the raw material – good, fresh fish straight from the quayside. Occasionally, when she was home for the weekend, Sal would help her mother in the smokeshed, but Elissa was never at ease on those occasions. She felt fear close in on her like an icy fog, forbade Sal to walk anywhere alone, even across the quay to the fishmarket, suspected every face that appeared in the smokeshed doorway, and did not relax vigilance till Sal was safely back under Lawyer Forbes's roof.

For rumour had it that things were not going well for Sinclair and Gibb. A shake-up in the board room. High-handed decisions, counter-manded one day, reconfirmed the next. Divisions, arguments, sack-ings. It emerged that the ice factory was not part of the Sinclair empire after all, but an independent company, split apart years back. Owned by Brodie Gibb and Another, a holding company in London, it was untouchable by the new director, though he tried just the same. Open war was expected to break out at any minute between Sinclair and Brodie Gibb and already bets were being laid in the Crown and Anchor on the possible outcome. Similar, as yet unsub-stantiated, rumours were rife about the other interests of Sinclair and Gibb: the rope factory, salt business, timber yard, ships' chandler's. But in all the confusion of gleeful speculation, one thing was certain: Sinclair was not the gentleman his father had been. He would not play the game by any rules but his own and if he lost, he would wreak vengeance on whoever crossed his path. Preferably the weak and the vulnerable. Young girls like Sal, or old thorns in the flesh like Elissa. People he saw as having done him wrong. Thwarted him. Taken what was rightfully his and not paid for it. Yet.

Elissa knew in her bones where the danger lay; knew that he would choose his moment, if it meant waiting weeks, months, even years. Knew he would not forgive her for taking the legacy his father had left her. Would not rest till he had clawed it back. But she would defy him. She would work and save and build and consolidate till she had the power to stand up to him, not as a penniless fishergirl from the gutting yard, but as a woman of influence and property. Already

283

'Mary's' handled twice the business it had done when owned by Sinclair's, and was twice as profitable. When Joseph's steam drifter was launched, they hoped in time for next year's season, they should make a profit there, too, and if predictions proved even half correct, a spectacular one. And that would be only the beginning. She would show Hugh Sinclair that the money he scorned and squandered could be put to better, more productive use. She would turn the money his father had left her into ten times the sum, out of gratitude and defiance.

Mary Noble shared her determination. 'I may be near seventy but I'm not dead yet and no murdering villain of a Sinclair laddie is going to scare me. Let him try, that's all. Just let him try.'

On that dour morning in March, a week before Sal's sixteenth birthday, work started before sun-up, even now in the tail end of winter, with a crust of ice on the water pails and glinting from the cobblestones underfoot. A thick sea mist hung in the darkness over the harbour entrance and from beyond the point the foghorn boomed its regular, mournful warning. But there were lights in the harbour basin, riding lights, working lights, the glow of open workshop doorways, lighted windows of offices in the Shiprow. The gas lights of the fishmarket strung their cheerful beams along the far quay and in their glow dark figures moved to and fro, manhandling loaded crans from hold to quayside, trundling trolleys piled high with fish boxes, shouting, bargaining over the open boxes of glistening fish. Dispatching these to the railway, these to the inner harbour, these to one or other of the big fish merchants, while yard boys scurried every which way, earning pennies if they were lucky, blows or curses if they were not, and the usual crowd of fishwives hovered, awaiting bargains or free handouts from their menfolk's leavings and the gulls gathered and screamed and swooped in the murky dawn.

The Noble household had been up since five and now, two hours later, old Gideon was installed in his usual chair beside the smoke chimney, the long-handled shovel for the sawdust beside him, an unlit pipe in his hand. His face was creased with concentration as he packed coarse fronds of tobacco from an open tin on his lap into the bowl of the pipe, pressing them down with square-tipped, arthritic fingers. Sal had given old Gideon the pipe two Christmases ago and it was his favourite.

Mary Noble was busy among the gutting lassies, checking their work, seeing the newest was up to scratch while at the same time shouting orders to the lad who swept the floor and ran messages, to the fish porters delivering the day's supply of raw fish, to Ina's lass tying tails with frowning concentration, and to Gideon himself to

284

'damp down yon second chimney. It's burning high' or to 'stir the ashes and add a wee bittie afore the smoke dies'.

Elissa was working beside Ina's Meg, tying her bundles with practised speed, one eye on the racks of smoked fish beside her, the other on the filling baskets, and at the same time running her eyes regularly over the whole building, checking for any change in the usual order, anything in the least out of place. They had a new, big order from a firm in Leith and it must be ready for the eight o'clock train if they were to fulfil their contract, a contract won against fierce competition, including an offshoot of Sinclair and Gibb. That fact gave Elissa particular pleasure, and made it imperative that they did not fail.

Then there would be the new fish to pickle and spear on to the tenterhooks for the smoke chimneys, the delivery baskets to make up, supplies of straw for the tying and sawdust for the fire to be checked and re-ordered. That last was proving a problem, for since the building of the second smoke chimney they had doubled their demand and it had to be the best oak chips or the flavour would be ruined. Their usual supplier had promised to do his best, but the load he had sent over this morning would scarcely last the day.

'Just to keep you going,' the lad had said. 'The rest will be along later.'

She would have to check that, too. They couldn't afford to interrupt the rhythm of the process or they would be way behind in no time. But there was enough for the time being and though the young lad who helped him was a wee bit feckless, old Gideon knew what he was doing.

Looking at her father-in-law now as he drew carefully on the filled pipe, Elissa felt her heart twist with compassion. Joseph's death had diminished him, shrunk him into an old man's shell, lined with grief and care, and though Daniel did his best to entertain his grandpa, it was uphill work. But Sal would be home at the weekend, and that would cheer him. And in spite of his inner mourning, he still knew his job.

'Right, lass,' said Mary, appearing suddenly at her side. 'I reckon it's time for a fly cup. My Gideon could do with one to wake him up, he's that slow this morning. I told you to damp down that second chimney, you old devil,' she shouted over the general chatter. 'We want them smoked, not frizzled to a cinder.'

'Where's that pesky lad,' grumbled old Gideon. 'He's the one as should do it.' Glowering, he laid down his pipe, creaked out of the chair, loaded the shovel high with fresh sawdust and tossed it viciously on to the glowing fire.

*

The explosion shook the windows of every house in the Square, or so the frightened Milly recounted afterwards, over and over. Shook and rattled them till she thought they would jump out of their frames and smash to the ground. Terrified, she ran outside, like all the other women. Then they saw the smoke and the flames.

'It's Mary Noble's smokehouse!' cried the nearest and they ran, as everyone else was running. With jugs and basins and pails for water and besoms to beat the flames. Anything to stop the fire spreading and to save those in danger. Shore porters, fishermen, office workers, yard boys, seamen from the vessels in the harbour, all flocked to Pocra Quay to help, making human chains of water buckets, from harbour water to burning timbers, while someone rigged up a hose pipe and pump and showered sea water on to the conflagration. The fire engine arrived, bells clanging, too late to do more than saturate the surrounding buildings to prevent the fire spreading, and to move the huddle of blackened, shocked and trembling survivors out of danger.

The blast had thrown them backwards, sideways, head over heels in a debris of fish boxes, fish and fish-guts, baskets, smoke racks, tenterhooks, and the deadly steel of a dozen gutting knives. Those nearest the big double doors had scrambled somehow to safety, dragging their friends with them, though none were unscathed. Ina's Meg had been tossed against the great wooden table and knocked unconscious, but Elissa, tripping over her in the smoke-blinded, fiery air, managed to drag her to the doorway before going back to find Mary who was screaming, 'Get up, you fool, get up!' and struggling to drag Gideon away from the blazing tower of the smoke chimney. The whole wall seemed to be alight, with leaping tongues of white and gold and blazing orange light mingled with billowing black smoke that stank of burning fish and something else. Something acrid and familiar. And the sawdust pile was mere yards away from the conflagration.

'Run, Mary,' shrieked Elissa, 'Quick! I'll bring Gideon.' She grabbed the old man's shoulders and tried to heave, though she knew even then that he was dead. If Mary knew it too she denied it, for she continued to shout and tug at his arm. A shower of sparks cascaded over them and Elissa smelled burning wool and hair. Hers? Or the old man's? What did it matter. All that mattered was to escape the searing, roaring heat, and the stifling smoke. To reach air.

'Help me!' she screamed as she and Mary heaved again at the old man's shoulders. Then miraculously men appeared through the roaring cloud of blackened flame. One swept Mary off her feet and ran with her for the doorway, two more grabbed hold of Gideon and followed, dragging his body between them, a third flung a blanket round Elissa, swung her up in strong arms and ran with her, through

286

the choking fumes and heat, to the blazing columns of the great double doors and out into cold, grey safety.

The shock of the cold air stung and burned and for a moment her eyes refused to focus after the blinding light of the fire. Then she saw the cool grey stones of the quayside, a bollard gleaming wet black in the pink-tinged morning air. A pink edge to the dark cloud overhead. More on the water. But the light came from the flames, not the sun. The harbour water was black and cold, but the million cat's paw ripples each had a touch of fire. Suddenly she shivered, with memory and fear.

'Mary? Where is Mary?' She fought and struggled to free her arms while her rescuer clutched and slapped and squeezed and held her imprisoned in a sizzling, acrid smell of burnt wool.

'Hush, lass. They're all safe. But for God's sake hold still while I kill the flames. Unless you want to burn your skirts away till you stand naked for all to see. And you a respectable married woman.'

She was quiet then, shuddering with shock. When she spoke again it was with awe and a sudden, overwhelming shyness. 'I am sorry. I did not realise. Thank you. But . . . but . . . please let me go. I must find what has happened to them all. Mary and Gideon and Ina's Meg. Ina will never forgive me if . . .'

She looked this way and that, in mounting desperation, searching for familiar faces. At the back of the crowd she thought she glimpsed a figure in a tall hat and tweed Inverness cape, the glint of a sneering, triumphant smile, a gloved hand raised in mocking salute; she blinked her eyes to clear them and he was gone. Oh God! Suppose one of her girls was still inside the smokeshed? She tried to run back towards the flames but strong arms grabbed her.

'Please let me go. I must find them . . .'

'They are all found, my little singing bird. All of them.' Someone's arm was round her shoulder, comforting. 'All the women are safe.'

'Thank God for that,' she said, leant her head against his shoulder and let the tears run. For one brief, blissful moment. Then she realised. All the *women*, he had said.

'I must go to Mary. She will need me.' This time no one tried to stop her.

It was only afterwards, when the men had carried Gideon's body home, with Elissa supporting Mary Noble in their wake, when the family had gathered, the neighbours come and gone, doctor and Minister likewise, when Sarah had been sent for and the family menfolk gathered, that Elissa found the time to think and to realise.

Someone had rescued her, carried her to safety from the billowing flames, someone familiar and in whose arms she had felt utterly at home. Someone who had called her his little singing bird. But she must have been dreaming, hallucinating with shock. Adam Grant

287

was on the other side of the world, in Australia. She shook her head to rid it of the puzzling dream, a dream too achingly sweet to be true.

The truth was far more cruel. Someone had deliberately set out to destroy her livelihood, her friends, and herself. Had spiked the harmless sawdust with explosive. Only one person could have done that. His gloating presence on the quayside proved it, unless that too was a dream. But dream or not, his villainy had claimed one more victim.

Gideon Noble was dead of a heart attack, the doctor said, and who could blame the old man when a harmless shovelful of sawdust exploded in his face? The smokeshed was burnt to the ground and nothing but a heap of smouldering ashes and blackened stone remained. Her livelihood had vanished with it. *But not her dreams.*

If Adam Grant could fly to her across half the world when she needed him, and disappear back again in the wink of an eye, then anything was possible.

The funeral was soon over. Coming so close on the heels of Joseph's it seemed like an extension of the first loss, a long, dreary time of mourning and fear. He was killing her menfolk, picking them off one by one: Adam banished, Joseph dead, and now old Gideon. Whom would he choose for the next victim? Her own Gideon Joe? Or Danny?

'Ma? Are you all right, Ma?' It was Sal, red-eyed but brave beside her. 'If you would like me to, I . . .' Sal paused, took a deep breath and said in a rush, 'I will give up my studies and come home, to help you to build up the smokehouse again.'

Elissa hugged her with gratitude and love, but she said through her tears, 'Thank you, Sal. It is sweet and loving and generous of you to offer, but I know how much your studies mean to you – and I would not dream of letting you do anything of the kind. You know how your father longed to see you a "bajan" at the university. And so do I. So that is settled.'

'But you will rebuild "Mary's", won't you? With the insurance money?'

Sal sounded so vehement and earnest that Elissa looked at her in surprise. She had not realised the girl felt so strongly about the smokehouse. Had even thought she disliked it.

'I have not really had time to think – ' she began, but her daughter interrupted.

'You must build it up again at once. I don't know what happened, Ma, but it was not an ordinary accident, was it? Whoever caused it, you must not let them beat you. Poor Grandma loved the place so much. And Grandpa.'

Sal is right, thought Elissa as she listened to the commiserations, the reminiscences, the words so kindly meant. In her lowest moments she had wondered whether to take the insurance money and merely

288

bank it. Add it to Joseph's savings to use for the steam drifter when required. But suppose it was not enough? And what of Sal's career? And Gideon's? And eventually her beloved Daniel's? What of her promises to Joseph, her dear, dead husband and father of her children? What of Mary Noble's grief? Sal was right: the smokehouse had been Mary's sustaining pride.

Retirement and domestic quietude had seemed blessedly desirable in Elissa's first grief and shock, but she knew in her heart that it would not do. She had obligations, had made promises she could not break. *Joseph, why are you not here to help me?* She scanned the room, counting the remaining men of her household: Joseph's brother Samuel, simple-hearted but kindly; his younger brothers Saul, Abel and Zach, all experienced fishermen now and willing enough. They would help her if she told them what was needed. They were strong and capable workmen. After all, they had all helped when she and Mary Noble had first taken over the broken-down, abandoned smokehouse and had rebuilt, repaired and furnished it, even to painting the signboard above the door. Gideon Joe was fifteen and growing, still grumbling about the indignity of being cook on the *Optimist*, the old family yawl, but pulling his weight. He had to; any backsliding and his uncle Samuel threatened to put him ashore at the nearest port. But Gideon Joe would make a good fisherman one day and he would lend a hand with 'Mary's', and though Danny was a mere seven, she knew he would expect to help too.

The herring season would not begin for another month at least. In that time, could they rebuild the smokehouse? In the wakeful loneliness of the small hours, Elissa knew that they must. Not only for poor Mary Noble's sake, but for her own defiant pride.

If it meant delay to the steam drifter, then so be it. She would talk to them all in the morning and take the first, decisive steps.

The *Elissa Downie* was launched a year later, in March '99. In memory of Joseph, the celebrations were lavish, the hospitality generous. All their friends and neighbours were invited as well as family, and as a precaution Elissa had hired a group of friendly shore porters, all known to her, to mingle with her guests, deter gatecrashers and keep watch for sabotage of even the smallest kind. Though investigations had been thorough, suspicions strong, no proof had ever been found to pin the blame for the smokehouse fire on to anyone. But Elissa needed no proof. She knew her enemy was at the bottom of it and might strike again at any time: and what better time or place than the launch of a steam-driven herring drifter, the first the port had produced?

There had been steam trawlers in plenty, but a drifter for the herring fishing was another matter. If successful, it could revolution-ise the herring fishery, as steam had revolutionised the deep-sea trawlers, and in the process make its owners a small fortune. So she warned friends and family to keep an eye open for anything sus-picious, hired her private guards and would have crewed the new steamer entirely with family if there had been an engineer amongst them. Unfortunately, they had grown up with sail and though they could find and trap the herring shoals with the best of them, not one knew the workings of the engine which would drive the new drifter, independent of wind or weather. One day Gideon Joe would take over, but not until he had served his apprenticeship, which, in spite of his protests, Elissa was determined he should do.

'You may be sixteen,' she told him, 'but you are not sufficiently experienced in ordinary seamanship yet, let alone able to handle a new and untested steam engine. Suppose it blew up in your face? We need someone who knows what he's doing, then you can watch and learn for yourself.'

Knowing that in this matter Lawyer Forbes would not be qualified to help, Elissa consulted Brodie Gibb. Since Joseph's death he had been a frequent visitor to the house in the Square, sometimes with Bethany and 'wee' Georgie, though Georgie at thirteen was far from 'wee', but more often alone. He came, he said, to offer sympathy, advice and help to his wife's family, now that both Joseph and old Gideon were dead.

'Samuel and the others are not bad lads,' he told Bethany when she complained he was forgetting which house he lived in, 'but they've not a full set of brains between the four of them. The lad Gideon Joe's bright enough, when he puts his mind to it, but he's inclined to be wayward and impatient, like most lads his age, and until he grows out of it, the womenfolk are needing an older man's advice now and then. With your sister Phemy's husband away in Buckie it's only Christian kindness to help.'

Brodie Gibb adjusted his tie in the gilt-edged mirror above the parlour fire and straightened the starched white corners of his collar. He was studying the symmetry with a half-smile of satisfaction when he saw his wife's face behind his shoulder in the glass. She was still a fine-looking woman, he supposed; if you liked plenty of flesh and loud laughter, but her features were coarse and hard, her expression dissatisfied. She led a comfortable enough life. She had servants to do her work for her and a good house in a good area. What more did she want? She had money to spend – too much of it, in his opinion – and was always gadding about to the theatre or a concert or some such idleness with her town friends. The Square folk weren't good enough for her any more. It had to be Mrs Captain this or Mrs Sherriff that or a string of shopkeepers' wives. Only she didn't call them shopkeepers

They were merchants or tea-traders, pronounced in a special voice to tell you how important they were. But that didn't satisfy her either. Nothing did. Especially not her husband, who provided and worked for every stitch of clothing on her well-fed, discontented body.

Brodie stared back at her, in the glass, and his eyes mirrored her own antagonism, though he could not match the spite.

'Since when have you been the helpless woman's friend?' jeered Bethany. 'You've never done a kind deed in your life unless there was money in it. How are you lining your pocket this time? Taking a cut of Milly's egg money?'

Since the reopening of 'Mary's' Milly had taken over the garden shed, and kept half a dozen hens there, with the fish baskets and coiled lines. One of the Bain boys had given her the chicks.

'Or maybe you're after bigger fish?' she taunted him. 'Like a half share in that blessed steam drifter?' When her husband pushed past her and into the hall she followed and stood in the parlour doorway, arms folded and leaning against the doorpost, watching as he put on his overcoat.

'Or is it the widow you're after? Preening and prettifying yourself in the looking-glass like a love-sick girl. It's pathetic. She may be needing a man in her bed, but she's not that desperate. No one could be.'

For a moment she thought he would strike her, but he would not give her the pleasure. Instead he said, with quiet venom, 'I see now why no one else would have you. You sour-tongued old bitch.' He wrenched open the street door and slammed it behind him.

Bethany flung it open again with a yell and something crashed on to the path behind him, in an explosion of shattering glass. 'I wish I'd never married you,' she shrieked in impotent fury.

So do I, thought Brodie for the thousandth time as he walked briskly along Marine Terrace in the direction of the harbour. I should have chosen the Downie girl. After her man drowned, I should have offered myself. Then I'd maybe have children of my own and a happy hearth. The Downie girl was free again and more desirable than ever, with a good, sound business and a bit of money put by. He would offer for her tomorrow, if he was free. If he wasn't tied for ever to that . . . that cow.

But his wife did have her uses. She had a good ear for gossip, most of it of the sniggering kind, but not all. Especially when she'd spent the day with a trawler captain's wife or two. Brodie Gibb had picked up several commercially valuable pieces of information from his wife's chatter and his own inquiries had filled in the rest. In fact, over the years he supposed he owed Bethany quite a lot, one way and another. Which was why he could be of such help to Elissa Downie

Noble and her family. Already he had steered her in the direction of the right suppliers of everything she needed for the first, trial trip. She deserved his help, poor, helpless widow that she was, and she always made him welcome. Not in any improper way, but like a grateful and appreciative friend. Elissa Downie Noble had always been an attractive woman, and in widowhood was even more so. It would have been a pleasure to help her, even without the business connection. As it was, his visits were doubly enjoyable.

'An experienced engineer? Leave it with me, Elissa, and I'll find you the best. Someone trustworthy, loyal and absolutely reliable. And preferably, he added under his breath, someone who hates Hugh Sinclair's guts.

Fortunately, there were plenty of those, but to make doubly certain Brodie Gibb had consulted his sleeping partner, via the London office before making his recommendation and was able to report with kindly triumph that Mr Scott would arrive the day after the launch to take up his position.

'Tell him to call at the house first,' said Elissa. 'Samuel's a fine captain but he's not so good at explaining the money side of things. I'd best do that myself.'

He opened the door and came in without knocking.

Danny was at school, the menfolk already aboard the *Elissa Downie* and Milly had gone with Mary to lend a hand at the smokehouse until Elissa came to relieve her. Elissa had set the simmering kettle to the side of the hearth, ready to make tea should her new engineer need it, had removed her work apron, tidied her hair and made herself suitably presentable and, she hoped, authoritative to deal with a new employee. She still wore widow's black, not just in Joseph's memory, for it was over a year since he had died, but because it reminded her constantly of her obligations and gave her the confidence to pursue them. Also, though she would have been ashamed to admit it, black suited her very well. With a cameo brooch at the neck of her neat-fitting bodice, deep tucks at the hem of the heavy skirt and a belt which emphasised her trim waist she looked elegant, feminine and capable.

The plans of the *Elissa Downie* were spread out on the cloth-covered table-top, together with the account book in which Elissa had worked out a rough guide for dividing the profit: a third for the boat, a third for the nets, a third for labour. They had discussed for hours whether the engineer should be paid a wage or a share, one side arguing for the old, established share system, the other pointing out that there were no engineers on a sailing ship where everyone lent a hand with the nets when needed – 'and you can't expect yon engineer laddie to

292

leave the engine to itself and haul in the nets, can you? We might end up in Greenland, or grounded in Greyhope bay.'

It was something Joseph must have considered, but he had left no indication, and in the end Elissa decided the man would be paid a wage for the trial trip – that way his money would be guaranteed – and afterwards they would review the situation. If there was an afterwards, for no one yet knew how the new drifter would perform. Suppose the engine failed, the nets were lost or destroyed? Anything could happen. Though Zeb had not been able to come home in time for his brother Joseph's funeral, he had been at his father's and his reports of the Lowestoft vessel, though cautious, had been encouraging. She must remember to write to him and inquire how they paid their crew.

It was at this point in her thoughts that she heard steps approaching on the path outside and the door opened, letting in the crisp morning air and a wedge of thin sunlight. She looked up to see only a dark outline against the light of the Square, but when he stepped forward from the gloom of the little entrance hall into the light of the kitchen and straightened to his full height she pushed back her chair, scrambled quickly to her feet and gripped the wooden chair back with white-knuckled hands.

He was dressed in a seaman's woollen jersey, short, brass-buttoned jacket, thick serge trousers with woollen stockings and supple leather boots to the knee. He was more heavily built than she remembered, more muscular. His hat was pulled low to shade his eyes and a speckled blond beard covered the lower part of his face.

'Thigh-boots are fine for the fish, but a darned nuisance in the engine-room,' he said. 'Mr Scott, reporting for duty.'

CHAPTER 26

She stared at him as if at an apparition.

'I was sorry to hear about your husband,' he said, removing his hat. 'He was an honest man. Like his father. May they both rest in peace.'

It could not be him. She was dreaming. Hallucinating, as she had done in the raging confusion of the smokehouse fire a year ago. Dear God, was she going mad? She must do something. Find her voice before she lost her reason.

'Mr Scott. You are Mr Scott, the engineer? From London?'

'Yes and no.'

'What sort of an answer is that?' she cried, suddenly furious. How dare they play tricks with her. Torment and frighten her.

'It is a stupid answer, Elissa, and I ask your forgiveness.' He tossed his hat aside, shrugged his shoulders and spread his arms wide. 'But I could think of no other way to come to you.' When she did not move, but continued to stare at him as at a ghost, he added, 'I would have come before, but you were sorrowing. I did not want to intrude. Besides,' and here his face darkened with remembered hurt, 'you had rejected me. I waited a whole extra week in London and you did not come.'

'You know why I couldn't – ' she protested, but he carried on, heedless.

'And I had built such hopes on *Singing Bird*. She's a lovely vessel, sleek and swift, and the cabin was built especially for you, just as I promised. When I eventually sailed, a week behind schedule and mortified, I swore that anyone who could reject such devotion did not deserve a second chance. Was not worth another thought. But thoughts don't always behave as you wish them to. I confess I have visited Aberdeen now and again, to find out how you were faring, you and Sal. And to attend to certain business interests here.'

'Business?' Elissa's mouth was dry, her heart pounding hard. Why had he come?

'Aye, business.' His eyes gleamed suddenly with satisfaction. 'I knew well enough who had ruined everything between us and when you sent me packing – '

'Adam, you know I – '

'Couldn't do otherwise? Aye, I know it, but what sort of comfort is that to a man in an empty bridal bed? So I decided there and then to take my revenge on the man who had robbed me not only of seven years of freedom, but of a wife and a daughter. If he thought he would escape unpunished, he was an arrogant fool. So I laid my plans, slow and sure, and I'm almost there.' He grinned, but only for a moment before his brow darkened again.

'That business with the burning smokeshed confirmed it for me. I might have relented if it had not been for that. Left him a crumb or two. But to plan cold-blooded murder, and you so newly widowed . . .'

But Elissa could stand no more torment. 'Why are you here?'

'When I heard from Brodie Gibb that you wanted an engineer, I saw my chance. Surely after a year of widowhood, I told myself, she will consent to speak to me? So here I am. Mr Scott. Engineer. Fully qualified and with years of experience. Ready and willing to put the *Elissa Downie* through her paces. After all,' he finished softly, 'it is the least I can do for my daughter, and for her dear mother, the one true love of my life.'

He took a step towards her. *In a moment, he will kiss me and I will not have the strength to stop him. Will not want to stop him . . .*

The kettle lid danced under bubbling steam and the small sound in the silence broke the spell.

Elissa turned away in confusion; sat down at the table and began to turn the pages of her account book, seeing nothing of the columns of figures, while her pulse calmed and she schooled her tumultuous thoughts into some sort of order. What was she doing, imagining his kisses? There could be nothing between them. Nothing. Too many years had passed. He had his own life in Australia, and she had hers. Here, where the family's fortune depended on her.

'So this Mr Scott I was promised does not exist?' she said, not looking at him.

'It is a name I use now and then, for business purposes. Especially in Aberdeen.'

'But what is wrong with your own name, Adam?'

'Nothing. Except that there are people who never forget names: you must remember that, if you value your life, and mine. I will be Mr Scott and only Mr Scott, to you and to everyone else, when I work the drifter for you.'

'But you can't, Adam! You have work of your own. Your business in Australia. Your cargo boats and steamers. How can you take a month's leave to work for me? I don't understand what you are doing here at all.'

'No,' he sighed, his back to her. He sounded suddenly deflated and sad.

He stepped to the small window which looked out on to the Square and, affecting to study the view beyond the net screen and the geranium plant, said, 'I will try to explain. I have done well, as I vowed I would do. At first, for your sake and then, when you rejected me, for my own pride and, I confess, to show you what you had thrown away. Not a praiseworthy motive, and it soon disappeared in the single, driving need to pay Sinclair back for what he had done to us. I was not sure then how I would do it, only that I needed money and power, in the same world he moved in, to do anything at all.

'Now I have ships, warehouses, a thriving shipping company in Melbourne. I have an office in London, too, and a regular service between London and Melbourne. Some time ago, on one of my London visits, I came across Brodie Gibb in the course of business. He put me in the way of a good investment and we have kept in touch ever since. He knows me as Mr Scott and I doubt he recognises me or remembers that I once worked for his curing yard in Gremista. We found we shared a mutual interest, and a mutual enemy. He undertook to handle the Aberdeen end of things for me, and still does.'

Elissa listened, motionless and totally absorbed. The feckless, light-hearted and laughing Adam she had once loved had matured into a man of rock-hard determination and a singleness of purpose she would not have dreamed possible. Yet under the pride of achievement and the confidence of success, she heard a sadness which twisted her heart with compassion. Fate had done that to him. Fate and Hugh Sinclair.

'Then, when I heard about the *Alice May* and Joseph's death, thought it was time to come and see for myself. And I saw just what villainy Sinclair is capable of. I vowed then that I would finish what had begun – and ruin him completely. For your sake, my love. And for mine.'

Elissa shuddered and looked up at him with sudden fear. 'Take care, Adam. You do not know how dangerous he is.'

His face was grim with purpose, his blue eyes hard and resolute.

'Oh, I think I do. And it is because I do, that I will ruin him. Absolutely. If it takes me the rest of my life. But first,' he said suddenly light-hearted, 'I intend to cast away care and enjoy myself with that beauty of a steam drifter you have just launched.' He turned away from the window and came to stand beside her at the table. 'I confess I am dying to put her through her paces and when the trial is completed to your satisfaction, Mrs Noble, I promise you the real Mr Scott will take over. Except that his name is Ross and he is waiting at the quayside now.'

It was six weeks before Adam declared himself satisfied with the workings of the engine and with the crew's understanding of it. Mr Ross took Adam's place and the *Elissa Downie* set forth for her first herring summer, taking the Noble menfolk with her, including Gideon Joe, swelling with pride at his first real voyage, and at the same time mortified that he was only to be the cook.

'Just see you keep your eyes open, lad, and learn all you can,' Adam Grant had told him. 'Then maybe Mr Ross here will consider you suitable to be his assistant one day. And if that's not to your liking,' he added, with a wink at Samuel behind the boy's back, 'you can always go back to the *Optimist*. Someone has to keep the old yawl seaworthy and working for her keep. So if you're wanting to run before you can walk, you'd maybe best stick to sail where you can do least harm.'

When Gideon Joe grumbled to Grandma Noble that he wasn't a child so why did folk treat him like one, and it was time they let him take his father's place and do a man's job, Mary sympathised.

'But you're still young, lad, with time to learn. You've started at the bottom, like everyone else, and you must work your way up, slow and steady, like your father did. That's the best way, and that's what he wanted for you. You have to learn, see? How quickly you do it is up to you, so there'll be no time for sulks. Think yourself lucky you've a chance on a fine new drifter. With a stew pot and a kettle and a good dollop of common sense you'll manage the cooking fine. Then you can look about you and learn about yon engine in a book and in no time you'll be handling it yourself.'

'Thanks, Gran,' said Gideon Joe in a small voice and had the grace to look ashamed.

On the morning after the *Elissa Downie* sailed, Adam met Elissa by arrangement under the archway of the Regency Screen which separated St Nicholas churchyard from the bustle of Union Street. Where she had been standing with little Gideon Joe on that dreadful day when Adam had come back from the dead. Had he chosen the place deliberately? Or merely because it was a convenient, central meeting point? It must be the latter reason, she decided, for weren't they going to discuss the performance of the new steam drifter and go over the accounts? But when she arrived at the meeting place to find him waiting, he took her arm and steered her through the crowds towards the corner of St Nicholas Street and the tram terminus. Soon, they said, the trams were to run on electrical current, without need of horses, though Elissa could not imagine how that would work. Two pairs of strong horses was one thing: a sort of toasting fork with a long handle running on an overhead wire was quite another. But that was in the future: the trams were still horse-drawn and familiar, the upper deck open to the sky and gained by climbing an elegant outside stairway from the deck below. Two such vehicles were standing at the terminus, one of them steadily filling with passengers. The upper deck was already half full.

'We will take the tram to Queen's Cross, then walk,' he told her. 'That is, if you don't mind walking?'

She shook her head. She felt at the same time awkward and excited, a half of her saying over and over, I am a respectable middle-aged widow with a family to work for and he is one of my employees. Nothing more. This is a business meeting. Purely business. While the other half of her whispered, thirty-five is still young. I am young and lonely and unattached. Anything might happen. Anything at all.

They sat side by side on the top deck of the rattling tram, the respectable citizenry of Aberdeen all around them and the respectable shop fronts of Union Street flowing past at their feet on either side. Elissa smothered a smile of self-mockery: how could she have hoped for anything romantic on a city tram? Except that the upper deck was a little romantic, if one discounted the wind snatching at one's hat and hair, the dust in one's face and the lurching which could throw one passenger against another without warning. It was romantic to ride above the world for a while, to look straight into an upstairs window, or down on to the heads of the crowds: so many hats of so many shapes and colours, moving and parting like a myriad multi-coloured ants scurrying about important business. But the horse-drawn tram was businesslike, too. Proceeding by timetable along a predetermined route.

In fact, this businesslike progress along the city's businesslike thoroughfare was not romantic at all, except in her imagination. She glanced to her side and below her and saw they were passing Gordon and Smith, Family Grocer and Provision Merchants. *Finest kitchen salt, fourpence a stone. Best Black Tea – Broken leaf, with good body and flavour – One shilling*. The surroundings were entirely appropriate for the occasion. Any minute now he would tell her how many tons of coal the new drifter had consumed per sea mile.

'I want to see if our house is still there,' he said suddenly, looking not at her but at the stiff back of a bombazine-clad matron in a fierce crêpe-swathed bonnet two seats in front of them. 'And to walk in peace with the far hills to look on and the town's din behind us.' He kept his face averted and she could not read his expression.

'I must not be too long.' She kept her voice deliberately cool and calm. 'Danny will be home from school and there is his homework to

298

supervise and Milly will be tired after helping Mary in the smoke-house today, instead of me. And – '

'And I am here beside you and need your full attention.' He reached for her gloved hand and his own closed over it, holding her captive. There was something in his voice which stripped her of her tenuous control and left her blushing and awkward, as she had felt all those years ago, when they first met. Her surroundings retreated into harmless background. Oblivious to everything else, they sat side by side, not looking at each other, a respectable widow in black, and a middle-aged, bearded sailor with a serious expression, while he continued to hold her hand and they progressed sedately up the busy length of the city's main street in full view of anyone who chose to see. But whoever might see them together, this time she had no need to feel ashamed. She was a widow and free.

For the first time the thought emerged in all its possibilities. She had known it was there, but had not acknowledged it fully until now. She had not wanted to. She had mourned Joseph's passing and still mourned him; missed his company, the warmth of his body beside hers at night, the easy exchange of daily trivia, the reassurance of his presence between her and the world. Now, for the first time since Joseph's death, the prospect of another man's company stirred her to interest, and expectation. But while her heart turned towards Adam, her head whispered caution.

Just because they had loved each other once, in that far distant time, did not mean they would do so again. She knew nothing about him. Except what she had always known: that there was an invisible bond between them which even her years of marriage to Joseph had not snapped. But Adam had an unknown life in Australia; another in London. Perhaps a wife and family. Today he was a stranger, sitting beside her in a city tram, bowling westward along Union Street, away from the harbour and the familiar life of the Square and into the unknown.

The tram reached its terminus. The passengers collected their various belongings and alighted on to the cobbles. When it was their turn, Adam descended the curved outside stairway in front of her, then handed her down the steps after him.

'Mind the tram-rails,' he warned. 'And mind your manners too. The Queen might be watching you.'

For a moment she thought he meant it, then saw his face. They were on the fringe of the city, the tram route behind them, and in front of them, the tree-lined vista which led westward towards the hills and eventually, fifty miles inland beside the banks of the Dee, to Balmoral Castle.

'Only if she has nothing better to do with her time, Mr Grant. And exceptionally good eye-sight.'

'True. Shall we walk, Mrs Noble?' He offered her his arm. 'It is a pleasant enough day for walking and not much more than a mile. Two at the most.'

She would look upon it purely as a business outing. An excursion for the engineer who had put her new steam drifter so competently through her paces. There were things she wanted explained to her, points she wished to check. What better way to do it than to stroll in peace in the countryside, with no more pressing business on her mind?

The stone gateposts were just as she remembered them, if more weatherworn, and where the dirt track approached the gates it split in two, just as before, one branch going south-west, the other to the north. They stood for a moment in the entrance, seeking a glimpse of the house, but the driveway curved through such a density of rhododendron bushes and other greenery that they could see nothing.

'Never mind. If you are good, I might lift you up to peep over the wall as I did before.' He offered her his arm again and sedately she took it. In silence they followed the same bridle path, around the boundary wall.

Beyond the wall the garden was more overgrown than last time, the trees taller, the ivy thicker, the rhododendrons more profuse, some in luxurious flower, their stiff, dark leaves the perfect setting for a dozen different shades of pink. In places, the wall had crumbled, the topmost stones fallen to the ground, where grass and weeds had covered them. Willowherb and bracken, tall Scottish thistles and clusters of sweet-smelling clover. Brambles smothered one stretch of fallen wall, replacing one barrier with another, but through the tangled stems the house showed square and solid in the light May air.

'Still occupied anyway,' said Adam, 'I must find out who owns it. Though the town seems to have crept nearer. Surely that row of houses was not there the last time we came?'

She followed his pointing finger to where the distant road dipped over a horizon broken by several small square blocks. 'I didn't notice.' Her voice was carefully polite and colourless. Whyever had they come here?

'No.' They walked on in silence, awkward with each other, the crumbling wall of Fairfields at their right hand and ahead of them the open country with, in the far distance, the low, pale line of the hills. A blackbird sang in the trees over the wall, another answered and from one of the fields on their left came the dreamy lowing of cows. Sadness washed through her and yearning, for lost youth and lost love.

After too long a silence, he tucked her hand closer under his arm and said, 'I think we have some catching up to do, don't you?

Suppose you tell me first about my daughter Sal? And then, with your permission, Mrs Noble, I should like to kiss you.'

The Friday after the *Elissa Downie* put to sea to fish in earnest, Sal could hardly contain her excitement. She had noticed a strange vessel in the harbour on Monday morning, when her Uncle Samuel had walked with her along Trinity Quay to the Green and Correction Wynd where Lawyer Forbes had his town house, but had thought no more about it. Now she realised and for once, was impatient for tomorrow and her usual visit to the Square.

Sal had grown used to the Forbes house and to the quaint curves and antiquities of Correction Wynd. She knew that Mrs Forbes thought it unfashionable and melancholy with its view of St Nicholas kirkyard, but the house had been the Forbes family home for three generations and the lawyer refused to budge. Though lately, she had heard Mrs Forbes brag to her lady friends that they had taken a house in the country, for the summer months when town became too crowded and uncomfortable. But the town house was convenient for Mr Forbes's work, as well as for Marischal College, and Sal loved it. In its quiet and studious respectability it was so different from the constant crowded bustle of the Square and she and Adelaide had a whole room to themselves for their studies. On occasions Adelaide's brother Thomas brought his friends home and though Sal, or Sarah as she preferred to be called in her new role as student, was usually far too shy and tongue-tied to speak, she listened enthralled to their sophisticated discussions of some aspect of philosophy which had been touched on in the morning's lecture, or, equally enthralled, to their high-spirited knock-about rendering of some student ballad or scurrilous sketch.

Increasingly she grudged the time spent in the Square, with its hard work and narrow horizons, but on this particular Saturday she had an assignation which even a personal invitation from Thomas Forbes himself would not have made her break.

She had had an answer to her letter. The secret letter which Adelaide had posted for her more than a year ago, after her father died, and which she had almost forgotten in the long months of mourning and the excitement of her new life with the Forbeses. She had asked for any reply to be sent to her, care of Adelaide, and when it came, though Mrs Forbes had been annoyingly persistent in her curiosity, Adelaide had refused to hand over the folded and sealed paper to anyone but Sarah herself.

'It is from her uncle,' she declared in answer to all questions. 'The one who works for the Lord, with the Bethel ships. They go all over the world now,' she had finished, anticipating argument and defying contradiction. 'I said Sarah must have her letters directed here, Mamma, now that she lives with us. I knew you would agree.'

When Adelaide spoke in those decided tones, Mrs Forbes knew better than to dispute the point. She had been worsted in argument more than once by her youngest daughter who had developed an irritating habit of quoting Greek or Latin tags which Mrs Forbes could not understand. Not only that, but she and Sarah Noble spoke Latin to each other 'for practice' and Mrs Forbes had no way of telling whether it really was the practice they said it was or merely a secret code.

The note, for it was hardly more than that, asked her to call at the Seamen's Mission the following morning, to collect a packet. On this particular Saturday it was Cameron's turn to escort her home, though at fifteen Sarah privately considered him more of a burden than a protector. If they ran into any sort of trouble, which fortunately she didn't think likely on a fine May morning, she would have to protect him rather than the other way round. He was a thin, gangly boy with an abstracted expression and the sort of pale red hair which looked as if it had faded in the sun. But Sal liked him well enough and on occasions they helped each other with Latin exercises. So, at the foot of the Shiprow, knowing how nervously conspicuous he always felt when they reached the harbour area, she told him she was quite capable of going home from there alone.

'But don't hurry back too soon, Cameron, or your mother will want to know why.'

She watched him out of sight round the curve of the Shiprow, then turned her face to the sea wind and the quay. She wanted to see whether that strange vessel was still where she had seen it, in the deep-water harbour, though she supposed it was unlikely after so many days. And anyway, just because a letter had come for her at last did not mean that her godfather had brought it himself. Sure enough, the *Laverock* was still there, where she had last seen her, gleaming with new paint and every brass fitting down to the last humble screw sparkling gold in the sun, but though she lingered as long as she could spin it out without embarrassment she saw no one remotely resembling the fair-haired hero she remembered in her dreams.

With a sigh of disappointment she turned away and retraced her steps along Waterloo Quay in the direction of the Seamen's Mission. Two men watched her go. One, with protective appreciation, from the deck of the *Laverock*, the other with less innocent intent, from the first-floor window of the office of Sinclair and Gibb, Shipping Agents. Except that at that very moment a lad with a ladder and a large pot of paint was busy obliterating the sign under thick strokes of green, and under the unsuspecting nose of Hugh Sinclair himself.

Sal spoke to the man at the Mission, fortunately someone she knew by sight from South Square and who knew her, and took charge of the packet. She did not want to open it in front of his curious eyes and thus advertise its contents to the whole harbour, so tucked it under her arm and left, with a thank you for his trouble.

'No trouble, lass. That was a sad business with your father. Tell your ma I was asking for her. And mind how you go,' he called after her. 'There's always riff-raff hanging around the harbour of a Saturday.'

She met the first specimen as soon as she stepped into the street.

'Miss Noble, I believe?' The gentleman who barred her way smiled a predatory smile and nodded the briefest of bows. 'Or should I say, Lissa Downie's Sal?'

'No, you should not,' declared Sal angrily, though she felt her heart quicken with fear. She knew who he was, remembered him from that day on Torry shore when he had abused her own father. Grandma Noble said he had killed him. She tried to pass, but he moved to block her path.

'Not so fast, my pretty. I believe we met at the Jubilee celebrations?'

'Then your memory is failing. I do not know you. Or want to.'

'But I would like very much to know you, my dear.'

Before she realised what he meant to do he had gripped her by the forearm with a strength that made her gasp.

'Let me go!'

'All in good time, Sal. All in good time. Let us walk a little together first, so you can tell me all about yourself.' He tried to propel her forward beside him, but she dug in her heels hard and hung back.

'Let go of my arm this instant !' She squirmed and tugged, but he held her firm, while the smile spread and spread.

'A girl of spirit, I see. Just like her mother. The last time I offered you a ride in my carriage you refused me. I hope you will not do so today. It is . . . just . . . around . . . this . . .'

'Corner?' supplied a voice behind him and he whipped round his head to see a man his own age, but with none of his own languid elegance. This fellow wore seaman's clothes, serge trousers, thick oiled jumper, brass-buttoned black jacket threadbare at the elbows, with a black felt cap and villainous beard. He also wore an expression which made Sinclair's eyes dart from side to side in search of support and, finding none, remove his hand from the girl's arm.

'Was this fellow bothering you, Sal?' asked the newcomer. 'Because if he was . . .'

'He has stopped now,' she finished, moving to her rescuer's side and smiling up at him.

'You'd best make yourself scarce,' he ordered Sinclair, 'before I call yon lad over to use the rest of his paint on your ugly poxy face.'

Sinclair's eyes looked past them along the quay to the signboard of his office and his face paled.

'I don't know who you are, fellow, but you'll pay for your insolence,' he snarled. 'As for you, Miss Noble, we will postpone our outing to some other time.'

'Over my dead body you will,' growled the other. 'You lay so much as one finger on her. Ever. And you'll suffer for it. You have my word on that. Now move. Or do I have to help you on the toe of my boot?'

Together they watched Sinclair stride away, not to the invisible carriage, but back towards the now unnamed office where the lad with the paint pot and ladder was already making his escape.

Adam grinned. 'Don't worry, lass, he'll not catch him. Young Tom can outrun a buck kangaroo, no bother. And he'll be back again when the coast is clear. Now I will walk to your door with you, to make sure you get home safe. One thing, though. Best not mention your encounter to your ma. It would only worry her. But you watch out for that fellow and keep well out of his way. Promise?'

'I promise.'

He offered his arm and she took it happily, knowing anyone who saved her from Sinclair was her trusted friend. Up York Place, into York Street, along past the shipbuilding yards they walked together in companionable silence. Then he said, 'I see you collected the packet. Have you opened it yet?'

'No, I wanted to save it till I got home.' She looked up at him shyly. 'Are you my godfather? Adam Grant?'

'I might be. But while I am in Aberdeen I'm plain Mr Scott. I grew this beard specially, and I'd be grateful if you would keep my secret. I don't want the likes of your molester friend finding me out. And before you ask, there's a good reason for it. Your mother knows it and understands. It's books in the packet, by the way. Your ma told me which ones you need, but if they're not right you can take them back to the shop and change them. And there's money inside the Greek one. Money for your studies.'

'You are very kind to me,' she said, but there was a question in her voice.

'And why not when I have no children of my own, more's the pity. A god-daughter is better than no daughter at all, even if she does live on the other side of the world.'

'No,' said Sal seriously. 'It is you who do that.'

'A true daughter of Victoria,' he laughed. 'And there's me forgetting this country is the centre of the universe. But here we are at your own door. I'll say goodbye and leave you.'

'No! Please stay. Come in and say hello to Ma. That is, if she is at home.'

Before he could protest again, the door opened and Elissa stood on the step, her face alight with happiness.

'There you are, Sal, at last. I was beginning to wonder when . . .' Then she saw Adam and stopped, her face suddenly pale. 'Is everything all right? The drifter has not . . .?'

'No, the drifter is fine. At least, she was when I last heard. But I met your lassie on the road here and thought I'd take the opportunity to look in and say goodbye.'

'Are you going so soon? You did not say.'

'No, but I have sudden urgent business in London. When it's sorted, I'll be back.' His eyes looked deep into hers and she read the promise they held. With a private smile, Elissa turned and went back into the house, saying over her shoulder, 'Well, come in the pair of you. You'll take tea with us before you go, Mr Scott. Or a dram.'

Sal, watching them together as they drank tea and chatted easily of this and that, felt suddenly excluded. He was her godfather after all. All those years when he had sent her presents, her parents had ignored him. Now he had suddenly appeared out of nowhere and her mother was behaving as if . . . as if he was her special, private friend.

'I am sorry you have no children of your own, godfather,' she said, determined to take her part in the conversation. 'It must be very sad for your wife.'

There was a stillness in the room as if even time had stopped. Then with a sigh of defeat, he said, 'Yes.' The one small word seemed to hang in the air for ever, betraying its secret over and over till every spark of happiness was extinguished.

'Would you like more tea, Mr Scott?' said Elissa when she could trust her voice to speak.

'No, thank you. I must be leaving if we are to catch the tide.'

'Sal, dear. Run over to Mrs Bain's, will you, and fetch Danny. I know he would like to say goodbye to Mr Scott.'

Sal hesitated, knowing she was being got rid of, but unable to think of an excuse to stay. Instead she said, 'I'll be as quick as I can,' and ran.

'Why didn't you tell me?' she said into the silence.

'You know why. I wanted you, as I have always wanted you. And it is not how you think,' he said bitterly as she turned away from him. 'My wife lives with her mother. We have not shared a house, or a bed, for years. I think I only married her because you refused to come away with me, though I was fond of her and still am, poor girl. We had a baby son who died. She almost died too, and afterwards her mind was not what it had been. She refused to let me near her and still does. Though I send money regularly to her mother and visit whenever I can. I feel responsible for her.'

'The poor woman,' said Elissa, her voice full of compassion. 'How terrible for her. And for you.'

'I should have told you, but I had not the courage. I thought . . .'

'You thought I need never know? When I wanted to know everything about you, to share your life completely?' She looked at him with bleak honesty. 'I confess I thought of asking you about a wife, but I too had not the courage. If I had asked and known . . .' She shrugged and said with a sad smile, 'I chose ignorance, deliberately, for my own ends. But I should have known better. It does not do to hide the truth.'

'I love you,' he said with stark simplicity.

'And I love you.'

He stood up, took a step towards her.

'No, Adam.' Her voice was desolate, but firm. 'It is too late.'

Before he could plead with her, two figures flashed past the window and the door to the street flew open. Danny shot across the room and catapulted between them.

'Can I come with you, Mr Scott? Can I come to London on the *Laverock* with you, and back again?'

'I might not be coming back, Danny. Not this time anyway.'

'But I thought you said . . .' began Sal, then seeing her mother's face her voice died away.

'Mr Scott has had to change his plans,' said Elissa quietly.

'Then next time,' persisted the boy. 'Promise you will take me next time?'

'I might,' said Adam, 'though I do not promise. Promises must never be broken, remember that, and my work with the steam drifter is finished. But I give you my word that if your mother tells me . . .' His eyes met Elissa's above the boy's head. 'When your mother tells me,' he repeated slowly, 'that I am needed, then I will come back. Willingly. And on that happy day, lad, you may stand in the wheelhouse with me, and steer my ship.'

'You will tell him, Ma, won't you? Sal, make her tell him. Ma, say you will,' clamoured Danny till in spite of her desolation Elissa managed a smile.

'Mr Scott has business of his own to see to, Danny. He will come back when he is free.'

CHAPTER 27

The start of Sal's college career was for ever after to be associated in Elissa's mind with the end of Gideon Joe's, and with her own desolation.To have glimpsed happiness and to have it snatched away so soon was cruel. Not Adam's fault. She could not have expected him to stay unmarried for her sake. But cruel just the same and Gideon's rebellion did not help.

In that winter of 1899 Gideon was a restless sixteen-year-old, his ambition, like his body, grown too big for the constriction of the tiny galley on the family's first steam drifter. Since her launch into Aberdeen harbour with such pride and ceremony in the spring, the *Elissa Downie* had proved her worth ten times over. A sister ship was already on the drawing board and, if all went according to plan, would be launched in the spring of 1901, but the prospect only fuelled Gideon's roving ambition. He wanted to be captain, if not of the new drifter, for he acknowledged his Uncle Samuel's superior claim to that honour, then of the *Elissa Downie*. When his mother fenced off his repeated demands with 'All in good time, Gideon', or the infuriating 'We'll see', he grew increasingly frustrated. He was the eldest son, wasn't he? Why couldn't he take his father's place?

'You can, Gideon dear, when you have served your apprenticeship,' soothed Elissa for the hundredth time. 'But first you must learn all there is to know about seamanship and especially about these new and complicated engines. Listen to all Mr Ross tells you and be patient.'

But patience was not one of Gideon's virtues. Driven by the restless energy of lusty good health and hampered by his own inexperience and the confining reins, as he saw them, of a close-knit family business, even his new promotion to engine-room assistant did not satisfy. He had been born into fishing, hadn't he? Known the industry since he was so high. Could bait a long-line in his sleep, hear a herring shoal a mile away, was equally at home on land or sea. He knew he would be master of one or other of the steam drifters one day, but he wanted that pinnacle of achievement now, not somewhere in the distant future when, as people kept telling him, he had worked his apprenticeship like everyone else. He was not 'everyone else'. He was the eldest son of a widowed mother and impatient for status and reward. Sal had won her precious bursary and with it her independence, so why shouldn't he?

The conflict did not make for easy relations with his mother who, as virtual head of the extensive household, aimed to maintain the same standards of discipline and obedience which old Gideon had demanded and which his widow Mary expected in her dead husband's honour. Mary had aged ten years since old Gideon's death and spent most of her time at the fireside, knitting interminable seaman's stockings for one or other of her sons or grandsons and staring into the embers. She had worked for a year or so in the rebuilt smokehouse 'just to help you get on your feet again, lass', then she had handed over 'Mary's' to Elissa.

'Nay, lass, it was your idea in the first place, and it's not the same without my Gideon. You'll get it anyway, when I'm dead, so why not now? I'm not wanting it any more. Maybe your Sal will help you instead.'

But by the autumn Sarah, as she now preferred to be called, had won her bursary, and had her sights on a different goal; Elissa had to find her help elsewhere. As the trawling industry flourished, with fish catches increasing more than five-fold in the last three years, so did the new 'Mary's', which now employed double the staff they had started with. As well as that, Elissa had taken Lawyer Forbes's advice and invested a part of her unexpected inheritance in her brother Tom Downie's new ice factory in Commercial Road. The trawling industry needed ice. Brodie Gibb's factory could not keep up with the growing demand and the new venture was already turning out twenty tons of transparent ice a day. On top of that, with the introduction of steam, the herring catches had increased beyond all expectations – and the profits of the curing yard with them. Ina's Fergus was doing well and, with two of his sons already in the business, looking to expand. Joseph's small investment in that particular curing business was paying good dividends. Curing, fishing, 'Mary's', ice . . . Elissa was glad she had so much to occupy her mind which might otherwise have betrayed her into despair. It would have been better, she thought, if Adam Grant had not come back, not walked with her, kissed her, loved her; reminded her so sweetly of what she had once had and could never have again. And yet, she would not cancel out the memory even if she could. In her bleakest hours, the thought of his arms around her was some private comfort in her loneliness. Then she would turn with increased vigour to her work.

On the rare occasions when the thought of the family business ventures woke her in the small hours with visions of disaster – a sudden glut like in '84; an equally devastating dearth, for who could tell from one day to the next where the herring shoals would be; or a storm so bad that it sank every vessel they owned – she would remind herself that, thanks to 'Mary's', they had a foot firmly planted in both camps. If the herring shoals failed and the curing yard with them, there would still be Tom's ice factory, and 'Mary's'.

In fact, it might be wise to expand the smokehouse; try and get a lease on the adjoining land and build on to the existing structure; or move to new, larger premises. But at this point fear always brought her up short. Hugh Sinclair had not been seen in the harbour for some months. Rumour had it that the firm of Sinclair and Gibb was beset by debts: except that it was no longer Sinclair and Gibb. On that desolate day when Adam Grant, married man, had walked out of her life, gleeful reports came scurrying in of signboards being painted out, new ones put up in their place, only to be viciously torn down again, while 'You could hear yon fellow Sinclair swearing and cursing from here to Timbuctoo.'

Later it transpired that Brodie Gibb had removed himself from the partnership, together with his manifold commercial assets, and had taken Lawyer Forbes with him. The details were not known: what was known was that they had been clever, and devious, enough to do it without leaving Hugh Sinclair anything but the original shipping company of half a dozen trawlers, 'and most of them no doubt pledged already for gambling debts' and not a thing he could do about it. The signboard when it was eventually replaced read *Sinclair's Shipping Company* in large defiant letters, but it was empty boasting. Without Brodie Gibb's business acumen and stolid grasp on the tiller Sinclair would founder soon enough. It was only a matter of time.

But in that time the lust for vengeance could flourish and devastate. Elissa had not forgotten the havoc one small shovelful of treachery had caused. The horror was indelibly etched into her memory: Gideon dead, Mary Noble distraught, all her girls blackened and terrified. She was afraid that if she was rash enough to extend or build up her premises, the act would inflame Sinclair to further vengeance. For the moment, it might be wise to do nothing, but if the adjoining land did become available, she knew she would take it; as long as it did not involve borrowing beyond their capacity to repay.

Careful management of every penny, earned or spent, had brought them to where they were, and at least her night-time worries did not include the burden of intolerable debt. She had tried to explain this policy to Gideon Joe, without much success. If the business was making money, he argued, why not spend and enjoy it? Increase his wages for a start.

In the last year, since he had realised he was not going to remain the puny, undersized creature he had hated, but grow as tall as his father had been, maybe taller, Gideon had stopped regarding girls as tormentors and bullies, and begun to look on them with a different interest. As they began to look at him. Meg Duthie's daughter Liz for one. But a man needed a bit of money in his pocket to walk out with a girl.

'Be reasonable, Ma,' he cajoled, when he found her alone in the scullery on a dour day in December, peeling potatoes for the evening meal. 'You are always telling us to put a bit by, but how can I do that with what I'm paid?'

'You have all you need, Gideon. Carry that pan through to the range will you, dear? It's awful heavy when it's full.' She followed him into the kitchen where Milly was ironing one of her brothers' shirts on the table. Elissa noted two already ironed and folded on one of the chairs and on another chair, a deep pile of creased and waiting linen. Only two done, and Milly had been at work for at least half an hour.

'Don't overtire yourself, Milly,' she said gently. 'Remember you promised me?'

'I'm not tired, Elissa, really I'm not. And I want to get it all finished before I go out.' Her cheeks were pink as she added, 'I said I'd look in at the Bains to see the new baby.'

And the new baby's Uncle William, thought Elissa and smiled. 'Then you'd best leave all that till later. I'll be needing the table anyway.'

'There you are,' said Gideon triumphantly. 'Milly's visiting the new little Bain laddie, but I can't because I've nothing to take. So you see why I need a rise, don't you, Ma?'

'If it's Nellie's baby you want it for, whyever didn't you say so?' said Elissa, reaching under her apron and finding a coin. 'There. Wish the wee lad luck with that.'

'Thanks, Ma,' muttered Gideon, looking less than happy. He would have to visit the infant now, have to hand over the coin. Worst of all, his mother knew it.

'If ever you want more, Gideon, for a specific purpose, you have only to ask.' She spoke gently, lovingly, but he felt his cheeks flush and frustration boil up in defiance. He did not want money doled out to him coin by coin as if he was Danny and not to be trusted.

'Oh yes? And have to justify every penny afterwards? I'm a man, Ma, not a child. I need a man's wage.'

'And will have it – when you earn it.' That was his Uncle Samuel, interfering as usual. Why did he have to come in at that crucial point? Gideon was sure he could have worn his mother down eventually, but not with his uncle in the room. Uncle Samuel backed up Elissa unquestioningly, in everything.

Whether it was the usual argument with her over when Gideon Joe

310

would be allowed a share of the profits instead of only a wage, with his gran over when he would stop wasting time with the lads and get a bit of useful book-learning into his head like his sister, or with one of his uncles about who had authority in the house (Gideon Joe considered that as the eldest son of the eldest son, he had more than anyone), Elissa could never remember, but something triggered the showdown on that momentous December day. Words were exchanged, threats uttered, and Gideon slammed out of the house in frustrated fury. He left as an apprentice on the family drifter; and returned hours later, sheepish but excited, with the news that he had signed up as a volunteer for South Africa and the war against the Boers. He would be leaving for the south in two days' time.

'At least they'll treat me like the man I am. Then perhaps when I come back you'll do the same.'

That was the beginning. Or the end. Or both. It did not much matter. The deed was done and could not be undone.

The new war, thousands of miles away in a foreign land, was barely three months old, and had seemed at first much like the others. Not a European conflict and presenting no obvious threat to the fishing on which so many thousands of citizens depended for a living, it was of interest principally as a spectacle to be seen in the Bio-Tableau at the Palace Theatre, or as a diverting feature in the daily newspapers. The continuation of the tramline from Union Street to Ferryhill and the proposed extension to the fishmarket were of more immediate interest: until casualty lists began to appear, with head-lines proclaiming DEAD IN HEAPS. British dead.

Further reports streamed in of major defeats for the Queen's army at Stormberg, Magersfontein, Colenso: places no one had heard of before, but which were now identified in detailed maps in daily newspapers from Land's End to John o' Groats so that even the most provincial-minded citizen could not fail to learn that Queen Victoria's army had been defeated, not once, but several times, by a rabble of rebellious Boers.

Casualty lists of dead and wounded appeared daily in the news-papers and in the resulting outrage patriotic landowners and city gentlemen up and down the country raised private companies of volunteers. Recruiting stations sprang up the length of the land. War Funds were started, and Funds For Those Left Behind.

A lively meeting in Footdee criticised the local Member for his attitude to the war and his conspicuous lack of patriotism. For someone who had volunteered immediately for the Greek war, what was he doing hanging back from this one? On that dour December day, young Gideon stormed out of his house and, via one or two quayside bars, into the vociferous crowd of fishermen who were by that time jeering at the Member for his cowardice. It was a short and

311

natural step when the meeting dispersed for Gideon and a few of the livelier lads, buoyed up by the patriotic fervour they had demanded in vain from their Member, to show him the course of action he should have taken: they marched to the barracks in King Street and, adding a couple of years to their ages where necessary, volunteered for service in the war.

By the time he had sobered up it was too late. Gideon had signed the paper and only time – or death – would release him.

Two days later the party of reservists and recruits of the Gordon Highlanders marched from the Castlehill Barracks to the Joint Station, two pipers at the head of the column and much of the populace of Aberdeen cheering them on their way. At the station the pipers played 'Highland Laddie' as the men piled into the train which would take them to Edinburgh, *en route* for the front. The doors slammed, the whistle blew, and the crowds cheered and waved the train out of sight with much patriotic emotion.

'The fool,' mourned Mary, over and over. 'He had not even the sense to sign up for the navy, instead of being unloaded in a foreign land with all the other innocents to be ambushed and shot at and – '

'Don't!' cried Elissa. 'Don't imagine such horrors. Pray instead that he comes home safe. And soon.'

I am sorry, Joseph. I should have stopped him, but I didn't know until it was too late. He had signed the papers and what could I do? Without you here to help me. Dear God, please watch over him and keep him safe.

Hitherto she had shrunk from the appalling details of this far-away war in an unknown land, but from the day her son left she scoured the daily papers with avid attention for any item however small that might link her to Gideon. She noted the name of his troop ship followed its inexorable progress south, and, trembling with apprehension, made herself read the casualty lists over and over again in case her son's name might be there. She knew it was silly, knew it would be at least ten weeks before he reached the Cape, but she could not help it. As long as his name was not in the list, then Gideon Joe was safe.

If Sarah felt a similar anxiety for Gideon she did not show it: if she mentioned the war at all it was to argue the case for the Boers which as Elissa told her with more than usual sternness, might be an interesting academic point to be discussed with her fellow students in the safe little cocoon of the college, but was hardly appropriate when her own brother was loyally fighting for his Queen and country.

'If women had the vote, there would be no wars,' was Sarah's daring retort which earned her jeers from the male members of the family and a warning frown from her mother. Though during the week Sarah lodged with the Forbeses in Correction Wynd, she came home to the Square at the weekend: but she came home with increasingly subversive ideas, particularly where the rights of women were concerned. And now, apparently, the rights of the Boers.

'Queen Victoria's a woman and it's her war,' pointed out Samuel and all Sarah could think of was to say, with lofty disdain, 'That's different.'

'Why?' demanded Danny. 'Gideon's papers had the Queen's name on them. Gideon showed me. She tells the soldiers to go and fight so why is it different?'

'Because.' Then because it was Danny asking she relented. 'Because the Queen has to do what Parliament tells her and Parliament is full of men who like to fight wars. Or to send other people to fight wars for them.'

'People like Gideon.' Danny was the only one in the Noble household to remain serenely unconcerned by his brother's departure. In Danny's eyes Gideon was a hero, gone to fight for his country, and when he was old enough he, Daniel, would do the same.

'I hope the war lasts till I'm big enough to go too.'

'Thank God he is only eight,' breathed Elissa and old Mary, hearing her, nodded in agreement as her lips moved in silent prayer.

Samuel, seeing Elissa's distress, said, 'Nonsense, Danny. A fine wee sailor like you. You'll be too busy captaining our new steam drifter to have time for a war. With Gideon away at the Cape playing soldiers someone will have to do it, and there's only you.' He winked at his brothers who said, 'Aye, Danny, Sam can't do it. He hasn't the brains. Or Saul. Or Zach. As for Abel . . .'

There was a gleeful roar in which Danny joined. '*His wife won't let him.*'

Abel had recently married a forceful young lady four years older than himself and been removed to her parents' house in South Square. Elissa would have preferred the young couple to stay with the Nobles, for she sorely needed an extra pair of female hands, and whatever else they said about Abel's Bess, she had a good pair of biceps on her and a rare speed with the hooks, but Abel's departure did ease the crowding. Especially with Mary Noble not as strong as she was, and Milly ailing.

That winter was a long one. Towards the end of March, Milly took a cold on the chest which moved deep into her lungs which, in the down-to-earth doctor's words, 'were scarce strong enough to keep her alive at the best of times, being eaten away already with the consumption'. He gave her a month at the most to live. Elissa made up a bed for Milly in the parlour, out of the way of the bustle of the family kitchen, yet close enough to feel part of it, and, delegating all other responsibilities to family or friends, set about nursing her young sister-in-law with all the devotion she had given to her Aunt Sarah, but with ten times the love. Sweet, mild, uncomplaining Milly asked for nothing from anyone, and was overwhelmed by offers of help, gifts of flowers, books, honey for her throat, sweet syrups, and so many visits that Elissa had to ration them lest her patient die of kindness.

'It is the overcrowding,' declared Sarah when she was told the news. The shock had robbed her of coherent thought and she babbled the first thing that came into her head. 'Overcrowding and poverty breed disease.'

She had arrived home on Saturday morning, as usual and unsuspecting, to be met by the news of Milly's illness, and was still in her outdoor clothes. Milly was resting in the parlour, Mary and Elissa were in the kitchen, Mary at the fireside, stirring a special broth she was making for Milly and Elissa ironing at the table. It was always difficult for Sarah on these weekend visits to move back from her student life into the life of the Square and today the shock of her mother's news disastrously mingled the two.

'Poverty?' cried Mary Noble indignantly. 'It isn't enough that my daughter is dying of consumption but you have to tell me to my face that it's because we're poor? And the Nobles with the best house in the Square and the best table? When have you lacked for anything in this house, my girl? Tell me that? Poverty indeed. If that's the sort of rubbish they fill your head with at that college of yours you get it emptied again, quick. And ask for your money back while you're at it. Poverty! My Milly lacked for nothing and nor did you, you ungrateful wee besom. Private lessons for yon gibberish you call Greek. Private lessons for Latin. Money for boarding with townsers when you could just as easy sleep in your own bed at home. And you call that poverty? If my Gideon was here now, or your own father, you wouldn't stand there in your fancy town clothes and – '

'Hush, Mary, hush. Sal meant no harm.' Elissa stood the iron on its heel and put her arm around her mother-in-law's shoulders. 'She is repeating new ideas without thinking, that is all. Sal's fond of Milly and she's had a shock.' She flashed a warning glance at Sarah who looked shamefaced.

'I am sorry, Gran, I didn't mean it,' she said humbly. 'At least, I didn't mean that *we* were poor. For it is certainly true that in many city tenements overcrowding and poor sanitation – '

'That is enough,' interrupted Elissa before poor Sarah could wade even deeper into insult. 'Gran does not want to hear a lecture on the Glasgow slums. She is worried and grieving for Milly who will wake at any minute and certainly does not want to see angry faces or discord. She needs loving reassurance and gentleness, which I know you will give her when you have had time to compose yourself. I

314

know it was a shock for you, Sal dear,' she finished gently, 'but we could not keep it from you any longer.'

'No, Ma. I see that.' Sarah was fond of Milly, who was more of a sister than an aunt to her, and the realisation that she was dying was hard to accommodate. It made Sarah feel old and selfish and guilty for enjoying her own vigorous health and the exciting and always stimulating college life which filled her weeks away from the Square. But by the time Milly woke, Sarah had composed the turmoil of thoughts and emotions enough to carry the tea-tray in to the invalid with almost her usual smile and her usual supply of light-hearted and undemanding chatter, until the next visitor arrived and, saying 'I'll come again soon, Milly', she slipped quietly out of the room.

Friends and family surrounded the invalid with loving visits and she was alone only when she slept, though even then either Mary Noble or Elissa sat beside her bed. Poor Willie Bain called every day and sat tongue-tied, big hands clasped together between big-boned knees, his brown eyes baffled and yearning. Then Mary and Elissa would leave the two together for ten minutes or so before bringing in tea. Willy would drink one awkward cup, mumble his goodbyes and leave, with the never-varying phrase, 'See you tomorrow then, Milly.'

'Let the poor lassie have what pleasure she can,' said her mother to Elissa one April afternoon, as they waited in the kitchen for the simmering kettle to boil. 'She has little enough time left. Sometimes I think she only hangs on to life so she can see that great gawk of a Willie Bain again.'

Elissa, collecting cups and plates for the usual tea-tray, felt her throat choke with emotion. Poor Willie. He might be a 'great gawk' as Mary said, but it was brave and loving of him to come so faithfully. It was lucky the herring season had not begun yet and the men were still at the long-line fishing, in home waters. She hoped they did not have to leave for the herring fishing before ... but she could not formulate that final thought, especially in the wholesome warmth and bustle of the family kitchen. It was bad enough with Gideon away: but the kitchen without Milly was inconceivable. Then it struck her, with heart-jolting force: Milly was a mere five years older than Gideon, more like a sister than an aunt. If Milly could die so young, then ...

'And her such a fragile wee thing,' continued Mary, setting down the newly filled teapot on the cloth-covered tray. 'Always was, right from the cradle. I remember my own ma saying, "You'll never rear that one, Mary," but we did, bless her, and kept her for twenty-one years. My Gideon thought the world of Milly, but soon they'll be together again. Before the week's out, the doctor says.'

Mary's face was bleak with loss, but she took up the tray, composed her face, and returned, bravely smiling, to the sick room. Marvelling at the older woman's composure and unshaken faith, Elissa humbly followed.

Mary Noble sat beside her daughter's bedside, knitting more and more slowly as the life ebbed out of the child. Though Milly would be twenty-two in May, if she lived, she was still a child to her mother and brothers, still a frail little sister in Elissa's eyes. But it soon became plain to everyone, even poor tongue-tied and suffering Willie Bain, that Milly would not live. With dread, Elissa watched the flesh shrink, the eye sockets grow huge and dark, the cheeks flush with unnatural red, the bones of forehead and wrist grow prominent under the parchment skin.

'Keep the younger children away from her if you can,' warned the doctor. 'I know it is not always possible with a large family, but there might be infection and young chests can be weak.'

Elissa did her best, but Milly loved her little nieces and nephews, as she did the children of all her friends in the Square, and it cheered her day to see them, especially Danny. Danny was given the special job of fetching in coal for Auntie Milly's fire and never had to be reminded. Then he would stay to tell her about his school-day or his friends until Elissa removed him with the warning that Auntie Milly was poorly and must not be tired. But in spite of the worried faces, the warning finger on the lips, the bowls of soup which came back almost as full as when they left the kitchen, Danny remained cheerfully confident that his Auntie Milly would get better soon. Even when her strength dwindled till she could scarcely open her eyes or find the breath to speak and Elissa had to lift her head and feed her with a spoon, just as she had done for Aunt Sarah all those years ago. Unlike Aunt Sarah, Milly's weakness did not sharpen her tongue, merely softened it.

'I am sorry, Elissa,' she whispered on an evening in late April, when Elissa held the teaspoon of warm milk to her lips. 'I cannot manage any tonight. Please forgive me. I am sorry to be so much trouble.'

'You are no trouble at all, Milly,' soothed Elissa, fighting back the tears.

'Is Ma there?'

The voice was barely audible, the searching hand suddenly urgent. Elissa flashed a glance at Mary Noble who was out of her seat and at the bedside in a moment. She took the frail hand in both her strong work-hardened ones and said, 'I'm here, Milly love. I'm here.'

With a sigh of contentment, Milly lay back on the pillows, eyes closed. 'I'm so tired, Ma . . .'

When Danny came staggering in with the loaded coal bucket, he crossed the floor with exaggerated caution so as not to make a noise

316

then something in the silence alerted him and he stopped, his eyes wide with fear.

'Is Milly asleep? She didn't say goodnight.'

'No, Danny.' Elissa held out her hand and drew him close against her knee. 'She didn't have time. She . . .'

'Is Auntie Milly dead, like Grandpa was?'

'I am afraid so.' She tried to draw him into her arms to comfort him, but he pulled away, his face creased with fury, and stamped his foot over and over, shouting 'She's not dead, she's not. You're telling me lies.'

Then he flung himself on to the bed and sobbed. After a moment Mary Noble gathered the child up and carried him to her chair where she rocked him to and fro, murmuring some sort of comfort while Elissa stood where she was, beside the bed, looking down at Milly's peaceful face, her own cheeks wet with silent tears.

Danny had cried when his father died, howling his misery in uninhibited grief, and again when they buried old Gideon, but it had not lasted long. Unlike poor Gideon Joe who had shut himself into his room and wept in secret for hours at a time. But Gideon Joe was hundreds of miles away, beyond her care or comfort, in an unknown foreign land. How would they tell him about Milly? She supposed a message could be sent somehow but what good would it do? It would be kinder to write gently herself, after the funeral. Lawyer Forbes would know how to find out the right address. But Zeb must be told – the Mission would do that for her – and Bethany. Bethany had visited only once since her little sister took ill, but she had a right to be informed. Zach or Saul could take a message to Marine Terrace. Then there was Phemy with her family, away north in Buckie. And Sarah. Studies or not, she would need Sarah to help her. And Willie Bain must be told. The poor lad must not hear, like everyone else, second-hand, on the flourishing grapevine of the Square.

She looked to where Mary Noble held Danny in her arms, both weeping, both comforting and grieving together. For the moment they had no need of her. Elissa sank to her knees, said her silent goodbyes to her sister-in-law and closed her own eyes in prayer for Milly's soul. Then she kissed the cool forehead for the last time and slipped quietly out of the room.

In the privacy of the little entrance hall she leaned her back against the closed door of the parlour and let the tears overflow. If only she had someone to comfort her as Joseph would have done. Or Adam. *Adam, my darling, if only I could write to you, pour out my sorrows, but I must not . . . It would not be fair . . .* Why was life so lonely, and so cruel?

But self-pity was a luxury she could not afford. She straightened, brushed a sleeve across her eyes, and with a sigh of desolation summoned the courage to do what must be done.

To Mr Adam Mackenzie Grant c/o the Scott Mackenzie Shipping Company, London. To be forwarded.

Dear Uncle Adam, I am writing, as I promised you I would, to give you news of the family. I know my mother will not write herself to tell you, but I know that, as an honorary member of the family, you would like to be told. My Aunt Milly died yesterday and the house is full of sadness. You met her yourself so you will know what a dear, sweet, loving person she was and how badly we miss her. Especially Ma who has to look after everybody and has no one to look after her since my father died. It is lonely for her and worrying as well since my brother Gideon took it into his head to fight for Queen and Country against the Boers. Not everyone agrees that the war is justified, as you will know, and there is a particular group of the student Liberal Party whose members have most interesting debates about the subject though too many of the university societies are still banned to women. Women have their own groups, in retaliation, and we have debates on all sorts of interesting subjects, including women's suffrage, and the war. But I am also working hard at my studies and I am very grateful for the money you send me for books. The Elissa Downie did really well last season and Ma is already planning to order another steam drifter if the profits are big enough which Uncle Brodie Gibb thinks they might be. If she does, will you come and test it for her like you did before? I will write again soon. Your loving god-daughter Sarah Downie Noble.

In October, Elissa heard from Gideon Joe. From Bloemfontein. It was a short letter, formal and direct.

Dear Mother, and Everyone. We arrived here five days ago, by train, from Cape Town. It is very hot. Some of the men have heat-stroke already. The town's water supply is bad and drinking water is scarce. There has been an outbreak of typhoid in the town but they tell us it is over now. However, we have had to dig many graves since our arrival and it is hard work in the sun. When the new horses arrive we will move again so I hope it will be soon. I hope the family are all well and especially Milly. Your obedient son, Gideon Joseph Noble.

The letter was dated 1st May. Five months ago. The day of Milly's funeral. She wondered if her own letter had taken as long to reach Gideon. Had it reached him at all?

Elissa knew the progress of the campaign by heart. Every day

318

while the men were away at the herring fishing and those left behind went about the usual tasks of their busy lives, she found the time somewhere, between the demands of 'Mary's' and of her household, to read the daily paper: not for the shipping notes or the reports of the herring catches, but for news of what she had dubbed in her own head 'Gideon's war'. Had read of the typhoid epidemic, the thousands of deaths from that cause alone, the hundreds of killed and wounded; the battle to relieve Mafeking, the advance into the Orange Free State; the capture of Johannesburg and Pretoria; had found all these unknown places marked on the helpful ink-drawn maps which the newspapers provided and followed every report of continuing resistance, ambushes, attacks. And though she had seen her son's name nowhere in those daily lists, men did disappear, letters did get lost. Only yesterday there had been mention of an 'unknown soldier' reported missing weeks ago and only now identified and 'presumed dead'.

All that longed-for, disappointing letter told her was that Gideon had been alive five months ago, in a typhoid-ridden town with, if he survived that danger, the prospect of one long march into battle after battle, in an alien country where even the water betrayed them. Gideon who had been brought up at the sea's edge, where the wind blew cold and clean. *Please God keep him safe.*

There were no more letters.

'Gideon never was much of a hand with the pen,' Sarah offered in a brave attempt at reassurance, but her eyes mirrored her mother's anxiety. One of the boys he had volunteered with, a Christie from South Square, had been killed at Ladysmith. Sarah had seen it in one of her mother's newspapers and knew her mother must have seen it too, though she made no mention. Her brother was a pest sometimes and a fool to have volunteered, especially for a war which so many right-thinking people disapproved of, but all the same Sarah did not want her brother shot and especially not by one of the Boers whose cause her college friends defended.

Since Gideon's letter she had changed her mind on that point, as, she acknowledged privately, she had done on many things, but with such a flood of new ideas coming in every day, how could she help it? It disquieted her to hear such apparent subversion from the older students whom she idolised for their intelligence and brilliant conversation. Everyone in the Square was all for teaching those Boers a lesson, the sooner the better, so their brave lads could come home again. But when she tentatively said as much to her college friends, she was jeered as a jingoist and even, patronisingly, 'an ignorant little Tory'. This last insult came from Ben and was doubly hurtful. Ben Lucas was in his final year, like Adelaide's brother Thomas and the others she had met on that long-ago day of the Queen's Diamond

Jubilee, and though Sarah was now a student, as he was, with a scarlet academic gown and a black trencher, he still treated her like a schoolgirl to be teased or patronised or patted metaphorically on the head now and then, out of kindness. As he was doing now.

They had all been attending the Literary Society meeting, as they did most Friday evenings, but the lecture room was emptying fast as, the meeting over, students dispersed for home or their digs or one or other of the city hostelries. Only a handful remained, unwilling to break up the camaraderie of the meeting, and most of them were what Sarah privately thought of as 'Adelaide's set'. She and Adelaide were Arts students and most of their classes were in King's College in the Old Town, which meant a good half-hour's walk every morning and the same back again. The Science classes were held in Marischal College in Broad Street, just off the Castlegate, but depending what course was being taken many students had classes in both places and the walk between the two was nothing. Men and women students of all disciplines belonged to the Literary Society, one of the few that admitted women, and their meeting on a Friday evening was a grand way to round off the week and to meet friends, especially if one could persuade the janitor not to lock up the moment the meeting was over, but to let them linger on 'for informal discussion' as Ben Lucas had solemnly put it to the janitor in question, adding a coin in the palm to help the man's understanding. But on this occasion, as far as Sarah was concerned, the informality had gone too far.

'If I am ignorant it is not for want of seeking information!' she flared, hot-faced with shame and fury. 'But any questions we poor "ignorant" females try and ask are laughed aside as not worth answering. We even have to sit in separate seats with a row of empty chairs to keep us at a safe distance from Your Precious Lordships. Now I know why. It's because you're so pig-ignorant yourselves you're afraid we might find out if we come too close. In debate, we are not allowed to speak in case we show you up for the bone-headed puffballs that you are. And you have the nerve to call me an ignorant little Tory.'

'Withdraw the "little" Ben, before she wallops you,' called one of his friends, which incensed Sarah afresh.

'Just the sort of juvenile wit to be expected from an overgrown schoolboy. Run home to your nanny, and pull the wings off flies.'

'Somebody tell me, what did I say?' pleaded Ben, rolling his eyes heavenwards in a pantomime of innocent bafflement.

'Nothing,' retorted Sarah, scarlet with fury. 'As usual. All you ever do is mouth the same thoughtless platitudes you accuse me of, only yours are gleaned third-hand from the Liberal Party. Just because they are different from mine doesn't mean they are superior. Not if you can't support them with valid argument anyway. And you can't. You can't string two coherent sentences together to save your life!'

'Phew,' whistled Ben softly. 'Will you be my campaign manager when I stand for Parliament?'

'I'd rather pelt you with rotten eggs from the crowd, you arrogant . . . tortoise!'

She had meant to imply his deliberate blindness to reality, but her choice of epithet convulsed the room and after a moment's still-simmering fury, Sarah joined in the laughter. But not for long. The subject was too important to her, her feeling of humiliation too strong. Abruptly she stood up and pushed her way to the door.

'Sarah!' cried Adelaide. 'Where are you going?'

'Home.' The door slammed behind her.

'Now look what you've done, you idiot,' said Adelaide, glaring at Ben. 'You always take things too far. Can't you see she's upset?' She snatched up her hat and hurried after Sarah.

'I'll have to go too,' said Thomas. 'I promised the mater I'd see the ladies home.'

'We'll come with you,' said half a dozen voices and the informal meeting dispersed.

Ben caught up with her at the top of Upperkirkgate, a trim, neat figure walking too fast, head held unnaturally high. She did not look at him, nor at Adelaide who arrived a moment later with a trail of friends.

'I am sorry,' said Ben humbly, adapting his own stride to hers. 'Please forgive me. I did not mean to offend or upset you.' When she made no answer, but strode on, staring resolutely ahead, he took hold of her hand and drew it under his arm. At least she did not withdraw it and after a careful moment he said, 'That is better. I was afraid you might trip and fall. Or lose your way. The streets are annoyingly dark when there is no moon and gas light is a poor substitute.'

'You cannot steer a ship by gas light,' said Sarah, still not looking at him though the tension had eased in her voice. 'That's what my grandfather used to say. He hated anything new. I think he was afraid of what he did not understand.'

'Like all of us,' said Ben with relief. 'Me now, I don't understand the stars or how one can possibly steer by them. I know the Great Bear, of course, and Orion, and I can sometimes spot Cassiopeia on a good day, or do I mean night? But if I had to steer by them I'd be lost in no time.'

'No, you wouldn't. It is easy when you know how.'

'Like so many things. But, you see, I don't know how. Perhaps you could teach me some day?'

There was silence, except for the sound of their feet on the cobblestones, a burst of distant laughter from the direction of St Nicholas Street and the voices of Adelaide and the others, some way behind them. Then Sarah's last resistance snapped and she accepted the olive branch.

'I might. If you will talk to me properly, without teasing and condescending as if I could not possibly understand. I might not understand even then, but I would like you at least to give me the chance.'

'Have I really been so insufferable? I am truly sorry.'

'It's not your fault, I suppose,' said Sarah thoughtfully. 'You see, where I come from, women are not silly little decorative creatures to be pampered and teased and indulged by clever men who go out into the world and make money. Women work too and their men depend on them for their livelihood as well as for their domestic comforts. It is a different world from your world. You could not be expected to understand.'

When he didn't answer, she said quietly, 'Don't think I have not noticed how no one asks me about my family. They are afraid I might admit I am a fisherman's daughter and they will not know where to look or what to say. My mother was a herring-gutter before she married. They would faint with embarrassment if I told them that. Adelaide knows, of course, and her mother, but "we do not talk about it".' Here Sarah gave a shrewd imitation of Mrs Forbes's distressed gentility. 'But I am proud of my family, and of my mother.' She might as well have added 'So there!' for the defiance was plain.

Ben grinned in the darkness. 'I would like to meet your mother. She sounds a formidable woman.'

'Why do you say that?' Sarah realised as soon as she had spoken, but it was too late.

'You know why, Sarah Noble. She must be, to have raised a daughter like you.'

Sarah was glad of the darkness for she felt her cheeks blush at the compliment. If it was a compliment. She turned her head in suspicion, but he was looking straight ahead, his face expressionless.

Before she could think of anything at all to say, they were in Correction Wynd with the railed wall of St Nicholas churchyard on their right and on their left the small-windowed, many-storeyed buildings which included the Forbes house.

'I would like to visit your family one day,' said Ben, as they neared the doorstep. 'Would you invite me?'

But the thought of Mrs Forbes and her inevitable prickles of disapproval had put Sarah on the defensive, as it always did.

'You sound as if they are exhibits in a zoo.'

'That is unfair, Miss Noble. You take umbrage at the slightest

322

opportunity. I had thought you a fair-minded person, without prejudice, but apparently I was wrong.'

Before Sarah could answer, the house door opened and Mrs Forbes herself stood in the doorway.

'Adelaide. What time is this to be coming home? I hope Sarah did not delay you. We keep respectable hours in this house as I have told you many times.'

'Yes, you have, Mamma,' said Adelaide cheerfully. 'But you see it is not late at all and the meeting was so interesting. We were discussing Greek tragedy. The word as you know comes from the Greek for goat-song which is another source of debate in itself, but we were arguing about whether the *Oresteia* can be said to have derived from the Homeric hymn cycle, or vice versa. You see, Mamma,' she continued gleefully, knowing her mother didn't understand a word of her impromptu babble, 'it depends whether you believe in a single authorship or in a combination of – '

'Yes, yes,' interrupted Mrs Forbes quickly. 'All very interesting no doubt, but you should have been home half an hour ago. Goodnight all of you. Not you, Thomas. You come inside. It is late enough already.'

'I will not be long, Mamma,' he said, with a cheerful wave, edging backwards the way he had come. 'We are just going round to Arthur's.'

Ben whispered in Sarah's ear, 'You see? I like zoos. And I'll visit yours any time you invite me.'

This time, she turned her head and smiled. But afterwards, in the attic room she shared with Adelaide, when they had doused the candles and their murmured recollections of the day's events had died at last into drowsy silence, Sarah knew that she would not invite him. At least, not yet. The gulf between her family and his was too wide and for all his friendliness and open-minded interest, she knew he would not understand. How could he, when all he knew was the comfortable, middle-class, professional life of confidence and comfort which he and all his friends had known from the cradle?

He was a townser, she reminded herself, relishing the childhood insult of the Square with all its sneering pity and hostility. But behind the condescension, she realised, there had always been an undercurrent of envy and unease. The townsers led a different life: a life barred to the Footdee folk, who were too fiercely proud to want to join it anyway, but a life with tantalising glimpses of novelty and riches, freedoms and ease. Aunt Bethany had shouldered her way into the fringes of that world, though Sarah knew her aunt would never truly belong, and, she supposed, she herself had a toe-hold now that she was a member of the university. She knew she was not the only

323

working-class girl student, but most of those were from the country, from a farming background, and had little in common with her. Besides, they were not in Adelaide's 'set'.

Lying in her coom-ceiled attic room with its tiny skylight, which reminded her comfortingly of home in the Square, Sarah reflected that there were similar rooms in farm cottages and fishermen's cottages the length of the land as well as in the town houses of professional men and the same stars shone through each skylight, whether rich or poor. The thought was a reassuring one.

I might ask him one day, she thought as she snuggled deeper under the bedcovers. When I am sure he wants to come for the right reason.

Sarah's college friends increasingly worried Elissa. It was all very well for Sarah to go to the university, laudable for her to want to be a teacher – Elissa was proud to have a student daughter, as Joseph would have been, and would be ten times more proud if she achieved her aim – but Elissa did not want her daughter to grow away from the life of the Square. Did not want her to be beguiled into a different, alien life where her own family could play no part. It was bad enough to have lost Gideon Joe, for though she had heard no news one way or the other she felt in her heart that even if her son did come back one day, he would not be the same Gideon Joe who, whistling with bravado, had swaggered out of the house a year ago, to march to the railway station with all the other thoughtless young lads on that awful December morning of '99.

Though Adelaide Forbes was a delightful and interesting girl, some of Sarah's other friends sounded decidedly suspect. Too full of book-learning and ideas that had no connection with real life. At least amended Elissa in the interests of fairness, for what did she know about the lives of townsfolk, no connection with the lives of her family and friends in the Square. Sarah who had been a friendly and gregarious girl in childhood, had brought none of her new friends home to meet her family and Elissa began to wonder uneasily if perhaps her daughter was ashamed of her home. Or it may be only that time was too short, she reassured herself. For Sarah always brought home a mound of books to study and was up till all hours working at the kitchen table when everyone else had gone to bed.

At least, her daughter was used to that. Which made Sarah's accounts of this Women's Debating Society of hers all the more baffling. Arguing about the rights of women to a vote, about whether women were fit to hold public office, about 'man for the field, woman for the hearth' as if it had not occurred to anyone that men and women could work together. As for women being too frail . . . Which of Sarah's new friends knew what it was like to go to bed at three

324

and rise at five? To knit and scrub and cook and wash for a family of twelve? To bait hooks and mend nets, gut and clean and pickle and smoke the fish the menfolk caught, or gut and salt and pack into barrels, to handle the family finances and sell the family fish? And as well as all that, to find time for loving? Which of them lived with fear as a constant companion? Fear for their fathers, husbands, brothers, sons? Which of them could do all those things *and* study for the university as Sarah had had to do? Those girls didn't live in the real world. At least Sarah knew the difference between one life and another. Why didn't she explain?

But Sarah and her friends were too preoccupied with what they called Women's Suffrage to see that women like old Maggie Bain and her friend Bessie Guyan, even the twittering Ina Duthie, together with most of the women in the Square, had all the power they needed already, where it mattered. Sarah had only to look at her own grandmother to see that. Mary Noble was a true matriarch who kept the family purse (or had done, till her husband died and she handed over to Elissa), oversaw the family business, and in her husband's frequent absences at sea, ran the family home, as did all the other women in the Square. Why should they concern themselves with a Parliament five hundred miles away, in England?

'Because,' argued Sarah, on that grey Saturday morning, 'that is where the ultimate laws are made. By men.' They were in the family kitchen which was bright with warmth from the cheerful fire and an appetising smell of fresh griddle scones and butter sweetened the air.

'The ultimate laws,' corrected Elissa quietly, pouring tea from the earthenware pot, 'are made by God. You should remember that.'

'I do. But I'm talking of the laws of the land.' She took the teacup her mother had just filled and handed it to her grandmother. 'And I don't believe God intended families to crowd into one damp, insanitary room so that the children could die of dysentery or consumption. Men arrange that so that they can line their own pockets with the profits of cheap labour.'

'I thought you went to college to learn how to be a teacher, Sal,' put in Brodie Gibb, who had called round to discuss the progress of the second steam drifter and had lingered to drink tea and talk companionably with old Mary and Elissa. He helped himself to a third and fourth scone from the plate Sarah offered him. 'Not to be a revolutionary.'

'I did. And I have not changed my mind.' She paused fractionally before finishing, with a touch of bravado, 'But new ideas are interesting. Don't you agree, Brodie?'

Her uncle looked at her in astonishment. Then at Elissa, whose eyes reflected his own surprise. 'I am your uncle, Sal, not your brother. I prefer to be addressed that way.'

'I know, but . . . but surely now that I am eighteen we are on an equal footing.'

'Equal? I am three times your age, lass.'

'Maybe, but we are both adults, so there is no longer any need for hierarchical forms of address.'

'There may not be for you, lass, but I assure you there are for your mother and me. Kindly remember that.'

'Sorry, Uncle Brodie.' Sarah had the grace to look shamefaced. 'I was just trying it out. You see, Adelaide calls her parents by their Christian names . . .'

'Not to their faces, I hope?'

'. . . and so do lots of others,' continued Sarah quickly. In truth the distinction had not occurred to her. 'It is the modern thing to do.'

'Modern or not, I forbid it in this house,' said her mother, but her smile was an indulgent one. 'All these new-fangled ideas. I don't know what they'll think of next. But I do know that if I had tried such a thing I'd have had a sore behind for my pains.'

'Aye, lass,' grinned Mary Noble, from her usual chair at the fireside. 'Your Aunt Sarah was a stickler for discipline and you'd have got a right skelping. So would Joseph. My Gideon wouldn't put up with disrespect from anyone, least of all from his own children. You remember that, Sal.'

'Yes, Gran.'

'There you are,' beamed Mary Noble. 'She learns quick, that lass. I was afraid she would call me Mary to my face.'

'Oh no, Gran!' cried Sarah in horror. 'I wouldn't dream of . . .' Then she stopped, her face reddening, as the inconsistency struck home.

'So the equal footing is sometimes unequal, is it?' teased Mary, then, when Sal frowned, searching for some sort of answer, she held out her hand to her granddaughter with a smile.

'Come here, lass, and give your old gran a kiss.'

Smiling, Sarah took her grandmother's hand and let herself be drawn close, then kissed her on the cheek.

'Sorry, Gran. It's just that the men have a Political Society and a Debating Society where they discuss all sorts of things, but we women are not allowed to join. So we have our own groups instead and everyone suggests things to talk about. Not about fishing or shipping or exports, but politics, history, philosophy. All sorts of things. And it's all so interesting and exciting.'

'I know, lass. But now you are at home do you think you could forget all these college ideas and be my own Sal again, just for today?'

'I'll take you to the shipyard to see how the new drifter's coming along if you like,' offered Uncle Brodie. 'Your ma and I were just going.'

'Can I come too ?' yelled Danny, erupting out of nowhere in a gust of exuberance.

Elissa looked questioningly at Sal, who shrugged.

'I suppose he'll have to tag along, the little pest.' But she ruffled Danny's already tousled hair and grinned, all intellectual argument forgotten.

They were walking along York Street in the direction of the great double doors of Hall, Russell's when Brodie Gibb said, 'By the way, Elissa. Did I tell you about my new partner?'

'No,' she said, unsuspecting. The air was crisp and clean under a gusty, cloud-scudding sky, and there were white cat's-paws on the harbour waters. Gulls tossed like snowflakes above the fish quays and in York Street the hard ground echoed with the sound of their sensibly shod feet.

'I'm having the new sign made specially,' said Brodie. 'Royal blue and gold with a winged horse for an emblem. That's for speed of delivery. It ought to be a train by rights, but a winged horse looks better on a sign. The Pegasus Company. Old Easton Sinclair was shrewd enough to keep the principal parts of his empire separate, especially in the last year of his life, so that son of his couldn't automatically milk the lot, and when Easton died and Hugh tried to get his hands on this venture and that, he found he couldn't. And why not? Because they didn't belong to Sinclair's any longer.'

'Who did they belong to?' asked Elissa, though she knew the answer before it came.

'To me and my partner. Or if they didn't then, they do now. To the new firm of Scott, Mackenzie and Gibb.'

Mr Scott. 'I decided to ruin him and I'm almost there.' Who else could Brodie's new partner be but Adam? Elissa's head, with her heart, was in turmoil. But it was Sarah who asked, 'So Mr Scott is your partner, Uncle Brodie? But he lives in Australia. How can he be in two places at once?'

'He travels,' said Brodie with a wink. 'And sometimes he travels as far north as Aberdeen. Not often, but now and again, just to see what's what and to keep me up to scratch.'

'When will he be coming to Aberdeen next?' Again Sarah put the question Elissa could not bring herself to ask.

'Soon, my dear,' said Brodie with a gleam of satisfaction. 'I hope, very soon. There are papers to be signed, formalities to go through. Mackenzie Holdings has been a major shareholder in the firm for some years, a sleeping partner, as it were, in London, and has been building up quite a sizeable stock. Now it turns out that Mackenzie and Scott are one and the same person and between us we plan to put Sinclair out of business once and for all. And not a jot Sinclair can do about it.'

327

He laughed aloud, then frowned as a thought struck him.

'But you'll need to keep good watch, Lissa lass, and keep your wits about you. He doesn't know the whole of it yet, but when he does, I reckon Sinclair will not take defeat without a protest. And knowing him, he'll take it out on those as can't fight back. He's not forgiven you, lass, for that business way back, so be on guard. Ah, here we are at Hall, Russell's. I'll have a word with them, too, if you like. Tell them to keep their eyes open. As for you, Sal, you take good care of yourself. He always did have a predatory eye for the young and vulnerable and you're a nice-looking lass. Like your ma.'

CHAPTER 28

The news broke a week later. Sinclair had borrowed money against all six of his trawlers and at least two of them had been pledged twice over. The man who held the promissory notes had decided to collect his debt.

The man known as Mr Scott, full-bearded and severe, arrived at the office on Waterloo Quay, with appropriate timing, on the first day of the New Year, together with a pair of bailiffs, two nervous-looking police officers, Lawyer Forbes and his assistant and all the paraphernalia of the debt-collector's art.

Hugh Sinclair, naturally, was not in the office and nor was anyone else, it being New Year's Day. But a small consideration like that could not stop the processes of law. As everyone agreed, Sinclair was no doubt still sleeping it off at his club and one of the policemen was sent to fetch him. The other, under protest, broke the door down.

'After all,' as Lawyer Forbes pointed out to him, 'the office does, to all intents and purposes, belong to this gentleman here.'

Once inside, the said Mr Scott inspected the premises: clerks' office and accounts office at the back, one large room at the front the panelled door of which proclaimed *Director* in large gilt letters with, underneath in forbidding black, *Private*. He opened the door and stepped inside. Stale air, tobacco smoke, a smell like a much-used public bar. The shutters were closed on the two tall windows and at a nod from Mr Scott one of the bailiff's men set about opening them.

'And a window, if you can. The air in here is foul.'

Pale winter light flooded in through the unshuttered windows to reveal the imposing portrait above the mantelpiece on the inner wall, an oil-painting in a heavy gilt frame of an impressive figure in civic regalia and a neat, grey beard who turned on them a forbidding, godlike stare.

'Alexander Christie Sinclair,' said Lawyer Forbes in the respectful tones of someone in the presence of royalty. 'Old Easton Sinclair's father. What he would have to say about this sorry business does not bear thinking about.'

'I can imagine,' said Mr Scott, with a frown. He cast his eye over

329

the remaining walls. 'What pictures used to hang over those lighter patches?'

All heads turned to study the paler rectangles which marred the heavy green wallpaper at regular intervals.

'Mostly ships,' said Lawyer Forbes. 'If my memory serves me aright. One or two of them were rather good. *The Battle of Trafalgar. The Cutty Sark.* That sort of thing. And there might even have been a small Turner among them. One would assume that as they hung on company walls they were company assets, but of course they may have been owned privately.'

Mr Scott did not trouble to answer. No doubt it was the lawyer's job to point out the various aspects of the case, but it was obvious to him as to everyone else that the pictures had been sold to raise cash, whether for private or for company use did not much matter. He turned his attention to the rest of the room.

The oak refectory table which took up a large part of the room had a dusty, unused look about it. The blotters were yellowing at the edges, the ink-wells dry, the chairs which were pushed in against the table on three sides looked as if they had taken root in the neglected floorboards. But on the fourth side, facing the door, a high-backed chair with carved wooden arms was pushed back at an angle, as if its owner had recently left it, and a litter of papers, an open ledger and two or three accounts books, sprinkled liberally with cigar ash, were strewn over the adjacent table top. There was also a brandy bottle, empty, and an overturned glass.

Mr Scott picked up the glass by the stem, between finger and thumb, and handed it to the lawyer's assistant who happened to be nearest.

'Get rid of that somewhere. And the bottle. No wonder the place reeks like a monkey's armpit.' Then he sat down in the director's chair, scooped the papers together into a tidy heap and began to go through them, glancing over each one before passing it to Lawyer Forbes. 'While we wait, we might as well make good use of our time. I don't suppose the fellow is in any hurry to get here.'

He wasn't. It was two hours before Hugh Sinclair arrived and then under protest and in a predictably villainous temper. They heard his oaths when he was still in the Shiprow and the slam of the street door below them made the whole building shake.

'Who the devil are you? Get out of that chair before I kick you out, you filthy blackguard. Shift!' he hissed between teeth clenched on the pain of a skull-splitting headache. 'Before I whip you to shreds.' He lashed the predictable Malacca cane down on to the table, sent the papers scattering with a vicious back-hand swipe and raised his hand to strike again. Two police officers and a bailiff grabbed his arm while another hooked an arm round his throat from behind.

'Easy, Mr Sinclair, easy,' said one of his captors, while Mr Scott sat unmoved and unmoving in the director's chair, his unwavering eyes fixed on Sinclair's face.

'It would be wise to hand over your cane, Mr Sinclair,' dared Lawyer Forbes.

'Unless you particularly want to appear before the magistrates on a charge of unprovoked assault,' added Mr Scott in a voice of calm reason which inflamed Sinclair to further fury.

'Unprovoked? When a scurvy villain breaks into my office and steals my private papers? You deserve to be whipped from here to kingdom come and I intend to do it.' He fought and twisted and lunged, but to no avail. The length of the solid table still separated him from the interloper who continued to stare at him with that infuriating, unwavering gaze.

'Your office? I think not.' Mr Scott retrieved the nearest of the scattered papers, lifted it and let it fall from his opened hand. 'Worthless. Except as evidence of your imminent bankruptcy. You see, Mr Sinclair, you have borrowed far too much money and unfortunately, in your arrogance, you have neglected to pay any of it back. I do not like that. It is my money you have borrowed and I am tired of paying for your cigars and brandy and loose women and gambling debts. You can pay for your own profligacy in future. And you can pay me back what you owe me.'

'I owe you nothing, you miserable drunken oaf!'

'I am afraid that you do. And it is you who are the miserable drunken oaf. Or if you aren't miserable yet, you will be. When I tell you that I own all your lavish promissory notes, with your pledges of this trawler and that trawler, and even, I see from my records, your last remaining shares in your father's company. In fact, Mr Sinclair, it is you who are the interloper here, not me. And before you fume and swear and threaten your usual arrogant vengeance, I will tell you that I have worked and planned for years to enjoy this moment. Ever since a certain evening in a certain curing yard in Gremista?'

There was a sudden silence in the room. Sinclair had stopped all struggle and was staring fixedly at his adversary, trying to see past the disguise of the unkempt beard and sunburnt, weatherbeaten face.

'Perhaps I should introduce myself,' said Mr Scott softly. 'These gentlemen here know me as plain Mr Scott, but that was a precaution on my part, knowing your capacity for remembering names. But the need for secrecy is past. I am Adam Grant, of Melbourne, Australia. You very kindly arranged my passage there, as I am sure you will recall?'

Sinclair turned the colour of rancid milk and when at last he tried to speak, no sound emerged.

'I am not surprised that you are speechless,' said Adam. 'If I were

331

you, I would remain that way until you have something useful to say. But before you throw your contrite self upon my mercy, as I am sure you are about to do, I will tell you that I intend to be lenient. Naturally I will take over the company and the company's shipping in its entirety, with the lease of this building and all its contents. Unfortunately, that will still leave a debt outstanding. However, I intend to, let us say, "lend" you that money to buy a small annuity which, with care and prudence, should support you in an honest if more penny-pinching style of life. Lawyer Forbes has already made the arrangements.' Here he nodded towards the lawyer who cleared his throat and consulted a paper in his hand.

'The payment will be made to you, via your bank, Mr Sinclair, on the first of every month, always supposing that you release all papers, documents, goods and chattels and vacate these premises without further hindrance or objection, now or in the future. The payment will be terminated immediately and without notice if you attempt in any way to harm either my client Mr Adam Grant or Mrs Elissa Noble or any member of his or her families or their property, livelihood, goods or chattels. In such an eventuality, my client will immediately seek repayment of all outstanding debts, with interest calculated as from today.'

'My advice to you, Sinclair,' said Adam Grant with a grin, 'is to behave yourself and go abroad. Money goes so much further on the Continent. Try Monte Carlo. Who knows? You might even win.'

But Sinclair had found his voice. 'Adam Grant. I remember you, you scum of the earth. Prison was too good for you. I should have had you hanged, and your doxy with you. But don't think you'll get away with this, either of you. I'll get even with you one day. I will make you suffer till you beg me for mercy.'

'Take note, officer,' said Adam. 'The fellow is uttering menaces. Note the names of all witnesses, with time, place and date. And I believe that sword-stick constitutes part of the estate which now belongs to me. Take it off him, will you, before he kills someone with it, and relieve him of any keys, though naturally I shall have the locks changed immediately. One cannot be too careful. Goodbye, Mr Sinclair.'

'*May you rot in hell.*'

The Noble household was holding open house, as usual at the turning of the year. Hogmanay had passed in a constant ebb and flow of visitors and, though many had not left till well into the small hours, more were expected today. Elissa had lit the parlour fire before her first, early morning cup of tea, in order to have the room nicely aired and warmed through for the expected visitors, and the kitchen fire had been built generously high for the boiling of kettles and cooking pots and the heating of griddles. Then she had whisked round both rooms, removing dust and debris from the previous night till all was spick and span again. The house had been scoured and dusted, polished and swept from top to bottom in the preceding week; brass gleamed, glass shone, wood smelt aromatically of beeswax and the table linen had been starched and pressed to even old Mary's satisfaction.

'We can't have folk coming in here and finding fault,' she had grumbled when Sal had suggested it wasn't necessary to go to quite so much trouble. 'There's that wife of William Downie's for a start, always pretending to be frail and meek and then coming out with some poisonous remark about dust on the poker, or fly-spots on the window-glass. And old Bessie Guyan's no better and her own house not fit to keep a pig in.'

Sal did not answer. The mention of her Uncle William had, as always, subdued her. She had seen him only once since she went to college and on that occasion he had hoped, sanctimoniously, that she would not let overweening pride and ambition lead her astray. Then he had recommended, for all the world as if he were the Minister himself, a day's fasting and humility at least once a week, to remind her of her true station in life. As a fisherman's 'acknowledged daughter'.

Suddenly on that New Year morning, the phrase came back to her with all its disturbing undertones. One day, when she was brave enough, she would ask Uncle William what he had meant. But not today. Today was for enjoyment and laughter. Everyone would come calling at some time or another: Uncle Tom and his family, Uncle Davie and his family, a string of Noble relatives of one kind or another, friends from the Square, everyone. Only her brother Gideon would be absent, Gideon who should have first-footed them at midnight, though Uncle Samuel had done it well enough. She wondered what Gideon was doing, and where he was? Then forgot even that worry in the bustle of the first guests' arrival.

Several of the Bain family, William Downie and his wife Katrine, assorted friends of Samuel and his brothers, followed by Brodie Gibb, 'wee' Georgie, and Aunt Bethany, larger than ever in purple brocade with an ostrich feather in her bonnet and a collar and muff of black astrakhan.

'See this,' she said, thrusting the muff under Sarah's nose. 'That's fur from Russian lambs, that is. Real expensive.'

'Poor lambs,' said Sarah, more to annoy her aunt than for any other reason.

'Rubbish,' retorted Bethany. 'Astrakhan's high fashion. All the best folk in London wear it. If they can afford it.' She looked triumphantly

333

over the assembled company, who couldn't rustle up a piece of fur between them, let alone a rare and curly black kind from Russia. 'I'll maybe hand it on to you, Sarah, when I'm tired of it. Fashion's always changing and it looks real dowdy to wear last season's clothes.'

'Thank you, Aunt Bethany,' said Sarah, straight-faced, and winked at her mother behind Bethany's back. 'Would you like to put your wrap and muff in the bedroom?'

'No, I would not. How could folk see it if I took it off? Besides, it's awful chilly in the parlour. It always was a nasty, damp kind of a room. I mind the day of your ma's wedding when you was – '

'Sarah,' interrupted her mother. 'Come here, quick. You see those people coming across the Square? Are they anything to do with you?'

Through the rapidly misting window-glass Sarah saw a bunch of some half a dozen young men, arms over each other's shoulders, reeling and weaving in a meandering course towards them. A snatch of one of the bawdier student songs came clearly over the crisp air and Sarah prayed suddenly and with unholy fervour that her Uncle William would not hear. It was a futile prayer.

'I think . . .' Sarah swallowed. 'Yes, Ma. They are students from the college. Though why they are coming here I cannot . . .'

'Sarah!' they sang in wavering unison. 'Little Miss Sarah! Come out and give us a New Year kiss.'

Sarah cringed in shame and would have sent them all packing had not her Uncle William spoken first.

'Disgraceful debauchery. I knew it. I saw it all along. Didn't I warn you of this, Elissa, years ago? But would you listen? Oh no. You and your paramour laughed in my face. But now you see the truth of my words. There, before you, in this disgraceful display of lewdness, drunkenness and . . . and . . .'

But the rabble had reached the house.

'Happy New Year, one and all,' roared a voice from the doorway and Ben Lucas, Thomas Forbes, and several assorted friends in various stages of drunkenness tumbled into the room behind him. Ben held an unstoppered whisky bottle in one hand and with beaming generosity offered it to the nearest man. 'Here you are, sir. Drink my health and I'll drink yours.'

For a moment Sarah thought her uncle would explode with outrage, but when he spoke it was with cold and concentrated venom. 'Get out of this house, you drunken, profligate scum.'

Suddenly Sarah's eyes blazed with an equal fury. 'This is not your house, Uncle William. How dare you decide who may or who may not come into it. We keep open house here and welcome all comers, even sour-faced, mean-spirited, unchristian killjoys like you.' Deliberately, she turned her back on her apoplectic uncle and took hold of

Ben's hand. 'Come in, Ben, all of you. Ma, this is Ben from the college, and I think you know Adelaide's brother Thomas and – '

'Elissa!' ordered William in a voice of thunder. 'Are you going to allow your daughter to – '

'Do be quiet, William,' interrupted Elissa. 'Can't you see you are embarrassing everyone? And Sarah is quite right. It is not your house.'

'I knew it. I knew it all along. Blood will out. Immorality. Fornication. Drunkenness and sin. But when the next bastard child is born don't come to me for help. Katrine, we have stayed long enough in this den of vice.' He grabbed his wife by the forearm and propelled her forcibly outside into the Square. 'Wine is a mocker, sir,' he roared at the astonished Ben. 'Strong drink is raging.' Then turned on his heel and strode home in dudgeon, pulling his wife half off her feet behind him.

'Phew,' said Ben, fanning his face with an empty dinner plate. 'Who was the hell-fire and damnation fellow? A friend of yours?'

'My uncle,' mumbled Sarah, blushing. Then, remembering the cause of the whole affair, she said, 'And what do you think you are doing, Ben Lucas, reeling in here at this respectable hour uninvited and obviously as pickled as a cran of herrings?'

'We,' said Adelaide's brother Thomas with the careful pronunciation of the very drunk indeed, 'are paying a social call on our dear friend and fisherlass . . .' He had great difficulty with that word, Sarah noted with bleak satisfaction. 'Sarah.' Having managed a whole sentence with comparative success he promptly subsided into unconsciousness in the nearest chair.

'We have been up all night,' explained Ben, beaming benevolence on all around him. 'Have a drink,' and he offered his whisky bottle to Sarah.

Elissa intercepted it. 'In that case, coffee would be far more appropriate. Or tea. With a good slab of plain bread and cheese. Sarah will see to it, won't you dear? And don't worry about your unorthodox welcome, Ben, if I may call you Ben? My brother is not used to young people, having none of his own. You are all most welcome. How is your mother, Thomas?' But Thomas was patently and noisily asleep. 'Oh well,' shrugged Elissa, smiling. 'It is not important. Now, while we wait for Sarah's ministrations, who would you like to meet?'

But they were not to be allowed a choice. A female galleon in shimmering purple brocade and what looked like a hundredweight of astrakhan fetched up against them, baring a generous set of teeth in a flirtatious smile.

'So you are one of Sal's college friends, are you? She never tells me nothing about you, but then with her having to work among the fish

335

when she's any spare time she's no time for leisure, like me. What's your name? I maybe know your parents, with me meeting so many important town folk one way or another. We've a box at the theatre, see, and – '

'This is my sister-in-law, Mrs Gibb,' interrupted Elissa. 'I am afraid I cannot introduce you, Ben, except as Ben.'

'Ben Lucas,' supplied the young man and extended his hand. Bethany took it and held on to it, looking coquettishly into its owner's face.

'Lucas,' she simpered. 'I'm not just sure, but maybe . . . would I have met your ma at one of they charity mornings for the Boer war?'

'I doubt it, madam. My mother died many years ago. My father and I have a housekeeper.'

'Well, I wouldna have met her,' declared Bethany, releasing Ben's hand. 'We don't meet that kind of folk, Brodie and me.'

Sarah, to her renewed mortification, arrived with a trayload of suitable refreshments just in time to hear this outrageous statement. Deliberately she pushed between her aunt and her friend, using the tray as a barrier.

'Brodie Gibb?' said Ben with surprise. 'The other half of what used to be Sinclair and Gibb?'

'Aye, that's my Brodie,' said Bethany, over her niece's shoulder. 'Hurry up with that tray, Sal. You're stopping me talking to your friends.'

That, thought Sarah with feeling, is exactly what I am trying to do. But there was worse to come. At that moment a flurry of movement at the door alerted Elissa who, with a murmured excuse, went to greet the new arrival, whoever it might be.

In the doorway stood a clean-shaven, neatly barbered, sun-tanned man of around forty, in a well-cut jacket and trousers, dazzling white shirt with gold cuff-links and, looped across the neat buff waistcoat, a heavy watch chain, also of gold. A look of triumph lit his handsome face.

'Happy New Year, Elissa,' he said and kissed her, decorously, on the cheek. 'May I come in and wish my god-daughter the same?'

Before Elissa could find the words to answer, or still the furious pounding of her heart, a voice rang out loud and clear across the throng.

'Bless me if it isn't Adam Grant! Large as life and twice as handsome.' Crowing with delight Bethany thrust through the crowd to throw her arms around the newcomer and aim her greedy, red-rouged lips at his unwilling mouth.

He jerked away his head with a second to spare and the scarlet smear daubed his cheek while he peered through the maze of ostrich feather in search of rescue.

336

'Come in, Adam. Sarah is just over here.' Elissa tried to pull Adam to safety, but Bethany was having none of that.

'You always was a greedy bitch, Lissa Downie,' she hissed in a furious undertone which reached every corner of the room. 'But this time he's mine. So you can keep your thieving hands off him.'

'It was Elissa I came to see,' Adam told her, with quiet finality. 'Elissa and her daughter. My god-daughter.'

'God-daughter? That's what you call it now, is it? Well, I can tell you there's folk call it something a deal plainer than that. Folk not a million miles from this room, and if you and that bitch think you can – '

'Hold your tongue, woman,' said Brodie Gibb, appearing miraculously at her side and gripping her arm with surprising strength for a man his size and age. 'Before you disgrace yourself and me by your behaviour. You sound like a drunken fishwife in a dock-side brawl. What will Sarah's friends think? And young Mr Lucas the son of a circuit judge.'

That stopped her. She took a deep breath, let it out again in a snort of derisive dismissal aimed in the direction of Adam Grant, heaved her shoulders under the weight of astrakhan to shake it and her disordered clothing to rights and turned her back on the interloper. Brodie gave him a brief nod of recognition and apology before leading his wife away.

'I'll introduce you to him, Brodie,' she was babbling excitedly. 'You can tell him you know his father.'

'Adam,' breathed Elissa in fear. 'Is it safe? What have you done with Mr Scott? Why have you come back?'

'You ask too many questions, my dear, sweet – ' but she gave a quick shake of the head.

'No, Adam. Please. You are my daughter's godfather, that is all. How is your wife?'

She asked the question deliberately, firmly, in a hostess's unemotional voice, reminding him of the barrier which separated them, and must continue to separate them, whatever the longing and the pain.

He understood the words behind the words and some of the joy drained out of his face. 'She is well. At least, she is well in body, though still troubled in her mind.'

'Is your wife ill?' asked Sarah, appearing at his side. She added in a swift aside to her mother, 'It's all right, Uncle Brodie will keep her in check.'

'Sal! I swear you look lovelier every time I see you,' grinned Adam and kissed her. 'Thank you for your letter. And Happy New Year.'

'And so do you,' she teased. 'Now that you have shaved that disgusting doormat off your chin.' She wiped his cheek with her handkerchief to remove the last trace of Bethany's contact. 'There. You look quite handsome.'

'Only quite? Thank you, madam.'

'But your wife?' persisted Sarah. 'Is she really ill?'

'No. Just troubled in her mind. She has discovered religion and says she is at a turning point in her life and cannot quite see her way clearly. But she will. One day.' His eyes sought Elissa's. 'We will talk about it later.' He put an arm around Sal's waist and said, 'But I haven't come half across the world to discuss my wife at home. How about introducing me to these college friends of yours, before your Aunt Bethany gobbles them all up, bones and all.'

Elissa, watching them together, felt her heart twist with love and fear. Bethany had come too close to giving away the secret of Sal's parentage: she had stopped because Brodie stopped her, or because she wanted to save the one weapon she had against Elissa for future use. But one day she would use it. Elissa shivered with apprehension. The Square knew, had always known: the revelation would startle them as a reminder of what they had forgotten, but that was all. It was Sal she feared for. Sal and Adam.

Was it really wise of him to cast off his disguise as the threadbare sailor Mr Scott and to walk among them as the prosperous shipowner that he was? What if Hugh Sinclair saw and recognised him? To her own eyes Adam, without the protective beard, looked the same handsome, blue-eyed, fair-haired demigod who had risen in gleaming leather thigh-boots from a silver sea of fish and captured her heart all those years ago in Shetland. And who had bounded to her aid in the darkness of that dreadful night on the shore. The night which had separated them, for ever. *For ever.*

But more guests were arriving. She nailed a smile to her face and prepared to welcome and entertain them.

'I was right,' said Ben Lucas much later, when Sarah eventually managed to shoo him and his friends out of the house with instructions to 'Go on home and sleep it off before your families send out the search parties.'

'Right about what?' demanded Sarah, barring the doorway so they could not wheedle their way back in. She felt like a wrung and tattered dish-rag after the social anxieties of the past few hours: her Uncle William had been abominably rude and as for her Aunt Bethany ... Sarah's cheeks flushed yet again at the memory ... and 'wee' Georgie with his endless boasting about how many fish boxes he could lift at once ... Her only hope was that Ben and his friends were so drunk that they would not remember a single thing when they woke up tomorrow.

'I said your mother must be a remarkable woman. And she is.'

But Sarah was still smarting under too many embarrassments. 'You mean a remarkable zoo-keeper, of course.'

'No I do not, you silly, prickly hedgepig. I mean your mother is beautiful. Calm and strong and sure and serene. I would trust her with anyone and anything. Absolutely. But Sarah . . .' He leant his head closer to hers, supporting himself with a hand on the door lintel. 'Dear Sarah, why is your mother so sad?'

The question shocked her out of all embarrassment. 'I don't know. I . . . Perhaps because she is a widow and my brother is away at the war and . . .'

Ben straightened unsteadily and relinquished the door's support. 'If I were twenty years older,' he said, with gallantry, 'I would make sure she did not stay a widow. I would make it my life's aim to banish sadness from her eyes for ever. As it is,' he said in quite a different voice, 'I might have to settle for peeling off those pesky little prickles on her daughter's character, until I find the soft, warm, glowing heart inside. Goodbye, Sarah. Happy New Year.'

Before she realised what he meant to do, he kissed her, not on the decorous cheek, but deliberately, generously, on the lips.

CHAPTER 29

Adam Grant stayed a week. Of careful business dealings. In company. Then another week. He visited her every day, at the smokeshed or the shipyard or the house in the Square; told her of his meeting with Sinclair, 'of his joy at finding revenge at last, asked her to go with him to the office on the quay, the office which had once been Sinclair's and was now his. But Elissa refused.

'I can't. Nothing will persuade me to go near the place where that evil man has spent so much of his time. I am sure I would feel him watching me wherever I went.'

'But he is in London, Elissa. Perhaps even across the Channel in France by now. He will not come back. At least, not yet, and if he does decide to show his face again, we will have good warning of it. I will make sure of that. Besides, I have had the place scrubbed and painted, polished and scoured till even the accounts clerk did not recognise it. You would think it a different place, Elissa, a cheerful place of light and air.'

Nothing he said could persuade her. She was glad Adam had triumphed, glad he was head of the shipping company, but she would not set foot in the building which had once held Hugh Sinclair. She did, however, consent to visit the *Singing Bird*, though with Daniel firmly at her side. She did not trust herself alone with Adam. She knew he had built the vessel for her, knew every detail in the captain's cabin had been chosen to please her, the panelled bed, the mahogany table, the hanging lamp, the brass-rimmed porthole; she admired the neat little galley, the saloon, the graceful lines of prow and stern, the wide, clean decks fore and aft. Adam Grant showed her over the entire vessel, always with Daniel's exuberant company to chaperone them, but companionways were steep and she could not refuse Adam's helping hand, nor his steering arm at her waist.

For though she had meant to keep him at a distance, to treat him with no more than cool courtesy as she had on that eventful New Year's Day, her resolution slipped with every passing hour. It was such joy to have a sympathetic companion with whom to share her troubles, to discuss her various business ventures, the new steam

340

drifter's progress at the shipyard, Sal's studies and Danny's school work. Someone to reassure her about her absent son Gideon, to soothe and comfort her, and where was the harm in a sympathetic family friend?

Of course she knew the harm: sometimes, in the grey small hours before dawn, she felt guilty about that. But surely virtue deserved at least some small reward? They grew closer every day in friendship until she thought she could not bear it when he left.

'I must go, Elissa,' he told her towards the end of the second week. 'I have my business ventures to see to in Melbourne. I have a good manager and a loyal work-force, but they need to know the boss is watching them and I have been away too long. Besides . . .' Here he lowered his eyes to the charts he had been showing her in the captain's cabin of the *Singing Bird*. He had spread them out on the mahogany table with its brass rail to stop things flying off on to the floor in rough seas and they stood decorously side by side, studying them. One of the crew had offered to show Daniel the wheelhouse and Adam had accepted before Elissa could answer. She could have forbidden it, even then, but she had said instead, 'I will come and find you, Daniel. In a few minutes' time.'

'Besides,' repeated Adam, not looking at her, 'I have matters to discuss with my wife. I had not meant to tell you, but you have been so open and honest with me that I must. My wife talks of entering the Catholic Church. She has begun to take instruction.'

Shock washed every other emotion from her face and heart. The Catholic Church. A divorce was bad enough for a Presbyterian, but for a Roman Catholic it was unthinkable. If his wife went ahead with it, how would Adam ever be free? As the last drop of hope drained out of her, there was nothing at all to say.

'I am sorry. I should have told you earlier, but I could not bear to spoil our time together. Please don't look so stricken, my love. She might still give me my freedom, before . . . And the Jesuits are marvellous advocates. Believe me, Elissa, if anyone can find a way, they will.'

He turned to her with sudden urgency. 'One day we will be together, you and I. One day we will be man and wife, I promise you. That is, if you will wait for me ?'

'I will wait,' she said, though her voice trembled. 'But only . . . only if you promise this time not to drown before you come back to me.'

He snatched her to him and kissed away all protests.

When at last he set her free, her voice trembled with joy and sadness. 'If my brother William were to see us, he would damn us to eternal hell-fire.'

'I understood it was God who provided that, not William Downie. Besides, the porthole is small and, in case you had not noticed, gives

341

a view of no more than a strip of harbour water and the hull of that whaler over there. Surely you don't suspect him of hanging over the ship's side to spy on us?'

Elissa managed a smile, but it was a small and desolate one. 'I will miss you, Adam.'

'I will be back. If I can, I will come for the launch of the new drifter. If not, I will send Mr Ross to help you. But I promise you, my darling, I will come back.'

'No, Adam. I don't think I could bear it. Not unless you were truly free.'

'But I must come. If only to make sure your friend Brodie Gibb is not fiddling the books.'

'That is no reason. Brodie is tight-fisted and shrewd and he strikes the hardest bargain in the north-east, but unfortunately I believe him to be absolutely honest.'

'Aye lass, so do I. Or I wouldn't sail half across the world and leave him in charge of my fortune. And I believe you to be honest too, my love, when you say you will wait for me.'

'Until you are free.' Desolation hung in the air between them.

'Dear God, I wish I could whisk you away with me on to the high seas and keep you captive, for ever. Then what nights of loving we would have.'

'You promised me that once, long ago,' she said, with sadness.

'I did not allow for life's misfortunes.'

There was silence between them before they turned to each other with sudden, yearning need.

'Goodbye, my dearest,' said Elissa at last, drawing away from him and brushing the tears from her eyes. 'I must go. Danny will wonder where I am.'

'Goodbye, Mrs Noble.' Gravely, he took her hand, then raised it to his lips. 'I promise you the next time I return it will be to make you my wife.'

Adam Grant sailed for Melbourne on the morning tide. A week later Queen Victoria died.

In memory the months merged into one unmeasured time of bleak skies and melancholy. Elissa supposed the sun had shone, the birds sung and the plants burst through the frozen earth and burgeoned green and blooming, but all she remembered years afterwards was black crêpe and mourning against an ever-rolling background of anxiety and endurance and a heart that never ceased to ache with yearning. She supposed babies were born to happy parents, lovers loved and laughed together, married couples were content: but in spite of the success of her enterprise – two steam drifters now and

342

already talk of a third – and the sure knowledge of Adam's love, whatever the outcome; in spite of Danny's health and high spirits, his loving hugs and unembarrassed kisses, anxiety shrouded all her days. Anxiety for her son Gideon, caught up in that far-away, futile war, and for Adam, whom she had loved and lost and found and lost again, and who risked his life daily, as all seamen did, on the oceans of the world.

In two more years she would be forty and there were too many deaths: Joseph, old Gideon, Milly, the Christie boy in the Cape – only one of the thousands of listed dead or wounded – and now the Queen herself. After a reign of sixty-four years, there were few who could remember a life without Queen Victoria on the throne. For Elissa and many like her the old Queen's death was a personal grief, and the months of official mourning prolonged the melancholy. Which in memory only cleared with the news a year later that a settlement had been reached in the Cape.

Surely now the cloud would lift and Gideon Joe come home?

They received his second letter in mid-June of 1902. Undated, it said merely that he had been discharged from the army and was on his way home. He arrived a week later, with a cabin trunk, a couple of carpet bags, and a young woman in a faded straw bonnet and faded, but serviceable travelling clothes. She carried a large canvas bag and a small bundle bound up in clean linen.

Elissa fought to smother the exclamation of dismay. Gideon Joe was unrecognisable as the jaunty lad who had left home with such bravado in that December of '99. Gaunt, haggard, his bleak eyes haunted with God alone knew what memories, he had the look of a man fighting down madness, or despair.

'Gideon my darling boy, welcome home.' She hugged him tight, as she had done when he was a child and had not minded. It was like embracing a bundle of lifeless bones. He stood without emotion, waiting till she should set him free and she bit back the tears of compassion and horror. What had they done to him?

'We have been so worried for you, Gideon.'

He allowed his mother a moment's indulgence before drawing away. 'As you see, Ma, I am fine. Or will be when we are inside. We'll bring the luggage in later. Give the neighbours something to talk about with all those strange labels on the cabin trunk.' The words were a pitiful attempt at jollity, the voice empty of all emotion.

'Of course. What am I thinking of?' Flustered, Elissa called into the kitchen, 'It's Gideon. He's home.' Then held wide the door and stepped back to allow them over the threshold. 'The men are away at the fishing, but they should be back at the weekend. And Sarah, too.'

343

Gideon Joe was too thin, though there was muscle under the taut, tanned skin, and he had lost all trace of adolescence. When he squared his shoulders and looked at her with those dark and haunted eyes she saw a grown man and had to remind herself that he was only just nineteen. As for the woman, she looked older, with unremarkable features, nondescript colouring and a general air of anonymity, but her face was kindly and she seemed pleasant enough. As she had not spoken a word it was difficult to make any other judgement. Then the woman stepped past her into the kitchen and Elissa saw what she carried in her arms. In the shadows of the doorway Elissa felt the years flip over and propel her into the next generation.

Gideon Joe looked round the faces in the family kitchen and said into the silence, 'You might at least say hello when I have travelled all this way. I told Mrs Dobson you would be pleased to see her.'

Elissa looked from her son to the woman in bafflement. 'Mrs Dobson?'

'Your son asked me to come home with him, madam,' she said, with a dip of the knee. The woman was actually curtseying to her! 'But I won't stay. My husband is waiting for me and now that I see things will be all right, I'll leave you. If you don't mind, Gideon?'

'No, Nellie. Away you go. And thank you.' Gideon touched cold lips to her cheek, then turned his back as Mrs Dobson handed her bundle to Elissa.

'Then if you will excuse me, madam, I'll say goodbye. I've done what I could, and gladly, the poor wee mite. You'll find everything you need in the bag.' Before Elissa could gather her wits to protest, the woman had hurried from the room and out of the house. Elissa followed her to the doorway, watched her scurry across the Square to where a man in a dark overcoat stood waiting. Then they linked arms, moved round the corner into New Pier Road and vanished. At that moment the bundle in her arms stirred, squirmed and gave a pitiful, bleating little cry.

It was Daniel who recovered first. 'It's a baby, Ma,' he cried in delight. 'Gideon's had a baby. It is your baby, isn't it, Gideon?'

Silently, his brother nodded.

'Then where's its ma? What have you done with its ma, Gideon? It wasn't that Mrs Dobson, was it?'

Gideon shook his head. Then he straightened, fixed his eyes on a point somewhere in the shadows above the grate and said, in a voice without emotion, 'My wife died in childbirth. Three weeks ago. They buried her at sea.'

Elissa bit her lip in dismay. 'Gideon, my dear, I am so very sorry.' She felt utterly helpless, without words or deeds that could heal her son's suffering. Mary Noble came to the rescue.

344

'What's done is done, and nought we can do about it. The Good Lord in his wisdom knows what's best. May the poor lassie, whoever she was, rest in peace. And she'll rest the calmer if she knows her wee bairn is in loving hands. Give the child to me, Lissa, while you see what's in yon carpet bag. We'll need to see about milk for a start.'

Elissa handed the child to her mother-in-law who was as usual in her chair beside the fire and Danny joined them, obviously fascinated by the tiny scrap.

'Well Gideon, lad,' demanded Mary, 'aren't you going to tell us, or do I have to strip the poor wee mite naked and look for myself? Am I holding your daughter or your son?'

'Daughter,' said Gideon, without turning his head.

Mary heaved a sigh of satisfaction. 'Good. A daughter's far more use, what with all the work you menfolk make. What's her name?'

This time there was no answer. Gideon was looking round the kitchen, searching with sudden urgency. Mary Noble, his mother, his brother Danny.

'Where is Milly?'

'She is in heaven, with Grandpa,' said Danny. 'She went to heaven ages ago, didn't she, Ma?'

'I am so sorry, Gideon. I thought you knew. I wrote to tell you. Lawyer Forbes found me the address and . . .'

But Gideon's face had turned white, his mouth trembled. 'I thought she would be here. I meant to give . . .' He covered his face with his hands and his shoulders shook with sobs.

'Hush, Gideon, hush,' soothed his mother. 'It has been a shock for you, I know, and coming so soon after your wife's death. Why don't you come into Sarah's room and lie down for a while, then I want you to tell me all about your poor, dear wife. She must have been a sweet girl and such a pretty one too, if her baby is anything to go by.' Gently, firmly, she led him out of the kitchen to the small back room, no more than a large cupboard, which was Sarah's precious territory, made him drink a measure of whisky, settled him under a rug on the narrow pallet bed, sat beside him, soothing and talking gently of harmless, childhood things until at last the tears ceased; he closed his eyes and sank wearily into the deep sleep of the emotionally, physically, utterly exhausted.

'I reckon you'll have to bring her up yourself,' said Mary Noble when Elissa returned to the kitchen. 'Poor wee nameless lassie.'

Danny said eagerly, 'I'll help you look after her, Ma. She can be my little sister.'

'Really she is your niece, Danny, and you are her uncle.' She looked down thoughtfully at the sleeping infant as Mary rocked her gently in her arms. 'But niece or sister, the little thing ought to be baptised.'

Cautiously, Danny touched the child's tiny fist and the minute

345

fingers uncurled, to close again around Danny's finger. Startled, he looked up at his mother with a mixture of wonder and delight, then studied the baby's sleeping face.

After a moment, he said gravely, 'I think I will call my niece Poppy. It is a pretty name and she will like that.'

'Poppy,' repeated old Mary thoughtfully. 'A funny kind of a name, but nice enough. Poppy Noble.'

'I think it an excellent choice,' said Elissa. She took the child from Mary's arms and held her up to look at her, face to face.

'Hello, Poppy. You are going to live with us, now. My first little granddaughter.'

'She is my niece,' said Daniel, with an air of new responsibility, and held out his arms for the child.

'Take care, Danny. Don't drop her.'

He turned on his mother a look of withering scorn. 'As if I would.'

Elissa watched her son with smiling indulgence as he seated himself carefully in the chair opposite Mary Noble's and began to croon softly to the child.

'He'll make a fine father, one day,' said Mary Noble, nodding her satisfaction. 'Not like some.'

Elissa was to remember that in the weeks to come and to marvel at the old woman's prescience.

On that first day, Gideon Joe slept solidly for eighteen hours. When he showed no sign of rising by seven the next morning, fear made her open the door a fraction and peer through the gap. He lay as she had left him, his chest gently rising and falling under the woollen blanket and she closed the door in relief. She did not know what she had feared, but so far he was safe. Two hours later, newly shaved and washed, he appeared at her side in the scullery where she was scrubbing away at several salt-encrusted linen squares. Sea water was notoriously bad for washing, but once the napkins had been boiled they would be fine.

'I am sorry, Ma.'

'What for?' She turned to him in genuine surprise. 'Where else should you come when in trouble but home to your family? But you've had nothing to eat since you arrived. There's porridge ready for you on the fire, the table's set and if you give me a minute to dry my hands, I'll make you a fine pot of tea.'

'I meant, I am sorry I went away like I did. I should have stayed at home. I know that now.'

'Put it down to experience, Gideon. Now not another word till you've put that porridge inside you. You need more flesh on your bones if you're to manage the engine room of the *Millicent*. We have two drifters now, did I tell you? And Hall, Russell's are working on plans for a third. Adam thought we should try something a little

346

different this time, so if you have any ideas on the subject, I'd welcome them.'

All the time she was chattering, Elissa was busy ladling porridge, making tea, cutting bread from the fresh loaf on the table, while Gideon Joe stood in the doorway to the scullery, looking lost and bewildered.

'Adam?'

'Adam Grant. You won't remember him, but he is Sarah's god-father. He lives in Australia, but sometimes he visits Aberdeen. He is Brodie Gibb's partner now. But I'll explain all that later. Sit down here, and get that inside you,' ordered his mother, as she had spoken to him in childhood. 'Mary has gone round to the Bains with the wee one, to show her off to the neighbours, and Danny has gone with them, as watchdog. He has appointed himself your wee daughter's guardian,' she finished and added gently, 'She is such a pretty little thing. Does she resemble her mother?'

She thought he would refuse to answer, but when he had eaten in silence for two or three minutes, he laid aside the spoon and said, as if talking to himself and staring, unseeing, at the window, 'Charlotte was so beautiful. When I first saw her behind the counter of her father's shop in Johannesburg I thought I was dreaming. No one could be so pretty outside a fairy tale. She wore a little frilled white apron over her dress – a yellow dress with little blue flowers on it.'

'Forget-me-nots?' suggested his mother gently.

'Yes. Forget-me-nots. And her hair in golden ringlets. I'd never seen a lass so pretty. As soon as I could persuade them to give me leave, we were married. Then I was told I could come home. We thought we would be home before . . . before the child was born . . . but there was some sort of delay, I don't know what, and before we got to London, Charlotte . . . The ship's doctor did what he could, I am sure of that, and everyone was very kind, but . . . They buried her at sea. Poor Charlotte, she was frightened of the sea and I can't help thinking of her, endlessly rolling and tossing in that dreadful canvas shroud, and so terrified, and me not there to comfort her.'

'Not terrified, Gideon. Not any longer. She is at peace. You must remember that, and pray. This evening I will enter your marriage into the family Bible, and record poor Charlotte's death. Will you help me do that? Then we will all say a prayer for her soul. And we will ask the Minister to put a memorial stone in the kirkyard. I think that would be the right thing to do, don't you?'

For the first time since his arrival home, Gideon showed a spark of interest. 'I hadn't thought of that, Ma. I could go and see the Minister this afternoon.'

'Then after that,' said Elissa with relief, 'Samuel can show you over the *Elissa Downie*. They should be back in port by midday.'

347

They learnt a lot in the days that followed. Gideon confessed that when the recruiting board found out he was a fisherman, they assumed he was a ship's carpenter. When he told them he was an assistant engineer, they shrugged and made him an army cook instead.

To Danny's crestfallen question, 'So you weren't a soldier after all?' he replied, 'Of course I was. Don't you know an army marches on its stomach? I had to march with them and fill the stomachs when they got empty.'

'But you didn't kill anyone?'

'I hope not. My cooking wasn't as bad as that.'

'I meant the enemy, Gideon. Didn't you have a gun and shoot the enemy?'

There was a moment's stillness before Gideon said, 'There was too much killing already, without me joining in. I saw the results. Sometimes I helped to carry stretchers.'

'War is not a game, Danny,' said Elissa quietly. 'Gideon did what he was told to do, and I am sure he did it well. But he does not want to talk about war, do you Gideon? It is all over now, thank the Lord. Let us talk instead about the new King's coronation.'

'Aunt Bethany is spitting mad,' volunteered Danny. 'She says if the Lord Provost gets to be invited to London, then why not Uncle Brodie and her? She says her Brodie is twice as rich as the Lord Provost and she's bought her clothes specially.'

'She'd have done better to spend her money on a teapot, like I did, silly creature,' said Mary Noble. 'Always thinking she's better than she is. But Bethany always was a daft kind of a lass when it came to clothes and showing off. No common sense, that one.'

The teapot in question held pride of place on the parlour dresser. It was a white china affair with portraits of Queen Alexandra and King Edward VII in a pretty painted garland of twined roses, thistles and shamrock leaves. Elissa had not the heart to tell her mother-in-law that the date on the teapot might well be wrong. She had heard a rumour only that morning that the King's illness might mean postponing the coronation till later in the summer, but what was the point of spoiling Mary's pleasure, especially for a mere rumour? And if the rumour proved true, then she would find Mary another, matching teapot with the new date on it, to remind her grandchildren of a special piece of history.

But the thought of grandchildren reminded Elissa of her own little granddaughter. She wished Gideon would acknowledge the child; talk to her, cradle her, play with her as Daniel did. But she had yet to see Gideon even look at his daughter, except accidentally, if he came upon the child unawares. It troubled her, though when she mentioned

348

it to Mary, she said only, 'It's the shock, Elissa. He's grown up too fast, poor lad, but he'll get over it one day. At the moment all he can think of is that dead lassie of his. He has no time for the live one.'

And no time for the steam drifters either. At least, so it seemed to his mother. His Uncle Samuel had taken Gideon off on that first Saturday afternoon to show him over the vessel, reacquaint the lad with the working of the engine and the general layout, but when he offered to take Gideon along when they moved to the east-coast fishing grounds on Monday, Gideon refused.

'Next time, maybe. I want to get my bearings first.'

It was the same when they showed him over the *Millicent*. Polite approval, but no enthusiasm.

'We still have the old fishing yawl,' suggested Elissa in desperation. 'Your Uncle Abel takes her out sometimes, just to keep her seaworthy. Would you like to go with him, till you get your sea-legs again?'

'You'll have to ask his wife first,' teased Danny. 'She's that strict she keeps Uncle Abel on a lead and he has to sit up and beg before he gets his dinner.'

'Daniel! I've told you before, you are not to say such things about your Aunt Bess.'

'But it's true, Ma. Leastways, its true that Uncle Abel has to ask permission for just about everything. Sam says she ...'

'Enough. I'll listen to no more such nonsense. Abel and Bess are coming round here tonight, Gideon, so you can ask them yourself. I reckon a sea trip would do you good; ease you back into the way of things. These last two years have been busy ones for all of us and there's plenty for everyone to do. I'm glad you're home again, Gideon, to help me.'

Gideon did not answer, but he did agree to go with Abel, just once, in the old fishing yawl.

'We'll try a bit of long-line fishing, lad,' said Abel. 'See if we can catch a wee bit haddock for your tea. Would you like to come along too, Danny? We'll not be away more than twenty-four hours.'

Danny, who would have jumped at the chance a month ago, refused.

'No thank you, Uncle Abel. I have to help Ma with Poppy. You see, she is my niece.'

Even that reminder of responsibility had not turned Gideon's attention in his daughter's direction. With a leaden heart, Elissa watched and waited. If only Adam were here, he might be able to talk to the boy, man to man. But Adam was not here. She had not heard from him for months, woke sometimes in the night with terror at her heart, imagining him dead, drowned, murdered by Sinclair, ruined. The light of day and her own determination usually restored sanity and hope, but she longed for a man's support and love. If Adam were here he might be able to help Gideon. No one else could get near him. Certainly not his sister.

Sarah came home for the weekend the day after Gideon's disastrous arrival.

'Who has been using my room?' she demanded before anyone had a chance to tell her what had happened in the last twenty-four hours. 'I told you I wanted nothing disturbed and my papers are all muddled. Someone has moved my books and – '

'Gideon is home,' interrupted her mother, and added with brutal simplicity, 'With a three-week-old baby daughter and no one to look after the child. He buried his wife at sea. See you remember that when you meet him.'

Sarah had been suitably subdued, to the point of offering to vacate her room in Gideon's favour, but made no attempt to hide her relief when her offer was refused.

'Gideon will sleep upstairs with the others, when he's ashore,' said her mother. At that time she had still thought it possible.

Sarah was shocked by her brother's appearance, embarrassed by his grief and by his mewing, helpless baby. When she had done what she could in the way of welcome and commiseration, she tried to jolly him into his old self again.

'You'll feel better, Gideon, when you are back at sea. Remember how you always loved steam engines? And begged and begged to be allowed to handle one? Well, we have two steam drifters in the family now and once you're settled you can have first pick. Or wait for the new one. It's only at the drawing board stage at the moment, but next year, maybe . . .'

'I'm not sure I want to go back to fishing.' The words had been as colourless as all Gideon's words since he came home, but there was a new edge of certainty to them.

'What do you want to do?' Sarah had asked in astonishment. 'You nag and nag for a steam engine and when you're offered one on a plate, you refuse it.'

'Sarah,' said her mother in warning. 'Give your brother a chance. He only arrived home yesterday. He needs time to adjust.'

'I don't see why. He's a fisherman, always has been, and never wanted otherwise. He was a good fisherman, too,' she conceded. 'Impatient, but good just the same. You know you were, Gideon, so what has changed?'

Gideon did not reply. It was as if any question, even one as small as 'Would you like a cup of tea?', was too much effort to answer. As if he inhabited a different world inside his head, and the gulf between that world and the real one was unbridgeable.

Patience, Elissa told herself over and over. We must have patience.

350

But as the days and weeks passed and she saw no change, even hope began to fail.

'Would you like me to speak to your Uncle Tom?' she asked him in desperation. 'See if there is a suitable job going in the ice-plant? After all, we own shares in the place so it would be no imposition.'

'I'll maybe talk to him myself, Ma. Tomorrow.'

Gideon was true to his word, but when Tom had shown him over the plant, explained the whole process from the delivery of the ammonia to the finished transparent ice, and finally offered him a job in the office where he could learn the business from the inside, Gideon had thanked him, and refused.

'I'm sorry, Ma, but it does not interest me.' He hung his jacket on the back of the door and slumped into the empty fireside chair.

Mary was out somewhere, no doubt gossiping with a neighbour, and Danny was nowhere to be seen, though she knew he would be back any minute, in time for Poppy's tea-time feed. Danny was a conscientious uncle. Remembering his devotion, Elissa was about to snap at Gideon to pull himself together and start to work for his living when he added in a voice so low she had to strain to hear him, 'Nothing interests me any more.'

'That is natural enough, Gideon,' she said carefully, her eyes on the pan of milk she was warming for his little daughter. 'You have suffered a deep and dreadful shock. I know what it is like to lose someone precious and most dearly loved. I know the feeling of emptiness, cold and dark is always with you. As if the world can hold no more comfort. But you must not let grief overwhelm you. What of those left behind, who love you? What of your little daughter?'

There was a long pause in which the only sounds were the soft murmur of the fire and the hiss of milk bubbles against the side of the pan. Then Gideon said quietly, but with stark decision, 'I think I must go away, Ma. I don't know where, but away from here, and home. It is not that I don't love you. I do. I love you and all my family. But I need to start afresh somewhere. I can't explain, but I know I want to be anonymous, somewhere where no one knows my grief or my failures. Believe me, Ma, I have tried to take up where I left off two years ago, but it will not work. I have changed, Ma. I have thought and thought about it, over and over, and always the answer is the same. I must go away.'

'And Poppy?' The words were both a reminder and a reproach.

'She will stay here with you, where she belongs. Please?'

For the first time Elissa felt something of what old Gideon must have felt all those years ago when his son Zeb turned his back on his family and went off to seek his fortune in the enemy camp. Gideon's duty lay here, with her. He should be taking his father's place, not

351

wandering, rootless, into the unknown on some selfish whim of his own. But all she said was, 'I am sorry to hear it, Gideon. I had hoped you had come back to stay. Where you belong. But if you must go, then you must. And don't worry about Poppy. She will find a loving home here as long as she needs it.'

'Thank you, Ma.' He stood up, put his arm round her shoulder and kissed her cheek. 'And don't worry about me. I think I might go to London, but I will write from time to time, to keep in touch.'

'You know your Uncle Brodie has a branch in London? I will give you the address.' Then, as she saw reluctance close over his face, she added, 'Merely as a precaution. In case you need to send a message home. And your Uncle Zeb, though I doubt you'd remember him, can be reached any time through the Seamen's Mission.' She would have liked to add Adam's name to the list, but feared Gideon would feel stifled if she said another word.

'Thanks, Ma. And I'm sorry.'

He left at first light, before even Elissa was awake. She stood in the doorway of the coom-ceiled room across the landing from her own, with the baby in her arms, and saw that his corner of it was stripped bare. It came on her then with the bleakness of loss that he had not once looked at his child.

CHAPTER 30

The King's coronation on 9th August passed Elissa by. She could muster no enthusiasm for the general celebrations, except, as she had promised herself, to search out and buy that matching teapot for old Mary who took a gratifying delight in showing the pair off to anyone who would look.

'See the dates? June on one and August on the other. That's because of the King's appendix. Nearly died, seemingly, but he didn't and I've two fine teapots to prove it.'

Mary was a great help to her, especially with the infant Poppy. But if Elissa was to continue to manage the smokehouse as well as overseeing the management of the steam drifters and the building of the third one, then she would need to find a nursemaid for the child. One of the many Bain offspring perhaps: Ina's youngest daughter Pearl was a sensible sort of a girl, or Jess's Mag. If only her own daughter Sal spent more time at home . . .

Elissa pushed the disloyal thought back where it came from and stamped on it, hard. Hadn't she herself urged Sarah to go to the university? Supported and encouraged her when her spirits flagged, as they inevitably did from time to time? Told her repeatedly how proud they would be when Sarah graduated? Of course the girl had to spend every waking hour at her studies. Of course there were books and lectures and suchlike at college which were not available to her at home. Of course she must spend more and more time at the Forbes house, which was so much nearer to the college than the house in the Square. How else was she going to keep up with the others and achieve her aim? But Elissa missed her just the same. She would have liked her daughter's company in these months of loneliness and burden. The menfolk came and went, as they had always done, according to the fishing seasons, old Mary endured, a fixture now at the fireside, and in spite of her orphaned and deserted state, little Poppy thrived. So did the herring fishing, which prospered as never before.

Since their introduction, the steam drifters had altered the lives of the fishermen beyond imagination. They might cost three times what

353

a sailing Zulu cost, but once they were in operation they were worth every penny. No more did the fleet have to wait, often for hours and with a full catch, for a wind to blow them home, while the gutters stood idle on the shore and the fish rotted. They could move in and out of harbour by their own power, independent of wind and wave, and search out the elusive shoals further and further afield.

This was increasingly necessary, and for a longer season. With such large, expensive boats it was not economical to lay them up for the winter and resume the line-fishing. Instead they followed the herring shoals for nine months of the year. But the new drifters were more comfortable by far than the old sailing drifters, having a wheelhouse for the helmsman, better living quarters and a good galley. The Noble steam drifters, *Elissa Downie* and *Millicent*, were strongly built wooden vessels, fifty tons apiece, greedy for coal, but with a fine turn of speed.

The third, which Elissa named the *Charlotte* in memory of her unknown daughter-in-law, was launched in June, a week after Poppy's first birthday. The following week, the entire Noble family, uncomfortable in their starched and polished Sunday best, walked to the city's Marischal College to see the first of their number receive her MA degree. The ceremony was entirely in Latin and incomprehensible, but what did that matter? There was their own wee Sal, 'Sarah Downie Noble' as the black-gowned official intoned, walking on to the platform in front of all the company in her academic gown, to be 'capped' and handed her precious rolled parchment. Elissa was glad that Adelaide's turn had come, alphabetically, first, so that she knew what to expect and could savour her daughter's moment of glory to the full. Or almost to the full. For she had hoped until the last second that Adam Grant would appear to see Sal achieve her aim. Remembering his promise, she knew what his absence meant and it was one more disappointment to add to the slow river of sadness which carried her steadily through her days. Sadness for Gideon, for his little motherless daughter, for her own lonely state. It was a pity Gideon had not been at the ceremony either, but then again perhaps it was for the best. Gideon had never really understood his sister's hunger for book-learning. But it was thanks to the graduation ceremony that they at last heard word of her absent son.

For afterwards, in the quadrangle outside, students and their families milled around in a chattering maelstrom and Elissa's sadness vanished in the spontaneous outburst of happy congratulations and laughter.

All the Forbes family were there to see Adelaide receive her degree, including her brothers: Thomas, together with many of his old college friends, and Cameron, no longer the timid, spindly, anaemic youth she remembered, but a pleasant-faced young man of nineteen with

354

warm brown eyes and copper-coloured hair. Having patiently, doggedly and with unwavering resolution worn down his parents' opposition, he was studying art at the Slade, in London.

'How are you, Mrs Noble?' he said, shaking Elissa's hand. 'I am glad to meet you, and to see that Sarah had succeeded so well. You must be very proud of her.'

'We are, just as your parents must be of Adelaide,' smiled Elissa.

Cameron grinned. 'I suppose they might just come round to the idea, one day. Though Mamma would far rather be at Addy's wedding than at her graduation. But before I forget, Mrs Noble, I have a message for you. I saw Gideon in London. He said to tell you he is well. And to give you this.'

Cameron handed Elissa a small parcel, the size of a shoe box. Inside was a wax doll with wavy brown hair, a long frilly dress and pantaloons threaded with blue ribbon. There was no name on the parcel, no note inside, but it was the first acknowledgement Gideon had made of his little daughter and it had completed the happiness of the day. Gideon was alive, his grief healing. One day, Elissa knew with absolute certainty, Gideon would come back to them. It was just a question of time.

Time, it seemed, was on Sarah's mind, too. When the precious new degree certificates had been passed around the group over and over, Sarah rolled hers up again, told her mother that Adelaide had decided to stay on at the college to work for a post-graduate degree and said that she, Sarah, would like to stay too.

'Just for one more year. To study to be a teacher. We can afford it, can't we, now that business is so good and after all, that was my purpose all along. You would not want me to give it up now, would you? Not when I am almost there.'

'Of course not, Sarah,' said her mother, with resolute cheerfulness. 'Your father would have been so proud of you today, as I am. So see you finish the course with flying colours and don't worry about the fees. They are my investment in a clever daughter. Who knows? You might be headmistress of your own school one day.'

Sal laughed. 'I suppose I might. Ma, would you mind awfully if I didn't come home with you just now? You see Thomas and Ben and some of the others are giving a party for Adelaide and they have asked me to go too.'

Elissa fought against disappointment, and hurt. She had planned a small celebration for her daughter, at home. Had invited friends from the Square.

'Don't look so worried, Ma,' bubbled Sarah, bright-eyed with excitement. 'It is at the Forbes house so it will be quite respectable. And you need not worry about me coming home late. Mrs Forbes says I can stay overnight, with them.'

'I will see your daughter comes to no harm, Mrs Noble,' said Ben Lucas, appearing beside her. He was a lawyer now, in his father's firm, still a junior, but working hard and apparently enjoying it.

'I am sure you will, Ben. It is just that I had hoped – '

'I will come home tomorrow morning, Ma, I promise you,' interrupted Sarah. 'But I haven't seen Ben and Thomas and the rest of them for months and we have so much catching up to do.'

When she saw her daughter's eyes sparkle like that and heard the bubbling exuberance in her voice, what else could Elissa do but agree? But she knew, even as she gave her permission, that one more link had been broken, and the gap between home and college widened.

A month later the packet arrived: a gold locket on a chain for Sarah Downie Noble MA, with a card of congratulation *from your loving Godfather (retired)*, and a sealed note for Elissa: *The road is longer than I thought, but never lose hope. Remember your promise, and mine. A.M.G.*

Another year passed and Sarah had a new certificate, this time a teaching diploma.

'And worth every penny,' reflected Elissa on a fine summer evening two years after Gideon's flight. The house door was open to the Square and the Nobles, like dozens of other families, had carried chairs and benches out into the sunlight to enjoy the evening sky and the warm air. Beyond the eastern side of the Square the waves broke in lazy rhythm on the sand – vast golden swathes of it, where gulls and oyster-catchers strutted, washed themselves in the shallows, or lazily rode the ripples.

Elissa liked to listen to the sea when it was calm and peaceful, as it was now.

The gardens inside the enclosing Square sparkled with colour and when the breeze stirred she could smell roses and lavender as well as the usual sea-tang and the lingering trail of wood smoke from 'Mary's' beyond the wall at Pocra. The Bains' cat was sunning itself three doors away and across the Square, on the eastern side, she could see her brother William and Katrine, sitting decorously straight-backed side by side, on identical wooden kitchen chairs. They were both reading.

Elissa wondered idly whether to stroll over and attempt a conversation, but decided against it. Since William's outburst against Sarah seven years ago, relations had been cool: that business with Sarah's student friends on New Year's Day had sent it plummeting to freezing. Seven years. The number had a Biblical ring to it. She wouldn't be surprised if William chose to 'forgive' her and her erring daughter when the right public opportunity arose, but it was not worth sacrificing such a tranquil evening to put it to the test.

She wondered where her brother Davie and his family had escaped to? Probably Tom and Kate's house in Ferryhill. Tom was generally considered to be a rich man, though neither he nor his wife Kate went in for ostentation. He could have afforded a turreted mansion in the west end, but chose instead a sensible terraced house with two main floors, an attic and a basement. The house was plenty big enough for a family of seven, within walking distance of the fishmarket and with a view of the harbour that gave him his livelihood. Elissa suspected William had not forgiven Tom for that: or for walking out of the meagre family business and making himself a fortune. Knew that Tom would gladly have shared his wealth with William and knew equally well that should Tom dare to offer, William would refuse. Poor William. She feared he had forgotten how to be happy.

On the flagstones in front of her, Daniel, now a sturdy thirteen-year-old, was playing a game with Poppy involving several polished blocks of wood which he had made himself. Daniel was building them into towers and Poppy was knocking them down again, with squeals of laughter. Daniel still took the duties of an uncle seriously and his niece adored him.

In a basket chair on Elissa's left, Mary Noble was, as usual, knitting and at the same time keeping an eye on everything that was happening in the Square. Beside her, a plain straw hat shading her eyes, Sarah was absorbed in the latest book Adelaide Forbes had lent her. Probably something political. Adelaide, reflected Elissa with a slight pursing of the lips, had developed into a forthright and outspoken young lady with ideas that were sometimes too advanced for decency, but she was a good-hearted, generous girl and Sarah's devoted friend.

As for Sarah, Elissa regarded her with loving pride. At twenty-two Sarah was a grown woman, but what a pretty one. Though perhaps 'pretty' was not quite the right word. Striking? Elegant? Even beautiful? Certainly her daughter dressed with a plain, uncluttered elegance which set off her fair hair, clear complexion and tall, shapely figure to perfection. Elissa knew there were tongues in the Square that whispered, 'Twenty-two and not married? That's what comes of book-learning,' and 'What lad in his right mind wants to marry a walking dictionary?' But Sarah seemed content.

She and Adelaide had had to work hard to get into college, and harder still when they were eventually admitted: there was still such a bias against girls taking a university course that they could not afford to be less than good at their studies. Now, armed with her new certificate, Sarah had secured a teaching post in a country school

357

north of the city, and would start when the schools resumed in August.

All along Elissa had feared how Sarah might change when she went to college. She had heard some of the arguments against educating girls – Sarah had reported them with great indignation. But the main theme seemed to be that too much education made girls unfeminine and unfitted for the domestic life which was their natural milieu. Looking at her daughter, Elissa smiled at the idiocy of that argument. Sarah had absorbed all sorts of arguments – many of them contradictory – with an enthusiasm and thirst for more that certainly enlivened her, sometimes made her argumentative, even dogmatic, but in no way took away her femininity.

Though Sarah had changed. Elissa had feared the girl might turn her back entirely on her family when she moved into that other, wider world of college folk and townsmen, but though Sal had grown apart from them in many ways, spending longer and longer in that other world of which they knew nothing, she still came home to the Square. Not as often as Elissa would have liked, but she came. However, she had certainly grown more self-assured, more capable of putting forward her own views, and was well informed on all sorts of topics, in particular the arguments of the Women's Suffrage movement and their supporters in the Liberal Party. Her own wee Sal had entered college as a naïve, excited girl, ill-educated and eager. Now, after years of instruction, Sarah had cast off the shell of the ignorant fishergirl and had emerged a confident, interesting and cultured young woman. Elissa looked forward to and enjoyed Sarah's visits and the time they spent together.

But now Sarah was to go even further away from her, to a post in an unknown school: she would not see her daughter for weeks at a time, maybe months. Recently, Sarah had acquired a bicycle and, since the spring, on many weekends when she might have come home to the Square, she had gone instead on cycling outings with her friends, usually with food to last them the day and sometimes the whole weekend: in her bleaker moments Elissa saw those cycling trips extend to cover every holiday in the year. But Sarah always arrived home again fresh-faced, bright-eyed and bubbling with vitality, whatever distance she had covered, and Elissa had not the heart to puncture her happiness by saying 'I would have welcomed your help in the smokeshed today' or 'You might have taken Poppy to play on the sands.' Sarah was a qualified teacher now and belonged to a different world. Boasting was not in Elissa's make-up, but she felt her heart warm with pride when she thought of Sarah's achievements and knew Joseph would have been as proud as she was of their clever, talented and attractive daughter.

No, she corrected herself. Of Adam's daughter.

In the past year she had tried not to think of Adam. He had said his wife had 'gone religious', that there was no part in her new devotions for a husband, that somehow those clever Jesuits would find a way round the obstacle, but since that brief note after Sarah's graduation she had heard nothing from him. Of course, it was her own fault. She should not have forbidden him to return until he was free. Should have set aside her inborn principles and taken him as he was: just as she had done in their first, sweet time of loving in that Shetland summer before Sal was born. But they had both been young and free then. Now everything was different. How could she deliberately take another woman's husband? Such a sin would have cancelled out any happiness they found together. But why did virtue have to be so lonely?

Brodie gave her news now and again. 'I saw Adam in London ... Heard from Adam the other day ... Selling some of his Australian stock ... Reorganising ... Paid a brief, turnaround visit to the office, but wouldn't stay. He sent his regards.' Regards? It seemed such a cold message; until she told herself it was merely caution on Adam's part. To protect them both. Once, heart-stoppingly, Brodie had reported, 'Do you know who I thought I saw in London, Lissa? That villain Sinclair. I swear it was him. Collecting his remittance money, likely. Or gambling it away.'

That had upset her. Since the man's hurried departure from Aberdeen she had put him firmly out of mind. He had gone to the Continent, to stay there. But if he was not on the Continent at all, but in London ... Dear God. Gideon was in London. So was Adam from time to time. She reassured herself over and over that London was a big place, that there was no reason at all why they should meet, yet the anxiety remained.

But on this tranquil July evening, Elissa put aside all fears and looked at her family with pride and near contentment: old Mary, Sarah, Daniel, Poppy. Had it not been for Gideon's continuing absence, she might have been truly happy. Joseph's brothers were away somewhere, inspecting the grand ocean liner that had newly docked amid the usual squealing excitement of the local children, or pottering over their nets or courting: it was rumoured that Samuel had overcome his lifelong shyness enough to actually speak to a girl and now she was walking out with him.

'And no, I don't mean the other way round,' Ina had told her. 'If Jess's George's Harriet hadn't asked him outright, he'd never have had the courage to say a word.'

Dear Samuel. Elissa had grown fond of him over the years. But if he did marry Harriet Black and bring his wife to live with them, how would they manage? Who was to say Saul and Zach wouldn't follow suit? The house was more than full enough as it was. In the last two years, since Poppy was born, she had felt a return of the old yearning for a house of her own, with space and privacy. Besides, she would dearly like a house with an indoor water closet and a bath that you didn't have to fill and empty by hand. Bethany had both: a huge white enamel bath with splendid brass taps and lion's feet for legs, and a mahogany panelled throne to hold the flower-painted lavatory cistern.

Suddenly, vividly, she remembered a Sunday afternoon in Shetland, when she had made their little hut spotless in readiness for their visitors. She had put wildflowers in a jam jar, for Adam, and Bethany Noble had tried to make her say the commandments. *Thou shalt not covet* ... Ina had rescued her and Bethany had dropped the stitches of her knitting.

Thou shalt not covet ... All those years ago Elissa had coveted Adam, whom Bethany regarded as her own. And now here she was coveting Bethany's indoor plumbing.

Smiling at her own foolishness, Elissa concentrated on the frilled hem she was turning on a white cotton pinafore for Poppy. She tried to dress the child in clothes with the sort of feminine touches she imagined poor Charlotte would have wanted, while at the same time keeping her sensibly and suitably clad.

'What are you smiling at?' demanded Sarah, looking up from her book. 'Have I got ink on my nose again?'

'Not that I can see, dear. I was day-dreaming, that's all.' Of Adam, but she could not tell Sarah that. 'I was thinking, if Samuel does marry Harriet Black, do you think the house will be big enough for everyone?'

'No, of course it won't be big enough, Ma. It is overcrowded as it is. Like most of the houses in the Square. I have told you before, overcrowding breeds poverty and poverty breeds disease. Which is why the life expectancy of the poor is so much shorter than that of the rich. Besides,' she finished, returning to her book, 'the rich have better plumbing.'

Elissa and Mary exchanged glances and simultaneously smothered a smile. Sarah did not like to be laughed at, especially in her serious moods.

'You may be right, dear,' ventured Elissa carefully. 'What would you advise me to do?'

'Tell the uncles to find their own houses. And put in a water closet.'

'Nonsense,' said Mary Noble sharply. 'My family lives with me and always has done. What is the world coming to if I can't keep a roof over my children's heads? As for poverty, who says we're poor? I've told you before, it wasn't poverty as put you through five years of college, my girl, and you not paying back a penny into the family purse. And it isn't poverty as keeps us in the best house in the Square,

360

neither. Overcrowded indeed! If we want more space, we'll lift the roof and add another floor and I tell you now, you'll not move me out of the house I was born in, nor my children neither. Elissa!'

'Yes, Mary?'

'You'll go round to the sanitary man first thing Monday and order us one of Sal's closet things, though what's wrong with our outside privy beats me. That seat's real mahogany and you'll not find a better in the whole of Scotland, not if you was to go to Balmoral Castle. Poverty indeed. You want your head seen to, Sal. It's addled with all those words you've stuffed into it.'

Later, when Sal, soothing and apologising, had followed her outraged grandmother into the house to see about making tea, Elissa sat quietly sewing and talking to Joseph inside her head, as she sometimes did when she was lonely, about the family and the family business. *Sarah is a good girl, Joseph, in spite of the things she says. She didn't mean to upset anyone. She doesn't always think before she speaks, that's all. And Mary is right. Our drifters have earned every penny spent on them. Ten times over. And the smokehouse continues to make a handsome profit. I hardly dare to put it into words, but we are certainly not poor. So far this year the season is going well and Fergus says the profits of the curing yard should be way above last year's, and those were good enough. Even the ice factory is flourishing, with the trawler fleet still expanding and their catches with it. At least . . .*

She paused, remembering Tom's warnings. Since the introduction of the so-called otter trawl, catches had increased by twenty per cent. Last year, the average weight landed per vessel, Tom said, had been double what it was in '86. But in the last three years the number of trawlers registered in Aberdeen had also doubled: one hundred and seventy-eight now instead of a mere forty in '86. With so much fish on the market, warned Tom, prices were sure to fall. That could affect 'Mary's', possibly the ice factory too. But not the herring drifters, surely? The trouble was, a drifter's expenses had to be paid whatever the size of the catch, so that was seven hundred pounds gone for each vessel before they could begin to see a profit.

But we are doing well enough, Joseph. I remember what you said, dear, and I try to do what you would have done yourself, in my place. If I am in doubt I ask Brodie's advice, or Lawyer Forbes's, and they keep me right. But I wonder, is Sal right about a bigger house? With room for everyone and a garden for Poppy to play in? I know you wanted us to have one, one day.

Suddenly into her head came a vision of the house at Fairfields, with its crumbling boundary wall and its overgrown garden. What a place that would be for Poppy and her little friends. But not while Mary Noble was alive. She would not hurt her mother-in-law for all the houses in Scotland. Unless perhaps the promise of electric light, an indoor water closet and a bathroom might persuade her? And if

361

she promised all the uncles could come too? Fairfields, she remembered, had three rows of windows on its ivy-covered façade. Adam had lifted her up to see over the wall and she had counted them. Adam. Dear Adam.

But she could never bring up the subject with Mary. The old woman would think they could not wait for her to die.

Elissa was counting the stitches of the next section of frill on her granddaughter's diminutive pinafore, when, out of nowhere, a shadow fell across the white material and Elissa looked up, shading her eyes against the burnished sky. A silhouette against the brightness. A man's silhouette, tall, broad-shouldered. Then her eyes focused and she scrambled to her feet with a cry of joy.

He held out his arms and she ran to him, felt his arms close tight around her, lifted her face to his, and the years of waiting fell away in one, blissful, endless kiss.

William's voice came clear across the Square. 'Disgusting. And in broad daylight. An outrage against decency and God. Inside the house, Katrine, at once. You shall not look upon such lewdness.'

But even the slam of his door could not separate them. Impervious to William, neighbours, children, everything, they kissed away the lost years in joyous reunion.

It was Danny who brought them back to earth. 'Ma! Ma! Sal says where's Poppy's clean pinafore? She's spilt milk all down the one she's wearing and it's sopping wet.'

Elissa turned a radiant face towards the doorway where Sal stood white with shock, the squirming Poppy in her arms. 'I don't know, Danny,' she said, untroubled, and turned back to Adam, but he was staring at Sal in disbelief.

'That child isn't yours?'

'No, of course not.' Then as she saw her mother's face and the way Adam looked at her and their hands clutched tight as if they would never let each other go, she blushed and looked away. 'But there is no reason why it should not be, is there? Or do you think no man would look at me now I have a university degree?'

Adam exchanged a glance with Elissa, raised a questioning eyebrow, then, one arm still around Elissa's waist, said, 'I reckon I'm needing one of those university degrees myself. For it would be a clever man indeed who could tell your mother and you apart. You've grown beautiful, Sal, while I've been away. Not that you weren't always the best-looking little lass in the Square. And the cleverest. Come over here, and give your godfather a kiss, then you can tell me all about that wonderful degree of yours.'

Later, he told Elissa about the annulment. 'They decided I was already "married" to the mother of my child in Scotland and that my marriage in Australia was never valid. Especially as I am a Protestant

362

and my wife is now a Catholic convert. I think she will enter a convent one day. It is certainly her intention, and for the first time in many years she seems happy. As I am. She actually gave us her blessing.'

When old Mary did the same – 'You were a good wife to my Joseph, but you've mourned him long enough and it's time you had a man in your bed again' – Elissa's happiness was complete.

Elissa and Adam were married a week later, quietly, in St Clement's church, with only Sarah, Mary Noble, Danny and Poppy to witness the ceremony. The uncles were away with the herring drifters and Elissa refused to call them back.

'They can drink our health when they come home. I want a quiet time alone, with my husband. No wedding party. No noisy celebrations.'

'And you shall have it, my love,' murmured Adam, his voice warm with promise. 'I am taking you away, to a place I have found, a place where we can be as quiet and as alone as we choose.' He refused to say anything more, except to tell Mary that he was taking Elissa away for a few days and hoped she would be able to manage house and family without her.

'Manage? Do you think I am dottled? I've managed more than a couple of pesky bairns in my time and Sal will help me, won't you, Sal?'

'Yes, Gran.'

Since Adam Grant's miraculous arrival home, Sal had been unusually subdued and withdrawn. She had always thought of Uncle Adam as hers, and now here he was, ignoring her, drooling over her mother like some love-sick adolescent. It had altered all her percep- tions and it made her uncomfortable. She was reluctant to admit that she felt jealous – why should she be jealous of two middle-aged love- birds who ought to know better? She had friends of her own. Young men who admired and courted her. She didn't want any of them, but if she did, she could have her pick.

No, it was not jealousy. A little bit, perhaps, if she was honest, but not much. It was an uneasy feeling that something was not quite right. There was a mystery, a secret, something they were keeping from her. One day she would find it out, but in the meantime she supposed she would have to make the best of it. Adam Grant was decent enough and though she didn't understand how he had managed to have his marriage to that wife in Australia annulled, she believed him when he said he was free. As for her mother, the memory of Ben's words on that momentous New Year's Day came back to reproach her. 'Why is your mother so sad?'

If Ben saw Elissa now he would not ask that. Her mother was radiantly happy, all the world could see that, and why should she not be happy, after so many years of loneliness? Moreover, now that Adam was here to look after her mother, Sarah was free to leave home with a clear conscience. Go where she wanted, work where she wanted. Even London one day, if she chose. Her brother Gideon was in London, Cameron Forbes had said so, but more important than that, Mrs Emmeline Pankhurst and her valiant band of Women's Suffrage campaigners had their headquarters there. Of course, there was her gran . . . But Sarah would still come home, now and again, to visit.

For the first time since Adam Grant's reappearance, the frown left Sarah's face. She would tell Ben the good news in the morning.

Adam had hired a motor car. A Daimler. For a quiet getaway that was a monumental mistake. The whole of North and South Squares turned out to investigate the splendid machine when the driver pulled up in North Pier Road and sounded the brass-funnelled horn to announce his arrival. Elissa was to drive to church in style.

The sun shone, a soft breeze blew from the sea, bringing the clean scent of seaweed and salt spray, and all round the Square the little strips of garden were bright with summer flowers. Elissa wore a high-necked blouse of white tucked cotton, with long sleeves, tight below the elbow but puffed full at the shoulder, and a plain skirt of soft blue merino wool, with a neat buckled belt which emphasised her waist. A matching blue bolero jacket and plain straw hat completed her ensemble, though Sarah had insisted on winding a blue chiffon scarf around the straw and pinning it in place with a posy of white rosebuds. Sarah herself wore a plain grey jacket and skirt and unadorned straw boater, though little Poppy's skirts were so frilled with lace that they stuck out almost horizontal and Danny warned her to keep out of the wind, in case it snatched her up and blew her over the rooftops, like a puff of thistledown. After that, Poppy kept tight hold of his hand.

Mary Noble had unearthed her finest finery and looked majestic in black bombazine with strings of jet beads and a black veil on her bonnet. But it was undoubtedly Mary's proudest hour when she was helped up into the motor car, took her place beside Elissa on the upholstered back seat and allowed the driver to tuck a travelling rug over her knees, as if she had been used to such attentions all her life. Poppy was allowed to ride with them, though Sarah and Danny walked along beside the running board, with the rest of the youth of Footdee. Along York Street, York Place, St Clement's Street, to the gates of the kirkyard, where Adam was waiting, in morning coat and neat striped trousers, of the best quality the city could provide. Elissa thought she would melt away with happiness as he handed her down from the motor car and they walked sedately into the church.

During the short ceremony inside, a running war took place outside, between the more daring of the fisherlads and the uniformed driver who strove to defend the precious territory of his Daimler, as some climbed the running board, others swarmed over the back, another tried to sound the horn. But they all scattered with squeals of excitement when Adam and Elissa emerged, arm in arm, from the church porch and Adam tossed a handful of coins into the road, for them to scramble for.

Then he handed Elissa into the car, climbed in beside her and ordered the driver to start up the engine. In the kirkyard entrance Sal and Mary Noble and Danny, with Poppy in his arms, waved and shouted their good wishes and goodbyes while the black polished Daimler moved off in a splutter of exhaust fumes towards the Castlegate, pursued by a straggle of cheering small boys.

'Where are we going?' asked Elissa when the car did not stop, as she had expected it would, at one of the city's hotels, but continued its chugging course the length of Union Street into Albyn Place and westward.

'Don't you know?' he teased with an air of such suppressed excitement that she should have guessed. As it was, they were almost at the gates before she realised. The driver sounded the horn, a lad appeared from nowhere and the wrought-iron gates creaked open to let them in. Through the entrance with its weather-worn twin lions keeping dual guard, along the twists and turns of the gravelled drive which wound its shadowed way between dense green foliage and taller, statelier trees to emerge without warning into a sun-filled space with, on one side, the creeper-covered walls of the house with its rows of windows and porticoed front door and on the other, a green lawn with flower borders and a tangled shrubbery beyond. The grass had been newly cut, though both flower borders and shrubbery looked decidedly untamed. But the effect of sunlight and summer profusion was enchanting.

'Well, Mrs Grant?' said Adam, handing her down from the motor. He dismissed the driver with a nod of the head, watched till the motor was out of sight round the first bend of the drive, then cupped her face in his hands and kissed her, with tantalising gentleness, before whisking her suddenly up into his arms, shouldering the door open and carrying her over the threshold into the cool peace of the entrance hall. There he set her down on her feet and kissed her again, this time with a fervour that left her bright-eyed and breathless.

'I have ordered us a wedding breakfast,' he murmured, his breath warm on her ear. 'Are you hungry, my love? Or would you prefer to see over the house first?'

'I think the house first, Adam. Though perhaps I should warn you: I am very hungry indeed. For you.'

'What a disgraceful admission for a respectable married woman. Whatever would Uncle William say?' Laughing, he took her hand and led her sedately across the entrance hall to the first doorway.

'The drawing-room.'

Dust motes danced over neglected parquet floors, sunlight slanted through dusty windows. A butterfly wing, gleaming velvet gold and burnished bronze, trembled in a cobwebbed corner. A window-sill was white with droppings from a swallow's nest under the eaves. In the fireplace under the pillared marble mantelpiece a litter of broken twigs and soot indicated nesting birds in the chimney. But in spite of its neglect, the room breathed tranquillity and peace.

More doors stood open on either side, revealing neglected pieces of abandoned furniture, a chair in one room, a broken-springed sofa in another.When they reached the back regions, through a green leather, brass-studded door into a linoleumed passage, more open doors exposed a chipped enamel basin on scullery flagstones, wooden washboards, bleached white and twisted by years of use, beside a huge double sink on massive wooden legs. A butler's pantry and a wine cellar, both empty. But in the stone-flagged kitchen the huge range was glowing, the room warm, and on the scrubbed deal table were laid out plates and dishes under a veil of protective muslin. Two wooden ladder-back chairs completed the furnishings.

'Our supper,' said Adam. 'When we need it.' He lifted a corner of the muslin cloth to reveal a dish of strawberries and the edge of a glazed and clove-stuck ham, then dropped it again and turned away. 'But first we must finish our tour.' He led her back into the cool of the entrance hall and for the first time Elissa noticed the scent of roses and traced it to a Chinese vase in the shadows at the foot of the stairs.

'Come, my love,' said Adam softly, and led her up the wide, uncarpeted stairway, round the turn at the half-landing where the stained glass of a floor-length window cast a many-coloured mosaic over the floorboards, and up again to the first-floor landing and a short corridor stretching to left and right. All the doors stood open, revealing the same neglected contentment; all except one.

'This, I think, is ours.' He turned the handle.

The door opened on to a transformation. Polished floorboards, an Indian carpet in glowing bronze and gold and green and red, and a four-poster bed with velvet hangings of a rich, imperial crimson. The twisted gold ropes which looped them back ended in tassels of more

366

gold. Through the gap in the curtains Elissa saw white linen pillows and starched white sheets under an embroidered counterpane of wildflowers and birds and butterflies in a myriad delicate colours. The two tall windows looked out on to the garden where the shadows were already lengthening and softening into evening.

Quietly, Adam closed the door behind him.

'Well, my love?'

'It is all enchanting, but . . .' She lifted her arms above her head, which in turn lifted her breasts most provocatively, and slowly unpinned her hat. 'Where is everybody? We have seen no one since we arrived.'

'No. Because there is no one. Only you and me.' He took a step towards her. 'For a whole, blissful week. This is what I promised you, all those years ago, remember? A house like the one where my mother worked, with lawns and flowers and upstairs a four-poster bed with curtains to draw close about us and keep the whole world out? You spurned my steamship, though I built it specially for you. Please say you will accept my mansion?'

'Yours?' Her voice held disbelief and shock. She had thought the place hired, from an absentee owner.

'Ours,' he corrected. 'I had meant to have it furnished and immaculate before I brought you here, but I found I could not wait a day longer. I apologise for the dust, but I had not the patience to do more than prepare the two rooms we need – I brought the furnishings with me from Bombay, on that splendid liner Danny so admired. I have waited far too long for you already, my stubborn, faithful darling. Later, we will put everything to rights. But at this moment, my little singing bird, we have far more important things to discuss than housekeeping.'

Gently he took the bonnet from her hand and dropped it on to a chair, then unfastened the first of the small pearl buttons of her blouse. 'One . . . two . . . three . . . four . . .' he counted softly until he reached the last one and peeled the garment slowly from her shoulders. 'If you knew how I have dreamed of this moment through all those lonely, yearning years . . .'

Later, when she woke in the tumbled warmth of their marriage bed with his arms close around her and his sleeping head against her shoulder she looked up at the dark roof of their canopy, then at the dark, warm folds of the closed bed curtains and thought she had not felt so safe and so loved and so blissfully content in all her life. Somewhere in that wilderness garden, a solitary bird sang an evening melody: there was no other sound but her own heartbeat, and Adam's breathing. She turned her head on the pillow to look at him and saw his eyes open, blue and bright and gloriously hungry. With a soft laugh, she moved closer, her hands exploring the warm, smooth planes of hard muscle and soft flesh which she remembered from that long-ago time in Shetland and had thought never to embrace again.

'So you will accept my mansion, Mrs Grant?' he asked her when, much later, they sat at the kitchen table in the warmth of the lingering fire and ate their belated wedding breakfast of cold roast ham, fresh bread and cheese and a blue and white china bowl full of strawberries.

For the first time since Adam's return, a shadow touched her face.

'Of course, Adam, but . . .' She looked up at him, her eyes full of love and gratitude and apology. 'What about Mary? She will never move and I cannot leave her.'

'Then we won't leave her, my love. This shall be our *holiday* house. Remember how she loved the Daimler? She will be delighted with her very own house in the country to boast about, especially when she sees the bathrooms we will install. I want all your family to come here. Sarah and Danny and Poppy and the uncles and anyone else who wants to. You did not think I would forbid them, did you?'

'I thought . . .'

'That I might want you all to myself? And I do, my darling. Why else do you think I planned this week together now – so if ever the family gets too much for us we will send them back to the Square and have another week together and another. As many as we like.'

Elissa laughed and fed him a single, sugar-dusted strawberry.

He caught her wrist and held it, looking deep into her eyes. 'Besides, my dear, sweet singing bird, I am a sailor, with a shipping line to run, and offices in London and Melbourne. I cannot always be here. I would not want you to be lonely. Except, of course, for me.' He leant forward and kissed her, with the taste of sugar on his lips.

A long time later, waking briefly in the small hours with Adam's arms enfolding her, Elissa thought of the empty rooms all around them, waiting to be filled. A holiday house. Mary would like that. She smiled with contentment and slipped back into sleep.

And Sarah would be delighted.

CHAPTER 31

Sarah did not wait to welcome her mother and Adam home, but left for Braehead school on the morning they were expected back. Partly from embarrassment; partly – a very small part, of which she was suitably ashamed – from a desire to show her mother that she could manage perfectly well without her; and mostly from the wish to start her new life without goodbyes which might shake her composure, and without well-meaning but inappropriate advice.

'Goodbye, Gran.' A quick hug. 'I'll be home in October, to see you.'

'Goodbye, lass. I'm right proud of you.'

That was all and all she wanted, though Danny and Poppy waved from the doorway till she was out of sight, her carpet bag in one hand, her bundle of books in the other. She wore a plain grey skirt, with a neat brown leather belt, grey fitted jacket, high-necked white blouse, brown leather ankle boots and an unadorned straw hat, and was unaware that as well as looking neat, efficient, and demure – the effect she hoped for – with her shining blonde hair, graceful figure and clear blue eyes, she also looked enchanting.

She took the tram to the edge of town, then walked the three miles north to the village – though it scarcely warranted that description – of Braehead, feeling nervous and excited in about equal measure.

The schoolhouse was small, but ample for the three dozen or so pupils from the surrounding farms and cottages. It stood in its own grounds, on the edge of a copse: pine and silver birch and rowan. There was one large schoolroom with a central stove and a desk for the teacher, and a smaller room opening off it, for the older pupils. At the back of the building were the headmaster's quarters, where Mr Kirk and his wife lived, with their children, Henry who was ten, Helen aged seven and a puny, whimpering scrap of a child, Lillian, who Mrs Kirk said was a year old, but who looked to Sarah half that age. A maid of all work slept in one of the coom-ceiled attic rooms and Sarah was to have the other.

Mrs Kirk explained on her first evening, as Sarah ate a simple supper with them in the schoolhouse kitchen, that really she and her husband could have managed the school perfectly between them, had the authorities allowed it – Mrs Kirk had been the assistant teacher herself until her marriage – but the place of a wife and mother was firmly in the home. Besides, her teaching days were in the past now and since the birth of Lillian Mrs Kirk had been ailing and had not the strength she used to have.

'Nor, I confess, the patience, dear,' she said, with a sweet smile. 'It is so unfair on the children to have a teacher whose mind is elsewhere, don't you agree? Your predecessor,' and here her cheeks flushed with what could only be embarrasssment, 'had, shall we say, too many outside interests.'

This was not true. Sarah found out within the week that her predecessor had had only one interest: a young and lusty farmer who had 'got her into trouble'.

'A nice girl,' said Mrs Kirk with an apologetic smile, 'but a little foolish. Your references say you are serious, hard-working and conscientious. I do hope you will not find us dull.'

'Of course not, Mrs Kirk. As you know this is my very first job and I have a great deal to learn. No doubt I will make mistakes, but I hope you will forgive them, and guide me?'

'My wife will do all she can to advise you, Miss Noble,' said the headmaster. 'I myself take the older pupils, as well as coaching the most promising for the university bursary competition.'

'I would be happy to help you with the coaching,' said Sarah eagerly. 'I won a bursary myself and . . .'

'I think you can leave my job safely in my own hands, Miss Noble. Your job is with the younger children, as I was about to explain. The three Rs as they are incorrectly called. Reading, writing and arithmetic. The cornerstones of all knowledge without which not even the smallest edifice of learning can be built.'

'Yes, but – '

'In the past, under my wife's excellent tuition,' he continued, without raising his voice yet by the drawing together of his eyebrows implying both rebuke and warning, 'I think I can say in all honesty that no child, even the most inadequately equipped, completed the third year without being numerate, literate, and able to express both accomplishments in passable copperplate. If you are able to achieve the same, Miss Noble, I will be well pleased.'

I'm sure you will, thought Sarah with simmering rebellion. *I will have done the greater part of your work for you.* She looked at him coolly, noting the pale, thinning hair, the sort of freckled skin that goes bright red in the summer sunlight, eyelashes that would have looked better on a cow, and a pair of eyebrows which to her disillusioned eye resembled two clumps of straw stubble in a neglected winter field. His eyes were sharp, his *amour propre*, she suspected, very dear to him. He was a large fish in a local puddle and did not relish an intruder, unless that intruder was content to remain a harmless tiddler. But his wife was sweet-tempered and had offered the new assistant nothing but kindness.

'Yes, Mr Kirk,' said Sarah meekly. 'Naturally I will do my best.'

At first she enjoyed it: the chorus of 'Here, Miss Noble,' when she checked the register; the chanting of multiplication tables, the laborious chalking on slates of simple addition sums, or the letters of the alphabet; the praise for George Henderson's writing or Mary Esson's sums. The confidences: 'We have a new baby, miss,' 'My cat's had kittens,' 'My uncle's dog bit Auntie Ina and Auntie Ina bit my uncle, to see how he'd like it.' The tale-telling (discouraged), the occasional presents timidly offered: an egg – 'I found it, miss, in the barn this morning' – or an apple or an extra peat divot for the fire. It all reminded her of the long-ago days in the family kitchen, when she had 'taught' her brother and wee Georgie and Cameron Forbes and various other children of the Square. Her brother was now somewhere in London, working for a mercantile company, so Cameron said, and Cameron himself was beginning to make a name for himself as a portrait painter. As for wee Georgie, he was six feet tall, built like a tree trunk and working happily as a trawlerman off the Dogger Bank, despite all Brodie Gibb's efforts to slot him into a safe shore job.

And she, Sarah Downie Noble, was teaching small children the alphabet, just as she had been doing when she was a child herself, all those years ago.

But it was a start, she reminded herself. Her first job. With a good reference, she might find a post in a city high school next. Teaching older children, with inquiring minds; children whose horizons stretched beyond the peat stack and the byre. She had brought some half a dozen college books with her, Greek and Latin which, in her innocence, she had thought she might be called upon to use, and one or two more daring books which Adelaide Forbes had lent her, on contraception and free love. Also some privately printed pamphlets putting forward the views of the Suffragists. Her friend Adelaide was on the committee of the Aberdeen Women's Suffrage Association. These last she kept prudently hidden away among her clothes in the small chest of drawers in her room, but the Greek and Latin texts she left conspicuously on view, with her Bible, on the stool beside the bed.

Mrs Kirk urged her repeatedly to spend the evenings with the family at the fireside, but after that first evening, Sarah refused.

'This is your home, Mrs Kirk. I see your children in school and they do not want to see me at home as well. Besides, I do not want to intrude into the family circle. Your time together is too valuable.'

That, she thought, was a polite way of putting it. In truth, the idea of sitting at the table in silence, while Mr Kirk smoked his foul pipe

371

and pored over the newspaper, grunting his disgust at one item after another, the children sat obediently in a corner, exercise books open at the prescribed page, and Mrs Kirk whispered encouragement to them in the intervals of turning a bed-sheet sides-to-middle, or cutting down one of her husband's threadbare shirts for her son Henry, filled her with dread. She found more stimulating entertainment in her own room with a Women's Suffrage pamphlet, or outside, strolling the river path to the little bridge and back again, or, on a clear evening, as far as the farm at Braehead, where the soothing gurgle of hens in the barnyard, the lowing of cows in the home field and the soft purring of the grey tabby as it rubbed this way and that against her ankle restored her spirits and her hope.

Doug Webster, the farmer's eldest son, sometimes left whatever he was about in the byre or the hayloft and strolled over to chat.

'How's my young brother Willie doing, Miss Noble? Has he learnt his three-times yet?' Or 'Mind and tell me if he plays up and I'll skelp his backside, the wee devil. He's always up to mischief, that one.'

But Sarah could cope with the boys: she had had enough practice in her own family for that. It was the girls that troubled her. She wanted to wake them up, to stir them to enthusiasms beyond the cooking pot and the cradle, to widen their horizons. In the playground she watched their skipping games and ball games and hopscotch; she heard their halting attempts at reading, corrected spelling, guided faltering hands in the careful loops and curves of joined-up writing, applauded their successes, shook her head sadly over misdemeanours or forgetfulness, and felt herself grow more and more frustrated by the rigid pattern of The Syllabus According to Kirk, as she called it in private. Thou shalt not allow a new idea to enter the classroom. Thou shalt not enlighten. Thou shalt go through the prescribed motions and no others. She amused herself by inventing new commandments and once, daringly, wrote them in a letter to Adelaide, though until the letter was safely posted she lived in fear that it might be discovered and read.

After that satisfying catharsis, she felt more cheerful and when Adelaide replied, commiserating humorously with her dire predicament and suggesting that Sarah devise splendid new methods of her own which would incorporate the things she was required to teach, but teach them in a more interesting way, she seized on the idea with enthusiasm ... Of course such a thing was not possible yet, for she knew she must tread with caution, but one day. *We will plan your strategy together in the tattie-picking holiday*, wrote Adelaide. *I am arranging a splendid bicycling tour for the usual crowd and naturally you will come too. If you must earn your honest crust in such an intellectual backwater you deserve at least one weekend with more stimulating company. Possibly even two – if you are good.*

The prospect lifted Sarah's spirits as nothing else could have done. Of course she would have to spend some time in the Square, if only to say hello to Gran, but her first free weekend was spoken for, and possibly her second.

The following morning, still bubbling with exuberance, she 'borrowed' a trug of new potatoes from Bessie, the maid of all work, dealt the youngest ones half a dozen tatties each and proceeded to teach simple addition sums with their aid – until Mr Kirk emerged from the inner sanctum reserved for himself and the top class, to see what the giggling was about and told her sternly to 'Replace those vegetables in the kitchen, where they belong'.

She had the strong impression that if she not been a grown woman of twenty-two he would have ordered her to 'Hold out your hand' and she would have felt the sting of the tawse on her guilty palm. Mr Kirk's tawse was an awesome black leather strap of legendary terror.

Obediently she returned the trug to Bessie, with whispered thanks, and hurried back along the linoleumed passage to the schoolroom where her children now sat in nervous rows, repeating the four times table at the direction of Mr Kirk's ruler. The youngest, their eyes round with apprehension, opened and shut their mouths in baffled imitation of their older brothers and sisters till the final 'Four twelves are forty-eight'.

'The three Rs, Miss Noble,' warned Mr Kirk. 'That is all we require.' She thought she heard him add *sotto voce*, 'Not shopkeeping or agriculture,' but it could have been wishful thinking. Then he strode back to his own room, leaving the door conspicuously open.

After that, she concentrated dutifully on the blackboard and the slate, until the longed for tattie-lifting time arrived, and freedom.

'My but you look fine and healthy, Sal, with a good colour to your cheeks,' beamed Mary Noble when Sarah arrived home on a bright Tuesday morning in October.

'I am, Gran.' That was the bicycling, but with her mother and grandmother looking at her with such happy indulgence, Sarah did not want to dwell on that particular subject.

Sarah knew her mother assumed the bicycling parties were all female, but she had never directly asked Sarah: if she had, Sarah would have told her that there were as many men as girls, but she had not asked. Nor had she asked about their picnics where they spread rugs on the grass at the riverside, in a woodland glade, on a rocky outcrop, or in the neglected garden of a deserted croft. Men and girls sprawling full length together, arguing, laughing, plotting the stages of the campaign they would one day put in motion, when the time was right. Sarah preferred to keep her two lives separate: it was less complicated that way, less prone to argument and hurt. Besides, she planned to spend no more than three days in the Square before taking off again.

'And are you happy, Sarah dear?' asked her mother.

'I think so.' Very happy, remembering the weekend, but that was not what her mother meant. 'I like the school and the countryside and the village, not that it is much of a village. Half a dozen cottages and a wee shop. And the Big House where Mrs Duff lives, though she spends the winter months in London, so I have not met her yet. And next summer, if I'm still at the school, we are going to take all the children to the beach for a picnic, so you can come to the sands and wave.'

'And why shouldn't you be still at the school?' demanded Mary Noble. 'Is that headmaster of yours not pleased with you?'

'It's only a temporary post, Gran,' reminded Sarah, avoiding the question. 'I am still on probation and Mr Kirk is very strict. But Mrs Kirk is a kindly woman, though far too docile. All the women are, as far as I can see. And they pass it on to their children. They need to be stirred up, as Mrs Pankhurst and her followers are stirring up those self-satisfied dinosaurs in the Houses of Parliament.'

'It does not do to stir up a settled community, Sarah dear,' ventured Elissa. 'Especially when you are a newcomer.'

'Someone has to do it. And if the mothers won't listen, then the daughters must.'

'Just remember how impressionable children can be. I hope you won't confuse the poor little things with too many contradictions.'

'There is no contradiction in teaching girls to speak for themselves, is there?' retorted Sarah, feeling the usual exasperation creep back: why must they be so complacent and unquestioning? 'Nothing wrong with giving them a little basic understanding of our iniquitous parliamentary system?'

'Yes, yes,' interrupted her grandmother. 'But all that little lassies really want to do is play with their dollies or their skipping ropes. Look at wee Poppy. She carries that doll of hers everywhere and there's no harm in that. You keep your speechifying and your politics for folk with nought else to occupy them.'

'But all women ought to occupy themselves with – '

'Wheesht, Sal. You're not in school now, and I've such news to tell you.' Old Mary's eyes were bright with excitement. 'You'll never guess what your ma and her Adam have gone and done.' Mary had been bursting to tell Sarah ever since the girl had come in the door. 'They've bought us a house in the country, so's we can all go and have a fine holiday together next year, when the new plumbing's done.'

'A country house?' Sarah turned on her mother in dismay. Gran

374

must have got it wrong, misunderstood somehow. 'You can't have done. I don't believe it.'

Sarah had thought about the changes her mother's marriage might bring to the household in the Square, but never in her wildest flights of fancy had she considered a country house.

The idea appalled her, though she could not have put into words exactly why. She only knew that it did not fit the pattern: it was wrong for her, for her family, for all the traditions of her upbringing in the Square. An upbringing to which she clung defiantly in moments of heated political argument, and which she conveniently forgot on other more social occasions. To be truthful, as she occasionally, in private, forced herself to be, she was both ashamed and proud of her background in more or less equal measure. Though lately, she recognised, the shame had diminished and, certainly with Ben Lucas, she was able to discuss the patterns of life in the Square without the edge of belligerent defiance she had once found necessary.

'That chip on your shoulder will soon be no more than a grain of sawdust if you're not careful, Miss Noble,' Ben had teased her only yesterday, when they were freewheeling down the road past Potarch and the white-flecked, sun-sparkling sash of the River Dee, her hair streaming loose behind her and her cheeks whipped pink and glowing by the autumn wind. Ben was her good friend, she loved his company, but the difference between their backgrounds would always be there, whatever he said. It was part of the attraction, for both of them, and she wanted to preserve that difference intact. Not have it eaten away by her mother's social ambitions.

'Why not, Sarah?' said Elissa, with an air of sweet reason which Sarah found both patronising and smug. Her mother was like a cat who had drunk several bowls of the best cream and was too replete to see anything beyond her own sleek whiskers. 'Surely it is not unheard of? Your friends the Lucases, for example, have a holiday lodge at Dinnet and I know for a fact that the Forbeses – '

'That is not the point,' interrupted Sarah, with a mixture of panic and fury. She felt the solid foundation of her life shifting under her feet, leaving her suddenly vulnerable. 'They are different.'

'In what way?' said Adam quietly. He had come into the room unnoticed and now stood behind her mother, his arm at her waist. He looked different somehow, with an air of new authority. As if he was suddenly master in the house instead of only her mother's new husband. Years ago, she remembered, her parents had not even spoken his name. A phrase from the past flashed vividly into her mind: *the hell-hole man*. That was Adam Grant, whom she had been forbidden to speak to. And now here he was, taking her father's place and criticising her.

'Are these friends of yours a different species from us, Sarah?'

'You know perfectly well what I mean, Adam.'

On her mother's marriage, Sarah had announced that she would call her mother's husband by his Christian name. 'Stepfather is so cold and formal and I can't call him Uncle any more. It sounds silly.' Neither Adam nor Elissa had disputed the point, which was disappointing. Sarah had prepared some devastating arguments and, remembering that old disagreement about hierarchical systems of address which she had lost, would have enjoyed using them.

'For an educated girl, Sarah,' retorted Adam, 'you are remarkably incoherent. Explain yourself.'

'I am no longer a girl, as you so disparagingly put it, but a grown woman of twenty-two.' *And should have been married years back.* She heard her Aunt Bethany's sneering voice and straightened her shoulders in defiance. 'The difference is obvious. The Lucases are gentlefolk, born into that sort of life. It is natural for them to live as they do.'

'And?' prompted Adam.

'And we are not,' she said, though she felt herself blushing at the feebleness of her argument and avoided his eye. 'It is social-climbing to ape one's betters and to try to buy one's way into a different social stratum.'

'Is that really what you think, Sarah?' said her mother. 'When you told us yourself that this place was too small for us, too overcrowded, without proper plumbing? That we would all die of poverty and disease?'

'I said the house was overcrowded, that's all. I didn't mean everyone had to move.'

'Everyone needn't move, Sarah dear. Samuel and Harriet will stay here when they marry, and so will anyone else who wants to. I expect there will be plenty of toing and froing between the two houses.'

'Two houses! That's even worse.' Sarah saw her whole background turned suddenly upside down and was shocked to her fisherlass roots.

'Worse?' said her mother in astonishment. 'To have space for everyone and, by your own argument, better health? I really don't understand you.'

'No,' growled Adam, 'and nor do I.'

'I did not expect that you would,' snapped Sarah, though she knew as she said the words that they were patronising and rude. That was the trouble with public speaking: out of self-defence one learnt to deflect criticism with a put-down of one kind or another. Sarcasm, personal gibes, erudite quotations way above the audience's heads. Anything to avoid answering an awkward question. She had become rather good at it. Everyone said so.

376

'And why is that?' persisted Adam, with an inflexibility which was already beginning to unnerve her. 'Though I do agree that it is hard for us to understand someone who says one thing and does another. Someone, for instance, who betters himself by education and influence but forbids others to do likewise. A hypocrite might behave like that, or a bigot, but not an educated, thoughtful and compassionate adult. So please tell your mother and me why we are incapable of understanding?'

'Because ... because ...' Sarah was floundering for an answer when she remembered another, similar occasion, not two days ago, Ben's amused eyes watching her, his wink of encouragement. 'Because we do not need to move at all,' she finished, knowing she had changed the argument, but pleased with the tactic just the same. *If you are losing on one ground, skip to another.* 'We have a good enough house here and as Grandma pointed out years ago, we can always build upwards, add an extra room or two. Where is the need to move anywhere, even for a holiday? The air here is clean, the seashore always available, with bathing huts and sand. What more could anyone want?'

'Is that why you bicycle as far away from here as possible, Sal?' said Adam, with a teasing gleam in his eye.

Sarah blushed, but stood her ground. 'Don't call me Sal. I grew out of that name years ago. And any fool knows you can't bicycle on sand.' Before the inevitable rebuke from her mother, she went on recklessly, 'No one in the Square has a country house. It's plain social climbing; showing off to the neighbours, like that Daimler you hired for the wedding. You're getting worse than Aunt Bethany. At least she is not hypocritical enough to pretend her motives are something else.'

'You will apologise for that remark, Sarah,' said Adam quietly. He tightened his arm round Elissa's waist and she leaned gratefully against him.

Sarah knew they cared for her, in spite of their obvious absorption in each other, knew they thought only of her good; but she had grown beyond their old-fashioned world of the harbour and the herring fleet. Her own world was wider, the free world of far-ranging ideas and causes, a new world they could not begin to understand. She narrowed her eyes into obstinacy, knowing she was in a corner, knowing she was wrong, yet refusing to give ground. That was what she was best at; Ben had said so and several of the others. 'That's your strength, Sarah,' they had told her. 'Build on it.'

That was all very well for the public platform, but here in her own home it was not so easy to sustain. She glanced at Gran, bemused now and anxious, at her mother who looked troubled, but years

377

younger and glowing with love; at Adam Grant, unusually stern, his arm still around her mother's waist. They were all looking at her, all waiting.

Suddenly she capitulated. 'I am sorry, Mother,' she said, eyes lowered. 'I did not mean it.' She looked up, managed a smile, and spread her arms in surrender. *When you lose, lose gracefully.* That's what Ben had told her. 'It was a shock, that's all. I expect I will get used to the idea in time. And if everyone agrees . . .'

'I think it's grand,' said Mary Noble. 'Me with a country house . . . I can't wait to see our Beth's face when she hears. She'll be purple with fury.'

Sarah caught her mother's eye, then Adam's, and tension vanished in their shared laughter. When Danny arrived, with little Poppy, and demanded what they were laughing at, Sarah said generously, 'Me.'

They went to see Fairfields that afternoon. While the adults moved wonderingly through the light-filled, cobwebbed rooms Danny and Poppy explored the garden, with excited cries when they found a bird-bath, a broken balustrade, a flight of moss-covered steps. Only Sarah remained obstinately unmoved by the beauty, the space, the tranquillity of the deserted building and its unkempt garden. She stood on the terrace under the rows of blank windows and refused to explore either house or garden. She was still there when the others emerged, smiling, from their preliminary tour of the house.

'I am sorry, Ma, but I still do not see why we need a country mansion.'

'Fairfields is neither in the country, nor a mansion,' pointed out her mother carefully. 'It is a large family house on the edge of town. A house that has once been beautiful and will be so again, when it is lived in and loved. That is all.'

Sarah turned her back and moved away from the group, her face averted. They would never understand. How could they, with their smug and limited horizons? It was a waste of time to try to explain.

Her mother followed her. 'What is it, Sal? What is troubling you?' Her voice was gentle and concerned and after a moment Sarah gave in.

'The contrast between what we have and what others lack. This place, for example, would house half a dozen families in comfort. There are slums in London, Ma, and in Glasgow, worse than anyone could imagine, and no one does anything about it. If women had the vote they would change that. Make it a crime for a landlord to house his tenants in places he wouldn't think fit for his dog. But as long as we are ruled by landowners, by the rich, well-born and well-connected whose aim is to preserve the privileges they were born into at whatever cost, we will see no improvement in the lot of the poor.'

'And are the poor not to be allowed to improve themselves?' asked Adam, joining them. 'As you have done by your education? As we have done by honest work?'

She turned to face them, her eyes brimming with frustration. Couldn't they see how she was torn in two? The Square and all its inborn traditions pulling her one way, the university and the big wide world the other?

'Of course they are, Adam, but it is not as simple as that. There are so many different arguments that you can't begin to understand. Sometimes I think people can argue the case for anything at all, if they have a persuasive tongue. Then half of me swings one way, half the other, until sometimes I . . . I feel I don't know my way any more!'

'Just remember what your ma taught you about right and wrong,' said Adam quietly, 'and don't do anything you would be ashamed for her to know about. That's simple enough, isn't it?'

Simple, and naïve. But Sarah nodded. There was no point in arguing.

Adam took a spotless handkerchief out of his jacket pocket and gently dried her eyes. 'You think too much, that's the trouble, lass. Give your poor brain a rest, just for a wee while, and use your eyes instead. Now this poor old place, for instance. It's a strange kind of logic which says we ordinary working folk mustn't patch it up and make it habitable, because Lord Someone-or-other five hundred miles away in London is letting his slums rot away.'

'That's not what I said,' protested Sarah, then, seeing his face, she reluctantly smiled. 'I'm sorry. I suppose I was being a little silly. And I agree, it is an ideal family house, with room for everyone.'

'Good. Now we can get on with the purpose of the visit.' Adam tucked her arm under his, then, with Elissa on his other arm, led them up the front steps and into the house. 'It is your turn, Sarah, to choose which of these dusty old rooms you would like for your own.'

Sarah chose; though she doubted she would ever use it.

For the rest of the term Sarah threw herself into her work with single-minded purpose. If she was to be a teacher, then she would be a good one.

In her teaching days, Mrs Kirk, the headmaster had told her, had produced literate, numerate calligraphers by the end of the third year: Sarah vowed to do it by the end of the second. They were dull children on the whole, but with one exception, Milly Thomson, she thought her goal was possible. Milly managed her times tables well enough, and could recognise most of the letters of the alphabet, so she must have some sort of a brain, but her slate work was disastrous. Sarah decided to give her extra help in the spring term; try and find out the problem. She might even discuss it with her own mother – Elissa had beautiful handwriting and had taught them all to write properly. It would be a small way of sharing her new life, thought Sarah with affection, and one that ought not to prove too contentious.

Sarah went home to the Square for Hogmanay but with all the family bustle and celebrations there was no time for talk of Braehead school beyond the usual 'How are you getting on, Sarah?' and her usual answer, 'Fine.' She was still at home, three days into the New Year when Grandma Noble died in her sleep.

Elissa found her, in the box-bed off the kitchen which Mary had shared with old Gideon for forty-three years, when as usual she took her a cup of early morning tea. At first she thought the old woman was sleeping, then she touched her shoulder gently to wake her, and realised the truth.

In the empty silence of the kitchen, Elissa knelt by the bed and wept for the woman who had been mother and friend to her for over twenty years; then she whispered her private prayers of grief and farewell, kissed the dear, lined face, dried her eyes and went to fetch Mary's oldest surviving son, Samuel. Mary Noble had lived her allotted years, borne many children, brought ten of them safely to adulthood, and seen the first of her great-grandchildren born. Elissa knew she was content to die and had been impatient to join her own Gideon for some time, but the knowledge did not make the loss any easier to bear.

Almost the entire family, including Zeb summoned from the Mission and Phemy from Buckie, gathered for the funeral. The whole Square attended and the Noble household was fuller than it had ever been, and more crowded even than for old Gideon Noble's funeral seven years back, for the family had expanded since then and their friends' families with them. Only Gideon Joe was absent. No one knew how to contact him.

Sarah was devastated, for she had loved her grandma deeply. The loss made her feel suddenly old and bleak and lonely. Daniel wept openly while at the same time, when Poppy cried in sympathy, telling his little niece that her great-grandma had gone to heaven to be happy with Great-grandpa and Auntie Milly 'and your own Mummy'.

Both Adam and Brodie Gibb had sent messages to London, trying to find Gideon, but to no avail. Lawyer Forbes contacted his son Cameron who promised to do his best, but they heard no word. Elissa mourned her son's absence, but Adam kept always at her side, comforting and sustaining her, while his own sorrow showed plainly in his grave and dignified face. Elissa was proud of him and deeply grateful.

When they had all gone again, the house seemed strangely empty, the fireside chair which had been Mary's a bleak reminder. Suddenly Sarah realised that the last anchor holding her in the Square was gone. Her mother had Adam and did not need her. Sarah could go her own way with a clear conscience. As her brother had done.

'Eat up nicely, Poppy dear,' her mother was coaxing on the morning of Sarah's departure. 'No, not like that. Try the spoon in your other hand. There, that's better.' She leant over the child, guiding her hand, then looked up at Sarah with a smile. 'When she's older, perhaps you would like to try some of your new teaching methods on Poppy?'

'How did you know I . . .?'

'I didn't. But I know you. And, from what you have let slip, I think I know what an old-fashioned place a country school can be. With an old-fashioned teacher at its head. Though there is still a great deal of sense in the old methods and you must admit, they get results. So go carefully, my dear.'

'Thanks for the warning, Ma.' Sarah hugged her with spontaneous affection. 'And I will try, I promise.'

It was three weeks into the new term when Sarah lost her patience, and her temper, for the first time.

'No, Milly, *not* like that!' She thumped her fist down on the desk so hard that she felt the bruise for days after. 'How many more times do I have to tell you to hold your pencil properly?'

Milly looked up at her with brimming eyes. Her nose was running and mousy strands of hair had escaped from the tightly drawn-back plait which was tied at the end with a piece of whiskery string. 'Sorry, miss.'

'Miss *what?*' She heard the headmaster's door open and knew he was watching to see what the noise was about, but Sarah was already ashamed of herself and fishing out the handkerchief she kept in her desk for such emergencies. She offered it to the child.

'Dry your eyes, Milly. Then we'll try again.'

'Sorry, Miss Noble,' sniffed the child and dried the tears from her eyes with one hand while the other clutched the offending pencil for all the world as if it were a spoon and she was trying to eat porridge with it.

A spoon. Sarah's eyes brightened as a sudden idea struck her.

'Now blow your nose, Milly. Put the pencil down and use both hands.'

She heard the headmaster's door close again and let out her breath in relief. 'Now, Milly, give me back the handkerchief and pick up your pencil. Would you like to try it in the other hand today, for a change? Look, I'll guide your hand for the first letter . . . There. Now see if you can copy that by yourself.'

She stood beside the child for ten minutes, watching the first, halting efforts change into confidence and, by the fifth attempt, produce a perfectly formed 'M' followed by a creditable 'i-l-l-y'.

'Well done, Milly. Now I want you to copy what I have written on the blackboard, just like you were trying to do before.'

'With this hand, miss? I mean, Miss Noble?' Mary cast a fearful glance towards the headmaster's door. 'Mr Kirk said if I did I'd get the belt.'

'Not this afternoon,' promised Sarah, praying fervently that the headmaster's door would stay shut. 'Not when I show him what excellent work you have done.'

That evening, she sought out Mrs Kirk and confessed.

'I told poor little Milly Thomson to hold her pencil in her left hand and look what she produced.' Sarah opened the copybook at the latest page, then flicked back. 'Compared with this, and this.'

'Oh dear,' said Mrs Kirk. 'It really does look as if you are right, Sarah. I did wonder, but the headmaster said . . .' Her voice trailed into silence.

'I am sure I am right. The child is naturally left-handed and will achieve far better results if she is allowed to follow her instinct. Think what torture it would be to us to be made to learn with the wrong hand.'

'Yes. But I wonder . . .'

'You wonder what Mr Kirk will say when he finds out that I have countermanded his orders? I had thought you might be prepared to speak for me, Mrs Kirk, but in the circumstances, would you like me to tackle him myself?'

'You know so much more about it, Sarah,' said Mrs Kirk with an apologetic smile and when the ailing Lillian obligingly wailed from somewhere upstairs, Mrs Kirk hurried off to see to her, with obvious relief.

'Oh well,' sighed Sarah. 'Here goes. God grant me diplomacy, and half a hundredweight of grovelling humility.'

She managed it somehow, offering up her own ignorance, inexperience, memories of feeding her younger siblings. 'She tries so very hard, poor child, for such meagre results and I thought she might feel more at ease, Mr Kirk, if she gave her right hand a rest. When you study the results, I think you will agree that they are encouraging, even remarkable.'

She dared to cross the room at that point, to stand beside him at his desk, and to put the open copybook down in front of him.

'This is the writing she did this morning,' and she indicated the pitiful spider-crawls on one page. 'And here you see the afternoon's left-handed efforts.' She pointed to the almost perfect page, then stepped back to a more respectful distance.

When he eventually raised his eyes, after a good five minutes' brooding silence, it was to say, 'Very well, Miss Noble. It is most irregular, but you may tell Milly Thomson she is allowed to use her left hand if she prefers it. Oh, and Miss Noble . . .' This when she was already turning to go.

She stopped, turned back, said politely, 'Yes, Mr Kirk?'

'Thank you. You have done well.'

The rest of the school year passed with minor skirmishes and eruptions, but nothing serious. Or so Sarah thought.

One balmy Saturday half-way through the summer term, Bessie came scurrying to wake her at seven in the morning to say that 'a party of young persons' was at the scullery door and would Miss Noble come quick, 'Afore the master hears them or there'll be the devil to pay.'

Sarah, who was already up and dressed, had scurried downstairs to find Adelaide, Ben Lucas and half a dozen others, with bicycles and bulging picnic baskets strapped to handlebars, crossbars, or behind saddles.

'We've come to take you out for the day,' said Adelaide, beaming. 'And don't say you haven't a bicycle, because Ben has brought one for you.'

Ben grinned and indicated the tandem which he had propped against the scullery wall. 'I am even prepared to let you take the rear saddle,' he grinned. 'If you are good.'

Of course she had gone; quickly, before Mr Kirk could forbid it. Saturday was a free day for her to use as she chose, she had reasoned, and Bessie had been asked to explain on her behalf.

How was she to know that Bessie had told them, 'Miss Noble went off on a bicycle with a man. For a picnic. No, she didn't say where.' Or that the farmer at Braehead had seen the party sprawling on the river bank, drinking lemonade, which he called 'strong drink', and laughing, 'while Miss Noble stood on a rock in her bare feet and shouted at them.' Or that Maggie Esson had embellished the story till 'that Miss Noble' was paddling in the river with her skirts up above her knees and teasing the men. 'Disgusting, it was, and her supposed to be a teacher. If you ask me, she's nought but a coarse-living fisherlass, for all her fancy book-learning.' Maggie fancied Doug Webster of Braehead and was jealous.

At the time, Sarah knew none of this and spent a glorious day with her city friends, talking, arguing, discussing this and that. She returned bright-eyed and eager, her spirits quite restored, in time to wash and change before the evening meal.

Mr Kirk said the usual grace, they ate in the usual silence, but afterwards, instead of taking his usual chair beside the fire, Mr Kirk said, 'May I have a word, Miss Noble, in private?'

'I would prefer it, Miss Noble,' he began when they had adjourned to the small schoolroom which was the headmaster's sanctum, 'if in future you ask permission before you go gallivanting off into the countryside with strangers of the opposite sex. I am, after all, *in loco parentis*.'

Sarah took a deep breath, opened her eyes in what she hoped was beguiling innocence, and said, 'If I have done anything to offend you, Mr Kirk, I am truly sorry. My friends – and they are all friends, known to my parents for many years – arrived early in order to make the most of our summer daylight hours and I did not wish to disturb the household by what I thought would be unnecessary goodbyes. As for *in loco parentis*, I am a grown woman, Mr Kirk, and Adelaide Forbes is almost a sister to me. Her father,' she added, looking earnestly into Mr Kirk's face, 'is Lawyer Forbes of Correction Wynd. He is most satisfied that I have found my first appointment under your expert guidance.' She lowered her eyes to her obediently folded hands and added, as an apparent afterthought, 'He has worked very closely with the Schools Inspection Committee.'

There was a pause before Mr Kirk said, 'Very well. But this is a small community, Miss Noble, where trivial misdemeanours can become large ones overnight. I advise you to remember that, and to be circumspect in all you do. In future, Miss Noble, whatever hour of the morning, you will have the courtesy to consult me before you embark on ill-advised picnics.'

Pompous old killjoy, thought Sarah as she walked demurely from the room. Afterwards, she had the grace to admit that he was right, but by then it was too late.

It was a picnic, the school summer one, that was Sarah's undoing. She could not explain what made her do it, except a fatal combination of high spirits, sunlight, devilment, and deep conviction.

She made her preparations slowly, secretly, over the preceding weeks, disguising everything as conscientious and dedicated teaching of the three Rs. In this, Milly Thomson was her unwitting but devoted accomplice. Solemnly Sarah cut out large cardboard squares, Milly inked a beautiful capital letter on each one, and they were used as models in the classroom for the children to copy. Together they made similar, smaller squares for the small letters. Sarah never used more than four of the squares in the classroom at once, keeping the others neatly stored flat in the drawer of her desk. The children dutifully scraped chalk over slate, chewed pencils, smudged ink, produced drunken, misshapen versions of their model letter, over and over, until Miss Noble said the magic words: 'Well done, Maggie,' or 'That's very good, Ian.' Or Doug or Willie or Ina or Bess.

In the playground she made them march, left, right, left, right, then form in a double line, fifteen at the front, fifteen at the back. Then change places, raise their arms in the air, drop them, change back again. Repeat. Over and over until she was satisfied.

The seniors did not take part, being engaged with higher things in the headmaster's room.

Messages were sent home via the pupils. The children were to assemble at the school by nine in the morning, rain or shine. If rain, they would travel to the estate's biggest barn in the pair of well-scrubbed dray-carts kindly lent by the Big House; if fine, in the same carts to Aberdeen beach, three miles away.

There would be games and races, cakes and sticky buns and an ice-cream cornet each to round off the day. Mrs Kirk would not go, being still delicate, but Miss Noble and Mr Kirk, with two or three volunteers from among the parents, would be responsible for the children's safety, well-being and good manners. Mrs Webster of Braehead farm was in charge of the picnic and the milk had been donated by the estate cows.

The day was clear, the sun bright, the children excited, but not over-exuberant, and the beach perfect. Several other schools had chosen the same day to visit the same spot and the long golden blade of the shore was lively with scurrying groups of raucous youngsters, swirling and gathering like sheep before driving sheepdogs, darting ankle-deep into the frothing surf and leaping back again with cries of glee or terror till the shouts of teachers and pupils alike mingled with the harsh cries of the herring-gulls, dipping and swooping on constant look-out for food, and the regular suck and draw of the waves on the sand. Milly Thomson daringly tucked her dress into her knickers and squealed with delight as she hopped in and out of the shallows.

Sarah was blissfully happy. A mile or so along the sands to the south she could just see the curve of the north breakwater and the entrance to the harbour, with the low row of roofs which marked the Square where she had been born, and her mother and grandmother before her. There was a comfort and continuity in knowing that: it gave her dignity and an honest stake in life. To her left were mile after mile of well-known sand and headland, past the mouth of the Don and on again, to Black Dog, Newburgh and the north. She was on home territory now and felt confidence flooding through her.

'Please, Miss Noble. What's this shell called?' 'What's this sea-weed?' 'What's this?' 'What's this?'

She knew all the answers, and more. And when the first rush of interest flagged, she set competitions for sand-castles; organised races, treasure hunts, counting games, until at last she threw herself flat on the sand in mock exhaustion and cried, 'Please Mrs Webster, produce that splendid food before I die of exhaustion.'

Mr Kirk joined in none of the games, but leant on the nearest breakwater watching and smoking his pipe.

After the picnic was eaten, Sarah decreed twenty minutes' quiet, 'to aid the digestion and stop you all being sick. But if you sit absolutely still, and don't wriggle or speak or poke your neighbour, I will tell you a story. Once upon a time, long before you were born, there was an old woman who lived in a vinegar jar – '

They listened entranced, even the youngest ones, and perhaps it was the sense of power their concentration gave her that scattered her last shreds of prudence. The story over, she roused them briskly to their feet.

'Now children, before we pack up and go home, we will thank Mr Kirk and Mrs Webster and the other parents for the splendid treat they have given us. Milly, fetch the cards.'

Milly ran to the first wagon and reappeared with an armful of cardboard squares which she handed out to the children. There was much shuffling and swapping between them before they were satisfied, then Sarah cried, 'Are you ready? Then off you go. Left, right, left, right . . .'

They marched this way, that way, round about and back again on the firm sand and finally lined up to face the shore in two perfect rows.

Then at a signal from Sarah the front row lifted high their cardboard squares in wavering unison to spell BRAEHEAD SCHOOL. One or two of the letters were upside down, but the message was clear enough. A nod and the four smallest children held up SAYS. Another nod and they all roared 'Thank you, Mr Kirk.' Another nod. 'Thank you everybody for a lovely day.'

The headmaster beamed, the parents beamed, the numerous bystanders beamed and all was momentarily well.

Then Sarah nodded again, the front row of cardboard squares was lowered, the back row of children, all girls, raised theirs and this time their young voices rang out with the message on the new cards:

'VOTES FOR WOMEN.'

CHAPTER 32

The next day the school closed for the summer, the children scattered to their various crofts and farms and labourers' cottages to work with the adults at the harvest or the wash tub or, in Milly Thomson's case, in the village shop, and Sarah was formally told that her work had been 'satisfactory on the whole'.

'Goodbye, dear, and thank you,' said Mrs Kirk, a tremor in her voice. She added, in what sounded almost like apology, 'For a beginner, you have done very well. People don't always appreciate . . .'

But Mr Kirk had joined them.

The headmaster nodded in dismissal. No smile, no commendation. If he knew what her future was to be, he gave no hint, though from the frown of his straw-coloured eyebrows it was not a rosy prospect.

'You will hear from us in due course, Miss Noble.'

Sarah had no choice but to go home. Go to her mother's precious country house, at least for a week.

Her mother had written that the plumbing work was finished. *How your dear gran would have admired the huge, claw-footed bath and wash-handbasin that Adam has installed upstairs and all with splendid brass taps. I do so wish she could have seen it before she died. But perhaps the anticipation was pleasure enough? I hope so. I miss her company dreadfully, especially when Adam is away (as he is often in the course of business) so it will be lovely to have you home again, Sarah. You will see a big change in Poppy who is a bright little girl and eager to learn. You might like to see what you can teach her in the short time you are at home . . .*

Short time. There was not much anyone could teach a young child in a week. Sarah felt a moment's guilt, then thrust it aside. She had her own work to do and little enough time in which to do it before the new term began at Braehead. If indeed it did, for her. The uneasy memory still lingered of the summer picnic and the ride home in ominous silence.

As soon as you come home, Sarah, we plan to move into Fairfields for the summer. Everyone has promised to help us and it will be quite an adventure

387

for us all. I can't tell you how much I am looking forward to seeing you again . . .

Damn, thought Sarah with daring. 'Damn' was a word Adelaide had taken to using, with great bravado, though only among her friends. Sarah would have to stay at least a week, but ten days was her absolute limit. Adelaide had invited her to go with her to London, to a cousin's house. A married cousin, Cecily Barrett, who was something on the London committee of the Women's Social and Political Union which had been founded by Mrs Pankhurst only two years ago but was, according to Adelaide, making great strides in the cause of Women's Suffrage. The WSPU was also, again according to Adelaide, most encouragingly militant and determined to get things done. They needed all the help they could get and an educated, enthusiastic girl like Sarah would be made most welcome and, far more satisfying, be given plenty to do. Especially as she could take her learning back with her to Scotland and spread the word there.

But first, she must go home.

The 'flitting' was like another summer picnic. Half the Square joined in, with the Bains, the Duthies, all Elissa's friends and neighbours offering help, encouragement or advice. Ina, Jess, Meg and Suffie rolled up their sleeves beside Elissa and set to to scour the place from top to bottom on that first Saturday.

Elissa, swathed in a huge apron which almost reached her feet, was black-leading the range and Sarah, 'being an ignorant kind of a lassie when it comes to housework' had been given a mop with its head tied in a duster and told to rub up the floor-tiles in the hall. Poppy was helping her. Various of Ina's brood and Jess's brood and other assorted offspring had been dispatched about the house on similar missions, with dusters, sweeping brushes, mops, pails of water. Someone found a dead mouse and threw it at someone else and their joyful squeals and shrieks of mischief echoed up and down the wide staircase and the length of the empty corridors.

At the bottom of the garden, the menfolk were busy with a bonfire to burn up all the garden rubbish. Then, when Elissa gave the word, they would fetch in the fuel and light the kitchen range.

'If we had Bethany with us it would be just like Gremista,' said Ina, 'when we had to scrub out the hut for the herring-gutting. My, but these shelves are filthy.' She was standing on a chair at one end of the kitchen, with a bucket of soapy water in one hand and a dripping cloth in the other.

'Wouldn't make any difference if she was here or not,' grunted Jess, on her knees on a rubber mat and scrubbing away at the kitchen flagstones. 'She was a right lazy cow, even then, always telling other

388

folk what to do and doing nought herself.' She heaved herself to her feet, picked up the pail of dirty water and tossed it through the open door into the yard. 'I reckon this floor hasn't seen a good scrubbing brush for . . . Well, talk of the devil. Look what the wind's blown in.'

Picking her way carefully round the corner of the house, bunched skirts held up in gloved hand to avoid the weeds, was a vision in brilliant green taffeta, a parasol tilted precariously over one shoulder in an effort to prevent its silken tassels tangling with the ostrich feathers on her hat.

'I see you've come to help us, Bethany,' challenged Jess. 'I like your working clothes. Real practical. Our Lissa's needing the chimney unblocked so maybe you could give it a poke and a stir-around with that umbrella thing, then there's the ashes to be cleaned out. You could put them in your hat.'

'I've come to pay a morning call, you daft cow,' said Bethany. 'But the front steps was covered in soap and I'm not spoiling my new boots – handmade suede these are and expensive – so I came round to find someone to put a carpet down.'

'Lissa!' cried Jess with glee. 'There's a lady here wants your front step carpeted afore she'll set foot in the place.'

'What a shame,' said Ina, clambering down to floor level. 'We're clean out of carpets.' She tossed the contents of her bucket past Bethany with a foot to spare and grinned. 'Good job I can see straight, or yon hat of yours might have got a wetting.'

'We were just saying,' said Jess, 'that if you was here, it would be like first day at the herring-gutting, in Gremista. Right quarrelsome you used to be, even then.'

Bethany turned her back. 'Some folks has no manners and never will have. I came to see my sister-in-law . . .' Her voice faded as she noticed the group of men at the foot of the kitchen garden. Adam Grant was among them.

'Were you looking for me?' said Elissa behind her.

'Not particularly.' Bethany turned to confront her with hard eyes. 'I came to see what sort of a place it was that you and your precious Adam were boasting about. A country house, I was told. Looks more like a country ruin to me. I wouldn't live here if you paid me.'

Sarah, coming into the kitchen to report progress, heard the sneering voice and moved swiftly to her mother's side.

'Aunt Bethany must have come about the housemaid's job, Mother.' She smiled inquiringly at Bethany. 'Five pounds a year, live in, and uniform provided? Was that the one?' Then she caught her mother's eye and winked.

'Oh dear, I am sorry,' said Elissa. 'The position is already filled.' Then she and Sarah burst into gleeful laughter.

389

'You think you're right clever, don't you?' snapped Bethany. 'You and your fancy schooling.'

'Don't be so stuffy, Bethany. It was only a joke. We are all on holiday today, a picnic outing from the Square. We will be having the picnic later, on the grass. Stay and join us.'

'Me? Sit on the grass like a charity child? In my best clothes? You always did have daft ideas, Lissa Downie, and you've grown dafter with age. And you can tell your precious Adam that he's wasted good money on this place. It's not fit to keep a dog in.' She turned her back and flounced off in the direction of the front door and the drive.

'So much for my country mansion,' sighed Elissa.

'Envy,' said Sarah. Then she grinned. 'And lack of taste.'

After that, mother and daughter got on swimmingly. Something in the feel of the place, the happy mix of people of three generations and a dozen different occupations putting the place to rights together, the splendid picnic made up of contributions from everyone, shared equally between them, the lemonade and cool ale and tea made from the great iron kettle which took an age to boil on the newly lit range, but when it did boil, did so triumphantly in a splendid jet of rattling steam; something in the way Adam looked at Elissa and then at Sarah, as if the three of them belonged together, and in the way that Poppy looked up at her uncle Daniel with absolute, loving trust; all these things, with the men's laughter and the women's chatter and the children's squeals and clamourings, combined to weave a perfect afternoon.

Later, they unloaded the dray-cart, carried mattresses, cooking pots, bedsteads into the house, distributed the bare essentials for the first night's occupancy. Elissa's bedroom was as she and Adam had left it after their week's honeymoon, though she had brought with her the wooden kist which had accompanied her to Shetland on that first herring summer, and which held her best table- and bed-linen, and some of her clothes. There would be time later to divide the family treasures; the first requirements were somewhere to sleep, somewhere to eat, and a good water supply. The latter, at least, was there in plenty: from the great brass taps in the scullery's double sink to the pairs of similar taps in the bathroom on the first floor and in smaller basins in three of the six bedrooms. There was a water-closet beside the bathroom, an earth closet in the outside privy and a pump in the yard outside the scullery door.

At the end of that exhausting, satisfying day, they all gathered in the kitchen for the ham, cheese and bread that remained from the picnic, passed round the whisky bottle and made tea or hot toddies for anyone who chose. Then those who were leaving piled into the empty dray-cart and set off back to the Square in the evening light, tired, but contented, and waved on their way by their grateful friends.

Only Adam, Elissa, Sarah, Daniel and Poppy remained.

They stood in silence, Poppy clutching Daniel's hand, Sarah with her arm through Elissa's, Adam's arm around Elissa's waist, and watched until the slow, creaking shape of the dray-cart reached the gate, bowled safely through and out of sight. Still they watched, listening to the returning silence; saw the silent spread of an owl's wings lift from a distant fencepost, move in dark flight across the twilight. The dart and weave and swoop of bats above the terrace. The smell of the dying bonfire lingered on the night air, with the more acrid smell of coal from the kitchen range.

Unexpectedly, and against all her principles, Sarah realised she was happy. Utterly, uncritically, primevally happy.

The letter arrived the following day: ... *unsuited to a country environment ... too high-spirited ... too independent ... too apt to act on her own initiative without prior consultation ... indoctrinating her charges with unsuitable ideas ...* and the final insult: *obviously finds it difficult to conform ... In the light of these serious and justifiable criticisms Mr Kirk could not in all honesty recommend Miss Noble's re-employment at his school.*

It was only later that she learnt the whole of it: the whispers, the gossip, the suggestions that she was 'after' Doug Webster, that she flaunted her legs with immoral abandon. Even on the occasion of that happy picnic, apparently, she was supposed to have sprawled 'lewdly' with her clothes in disarray as a provocation to the menfolk and a disgraceful example to the young in her charge. No mention of the fact that she had taught a bunch of turnip-heads to read and write like gentlefolk, or equipped even the stupidest of them to count his money to the last halfpenny and not be cheated. Not a hint that she had helped them to *enjoy* school.

Sarah was alternately mortified, furious, and despairing: if this was the face of official education she wanted none of it. She knew she was a good teacher and as for immorality ... the most immoral thing she had done was to ride on the back seat of a tandem, in an ankle-length skirt deliberately designed for modesty and convenience, behind an unmarried gentleman she had known for years, and in the company of half a dozen other people of both sexes, in broad daylight.

Whether it was the odious Mr Kirk's mind that was murky as a sewer, or whether the collective hostility of an inbred and stupid community had swayed him, Sarah could not decide. But after the first shock and outrage and when the first pain had dulled, she did know that they were wrong. Sarah Downie Noble was a good teacher: if they were too stupid to recognise that, then it was their loss.

391

But she would miss the children, especially Milly Thomson.

When her mother asked what news she had heard, Sarah dissembled: 'They haven't settled the placements yet for the autumn. I may be sent to a town school this time. It depends where the vacancies are. They are going to let me know.' Then, as it seemed as good a time as any, she added, 'I shall go to London while I am waiting to hear from them. Adelaide has invited me, and I have always wanted to see the place for myself.'

At first, London was disappointing. Sarah did not know what she had expected, but it had certainly been more than the earnest coffee mornings, the poring over parliamentary reports and constituency reports and schedules of election meetings. No one explained to her why they were doing it, even Adelaide assuming that she knew.

The house was disappointing, too. A tall, ugly, ostentatious building illustrating the worst excesses of late-Victorian architectural boasting, though, as Adelaide assured her, in the very best part of St John's Wood. But to Sarah's eyes the trees looked tired and dust-laden, the gardens parched and drab, with none of the clean green brilliance she associated with summer flowers and hedgerows. The air, Adelaide explained in a warning whisper, was always sooty from the thousands of smoking chimneys all over London, and always dusty from the bowling carriage wheels and scuffing heels of the residents.

'You can't expect a place the size of London to be as clean as Braehead, so for Pete's sake don't mention it, unless you want to be branded Country Bumpkin on your first day.'

But whether she was branded so or not, it was exactly how Sarah felt. Just as she had felt all those years ago when she had first gone to stay with Adelaide's parents in the house in Correction Wynd and had found the contrast with her own life in the Square so awesome and unsettling. At least her years at the university had introduced her to and familiarised her with different layers of society, but even so the transition from Braehead school to St John's Wood was to jump half a century.

Adelaide's cousin believed in the latest style: of clothes, food, conversation, politics. Even house furnishings, though here her husband's more conservative tastes kept her in check and it was only in the breakfast room that modernity was allowed in the form of a plain, functional table with unusual legs and a set of chairs no doubt pleasing to the aesthetic sense, but decidedly hard on the spine and 'lower back'. Sarah had learnt early on to bag a place on the window seat for the Suffrage meetings: at least the cushions were comfortable.

Mrs Barrett was a stylish, well-groomed and intelligent woman of forty-seven. Not much older than Elissa, thought Sarah with interest, but worlds away in style and experience. Sarah doubted Mrs Barrett had ever seen a herring, let alone gutted one, and certainly had never scrubbed her husband's back in a hip-bath in front of the fire. The thought made Sarah snort with suppressed glee until Adelaide dug a warning elbow in her ribs.

Mr Barrett was 'something in the City' and rarely seen, but his daughter Flora, a withdrawn, supercilious girl of about Sarah's age, with pale hair in a long plait, was always at her mother's side, though usually her tasks consisted of pouring coffee or tea, fetching whatever book or paper or report her mother wanted, and taking notes when required. On the rare occasions when she did speak, it was always sensible and to the point. Not like several of the other women who tended to squawk and chatter like a clutch of barnyard hens at times, particularly when discussing what they called 'tactics'. Women in pearls and little diamond brooches and beautifully arranged hair under elegant bonnets of the latest fashion, though one or two of the younger women wore manly shirts and long, plain, no-nonsense skirts with leather belts. One side supported ladylike lobbying of Members of Parliament known to them, a tactic they called 'democratic persuasion'. The other, more vociferous side said reasoned argument had been tried for long enough with no result: it was time to Act.

Sarah longed to ask what they meant by that, but again she had the impression that everyone else knew what they meant already. Either that, or they meant nothing at all and were merely indulging in an exciting new game. Sometimes Sarah found it hard to believe that these leisured, pampered women knew the first thing about the reality of most people's lives: of her own mother's for instance, or her grandmother's. Even of her own. When they talked so bravely of votes for women did they mean for themselves alone, for the leisured and the land-owning, or for every woman, from the lowest herring-gutter to a duchess of the realm? And when they said it was time to Act, what were they actually going to *do*?

At the end of the first frustrating week, she waylaid Flora Barrett under the stained-glass window at the turn of the stately stairs and asked her outright.

'What are we going to do? Why, plan the campaign, of course. Every Liberal candidate is to be barracked. Every election meeting covered.'

'Covered? I ask,' said Sarah quickly, blocking her way before the girl could continue downstairs, 'because I have travelled all the way from Scotland on purpose to be informed. The movement has too few supporters in the north and I intend to take back, and spread, any knowledge I acquire. For the good of the cause.'

'In that case,' said the other, moderating her scorn, though only fractionally, 'I will put it as simply as I can.'

Whether because Sarah had come so far, because she had come from such a benighted place as Scotland, or because she was obviously a simpleton Sarah was not sure.

'As you know, or should know,' continued the girl, 'there is to be an election. Whenever and wherever a candidate speaks, we intend to place in the audience a group of our people, two is the minimum, more is better, who will question that candidate on his party's policy towards Women's Suffrage. Question, and press for an answer. There will be heckling, possibly even physical removal, so our people need to be well schooled and well prepared. But we will ask, and we will be heard. Now you must excuse me.' She stepped to one side, making to push past Sarah and continue downstairs. 'I have work to do.'

'You should talk to her properly, Flora,' said a familiar voice and Ben Lucas appeared in the hallway below them. 'Sarah is a fine public speaker, and obstinate as hell. She swats the hecklers like so many pesky flies. Isn't that right, Sarah?'

'Ben! What are you doing here?' cried Sarah in delight and sped down the stairs to take him by both hands and be kissed exuberantly on the cheek. Then, remembering her dignity, 'Shouldn't you be minding the shop at home? Or has Daddy given you the day off?'

'Day? What would I do with a mere day? I have a whole month, though I've used a good chunk of it already, one way or another. Is Adelaide here?'

'More or less.' Sarah's spirits had soared to jubilation at the sight of Ben, his hair ruffled by the straw boater he now held in his hand, grey flannel trousers and blazer proclaiming his holiday status and the usual silk cravat at his neck declaring he took trouble with his appearance even when in pursuit of summer pleasures. As he seemed to be now. He grinned up at Flora Barrett, the light through the leaded window on the landing patterning his face and hair with reflected red and green and blue.

'La Belle Dame sans Merci. As always, Flora.'

'As you two obviously know each other, I'll leave you to it,' Flora snapped and pushed past them at the foot of the stairs to stride in obvious dudgeon along the passage to the library door.

'And about Adelaide, in case you are still interested, it's "less" at the moment,' she called from the doorway. 'Mother sent her to Westminster, officially to collar her MP and ask awkward questions; unofficially to study the set-up.' She disappeared into the library. The door did not actually slam behind her, but it made enough noise to raise at least one eyebrow.

Ben shrugged. 'Funny girl. Didn't know you and she were friends.'

'I don't think we are. But what are you doing in London, Ben? You didn't say you were coming.'

'I didn't know. My father fixed it up behind my back and only told me last week. I'm staying at my uncle's place so he can look me over. If he likes what he sees, I might find myself condemned to work for the old codger in Lincoln's Inn one day.'

'Oh.' Sarah's spirits sank as swiftly as they had risen. At Braehead it was the promise of weekends with Adelaide and Ben and the others which had kept her sane. And if she was not to be incarcerated at Braehead, then it would be somewhere worse. But if Ben was in London . . .

'You look as if you need cheering up, Sarah. If you are not doing anything, or being sent anywhere, how about taking a cab to St James's with me? I have an errand to do for my father, and afterwards we could look for Adelaide in Westminster. If we don't find her, no matter. I fancy a walk along the embankment anyway. The river traffic is fascinating.'

Sarah fetched her coat and hat, but it was while adjusting the latter, a plain straw boater, to the most flattering angle in her attic bedroom mirror that her conscience pricked. When Sarah had left Fairfields after only a week, explaining that she had an invitation to London with Adelaide, her mother had been disappointed, but had tried to hide it under the hope that Sarah might come across her brother Gideon.

'Please keep a look-out for him, Sarah. You could contact that nice Cameron Forbes who might be able to help. Adam has asked at all the big shipping company offices to no avail, and Cameron is my last hope. Only if you have the time, of course, but if you could, I would be so grateful. And he is your brother. Gideon has been away for three years now and it is long enough.'

Guilt had made Sarah promise, but so far she had done nothing about it. Now, the mention of Ben's errand for his father reminded her. If Ben was to be in London too, he might help her in her search. After all, he knew Cameron, and if that led nowhere they could try the shipping offices together. Just because Adam knew nothing of Gideon's whereabouts did not mean that nobody else did.

Ben's father's 'errand' proved to be at a wine merchant's in St James's Street, where, in a splendidly panelled eighteenth-century office, Sarah sat obediently on the wooden chair indicated while Ben tasted, selected and placed an order for several cases of port and as many of claret. The wine merchant treated Sarah with an old-world courtesy which managed at the same time to imply sorrowful reproof. Even the offer of tea, refused, underlined the message that wine with all its mysteries was a man's domain. Sarah inwardly fumed, but for

Ben's sake outwardly complied. She countered avuncular courtesy with a demure smile of such meekness that Ben's eyebrows shot up in astonishment. By the end of the transaction that smile had melted the Ancient's disapproving heart so completely that he escorted them to the outside door himself.

'Goodbye, Miss Noble. And to you, Mr Lucas. Your order will be dealt with immediately, I assure you.'

It was as he held open the door for young Mr Lucas's charming companion to step outside that Sarah saw someone vaguely familiar mounting the steps towards them. A man of fifty or so, with a dissipated look about him in spite of his 'good' clothes and swaggering walking cane. Then he looked up. She saw his face and clutched Ben's arm in shock.

The twisted nose was unmistakable, the sneer etched deep and sinister around his mouth.

'Quick, Ben,' she gasped. 'Hide somewhere.' But it was already too late.

CHAPTER 33

'Miss Sarah Downie Noble, I believe? Charmed to meet you again after so long. Your mother is well, I trust?' When she deliberately ignored him, turning instead to the Ancient with murmured thanks for all his help, Sinclair's pale eyes gleamed cold and hard. He gave a mocking bow and stepped to one side with a flourish. 'Allow me.'

Sarah stayed where she was inside the doorway, her arm tight through Ben's. She would not pass so close to the man for all the world. What he, or she, would have done next Sarah would never know, for from the mahogany gloom behind them the Ancient spoke.

'Mr Sinclair. Unless you have come to clear your outstanding debt, I would respectfully remind you that your presence is not welcome on these premises.'

'Respectfully? Let me *respectfully* tell you, you ignorant old fool, that my father and his father before him kept this firm in business single-handed, when others less loyal were leaving in droves. Your precious *premises* are still as mouldering and decrepit as they always were, so if you know what's good for you you will *respectfully* supply me with a case of your best port before you go completely bankrupt. Send it round to my rooms this afternoon.'

'Certainly, sir. When your debt has been cleared. I am afraid I must insist that until such time I – '

'Insist? *Insist*? You poxy, jumped-up office clerk. How dare you presume to tell me what to do.' Sarah and Ben forgotten, Sinclair pushed past them into the dark-panelled sanctum to confront the pained, grey-faced but resolute Ancient. 'I demand that you supply me. Dammit, I'll have *two* cases for your insolence. Two cases of best port. *Now*. As of right.'

He raised his stick to threaten the old man and two assistants appeared out of nowhere to restrain him while Sarah stared in fascinated horror.

'I think retreat is called for,' murmured Ben at her side and propelled her through the door into the safety of the street, then at a brisk stride towards the corner where St James's Street met Pall Mall. But he was not quite quick enough. They were almost at the corner when a tumbling, sprawling figure was ignominiously ejected from the wine merchant's despised premises behind them, followed by the clatter of his hurled walking cane.

'This is your fault, Sarah Downie Noble,' the voice clawed after her with concentrated venom. 'Yours and that mother of yours. But you'll not escape me. I'll make you pay one day.' The evil words cut through the noise of the wind and the rattle of wheels in Pall Mall to strike real fear into Sarah's heart, before Ben managed to flag down a hansom cab and bundle her inside.

'Houses of Parliament,' he ordered, then collapsed on to the seat beside Sarah and said, 'What on earth was all that about? I take it you knew the fellow?'

'By sight, yes.'

'As he knows you, apparently.'

Sarah shuddered. 'It is a long story, and I suspect I do not know the half of it. All I do know is that my father and Brodie Gibb and Adam Grant between them managed to ruin Mr Sinclair, though I gather left alone he would have done it for himself soon enough. He caused my father's death – you maybe heard about it? – and I know he hates us. Particularly my mother. And now, apparently, me.'

'Don't worry about it,' said Ben. 'You have a witness that he uttered menaces. And you have a good lawyer.'

'Yes. Lawyer Forbes is a family friend.'

'I was not thinking of Lawyer Forbes,' said Ben, slipping his arm around her waist. 'You forget, I am a lawyer myself. And, I think, a good one.'

'I'll remember that, when I find myself in jail.' Sarah straightened her back and with one gloved hand, removed Ben's warm, ungloved one from her waist. 'Thank you for your support, but I am fully recovered now. Tell me what you think our plan should be when we reach the Houses of Parliament.'

'You are a hard woman, Sarah Noble,' sighed Ben with a comical grimace indicating resignation and thwarted ardour.

'No. Just a determined one.' She grinned at him with affection. 'And Adelaide is another. What is the betting that she has wangled her way inside the holy of holies already?'

Adelaide had. First the Strangers' Entrance, then through awesome corridors of power to the Octagon, or Central Hall.

'Where I demanded to see my MP,' she finished with triumph. 'Only the lazy fellow wasn't there. Summer recess, they told me, as if addressing an idiot. Of course I knew that before I went, but I wasn't going to tell them so. I looked around me in simulated awe and stupidity till I'd seen what I wanted, then promised to come back when Parliament resumes in the autumn. But I reckon it would be easy as pie to stage a demonstration in the Octagon, if we could get enough of our members inside. They would have to filter in in ones and twos, nothing too overt, but once inside, we could cause quite a stir.'

Adelaide was reporting to her cousin, Cecily Barrett, in the small breakfast room they usually used for the purpose. Flora Barrett sat at the table, taking notes, while Sarah and half a dozen other women listened with close attention and varying degrees of excitement. Next they were to be told about methods of self-defence. But when they moved on to specific plans, autumn election meetings to be disrupted, marches to be organised through London's streets to Westminster, Sarah's excitement dwindled to bleak despair.

In two more weeks she would be home again, if not at Braehead school, then in some similar establishment. Unless the vengeful Mr Kirk had managed to blacken her name beyond redemption. Oh God, suppose he had? How would she ever face her family? But whether employed or not, she would be five hundred miles or more away from the centre of the Suffragists' activity. And from Ben.

'You, Sarah!' Mrs Barrett's crisp voice broke into her melancholy. 'You will do what you can on your home ground. I realise that with small resources you may not achieve much, but I will tell Mrs Duff that she may count on you. Supporters are thin on the ground in your area and she welcomes any help she can get.'

'Mrs Duff? Not Mrs Athena Duff?'

'Indeed yes. An admirable woman, staunch and sensible. You can rely on her absolutely. As to the programme, Adelaide will keep you informed.'

That was all. No prospect of immediate action, no protests, no banner-waving. Only plans and more plans. And at home, the elusive Mrs Duff with her Big House and her London seasons. If she were to hear of the disgrace of the latest assistant at Braehead school, at least she might not altogether disapprove of the summer picnic incident. But what good would it do? It would not get Sarah her job back. None of this campaigning and banner-waving could do that.

Sarah, disillusioned, allowed herself to be persuaded by the ebullient Ben to play truant and explore the city with him. The embankment, the Tower, the Pool of London, the East India docks: all with the ostensible purpose of tracking down Gideon. Though when Ben and Adelaide arranged a rendezvous with Adelaide's brother Cameron for the same purpose, in a café near his Hampstead studio, the four of them spent the evening drinking cheap wine and talking about Cameron's art and his recent painting trip to Venice.

It was only when they were leaving that Cameron said, 'By the way, Sarah, Gideon asked me to tell you he is fine. Living and working here in London, though not quite ready to be found. He wants to make his mark first. But he said to tell your mother that he has not forgotten her, or Poppy, and will come home when he can.'

'Then you can tell Gideon from me,' flared Sarah, suddenly furious, 'that he is the selfish, stupid pig he always was. Tell him I am not a postman and he can take his own rotten messages. Tell him, from me, to stop moaning and grow up. Tell him . . . tell him that if he can't be bothered to spare a thought for his own little daughter, he might at least write to Ma who is bringing her up for him. Tell him I don't care if I never see him again, and nor does Poppy – she's never seen him anyway. But Ma cares and he's hurt her long enough. Have you got all that, Cameron?'

'I think so. Anything else?' said Cameron, impassive.

'Yes. Tell him to go to hell.'

'Phew,' whistled Ben admiringly.

'Pretty good,' conceded Adelaide. 'A bit repetitive, perhaps, but a good start. Mind and remember it word for word, Cameron. He deserves it.'

Sarah merely glowered. How dare her brother send her messages via a third person when they were in the same city? She did not regret one word of her reply: Gideon Joe had had it coming to him for too long.

'What is Sarah's miserable brother doing anyway, Cameron? Surely you can tell us?' demanded Adelaide. 'Or is it something unmentionable, like opium-smuggling, or ladies' hairdressing?'

Her own brother grinned, but he shook his head. 'Sorry. I promised. But I think I can say he is doing well.'

'And so are you, Cameron, by the sound of things,' said Ben Lucas. 'Portraits of the rich and famous. Commissions to paint debutantes. You'll be doing babies and little lapdogs next.'

'Very probably,' said Cameron, straight-faced. 'Would you like to make a provisional booking for a portrait of your first-born?'

'That very much depends on the child's prospective mother. What do you say, Sarah?'

'Don't count your chickens before they're hatched,' she snapped.

'Oh well,' shrugged Ben. 'That's that. I don't think Cameron does chickens.'

The incident ended in laughter, but for Sarah the niggle remained, with the usual residue of annoyance and fear. Not for Gideon: she didn't care a damn what happened to him. 'Damn', she had discovered, was sometimes a most satisfying word. But she did care about Ben Lucas. She was fond of Ben, very fond, though she did not want to marry him. Not that he had ever mentioned marriage. But why couldn't men be content to be good friends without always wanting something more?

'Do you ever think of marriage?' she asked Adelaide on her last night in London as they lay in the darkness, in the attic room under the eaves, waiting for sleep. A room like their room in the Forbes house in Correction Wynd; like the attic room in the Square at home. Only this room was higher-ceilinged, with new linoleum on the floor, freshly whitewashed walls, lavender bags in the drawers of the chest and a folded paper fan in the grate. Adelaide told her it had once been the night-nursery and the two narrow pallet beds certainly suggested children rather than adults. Sarah's feet stuck out at the end, but as the room was heavy with collected summer heat that was no disadvantage.

'Marriage is old-fashioned,' murmured Adelaide, half asleep already. 'Invented to preserve the social order. That's what Ben says anyway. Especially when Flora is being particularly odious.'

'But . . . but what has Flora got to do with it?' Sarah was mystified: Flora and Ben hardly spoke to each other.

'Didn't you know? Her ma and Ben's ma were at school together. Practically sisters. They paired off Flora and poor Ben in their cradles and he's been trying to escape ever since. Flora is venomously jealous, so watch out.'

Sarah was silent, readjusting all her ideas. Then she said carefully, 'Will Ben marry her?'

'Not if he can help it. Nobody would, in spite of her fortune. But it's no good asking me these things, Sal. I don't believe in marriage. Two people voluntarily bound by the chains of a convention designed to constrict something that should be unrestricted and free.'

'Yes, but . . .' Sarah hated it when her friend talked like a textbook, particularly a textbook she, Sarah, had not read. 'What about children?'

'What about them? Nasty, noisy little brats.'

'Don't you want any of your own? Or a husband?'

'Which? Or do you mean both? It is perfectly possible, my dear Sarah, for an intelligent woman to lead a happy and fulfilled life without marriage – look at my sister Madeleine – and it is equally possible for an intelligent woman to have a child without the impediment of a husband, if she so wishes. Possible, but not, alas, advisable. Not in these benighted times.'

'Adelaide. Can't you ever be serious? Do you mean to say you never want to get married?'

'Never say "never". But not at this moment, no. All I want is to go to sleep.' With that she hauled the bed-sheet up over her face and ostentatiously turned her back.

But Sarah lay for a long time, wide-eyed in the darkness, watching the night sky darken and pale again towards dawn. It was a darker sky than at home and at the same time not so dark for there were gas

401

lights in the street below and passing cab lights which sent an eerie glow across the ceiling from time to time. But the stars were not so bright, nor the sky so clear, and there were too many people crowding around her in their unknown thousands, out there in the alien darkness.

Suddenly, she had had enough of London and Suffrage and clever ideas. She wanted to go home.

Apparently Mrs Duff had put in a good word for Sarah, whether because of Adelaide's London cousin, Mrs Cecily Barrett, or for her own private reasons Sarah never knew. But the result was a less than cordial note from Mr Kirk and a frozen reminder that she was expected back at Braehead school for the autumn term after all.

She received the news with a mixture of relief and dread, but at least her mother did not question her about it, being engrossed in a letter of her own. They were lingering over a cup of tea in the comfortable kitchen at Fairfields, the door standing open to the yard where half a dozen hens grubbed contentedly in the overgrown cassies. The hens were Poppy's responsibility and she loved them dearly. Beyond the yard was the kitchen garden which Danny was helping Adam and anyone else who volunteered to put to rights, and beyond that the overgrown shrubbery and the trees which mingled with the boundary wall to encircle the property. At the front of the house, facing east, the shrubs were clipped and the drive reasonably weed-free; on the south, the lawn was coming on well, and the herbaceous borders had begun to look more like flowerbeds than mere extensions of the tangled shrubbery; but Elissa preferred to begin the day in the kitchen, even though the yard was in shadow till the sun rose high enough to clear the gable end. Shadow was welcome when the kitchen range heated the place to tropical temperatures. Adam said it was worse than Melbourne in high summer.

This morning, Adam was away with the others to the harbour, where Elissa herself should have been, but since her marriage she had appointed her friend Ina full-time manageress of the smokeshed so that Elissa might have more time for her husband and family. As Elissa had anticipated, she hardly knew from one day to the next who would be at Fairfields, who in the Square, but the new freedom and the happiness seemed to envelop them all, family and friends alike. Even Sarah had conceded that Fairfields was 'nice enough'.

Only Bethany remained scornfully aloof, declaring 'I can't be doing with all this prancing about and showing off. Some folks think they're Lady Muck just because they've an inside toilet and an extra bedroom. I call it greed myself. Greed and vulgarity. But she'll get

402

her come-uppance one day, you'll see. She and that stuck-up daughter of hers.'

Sarah felt anything but 'stuck-up' as she folded the frosty letter and tucked it away in her pocket. If her mother asked, she would say it was merely confirming the day she was expected back. But Elissa did not ask. She was too excited by a letter of her own, from her errant son Gideon.

Among other things, it informed them that he was working for an import-export company which handled a wide range of goods and required him on occasions to travel abroad. However, he planned before too long to come to Scotland when, naturally, he would pay them a visit.

Naturally, sneered Sarah under her breath, but she was happy for her mother whose joy was plain for the whole world to see. Except when she reached the postscript.

'Oh dear. Sarah, you had better listen to this most carefully. Gideon writes, *Rumours are going round the business world that Hugh Sinclair has run up intolerable debts. One or two of our clients, wine merchants in particular, are in financial trouble as a result and a general warning has been put about to call in all credit. Remembering his antagonism, I thought you ought to know, Mother. In case he turns up in Aberdeen to ride out the storm. Your loving son, Gideon Joseph Noble.*

Loving son indeed, thought Sarah indignantly, then the full import of his postscript struck her. She remembered the incident in St James's and shuddered. But why should the man come north to Aberdeen? There was nothing for him here. He would be far more likely to go abroad.

'If he does come, he won't annoy us,' said her mother, reading her daughter's thoughts, but there was a note of uncertainty in her voice. 'Adam told me the allowance stops if he troubles any of us, in any way at all.'

'Don't worry, Ma,' she said. 'You have Adam to protect you, and I shall be perfectly safe at Braehead.'

It was the only recommendation she could think of for the place as she faced her return.

'After your disgraceful display at the summer picnic, Miss Noble,' were his welcoming words that first evening, when she had been summoned to the sanctum, a mere five minutes after her arrival, 'I had expected the authorities to remove your influence from our children forthwith. However, Mrs Duff thinks otherwise and who am I to question her decision?'

God himself, supplied Sarah, under her breath, and God in an almighty huff. But she kept her expression meek.

403

'I am sorry if my exercise in modern politics did not find favour, Mr Kirk,' she offered. 'I thought the contemporary touch might be . . .' But seeing the look in his eyes she did not trouble to complete the sentence and fixed her own eyes, for safety, on the polished surface of his desk.

'The three Rs, Miss Noble. Nothing else. Now do not keep Mrs Kirk waiting any longer. This is a well-regulated household, Miss Noble, and the broth has been ready a good half-hour. Punctuality, Miss Noble, and consideration for others. Remember you are on probation. I shall be watching you.'

And he was, from the moment the first child arrived in the morning, with its peat divot or peck of meal or baked potato to keep warm on the stove, till the last one left at the end of the school day and she barred the door behind it. Watched her as she came downstairs in the morning; watched her at mealtimes; from behind the parlour curtain when she went out for a stroll in the evenings; through the open door of his sanctum at any hour of the school-day. She even suspected him of standing in the garden and studying her attic bedroom window to see when she turned out the lamp.

After the first week of intense irritation, she learnt to ignore him. She was a good teacher, even he must concede that, and if he had nothing better to do than watch her, then she would show him something worth watching.

Her children excelled: mental arithmetic, multiplication tables, addition and subtraction; cursive script, capital letters, even italic writing in good black ink. They could read aloud, write a letter, copy poetry or prose, and one or two of them had progressed to what Sarah thought of as Real Books. *The Water Babies* and *David Copperfield*. Only in needlework did she feel inadequate and Mrs Kirk helped her with that. But the better the children's work, the more dissatisfied Sarah grew: it was too easy, too insular, too lacking in challenge. And still the headmaster watched her, like a hawk pin-pointing its prey.

In self-defence, she took to going home to Fairfields every second weekend. Mr Kirk could not prevent it, and it gave her a welcome rest from the ever-present eyes. Though increasingly she felt the eyes followed her even there. She was sure someone watched her as she walked the last stretch from Queen's Cross. Felt eyes on her back as she turned in between the familiar gateposts. Was the wretched fellow checking that she went straight home, instead of looking for custom on the quay?

But she did not always go to Fairfields. One weekend in early October she went to the house in the Square instead. Uncle Samuel had married his Harriet the previous winter and now Harriet ran the household in Elissa's place. But she was an amiable girl, already five months pregnant, and welcomed her step-niece with easy friendship, as she welcomed all of his various relatives, young and old. She had known most of them from her childhood anyway.

When Sarah arrived, most of the menfolk were at home, engaged in last-minute preparations before the East Anglian herring fishing began. Another week and the Square would be emptied of menfolk, leaving only the too old and the too young. The girls were in a state of excitement, too, those who were off to the herring-gutting in Yarmouth. Many of them were Sarah's old school-friends and contemporaries, and for a moment she felt a pang of real envy that she was not going with them, to the cramped quarters in Yarmouth Rows, and the wind-whipped, spray-dashed gutting yards where sodden binding-rags froze to chilblained fingers and even the thickest-soled boot could not keep out the cold. The girls were already chattering of the fun they had had last year, the better fun they would have this, the lads they would meet, the parties they would give, even the presents they would buy with the money they earned.

Sarah felt suddenly isolated, a stranger in this familiar, welcoming crowd. She had not once been to the herring-gutting: all she knew was hearsay, from her ma and her grandma and now her own friends. She was tempted to beg for a place, any place, so that she might go with them to freedom instead of returning to the prison of Braehead school. But what use would she be? She had not gutted a fish for years; doubted she even remembered how. She had chosen her world years ago and it was too late to go back.

'Cheer up, Sarah,' said a voice from the doorway and she looked up to see Adam Grant, in thigh-boots and knitted gansey like the others, a broad grin on his face. 'It isn't the end of the world just because the menfolk are leaving.'

'It's not that that's grieving her,' said Samuel's Harriet, with a broad wink. 'It's because all the lassies are running after them, to grab the best for themselves. Isn't that right, Sarah?'

'It might be, if I wanted one of them,' said Sarah, with an effort. 'As it happens, I don't.'

'I've heard it's a townser you've fixed your eye on,' teased Ina's Bess. 'A lawyer laddie with a house in Queen's Road and a fine office in Golden Square.'

'And he had to hop it to London, to escape her clutches,' giggled one of Jess's brood.

Sarah blushed and turned her back in annoyance. Why couldn't they mind their own business? But then the Square never could. One person's business was everybody's. Whether it be tittle-tattle or truth. For the first time, Sarah glimpsed something of her mother's reasons for moving to Fairfields.

'Rubbish,' she snapped. 'I've better things to do with my time. As you should have.'

405

'Aye, but we're not all as clever as you, Sarah Noble,' said one pert lassie who was barely fifteen. 'Me, I'd rather have a man in my bed than a book.' This was greeted with shouts of delighted laughter from men and girls alike.

'Ignore them, Sarah,' grinned Adam. 'They haven't a brain between them. Take a stroll with me, instead. I see little enough of you these days and I'm away to London again on Monday. We can take a look at the *Millicent* in passing and then, if you can spare the time, we'll call in at the smokeshed and see how your ma's getting on. She'll have a busy time of it with the lassies away in Yarmouth.'

Gratefully, Sarah accepted. The high spirits and the ribbing had made her feel excluded; a visitor, when she should have been an equal. As they turned the corner from North Pier Road on to the stretch of Pocra Quay which fronted 'Mary's', she felt the now-familiar sensation of watching eyes at her back. Involuntarily she glanced over her shoulder but there was no one in sight. Only the usual stretch of quay, the pilot's tower and the long arm of the north pier reaching eastwards into the grey North Sea. Waves were breaking in monotonous rhythm against the barnacled timbers, throwing grey spray high into the morning air. An innocent enough sight. So why had her spine tingled and her senses sprung to the alert? She was growing paranoid. Mr Kirk could not possibly have followed her here.

The big double doors of 'Mary's' stood wide to the fresh sea air and inside groups of aproned and rubber-booted women worked cheerfully at the various scrubbed wooden slabs, beheading and gutting, tossing, spearing, threading on to tenterhooks, while two or three lads fed them a steady supply of overflowing fish baskets to replace the empty ones and the sawdust-covered floor grew steadily wetter and more slippery as the fish-guts overflowed their barrels and were trampled underfoot. Ina Bain was over by the smoke chimneys, talking to the man whose job it was to feed the fires, or damp them down.

At a side table, Elissa, sleeves rolled to the elbow, long, wide apron tied twice around the waist and strands of hair escaping from the bright bandanna she had bound around her head, was engaged in showing an anxious fourteen-year-old how to tie the tails of a trio of smoked haddock just so.

'Thank goodness you've come, Sarah,' sighed her mother wearily. 'If I've shown Eppie once, I've shown her a dozen times. Not too tight. Not too loose. Twist and bind and knot. You'd think it was simple enough, but can I make her see it? You try, there's a dear.' She said, in a quick aside, 'I can't employ her if she doesn't learn and her poor mother needs the money.'

'Sarah is a teacher, Eppie,' she told the girl. 'So listen to what she says and do it.'

'But Mother, I haven't . . .' Sarah's voice died. What was the use of reminding her mother it was years since Sarah had worked in the smokeshed, years since she'd handled a smoked fish, or any kind of fish that wasn't already prepared for cooking. But her mother was leaning wearily against Adam's shoulder, his arm was around her waist and he was leading her to the chair that had once been old Mary's, beside the smoke chimneys. The two of them were already in a private world.

'Right, Eppie,' she said with more confidence than she felt. 'You see that wooden slab over there?'

'The dirty one with all the fish-guts and stuff?'

'That's the one. If you don't watch me and concentrate and get it right first time, you will scrub that slab, for no pay, for the whole of next week. Understand? Now watch me carefully and do exactly what I do. We will take it very slowly.'

That was for her own benefit, to allow her fingers to remember their lost skill. And they did, with a soothing, satisfying rhythm which took her back to the simpler days before she had discovered the world beyond the Square. It was good to know she could still find the way back. Gut fish with the others, if she wanted. Follow the herring.

When they eventually left, she and Adam and Elissa together, the watching eyes had gone.

One Saturday in early November she received a letter from the elusive Mrs Duff, from her London address. There was to be a Grand March from Caxton Hall in February. All who supported the Cause were required to be there, if humanly possible, and it would be to Miss Noble's education and advantage to attend. If Miss Noble required leave of absence, Mrs Duff would be happy to arrange it with her headmaster. By the same post came a note from Adelaide, giving her the same information. *Cousin Cecily will put us up, as before, and all the girls are going as well as some of the men, to give us moral support. Do come if you can. We could travel down together.*

Sarah was in an agony of indecision. Of course she wanted to go, but would it be worse if she asked Mrs Duff to beg leave on her behalf? Or if she bearded the headmaster herself, in his holy of holies? Either way she would suffer: he still watched her, still hadn't forgiven her for the summer picnic and if she suggested a protest march, he would probably sack her on the spot. Her only hope was if the meeting were to coincide miraculously with a school holiday. Or a measles epidemic.

407

In the end she penned a polite note in reply to Mrs Duff, saying she would use her best endeavours to attend, always supposing she could secure the necessary leave of absence. She posted the letter herself, in the village shop, where Milly was helping her mother, as she always did outside school hours. Then she took her usual walk through the woods at the back of the school and home along the river bank, waving to Doug Webster as she always did when she passed the farm. By the time she turned in through the school gate she knew the eyes still watched her: that settled it. She would wait till the last possible minute to ask Mr Kirk's permission. If at all.

Every weekend now was spent in a state of heightened excitement: when she went home, she spent most of her time with Adelaide and the usual group, talking and planning. Ben was as interested as Sarah in the proposed march which was to be from Caxton Hall to Westminster and coincide with the State Opening of Parliament.

'I'll get my uncle to find urgent business for me in London,' he offered. 'Then I can do the thing properly. Bail you out, visit you in prison, that sort of thing. Which reminds me, Sarah. Have you tackled the jailer yet? Or shall I do it for you?'

'No! Don't you dare,' she cried in horror. 'Already he thinks you are Bad Company.'

'And he'll think I mean to Lead you Astray? Not a chance, unfortunately.'

'Don't worry, Sarah,' soothed Adelaide. 'We'll think of something. Or Mrs Duff will.'

Which is why, when the note arrived by messenger, that Friday evening, not half an hour after Sarah had shaken the November mist from her coat and hat and settled gratefully into the fireside chair, with a cup of tea in her cupped hands, she showed no surprise. It was only a week since she had last come home to the Square, but Braehead school was becoming increasingly claustrophobic under Mr Kirk's unflagging vigilance and she found more and more reasons to leave after school on Friday and have two days' blessed freedom with what remained of her family. The men were away south with the herring fleet, and many of the girls with them, so the Square was emptier than usual and Elissa had chosen to close Fairfields for the rest of the herring season and move back into the old house, in order to be nearer her work, which always seemed to increase when the men were away. The dark winter mornings were unpleasant at the best of times, but the journey from Square to smokeshed was so much shorter and more convenient.

'Who's it from?' demanded Harriet eagerly. As one who never wrote or received letters herself she regarded such things as inevitable bearers of good fortune, or death. 'Is it from your young man?'

'No it is not.' But she could not keep the excitement from her voice.

Dear Miss Noble, she read, *I would consider it a favour if you would call upon me at the above addresss at 11.00 a.m. tomorrow morning to discuss something to our mutual advantage.* The letter was signed *Athena Duff.* and the address was c/o a Colonel Wellington in Rubislaw Den.

'It's from a lady who is arranging something for me, that is all. Mrs Duff, Ma. The one I told you about.'

'I thought she spent her winters in London, Sarah?' Elissa looked up from her knitting in surprise.

'She does, but I believe she is planning some sort of grand event in the spring and I expect she is here to make the necessary arrangements. Anyway, I have to see her tomorrow at eleven.' She passed her mother the note to read. 'So if Adelaide comes looking for me, could you explain? I don't expect to be long.'

'How exciting. Do you think she is going to ask the school to a garden party at the Big House? A spring party, when the rhododendrons are at their best?'

'I don't know, Ma.' Suddenly, Sarah was too ashamed of herself to elaborate and when Poppy climbed on to her auntie's knee demanding a story, she welcomed the interruption with relief. She knew that if she mentioned Suffrage the arguments would begin and it was so much simpler to keep her two lives apart.

The room was stifling, the air thick with the aroma of good beef stew from the iron pot on the range, the kettle simmering contentedly, the coals glowing, her mother's face calm and beautiful in the firelight as she bent her head over the knitting. Something white? A woollen vest, probably, for Adam or Daniel or one of the others. Or a shawl for Harriet's expected baby. Harriet was knitting a large and whiskery stocking which could only be for her husband Samuel's enormous sea boot. One of Harriet's younger sisters was whispering and giggling with young Pearl Bain who was supposed to be washing Poppy's aprons in the scullery, and later, her mother's friend Ina would no doubt look in, to talk over the day's work in the smokeshed and the doings of the various workers and their families. News would be exchanged of the menfolk away, of the herring catches, the weather, the price of fish here at home.

Sarah was reminded vividly of a stark evening in the schoolhouse at Braehead and the contrast brought a rush of sudden love to her heart: love for her mother and her childhood home and the community in which she had grown up. And tomorrow, she would step from this warm, enclosing nest into the exhilaration of that other life outside the Square.

How blessed she was to have them both.

She wondered what she ought to wear to meet the unknown Mrs Duff?

The next morning was crisp with sunlight and a fresh sea breeze. Sarah looked into the smokehouse, on an impulse, to see how her young pupil Eppie was progressing, then walked quickly along Waterloo Quay towards the Shiprow. She had decided on the plain-but-feminine style and wore a dark grey woollen skirt and fitted jacket, which she knew suited her, with a high-necked, white tucked blouse and a straw boater trimmed with dove-grey ribbon. Her blonde hair, neat figure and eager step attracted many an appreciative glance, though Sarah was too preoccupied to notice. The meeting with the unknown Mrs Duff meant a lot to her, holding, as it did, the key to the secret world of Suffragist activity.

As she walked, Sarah studied the shipping of the inner harbour and Albert Quay, as she always did: her mother said it was important to keep track of the competition, and there certainly seemed to be plenty of it. Sarah knew the outline of every one of the Scott Mackenzie vessels by heart, with their names and pennants and individual colours: knew the blue and white flag of the Pegasus line, as Brodie Gibb had christened his new company of Scott Mackenzie and Gibb. Knew the more homely, functional, but no less distinctive line of their own three steam drifters, though she did not expect to see those in harbour. They were still pursuing the East Anglian herring shoals and if they did put into port, it would be for restocking and a quick turn-around before heading back south.

The London steamer was newly docked further along the quay ahead of her; the swinging derricks of a coal barge unloading; the noisy, heaving activity of a cattle barge; the regular ferry to the Islands waiting quietly at its usual mooring on Albert Quay. Add a couple of grubby tug-boats, several trawlers including two with the Pegasus line pennant, and a spruce passenger steamer of the White Star line, and it was a normal dockside morning.

She reached the stretch of quay where the London steamer had tied up to a pair of salt-rusted bollards. The companionway clattered down on to the quayside amid shouts and warnings from traveller and seaman alike, and the first of the passengers stepped ashore. They came in an untidy stream, pushing and grumbling like the cattle of that distant barge, and it was as she stepped back to avoid the crush that Sarah felt the old, unpleasant sensation that someone was watching her. She glanced over her shoulder, then to the upper windows of the nearest buildings before telling herself not to be so stupid. She was on home ground here, not at Braehead.

410

She took the tram to Queen's Cross, checked the time on the watch Adam had given her on the day he married her mother, and slowed her step to a measured stroll as she made her way along the Queen's Road towards the junction with Forest Road and the hallowed precints of the Den.

Rubislaw Den was the home of the wealthy, the successful, the well-born and the self-made: large detached houses with tradesmen's entrances and well-kept grounds, with wine cellars, billiard rooms, acres of Turkish carpets and dozens of uniformed maids to sprinkle sawdust over the precious pile and brush it up to fresh perfection in the small hours before their employers rose from their lavender-scented beds. Well-ordered households where it would not do to arrive early.

At Colonel Wellington's house the thought of the tradesmen's entrance gave Sarah a moment's pause, then she told herself firmly that she was a professional woman, calling upon her equal. She straightened the folds of her best worsted skirt, adjusted the points of her high-buttoned fitted jacket to her satisfaction, pushed open one of the tall iron gates and stepped through, closing it tidily behind her. Then she walked slowly up the curve of the drive to the front door. An undistinguished frontage with too much of the tappie-tourie about it for Sarah's taste; two respectable windows on each side of the front door, but a turret stuck on to one corner, with rounded windows in it and what looked like imitation gargoyles. There was even a military-looking parapet around the roof.

Sarah decided she preferred the Georgian simplicity of Fairfields any day, even if it was a touch decrepit. But no doubt Colonel Wellington felt at home here. She raised the heavy brass knocker and let it fall. Once. Twice. Then half turned to look back down the drive towards the gate. The garden was of the anonymous kind, clipped lawn, low bushes of this and that round its edges, a grey gravel path, trees at the boundary. The gate was out of sight, obliterated by a massive rhododendron bush.

As she waited on the doorstep she decided that she did not like the feel of the place, it being somehow depressing and dour. Something to do with rooks in the bare trees at the back of the house, the drab colour of the winter grass and the dusty, dull green of the flowerless shrubs. There was something in the silence, too, that was unnerving; and now that she looked more closely, the windows were less than clean. Any woman in the Square would have been ashamed of them. But no doubt Colonel Wellington was an elderly widower, with an equally elderly housekeeper and neither of them noticed such details.

She was about to lift the knocker again when she heard the sharp clip of footsteps on an uncarpeted hall. Parquet probably. She was

411

wondering if she would be expected to take off her ankle boots, which were new and rather elegant, so as not to mark the surface when she heard the handle turn and the heavy door swung open.

'Miss Noble, at last. Do come in.'

She had stepped over the threshold before she realised and by then it was too late. The heavy door closed behind her and she heard him shoot home the bolt.

CHAPTER 34

Sarah's heart turned over with fear, before every sense leapt alert with desperate calculation. Was anyone else in the house? Perhaps he had talked his way in somehow and Colonel Wellington was in the back regions? No, he would have come by now to greet her. If she screamed, would anyone hear? Was there a way out through the back scullery and if so was it locked?

But her face showed none of this. She even managed a cool, almost sardonic smile.

'Mr Sinclair. I did not expect to see you here.'

He was thinner than she remembered, his hair greyer and receding, his skin coarser, his eyes duller, and the lines on his face more marked. But the damaged profile was the same, and the etched sneer of the mouth. He must be Adam's age, she thought. No more than forty-five. He looked much older and somehow shop-soiled in spite of his brocade waistcoat and tailor-made checked suit; shop-soiled and dissolute. She felt her lip curl in distaste and turned her head away.

'You must excuse me. I have mistaken the house. I was looking for Colonel Wellington.'

'He is not here. To tell the truth, he does not exist. I thought that was rather a good touch, don't you agree?' He smiled with private triumph. A brief smile, instantly gone. 'And before you ask, Mrs Duff has been most regretfully detained in town.'

He is mad, she realised with a thud of shock. Mad and ruthless. He had laid a trap for her, deliberately, and with God only knew what evil intent, and she had walked straight into it.

'I did not realise you knew Mrs Duff.'

'I don't. But I have been watching you, my dear, for weeks. Watching and noting and finding out. Nice girls really should not tangle with politics, Miss Noble. It is so unfeminine. Leave that to men like Colonel Wellington.' He giggled. 'I think I chose well there, don't you? Very solid and respectable.'

'Wellington is certainly a distinguished name,' she said carefully and with all the calm she could muster. *Do not panic. Do not annoy him.*

'I thought so. That's why I chose it. I once had a housemaster called

413

Wellington. A perfect gentleman, but weak as water. I ran rings round him.'

'I expect you did.' Dear God, how was she going to escape? She half turned, put her hand on the door-knob behind her.

'Not yet, Miss Noble. You have only just arrived.' His loathsome hand gripped her arm, lightly but with enough strength to warn her not to struggle. 'When we last met, I fear we parted on less than amicable terms. I would like to correct that, so that we can become friends.'

This time she looked at him in genuine surprise. 'You caused my father's death. You would hardly expect me to forget that.'

'Not forget, no,' he said, with what she supposed was his version of a humble smile. 'But that was long ago. Let bygones be bygones, Miss Noble, and forgive. It was a genuine misunderstanding, I assure you. An over-reaction in the heat of the moment. The result of understandable anxiety and stress.'

'Nonsense,' said Sarah. 'It was sheer brutality.' Did he really think she would swallow such outrageous lies? 'If that is all you have to say, let me pass. I wish to go home.'

'Not quite all, Miss Noble.' He turned on her his shop-soiled, charm-the-ladies, apologetic smile. 'That disgraceful business in St James's Street was all a misunderstanding, cleared up long ago. Nevertheless, you may have heard a small rumour that I have, shall we say, fallen upon ill-fortune these past years? Certainly my lifestyle has not been as ostentatious as it used to be, but that is because during those years I have had time to reflect and to reform. It is because of this, shall we say, conversion of mine, dear Miss Noble, that I hoped you might find it in your generous heart to forget the past and begin again?'

'Begin? Begin what?' Misfortune, or drink, must have addled his wits completely. She tried to edge away, but the foul grip tightened on her arm.

'Why, friendship of course. I have always admired you, Miss Noble,' he continued, lowering his voice to an intimate murmur, 'and now – '

'Are we to stay in this dark hall for the rest of the morning?' she interrupted, more to stop whatever horrors he was going to suggest than for any other reason. 'That would be most inhospitable and such a shame with all this beauty around us . . .' She waved her free arm rather wildly to indicate the bare expanse of parquet, the closed doorways on either side, the stairway leading up to un-known shadowed horrors. 'I assume this . . . this lovely place is yours?'

'This?' He let go of her arm and looked around him, his face dark with brooding hatred. 'It ought to be. Would have been if my devil

414

of a father had not lost his senses and fallen victim to a pack of scheming rogues and a faithless woman. But we won't talk of that. Let us just say that I have a legitimate interest in the place. If I choose to entertain a friend here, an intimate friend, then that is my business. Wouldn't you agree?'

'It sounds . . . logical.' Always humour madmen, she remembered someone saying. Madmen and drunks. She glanced furtively behind her and saw the heavy bolt of the door was well and truly shot. No escape route there. And no rescuer, even supposing there was one, could enter that way either. 'Do you entertain many friends here, Mr Sinclair?'

'Not as many as I would like, Miss Noble.' He took a step towards her and it was all she could do not to flinch. 'And none as welcome as you are. Your mother and I have known each other a long time and though recently we have not been on the best of terms, there has always been a certain bond between us. I am sure you are aware of that?'

'I suppose . . .' She took a deep breath. 'I suppose you could put it like that.'

'A deep bond, Miss Noble. A bond I would have liked to make deeper still, but that villain snatched her from me. Then when I disposed of him, the other villain took her. I can't forgive that. You do see, Miss Noble, why I can't?'

'Oh yes. At least . . . I think so. But perhaps we could . . . could move away from this dark hallway and talk about it properly?' *Dear God, what am I going to do?* 'Is there a breakfast room, perhaps? Or a library? Somewhere where we could sit down?'

'Of course! What am I thinking of? You have come to visit me and must be suitably entertained.'

He turned the key in the nearest door and flung it open with a flamboyant gesture to reveal an empty, uncarpeted room, its floor-boards grey with dust and its chandelier tied up in a linen bag. 'The drawing-room, but not very comfortable at the moment, as you see. Your mother's fault. Perhaps this room . . .' He strode across the hall to unlock and open the door opposite. The same bare floorboards and shrouded chandelier, but a large white rectangle filling the middle of the room. 'Here is the dining-room, complete with table. Too big to remove, you see, without cutting it up. I sold the rest of the furniture, though they had to dismantle the sideboard to get it through the door.'

'Really? It must have been huge.' *But the windows are all bolted and no one can see me from the road.* 'Was it mahogany, like the table?'

That was a mistake. The table was completely shrouded in dust-sheets, with not even the castors showing, but he did not appear to notice.

415

'What does it matter what it was. It fetched a good price. But now there is nothing left to sell.' He spun on his heel and frowned down at her. 'Which is why I invited you here.'

'There are the chandeliers,' she said, to divert him. 'I believe such things, if they are as beautiful as yours undoubtedly are, fetch phenomenal prices at auction.'

'Chickenfeed,' he said, with a curl of the lip. 'But shall we go upstairs? It is brighter up there and I want to show you the master bedroom.'

'Before we do that,' said Sarah, in her best schoolmistress voice, 'would you explain to me exactly why you sent for me? I am afraid I don't quite understand.'

They were standing in the open doorway to the dining-room, he with his hand on the door, she hanging back, clinging to the comparative safety of the hall while her eyes searched this way and that for some way out of the trap. The parquet floor, she noticed with a detached part of her mind, was much in need of polish. She need not have worried about her boots.

Suddenly, he let go of the door handle and turned towards her. His shoulders were outlined against the pale rectangle of the dining-room doorway, his face in shadow.

'You wouldn't listen to me when I spoke to you in St James's Street. That was uncivil. But I understand now why you rebuffed me. Such moments should be private, not tainted by the common herd. Your friend explained that I should meet you alone somewhere, where we could talk without interruption. Where we could – '

Before he could finish the sentence and destroy her nerve completely, Sarah interrupted, 'Yes, yes, you are quite right. One should not conduct private business in the public street. But what is it you want to say? I confess I am baffled, but ready and willing to listen.' *Please God, send someone to help me. Please.* 'And could we perhaps go into the kitchen? I could make coffee for us? We could sit at the table and – '

'Your mother wronged me, Miss Noble,' he interrupted, frowning as he took a step towards her. 'Thwarted me, maligned me, turned my father against me. She deserves to be punished. Severely punished. Because of her and her paramours, I am penniless. Whereas she has money in plenty. I know she has, because I have made inquiries. I have watched and noted and calculated. She and her villain of a husband have shares and ships and a smokeshed like I once had.' Another step and she backed away, glancing wildly over her shoulder: behind her the drawing-room doorway, to her right the bolted front door, to her left the stairs and beyond them a red baize door which must lead to the servants' quarters. Oh God, which way should she run?

'Mine were taken from me, by fraud and deception. Just as she was.' He was still smiling, a fixed smile which failed to mask the devilish purpose behind it. 'By jealous, evil rivals without scruple or heart. One of those villains was her husband. Another was her lover. They thought I had forgotten all that years ago, but I never forget an injury. Besides, every morning I see the reminder in my own glass.' Here he ran a reflective finger down the ridge of his twisted nose. 'So you see it is always in my mind, waiting for the right moment. Which, it seems to me, Miss Noble, has arrived. Today I intend that you shall recompense me, fully, for the harm done to me.' His eyes gleamed in anticipation. 'I intend to enjoy every private minute of that recompense. And we are very private here, I assure you.'

'But . . .' Sarah swallowed, searched wildly for something, anything to deflect him, and said, 'I don't see what . . . I mean, which of my mother's businesses are you most interested in? The smokeshed is – '

'*All of them, dammit.* Don't you understand even yet? I shall take back everything your villains stole from me. Your mother is no longer the innocent young girl I first wanted, they saw to that, and I don't like used goods. No matter. She does not deserve me. But you are still innocent as she was when I first saw her. A little older perhaps, but just as attractive to me. I like my women young and untainted, ripening peaches waiting to be plucked. Alas, there are so few of them available, but you, my dear, you are perfect. You may be a fisherwoman's daughter, but you have grace and style. More than many so-called ladies I could name. You have no breeding or background, but I am prepared to overlook that. I have the breeding and this spacious, elegant mansion.' Was there an edge of sarcasm to his voice as he spread his arms to indicate the dusty neglect around him? She could not be sure. 'Your parents, my dear Miss Noble, have the wealth. What better partnership could there be?'

'Partnership?' She dared not take her eyes from his face lest he catch her unawares, reach out and pinion her. She measured the distance between them. It was too short.

'Let me put it plainly. You have what I lack. I have what you lack. Together we could both be satisfied. I had hoped to marry someone of my own class, but – '

'Marry!' This time Sarah could not keep the horror from her voice and his mask of control slipped.

'Don't deceive yourself, my dear. I intend to take my recompense whether you agree or not. But afterwards, providing you have pleased me, I am prepared, in my magnanimity, to make you my wife. I agree it would be a come-down for me, but I will not be the first gentleman to marry into trade. Beggars, as they say, cannot be choosers and it would be to your advantage. Everything I have would be yours, including my debts. But it would be your privilege, as a loving wife, to discharge those and a small price to pay for an alliance with the Sinclair name, and with me. Your family has money enough and to spare. As for me, everything you have would be mine, including your shares and your ships and your smokeshed.'

'I don't think so,' said Sarah carefully. 'Of course Adam would give me a dowry, but I have brothers and – '

'Adam Grant!' The name triggered an outburst of venomous fury. 'He is the author of all my troubles. All of them. And he shall pay. Oh yes. I have it all worked out. He and your mother will pay me to set you free. And if I do not choose to let you go, then they will pay me to make an honest woman of you. Simple really.'

When Sarah found no words to reply, but stared at him in growing dread, he said softly, with the supercilious sneer she had dreaded, 'So you see, my dear, if you will not humour me, I shall have to take what is mine the hard way. Because one way or another I assure you I mean to get it.'

Without warning, he lunged, caught her by the skirt; she twisted, jerked back, and in a tearing of cloth broke free, moving now this way, now that, while he edged her back towards the locked front door, away from the stairs, the kitchen door, from any escape.

'Aha!' he cried in triumph. 'She fights me!'

When he reached for her, she kicked out, in the way they had practised at Mrs Barrett's in London, 'learning how to resist arrest'. While part of her mind noted that hand-sewn suede boots were nowhere near as effective as the leather working variety, another part prompted a different tactic. She pushed her hand into his face, fingers splayed, dug her nails in hard, then whipped past him and through the nearest doorway. The dining-room.

Round the table with him close on her heels and panting now with lust and fury and excitement, blood-specked weals striping his cheeks; round a second time, then a third, still just ahead of his grasping hands, but he was fitter than she had expected, though his breath rasped hard in his throat, and her own strength was beginning to fail. *Three times around went my gallant ship and three times around went she* ... The words of the familiar song rang suddenly through her brain and she saw Braehead school and her children, singing. She felt light-headed with imminent hysteria. On an impulse she sang the words aloud – if he wanted a game then he should have one – and with a whoop of pleasure he joined in. *Till she sank to the bottom of the sea* ... On the final words she grabbed hold of the table's dust-sheet, dragged it off as she ran and flung it into the face of her pursuer.

He tripped, staggered, fell against the table edge.

In the moment's grace that gave her she was through the door into the hall, had pulled the door shut behind her and struggled to turn the heavy key in the lock. She thought he would wrench the door open again before she could lock it but instead he smashed his fist against the door panel, bellowing rage and frustration, and did the job for her. The key clicked home, her knees gave way, and she almost fell to the floor in terror. But she was on her feet again in a flash.

'You are a bad boy, Hugh Sinclair!' she shouted sternly through the door, despising herself with every word. 'You will stay in there till you promise to be good.'

Then she dragged back the bolt of the front door, wrenched it open, slammed it behind her and ran. Down the drive, out of the gate and into the arms of Ben Lucas.

'Hush, hush,' he soothed, holding her tight and looking searchingly over her head at the gateway and the concealing rhododendron. 'You are safe with me.'

'No. We must run. He'll escape in a minute and – '

'Ssh . . . I have a cab waiting. See.' Fifty yards away she saw the blessed sight of a hansom cab at the corner into Forest Road.

'Then we must get to it. Quick!' She pushed her dishevelled hair back from her face, caught up the torn portion of her skirt in one hand, to keep it from the dirt underfoot, and hurried with what dignity she could muster towards the hansom cab, and safety. But she was trembling all over, with fear and reaction and a burning, blistering shame. She felt tainted from head to foot, wanted to burn her clothes, to strip naked and scrub every inch of her body till her skin was raw. To put her head under the nearest pump and wash away every last loathsome breath of him.

Ben handed her up into the cab, climbed in beside her, told the driver to drive like the wind to . . .?

'Fairfields,' supplied Sarah and collapsed into draining, exhausted tears.

'It is all right, my love, you are safe now. Safe with me,' murmured Ben, his arms around her in comfort and reassurance. This time she did not rebuff him, did not remove his hands, and when eventually he kissed her, she responded with love and gratitude and an urgent, overwhelming need.

Fairfields was closed, but Sarah knew where the key was kept and let them in through the scullery door, while the cab waited for them at the gate.

The kitchen was dark and cold and empty, but full of familiar sights and comforting with memory. The huge range was dead, but still gleaming from its last polish. The tap at the sink filled the

419

earthenware basin that her mother used for mixing dough. The small looking-glass with one corner missing was still propped against the back of the pot shelf – her mother's small vanity: she said she liked to check there was no flour on her nose before she answered the door to visitors. And the onions that Danny had so proudly harvested before taking off to Yarmouth with the others, hung in neatly plaited strings from a huge iron hook in the ceiling. Dried herbs hung from another and, Poppy's contribution, a bunch of drying honesty, the pale discs gleaming ivory in the half-light and rustling in the cold air that blew in through the open scullery door. Sarah wanted it left open: she had a sudden horror of closed doors.

The long deal table was scrubbed white and clean, just as they had left it, the wooden kitchen chairs ranged neatly against the wall. Elissa liked space around her table when she was working. Remembering, letting her eyes range over the homely details, Sarah felt her mother's reassuring presence and was comforted. How could Sarah have been so horrible about Fairfields? It was a beautiful place.

'I must wash, tidy my hair and make myself respectable somehow,' she apologised, her voice trembling with delayed shock. 'I cannot go home to the Square like this. Mother would ask questions and I cannot bear to tell her. It was so humiliating and terrifying and ...' She shuddered, looked up at him with haunted eyes.

'Tell me!' ordered Ben, his face grim. 'Tell me everything. Remember the shame is his, not yours. Whatever happened.'

Suddenly she saw what he needed to know and her face relaxed into almost a smile. 'I had to fight – those tactics of Flora Barrett's group came in very useful – but I escaped and I am still ... intact. He wanted to ... he wanted ...' But the memory was too much. She sank into a chair, covered her face with her hands and wept.

He stood behind her, gently stroking her head until she quietened, then repeated gently, 'Tell me.'

Slowly, carefully, repeating every detail, she told him. At the end of it, she felt curiously cleansed and almost cheerful again. She sprang to her feet and crossed to the sink.

'And I locked him in,' she said, looking up from the basin where she was dousing her face in cold water. 'Do you think he will be able to escape?'

'Unfortunately, yes. But he will be punished. I will see to that.'

'My hero,' smiled Sarah, only half teasing. 'I wonder what he meant when he said my friend had told him to get me alone?'

Ben frowned. 'Don't worry about it. It is over.'

'Dear Ben ... But you haven't told me how you found me. You left it a little late, perhaps, but I forgive you.'

'I thought I arrived with exemplary speed, in the circumstances. Your mother told us of the note when Adelaide and I called round for you this morning. You are dripping water down your front, by the way.' He was leaning against the dresser, arms folded, ankles crossed, watching her. 'The address was of a house which my father's firm takes care of. I knew it was empty. Has been for two months now. The last tenant's name was Mrs Winthrop, a respectable widow now living with a daughter, in Bournemouth. The house used to belong to old Easton Sinclair. I remembered that incident in St James's Street and came to find you.'

She looked up at him with a trembling smile, her face tingling fresh and clean from the icy water. 'Came to find me indeed. You make me sound like a lost dog.'

'You looked rather like one. A bedraggled dog, probably a stray, and much in need of care and attention.'

'In need of a hairbrush and a basin of clean water,' retorted Sarah, her spirits returning. 'And a pin to hold up this torn piece of skirt. There must be a pin somewhere here.'

She crossed to the dresser where he was leaning, but when she reached past him to open a drawer he caught her by the waist and held her tight.

'I love you, Sarah Noble,' said Ben and kissed the tip of her upturned nose.

'And, much against my better judgement, I love you, Ben Lucas.'

'As a lawyer, I think I am entitled to require proof of that, don't you?'

'Then I suppose I have no option but to give it.'

The news was all round the Square by Sunday morning. That wastrel Hugh Sinclair had been found, shot by his own hand, in the basement billiard room of his father's old house in Rubislaw Den. Broke in by the window, seemingly, bolted all the doors, and shot himself. A neighbour heard the shot and found him, sprawled over the good baize cover of the billiard table with blood everywhere. Gambling debts, drink, opium, unmentionable diseases: rumour blossomed, flourished and produced a bumper harvest of explanation and innuendo. But whatever the reason for the suicide, everyone was agreed on two things: one, the billiard table would never be the same again, and two, the fellow was much better dead.

'I feel so guilty,' confessed Elissa as she said goodbye to Sarah at the door that afternoon. 'It is wicked to rejoice in someone's death, but I can't help feeling relieved all the same. With all the menfolk away, I was never quite sure he wouldn't try something, in spite of what Adam said.'

'No, Mother,' said Sarah solemnly. 'Nor was I.'

'All the same, I'm glad that nice Ben Lucas has offered to drive all of you into the country this afternoon and drop you off at Braehead, Sarah, on the way home. A nasty incident like that can be quite a shock and I don't like you walking alone in the dark at the best of times. The days are so short at this time of year.'

'Don't worry, Ma,' said Sarah, giving her a quick hug. 'I shall be quite all right.'

She saw no reason to correct her mother's impression that the afternoon outing involved a crowd of people: a drive in a motor car was much more enjoyable when there were only two of you.

CHAPTER 35

The Yarmouth season ended, the herring fleet came home, and Elissa took her family back to Fairfields. With the men home, and Harriet's baby, and the Square once more full of chattering girls exchanging tales of the herring-gutting, of the men they'd met, or hoped to marry, the house in the Square was full to bursting.

In the intervals of the winter work of scouring and refurbishing the drifters, disposing of New Year celebrations and generally putting the fishing world in order, the Noble menfolk, including young Daniel who was fifteen now and a fisherman like the rest of them, used what spare time they could find to get on with the repairs that still had to be done at Fairfields. Broken windows, loose slates, cracked guttering and blocked downpipes all had to be sorted and why pay other folk to do what they could do themselves? Adam Grant came and went, as his business affairs demanded, but since the news of Sinclair's death he had seemed more carefree and talked of winding up the Australian end of things for good.

By March the whole house was clean, dry, draught-proof and weathertight, still a little sparsely furnished, but every brass door-knob, hinge or tap gleamed bright as burnished gold. Elissa had young Eppie Bain to thank for that – Eppie had been promoted to housemaid, at her own request, and even the kitchen range was a beautiful gleaming ebony. It also burnt superbly and the heat from the basement kitchen permeated into all the rooms on the floor above, including the one which Elissa used as a family parlour, though from the labelled bells on the wall behind the kitchen door, it had originally been a breakfast room.

This room, on the left of the porticoed front door, looked east towards the sea, though little of that could be seen for the massed rooftops of the town. But there was a good view of the drive and the great iron gates which stood permanently open. It was here that Elissa did her household sewing, wrote up her accounts, taught Poppy her alphabet and simple sums, and watched through the long window for Adam coming home. He had a motor car now, a

Wolseley, which he boasted proudly was the twin of the one ordered for Her Majesty Queen Alexandra.

'Though she has a chauffeur to drive hers and I drive my own.'

Danny nagged him incessantly to be allowed to 'chauffeur' Adam, but so far Adam had resisted, though in a weak moment he had promised Sarah that she could take the wheel 'if those Suffrage friends of yours ever get the vote'.

There had been a big meeting in London, in February, and other, smaller ones, at which some of the women had been arrested. There had been reports in the papers. But fortunately Sarah had not been mixed up in any of it. They would have heard if she had been.

So it was that on a bright spring morning in May, when they had been back in their new house for five happy months, Elissa glanced towards the gates and saw with a blink of surprise a bicycle swerve round the corner and into the drive. Straw hat tied under the chin with a long bandanna, white blouse, dark jacket and long dark skirt: it could only be Sarah. Sarah who should have been miles away in a village north of Aberdeen. Elissa dropped the pinafore she was making for Poppy and hurried to the door.

'Sarah, how lovely to see you,' then, as she saw her daughter's face, red-cheeked from the fresh air and exercise, but set with determination, she faltered, 'Is anything the matter?'

'Yes, Mother. I have to talk to you. Can I come inside?'

Elissa who had been standing in the middle of the doorway, watching her daughter dismount and lean the bicycle against the house wall, stepped hastily to one side.

'Of course, dear.' She led the way into the parlour, indicated a chair and took up her sewing, as much to steady her agitated pulse as for any other reason. Why wasn't Sarah at school? Surely it wasn't a holiday? Sarah had seemed so happy when she was home at Christmas; not an argumentative word to anyone and the house had been full from basement to attic with family and friends from the Square. She glanced up at her daughter's face: strained but not thin, and her figure was if anything a little plumper. She didn't look ill, but something was obviously wrong. Fear robbed her of appropriate words.

'I was in the middle of letting down Poppy's pinafores,' she babbled into the silence. 'I should be at "Mary's", but Ina is looking after things for me till this afternoon. Poppy is growing so fast these days and – '

'Mother. Adam said I was not to do anything I would be ashamed to tell you about and I am not ashamed.'

The defiance in her voice suggested otherwise, and Elissa felt her heartbeat quicken.

'Old-fashioned notions of right and wrong are outmoded,' declared

424

her daughter. 'Biblical precepts were designed for Biblical times, to avoid disease, to keep the people in their rightful place, to preserve the social order. Civilisation has progressed beyond that . . .'

These are not Sarah's ideas, thought Elissa with alarm. These are someone else's ideas that she is repeating word for word, someone who wants to sway her to his or her will. Dear God – she realised what was coming before Sarah spoke.

'I have left the school. No. To be absolutely truthful, as I intend to be, I was asked to leave.'

'You went to the Suffrage march after all, without permission!'

'I went, but I had permission. Grudging certainly, but official permission. It was a splendid occasion, Mother. Such spirit, such excitement. I did not tell you because I know your feelings on the subject and it would only have led to argument.'

'But you told the children – and the school disapproved?'

'No, it was nothing to do with the Suffrage march. Though in a way I suppose it was.' A private thought lit up her face with remembered pleasure. 'But you were right about country folk, Mother. They are not receptive to new ideas. They are hidebound by the rigid conventions of their narrow and bigoted upbringing . . .'

Again someone else's words, thought Elissa with mounting dread.

'For such people the idea of a love free from the chains of convention is an affront which they cannot stomach. At least they did not drive me out of the village with stones: only with words.' Sarah lifted her chin a fraction higher and looked Elissa straight in the eyes.

'I am not ashamed. I am proud to tell you, Mother. I love someone. I am expecting his child.'

You have been with a man! Aunt Sarah's words rang through her head so vividly that for a moment she thought it was herself who had spoken. She had thought that memory safely buried, under twenty-four years of rectitude. Other memories tried to force their way through the barrier, but she thrust them back and with a huge effort of will she managed to control her voice to almost its usual calm.

'May I ask who is the father?'

'You may ask, Mother, but I will not tell you. I have talked it over with Adelaide who has pointed out my options. The first, abortion, is out of the question. The second, adoption, depends entirely on you. The third, which I favour, is to bear and bring up my child myself, unaided. There is no question of marriage.'

'The man is . . .?' But Elissa could not go on. The idea was too appalling.

'Is already married? That is what you were going to say? But I shall not tell you that either. It is immaterial. Married or unmarried, I would not humiliate myself by forcing a man to marry me, merely because I carry his child.' Sarah sat straight-backed and defiant on the very edge of her chair, hands folded in her lap. Only the white-knuckled fingers showed any strain as she said into the silence, 'The identity of the father is of no concern to anyone but myself.'

'Oh, but it is. *What about your child?*' Suddenly anger boiled up and overflowed in a scalding, searing stream. 'Will you deprive your child of a father for the sake of some selfish, modern theory that proves you are right and everyone else for generations has been wrong? Has your poor child no right to know its father? Or the father to know his child? How can you be so ... so greedy ... and so stupid?'

Sarah flushed with outrage, but before she could speak, Elissa regained breath. She did not know who put the words in her mouth, but they streamed out with all the venom of the woman she had striven for twenty-four years to forget.

'How dare you come to me, your own mother, with no shame, no penitence, no sense of any sort of wrong-doing and tell me to my face, with *pride*, that you are expecting a bastard child? You, who have no excuse of ignorance or neglectful upbringing. You who have known right from wrong from infancy, and been taught not to sleep with a man till sanctified by marriage. *How dare you?*'

'I dare because I love. Freely and without the artificial bonds of matrimony. And so does he.' Sarah was out of her seat now, glaring defiance.

'Who?' But if she had thought to trap the name out of Sarah, she failed. Frustration sparked her to fresh fury.

'You and your stupid ideas. You mouth them parrot fashion without the slightest understanding of what you are saying. Free love indeed. Can't you see, you little fool, that your argument is a man's argument? So he can take his pleasure and avoid responsibility? And you claim to support Women's Suffrage and women's rights. But it's not that at all, really, is it? You saw a man who was someone else's and you wanted him.'

'Just like your mother before you.'

The voice from the doorway brought them both to their senses with the shock of a pail of icy water. Smiling with triumph, Bethany Noble picked up her skirts between finger and thumb and with exaggerated care, stepped into the room.

'Had to let myself in. You didn't see me coming. Didn't hear the bell. Didn't hear much really, seeing as you was making such a din yourselves. I could hear you from half-way down the drive. It needs sorting, by the way. Weeds sprouting everywhere and great pot-holes. Do a lot of damage, pot-holes can, especially to a motor car. I wonder Adam allows it, but then he's only got one of they cheap Wolseley things. Did I tell you Brodie's buying me a Benz?'

426

As the silence stretched, Bethany chose a chair, spread her skirts and sat down. Elissa took up her sewing and attempted one, trembling stitch. Sarah remained standing for an uncertain moment, then perched uncomfortably on the edge of a hard-backed dining-chair against the wall.

'I've heard so much about this precious house of yours,' said Bethany, when it became obvious that neither of the other women intended to speak. 'So I thought I'd pay you a morning call. See how you've done it up since I was last here. You haven't improved it much, have you?' She cast her eyes over ceiling, faded wallpaper, threadbare Indian rug. 'I'd have thought living in a *mansion* you'd have furnished the place with better taste. You want to buy new things, not that old junk. But maybe you can't afford nice things like we can. With spending all your money on a ruin.'

She directed a challenging look at Elissa who refused to rise to the bait.

'But never mind that,' continued Bethany, with arch politeness. 'I interrupted you in the middle of an interesting discussion. What was it you was saying? Oh yes. Seeing someone else's man and wanting him. What man would you be talking about, Elissa?'

'It was private business,' said Elissa, white-faced. 'You had no business to listen.'

'Couldn't help it, when you was shouting like a pair of fishwives. Besides, I like a good argument. What was it about?' Bethany's voice was innocent, her eyes gleaming malice.

'A private matter, between Sarah and myself. Now have you time for a cup of tea before you go?' Elissa moved to the door, but stopped when her daughter spoke.

'What Mother means is that she is ashamed to tell you, Aunt Bethany. I will be happy to do so, but first, why did you say "Just like your mother before you"?'

'Something I remembered from way back, Sal, when we was with the herring fleet in Lerwick. There was this man, see, who was courting me, and your ma fancied him. Maybe that was what you was arguing about?'

Sarah swallowed the hook without noticing. 'No, Aunt Bethany. I told my mother I am expecting a child. That is all.'

'All?' cried Elissa. 'How can you stand there with that innocent expression and say "all". When there is no father for the child and apparently never will be?'

'It wouldn't be the first time it's happened, you sanctimonious cow,' snapped Bethany. 'You of all people should know that.'

'That's enough. You have always hated me, ever since Lerwick. How could I forget when I have this to remind me?' Elissa wrenched

427

back her sleeve and showed the long red scar. 'Bethany did that, Sarah, deliberately, and her tongue is as sharp as her gutting knife. Don't listen to her.'

'You hypocrite, Lissa Downie. Yes, I cut your flaming wrist and I wish it had been your throat. Making eyes at my Adam and carrying on behind my back. You think you're something special now, with your fancy airs and your fancy house. But you're no better than the rest of us and never were, for all your pious innocence and praying.'

'Adam?' breathed Sarah, her eyes wide with shock. Neither woman noticed. They were both on their feet, confronting each other like fighting cocks.

'I will not be insulted in my own house, especially by someone I did not invite. Kindly leave.'

'Don't you dare get on your high horse with me, Lissa Downie, and you not fit to tell honest folk how to behave, especially your Sarah. And don't you go having an abortion, lass, whatever your ma says. It does things to your insides.'

'I did not say . . .' began Elissa in horror, but Bethany ignored her.

'Much better find a mug who'll marry you, or get your ma to find one for you. She's had plenty practice.'

'Get out of my house,' breathed Elissa with concentrated fury.

'I haven't stayed my twenty minutes yet, and I'm enjoying myself,' taunted Bethany. 'Did you say you was fetching tea?'

'Adam?' said Sarah, more loudly this time.

'No!' cried Elissa, and Bethany grinned in triumph.

'Shame on you, Lissa, for telling such a lie. And to your own daughter.'

'But there is no point, Bethany. Why can't you leave well alone? Please?'

Deliberately, Bethany ignored her. 'Aye, Sarah. It was Adam Grant. And if you don't believe me, ask your precious ma about your father. *Your* father, mind. Not Gideon's.'

On that splendid exit line, Bethany Noble picked up her skirts, said, 'I'll not wait for tea after all,' and flounced triumphantly out of the house.

In the room she had left the silence stretched and stretched. A coal stirred in the fire in a spurt of sudden flame; the clock tick-tocked with relentless rhythm. Somewhere in the garden a blackbird sang and from the back yard came the faint clank of a bucket. Eppie was filling a pail to sluice the kitchen floor.

It was Sarah who broke the silence.

'Who is my father?' When Elissa did not immediately answer, Sarah said, with a note of contempt, 'Surely if I can tell the truth, without shame, you can do the same?'

Elissa took a deep, steadying breath. She would never forgive

Bethany. Never, as long as she lived. 'Your father was drowned before you were born.'

Sarah looked at her, challenging her mother to meet her eyes. When Elissa inevitably looked away, Sarah pounced.

'You are not telling me the truth, are you? *Are you?*'

'No, Sarah, I am not. But it is because some things are best left buried. It was not how you think. I thought your father was dead. Everyone believed it. So I married Joseph.'

'Before I was born? Or after? Yes. I see.' Her face was white with shock and outrage. 'You were just like me, weren't you? Pregnant to a man you couldn't marry. And you had the nerve to lecture me about morals. You hypocrite. You sanctimonious prig.' Then she realised. 'You said "thought" he was dead. Which means he wasn't after all.'

'No. There had been a mistake.' Oh dear God, thought Elissa with despair. There is no way out. No escape. 'Six years later, your father reappeared. I was already married then. Gideon was four.'

'It was Adam Grant.' Sarah looked at Elissa with loathing. 'And you have been carrying on with him ever since, first behind my fa ... behind Joseph's back, then behind Adam's wife's back till you could get him for yourself.'

'That is a lie, Sarah, and you know it. People make mistakes, mistakes they regret for the rest of their lives, but that need not prevent them living honourably, as I have tried to do.'

'Adam Grant is my father. Isn't he? *Isn't he?*'

Elissa flinched at the violence of her question. 'Yes. But he did not know it till years afterwards.'

'And you had the nerve to tell me he was my *godfather.* Holy Moses, what a pair you are! What a charade. What a farce. The two of you must have been laughing up your sleeves at my poor fa ... at Joseph.'

'It was not like that, Sarah. Believe me. I sent Adam away and he stayed away. You know he did. He is an honourable man.'

'Honourable? To carry on with another man's wife behind his back? To let another man bring up his child for him?'

'Joseph was your real father, Sarah. He loved you as his own daughter and it would have broken his heart to hear you now. Adam loves you too, in a different way. We did it for the best, Sarah. For your sake.'

'You disgust me, with your pious excuses and your virtue. It's one thing for you to have a child outside marriage, oh yes, but quite another for me.'

'Please, Sal, try to understand.' She was in tears now, begging. 'Please don't condemn us. Please – '

'I shall do what I damn well choose, *Mother.*' She spoke the word

429

like an insult. 'And I certainly won't take advice from a lying hypocrite like you.'

Sarah stormed out of the room, slamming the door behind her, only to open it again for a parting shot.

'And you can keep your precious mansion. I will never set foot in the place again.'

And she kept her word. For eighteen years.

PART IV

CHAPTER 36

1914

They had managed without her. Over the years the wound healed, but it left a lingering ache, like the ache of an arthritic shoulder or knee which strikes occasionally and without warning into sharp pain, then subsides again to dull normality.

Adam had been appalled, wrung with grief for Sarah and pity for Elissa; then the other way round; over and over. She knew Adam understood, forgave her anger, shared her anguish; knew that he grieved for Sarah and worried for her safety. Knew that he wrote to her occasionally, via Adelaide Forbes, though Sarah did not reply. Adelaide Forbes Ellis to be correct, for Adelaide, to everyone's surprise, not least her own mother's, had suddenly given up her post-graduate course in mid-term, slipped out of the active branch of Women's Suffrage, and married James Ellis of Ellis's department store in Union Street. She had become a model wife, hostess, mother and household manager, in a solid granite edifice in the more exclusive part of the Queen's Road, and, over the years, she had become Elissa's friend.

Adelaide gave them news of Sarah from time to time and undertook to send on Adam's occasional brief letters. Elissa knew Adam included her love with his, but she could not bear to write herself. The wound had gone too deep. She would never forgive Bethany for that. Never.

Bethany herself, puffed up with glee at her undoubted victory, chose to ignore Elissa completely, to the latter's relief.

Afterwards, in the tormented anguish of the months that followed, Elissa could not remember precisely when Gideon came home. Was it before they heard, via Adelaide, that Sarah had a daughter, or afterwards? Before, or after, she built the extension to 'Mary's'? Before she ordered the fourth steam drifter, to be called, defiantly, the *Sarah Noble*, or after? She only remembered the relief of Gideon's arrival, his pleasure at seeing the house for the first time, and her own pleasure in Yvonne, Gideon's quiet, sensible, rock-solid second wife.

Yvonne was a widow when Gideon met her, with a son Paul, two years older than Poppy. Afterwards, Elissa wondered if Yvonne had chosen the doll which had arrived so unexpectedly via Cameron Forbes, but she did not mention it. The showdown with her daughter Sarah had dented her confidence and left her unsure of how to speak to her son. Remembering the silent devastation of his grief for Charlotte she was nervous of doing or saying anything which might damage Gideon's new composure.

Apparently Gideon and Yvonne had come home to stay. The firm he worked for in London, an import-export business, was opening a branch in Aberdeen of which Gideon was to be the manager. 'But if there is any way in which I can be of use to you, Mother, in the family business, I would be glad to help.'

'Thank you, dear,' said Elissa. 'It will be good to have you back. But we'll talk about that when you've had time to unpack and settle down.'

Adam looked at Gideon shrewdly, noting the well-cut city jacket and trousers, the snuff-coloured waistcoat and polished leather shoes. The boy's hair was receding at the temples and he looked older than his twenty-five years. 'You'll be used to an office job, not a fisherman's?'

'Yes. I thought I might be able to help with the export side of things. I've made some useful contacts in London, and on the Continent.'

'Good. We might need them, lad, sooner than you think. Business isn't so brisk this year, though I hope it will pick up. We've had three splendid years in a row, so we can't complain, but if fish is going to be in short supply, we need to get the best price we can for what we do catch.'

'How is the market in Germany holding up? Or do you sell more to Russia these days? Whichever it is, we'll need to keep an ear to the ground. I've heard a few disturbing rumours lately, one way and another.'

'Then you'd best tell me, lad, so we can be prepared.'

Elissa watched the two men stroll off together into the garden, and smiled. It was good to hear them talking man-to-man; good to see Gideon accepting Adam's presence without animosity. But then, remembering Gideon's years of absence, her son was probably glad to have the responsibility of a widowed mother taken off his shoulders – not that it had ever weighed heavy on him. As for Poppy, Gideon gave her the attention a distant uncle might give, no more.

But Adam was genuinely pleased to have Gideon there. Poor Adam: he had taken Sarah's desertion hard, especially as it was the discovery that he was her real father that had caused it. Danny had done his best to cheer the atmosphere, and Poppy had been as affectionate and lively as she knew how, climbing on to her 'grandpa's' knee, asking him to tell her stories, telling him stories of her own, in turn. But there had still been moments when Elissa had glimpsed Adam's face in an unguarded moment and seen her own grief etched into the lines of care. Perhaps Gideon's return would go some way towards healing the hurt.

Gideon and Yvonne moved into rooms on the first floor, with young Paul, and Elissa gave them what had once been the library for their exclusive use. The room was still unfurnished, which meant that Yvonne could arrange it as she chose. She chose to install a piano, not Mary Noble's prim and unused upright one from the house in the Square, but a grand piano which Gideon ordered from London, and on which Yvonne played Chopin nocturnes, hymn tunes, Strauss waltzes and even, once, a lively modern dance called, apparently, the polka. Within a week she was giving Poppy piano lessons at Poppy's own request, while Paul sat on the window seat and drummed his feet against the wood in time to the music.

Poppy had taken instant charge of 'my new brother' but addressed Gideon as 'uncle' and Yvonne as 'aunt'. Elissa was too unsure of Gideon's feelings to correct the child and when eventually she found the courage to speak to Gideon about it, he shrugged and said, 'What does it matter? I have not exactly been a father to her, have I? Uncle will do fine.'

Yvonne was five years older than Gideon and soon proved to be as capable a housekeeper as Elissa herself. With relief, Elissa handed over much of the everyday running of the place to her new daughter-in-law and, with Adam so often away in London or at sea, devoted herself more and more to 'Mary's'.

Adam had not, after all, wound up the Australian end of his business: it was too lucrative and, as he confessed to Elissa, he felt sentimentally attached to it. 'I built it up myself, from nothing,' he explained. 'It's all my own work.' Not like the business he and Brodie Gibb had collected together, deliberately, through Hugh Sinclair's mismanagement and fraud. The Mackenzie and Gibb business flourished, in London and in Aberdeen, but Adam kept his own, Australian company separate. 'So I can sell it whenever I've a mind to,' he explained to Elissa. But she doubted he ever would sell. He had a good manager and reliable staff to run things for him, and he still sailed to Australia every two or three years, 'to see for myself'.

Elissa laughed, called him 'my part-time husband', but she understood: she felt the same about 'Mary's'. And though he asked her more than once to go with him on his trips to Australia, Elissa always refused. She used 'Mary's' as her excuse, but really she had no wish to see Adam's other life with all its painful associations. She was content with the life he shared with her at Fairfields, and in his frequent absences she had plenty to occupy her.

Just as Joseph had once been Fergus Mackie's partner in the curing business, so Fergus's wife Ina was Elissa's trusted friend and manager in 'Mary's'. With the new extension their output had doubled and they had taken on extra gutters and filleters. They had regular orders from as far away as London and supplied a dozen different hotels daily, in and around Aberdeen, with kippers for breakfast and smoked haddock for poaching gently in milk and butter, or for kedgeree. Last year they had adapted a part of the main building for smoking salmon, but so far only on a small and experimental scale: the three-month winter close season meant three months of idleness. But the finished product had met with approval. If the uneasy rumours which drifted back from the agents in Germany and the Baltic ports proved groundless, she might consider developing that side of things further. 'Mary's' had come a long way from the smoke-blackened cupboard in the garden shed of the house in the Square and, remembering the black tin box and the bank account it fed, Elissa knew that should the bad times come upon them, they had the means to survive, at least until they found their feet again.

On the day that Daniel brought his chosen girlfriend home to meet his family, the bad times began.

Daniel was twenty-three, a tall, well-built and muscular young man, with laughing eyes and rumpled blond hair that refused to lie flat. The previous year, 1913, he had been made master of the *Sarah Noble* and that year's profits had been the best ever. So far this year, with the fruitful autumn season yet to come, the catches had been lighter. But, argued Danny the optimist, as Scotland was experiencing a heatwave, perhaps it was just as well.

'The lassies have to work fast enough as it is, Ma, as you know yourself, and who wants a glut when it's eighty degrees in the shade? The fish would go off before they were even landed. As it is, we're managing fine. The *Sarah Noble* was leading shot again today. Thirty crans, and Tom tells me they fetched thirty-four shillings the cran.'

At the beginning of June, the *Singing Bird* arrived in Aberdeen, and when she prepared to put to sea again for the return voyage to Melbourne, Adam decided to go with her. 'While I still have the chance. If these rumours have any foundation, I'll need to make a few changes and I'd rather do it in person. Come with me this time, Elissa? Please? Yvonne will look after things till we get back.'

Elissa shook her head. 'No, Adam. Australia is your country: Scotland is mine. But come back to me soon.'

'I will, my love. I promise.' He kissed the palm of her hand in their own, private ritual, and folded her fingers over the place. 'That's to remind you, till I come home again.'

She waved to him from the north pier, as she always did, missing him already, but knowing that even when he was on the other side of the world he was still with her, locked close in her heart. The sea was calm, the sun unusually hot. Not a hint in the cloudless sky of the storms to come.

All through July the sun continued to bless them, thousands daily thronged the long, golden beach, the children splashing in the shallows, the more intrepid wading deeper, and the summer serenity seemed as if it would never end. There was a run on Panama hats at Falconer's and at Esslemont and Macintosh's the daintiest of summer frocks and muslin afternoon gowns were in constant demand. Why should Wimbledon and the lawn tennis tournament see all the elegance when Aberdeen could produce a summer just as idyllic for tennis on the lawn, or croquet? The motoring élite discarded their fur-lined leather overcoats in favour of a Motor Pattern Burberry and drove into the country with the summer breeze in their hair, all rumours of diplomatic troubles abroad forgotten.

On the first day of August, Danny called out before he had even reached the door, 'Top shot again. Thirty-five crans. Beat Uncle Samuel by two.'

Elissa hurried from her little parlour into the front hall and met him just as he stepped over the threshold. He caught her by the waist and swung her high into the air.

'So you see, Ma, I can earn a living as well as the next man, in spite of my misspent youth.' He put her down, protesting, kissed her on the forehead, then, one arm round her waist, he called to the girl who had been waiting in the shadow of the entrance, 'Come on in, Becky, and meet the best Ma in the world.'

'Flatterer,' laughed Elissa. 'What are you after this time?' Then she saw the girl and her laughter dried.

She was beautiful. Small, demure, perfect features, a sweet smile. Not at all the kind of boisterous hoyden he usually favoured.

'Good afternoon, Mrs Noble. I am very pleased to meet you. Daniel has told me so much about your beautiful house and garden.'

She was a lady, too. Well spoken and polite.

'Then perhaps Daniel would like to show you the garden, Becky, while I organise tea? You will stay for tea, won't you?'

'Of course she will, Ma. That's what we've come for. Ma's sponge cake is the best in Scotland, though Yvonne's oven scones take a bit of beating and as for young Poppy, you should have seen the black

437

shortbread she made last week. You could have soled your shoes with it. Isn't that right, Poppy?'

'That's not fair, Uncle Danny,' protested twelve-year-old Poppy who, like Elissa, had come running at the sound of Daniel's voice. 'Just because I went off to look for something and forgot. Anyway, you ate it. That proves it was all right.'

'No, it doesn't. It just proves what a tolerant, kindly uncle I am.'

Poppy lunged at him, Danny dodged laughing out of reach behind Becky, and the ensuing scuffle ended with all three of them strolling out into the garden together, Daniel with a girl on each arm.

Watching him from the open doorway, Elissa swelled with pride and love. Daniel had grown into a son any woman would be proud of, a loving, affectionate son without malice or guile. No wonder Becky, whoever she was, looked at him with such open admiration. But she seemed a pleasant girl, well-mannered and without affectation and Poppy obviously liked her. That was a good start. She watched them till they turned the corner of the house and for ever after she was glad she had lingered, for the picture was etched deep into her memory: her honest, handsome, happy son with an adoring girl on each arm and the afternoon sunshine in his hair. Etched so deep that nothing that came after could obliterate it.

They heard the news themselves, from the pulpit, the very next day. Sunday, 2nd August. Though they had been living in Fairfields for eight years now, Elissa still attended their old Footdee church of St Clement's from time to time, especially in times of crisis. Usually, if the weather was fine, they walked through the tranquil, empty Sabbath streets, past the closed doors of the Electric Theatre which showed moving pictures, past the new La Scala cinema in Union Street and the shuttered windows of F.W.Woolworth, with the wide street empty of all but church-goers like themselves and the occasional errand boy.

But on this particular Sunday, they found the city crowded with people. Yellow newspaper placards everywhere, newsboys shouting: 'Germany declares war on Russia.' It was unheard of to have a newspaper on a Sunday: that was warning enough, but in case anyone should still be left in ignorance of the gravity of the situation, the news was announced from every pulpit in the land.

In St Clement's church the congregation listened with unusual attention as the Minister did his best to explain the complicated chain of treaties and events which had brought the countries of Europe to this present and most serious state of affairs. In June, Archduke Francis Ferdinand of Austria had been assassinated in Sarajevo, by a Serb. Austria had demanded compensation from Serbia. Serbia had refused. Germany supported Austria. Russia supported Serbia. France was Russia's ally and could not escape involvement. Britain

438

was pledged to help France defend the neutrality of Belgium. Therefore, it was explained to the by now bemused congregation, everyone must be prepared for the real possibility of war. The rumblings and murmurings which had been gathering force on the Continent ever since the Archduke's death had finally come to a head. Germany had declared war on Russia and Russia was mobilising her troops. Prime Minister Asquith had had consultations at Buckingham Palace and already it was known that all Royal Naval Reserves were to be mobilised.

At this point everyone realised that, though war had not yet been officially declared, barring extraordinary feats of diplomacy, or a downright miracle, war was inevitable.

The congregation that emerged at the end of the service was a subdued one, fired by none of the usual cheerful camaraderie or urge to exchange news and gossip. There was too much else to think about. By unspoken agreement, when the Nobles left the kirkyard – Elissa, Gideon, Danny and the rest – instead of taking their usual route to the Castlegate they turned down Church Street to Waterloo Quay. They had a need to see the harbour, calm under the summer sun, to see the Sunday boats resting at their moorings, all the well-known, reassuring sights that were part of their lives. They paused at the corner to glance eastward to Pocra and the solid, well-maintained structure of 'Mary's' with the green and gold lettering over the door and the gold-glinting emblem of three fishes, bound by their tails, then, reassured, they turned right on to Waterloo Quay. Past the Newcastle and Hull steamer wharf and on towards the inner harbour, the harbour offices, the foot of the Shiprow, breathing in the familiar reassurance of sea air, pitch, smoking fish, seaweed, coal and the dozen other smells that made up the harbour. Then, their courage strengthened, they turned their backs on the sea and made for home.

Crowds still thronged Union Street, Union Terrace, Rosemount, but there was an air of sober reflection now, of anxiety, and in some, the feeling that they stood on the brink of a great and threatening unknown.

'What will it mean?' asked Elissa eventually, when their own, familiar weathered gateposts were in sunlit view ahead. She wished Adam was with her, for support.

'If the naval reserves are called up, then there's hardly a vessel in the harbour that won't lose at least one man,' said her son Gideon beside her. 'Some will lose two or three.'

Daniel, ever cheerful, said, 'Then the rest of us will have to work a bit harder, that's all.'

'What will you have to do, Uncle Gideon?' asked Poppy who, as always on a Sunday, walked to church beside her father. 'Will you have to go as well?'

439

'If there is a war, I rather think we will all have to do as we are told,' said Gideon. Yvonne, on his other side, looked worried – her first husband, a soldier, had died at Mafeking – but fourteen-year-old Paul said solemnly, 'I shall go and fight for my country, like my father did. As soon as I am old enough.'

'Then you'll have to grow a bit faster, laddie,' said Daniel, ruffling his hair. 'Folks say if there is a blessed war it won't last more than six months.'

'I hope you're right,' said Gideon. 'I reckon we'll all be in trouble otherwise.'

The trouble began the next morning, before war was even declared.

The news was all round the harbour before the sun was up – and in summer that was early. All trawlers were forbidden to put to sea. Several local boats had already been boarded, stripped of their fishing gear, and commandeered as minesweepers. Insurance men swarmed everywhere, warning anyone they could corner that any boats that put to sea would not be covered under their present policies. Several harbour officials and fishmarket officials had been called up as reservists. Several more trawl skippers had already reported for duty. The harbour was at a virtual standstill, except for the arrival in ones and twos of coastal shipping or trawlers from more distant waters. No herring drifters could put to sea unless they chose to take the risk and sail without insurance.

It was a grim outlook for everyone in the fishing trade, and for the city. When war was declared on the 4th it was merely a confirmation of what they already feared. With Europe in a turmoil, the Russian and German markets were lost, while all up and down the east coast, in neat rows three layers deep, stood hundreds of fresh-packed herring barrels waiting to be shipped, and now, in all probability, worthless. The curers would be ruined, and thousands of dependent workers with them: gutters, packers, coopers, carters, all would be out of work and penniless.

The white-fish trade was no better. With the insurance men pulling out, the trawler owners had no choice but to pay off their crews. The results would inevitably spread throughout the city and all related trades would suffer. Besides, the open seas were forbidden territory. Coastal trading only was permitted.

In those first few days, stray trawlers continued to arrive, including two unsuspecting German ones, flying the Union Jack, though they were soon enlightened and sent scurrying home. With a coastal drifter or two, there was still a little fish in the almost deserted market and what there was fetched record prices. Already food was growing scarce and costs rising. Several Aberdeen vessels were trapped in Baltic ports and there was still no word. But even if they did make their home port in safety, the export trade they plied would be finished. It was forbidden to export anything that might be of the smallest help to the enemy.

But while the harbour had been virtually closed, other parts of the city saw frenetic activity. As the mobilisation orders took effect, the barracks was crammed with reservists and volunteers, the military took over the railway system and when many of its doctors and nurses were called up, the hospital announced that in future only emergency cases would be treated. The fourth Gordon Highlanders were quartered at Gordon's College and the army commandeered the Beach Joy House and Beach Pavilion for their own use.

Out of a brilliant summer sky, chaos had fallen.

No wonder that picture of Danny strolling in the garden, with Poppy on one arm and Becky on the other, stayed so vividly in her mind. It was a picture of bright, untroubled innocence. A talisman to hold fast to in the endless, turgid, swirling, terrifying darkness that followed: a heart-rending nightmare of a journey the worst details of which, mercifully, memory would blot out. The contrast between God's glorious summer heatwave and the devastation that man's lunacy spawned under it had been a cruel joke. A double vision that saw black and white together, good and evil, life and ... Oh God, Adam was on the other side of the world by now. He had promised to come back, she held his promise in her hand, and he would come back, one day. Until he did, she must hold tight to the beauty, keep it strong in her sights while the darkness rolled over her. Only that way could she emerge again, whole.

The constant anxiety, the grief, the loneliness, the obstinate endurance in face of physical exhaustion and mental despair became a way of life, a garment that one wore day and night. Only the knowledge that others looked to her for strength, good sense and guidance saved her from collapse. That and pride. But she did not give in. Not even when they took her beloved Daniel from her, with Ina's sons and Tom's and Davie's, all the young men, so many sons and brothers and friends, swept up like day-old chicks and dispatched across the Channel or to distant seas to live or die as fate decreed. They went with pride and excitement, while their women wept.

But they learned to weep in secret. There was work to be done. Men's work in munitions, in fields, in hospitals, driving motor cars, all sorts of jobs women had not done before, but soon learned how to tackle.

William Downie, retired from the sea two years back, would have gone with the rest of them, and proud to do it, but he, like all the older men, had no choice. Despite his forty years of detailed sea knowledge and experience, they would not have him on a minesweeper. Sixty-one was too old for service; except in home waters, for the fishing, where the sea, and the danger, were just as great. The nation needed all the food they could produce.

With the markets – and the steam drifters – gone, the herring-curing business was done for, that was plain. So, after a hasty family conference, the Downie brothers, William and Davie, dusted down the family yawl, oiled its motor and took the Zulu to sea again for the line-fishing, with William Downie in charge and a couple of fifteen-year-olds still too young to 'Rally round the Flag'.

Fergus Mackie followed his example. With his curing business in ruins, he did the rounds of the shipyards, already thriving on government contracts, and offered his extensive carpentry skills, but too many others had been before him. So he overhauled the *Optimist*, scoured the Square for an experienced skipper to sail her for him and, with a pair of young cousins from the Square and an uncle with a wooden leg, put to sea himself, for the first time in his life.

'When the old tubs start leaking,' he told Ina, 'as they surely will, I promise I will set myself up as ship-repairer and general handyman on Pocra Quay. Until then I might as well see where our livelihood has come from all these years. Besides, Wallace Lennox is a good skipper. He knows what he's doing.'

Ina confessed to Elissa that the first thing that came into her head when Fergus told her was the comment Wallace's sister Suffie Lennox had made all those years ago in Lerwick. 'Pity he's not a fisherman ... but at least he'll not drown and leave her with rows of kids to bring up on her own.' But Ina, like all the women, had had to swallow her fear and endure. The country was at war, but the people still needed food. And though the fishermen ran the same risks as those on war service, it was no good telling them to stay on dry land. Men like Tom and Fergus and William Downie, those too old, or too young, or too medically unfit for active service, would rather follow the fish than be idle ashore.

They heard, through Adelaide Ellis, that Sarah was working as an ambulance driver, but Adelaide couldn't, or wouldn't say where. Gideon, at Elissa's request, wrote to Sarah to offer to look after her child at Fairfields until the war was over, but they had no reply. Then Gideon was summoned south, his experience in the export trade being, apparently, of use for the knowledge he had gained of various foreign ports. As he was to be based in London, Yvonne and Paul went with him.

'I know he would be safer here with you, Elissa,' she explained, 'but I want to keep him firmly under my thumb. He is a tall boy, and growing. I do not trust him not to falsify his age and enlist behind my back as soon as he thinks he could get away with it. I would hate him to do that to you, Elissa. I know you would blame yourself for ever after.'

Gideon did not tell them what his work was to be, saying only that it was 'Top Secret'. At least, thought Elissa with what optimism she could summon, he will not be sent to the battlefield. Not like the others.

One by one all four of their precious drifters had been commandeered by the navy and re-equipped with great steel nets for minesweeping. Two were detailed immediately for the Dover patrol whose job it was to lay steel net barriers underwater to keep the cross-Channel route free of enemy submarines and prevent them laying mines. Every six hours the nets had to be hauled in and repositioned for the next tide, baited with mines of their own for any unseen enemy intruder, while all the time the U-boats lurked underwater, seeking a way through the barrier to attack. Joseph's brother Samuel skippered the *Elissa Downie* and his brother Abel the *Millicent* with Saul as engineer. The men called their work cheerfully the 'Suicide Club'.

The fourth drifter, Daniel's, was stationed for a while at Leith, then Granton. After that ... But by that time Elissa had grown used to death.

The family Bible, in its sombre black leather binding, lay permanently ready on a side table in Elissa's parlour. After only two years of war, she had recorded the deaths of three of Joseph's brothers in thick black ink. 'Died at sea', with the date. Saul and Abel on the same day in 1915. Samuel a year later. Two more widows. Five more fatherless children.

Was Ina the first to be widowed? Or Suffie? Afterwards it seemed as if the black veil of widowhood descended on them all indiscriminately. The fishing fleet was attacked by U-boats soon after the city had been blacked out, to deter bombardment from the sea. That was when poor Fergus drowned, with the rest of his crew: Ina's distraught face, Suffie's anguish, Meg's furious tears.

'How dare the bastards drown my Wallace?'

Then Jessie Bain, her husband lost overboard when his sailing smack was spotted by a cruising U-boat and scuppered. He was sixty-seven.

'And they had the brazen gall to raid the larder first,' she wept into Elissa's shoulder. 'I'd given him a piece of cold beef I'd cooked special and they even took that. My George loved his bit of cold beef.'

Any minute now it will be my turn, thought Elissa, over and over, but no news came. She had heard from Adam three months into the war. The longest letter he had ever written her, describing how he had been in Australian waters when he heard news that war was declared. He had joined the naval reserves, offered himself and the *Singing Bird* for the merchant fleet. They had fitted her with guns and, as he put it, 'other bits and pieces', and now he was at sea. He could not tell her more than that, but she was not to worry. He finished, *Remember my promise, and wait for me. I will come when I can.* She had heard only once since then: a short note, telling her nothing, except that he missed her and sent his love. It was impossible to work out where the letter had been posted. But if ever she found herself worrying about the lack of news, she told herself that Adam had never been one for letter-writing, and as long as she heard nothing to the contrary, at least he was still alive.

'Mary's' struggled on, but there was little enough fish for smoking and what there was could be quickly disposed of. Most of the girls found other jobs, in munitions factories, engineering works, hospitals, even bill-sticking or newspaper-selling, and when, two years into the war, the nation ran out of volunteers and introduced conscription for all unmarried men between nineteen years and thirty, they took over all the jobs the men left behind them, even in coalyards, and farm labouring jobs on the land.

Daylight Saving Time was introduced, food grew scarcer. Then one day a white-faced, brave but frightened Becky called at Fairfields and asked to see Elissa.

'Daniel asked me to tell you, Mrs Noble, that he is well.'

'You have seen him?' Elissa fought down the sudden stab of jealousy and said, 'Where? When?' They had not heard from him for several months, but Elissa had long ago taught herself to cling to the reassurance of the last letter until a new one appeared.

'I am not really supposed to say,' faltered Becky with downcast eyes, 'but I have visited Daniel in Granton once or twice. This time, a week ago, he told me ... he told me they are sending him to the Adriatic, for minesweeping and patrol duties. I promised I would tell you, in case you were worrying.'

And now I shall worry ten times more, thought Elissa with dread, but she forced herself to stay composed.

'I am glad you did, Becky dear. And if there is anything else you need to tell me, anything at all, please come, as you have come today. But you look tired and a little drawn. Stay and have tea with me, unless you are busy?'

'No thank you, Mrs Noble. It is very kind of you, but I have work to do at the hospital. I am late as it is.' Then she was gone.

Becky Macrae lived with her widowed mother in Ferryhill, less than a hundred yards from Bethany's house. She had taken the tram, nevertheless it was a good distance out of her way, especially when she was due at the hospital. Daniel had told them Becky's father was a trawler captain, drowned in a winter storm when Becky was six.

It was good of her to have called, not easy to bear a message from son to mother in such circumstances. At the edge of her mind an idea was forming, but she slapped it down. Married or not married, they had a right to see each other if they chose, especially when war threatened everyone, every moment of the day or night, with the loss of a husband, lover, son.

That was the point when the mood of furious activity snatched her up and whirled her headlong. She brought them all to Fairfields. Brought the grieving mothers and widows and their children, organised them and drove them as hard as she drove herself. Food prices were rocketing. Eggs three shillings the dozen and a gallon of milk as much as one and sixpence. The war had taken their men and now was threatening to starve their children and all those left behind.

'We will dig up the flowerbeds and plant vegetables,' she told them. 'We will buy chicken-wire for a run, and keep hens. We will teach the townsers how to live on oatmeal and salt-herring, and we will work all the hours God gives us for our absent menfolk and their families at home. The children will help. If we have other work to do in the daytime, as most of us have, then we will work in the evenings. When it is too dark to work outside, we will work inside. Knitting, sewing, making dressings and bandages. We will collect moss. It is important to be occupied, and to do all we can to help our men.' And to obliterate the terrible fear that gnawed unceasingly day and night. Last week Ina's son 'Mackie' had been killed, torpedoed off Scapa Flow.

As for the men who remained, they rose before dawn and were gone for days on end. The fish were elusive, the seas dangerous, and the little fleet fished from a dozen different ports along the east coast. In the rare moments they had ashore, she saw how haggard William had grown, how careworn and stooped. His arthritic hands were scarred, the skin split and often bleeding. Davie's hair had turned grey overnight, every last trace of brown completely gone. They faced death every day: not just the usual hazard of the sea's caprice, but the added one of cruising enemy destroyers on the sea's surface and, below it, the invisible menace of the U-boats. They had already seen too many men drown: friends and sons of friends.

Increasingly, Fairfields became a house of women. Adelaide Ellis called whenever her work at the hospital allowed and they would talk about ordinary things: the hens, Poppy's schooling, what to do about the pot-holes in the drive, while anxiety stood over them like a waiting messenger of doom, a messenger they could not ignore. James Ellis was now an officer in the Gordon Highlanders, 'somewhere in France'.

'I can't talk to Mother,' Adelaide explained, her face white with strain. 'As soon as I open my mouth she starts weeping and wailing

445

as if James were dead already. I don't need that. I need strength and comfort.'

Elissa did her best to provide it. Then, at the end of each exhausting day, she would creep into her lonely bed and fight her own fears. Gideon she did not worry about: at least he was in London and, though she knew there were Zeppelin raids, Gideon would be safe. Adam, she told herself firmly, was on his own ship, in full command: he could take care of himself. Besides, he had promised her. It was Daniel her heart ached for.

Daniel would be in the Adriatic now, working out of Brindisi, patrolling the Straits of Otranto and dodging the Austrian gunboats. Please God keep him safe.

CHAPTER 37

She rose earlier and earlier, sometimes spending less than three hours in bed. For with Adam away, the bed was cold and lonely and there was work to be done.

First the smokehouse: Elissa had vowed that, whatever happened, she would do her utmost to keep the place going, so that when this dreadful nightmare was over there would be work for the girls again. Tom had hung on at the fishmarket, for much the same reasons, though on many occasions he put to sea with one or other of the fishing boats, if they were short of a crewman.

Then when she was not digging, hoeing, weeding, raking, harvesting or planting the garden, she was looking after the numerous offspring that her working friends left in her care. Elissa organised picnic raids into the country. A dozen or more women and children took the train up Deeside to scour the moors for sphagnum moss which they carried back in pillowcases or flour sacks to one or other of the city depots. There the moss was sorted and dispatched for use as a substitute for cotton wool. Hospitals had opened in several of the city schools for the war wounded, the sick and the dying, and normal supplies had run out long ago. She copied out the government leaflets on how to feed a family on salt-herrings and distributed them to the poorer tenements in town, often with a free barrel from the store at what had been Fergus Mackie's yard. And, in any spare hour that remained of the twenty-four, she knitted. Seamen's stockings, fingerless mittens, balaclavas, ganseys. She taught Poppy and the younger girls the patterns till they could knit unaided. She visited her friends in the Square, especially the widows and the bereaved mothers, and if they were not already involved in war work, she found something suitable for them to do. It was the only contribution they could make towards defeating the villains who had killed their loved ones.

Poppy started to have nightmares and when she woke screaming in the small hours, Elissa would take her into her own bed, for reassurance: her own as well as Poppy's.

The girl was asleep beside her when Elissa had the dream, a dream so vivid that she remembered every detail for years after.

She was in the country somewhere, it didn't matter where, on a hillside, with a busy little stream below them, the white water gurgling and swirling down the rocky gully and out of sight. The sun was warm in her face, and the trees on the distant hillside were clean and straight, all standing to attention and shining. There were children all around her, squealing and laughing, with Poppy in their midst. Then they parted and made a circle around something which they called her to come and see. She walked towards them, into the circle, and there was a huge pile of sphagnum moss, like a great green sand-castle. Then the moss quivered, shivered, heaved, and out of the pinnacle erupted a figure, bright-haired and dripping trails of moss, like seaweed. 'Hello, Ma,' said Daniel. 'I was top shot again today.' For a shimmering moment he stood tall, smiling at her. Then he turned his back on her and walked through the children and across the stream. Into nowhere.

Elissa woke sobbing, her eyes streaming tears and her whole body shaking.

'Hush, Gran, hush,' said Poppy beside her. 'It's only a nightmare. It will be all right in the morning.' That was what Elissa said to Poppy whenever she awoke, crying. 'Don't cry, Gran, please. It will be all right.'

But Elissa knew it would never be all right again.

Daniel Noble died on 15th May 1917 in the Straits of Otranto. They received the details with the citation for bravery which was to be Daniel's posthumous reward. His was one of forty-eight drifters grouped into eight divisions, each drifter with a crew of ten and a six-pound gun as their only defence. They were laying anti-submarine nets across the Straits when they were attacked by Austrian gunboats, nine of them, with overwhelming gun-power. The enemy signalled to them to abandon ship, but the *Gowanlea* in Daniel's division was having none of it, and nor was Daniel. When the *Gowanlea*'s captain, a Fraserburgh man, ordered, 'Full speed ahead,' and his crew with cheers of defiance trained their gun on the enemy gunboat, Daniel followed suit. Both gunners took aim and fired, and both hit their target.

After that, it was a bloody and unequal battle in which all the flotilla joined. The *Sarah* took a direct hit amidships, exploding a box of ammunition and dislodging the gun, as well as killing four and injuring three of the crew, but those who remained had managed somehow to keep the drifter afloat, to give what help they could to the wounded, and at the same time to get the gun working enough to fire another volley at the enemy. Skipper Daniel Noble had remained at his post throughout the engagement despite his own wounds, and when, the battle over and the *Sarah* plainly sinking, the *Gowanlea* came to offer assistance, Skipper Noble had refused to leave until all wounded had been safely transferred. He was still at the helm, in full command, when the drifter sank.

Several medals for bravery were awarded – the *Gowanlea* skipper won a VC – and Daniel Noble was singled out for conspicuous courage in the face of the enemy. He was an example to all of the true grit of the British sailor, 'The fighting spirit which will win the war, and,' hoped Admiral Jellicoe, 'win it quickly.'

That hope was a vain one, unless another eighteen months could be called 'quickly'. That same month of May they raised the recruitment age for men to fifty. More men left for the front, more women took over jobs they would never have dreamed of doing three years ago. The land girls wore rubber boots – nothing new for the herring lassies – but they shortened their skirts to a practical and no longer shocking knee-length. Ina, in the fury of her grief, found herself a job shovelling coal into a factory furnace. 'I imagine each shovelful is one of the enemy and I'm tossing him into hell-fire,' she told Elissa, her cheeks smeared with coal dust and her eyes bright with vengeance. 'That's for killing my Fergus, I say, and toss in another shovelful, and that's for drowning my Mackie who never did anyone any harm.'

Elissa understood exactly how she felt and insisted that Ina come and take a bath in the splendid brass-tapped bath-tub in Fairfields as often as she wanted, to scrub away the dirt and regain her strength for the next onslaught. To see a grown woman heaving coal sacks was no more than commonplace in the general chaos of the times.

The old order was being turned upside down, but Elissa no longer noticed. Her whole body seemed dyed deep in grief and if it had not been for Adam she feared she might have lost her reason. But Adam was always with her now: he might be half-way across the world, fighting on some distant sea, but she felt his presence with her always, spoke with him, mourned with him for her dear, dead Danny and all the other young men, dead before their time, while their mothers lived on, grieving. Danny's father, Joseph, was no more than a vague memory now: just one of the growing army of the dead, an old hand, dead twenty years and pushed to the back. It was Adam she felt at her shoulder when she entered Daniel's death in the family Bible, when she prayed for the peace of Daniel's soul, when she did what she could to heal poor Poppy's desolate heart. Poppy was fifteen, a lovely, open-hearted girl, who had loved her Uncle Daniel as a father, brother and friend.

It was something in the turn of Poppy's head and the yearning in her eyes that reminded Elissa suddenly of Becky Macrae. She had not seen the girl for several months, not since the day she called at Fairfields to give them Daniel's message. She ought to go to her, tell her if she did not already know, comfort her if she could.

A month after they heard of Daniel's death, Elissa put on her summer coat and a plain straw hat, left Poppy in charge of the house and took the tram to Ferryhill. She avoided looking in the direction of Bethany's house: Brodie Gibb must be nearing seventy but was still managing to keep some sort of control over what remained of the Mackenzie Gibb enterprise. The rope factory was still in operation, under contract to the government, but most of the trawlers had been requisitioned, like their own drifters – 'wee' Georgie was on one of them, now a minesweeper. She supposed Bethany was helping in the offices, but had no wish to see her.

The Macrae house looked depressingly empty, but when Elissa rang the doorbell, a maid eventually opened the door. Small, sharp-faced, suspicious, with a neat white apron and dour black dress, she could have been almost any age from fifteen to fifty.

'The mistress is away,' she said before Elissa could open her mouth to speak. 'I was to say if anyone called that she has taken her daughter into the country, for her health. And the condition she was in I'm not surprised, poor lass,' she added with unexpected sympathy. 'This war's a terrible thing. All the young men killed and the lassies left grieving.'

'Do you know when they will be back?' But the maid, her message delivered, had closed the door. She heard the bolt shoot home and the rattle of the chain as it was hooked in place. Poor Becky. She must be heart-broken. Her mother was wise to take her away from the harbour to somewhere without such haunting memories.

And the chaos continued. There had been Zeppelin attacks on the south and east coasts from early in the war, but now the smaller, faster aeroplanes took over and raided London while in Russia the upheaval came from within when a revolution overthrew the reigning royal family. Food grew more and more scarce and in London and the Home Counties ration cards were issued to everyone, from the King and Queen to the humblest boot-black in the street. Meat, sugar, butter, Elissa no longer noticed the details, picking up the ebb and flow of the fortunes of war as if by instinct. Sometimes the tide swung one way, sometimes another. The main thing was to hold fast to life and endure. One day soon she would hear from Adam. One day he would come home.

The King and Queen celebrated their silver wedding anniversary and in Russia, ten days later, the deposed Tsar Nicolas Romanoff was shot and most of his family with him. As if there had not been killing enough already, thought Elissa with weary despair. And the latest was an outbreak of influenza, here at home. A wicked and virulent influenza which picked out the weak and the vulnerable, the mal-nourished, the old, and killed them as effectively as any German bullet. Several of the old people in the Square died, and too many of the little children, before the murderous wave passed on and left the bereaved and the ailing to recover as best they could. Then suddenly, out of nowhere, came a lightening at the edges of the storm cloud, a new breeze of hope. Rumours began to spread of the end in sight, a victorious end. The Germans were retreating.

It was then, with peace almost within grasp, that the cruellest blow fell.

Elissa was in the garden on that misty October evening. There was wood smoke in the air and that special autumn smell of burning leaves and vegetation. She had spent the first part of the day in 'Mary's', as she usually did, then in the Square, then the hospital, where she wrote letters for some of the wounded, read to others, helped sort the new arrival of dressings and promised to deliver fresh vegetables from her garden on Monday. Now, she was digging the last of the potatoes with Poppy who, in long rubber boots and a short wrap-over overall, hair pushed up inside a knotted scarf, looked like any other land girl, digging for her country, when she spotted the messenger boy in the drive.

'Can you finish the row for me, Poppy?' said Elissa, straightening carefully so that the girl might not see her flinch. Digging always gave her a sore back, but she would rather die than admit it. 'I will be back in a few minutes.'

Then, keeping her steps carefully unhurried, she made her way across the vegetable plot to where the messenger waited. It was a letter from Adam, she knew it was. And she had waited so long.

She took the envelope from the boy, thanked him, waited till he was out of sight again round the bend in the drive. Half of her wanted to tear open the envelope now, in the garden where she stood. Half wanted to keep it forever unopened, feasting on the promised joy it contained. Excitement, dread, jubilation, terror churned and boiled inside her till she thought she would burst with the pounding force of it. But she managed to walk steadily and slowly to the scullery door and on into the kitchen. She placed the envelope on the scrubbed deal table, ran the tap for cold water. Washed her hands. She did not want any trace of mud on her precious letter. Then at last she took up a knife and slit open the envelope. With infinite care, she drew out the folded sheet of paper and opened it.

*

451

Poppy, coming into the kitchen half an hour later, found Elissa sitting upright at the table, her sewing in her lap, and staring unblinking into space.

'Is something the matter, Gran?'

Elissa did not answer. Poppy stood a moment in indecision, then reached hesitantly for the paper which lay on the table in front of her grandmother. . . . *missing at sea* . . . *believed drowned* . . . *Captain Adam Mackenzie Grant* . . .

'Oh, Gran darling, I am so very sorry.' She put her arms round Elissa's shoulders, laid her already wet cheek against her grand-mother's dry skin, but when she could get no response from the rigid, silent figure, she withdrew her arm, brushed the tears from her eyes with the back of her hand, then, after one wild, helpless glance around the empty kitchen, did the only thing she could think of: she made a cup of tea.

'Drink this, Gran,' she said gently. 'It will give you strength.' When Elissa ignored the cup, Poppy lifted it herself to Elissa's lips.

The hot tea triggered her grandmother to action. She pushed it aside.

'No. There isn't time. I must tie my fingers or I'll be late.'

Poppy watched in dismay as Elissa pulled and tugged at what she had thought to be sewing, but what she now saw was the skirt of Elissa's own petticoat. She heard the tearing of cloth as the material parted, watched, appalled, as Elissa laid one long, narrow strip on the table, then another.

'Don't, Gran . . .' she began, but Elissa turned on her a look of such blankness that Poppy bit her lip and was silent. Elissa began to wind the strips round her fingers, on and on, over and over again.

What was the matter with her gran? If only Ina would come back, or Jess or one of the others. Poppy put a shawl round Elissa's shoulders and prayed that someone would come to help her, soon, and all the time those fingers continued their restless winding, on and on. She had heard that morning that influenza was back in the city: perhaps Elissa was suffering from that? Fever did strange things to the mind. Made people delirious. But she knew in her heart it was not influenza. It was something far, far worse.

Jess and Ina put Elissa to bed. When she protested, Ina exchanged a glance with Jess, then said, 'Nonsense. We're all for our beds. You don't want to be late at the gutting, do you? What would the others say?'

Then they sent Poppy flying to fetch Dr Blair. He was out on his rounds. They would tell him the moment he came in. No, they couldn't say when that would be.

They waited two hours before he came. Two hours during which

Elissa continued to inhabit her own, private world, in a herring-gutters' hut at Gremista.

'How long has she been like this?' asked Dr Blair, an over-worked, still competent but despairing man of seventy who had been fetched out of retirement to do the work of ten. The influenza epidemic had been the last straw on an emotionally battered and exhausted back, but until someone could be found to help, or the war ended, his professional commitment would not allow him to give in.

'Since this afternoon, doctor. When the message came.' Poppy showed him the letter, on official paper. 'It is about her husband.'

'*Missing, believed drowned*,' read Dr Blair and looked over his half-moon glasses towards the bed. 'Poor woman.'

They were standing in the open doorway of the bedroom and through the unshuttered window they saw the first faint mist of moonlight touch the night sky. Poppy had lit only one lamp, on the little table beside the bed, and beyond its pool of light she saw the darkness of the folded shutters gleam suddenly with an eerie light. The October moon.

'Shock. Emotional exhaustion. It doesn't much matter what you call it,' sighed Dr Blair. 'The mind can take only so much punishment. I think your grandmother has taken more than she can cope with and has quietly switched off. Rest and careful nursing is all I can prescribe. And a sedative to help her sleep. I will look in again tomorrow, if I can.'

At the door, he took pity on Poppy's anxious, tear-streaked face. 'Don't worry too much, my dear. I have seen plenty of similar cases in the last four years and Mrs Grant is a healthy woman. She will recover in time.'

The listening women realised it was a measure of the seriousness of Elissa's illness that he did not trouble to lower his voice.

'Right,' said Ina when Dr Blair had gone. 'We'd best work out a rota between us. Who's not working tomorrow morning?'

CHAPTER 38

1924

'That's it!' cried Cameron Forbes. 'The exact look I wanted. Proud, with a touch of sadness. The indomitable spirit of womanhood.'

Elissa moved position in the hard-backed chair to ease her stiffening joints and saw him glance up from his palette in warning.

'Just another minute or two, if you can manage it, Mrs Grant.'

'Of course.' She was longing to stand and stretch her aching arms above her head, but it would not be fair on poor Cameron. Not with the portrait so nearly finished. He might have to start whatever bit he was doing all over again and take twice the time. Then she would feel guilty. It was not so very long ago, she remembered, that she had chastised him with a wooden baking spoon, on the behind. For stealing the cherries off a cake on the kitchen table in the Square. She had felt guilty even then. He was only a small boy, after all, and knew no better. A quiet child, with never a word to say for himself, and now look at him. Quite the fashionable painter, Gideon said, and not just in the north-east.

The trivial memory brought others. Grey memories, heavy with sadness. So many things had changed. Even this precious house. All those years ago, when Adam had first brought her here, the view from the morning room had been of green fields sloping down to the granite town and the harbour, with the sea's shimmer merging into the sky. Now, there were houses, row after row of them, in a forest of smoking chimneys. The sea was still visible, if you knew where to look, and the sky. But not the harbour. Not her past life. Except that the past was not merely a place: it was memories built into the soul. Inescapable. Strong as granite, and as doggedly enduring.

'Are you sure you are all right, Mother?' Gideon's voice was anxious, solicitous. He had spoken to her like that ever since he returned from whatever secret work he had been doing in London during that dreadful war. That had been after the Armistice, when everyone was happy and relieved that war was over, but by then things had got her down. She had not been herself.

Gideon had been so kind – giving up his own work at that export firm of his and taking over Adam's shipping company, as well as what was left of their own. She had told him it was not necessary, that Adam would be home himself very soon, but he had insisted.

'We don't want him to come back and find things in a muddle, do we?' he had told her and she supposed he was right. With the loss of the drifters and the foreign markets and the herring fishing just about ruined there had been a great deal of sorting out to do, and at the time she had not been well enough to do it herself. Gideon had done the sorting, and looked after 'Mary's' too, until she was strong and fit again.

'Yes, dear,' she said now. 'I am quite all right. Just a little tired.'

'How much do you have left to do, Cameron?' Gideon had been sitting in a chair in the bay window from which he could keep an eye on the garden as well as on the progress of the portrait which would one day hang in the place of honour on the boardroom wall. Now he stood up, crossed to the easel and stood beside the artist, looking over his shoulder at the canvas.

Elissa, sitting obediently still, watched her son with the mixture of love and bafflement and pain which he had roused in her for as long as she could remember. He had been a good-looking child and was still good-looking, in a quiet, understated way. Like his father, Joseph. Strange how she could not remember Joseph clearly, only see reminders of him in Gideon. Dark hair, dark eyes. He held himself well, too, which made his medium height look almost tall. Now, he was bending slightly to study the canvas over Cameron Forbes's shoulder. The two faces made a strange contrast. Gideon's dark and thoughtful, Cameron's sharp-featured, almost pointed, with a mat of auburn hair and a beard of the kind they called Vandyke, above a paint-spattered smock with Bohemian echoes. Whatever would Lawyer Forbes have said if he had seen his son now?

Gideon looked from the painting to the model and back again, seeing the same obstinate, proud-backed woman, thinner than she used to be, but still handsome. Still with the power to exasperate and dominate and wring the heart. No wonder she and Sarah had struck such sparks off one another. Then he saw the sadness behind the composure and remembered. He hoped to God they would all come.

'It's coming on fine, Cameron. Well done. Perhaps you would like to take a rest, Mother? I could have tea sent up. Or coffee?'

'Not tea, thank you. Tea will be served on the terrace when everyone has arrived. But I confess a rest would be welcome. If it does not inconvenience you, Cameron? I have been sitting in one position in this chair for so long that if I stay much longer I shall fall asleep and that would never do. Not with so many visitors expected.'

'Then we'll take a break. That all right with you, Cameron?'

Cameron Forbes looked up from his canvas, smiled at Elissa, nodded agreement, then continued to concentrate on the painting. Gideon's mother was a handsome woman. In her seat beside the elegant marble fireplace, a vase of arum lilies on the small table to her right, she looked positively regal, with the dark red woollen material of her skirt falling in such elegant folds. The white pleated blouse with the high-buttoned neck was reminiscent of Queen Alexandra and, thought Cameron, Mrs Noble had something definitely queenly about her, in spite of her humble background. Though he said it himself, it was going to be a splendid portrait. One of his best.

'May I see how my picture is getting on?' asked Elissa.

Without waiting for an answer she stood up, smoothed the folds of her skirt, an almost ankle-length one, and adjusted the neat-fitting waistband. Waists, in her opinion, should be where God meant them to be, not half-way down the hips and no waist at all. The full sleeves of her high-necked blouse narrowed below the elbow into long buttoned cuffs. Both elegant and practical, it was a style she had worn, with only minor alterations, for more than twenty years and she knew it suited her. Let the young ones chop their hair and their skirts, tug on their bust bodices and try their best to look like boys if they wanted to. Elissa had too much sense to follow their example, and too much dignity. Besides, whatever would Adam say?

'I don't think Cameron likes people to . . .' began Gideon, but Elissa waved a dismissive hand.

'Nonsense. Cameron doesn't mind, do you, dear?'

She touched the black velvet ribbon which hung almost to her waist, checked her lorgnette was in place should she need it, and crossed the expanse of polished floor to stand beside the artist.

Gideon exchanged a quick glance with Cameron, raised expressive eyes to the beautifully plastered ceiling and shrugged. He folded the newspaper he had been reading and laid it aside, with the gratifying headline carefully in view: OLYMPIC GAMES – LIDDELL WINS 400 METRES FOR GREAT BRITAIN. It was good to know things were returning to normal.

While he waited, with a certain apprehension, for his mother's comments – devoid of vanity, she had been against the project from the start, as a waste of good money – he turned his back on the room and stared out of the window at the lawn. One of the Bain boys was laboriously pushing a mowing machine over the far end of it, where the herbaceous border began. Considering it was barely six years since the place had been knee deep in turnips, potatoes, squawking hens and goodness knows what else, the garden was looking good.

Behind him, the silence stretched and stretched.

At last Cameron Forbes gathered courage. 'Well?'

He was saved by the sound of a motor horn at the gate. The Bain boy dropped the handle of his mowing machine and disappeared at a run round the corner of the house. They all listened. The motor crunched slowly up the invisible drive, stopped at the invisible front door. The high chatter of children's voices wafted through the open window with the scent of roses and fresh-mown grass.

Elissa's tensed shoulders relaxed again. Her brother Tom's brood. Or Meg Duthie's.

'Did you tell Yvonne about the children?'

'Yes, Mother. They are to play in the garden as soon as Poppy has everything ready. Look, there she is now, with the croquet hoops.'

A slim girl in a shapeless pale green garment with an extraordinarily short pleated skirt which barely covered her knees had emerged on to the lawn, carrying an armful of wooden mallets and metal hoops. She turned her head, freed a hand to wave, dropped half the mallets and pulled a comical face which made Elissa smile in spite of herself. What a pretty girl she was, even with that poor shorn head, and though she did not at all approve, especially of those flesh-coloured stockings which might as well be bare legs, that modern style of dress did suit her.

A string of children tumbled out after her, squealing and skipping. Two small boys made straight for the abandoned mowing machine and began pushing and shoving each other for possession of the handle. A small girl fell over. Another hauled her to her feet and dragged her, still wailing, to where Poppy was already marshalling her unruly flock into some sort of order.

Tom's brood, and Meg's. Her brother William was already here, with Katrine, both of them seeking peace somewhere upstairs. Ina and Jess were supervising in the kitchen.

'Perhaps you could check for me, Gideon dear, how many more there are still to arrive?'

'In a moment, Mother. We want to know what you think of the portrait.'

'Oh. I think . . .'

They held their collective breath.

'I think it is beautifully painted, Cameron. As good as anything in the Royal Academy. But it is not quite me.'

'What on earth do you mean, Mother?' demanded Gideon, frowning. 'I have never seen a better likeness. It is exactly you.'

Elissa stepped back a pace, raised her lorgnette, dropped it again. Shook her head. 'No, dear. I disagree. Why are my hands folded, white and slender, in my lap?'

'Because . . .' Cameron blushed with fierce embarrassment.

'Because that is how a lady's hands ought to be? That was what you were going to say, wasn't it, Cameron? Well, mine are not like that. Look.'

457

She thrust them towards him, palms upwards, then turned them over to show the calloused, work-scarred skin. 'No, don't turn your head away. Look at them, and look well. I want my own hands in my own picture, young Cameron. No artistic lies. Now, the background . . .'

Gideon opened his mouth to protest, but Elissa forestalled him. 'No, Gideon. I only agreed to this project because you said it would be an inspiration to the board to remember past achievements and aim even higher. And it won't inspire them if it's not true. So Cameron, you can leave the marble fireplace and the wee table, for they are true enough, and the room is lovely, but the lilies worry me. Lilies are beautiful, but they toil not neither do they spin. An idle model to follow, especially for a boardroom, don't you agree, Gideon?'

'Have you finished, Mother?' Gideon meant his voice to be sarcastic, but Elissa took his words blithely and literally.

'Not quite, dear. Just one more thing. I wonder I did not think of it before.' She crossed the room on light, quick feet to the bell-push beside the fireplace. Put her thumb to the button and kept it there.

The door opened. A middle-aged woman with sleeves rolled to the elbow, and a disrespectful look in her eye, said, 'What do you want? Interrupting me in the middle of my pastry. I'm doing wee tartlets and those scallywags'll eat the lot while my back's turned.'

'I'm sorry, Nellie, but I need my knitting. Can you send one of them to fetch it for me?'

'Knitting?' exploded Gideon. 'Mother, you can't expect Cameron to – '

'Not to knit, no.' Elissa smiled blandly at both of them. 'I shall knit, while Cameron paints. Being such a well-known and accomplished painter, he will have no difficulty painting the knitting in my hands. Nor in finishing the portrait in time. Will you, Cameron?'

Gideon took a deep breath, before saying carefully, 'The board commissioned a portrait to hang in the boardroom, Mother. A dignified, respectful and inspiring portrait. Not a . . . a picture of a wifie, knitting.'

'As I recall, the details were not specified. Certainly my portrait will be dignified and respectful. I can rely on Cameron for that. As to inspiring, that must depend on the eye of the beholder. Besides, have you ever known me sit idle, except here, in this chair, for that portrait? And I would like a Bible on the table instead of the lilies.'

'As well as . . .?' ventured the despairing artist.

Elissa relented. 'If you like, Cameron. After all, the lilies are the reward, are they not? And you have painted them beautifully. If you do my hands just like I want them done, I might even allow you to put fancy gold edges on the Bible and a lovely ribbon marker, for a treat.'

The door burst open and a breathless child of five or six years old shot across the polished floor and skidded to a halt at Elissa's side.

'There you are Auntie Lissa. And I didn't drop the stitches.'

'I should think not, Bella, and you the best little knitter I know.' Elissa bent to kiss the child's cheek. 'Thank you, dear. Tell Ina I will be out to help in twenty minutes.' When the child had gone again, Elissa resumed her chair, took up her knitting and said, 'Well, Mr Cameron Forbes. I am ready.'

Gideon made one last attempt. 'Would you at least tell us why, Mother?'

'Why what?'

'You know perfectly well what I mean, Mother. Why the knitting?'

Elissa looked at her son for a long moment, seeing the well-groomed businessman's exterior, the prosperous city suiting, the watch-chain and tie-pin, the cigar. Behind his shoulder stretched the newly mown lawn, with the coloured haze of the flower border in the distance, and the children playing.

Then the lawn changed to a wind-swept headland, the children to grown women, and she heard the sighing of a far-distant sea. When she spoke again, her face was stripped of all defence.

'A reminder,' she said quietly, 'of the long road I have travelled. It does not do to disguise the truth. Sarah will tell you that.'

If she comes.

The room was suddenly still; only the soft sound of brush against palette, her own breathing, the click of her needles, and from the garden, the happy chatter of children's voices and the sharper click of mallet inexpertly struck against croquet ball. It was a lovely room, tranquil, comfortable, with well-worn, faded covers on welcoming sofas and deep armchairs. Nothing that was not well used and well loved. A contented room. She felt the calm spread through her till all doubt was stilled and she knew, with sure faith, that this time her daughter would come back.

Gideon looked at his watch. 'Twenty minutes. Time enough for you, Cameron?'

Before he could answer, the door burst open and young Bella skidded to a halt in the middle of the room.

'Ma says to tell you, Auntie Lissa, that that blessed mannie from the paper's here and wanting to see you. And her scones just hot from the oven.'

'Then tell him to come back later. Say we're just going to have tea.

No,' she called after the child, who had already reached the door. 'Say he can interview Mr Cameron Forbes instead. The famous artist. In here. They can talk about the portrait together. It is much improved, Cameron,' she said with a sweet, disarming smile. 'The hands are just how I wanted them. And the knitting. But don't forget the Bible, will you? And don't spend too much time with the man from the paper or all the meringues will be finished. I remember you always had a taste for cream. We will be on the terrace.'

Before he could argue, she followed Bella out of the room.

It was cool on the terrace, under the stretched awning of green and white striped canvas, with the solid granite wall of the house at their back. A row of terracotta urns with trailing plants and flowers separated terrace from lawn where a rug had been spread for the younger children. On the terrace, basket chairs and wrought-iron chairs had been set out, together with a white-clothed tea-table in the shade of the awning. Several three-tiered cake stands held plates of scones, Nellie's tartlets, shortbread, meringues and slices of fruit cake. For the children Jess Christie, her brother Davie's widow, had supplied sandwiches and iced biscuits and Tom's wife Kate, as vigorous and indomitable as ever in spite of her years, had arrived with several quarts of home-made lemon barley water.

When Elissa emerged on to the terrace, narrowing her eyes against the sudden glare, a chorus of voices greeted her, then subsided into a sudden hush. The silence lasted while Elissa took her seat in the centre of the company, between Gideon's wife Yvonne and Tom's Kate. Her brother William and his wife Katrine, as usual, sat together and slightly apart from the rest, as if to indicate that though they were there out of family duty, they did not altogether approve and therefore preferred to cede their undoubted precedence to someone less scrupulous. In the continuing silence, Nellie Bain handed Elissa tea in a pretty bone china cup, one of the better leavings of the previous owners of the house. She was raising it to her lips when the continuing silence struck her, and she noticed that the children were grouped together in unnatural quiet in the middle of the lawn.

'There is no need to be quite so polite,' she said, smiling around her. 'Help yourselves, all of you, before the wasps arrive. Poppy, dear,' she called to the slim girl in the outrageously short green dress. 'The children may come and help themselves too, as long as they don't jog anyone's arm and spill tea everywhere.'

'In a moment, Gran,' called Poppy. Then she turned her back, faced the group of children who were bunched together in suppressed excitement, raised an arm, and gave the signal.

'Happy birthday to you, happy birthday to you, happy birthday Aunt Elissa, happy birthday to you.'

As the last exuberant note bounced through the treetops, from the french windows behind her emerged Ina, bearing a huge square sponge cake, iced and studded with glacé cherries, with a single, eight-inch candle triumphantly alight in the centre.

'We reckoned the wind'd blow it out anyway,' said Ina, 'and it'd take forever to light sixty of the blessed things.' She put down her burden in the middle of the tea-table and stood back to admire it. 'Well, hurry up, woman,' she said as Elissa stared at the cake, entranced. 'You'd best blow the candle out, quick, and make your wish, before one of those pesky little tykes does it for you.'

'In a minute. Just let me look. It is so . . .' Suddenly she thrust her cup into Kate's hands, scrambled to her feet and flung her arms round her friend. 'Thank you, Ina. It's a splendid cake.' Then she brushed a swift hand across her eyes and said, 'And there is plenty for everyone. But first, I must blow out . . . the . . .'

Her voice trailed into silence as she saw someone standing in the gloom of the french windows behind them, a huge, bulky shape too large to be Cameron Forbes drooling for his meringue. For a bizarre moment she thought it was a bearskin rug, come to life. Then she realised the huge head was not a head at all, but a straw hat, for all the world like one of the urns on the terrace and similarly overflowing with flowers and greenery. The bulk, as it emerged into the afternoon light, proved to be many layers of sky-blue chiffon, bunched into flowing folds and tied in place at the hips by a sash of yellow silk.

'Like a hoop round a herring barrel,' giggled Nellie Bain, but the ripple of merriment died in a gasp of indrawn breath as the late arrival stepped forward into full view. For, draped round the skimpy puff sleeves and the sturdy shoulders which threatened to burst out of them was what appeared to be a live fox, teeth bared and apparently clamped around its own tail. Between flower basket and fox was a fringe of unnaturally red ringlets and the plump, rouge-cheeked and red-lipped face of Bethany Noble Gibb.

'I'm not late, am I?' she said, to no one in particular, and stepped forward so that the whole company could see to advantage her silk-stockinged ankles and yellow silk strapped shoes. She carried a frilled yellow parasol, furled, which apparently she used for posturing purposes, for she leant on it now, in order to survey the company from centre stage. Still striking, in spite of her girth and her sixty-five years, still with that air of belligerent sexuality, she was a formidable sight. But before Elissa could sort out the turmoil of emotion which swept through her, Bethany had spotted the cake and the candle which still burnt with a tall and steady flame. Swift as thought, she bent over the table and blew the candle out, with one noisy puff.

'Dangerous things, candles, and me with my new chiffon. Happy birthday, Lissa,' she added, mouth smiling and eyes bright as bottle glass. 'Sorry I'm late, but your drive's awful rough for the wheels of

461

my Daimler. You should get it sorted.' Then, deliberately, she sat in the centre of the company, in Elissa's empty chair.

'That's Auntie Lissa's chair,' said one of the children indignantly into the silence. 'That old lady's not allowed to sit there, is she?'

'No, dear,' said Poppy clearly. 'But she is going to move.'

Everyone stared in silence at the intruder and waited.

'How was I supposed to know?' grumbled Bethany. 'My Brodie's on the Council. He'll likely be Lord Provost one day. I'm due respect, I am, and my Brodie richer than the lot of you put together.'

She lumbered to her feet and moved away, still grumbling, to join a new arrival who had appeared from the direction of the kitchen garden. He was standing alone, a discreet distance away from William Downie and Katrine. A tallish man, thin-chested, but with the air of someone who had once been bigger; with a jaunty Panama hat and a grey moustache and beard like the King's, though not so neatly trimmed. His shoulders stooped in the cheap linen blazer and the skin of his face was rough as leather and deeply lined. He must be Bethany's chauffeur, though from the way he bent his head to hers and the way she put her hand on his arm to whisper something in his ear, an over-familiar one.

Suddenly the years peeled back with heart-stopping speed and Elissa was in the herring-lassies' hut in Shetland with Will Masson banging on the door to rouse them all with his cry of 'Tie up your fingers.'

Will Masson. She had not seen him or heard of him for years. Apparently Bethany was up to her old tricks again. How dare she humiliate Brodie, and in public, uninvited, at Elissa's own birthday party.

With a huge effort of will, Elissa took the matches Ina indignantly offered, struck one, lit her candle, watched it flare up to its full height, then settle into a steady flame. For a moment she stood motionless, eyes closed in secret wishing, then blew it out. She resumed her seat between Yvonne and Kate, Yvonne squeezed her hand in reassurance and Kate handed her her teacup.

'Tell the old bat where to go,' Kate urged. 'Or shall I tell her for you?'

'No. I'll handle it.' Bethany was an old and formidable adversary, but Elissa was on home ground and angry. 'I am glad you were able to come, Bethany, in spite of not being invited, and in spite of your many other social engagements. No doubt they all fell through at the last minute? Or you could not find anyone to bribe for the necessary tickets? Or perhaps you just couldn't resist the idea of a free tea? I remember you often used to send poor Georgie to tea at my house, because it saved you money.' Georgie had died, like Daniel, in the Adriatic. 'And for other reasons not fit to mention in polite company.

462

I see you've brought one of them with you to share my hospitality.' She was tempted to add 'Uninvited', but years of training in the boardroom stopped her tongue.

It did not stop Gideon's.

'You, fellow! If you have come on some sort of tradesman's errand, the kitchen entrance is at the back.'

'Don't be daft, Gideon Joe,' glared his Aunt Bethany. 'You know Will Masson. He drives my car for me.'

'That's one way of putting it,' came a voice from the company, Meg's or possibly Ina's, but Bethany was in full flow and impervious.

'And before you say he's not invited, he's come instead of my Brodie. I was told the whole family was expected. So seeing as you didn't see fit to waste one of they pasteboard invites on me, we've come anyway, to represent the family like. I tellt Brodie a garden party was no good for a man in a basket chair, what with someone having to wheel him all the time and tearing the lawn up in chunks. Besides, he was seventy-eight last week and the sun would likely finish him off, so Will came instead. To see me safe home.'

Without a word, William Downie rose to his feet, offered his wife his arm, and led her in silence across the terrace and into the house. Elissa wondered whether they would retreat upstairs, to the comfortable sitting room she had put at their disposal, or whether they would carry outrage to its logical conclusion and go home. Once she might have listened in trepidation for the slamming of the great front door: today she found she did not care.

'Leave it, Gideon,' she warned, as he pushed back his chair. 'I said I will deal with it. All my guests are welcome,' she added in a voice deliberately calculated to reach the far herbaceous border as well as the open upstairs windows of the house behind her. 'As long as they behave themselves.'

She smiled, pretending this was meant for the children, but her eyes were on Bethany's glaring face.

'We are Lady Bountiful, aren't we?' she sneered. 'But there's one of your family who hasn't come, isn't there? In spite of you and your Gideon Joe ordering everyone to turn up to sing your praises at your precious party, your own daughter hasn't seen fit to put in an appearance. And I don't blame her.'

'Quiet, woman!' bellowed a surprisingly powerful voice from the corner of the house. All heads turned to see a white-haired old man in a basket chair on wheels, propelling himself along by his hands on the wheel rims. 'I knew you were up to your mischief, barging in where you aren't wanted. But you will hold your evil tongue, or *walk* home. As for you, Will Masson, get round the back where you belong or you'll be out of a job before sundown.'

'Hello, Brodie,' said Elissa, smiling. 'How nice to see you. Bethany

463

said you weren't able to come, but I am so glad you did. Ina, pour Brodie a cup of tea, would you, dear? And if you could see that he has something to eat, Yvonne? Now help yourselves, everyone, or we will be eating up the left-overs for a week. And Kate, dear. Hide two of those meringues, quick, while there are still some left. For poor Cameron Forbes. I am afraid I was a little hard on him.'

When tea was long over, appetites for both food and gossip satiated, when even the most determined child could not persuade Poppy to play any more games with them, and in the drawing-room, where her almost-finished portrait had been suitably shrouded, the proffered sherry found no more takers, people began to collect possessions and children and say their goodbyes, until tomorrow, when they would meet again at the ceremony. Elissa stood in the open doorway, in the shadow of the Grecian portico, its granite columns gleaming in the evening light, waiting for the remaining two or three to leave. She had promised Cameron one last sitting before the light was completely gone.

The shadows were lengthening fast. She saw the sharp-edged outline of the portico, a black shape on the silvery gravel path, its two outer columns elongated to grotesque proportions by the dipping sun and its two inner, blurred into the darker bulk of the house wall.These two were unpolished grey granite, from Rubislaw quarry, the two outer which supported the portico roof, a pink granite, polished to a marble sheen. All were equally anonymous in silhouette. She was wondering idly why that long-ago builder had not made all four the same, when she heard a low voice, close behind her.

'She told me, you know. About Sarah and you and what she'd said.'

Brodie Gibb had propelled his chair over the tiles of the hall on silent wheels.

Elissa collected her startled thoughts, but could think of no answer except, 'Who?'

He jerked his head back, indicating someone over his right shoulder, and she turned to see Bethany Noble, preening and simpering into the gilt-framed mirror in the hall. Bethany was arranging her preposterous hat, tweaking those appalling ringlets into position, turning this way and that the better to admire herself, and lingering longer than was necessary, her eyes straying too often towards the foot of the stairs, or perhaps the baize door beyond. As if waiting for someone to impress. Elissa wondered if that fellow from the newspaper had left? If not, he might well be Bethany's prey.

'She told me the day it happened,' went on Brodie, in a low, urgent voice. 'She was laughing herself sick with glee because she had given you, in her words, your come-uppance. She said other things, too. Wicked, hurtful things. I was ashamed of her. Ashamed I had married

464

a woman so spiteful and cruel, and sorry you had been hurt. I told her then that she'd get nothing from me. Told her I'd leave everything to Georgie. That was before he died. Afterwards, I didn't care who got it as long as she got none of it. Then you started your fund and I was so happy to be able to give it all to you. My greedy bitch of a wife was furious and still is.'

'Brodie, I'm so very sorry.'

'I know, lass. The worst of it is, I know she'll outlive me. Otherwise, you and I might have married. It's what I've always wanted, Lissa, ever since I saw you all those years ago, that herring summer in Shetland.'

'Dear Brodie,' she said, with careful compassion. 'But even if Bethany died, you know we couldn't marry. I'm not free. I have to wait for Adam.'

'But Elissa . . .'

'Hasn't that fellow brought the Daimler round yet, Brodie?' called Bethany from behind them. 'You'd best fetch it, Elissa, or we'll be here all night.'

Brodie turned on his wife a look of venom. 'You fetch it, woman.'

'What, and leave you alone with your fancy piece?' Then she threw back her head in a wild crow of laughter. 'A cripple and a dottled old wifie. You make a right pair. What would your precious Sarah say if she could see you now?'

'Goodbye, Brodie. I'll send someone for your car.' Elissa turned on her heel and walked back into her house. Across the hall, up the stairs, along the landing, and into her bedroom. Somewhere in that other world, beyond the turmoil in her own head, she heard a voice say sarcastically, 'That's right, don't bother to say goodbye to folks, will you?' and another voice said, 'Leave her be, you silly cow. No one asked you to come anyway.'

But Bethany had come. Elissa shut the bedroom door and leant her back against it. Had she expected to find Sarah here? What mischief had she planned this time? Or was it plain jealousy? And how dare she call Elissa dottled? Was it dottled to keep faith? To remember promises and believe them? She had let them persuade her long ago, when she stood over the unknown body on the Yarmouth shore and believed it to be Adam. Well, they would not persuade her again. They had been wrong then and they were wrong now. Adam would come back one day. Then she realised. That was why Bethany was jealous! Of course.

But what did it matter after all these years? What did anything matter? Sarah had not come. She closed her eyes on weariness and let the tension and the anger drain out of her, leaving only sadness.

When she opened her eyes again it was to look on the usual tranquillity of her faded bedroom. Faded because she had loved the old, parchment-coloured wallpaper at first sight, all those years ago; the elegant, threadbare curtains at the window, the worn Afghan rug; had loved them and kept them unchanged. *How you can live with that old junk beats me*, she heard Bethany's long-ago voice taunting. *You want to throw it all out and buy good stuff like mine, and you boasting about your fine new mansion. Looks more like a tip to me.*

But Elissa had never boasted. And she had slipped into the time-worn bedroom with a sense of coming home. As she did now. Like a child counting precious possessions, she let her eyes rove over the high four-poster bed Adam had given her, its tasselled hangings gleaming gold in the soft evening light; the simple white bedspread she had stitched and edged with crocheted lace herself, and at the foot of the bed, the plain wooden chest which had once held all her worldly goods.

Now, a polished mahogany wardrobe on the far wall guarded outdoor and indoor clothes, skirts and jackets for work, day dresses, evening clothes, with half a dozen different pairs of shoes. The matching dressing table in the wide bay window held drawers of lavender-scented undergarments, silk stockings, nightgowns. On its polished surface, in front of the triple mirror, was the set of silver-backed hairbrushes and hand mirror with two cut-glass and silver-topped phials for lavender water and eau-de-Cologne, which Adam had given her on their first wedding anniversary, the year they had moved into Fairfields.

Dear Adam. He was a generous and loving husband.

Beyond the dressing table, the window looked out over the garden where the children had played. A stray shaft of sunlight touched one corner of the room and the warmth of the afternoon still clung to faded walls and polished floor. A fire was laid in the grate, ready to light if the evening grew chill, but there would be no need.

As she often did in times of stress or loneliness, Elissa slipped off her shoes, turned back the cover, lay back on the pillows of the bed and closed her eyes, waiting for the sense of Adam's presence to comfort her.

A knock, some time later, roused her. The door opened a crack, and Bella, one of Ina's many grandchildren, tiptoed into the room. She carried a cup and saucer, very carefully, in both hands.

'This is to revive you, Auntie Lissa, and the painter mannie says can you come before it's dark. He's wanting to paint your knitting.'

'Tell him not just now, dear. It's late and I'm tired. Tell him to manage without me. Say I'll come if I can, but I have so many things to think about before tomorrow.'

When Bella had gone, closing the door with exaggerated care

behind her, Elissa lay back on the pillows, sipping her tea and thinking over the events of the afternoon. Her portrait was going to be what she wanted, and when he saw it finished, Gideon would be sure to approve. And it had been a lovely party: all those children playing happily together, laughing, running about with such energy and enjoyment. Poppy had done wonders with them. Dear Poppy. And all Elissa's friends had been so kind. She couldn't thank them enough. But she wished Sarah had come home.

Sarah. She tried to remember her daughter as she had once been, before the bursary scholarships and college, and Sinclair's money. If the Sinclairs had not come into her life, how different it might have been. Sal might have married a fisherman, be living happily in the Square or, remembering the turmoil and devastation of the war, here at Fairfields with the others. Sal might even now be a loving daughter and friend instead of . . .

Abruptly Elissa closed that line of thought. She was being maudlin. She had told Bella she had things to think about and the first thing, for her own peace of mind, was to work out why Bethany had come. Poor Bethany. Childless. Her adopted son drowned, her husband crippled. She had so few blessings. Whereas Elissa had so many. No wonder Bethany was jealous. Though she couldn't possibly think that she and Brodie . . . Elissa shuddered with distaste.

Uneasily, she remembered Brodie coming to her, two or three years after the war was over. She had already collected the government compensation and started on their plans for the future. He told her, to her astonishment, that he would have married her, if Joseph had not snapped her up first.

'I'd had my eye on you for a whilie,' he confessed. 'I should have offered for you before the child was born. At least then I'd have had children to follow after me. Instead, look what I got. And even my George has been taken from me. He was a good lad, my George.'

'Yes, he was,' agreed Elissa, while her mind raced with shock. She could not tell him she would not have touched him with a barge-pole, let alone married him, even if he was the last man on earth. Instead she had soothed and comforted him. 'They were all good lads, the sons we lost. And the husbands.'

'I wish I'd gone with them. Even the influenza passed me by. And now my hips are so arthritic they won't hold me up any more. What have I got left in life but money and a wife who spends it?'

It was those bitter words of Brodie Gibb's that had given her the first small idea.

'Suppose . . .' she began carefully. 'Suppose there was a better way to use that money . . .'

Brodie had been her first subscriber, head of the list with a sum designed to shock the close-fisted into generosity. Elissa, to Gideon's alarm, had matched it, emptying their account at one sweep. She had even sold their shares in Tom's ice factory. But Adam, like Joseph before him, had left everything to Elissa and there was nothing Gideon could do about it.

'We have a house, big enough for all of us, and Adam will not mind. We have "Mary's", which was more than your grandfather had when he started working life, and we have your skill and experience,' she told him. '"Mary's" will bring in enough to start us on the next venture. We have no need of more. Until Adam comes back, you will look after our export business and I will work for Daniel's memorial; for Daniel and for all the sons and husbands and fathers and brothers who died in that dreadful war. Together, we will succeed.'

And they had. Tomorrow morning she was to be made an Honorary Burgess of the city for the work she had done to raise money for the proposed new Infirmary. Tomorrow afternoon her portrait was to be unveiled in the boardroom of the Grant Noble Coastal Steamer and North-East Trading Company, of which a valuable subsidiary was 'Mary's smokehouse'. All her family and friends would be there – with one exception.

Aunt Sarah would say it served her right.

But the memory of Aunt Sarah jogged her conscience. She ought to go down and sit for poor Cameron after making him do so many alterations. She tossed back the counterpane and swung her feet to the ground, put on her shoes, tidied her hair at the dressing table. If she was to pose for that wretched picture again she had better try and look much as she had done in the afternoon. She heard the sound of a motor car in the drive: the man from the press perhaps. She had forgotten to ask if he was coming back. If it was him, he would just have to wait.

She went out on to the landing, closed the bedroom door behind her, and walked towards the stairs. She had her hand on the banister rail, her foot on the first step, when the front door opened and she felt a gust of evening air rise up to stir her skirts.

Then a woman's voice said, 'Hello, Ina. Is my mother in?'

Slowly, with measured care, her white-knuckled hand gripping the polished banister rail, Elissa descended the stairs. At the bottom she stopped and looked across the chequered hall, black and white squares alternating, regular as a chess board and highly polished. Poppy had put roses from the garden in a plain white jug on the hall table. The scent wafted towards her on the evening air from the open doorway in which stood a tall, slim figure, her face in shadow.

'Mother?' She took a step forward out of the shadow and Elissa saw her face: older, sadder than it had been, but still beautiful. She wore a beige jumper and short, pleated skirt revealing flesh-coloured stockings, neat strap shoes, and no waistline at all. Her brown felt hat seemed to have no brim and was pulled down low over her forehead, concealing her hair except for a small pale swathe over each ear. Elissa stared and stared, struggling to see in this smart city woman the daughter who had stormed out of her life all those years ago. She could not think of one word to say.

'The journey took longer than I expected,' said Sarah into the silence. 'I am sorry I am late.'

Eighteen years late. Shrugging off the past with a surge of joy, Elissa found her voice at last.

'But still in time, Sarah,' and she held out her arms to her daughter. For a moment she feared a rebuff, then Sarah moved hesitantly towards her and suddenly they were hugging each other and crying as if the long separation had never been.

But at last Elissa pulled away and, her arms on her daughter's shoulders, looked deep into her eyes.

'You have grown into a handsome woman, Sarah. Your father would be so proud of you. But what am I doing keeping you standing here in the hall like an unwelcome visitor? Come in and we will have a glass of wine together, to celebrate. Or would you rather wash first and unpack? The others will be down soon. Gideon and Yvonne and Poppy. You will stay a day or two, won't you? Stay as long as you like?'

'I have to be in London again on Monday, Mother, but I hope you can find room for us till then.'

'Us?'

'Didn't I say? I have brought my daughter Margaret with me. I told her to wait in the car until I had seen you. I wanted . . . I wanted to meet you myself, first.'

'To see whether I would let you over the threshold?' asked Elissa, with a touch of sadness.

'No, Mother. To say I was sorry. Sorry for what I said.'

They both knew what she meant.

'I didn't really believe it. I said it to hurt, I suppose. In revenge. I didn't want to believe that Adam Grant was my father.' She looked suddenly shamefaced and twenty years younger. 'I loved the father I had.'

'I know you did.' They looked at each other, eyes brimming, then embraced again, in reconciliation and understanding.

'And I loved Adam, too. He was the kindest of godfathers. I am sorry he died.'

'But he didn't, Sarah dear. They said "missing", that's all. He will come back, when he can. You must have faith, as I do.'

469

'Oh, Mother,' said Sarah, and shook her head in despair. 'Please don't . . .'

'Don't what? But never mind that. Come,' she said, taking Sarah's hand and drawing her into the little parlour beside the front door. 'If Margaret can wait just a little while longer? I want a few minutes alone with my own daughter, while I have the chance.'

When they were comfortably settled with the door closed, Elissa said, 'How have you managed all these years? I have been so worried about you. You and your little daughter. And her father?' She was afraid Sarah would resent the question, but the time for resentment was long past.

'The last time you asked me that question, in this same room, I refused to answer, didn't I? Now when I look at my own Margaret, I know that if she came to me and said what I said to you all those years ago, I would ask the same questions. I said dreadful things on that terrible afternoon, Ma, some I meant and still mean, but others I have wished unsaid too many times to count. You were right to do what you did. I know that now. Ben asked me to marry him as soon as he knew I was pregnant, but I said no. I thought they would think I had trapped him on purpose and I couldn't bear that. I was too proud.'

After a pause, Sarah said quietly, 'Ben was killed on the Somme. I loved him, Ma. Always. But I left it too late.'

'I am so very sorry, Sarah. He was a charming young man, friendly, courteous, always cheerful.'

'And Margaret takes after him.'

'Oh, Sarah, you can't know how glad I am to see you after all this time. I only wish your father was here too.'

'To welcome the prodigal daughter? I think I could do justice to a piece of fatted calf after that tedious journey and I am sure young Margaret could.'

'I am sorry, Sarah. Whatever am I thinking of? And the poor girl sitting out there starving all this time. She will think her grandma doesn't want to meet her, let alone feed her. I must see to it at once.' Elissa rose to her feet and moved for the door.

'No, Mother, don't go yet. I was only teasing.'

'Nothing of the sort. You are hungry and thirsty and if I know young people, your daughter – my granddaughter – will be more so. If she has not grown tired of waiting and driven to the nearest hotel. So let us go and find her first, then see about some food for everyone.'

She held out her hand, Sarah took it, and together they walked to the open front door. A small Austin motor car was parked some yards away and when Sarah called, its passenger door opened and a girl of seventeen unfolded long legs and climbed out.

'Hello, Gran. My name is Margaret, but most people call me Meg.' She grinned and held out her hand.

Elissa took it, and held it between both of hers, looking searchingly into the girl's face. Tall, like her mother, slender, fair-skinned, but with darker hair, she had clear, honest blue eyes, a small, freckled nose and an eager, almost excited expression. For some reason, a trick of the evening light perhaps, she saw herself as she was all those years ago, when, with all the other girls, she took the boat to Lerwick, full of happy expectation and dreams.

'Mother has told me so much about you,' she said, before Elissa could find words to speak. 'About the herring summer and the harbour and "Mary's" and this lovely place. About Grandpa and the uncles and godfather Adam and all the relatives I've never seen. I have been longing to meet you all. And especially you, Grandma. Mother says you were such a lovely, loving parent. The best mother anyone could have.'

Elissa's eyes brimmed with sudden tears and she put her arms round the girl and hugged her. 'Thank you. I am so proud of your mother. And of you, Meg. But you must come inside and meet the others. Poppy will be delighted to find an unexpected cousin and someone nearer her own age. She has spent the afternoon with a horde of kindergarten horrors, the dear girl, and is thirsty for more adult company. Paul will be arriving tomorrow morning – he is a fledgling lawyer in Edinburgh and couldn't get away today – and then our party will be complete. I am so very happy to see you both. Oh dear, I forgot!' Her eyes widened in horror. 'Cameron Forbes has been waiting for me all this time. I must go and apologise to the poor man.'

They found the drawing-room empty, Cameron nowhere in sight. His paints and other painting paraphernalia had gone, but the canvas on the easel was no longer shrouded. As they came in the doorway, it faced them across the long polished floor and Elissa saw herself as in a mirror glass.

'It is exactly like you, Gran,' said Meg. 'Mother told me you were always knitting. Is that for the ceremony tomorrow?'

'Is there anything you don't know about me, young lady?'

'Oh yes, hundreds of things. I have so many questions to ask you, Gran. About following the herring, and the curing stations, and the Square. Mother has told me lots of things, but I want to know everything, just as if I had lived it myself.'

Elissa turned her head to see Sarah's face but Sarah was staring at the portrait, with an expression she could not read.

'What do you think of it, Sarah? I told Gideon it would be a waste of money.'

471

'It is perfect. I don't know what it cost, but it is worth every penny.' Suddenly she laughed aloud. 'With you looking down at them from the board room wall no one will dare be idle for a single moment. You should double your profits in a year. That will please Gideon. But what I want to know is, will that knitting of yours grow longer, day by day?'

'Till it reaches the bottom of the picture and tumbles over the frame,' spluttered Meg.

Elissa, watching mother and daughter laughing together, felt contentment spread through her and wash away for ever the ghost of that other Sarah, Sarah Downie Robertson, who had cursed her as a whore.

Later, there would be time for questions, so many years to sort through and pick over, the whole of Margaret's life and as large a chunk of Sarah's. But now the rift was healed, there would be the rest of her life in which to do it.

When at last the excited household retired for the night, Elissa slipped into bed, settled comfortably on the pillows and waited for Adam to join her.

Sarah has come home, Adam, and has brought her daughter with her. A lovely daughter, friendly and eager. Full of wholesome curiosity. She reminds me a little of Poppy. But I wonder what will happen to them both with so many young men killed? Widows and spinsters, that is what the war achieved. Too many dear, brave women, who must learn to manage alone. There is Paul, of course. He is coming tomorrow, in time for the town ceremony. Poppy likes him, I know, and he is no blood relation. Yvonne says he is lucky to be alive. The war ended the week before he was eighteen. Daniel was not so lucky, my precious Danny. But he is with his father now, and his grandparents and uncles and so many young friends.

I wonder what became of Becky Macrae? I asked once or twice, but she never came back to Ferryhill. She loved Danny and would have made him a good wife. I hoped, once, to see their children. But Sarah has come home, with Meg, and I think, like me, you would approve.

I wonder if you will approve of my portrait. I think I look rather stern, but Meg and Sarah both like the knitting. I hope Gideon thinks it is value for money.

Goodnight, my darling, and come home soon.